The men and women of

THE WILD BLUE

ED NOVACK—Holding on to hope in a Hanoi prison camp, he faced his torturers, not knowing if rescue would ever come.

KATHY KELLY—She waited years for her man to satisfy her . . . then wondered where he had learned how.

MICHAEL McMANUS KELLY—A good Irish Catholic, he prayed to God to get his wings, then met his destiny not in Korea but in California.

(more)

The men and women of

THE WILD BLUE

===★===

DON PICARD—A man who loved machine above all things and planes above all machines

JOAN BROWN—A woman of many longings one flyboy wasn't enough for her.

JIM GARVEY—They said he went nuts and sho up a Korean airfield . . . so they knew he wa the right man for an even crazier mission.

Praise for

THE WILD BLUE

===★===

"Impressive . . . tells of the great challenges and sacrifice faced by those in the Air Force—the men who maintaine discipline and honor, the strength of families raised with an understanding that everyone owed service to thei country. A wonderfully American story wonderfully told.'
Hon. Barry Goldwater, Senator

"Impressive . . . after reading this novel, never wil you look up and watch one of their jets fly overhead without remembering something of this poignant American story."
Rave Reviews

The men and women of

THE WILD BLUE

==⊛==

LARRY WHITE—He flew for the sheer thrill of it, and no one thought he'd ever live to collect his pension.

RACHEL GARVEY—Her father said it wasn't feminine to fly . . . which made her want to soar all the more.

MILLARD WASHINGTON—A black man whose mother wanted him to preach, he chose instead to break the barriers of sound—and race.

Praise for

THE WILD BLUE

==⊛==

"Boyne and Thompson . . . write with candid authority and considerable finesse about the most elite and glamorous branch of the military."
Booklist

"THE WILD BLUE is as big as its locale. It's a tremendous work, exciting and provocative, and is an absolute must-read for anyone who has longed to wear wings."
Ernest K. Gann

THE
WILD BLUE
The Novel of the U.S. Air Force

Walter J. Boyne and
Steven L. Thompson

IVY BOOKS • NEW YORK

Ivy Books
Published by Ballantine Books
Copyright © 1986 by Walter J. Boyne & Steven L. Thompson

Library of Congress Catalog Card Number: 86-2636

ISBN 0-8041-0149-3

This edition published by arrangement with Crown Publishers, Inc.

Manufactured in the United States of America

First Ivy Books Edition: August 1987

FOR THOSE WHO SERVED

Millions of American men and women have donned Air
Force blue since 1947. To them and their families we
dedicate *The Wild Blue,* in the certain knowledge that
no written testament to their patriotism, courage, and
skill can describe adequately their sacrifices and service to the nation. Our freedom is their monument.

Walter J. Boyne   Steven L. Thompson

January 1986
Washington, D.C.

The Language of the Air Force

ADF: *automatic direction finder radio*

AFIT: *Air Force Institute of Technology*

AFR: *Air Force Regulation*

AFSC: *Air Force Systems Command*

AGL: *above ground level (measure of altitude)*

ASD: *Aeronautical System Division*

back seater: *designation for copilot or weapon systems officer in F-4*

Big Belly: *the modification to carry more conventional bombs in a B-52*

BOQ: *Bachelor Officer's Quarters*

BUFF: *nickname for the B-52 stands for Big Ugly Fat Fucker, or in polite society Big Ugly Fat Fellow*

BX: *Base Exchange*

CEP: *circular error probable: the average distance a bomb misses a target*

CinCSAC: *Commander in Chief, Strategic Air Command*

C.O.: *Commanding Officer*

C.P.: *Command Post*

DCA: *Federal Aviation Administration designator for Washington National Airport*

DCO: *Deputy Chief of Operations*

DFC: *Distinguished Flying Cross: Air Force decoration*

DOD: *Department of Defense*

ECM: *Electronic countermeasures*

ER: *Efficiency Report—a fitness rating*

FAA: *Federal Aviation Agency/Administration*

FAC: *Forward Air Controller*

FFF: *made-up acronym for fictitious automatic data processing system, the fast fault finder*

FNG: *Fucking New Guy: a recent arrival in Southeast Asia*

formate: *to fly in formation*

GAO: *Government Accounting Office*

GCA: *ground controlled approach: radar control from the ground*

GIB: *Guy in the back seat—the F-4 copilot/weapon systems officer*

Gooney Bird: *Affectionate name for C-47 aircraft*

G.S.: *Government Service, the civil service rating*

GUMP check: *Standard preflight check for gas, undercarriage, mixture, prop*

ICBM: *an intercontinental ballistic missile*

I.G.: *the Inspector General*

ILS: *an instrument landing system*

IRAN: *Inspect and Repair as Necessary: a maintenance system*

JAG: *the Judge Advocate General*

Jolly Green: *the large helicopters used for air-sea rescue*

MARS: *Military Auxiliary Radio Service*

MATS: *Military Air Transport Service*

MiGCAP: *MiG Combat Air Patrol: a formation designed to prevent MiGs from attacking*

NCO: *noncommissioned officer*

NCOIC: *the noncommissioned officer in charge*

O.D.: *olive drab, standard Air Force color for fatigues*

OER: *Officer Efficiency Report*

OMB: *Office of Management and Budget*

OSI: *Office of Special Investigation*

OWC: *Officers Wives' Club*

PACAF: *Pacific Air Force*

PCS: *permanent change of station: a move to another base*

PDI: *an instrument the bombardier uses to guide the pilot on a bomb run*

pipper: *the illuminated crosshairs found in gun sights*

POL: *Petroleum, oil, and lubricants: anything dealing with fuel, etc.*

PSP: *pierced-steel planking used to make runways and taxi-ways*

PX: *Post Exchange: an army term that survived in the Air Force for years*

R&D: *Research and Development*

R&R: *Rest and Rehabilitation—a G.I. vacation*

RIF: *Reduction in Force*

RPV: *remote piloted vehicles, drones*

SAC: *Strategic Air Command*

SAM: *Surface to Air missile*

SOS: *Squadron Officer's School*

TAC: *Tactical Air Command: light bomber equivalent of SAC*

TDY: *temporary duty: usually a detail away from home station*

TIC: *Troops in Contact: forces actually engaged with enemy*

TISEO: *a television electro-optical device for identifying enemy aircraft at a distance*

TMTS: *a fictional acronym for a Tri-Mission Tri-Service aircraft*

TWX: *a military telegram system*

VMI: *Virginia Military Institute*

VNAF: *Vietnam Air Force*

WSO: *weapon systems officer—the GIB in the F-4*

Prologue

THE
MISSING MAN

0915 LOCAL
8 September 1978
Arlington, Virginia
USA

The sun burned through the morning haze, transforming the bronze statues guarding the Memorial Bridge to gold and dappling the waters of the tidal basin. The funeral procession moved slowly along the bridge toward the entrance to Arlington National Cemetery, the shiny black hearse leading the procession glowing eerily in the diffused orange sunlight.

In the limousine immediately behind the hearse, Kathy Kelly turned to her left, glancing down the span of the bridge toward the Lincoln Memorial. "At least it's warm," she said evenly. "Remember how cold it was at John Kennedy's funeral?"

Next to her, Joan nodded, grateful to discuss the weather. The weather was always a safe topic. "It seems like yesterday. Where were you stationed then?"

Kathy squeezed her hand warmly. "You remember. We were at Edwards. Mike and Duke were working on some dumb bomber project. I think that was their second or third big fight."

The cortege moved up Memorial Drive, toward the Eternal Flame flickering by Kennedy's grave. The procession wound around the corner in a long arc behind the hearse, ants following a big black beetle.

On the opposite side of the drive, separated by the carefully tended parkway, a smaller procession was leaving. Arlington Cemetery was always busy.

Kathy leaned forward and touched Louise's gloved hand. Sitting in the limo's rear-facing seat, Louise had been staring out the window to the right, looking worse with every passing minute. She started slightly at Kathy's touch.

"Louise. Are you all right?" Kathy's concern was evident.

Louise always seemed the strongest of them all. She patted Kathy's hand and smiled thinly. "I'm okay. I was just thinking how many times we've done this."

Joan Brown shook her head. "Too many times," she said slowly. "Do you remember how you helped me at Castle? I'll never forget it."

Neither Kathy nor Louise answered. There was no answer. They sat and waited.

The procession moved slowly, a long line of headlights reaching back toward Fort Meyer. A car passed the line, honking furiously at being delayed. The driver looked dismayed when he realized it was a funeral.

0917 LOCAL
8 September 1978
National Airport
Alexandria, Virginia
USA

"Good morning, General."

"Larry. Good to see you."

"And you, sir. It's been a long time."

"Too long, eh?"

"Yes, sir."

"Well, tempus fugit. And so should we. This your bird?"

"One of 'em, General. Our first, actually, and it will get us to Nashville in a hurry."

"I saw your ad in *Trade-A-Plane*; recognized your name right away. McNaughton has two corporate jets, but one was in Europe and one was on hold to go to Brazil, and I had to be in Nashville. Glad I could call you."

"Rog. Worked out well. We come to DCA a lot on charter, mostly for the real-estate association. Those guys need to be at all the hearings."

"Yes, well, what time is wheels up?"

"We're slated for ten o'clock, sir."

"Good. Say, Larry. Do you get much flying time?" Larry smiled inwardly. Old habits die hard. The query was couched in casual terms, but the old Air Force concern with flight currency was there. No old pilot wanted to trust his ass to somebody who wasn't current.

"Oh, a hundred, maybe one twenty hours a month. But it sure beats working."

"Yeah. I'd give my left nut for your job, Larry."

"Can't see it, General. You're the one who turned the Air Force into a paying proposition. I'm still just an airplane driver."

"Flying's what it's all about, Larry. Always was, always will be."

4

"Yeah. Maybe." Larry flushed with pride. The general might be simply stroking him, but still, a compliment from this man was worth a dozen fat corporate charters to Bermuda. "Well, I gotta talk to clearance delivery. Good talking with you, General. And thanks again for calling us."

"What are friends for, Larry?"

Larry White smiled and went forward between the leather-covered seats of his Lear 24F. The general was right. But then he was always right. That's why he was a retired general, and Larry was a retired lieutenant colonel. White settled himself into the snug seat on the left side of the dazzling blue-and-white Lear and nodded to Rick Thomas, his young copilot.

"All set?"

"Yeah, Larry. But we got a delay on the takeoff; they've got a flight of four F-4s making a pass over Arlington Cemetery in five minutes. Missing Man formation."

White swore under his breath. He hated late takeoffs, especially when he had a VIP on board. Maybe this particular VIP would know who was being buried, and he'd understand.

White slipped out of the seat and went back to the small cabin, where the general was reading a pile of typewritten notes. He was already belted into his swivel chair.

"Sir?"

"Yes."

"We've got a departure hold. Traffic's backed up because of a flyover. Some F-4s doing a Missing Man for a funeral at Arlington."

"Oh?"

"Yeah. You know anything about it?"

"A little." The general glanced at his watch. "It would be going off about now."

White glanced out the small cabin window, up into the clouds. It was a typical Washington summer morning, mostly haze, some low scud. Ignoring the activity on the ramp where his Lear was parked, engines running at ground idle, he scanned the sky, back toward Arlington, only a mile away. The F-4s would probably come from up the river.

"You know the guy they're burying?"

The general peeled off his reading glasses. He blinked slowly and looked out the window.

"Yeah," he said, "I knew him."

0930 LOCAL
8 September 1978
Arlington, Virginia
USA

They reached the grave site, one blank spot among acres of white crosses. People spilled out of the cars to move in a strange, weaving, practiced pattern which ensured that the family could reach their seats first, surrounded by a sea of supportive looks.

The widow went forward and sat down. On either side of her sat general officers, ramrod straight. About half the crowd was in uniform. Most were flyers.

The two other women held back.

Louise looked at the row of people at the graveside, their heads bowed, waiting for the chaplain to begin. Joan's head was bowed too. Her hands were clasped so tightly that her nails dug into her palms, almost drawing blood.

She had promised herself she would not cry. She did anyway. And she'd promised herself she would not lean on Kathy. She did anyway. The jets on approach to National howled low overhead—God, how she hated that sound, that awful spine-chilling hollow moan!—and the tears simply came, of their own accord. She'd done this more times than she could remember, for friends, squadron mates. And she'd never, ever cried. But earlier, as she'd slowly dressed, alone in Kathy's guest room, she'd looked at herself, gaunt, tired, and red-eyed, and known that this time, all those years were going to come crashing down in unstoppable tears. She cried not just for him, but them all. All those young men they'd lived with all those years. Tall, short, thin, fat, some no more than kids when they died in their damned mistress airplanes, others almost as old as the blackened remains of the man who lay in front of them. She knew it was somehow the effect of the booze and the detox process, the long, terrible drying-out, but she couldn't stop. She leaned on Kathy—Kathy, of all people!—and sobbed uncontrollably.

Kathy Kelly wore black; it suited her coloring more than most women's. The humid Potomac wind moved her veil sluggishly. A veil was a nice accessory, she thought. It should be worn more often. It shielded you, kept people from seeing your face. But no one tried to look. Like Joan, all the Air Force men and women around her were plunged into their own thoughts.

It was just as well. He'd want it that way. She knew that, and o did Joan and Louise. Kathy glanced at Louise. She was still beautiful, as she had been the day they'd met almost twenty years ago.

Louise Washington seemed not have aged at all, despite the wisps of gray in her hair and the tiny wrinkles in her skin. She did not look up to search for the airplane that Millard was flying. She knew he was there. That was enough for her. Somewhere inside the usual tiny, tense knot of fear coiled tighter as she realized that even this flight could be dangerous. They all were. There had never been a flight without tension; each time he climbed into a B-52 she was terrified, and she was never permitted to admit it. His leaves were precious things, for she could lie beside him, watching him sleep, and know that he was not going to get up at some godawful hour to fly. So often she had watched him slip out of her bed, quickly bathe and shave and step into a flight suit at an hour when most men were still sound asleep. He would kiss her lightly—almost absently, his mind already on the mission—and grab his flight bag to clump out of the house in the combat boots that left black heel marks on the tiles, perhaps never to return. She wanted it over. So she did not look up.

The service was brief. The Air Force honor guard went through its rifle drill, and the three traditional nerve-jarring volleys faded into the mournful brass sound of Taps.

From the north there came the rumble of a flight of four McDonnell Douglas F-4s, with their strangely angled wing and tail sharply defined against the eight trails of smoke streaming from their engines.

Before they reached the cemetery boundary, the number-two F-4 pulled up and out, leaving a vacant spot—the missing man—in the formation as it thundered over Arlington.

The pilots among the mourners looked up instinctively, even in these surroundings checking the formation, the airplanes, the pilots who flew them. The women winced as the fighters shook the ground. Kathy squeezed her eyes shut and allowed the thunder to wash over her. Louise simply shut it out. Joan balled her fists tighter and made no attempt to stop the tears.

Suddenly it was over. The F-4s were gone, the casket ready to be lowered into the grave and the flag that had honored it folded and presented to the widow. She sat for a moment clutching the flag while people came together near her, spoke meaningless words softly and touched her hand. She knew she ought to be praying for him, but her thoughts were about all of them, about Millard and Duke and Mike, Garvey and the rest.

7

So many, she thought, dear God, so terribly many. When th[e] news had come, she'd been stunned. The others could die i[n] flaming balls of fire, but him? It had not seemed possible. An[d] after retirement, to boot. She had learned long ago that nothin[g] in the Air Force was "fair." But it had not seemed fair. Th[e] crash had driven Joan, Louise, and Kathy together, as they ha[d] been driven so many times in the past to seek out one anothe[r] for comfort. She had often thought it ironic, because the three o[f] them had little in common except the Air Force, and what i[t] demanded of them.

Now it demanded this of them.

How had it come to this? Why?

0941 LOCAL
8 September 1978
"Alpha Two"
12,700 ft. AGL
Arlington, Virginia
USA

In the rear cockpit of the number-two F-4, Maj. Gen. Millar[d] Washington looked down at the dot of Arlington Cemetery, an[d] at the smoke trails from the rest of the formation drawing away t[o] the south. The intercom broke into his thoughts.

"General?"

"Roger, Captain."

"I'm going to stay high and go well south around the airpor[t] traffic to land at Andrews; no point in chasing the formation."

"Roger, okay by me."

"General?"

"Go ahead."

"How did you get permission to have a fly-by? He was retired, wasn't he?"

"Yeah, officially, but you know, you never really retire. Besides, he had a lot of friends. I TWX'd the Chief of Staff, and he arranged it. Probably had to go to the White House, or at least to the head of the FAA. The chief had orders cut for me to fly, this one time. Hope I haven't scared you."

The captain chuckled, said nothing. A diplomat.

Washington looked back; he wondered how Louise was taking it. She'd grown ever less fond of the Air Force. And she hated unerals. He allowed himself another moment of thought for the man in the ground and returned his attention to the F-4 and the way the young captain was flying her.

0946 LOCAL
8 September 1978
Arlington, Virginia
USA

The widow walked back to the limousine, holding the folded flag to her chest, eyes down, picking a path where her needle-sharp heels would not sink in the moist ground.

A gray-haired man joined her by the limo. He leaned forward and kissed her. She knew what to expect, and what was expected of her. She waited patiently for the words.

"He was a great man, honey. I was proud to know him."

"Thank you, Congressman; he'd be glad to know you were here. Thanks for coming." He nodded somberly and moved away. The attendant opened the door and she climbed in.

Around her, the groups of people entered their own cars. The mood was changed now; she could hear their rising conversation, promises to meet, even laughter. In the old days, there would have been a little buffet reception at home. She was glad he didn't have to do that. She was just going home to sort things out.

0949 LOCAL
8 September 1978
National Airport
Alexandria, Virginia
USA

"Sir? Larry?"

White blinked and cleared the F-4s from his mind. He leaned out from his seat across from the general and looked up the Learjet's little passageway at Rick Thomas.

"Yeah?"

"We can go anytime now, skipper."

"Great. Nice to get off the ground." Larry glanced quickly at

9

the general. He saw that he, too, had been affected by th
Missing Man flyover. His look was remote, his gaze still outside
Larry got to his feet and hesitated. It seemed that there was mor
to be said, somehow. A comrade had died and was being burie
at Arlington. There should be more to it. Larry didn't think c
himself as a romantic. Just a pilot. But there ought to be more
He was fumbling in his mind for what to say when the genera
pinned him with a diamond-hard look. "You know it all starte
right here?"

Larry just stood there as that familiar little twinge of uneas
shot through him. It was the feeling he got whenever he knev
there was something he should know and didn't. "Ah—no.
don't—"

The general was looking through him. He turned that search
light gaze on the window. "Right there. On that hardstand ove
there, where that New York Air DC-9 is. That's where it started
for you, for me, for the men in the F-4s, for the man bein
buried."

"I—I don't follow—"

The general ignored him. "July 26, 1947. Right there, Larry
Lt. Col. Hank Myers is in the cockpit and Harry Truman is in
back. It's hotter than blazes, but Truman sits there in his worste
double-breasted suit and everybody just sweats. Myers has no ai
conditioning, and he can't start the engines until the presiden
says so, and the president won't say so until the bill he has to
sign gets sent over from the Executive Office Building. You
know what the damn bill is?"

White shook his head.

"I'll tell you. It's the birth certificate of us all. The Nationa
Security Act. Truman is waiting to sign the damn thing, righ
there in his own Air Force airplane, the *Sacred Cow*. Used to be
Roosevelt's personal transport. Harry took it over. And he':
waiting to sign the act, to separate the Air Force from the Army
and create the real Air Force, and then get that thing in the air,
so he can go to his sick mother in Independence, Missouri.
She's dying. He loves that woman more than anyone on earth,
but he's the president, and he believes that means everything
comes before his own concerns. Not like the guys we have today,
Larry. So he sits there, sweating, not swearing at the idiots whc
are holding him up, just waiting.

"Finally the guy with the paper runs up the air stairs. The
president whips out his pen and signs the paper, then shoves it
10

ack and says, 'Let's go' to Myers. The first engine was turning efore the courier was off the stairs.

"Everything started right over there, Larry. Korea, Vietnam, e 47, the 52, the 58, ICBMs, the spaceships, the fighters, the orks. Not a hundred yards from us. Makes you wonder, doesn't ?"

White blinked. "Uh—" he stammered.

"She died, of course. They weren't even past the Mississippi hen the word came. Truman turned 'em around and the first ight of the U.S. Air Force was over. Aborted." He paused, ooking out over the ramp. "Makes you wonder."

Thomas called, "Hey, skipper, we better get moving. Taxiay's getting pretty jammed."

"Be right there, Rick." He tried to think of something appropriate to say. As usual, nothing came. He never was much with ords.

"He was a good man," White said finally.

The general looked out the window. The F-4 exhaust trails, ke dingy spoor of the nineteenth-century locomotive, were lmost gone. He watched them dissipating in the morning air for moment, then slipped his glasses back on and picked up his apers.

"Yes," he said slowly, "he was. The best. The very best."

Book One

—★—

THE
WILD BLUE

1

Michael Kelly slipped into the back pew, hoping he could remember the Act of Contrition. It had been a long time since he'd prayed. He glanced around the still-familiar basement church almost furtively. The holy-water fountains and the plaster Stations of the Cross still easily evoked memories of stormy and terrifying Good Fridays.

A pang of guilt stabbed through him. It had been six years since he had been to mass, seven since he had performed his Easter duty and gone to confession and communion. He'd been an altar boy, a good Catholic by any standards. But then those ductless glands had erupted in him. Along with the growth of pubic hair they brought at long last, they also brought the insoluble problem of how he could possibly be truthful in confession. How could he confess to the frail old father behind the screen what he wanted to do—and now, sometimes did—with just about every girl he laid eyes on?

He couldn't. Not then, not now. The drift away from the Church had been slow, but inevitable. He tried to substitute direct prayer for the confessional, but it wouldn't work. No Catholic could ever really believe that there was communion without absolution. So he was trapped. Rebellion was one thing. Damnation quite another. The only solution had been to ignore the whole thing.

He began to understand a little what it was that kept the people coming to mass. Every morning, rain or shine, the front pews were filled with little old ladies running the beads, shooting disapproving looks at old man Gerhardt and his sidekick Quigley, who were drunk together in Foley's Tavern every night, and hungover together every morning at mass.

When Kelly's urges began to get the upper hand over his faith, he would sit in this incense-laden sanctuary trying to work out his own personal deal with God, trying to maintain contact outside the varnished pine walls of the confessional. His fellow

15

altar boys, rough and raucous as they shared a bottle of stolen sacramental wine, would question the existence of God. Kelly never doubted it for a moment. He just wasn't sure if there was a need for God to have guys like Pops Trombley to intercede. A God surely wouldn't have put all that mindless passion between his legs and then expect him to ignore it, as Father Trombley so obviously did.

Early on, his prayers had been simple: Please, Dear God, keep Dad sober, or if he gets drunk, don't let him go to church. And: Please don't let Sister Kenelma deck me with her sweet right cross because I didn't do my homework.

Now he wasn't praying. Just talking, as he might have talked to a sober father or a loving mother. He was trying to work out a plan, to bring together the sense he had of being somebody against the continual hard knocks of being poor.

He thought maybe he could work out a deal. Maybe there'd be a way he could get to school, make a little money, come back and do a little something for the church. He'd heard that sort of reasoning at Holy Angels, and sometimes outside the confessional. Old Father Trombley was adder-deaf, and he'd repeat the poor penitent's sins in a loud voice, wringing out a little conscience money before giving absolution. As a result, there was always a long line waiting when young Father Hannegan was hearing confessions, and when Hannegan would leave, most of the crowd went with him, thereby infuriating Father Trombley. The next person to see him paid a heavy penance.

Kelly knew you couldn't pay God off—and in East St. Louis, God was the only one you couldn't pay off—but sometimes a little extra prayer, a little extra talk seemed to work. He felt sure he'd prayed himself into his first car, a clapped-out '31 Chevy he'd stolen from his uncle for fifty bucks. And a few times he'd prayed to get a girl into the back seat for a little serious loving until he suddenly scored and was then overwhelmed with the sense that he'd been sacrilegious. Still, the Chevy worked for him, gave him freedom and the opportunity for a little sex. It ran most of the time, and he liked working on it when it didn't. The only time he despised it was when Bill Roberts passed him in his father's Chrysler Highlander, with its plaid upholstery that was absolutely guaranteed to pull the panties off any girl foolish enough to sit on it. And he hated it when Dr. Francis Engle would drive his brand new 1948 yellow Buick Roadmaster convertible into the filling station and say, "Fill it up, young fella, and don't spill any gas on the paint." The fucker said it every time, and laughed every time.

Engle was triply affronting. He drove big new cars and lived in a big house and he never failed to ask, "How is my dear old friend, Dr. Kelly?" Knowing, of course, that if it were after noon, his dear old friend was drunk. Old Doc Kelly was a joke, a has-been: once the county coroner—a powerful politician in his own right—now he was a down-and-outer dispensing paregoric for other down-and-outers. The Engles lived in a stone house, air-conditioned, for Christ's sake, just like the movie theater. Doc Kelly and his family lived in a crumbling bungalow, yard overgrown, windows painted aluminum to keep the world out. That had been his mother's only response to their continuing slide into poverty and misery. She was a pathetic, lie-down comic, dispensing bitter defensive irony with the same fervor with which her husband now dispensed worthless medicine to those even more desperate than he. Of late, her favorite observation, her only attempt to explain her state was: "We're Irish, of course, Michael. But not lace-curtain Irish, not even shanty Irish. We're aluminum-window Irish." Whenever she said it, she'd laugh a laugh that tore Kelly apart. He tried to understand them, to understand what he should do, how he could help, but it never worked. So he talked to God instead.

The church was deserted except for the two little Italian ladies in the front pew, swathed in their customary black. Kelly felt in his pockets, found a quarter. He went forward to the candles guttering in front of the statue of Saint Joseph. He'd always liked Saint Joseph, who had never gotten a square deal either. It couldn't have been easy having a virgin for a wife and a god for a son. He dropped the quarter in the box, lit a candle, and ran quickly through three Hail Marys, three Our Fathers and an Act of Contrition. Then he got serious.

"Please, dear God: Let me pass that physical. Get me out of this town."

If Kelly hadn't had to wait for the bus on Collinsville Avenue to get to his night job at Bud Drummond's Conoco station, he might never have even had the chance to get out. He had to transfer from the Rosemont bus to the State Street line there on Collinsville, and that's where Sgt. Hank Bindle's recruiting office was. One afternoon he'd been standing there, exhausted already, awaiting the bus, when Bindle saw him eying the models of airplanes in the window of his office. He didn't waste any time.

"Like 'em son?"

"Yeah."

"Wanna fly 'em?"

"Sure. But you gotta be an officer, right?"

"Yep. But there's ways, son, there's ways. Got any college?"

"A year at Washington U. But I dunno if I can make it."

"Money?"

"Yeah. I work two jobs, and got a tuition-only scholarship. Probably have to quit."

"Don't, son. Tell you what. You stick it out for sixty credits, and I'll get you into the aviation cadet program. A year later, you'll be flying one of them P-51s, just like that model."

"No shit?"

"No shit."

The bus came a moment later. But Kelly wasn't on it. He was inside Bindle's office. When he came out, everything was different. And even though Drummond was pissed off about his being late for work, Kelly just grinned at him.

One more year.

Sixty credits.

He would do it. He had to. What else was there?

2210 LOCAL
20 November 1948
San Antonio, Texas
USA

Michael McManus Kelly, Aviation Cadet, Class 49D, stared into the huge mirror behind the bar at Rosa's, where over the course of a few Saturday nights he had discovered some important things.

First, Rosa's mirror taught him that he was different from most of the other guys in the program. He looked like them, he talked like them, he sweated through the classes and the flying and the hazing and the marching just like them, but he was different. He never asked "why?" He only asked "how?"

A lot of those who asked why were gone, washed out. Around here, at the self-styled West Point of the Air, there wasn't time for why. There was only time for "Yes sir," and learning how.

And that was at the root of the second thing he learned one night in the mirror at Rosa's.

He was happy. It stunned him to realize it. He'd been hustling his whole life, trying to protect himself, trying to break away from the endless rounds of denial and failure. And now, none of that mattered. What mattered was that he rolled out of bed every morning at 0530 and raced through days filled with the promise of something he'd never had in East St. Louis.

The future. These guys were giving him an honest-to-God shot at a future. All he had to do was work like a coolie, learn like an Einstein, and fly like a Lindbergh. When he'd first got to basic, he would march in the flight past upperclassmen who would shout, "You got it made if you don't fuck up!" He wasn't going to fuck up. He was going to have it made. In less than a year, he'd be a second lieutenant on flying status.

Less than a year. Less than a year ago, the left rear wheel of his '31 Chevy had floated off into traffic, the stub of its axle ground down to a needle point, taking with it his freedom. Less than a year ago, he'd been a faceless sophomore, nothing special in academics or athletics, and nothing special with women. Less than a year ago, he was in purgatory, in the special realm of the almost-damned; the gutted, cheated, used, and discarded town of East St. Louis. Now he was in San Antonio, where the wind tasted of parched sand and sage and the sky was almost always a clear dome of blue made to order for fliers.

He sloughed off his old life in purgatory like a useless suit. Two weeks after he entered flying training he felt as though he'd been in the Air Force his whole life, surrounded by guys who march straight, wore their hair short, and talked about flying in a language all but incomprehensible to the rest of the world. As the weeks ground on relentlessly and the guys who wondered if they'd make it didn't, he fought to excel with a concentration and a fury he never knew he had. Fear made him do it. Not so much fear of failure, but fear of the consequences of failure.

In the beginning, there had been only East St. Louis, and it reached out for him as it had for all the people in town, a sinkhole where no one came and no one left. Whenever he'd doze over his manuals, whenever he would flag from lack of sleep, he would think again of East St. Louis and come wide awake. Whenever some upperclassmen loaded him with demerits, forcing him to walk them off in long tours around the squad, dressed in full flying gear, he'd remember the stink of East St. Louis. Whenever an upperclassman would stop him in the hallway to recite the endless lists of nonsense verses—"How's the Cow? She Walks, She Talks, She's Full of Chalk"—the awful stockyard stench would return to him, and he would give them exactly what they wanted, because the alternative was East St. Louis.

And he had his own checklist. One he'd worked out with God. Before you took off in a trainer, you ran a GUMP check: gas, undercarriage, mixture, propeller. Before Kelly did anything, he ran a PDGLMWMW checklist. It was a simple prayer, the simplest he'd ever had: Please Dear God, Let Me Win My Wings.

The prayer became his talisman. When someone washed out, he'd mutter it. During a written test, he'd impress the letters into the wood of the desk. He scribbled it in the margins of his notes, marched to it, woke up to it. PDGLMWMW. In the fashion of the secret code that girlfriends used in sending letters to cadets— SWAK, sealed with a kiss, or PMRLH, Postman, run like hell—he would ink PDGLMWMW in the upper righthand corner of his rare letters to purgatory, then place a stamp over it. Nobody knew but him and God.

Maybe it was working, because here he was at Rosa's, two hoarded dollars crumpled in his pockets for a couple of Lone Stars and a taco, while other guys washed out every day.

It was worth the hoarding. Rosa's was an adventure for Kelly, a departure from the austere, pragmatic saloons of his hometown, where the shot and a beer were the preferred drinks, and food ranged from pickled hard-boiled eggs, streaked murky red like fetal slugs in a molding gallon jar, to sticks of sausage or bits of dried herring. The musty sump smell of stale spilled beer was the same, but instead of aging lath and peeling plaster, the walls were rough adobe covered with snapshots of young student pilots. Fading serapes obscured the cream stucco, scented with the kitchen's promise of gutty Mexican food. A bullfight poster, corners curled, took the place of the traditional Anheuser-Busch's Custer's Last Stand. Overhead, two fans turned slowly, mixing the stale blue smoke from the ceiling with the fresh gray smoke streaming upward.

As usual, he was jammed against a mahogany bar, polished only where elbows rubbed against it, part of a line of look-alike young cadets. Most were in sharply creased khakis. The rest wore short-sleeved shirts and slacks. The difference spoke plainly of who had money and who had none. Kelly was a have-not, so he wore his khakis, with pride. They were the best clothes he had ever owned.

Behind him, there was a rising tide of talk and laughter, and behind the bar was an absurdly bad painting. Hanging crookedly, a small hand-printed sign proclaimed it to be, "From the Odalisque by Ingres." The face of the naked woman lying on the couch was of a younger Rosa, eyes not yet hard. Like so much at Rosa's and everywhere else near Randolph, the picture had a story, part of the old Air Corps lore. The rumor was that Rosa's lover had been an artist and a Kaydet, back in the days when they flew DH-4s and Tommie Morses; legend had it that he'd fallen in love with Rosa, painted her, and then, when she'd spurned him, augered in somewhere in the desert south of San Antonio. Rosa, in her grief, was supposed never to have married. Everybody liked the story, even Rosa, but of course it was just a story. Rosa had married Toni, her *novio*, at eighteen, and they had four children. In wild extravagance he had paid a drunken artist to paint the picture when they opened the bar. Four years later Toni ran away with the first waitress they had hired. Rosa had not been sad. And she had certainly not tried to quash the story, since she made her money almost exclusively off the cadets.

Kelly pulled cautiously on the Lone Star, blocking the flow with his tongue. There was money only for two tonight, and he wanted to make them last. Rosa elbowed past him, sailing through the milling cadets like a Spanish galleon, two hundred pounds of doughy limbs and sleekly oiled hair, a platter of steaming jalapeño-ornamented enchiladas in one hand, four Lone Stars caught by the neck in the other. She materialized between two cadets, drunk on three beers, ready to fight over who was the best pilot. She scolded them, and they laughed it off. In a single fluid wide-hipped motion she dropped the platter before a kissing couple, and then, boss woman on her turf, turned to survey the needs of the crowd.

Kelly watched her in the mirror, as always fascinated by the flinty power of her eyes and the tricks she used to command the unruly swarm of young men and their dates. They talked about command at Randolph, but even his flight instructor, hardbitten First Lt. Robert C. Dendy, the man with the power to make Kelly or break him, could have learned from Rosa. Mike watched as she checked out the action in the crowd.

He turned to join her in the pastime. Without much money, it was all he could do. The likelihood of an unattached girl coming to Rosa's was remote, and the likelihood of her getting more than three feet through the door before being claimed was impossible. But still he scanned. After a moment, he saw Chick Coughlin, one of his tablemates, waving. He raised his own bottle and signaled him to come over to the bar.

Coughlin was a huge fullback from Boston College who was very close to washing out. Everybody knew that but Coughlin.

"Hey, Kelly, what's the word?" He slapped Mike on the back and nearly knocked him off the barstool. One of the reasons Coughlin didn't know he was so close to washing out was that everybody liked him. He was just too damn jovial.

"Nothing, Chick, same old shit. Any action downtown?"

"Hell no," he bellowed, "who wants to go out with a piddly ass cadet? The officers get all the action." It was the common complaint in their ranks, roughly equivalent in validity to the unwilling wife's headache.

Coughlin finished his beer and held it by the neck, waving it until Miguel hurried over with another. He gulped down half the bottle with a single swallow, watching Kelly as he did.

"Open throat. I can just open my throat and pour it in."

He grinned and demonstrated, finishing the bottle by tipping it over and pouring. He signaled again to Miguel.

"You ready, Kelly?" he asked.

"No, I'm nursing this one." He didn't add, "as usual." It was his standard style; he loved to drink, but he sent most of his money home, where he knew with acidic certainty that it would go only for such vital victuals as Crab Orchard blended whiskey and cigarettes. Still, it was part of the deal he'd made with God back in the basement at Holy Angels. He'd promised God he'd take care of his parents as long as he could, if only he made the program.

He watched enviously as Coughlin chugged down half of another beer, wiping foam off his face with the back of one huge hand. He blinked and grinned at Kelly, then jerked a thumb over his shoulder at the milling crowd.

"Hey. Did you know Brown was here tonight?"

"Our Brown? Duke Brown? Here at Rosa's? Bullshit. He wouldn't be caught dead here."

"No kidding. The sonofabitch is sitting in the corner with a good-looking broad. Word is, she's his wife. Half drunk, but a knockout."

Kelly swallowed the rest of his warm beer. The news that Brown was here was more unsettling than he liked to admit. Among the cadets, Mike was a kind of hero, even though he was a loner. He'd outfaced Cadet Maj. Morris Clampton, a spit-and-

lish ex-VMI junior who had heard about Kelly and decided to
ake an example of him. One morning he'd caught Kelly
ming out of the flight's latrine and braced him against the wall
 twenty minutes, screaming abuse at him from two inches
ay, his breath reeking of fried eggs, until he was simply worn
t by Kelly's indifference. Kelly walked his quad tours for
ampton and eventually the guy gave up, and went in search of
ner prey more rewarding. The other cadets of 49D figured
lly had some secret weapon, but of course it was only that he
ew what real badasses were like—Harry Williams and Tom
ackley, for instance—and Morris Clampton simply didn't rate
 their scale. Besides, Mike could hear the lovely liberating
und of T-6 engines running up outside while the cadet C.O.
lled at him. There weren't any T-6s in East St. Louis, and
lly never forgot it.

But there were guys like Charles Kingston "Duke" Brown.
uys like Doc Engle's son Francis. Guys whose own wealth,
curity, and status were a constant pricking reminder to Kelly of
aat he was not, and what he had not. Kelly hated them for the
uses they lived in, the girls they dated, the cars they drove,
d the snubs he was certain they aimed at him.

The worst of them had come upon his graduation from high
hool, when Doc Engle had thrown a big party for the class and
vited all the parents, including his dear old friend Dr. Joseph
'illiam Michael Kelly.

Engle and Kelly had been classmates at Illinois, and Engle
d never forgiven Kelly his brilliance. During World War I,
r. Kelly had been a well-respected surgeon in the Army at
ooks Field. He'd built a little hospital in Houston, then re-
rned to East St. Louis and politics, becoming the youngest
aroner in the history of St. Clair County. But his casual
inking had become serious in direct proportion to his success.
'hen the booze locked him deeply into failure, he responded by
inking harder. Dr. Kelly had steeled himself to go to Engle's
arty with Crab Orchard, then dosed himself with his customary
ae-ounce jolts from his calibrated cough-syrup bottle. Mike
uld tell at a glance how many drinks his father had had, just as
e could tell when he would fall down, and when he would
row up. It was all inevitable.

And so it was. Doc Kelly finally lurched into a waiter, cursing
im as he knocked down the tray of drinks before slumping into
white wrought-iron chair in the middle of Engle's immaculate
wn.

23

Mike could tell the incident had made the party perfect f[or]
Engle, who helped him steer his father through the thickets [of]
snapping eyeballs and smirking lips into the back seat of the o[ld]
Chevrolet. "Bad luck, young man," Engle had whispered, sot[to]
voce, "your father had a lot of promise. Let me know if I ca[n]
ever be of help."

When Dr. Engle had shown up next at Bud Drummond['s]
station to fill his Buick, Mike had not hesitated to palm [a]
handful of sugar cubes into the fuel tank. He wanted to do it f[or]
the three years he'd worked at Bud's, and the party made [it]
imperative. An eye for an eye. God would understand. Eng[le]
stopped coming into Drummond's after he took his ailing car [to]
State Street Buick; they told him the warranty was invalid b[e-]
cause he'd used bad fuel.

All through high school at Holy Angels, Mike sought a reaso[n]
for the way his life was running. It wasn't until he was [a]
freshman at Washington U. that he knew the truth. The tru[th]
was that no matter how you cut it, money and family counte[d]
over everything. The boundaries to his life were all ceilings, n[o]
floors. But in the Air Force, all that seemed to count wa[s]
performance. Money and family, he had thought, were meaning[less]
less.

Then Charles Kingston "Duke" Brown had appeared at Lieu[-]
tenant Dendy's table of would-be pilots, a spit-and-polish Arm[y]
version of Francis Engle. And when Mike had seen Dend[y]
almost piss all over himself to be nice to Brown—who was only [a]
second john, at least three years junior to Dendy, West Point [or]
not—he had begun to realize that even here, even among th[e]
T-6s, some things never changed. He knew that sooner or late[r]
he was going to collide with Brown.

He never thought it would be at Rosa's. It was a cadet join[t]
not exactly off-limits to civilians and officers and enlisted me[n]
but not friendly to them, either. Perched on the perilous limb [of]
almost-officerhood as the cadets were, between the safe harbo[r]
of the noncoms and the officers, they needed a place where the[y]
could lick their wounds and ignore their terrible temporary statu[s]
for a few hours. Rosa's was it. And for an officer to invade such [a]
place was almost incredible, an act of stupidity or bravado tha[t]
defied common sense.

Mike twisted his bottle around on the bar, making little we[t]
overlapping circles. When he said nothing, Coughlin, with th[e]
sensitivity of a mule, snorted and said, "You know his old man['s]
a goddamn general?"

"Nope," said Mike, although he did know, just as he knew—or thought he knew—how many girls F. Engle Junior had had in the back seat of that unbelievable Buick.

"Yeah," grunted Coughlin, fishing for a smoke in his shirt pocket, "I got the full ring-knocking story. He's class of '47 West Point, varsity baseball and boxing team, and his brother was class of '44, now a major flying B-29s. Pop's a retired Army three star." He patted his pockets, searching for a light. Mike pulled out his Zippo lighter and lit Coughlin's cigarette. Kelly didn't smoke, but had carried the lighter for two years, ever since he decided that it would be a great way to start something with a girl. It never had been, but still he carried it. As he slipped it back into his pocket, he ran his thumb again over the slick metal of the silver lighter. It was blank now. But in ten months, he'd have a pair of little silver wings soldered on it, with the words 2/LT M M KELLY engraved under them.

"Thanks," said Coughlin, blowing smoke through his nose. "Anyway, the whole goddamn thing makes me sick." He paused a moment, picked a shred of tobacco off his tongue and spit it at the floor. "Baseball and boxing. Shit. Too bad the bastard didn't go out for football. We'd have killed him."

Mike knew he should change the subject. He knew that Brown really didn't count. He knew that what counted were those little wings on the silver lighter. But something made him prod Coughlin. Something like whatever it had been that made him taunt Harry Williams and Tom Buckley once too often and led him to stagger home that day bleeding like a stuck pig, crying and feeling the place where Buckley's lunchbox had smashed chips out of his two front teeth. He ran his tongue over the caps the dentist had put in for him, when, unexpectedly, the Air Force had told him at his preentrance medical exam that people with busted-out teeth didn't become fighter pilots. It had taken him days of walking through dentists' offices in East St. Louis to find one to whom his dad didn't already owe money. Finally old Doc Prosser agreed to do it for a promissory note on eighty-five bucks. He was paying it off at five dollars a month, without complaint.

"What's he doing here?" Mike asked at length.

"Who knows? Rosa didn't want to let him in, but he kept smiling and pushing through. Maybe his wife wants to slum."

Kelly looked up into the mirror in time to watch a girl slap a cadet's face. She stood up to leave, and the cadet was on his feet, begging, almost tearful. It was tough to find a girl, tougher to

25

lose one. You never brought a girl to Rosa's on a first date. Only when you thought you had something serious going.

Kelly listened to Coughlin's monologue on the good deal the student officers had and watched the action in Rosa's mirror. He saw the arguing couple sit down, and there, behind them, was Duke Brown.

Brown was shorter than Kelly's five-eleven by an inch, and weighed about the same 160. He wore it well, with a stocky self-content that would have irritated Kelly even if his rich-guy gabardines had not. Brown had never been hungry, not for food, not for anything, not even for his wings. They wouldn't wash Brown out of the program even if he taxied a T-6 into the commanding-officer's living room. He was almost handsome, with wide-set blue eyes, warm and always calm, a square-cut jaw, and straw-blond hair with a roll well set with Vitalis. Three horizontal lines seemed to divide his face like venetian blinds, and they crinkled into a triplane smile or frown that intensified his expression. He was rigidly correct with the cadets, demonstrating a polite military courtesy that underlined the fact that they were otherwise invisible to him.

Kelly had come to detest Brown's coolness, his unvarying punctilio. It was a perfect armor, a secure stance reflecting the conviction of his superiority to all men, but especially to cadets and particularly to Kelly. He would be given his wings as a matter of course, as he had a beautiful wife as a matter of course and a gleaming green Olds 88, a Rocket 88 by God, as a matter of course.

The same reckless craziness that made him taunt Williams and Buckley had driven Kelly to test that coolness, that perfect courtesy as the training had chewed people up and spit them out, out to navigator training or even to enlisted status for the really unlucky. Brown had been impervious to it all. So Kelly had begun to probe the armor. He had begun to force Brown to notice him, to acknowledge his existence. At first it was a kind of game, in which he'd station himself where Brown would have to return his salutes. But Brown could snap a perfect, even charming countersalute without noticing whether the human in the subordinate uniform was a buck private or a senior cadet. So Kelly had begun using the pre- and postflight table sessions to draw Brown's attention.

Nothing had worked until the day he commented during the session after their first spin training that Brown had looked a little sloppy in recovery. The barb had been couched as a typical isecrack. But those blue eyes had zeroed in on him like crosshairs. he jaw had clenched and the triplane lines had frozen Brown's ace into something cold and almost reptilian. Kelly retreated ast, knowing suddenly he might get more than he bargained for. But before he did, he saw something puzzling flash across Brown's eatures. For a moment, it seemed almost like fear.

Ever since then, two weeks ago, Brown had been treating him vith icy reserve, using all the tricks to show Kelly his contempt or him. Dendy had ensured that Kelly had no chances to bait Brown again. Tonight was the first time he had ever seen Brown ff base.

The slight release of the single 3.2 beer stirred the reckless esentment within him. He felt the familiar flush of stupid, rsatz bravery welling up. He was powerless to halt it. His heart eat a little faster as he stared at Brown and his tablemates in the mirror.

"Hey, Chick," he said, interrupting Coughlin's droning litany.

"Huh?"

"Maybe I'll just go over and ask that gorgeous lady for a ance."

"Jesus, Kelly! She's his fucking wife!"

"So?"

"So you don't ask officers' wives to dance, buddy. Not unless ou want to blow the program." Coughlin swiveled and leaned n an elbow.

"I'll make you a bet, Chick. I'll bet you a buck that woman vants some attention. Look at her. She's eating it up. Every wingin' dick in the place is looking down her dress."

"Maybe be so, but—"

"But nothing. What the hell. Nothing ventured, nothing ained. See you later." Before Coughlin could reply, Kelly had lowned the dregs of the Lone Star and begun to work through he crowd to Brown's table.

Brown was sitting ramrod straight, wearing a crisp blue Haspel uit and some kind of regimental tie. His wife was beautiful. She ad long black hair, cascading down over a flame-red dress. Tanned from days at the club pool, she pretended to be oblivious o the circle of cadets all trying to look down her cleavage. She ung on the Duke's arm, flushed with excitement, dark eyes lashing. At her right was the French air force student from their able, Lt. Pierre Deschampes, inevitably dubbed either Frenchy r Lucky Pierre by the cadets.

27

They had not seen him approach. He sidled around behind the girl.

Deschampes looked nervous. The girl whispered to him, and he held out a pack of French cigarettes. She took one, and as Brown reached for his lighter, Kelly reached around and offered his Zippo.

The girl craned her neck and lit the cigarette. She blew a cloud of smoke and smiled thanks at him. "My pleasure, ma'am," he said coolly. His eyes were on Brown. "Good evening, Lieutenant. What brings you to Rosa's place?"

"Good evening, Mr. Kelly." Brown's iceberg smile never wavered. He placed his hand on the table, drummed the big West Point ring. The silence stretched just long enough to let Kelly know Brown wouldn't answer him.

The woman spoke. "We thought we'd like to see how the cadets were doing tonight. And thank you for the light." Her voice was husky, her accent a slightly slurred, genteel southern belle's.

"No problem, ma'am. Always glad to lend a hand to a lady in need of help."

"Joan—Mrs. Brown—is hardly in need of help, Mr. Kelly." Brown's tone matched his frozen demeanor. Sweat stood out just below his hairline. Mike had the sensation that he was in deeper than he wanted to be. It was too late. His damned mouth raced ahead of his brain. "Well, sir, I'd say in one area, she is."

"What area is that, Mr. Kelly?" Brown's voice was low and dangerous. Deschampes rested a hand on his arm.

"Sir, in the area of dancing, it appears to this cadet that Mrs. Brown is behind the power curve. I'd like to offer my services and welcome her to Rosa's by asking her for this dance."

Before Brown could spit his reply, Joan Brown laughed. It was husky and spirited, a feral laugh, the laugh of a sorority girl on a wild spree. "Oh, Duke! Isn't this just grand! You never told me these boys were such fun! Why, Mr. Kelly, of course I'll dance with you. Won't I, Duke?"

Brown opened his mouth. Then he closed it. And nodded. The horizontal lines on his forehead were thunderclouds rolling in.

Joan stumbled slightly as she rose. She grabbed Mike's arm and giggled dizzily. Oh Christ, Kelly thought, she's loaded. What the hell do I do now? Deschampes sent warning semaphore signals to Kelly with the black forest of his eyebrows. He squeezed Brown's forearm.

"Duke," said the French lieutenant, "I think perhaps we ought to be going. We all have much to do tomorrow, yes?"

It was too late. Brown would lose too much face if he left now. He understood the schoolyard calculus as well as Kelly. He had no choice now. "Let the lady dance, Pierre," he grated. "Then we'll go."

Kelly's neck burned as he stood aside to allow Joan to lead to the tiny dance floor. She couldn't push through the crowd, so he passed her, took her hand and led her to the small circle near the jukebox where cadets and dates were locked in slow-stepping embrace, concentrating more on pelvis contact than the music. As he took her hand and placed his on her back, he felt Brown's eyes drilling holes through him. He didn't allow himself to think about how stupid the whole thing was.

She looked at him, laughed, and pressed the warm richness of her flesh against him. He was instantly, embarrassingly hot. It had been a long time since he'd had a woman.

He concentrated on being casual and cool, trying to ignore her scented breasts and the slowly gyrating swell of her buttocks only inches below his hand. He cleared his throat. "So," he said, in an attempt to make conversation, "what do you think of our newly elected president?"

She laughed huskily again and tossed her hair. "Harry Truman? Why, he's an old family friend. My daddy's worked with him for years. But we never thought he'd be elected president." She laughed again. "And neither did he!"

He flushed and his mind went blank. Jesus. He was dancing with somebody who was a family friend of the president of the goddamn United States. How the hell did he get into this?

Joan read his discomfiture and smiled. "Do you come here often, Mr. Kelly?" She asked it in a neutral tone.

"Saturdays," Kelly said. "They're about the only time we have off."

She nodded, eyes hooded, and they simply danced a while. Cautiously, Kelly squeezed her a little closer. He wasn't going to make a pass at her, just dance with her as he would any other beautiful woman who knew Harry Truman personally. He felt slightly giddy, as he had the first time Dendy had shown him a split-ess in the T-6. She didn't seen to mind. They were shielded from Brown and Deschampes by the crowd.

"You're at my husband's table on the flight line, aren't you, Mr. Kelly?"

"Yes, we share Lieutenant Dendy. Deschampes is there too,

and a cadet named Coughlin. He's here tonight. Everybody here but Dendy."

"We've had Lieutenant Dendy over for dinner. He's got good sense of humor. You have to, to eat in our little place. think he mentioned you; he said that he'd never seen anybo try harder."

Kelly danced silently, flushed with pleasure that Dendy ha mentioned him, somehow angry that he'd been to dinner at th Browns'. He'd never dreamed of even seeing Dendy off the fligl line. Instructors were gods, and Brown was having him over fc dinner. He was probably glad to go, hoping to butter up Brow in case he worked for him later in his career.

Joan moved slowly to Glenn Miller's beat with him, eye mostly closed. Above them, the fans endlessly churned th cigarette smoke. Kelly began to relax. This was turning out oka after all. She was a good dancer, and so was he, and this wa after all, only a dance.

The crowd shoved them together. Kelly found himself onc again pressed lightly against her. This time, his heat couldn't b denied. And this time, Joan did not pull away. Instead, sh glanced up at him quickly, smiled languidly, and suddenl moved hard against him, pressing her pelvis against his.

Kelly was stunned. A little coquetry he could understand. Bu enough was enough. All the alarm bells that still functioned i his brain began ringing at once. This lady was danger, the screamed at him. A jumble of half-sense rattled through hi brain as his metabolism dueled for control of his body. Why wa she doing this? Why was he, for Christ's sake? Things wer rapidly getting out of control. And yet—

Joan moved suddenly to the left, catching him on the wron, foot. He stumbled slightly and ducked his head as he caught hi balance.

"Sorry," he mumbled hoarsely. She widened her smile, close her eyes, and stood on her toes in one swift motion. Before h could react, she stuck her tongue deeply into his left ear. As sh pulled back, she bit his earlobe lightly. The cool wetness of he tongue and lips sent a shock through him.

He opened his eyes wide and simply blinked as she relaxec back into his arms and picked up the beat again.

"Call me sometime," she said. Kelly swallowed. Had sh really said it? Or—?

"Do you hear? Call me, Cadet Kelly. You know Duke's schedule."

Kelly felt his gyros tumble. The room swam, even as he continued to move automatically around the jammed dance floor with her. He knew he ought to say something, but all his words were just gone. As he struggled, her expression changed; she had the satisfied look of a cat who's trapped a mouse.

While he tried to figure out what to say, he jostled for dancing room, elbow-to-elbow, with some Hawaiian-shirted cadet, and suddenly Joan stepped back from him. She eyed him for a long second, then slapped him, hard, in a spoiled little Bette Davis motion.

Kelly simply stared at her, dumfounded. He raised his hand to his stinging cheek. "What's that for?"

She cocked her head and snarled in her most penetrating voice, "You know very well what that's for, Mr. Kelly. You need to learn that gentlemen keep their hands to themselves."

"Hey—!" He said, reaching after her. But she spun on her high heel and shoved her way through the crowd back to the table. He stared after her. His stomach knotted. He stood rooted to the spot as the people swirled around him, ignoring him, lost in the music. His brain finally reengaged and he lurched forward, just in time to see Brown and Deschampes moving toward him.

They met just off the dance floor, jammed between two tables of curious cadets. Brown pushed aside an empty chair. His face was flushed, his eyes slitted, his hands balled. Deschampes hovered behind him.

"Outside, Kelly. Now." Brown's voice was like gravel in a grinder.

Kelly spread his hands. "Lieutenant, believe me, I never did a thing—"

Deschampes moved between them. Brown shoved him aside. He ricocheted off a table. The cadets jumped up and moved back. Suddenly they were the focus of attention.

"Nobody," Brown breathed slowly and dangerously, "cadet or not, lays a hand on my wife."

"Damn it, I'm sorry, but I don't know what happened. She just—"

Brown's nostrils flared. "You sonofabitch. Now you're calling my wife a liar? Step outside and take it like a man, if you can."

Kelly felt his anger rise in response to Brown's fury. He knew he had to be cool. His whole life rode on not busting out of the program by something stupid like this. But he was just reacting now, and he couldn't stop it. Brown would never believe what

31

she had done, and never believe that he had not responded. "Goddamn it," he growled, "I didn't lay a hand on her, and I'm not going to risk getting thrown out of the program for fighting about something I didn't do."

"Bullshit, Kelly. You copped a feel and now you're lying about it, like the guttersnipe you are. Go outside or I'll deck you right here." Brown stepped toward Kelly.

Deschampes took Brown by the arm. "Come on, Duke, let's go. You could get in trouble, too. He doesn't want to fight."

Brown halted a foot from Kelly, dragged to a stop by the Frenchman. He breathed hard, and shook off Deschampes's arm.

"Okay, Pierre, okay." He sneered at Kelly. "I guess we've got your number, Kelly. All talk and no action. Just what I'd expect of a sneaky redneck like you."

Brown kicked the table aside and turned his back on Kelly. It was too much. Kelly reached for those wide shoulders under that perfect suit. "Come here, you rich bastard—"

Brown's fist caught him squarely on the chin. As Kelly's head snapped back, the pain seared through him and he fell into a long, dark well. The last thing he saw before the light blinked out at the top of it was the slowly revolving fan. The last thing he felt was his tongue automatically checking those eighty-five-dollar caps. Before he knew if they were still there, he stopped feeling, tasting, or seeing anything. He only had time for one thought, and then he even stopped thinking.

Please Dear God, Let Me Win My Wings.

1015 LOCAL
26 November 1948
Mavis Auxiliary Airfield
Texas, USA

The tiny beads of sweat that stung Kelly's right eye formed somewhere up under the ill-fitting, uncomfortable flying helmet that had once been khaki and was now brown, stained dark by grease and sweat. The sweat drizzled down around the ragged rubber foam of the goggles, down the sunburned side of his nose, then with agonizing slowness and exquisite inevitability into his eye. He could spare not so much as a finger to mop his brow or divert the sweat. His left leg was stretched out applying full rudder to

32

stop the spinning, his left hand had the throttle full back, and his right had the stick full forward, rubbing the instrument panel. It was the sixth spin of the day, and it had gyrated his stomach and his bladder into potential disaster areas.

On the ground, the T-6 trainers were virtually indistinguishable, all low-wing silver monoplanes, but in the air they varied. This one was a dog. Kelly squinted as the Texas sun rotated past him; his thigh muscles began twitching under the load of the heavy rudder, and he silently cursed whoever had worn the heap out to this point. Then, at last, the wings suddenly leveled and the nose dropped, picking up enough airspeed to break the stall. He applied power and glanced at the altimeter—four thousand feet. The damned spin had started at six. Too much altitude lost to make Dendy happy. He winced and waited to be upbraided again about taking too long to break the spin.

When Dendy's dry, nasal voice crackled through his earphones, he ignored the spins. Instead, he said, "Let's go in and land, Mr. Kelly."

Kelly eased the throttle back, set up a five-hundred-foot-per-minute rate of descent, watching, as always, for a suitable field in case Dendy suddenly called for a forced landing.

"Mr. Kelly, did you hear me? I said let's go in and land!" Like all instructors, Dendy either ordered or sneered; this was a sneer.

"Yes sir, I'm letting down."

The stick banged against his leg.

"I got the airplane, mister."

Kelly glanced into the little convex mirror mounted in the upper canopy rail. Dendy's goggles were on his forehead, his expression inscrutable. He was looking around Kelly, out over the T-6's long nose. He picked up his mike and said, "Now, Mr. Kelly, I'll show you how an Air Force fighter pilot enters the pattern, and you may notice it's not with a pissant Piper Cub crawl."

Kelly relaxed. So. It was a new procedure. He hadn't been fucking up. For a minute there, he'd thought—

The airplane snapped inverted before he could complete the thought. Dendy brought the power back and the flat squares of Texas countryside loomed straight in front of Kelly. He grabbed the canopy rails to hold on.

The T-6 rolled on its axis, aiming straight down. Bits of dirt floated up from the floor, thrown up by centripetal force. The airspeed hit the 240-m.p.h. red line, then crept past it. The sound of screaming wind and creaking metal drowned out the

33

engine noise. Invisible sacks of lead shoved him into the seat as Dendy reefed back on the stick. His vision grayed with the G forces and his bile rose to his throat, threatening to get past his clenched teeth. Then the pressure abruptly ceased and the T-6 leveled, rolling again around its axis, the sun and ground trading places. He forced his eyes to remain open and forced the bile back.

Dendy rocked the stick.

"You got it," he said, as if he were tossing a pack of cigarettes to Kelly.

Kelly took the controls and looked around. They were on a perfect downwind leg for landing, the gear was down, airspeed and altitude—everything—just right.

"Fly the airplane, Mr. Kelly, don't let it fly you. You've drifted off your heading and altitude. Fly the goddamn airplane."

Kelly wallowed around the turn to the base leg; at the forty-five-degree point Dendy chopped the throttle.

"Power-off landing, Kelly. Touch down in the first third of the runway."

Kelly turned onto final approach, holding off on the flaps, keeping the airspeed at ninety m.p.h.

"You're hot, Mr. Kelly, you're hot."

Kelly dropped quarter flaps, adjusted the airspeed. The T-6 began to sink like a five-thousand-pound rock. He shoved forward on the throttle, but Dendy had it locked in an iron grip.

"You're low and slow, Mr. Kelly, low and slow. That's no way to be."

Kelly sucked up the flaps and lowered the nose to gain a little airspeed. It was going to be close. There was a fence about thirty yards from the end of the strip.

Dendy was silent.

Kelly desperately pushed on the throttle again. Locked tight. The ground rushed up, he flared the airplane, the excess speed streaming it along above the sage-strewn desert floor. As the airspeed bled off, the T-6 seemed to float, clearing the fence by ten feet. He touched down twenty feet inside the edge of the strip.

"Close, Mr. Kelly, but a cigar. After completely fucking up the approach you managed to salvage it. That's how a pilot learns in the long run."

Kelly had been so concerned about the approach that he'd almost ignored the touchdown. It was one of the best he'd done, a sweet three-point kiss of rubber and ground. They arced off the end of the strip, ess-turning down the gravel taxi-way.

"I got it," Dendy barked. He jazzed the throttle and booted the rudder. The T-6 did a dusty 270-degree turn, stopping at the edge of the taxi-way.

Kelly watched Dendy in his little mirror. The instructor unplugged from the intercom, climbed out of the back seat, and leaned into the forward cockpit, where Kelly sat. Mike swiveled his head to the left to look at Dendy.

Dendy's smoky black eyes gave nothing away. Little creases that spoke of some ancient bitterness bracketed his thin lips. He stared at Kelly a moment, then said, "Mr. Kelly, I'm tired of you trying to make my wife a widow. I want you to fly this sonofabitch by yourself while I catch a smoke down here and try to recuperate from your nearly killing us. Do you read me, mister?"

Kelly blinked back the sweat, and tugged at his goggles. He nodded.

Dendy turned away, then stopped and put a hand on the cockpit coaming. He leaned forward, squinting at Kelly. "You okay, son?":

Kelly nodded again. "Good. Don't disappoint me, mister. Three times around the patch, and then back to pick me up."

Kelly nodded once more, and Dendy bounded off the wing, striding across the sage desert, his parachute slung over his shoulder, his hand shielding the match he held to his cigarette.

This was it, the first solo, make or break time. Could he actually fly this monster by himself? Kelly's hands were lead weights, his legs tree stumps. On the panel, the oil temperature needle flickered ever so slightly, pulsing against the bottom end of the indicator. He inhaled deeply of the mixture of ancient sweat, hot metal, aromatic fuel, and grime that was the distinctive odor of the T-6. It was perfume.

Please Dear God, Let Me Win My Wings.

Dendy stopped and turned around, tossing the parachute down as a back rest against the wheeled fire extinguisher. He sat down, near a group of cadets all watching Kelly. The bus that brought them from Randolph stood nearby, baking in the sun, the enlisted driver asleep. But next to Dendy, Brown, Coughlin, and Deschampes watched intently. All first solos were worth watching, but the first solo in a whole class was an event. Kelly saw Brown smirk, and the adrenaline poured into his system. He fingered his jaw, still sore where Brown had clipped him. Time to go.

His left hand pushed the throttle forward, his right holding the stick back in his crotch. He tested the brakes gently, then turned the T-6 down the taxi-way to the run-up area.

Kelly's body was working the airplane flawlessly, while his mind remained detached, as if watching someone else. He took elaborate care with the preflight checks, savoring his sense of control. Nothing must go wrong with this flight. He waggled the controls, eased the throttle forward, and spun the airplane around to clear the area, checking the final approach. The mobile controller in his truck gave Kelly the green light. Cleared for the takeoff.

A strong crosswind blew out of the west, trying, as usual, to weathercock the mulish T-6 as he lined up on the runway. Heat poured off the desert floor in waves. Dust blew through the open canopy, swirled by the big prop. He ignored it and played the throttle, brakes, rudder, and ailerons precisely as he had been taught. The airplane bumped and jounced to the center of the rough runway, and he pushed the throttle forward, peering to the side of the huge cowling that blocked the view straight ahead. The big Pratt & Whitney radial roared to full takeoff power, and he danced on the rudders, keeping it straight down the center, letting the bumps dampen out as he reached takeoff speed. A little back pressure and he was climbing.

When he no longer had room to land and stop on the runway, he raised the landing gear, hitting the button that activated the hydraulics and raising the gear lever. He fed in elevator trim on the big handwheel next to the throttle. The stick lightened in his hands, and the T-6 lifted itself clear of the earth. He climbed at 110 m.p.h. When the altimeter told him he was five hundred feet above the ground, he made the turn to the crosswind leg. In the process, he glanced out to the side for the first time, watching the invisible wind provide him lift. He rocked the ailerons gently, felt the airplane respond to his touch. He turned downwind at one thousand feet, and quickly went through his checklist, first to clean up after takeoff, then to prepare for landing. When he was done, he looked around.

It was as if he'd never seen the world before. Everything was sharp and clear, the sky a cobalt blue, the ground a blinding yellow-white where the sun glinted off the mica sand. The air was sweet and cool. He gulped it in huge lungfuls, and with the Texas air tasted joy of a sort he had never known. It filled him until he had to yell it at the antlike men on the ground. He hollered and whooped and marveled at it all, at the sky, the airplane, at himself.

He was alone in the sky. And he was calling the shots.

He was making everything happen. *He* was.

As he flew abeam the end of the runway, he sobered and concentrated on the prelanding checklist, on keeping altitude and airspeed scrupulously on the dot, on exercising a precision that exceeded even his best efforts for Dendy. He still sweated, but he did not notice. He seemed to be in a cocoon of still, quiet air, in spite of the pounding engine, the hissing earphones, the wind buffeting around the open canopy and moaning over the bumps and through the crevices that festooned the creaky old T-6.

Without noticing, somehow, he was lined up on final, gear and flaps down, aiming for the point next to the battered sage-brush that marked Dendy's favorite touchdown point. He ca-ressed the airplane down, mind still somewhere else, still observing from above.

His first landing was perfect, a sweet three-point textbook touchdown that sang a song of burnished rubber. He glowed as he taxied down the runway and turned back. As he passed them, he shot the group of cadets by the bus a thumbs-up, and was rewarded with V-signs and applause. He noticed that Brown was gone, but before he had time to reflect on his absence, he was far down the taxi-way, ready for the second takeoff.

This time he sang out loud as soon the wheels left the gravel, boom-boom-booming out his own version of the choral portion of Beethoven's Ninth Symphony, crumpling it into his own ode to flying joy. For twenty-one years Mike had nothing to sing about, and now there was a fierce pride coursing through him, bursting to get out. He gave it voice, and all through the second orbit of the field, he pounded the side of the fuselage to supple-ment his ragged voice.

The second touchdown was average. He bounced the third one and had to use power to recover, landing far down the field in a series of jolting bumps. And then, suddenly, it was over.

Sobered and trembling slightly, partly from relief, partly from joy, and partly from fear of what Dendy would say about the last landing, he taxied back to where the tall, lean instructor was standing.

Dendy shook his head, stubbed out his cigarette in the dirt, then strode to the airplane, eyes on the ground. A wave of fear swept over Kelly. Had the landings been that bad? Had he failed again?

Please Dear God—

Dendy paused while climbing up on the wingroot. He glanced down at Kelly for a moment, his eyes impenetrable behind the issue sunglasses. Then he slapped Kelly on the shoulder and climbed into the rear cockpit.

King Arthur never created a knight with a more eloquent gesture. The wrenching knot of fear in Kelly's stomach dissolved. He began to breathe again.

He heard the tinny click as Dendy plugged into the intercom. "Okay, Mr. Kelly, I presume you know what you did on that last so-called landing?"

"Yes sir, I—"

"Don't tell me, Mr. Kelly, tell yourself. Let's go home, shall we? Why not show me a short-field takeoff this time?"

He botched the takeoff, too, pulling the airplane off the ground before it was ready to fly, than letting it dribble along back into the air like a duck running on top of the water to get airborne. It was horrible. But Dendy didn't comment. He allowed Mike to enjoy the glow of his first solo.

Once airborne and headed back to Randolph, the glow spread when Kelly recalled the look on Brown's face as he'd taxied out. Second Lt. Charles Kingston Brown thought he had it all: the rank, the car, the woman, the privileges, and he'd even gotten in the first—and so far the only—punch. But Aviation Cadet Michael McManus Kelly knew something about the woman. And, maybe more important, he was the first to solo. He'd never forget that. Nor would he forget what Joan had done. With luck, those two things would more than make up for one lucky punch.

**1935 LOCAL
29 November 1948
Offutt AFB
Omaha, Nebraska
USA**

Maj. William Kingston "King" Brown normally enjoyed meeting general officers. Many were friends of his father and had known King as a young Army brat, so there was always some personal interchange to add depth to his career portfolio in such meetings. But King did not enjoy the prospect of his first meeting with the lieutenant general whose office lay behind the door through which the clear sounds of rage emanated.

38

Lt. Gen. Curtis E. LeMay had been in charge of the Strategic Air Command for a little more than a month, and it was no secret that he did not like what he found when he took command. That would have been bad enough, but the worst sort of air accident that could happen in SAC had just happened, and everyone here at SAC headquarters in Omaha was spending the evening jumping through hoops. As a SAC command staff officer, King jumped as high as anyone else. In the staff meeting only recently finished, LeMay had asked him directly for the report he now held with the tips of his fingers to keep it from getting moist. Filthy Nebraska November weather made it bone-chilling cold outside, and inside, the wheezing wartime steam radiators, caked in sickly yellow paint, couldn't offset the wind howling past the windows. But King Brown sweated anyway. LeMay was a legend, and so was his fury when something like this happened.

Two B-29s had collided on a practice bombing mission. There were no survivors, and the wing commander could not be located. It was impossible for the situation to look worse to the new commanding general.

Well, not quite impossible. King Brown knew the report he carried would make it worse. With the Russians blockading Berlin, LeMay wanted to send the 301st Bomb Group to Furstenfeldbruck, Germany, as an immediate show of strength. But the 301st's B-29s would go as "show" only, not "go." King hoped LeMay wouldn't shoot the messenger who brought the grim numbers that showed why. He hoped, actually, that LeMay would send him away before reading the report. The fact was, the American bomber force—like the whole American military establishment itself—was no longer capable of fighting a war without six months' intensive preparation.

His report revealed that of the nearly nine hundred aircraft on SAC's strength, more than half were B-29s from World War II, with just a sprinkling of the newer B-50s and Convair B-36s. These raw figures were damning enough, but the real problem was the abysmal readiness state, the lack of training made apparent in a practice bombing raid on New York in which more than half the aircraft aborted. LeMay would very much not like that. Not on top of a collision.

Brown watched the pictures dance on the wall as the phone slammed down in LeMay's office. Whoever had been the commander of the 44th Bomb Wing (M) was on his way to Berlin as a C-47 copilot.

Luckily, King himself was clear of this particular mess. But as he sourly recalled the envelope in his pocket, he realized another one of a different kind waited to enmesh him, embroiling him with yet another three-star general—his own father. The letter was from Bob Dendy, an old student of his and now his brother Duke's flight instructor at Randolph. It was no accident that Duke was at Dendy's table, and a good thing he'd arranged it that way. The kid got airsick.

Airsick, for Christ's sake! The Old Man would go crazy if Duke blew flight school. Father orchestrated their careers with intense precision, and the script did not call for a Brown to fail at anything. In spite of his thirty years in the Army, Father saw the Air Force as the only military branch with a future. That was why Duke had been directed to transfer his commission to the USAF rather than the infantry, that was why King was in SAC, and that was all there was to it, as planned and ordered by Lt. Gen. Kingston Dupree Brown, United States Army (Retired) (Reluctantly).

Dendy wrote that while Duke did everything well, he was still sneaking brown paper bags on board and throwing up on every flight. He thought he was fooling everybody. Dendy was really worried about letting him continue, and wanted King's advice. It was the right thing to do on Bob's part; he'd learned the ropes well from King, and kept it quiet. King would take care of him well when he got his own stars.

The phone buzzed on the desk across from King, and the airman manning it answered it immediately. He spoke into it quietly, hung up, and stood up. He gestured toward the door. "You can go in now, Major."

Brown punctiliously went through the formal drill of knocking on the door and reporting. LeMay returned his salute and told him to stand at ease. Brown tendered his report.

While LeMay flipped it open, Brown studied the man who had masterminded the aerial crushing of Japan. He was as advertised by his legend. He was a shortish figure, wearing the new blue uniform, his three stars glittering on each epaulet. He had a face like an angry bulldog, but composed, with level, rock-hard eyes and a stubby unlit stogie in his mouth.

As he scanned the report, he manifested no emotion. Brown glanced around the room. It was utterly without luxuries; the office was strictly government issue, the desktop piles of paper neatly arranged, the telephone off to one side on its own table.

LeMay looked at the figures, then flipped to the back to read

40

ne conclusion, where Brown had called for tripling the number f training flights, and setting up a SAC-wide standardization nd evaluation system. His only response was to roll the stogie to ne other side of his mouth. He glanced up at King and said, Thanks, Major Brown. I'll read this in detail tonight. Please be ere at oh-eight hundred tomorrow. I'll want the staff to discuss our conclusions."

Brown saluted, did an about-face any training officer would pprove, and left. The chill of the outer office hit him like a cold hower. The sweat on his hands began to dry. As he walked nrough the confusion of the HQ offices, he noted the corpselike allor of several of the officers waiting to see LeMay and did not nvy them their fates. He was glad to get out with his hide.

Father would approve of how he'd handled his first session vith LeMay. But the meeting with LeMay was the easy part of vhat had to be handled tonight. The hard part was Duke.

King made his way through the building to his own office, a iny, cold cubicle decorated with photos of him and his crews rom the war. He dialed the base operator and asked for a long ine.

The woman's voice answered, "Hello?" and King grimaced. Vould Joan never learn the correct way to answer an officer's hone? Maybe Mother could discreetly slip in some instruction vhen they all got together again at Christmas.

"Joan. This is King. How are you?"

"King! Why, so nice to hear from you. Where are you, rother-in-law?"

"Offutt, sister-in-law. Listen, is Duke in? I haven't much ime. Things are cooking here. But I need to speak to him."

"Surely. Please wait a moment. I think he's in the bathroom."

Puking his guts out, no doubt, King thought glumly.

"King." Duke said it as he always did, with precisely the right mount of coolness tempered with deference, little brother to big rother.

"Duke. Look, I won't mince words with you. I got a note from 3ob Dendy. He says you're tossing your cookies in his ship. That ight?"

The line hissed.

"Duke? Are you there—?"

"Yeah. Wait a minute, will you?" King heard Duke press a nand over the receiver. It didn't quite conceal his conversation vith Joan.

"Honey? Look, this is private, brother stuff. I wonder if—oh.

41

Thanks. About five minutes, no more. You'll be at Sheila's. Okay." Duke came back on the phone. "All right, King. What' the problem?"

"That's what I want to ask you, kid. Are you really losing you lunch in the air?"

Duke hesitated. King could understand why. Neither of then was trained to accept personal shortcomings. Neither could imag ine such a thing getting back to the Old Man.

"Look, Duke. This'll stay with us. Father won't hear of it."

"Sure. Thanks, King. Well, fact is, I seem to get a little airsick."

"That's all? Nothing else?"

"No. Of course not."

King weighed the tones, analyzed the hesitation. Duke was a tough kid. Until he'd fallen behind scholastically at the Point. he'd been in the top five. But King knew how flying could send even the tough guys to the showers. Either you had it or you hadn't. It had never occurred to him that a Brown might not have it—whatever it might be that was required. Duke might be covering up for some real problem. If so, they all stood to lose by it—Duke, by washing out ignominiously, to be sent off to weather school or some damn thing; Dendy, for sticking with a washout too long, and finally King, for having a brother who couldn't hack the program. Three careers riding on Duke's stomach.

"Okay. We all get queasy in the air sometimes, kid. Must be the chow. Are you eating right?"

"Sure."

"Breakfast? You absolutely have to eat breakfast, even if you can barely force it down."

"Of course. Ham and eggs, every morning." King could now easily detect the edge in Duke's voice. Good. The kid was beginning to get the picture.

"Then here's what you do. Have Joan find a good pharmacist in town. Get some Mothersils. Take it just before each flight."

"Mothersils? In San Antonio? We're hundreds of miles from the ocean, King—"

"Seasick, airsick, it's all the same. I had a gunner who used the stuff in England. Worked like a charm. The guy got two Messerschmitts. Without his Mothersils, he was useless."

"Okay. Sure."

"Take it seriously, Duke. Dendy can't cover for you too much longer. And I can't expect him to. You understand what's at stake here?"

"Sure. Don't worry, King. I love to fly. Must be a bug I picked up down here."

"Yeah. Mexican food. Stay away from it while you're in training."

"Got it. I'll give the enchiladas a pass from now on."

"Okay, kid. Good luck. I'll check in again soon. Oh—and a little word to the wise, off the record. When you get through with those godawful 6s, look for some real fun. I think you guys might be among the first students to get P-80s in Advanced."

"No kidding? Say, that's great!"

"Right. Now, remember: Mothersils and breakfast, every flying day. And stop sneaking the goddamn barf bags on board. Dendy now's what's happening, and pretty soon everybody else will too."

"Understand."

"Rog. I have to go. There's a flap on here. Heard from Mother recently?"

"Last week."

"Father?"

"Two days ago. He's in Washington."

"Yeah. I know. Take care, kid. Remember: after these 6s, the real fun begins. Just hold on until then, and you'll be okay. Best to Joan. She's a brick."

"You bet. So long."

Duke replaced the receiver with exaggerated care. So. The real fun will start soon, eh? He pulled out his Camels and tapped one out absently. He stuck it in his mouth and lit up, thinking about what he would have liked to have said to King.

It would have been something like: I puke because I'm scared stiff, big brother. I've been terrified of these goddamn airplanes ever since that summer you came back with your Distinguished Flying Cross and took me for a ride in the Cub. I hate flying, I hate the Air Force, and, truth to tell, I'm not too keen on you, either, dear brother. It would have been delicious to have said all that, delicious but unbelievable. He was a Brown, after all, and Browns became generals by conquest, not candor. He had understood from the very first day Father had begun outlining his career path—in his third year at the Point—that he would either have to resign immediately or tough it out in the Air Force. He might even have considered resigning, had he not agreed with the Old Man's analysis: the Air Force *was* the future. The price

43

of admission was high, but he was a Brown, and he would p
it.

He thought of King's advice. If only it were the food
motion sickness, Mothersils might even help. But it was not.
was fear. Gut-wrenching, primal, unstoppable. He knew wi
deadly certainty that every time his airplane's wheels left tl
earth he was going to come back down in a flaming ball
aluminum, trapped, screaming to get out, alive and in unimagi
able agony until the very last bone-shattering impact. He saw tl
end at the beginning of every flight. He even dreamed it, nig
after night.

Joan thought it was simply the pressure, of course. And sl
puttered and fussed, trying in her own way to help. Trouble wa
the only help would come from within. He fought himself eve
flight. Actually, he didn't mind the flying itself, and the m
chines were even mildly interesting. It was simple: he was lock
in a death struggle with himself.

He grimaced and stubbed out his Camel in the ashtra
Everybody wanted to help. Like Joan, they were all bricks. The
were bricks everywhere. And they stacked up to walls. Higl
uncaring, unyielding, impossible walls behind which he cringe

Joan swung wide the door to their tiny apartment and peeked i

"Okay?" she asked. He wiped the frown from his face, strode tl
four steps to the door and pulled it all the way open. He kisse
her lightly, and tried to ignore the odor of whiskey she carried

"Fine," he said, "just fine. We were talking flying."

Joan wrinkled her nose. "What else *could* it be?" Duke ga
her his practiced flyboy grin. "Nothing," he said with gust
"What else is there?"

2

1645 LOCAL
17 February 1949
Wiesbaden Air Base
American Zone, Germany

The wind blew enough to press the swirling fog into a cold clo
of moisture enveloping the world. Second Lt. Larry White turne
up the brown mouton fur on his jacket, and flipped the yello
flashlight beam inside the cowling of the C-54. He had neve

44

een happier. If they had told him at Virginia Polytechnical Institute that he was going to wind up copilot on this beautiful Douglas airplane he never would have believed it. He loved flying school, but this was the absolute best: He got to fly every day, and when he wasn't flying he got to help run the maintenance effort. The Berlin airlift was barely four months old, and was beginning to stay even with the demands of the two million dazed Berliners who were sure they'd have to do April 1945 all over again. Maj. Gen. William H. Tunner was running the operation, and although White had never seen him, he was glad to be with him.

White was flying out of Wiesbaden, and he enjoyed even the most weather-burdened flights down the corridor to Templehof. When the visibility was good—maybe as much as a mile—he loved looking down at the gutted houses, the sere scars of the war. The streets were mostly clear, but there were still tank carcasses spotted here and there, and once in a while the tail of an aircraft. He couldn't believe the Germans he met at the base, polite, even jovial, could have endured the pervasive horror. They never talked about it.

He was a genuine green bean; most of the other pilots were World War II vets, some of whom had caused the damage, flying in cold B-17s at twenty-five thousand feet, dumping their five-hundred pounders into the wreckage below. Now many of them were recalled for the crisis and bitter to have their lives interrupted a second time, this time to feed the people they'd been trying to kill a few years ago. Shifted from crew to crew as the demand required, White learned quickly from the cross section of pilots what to do and what not to do. He was glad he really didn't like to drink; too many of the older guys drank even the night before they flew. Tonight he was flying with Capt. Barton C. Lautig, known as "Crash" Lautig behind his back in reference to the spectacular bouncing landings he'd done in equalification checks.

Lautig was a round little man, a menacing Edward G. Robinson type, swarthy, and given to sharp intakes of breath and bitter curses. He had been recalled to duty from his hardware store in Cheyenne, and he hated it. "Fuck the Germans, let 'em starve," was his motto.

The airlift operation, which had started on an ad hoc basis with a handful of C-47s, had become routine; aircraft flew at specified altitudes, from five thousand feet up to ten thousand feet, at specified airspeeds and intervals. Seventy C-54s, the best

45

cargo planes available, military versions of the DC-4, were load
every six hours, day and night. A steady stream of ten-ton trailɛ
brought supplies, coal the first priority, food, second, to th
airfields, where displaced persons from every country in Easte
Europe, fed better than they had been in years, loaded the carg
It took an average of one hour and twenty-five minutes to loa
and forty-five minutes to unload.

"Aren't you finished yet?" Lautig's voice was slurred.

"Yes sir, just rechecking while I'm waiting. Ready when yɛ
are."

Lautig climbed up the ladder into the hold, nodding brusque
to Estepp, the loadmaster and Finney, the flight engineer. They
been at briefing together earlier, and Lautig had studiously avoidɛ
talking to them. White followed behind, checking the straps
the load as he went, before slipping into the right seat.

Lautig leaned over, beery breath preceding him. "You ju
read the checklist and do as I tell you. Don't touch anythiɪ
until I tell you to. Got that?"

White flushed.

"Yes sir." It was uncalled-for; he knew his copilot duties, aɪ
knew they couldn't be done on demand; it had to be a teaɪ
effort. In direct defiance he began busying himself with switᴄ
positions, adjusting the lights, checking the radio frequenciɛ
Lautig looked out the window, his hand resting on the engiɪ
controls.

Finney worked with Lautig to get the engines started; thɛ
weren't coordinated and two of the four big Pratt & Whitnɛ
R-2000s backfired, belching rich blue-black smoke out the stack
and shuddering the slowly turning props to a halt. Finney flusheɖ
he knew he'd get ribbed by the crew chief and have to buy tw
rounds of beers. Backfires were the sign of the ham-handed, aɪ
they could be dangerous. They were running three minutes laᴛ
on engine start, and Lautig taxied into position too swiftly, th
nose wheel oleo compressing and nodding them when he hit th
brakes. White flinched as the wingtip swung just over the horɪ
zontal stabilizer of a parked C-47. A taxi accident was the kiss
death; better to fly into a mountain than to ding a wingtɪ
taxiing, according to officers'-club lore.

They went through the interrogation and response of th
checklist, and Lautig poured the coal to it, having some diffɪ
culty at first keeping on the centerline. White was busy cleaniɪ
up the airplane when they entered the cloud deck at thrɛ
hundred feet.

Something in Larry's inner ear swirled as he reached over to change radio frequencies. He glanced at his instruments and the artificial horizon was tilted at a crazy angle, the needle and ball had swapped sides. He looked at Lautig's instruments; the horizon was straight and level, but his ball was off center too. The rate of climb had dropped below zero, and the altimeter was beginning to unwind. The vacuum-driven instruments had failed, iced-up maybe. Lautig stared straight ahead.

White grabbed the wheel and booted in right rudder, yelling "I got the airplane!" He looked over his shoulder at Finney and yelled "Max power!"

Lautig whirled on him, shaking the wheel. "Let go of the controls, Lieutenant!"

White reached across the cockpit and slammed his fist down on Lautig's arm, pulling it free of the wheel. "You're spinning us in! Sit back and shut up."

Lautig subsided, and White watched the needles slowly trend back in the right direction. He set up a five-hundred-foot-per-minute climb, adjusted the power, and edged back on course. He figured they'd been maybe ten or fifteen seconds from going in. Finney leaned forward and punched his shoulder.

"Thanks, Lieutenant. I won't forget this."

Lautig took over when they were at altitude and flew the rest of the way into Templehof in silence. When they landed, he raced back down the aisle and left the airplane. The instruments were out, and it meant they had to deadhead back on another airplane. They didn't see Lautig again that day.

The next morning at Wiesbaden Larry got a call: report immediately to General Tunner's office.

Well, White thought, this is it. Lautig must have reported him for insubordination. He'd be lucky if he ever flew again. What the hell. He'd done the right thing; he'd saved the airplane.

He expected to wait at Tunner's office, a swirling madhouse of telephones, radios, teletypes, plotting boards, hustling airmen, and threadbare, servile German civilians. Instead, he was ushered right in.

Lautig was there, having told the whole true story. Tunner shook Larry's hand, and talked about a decoration. White's apprehension vanished, and Tunner asked him a lot of questions about what he was doing, how things could be improved, and especially about whether he thought guys right out of flying school could hack the course on the airlift. When they were through, Tunner laid a hand on Larry's arm. "Son, how would you like to be my aide when we finish up the airlift?"

White stammered. He was stunned, but for some reason, he didn't even hesitate to say, "Ah, I'd like that a lot sir, but if you don't mind, I'd prefer to stay on crew duty. I'm better off flying than when I'm doing anything else." After he'd said it, he realized by the arched eyebrows around him that he must have said the wrong thing.

Tunner just shook his head and smiled wanly. He knew the opportunity White was missing, and he knew why. White was a hardware freak, the kind of pilot who made the Air Force work whatever the conditions, whatever the odds. Men like White never became generals; they just made it possible for those who did. He said something reassuring and indicated that the interview was over.

When Larry left the general's office, he was dazed and happy. He meant to go straight back to the BOQ and dash off a letter to his wife Micky. But he was waylaid in the hallway by his C.O.

"White. Congratulations again."

"Thanks, skipper. When the general told me—"

"Right. Listen, Larry, here's the scoop. Lautig's taken himself off flying status, so we're short. Sorry to do this to you, but you're going to have to take up the slack. I've got you down on a mission in half an hour. Can do?"

"Sure, skipper. No sweat."

"Great. Your crew chief has the skinny on the briefing. Thanks again, Larry. I was sure you wouldn't mind."

White waved a salute, but the C.O. had spun around and hurried off down the crowded, noisy corridor. Mind? How could he mind flying the best airplanes in the world every day, as much as he wanted? Sometimes he felt like he was dreaming, he enjoyed it so much. The only snag was that Micky wasn't here to share it with him. Thinking of her, he realized that he wouldn't be able to get his letter off on the daily command courier to London, and so he'd miss a day with his letters. And he'd promised to write every day.

Somebody bumped into him and muttered a curt apology, scuttling off with a sheaf of papers. He grinned and joined the flow of hurrying figures, heading for the flight line.

She'd understand. She always did. That's what made her, in addition to being the most beautiful girl in the world, the best Air Force wife in the world.

Micky White leaned back in bed, Larry's letter folded in her hand. Outside, the cold rain made the Virginia night miserable. Inside her little apartment near Langley, the hissing steam radiator and Larry's letter made the night cheerful and warm. The first part of it had been a recital of his adventure with Lautig; the last part had been a wonderfully detailed picture of how he wanted to make love to her.

She was so proud of him, and wanted him so badly. He was such a strong, wonderful lover. But they'd been together so little; they were married and had six months at Dover Air Force Base, where he was away most of the time on long trips. Now it was Berlin; what was next?

She lay quietly, trying to feel movement inside. She knew she could not, since it was still too soon. He didn't know about the baby yet; she'd better tell him, so he could plan to be with her, and not off on some other crazy assignment.

It was going to be difficult to tell her parents. They hadn't wanted her to marry "an Army man"—they still hadn't sorted out that the Air Force was a separate service—and they'd be appalled that she was pregnant already.

Micky laughed aloud when she thought how they and their friends would be anxiously counting the months until the baby was born. The gossips would be so pleased if they could tar her with the old saw, "The second baby takes nine months, but the first one can come any time."

But Larry and Micky were safe from the gossipmongers; the baby would be born ten months after the marriage. It could easily have been ten months before, for she and Larry had steadied down to systematic lovemaking within weeks of their becoming engaged. He was considerate and tried to protect her with those awful rubbers, but she was glad they'd stopped using them as soon as they were married, gladder still that she was pregnant.

Still, his letter was a worry. She was proud of him, of course; from the moment she had seen him, standing so tall and straight at the dance, she had just *known* he was the kind of man who would do things like that. He was not the handsomest guy in the

49

world, maybe, but he had a twinkle in his blue eyes and he always seemed to be smiling shyly. It wasn't exactly right to say that he stood out in a crowd—especially at VPI, where they all seemed to be guys of about average height and weight, with cleancut regular features—but he had an air of such undeniable decency that Micky couldn't really help being attracted to him. (Besides, could she not say the same thing about herself? She was pretty, maybe, with her fine, bobbed straw-blond hair and her adequate if not stunning figure, but Lana Turner she wasn't, just as Larry wasn't Gary Cooper.) But his decency was sometimes too much, even for her; in college everyone had taken advantage of him, borrowed his old junker car, his notes, and his money.

Back then he had two things on his mind: getting his commission so he could fly, and getting her in bed. "In bed" was a euphemism; they made love wherever they could, on blankets down by the river, in the back seat of his rickety Ford, on the bench by her sorority house when the night was dark and they simply couldn't wait. Once they had even done it standing up by the door to the house; they hadn't intended to, the good-night kissing just got more passionate, and they somehow contorted together, her leg cocked up on his thigh, his back bent backward. Like their courtship, it was exciting in a way that not much else was at Mary Baldwin. She smiled, remembering. The housemother would have fainted if she'd opened the door. But maybe not; they were hardly the first young lovers at Mary Baldwin College.

She reread the first part of the letter. The implied danger didn't bother her; the other pilots in his squadron, like his flying instructors in Texas, all said he was one of the finest natural pilots in the service, so she knew he could handle that. But he didn't seem to know how to capitalize on the situation. He should have told Tunner, "Yes sir!" and become his aide. Micky didn't know too much about the military yet, but she had seen enough at Dover to realize that you had to have some pull to get ahead. Just being a pilot wasn't enough. Thank goodness her parents wouldn't read the letter. Both would be appalled at the clinical detailing of what he intended to do to her when he returned—often, she hoped—but Father would be furious with him for turning down Tunner's offer. He hadn't wanted her to marry him anyway, and had uncharacteristically lost his temper when she informed him of the engagement.

"He's just a shiftless soldier! I've seen them a hundred times, they come in the bank, want a loan, and don't have a cent in assets. Most of them drink and chase women and they bounce around the country like rubber balls."

Her mother was no happier; she'd had her heart set on a "Tidewater family" for Mildred. From high school on there had been a parade of "eligibles" trotted by, nice young men from good families all set up to be successful lawyers, doctors, politicians. And not one of them had stirred her as Larry had.

She'd met Larry at a dance; he came down with the VPI bus, and had hung back on the sidelines. She'd noticed him right away, but he wouldn't look her way, shuffling off to the punch bowl, kidding with his pals. But when their eyes did meet, something had happened. He smiled his little smile, walked right over to where she stood, took her gloved hand, and said, "You're mine for the evening, and maybe more."

She knew instantly by the way he said it that it wasn't a line he used with other girls. He had all the earmarks of a guy who'd nerved himself up mightily to cross that dance floor, and while she smiled back at him in the sudden silence that followed his slightly breathless, brave declaration, her heart simply went out to him. Here at last, she thought in a confused tumbling flash of insight, was a man who was more than a jock. Larry had looked poleaxed when she'd simply set down her cup of punch and taken his arm, wordlessly, and gently nudged him toward the dance floor.

It had been fine with her then, fine with her ever since. Except that he was gone so much. She had enjoyed the little taste of military life she'd seen—the customs, the support from the other families—but she enjoyed Larry too much to have him gone. Micky was a little dismayed at her own lust; she missed his strong lean body. And she missed his sense of humor, his boyish enjoyment of his sexuality. She wanted him now, and she wanted him permanently.

The Air Force was going to be a problem; she still didn't understand his total fascination with the airplanes. To her they were big, offensive trucks, smelly, noisy, dangerous. It was one thing to crawl into a nice DC-3 and fly up to Washington in comfort; it was another to pound around to all the countries of the world, freezing one day, broiling the next, just to drop off some stupid supplies.

Yet he loved it. All the men loved it. The Berlin Airlift was clearly worthwhile, and she was proud of his being there. But what was next? And what was left for her when he was gone?

She rubbed her hand on her stomach, as yet only nicely rounded. What about the children? The kids she had seen on base seemed happy enough, and heaven knew there were plenty of them. What about her own baby, or babies? Larry was talking about five or six. Her parents would faint at such a figure. They'd never discussed anything so intimate, but she knew they would prefer a genteel two; one boy, one girl, with twin beds for the parents until they got twin bedrooms.

Fat chance; she was going to be dropping kids for the next ten years if Larry had his way, and he would have his way, she knew.

What else was there, though? The second month he had been overseas, she had thought about going back to school, getting an advanced degree, but it was out of the question with the baby coming. If they could be certain of living here in the Tidewater she could work in Father's bank, or someplace else equally refined. And she had to do something; she hadn't realized just how little the service paid. There were lots of things to make up for it—having the baby wouldn't cost a dime—but there was no *real* income, no way to build up some assets.

She rolled over again, realizing she sounded like her father. Assets. She'd never heard the word in her six months at Dover; Air Force people didn't think about such things. But somehow, she had to help Larry get some for the family. If they had five or six kids, they'd have to educate them some way, and she wouldn't ask Father for the money. Not that he'd give it to her, even if she asked. He'd made that clear in his stiff little lecture before the marriage. They'd waited to get married until they both graduated and before Larry went off to Texas, but it had made no difference to Father. He'd made it clear they were doing it without his blessings. The way he'd carried on, you'd have thought she was going to marry a Negro. No. It was clear she'd burned her bridges with Arthur W. Goode, president of the Goode Bank of Custisburg, Virginia. It was equally clear that in his mind, she was no longer Mildred Drew Goode, his only surviving child, but some sort of wild hussy. If Tom had only not gone off and joined the Marines in '44, and not gotten killed at Iwo—well. He had, and that was that. The Goodes never really got over losing her brother; it had turned Father bitter and turned Mother into a nervous wreck.

Micky closed her eyes and wrenched her thoughts from the past. She missed Tommy as much as they did. Maybe more. But he was gone. She had responsibilities now. She had the life within to think of. And she knew that somehow this matter of refusing Tunner's offer boded ill for the well-being of the White family. With the same certainty that had put her on Larry's arm at the dance, she knew that it was going to be up to her to keep the White family healthy. A year before, she might have been daunted by it. Now, inexplicably, she relished the challenge.

Larry always kidded her that she'd been the world's greatest saleswoman, selling herself to him. Maybe she'd try that; the problem was what to sell, and to whom to sell it. Not to her Air Force friends; if they couldn't get it in the commissary or the PX, they couldn't get it.

All any of us want, she thought dreamily as she began to drift back to sleep, is love and money. Some of us get one, some the other; why not both?

She wanted both, and she wanted them both from Larry. If only he'd stick around, she'd get all the love she could handle from him. But the money she'd have to find elsewhere. Her mind coiled around the prospect with curious warmth, and, following the coils off into the mists of what-if, she slipped into a sleep deeper than she'd found since Larry left. After a few moments, her fingers relaxed, and his letter fell to the floor.

3

0725 LOCAL
27 July 1948
Lackland AFB
San Antonio, Texas
USA

"Hey, Joe. Lookit this. You see this?"

Kugler put down his coffee. "What?" He allowed himself the luxury of displayed irritation. Roscoe always interrupted his 0700 coffee and doughnuts, usually by reading him something out of the San Antonio paper.

Roscoe leaned closer, partly to make it easier to read over the hubbub in the NCO mess, partly because of the story itself.

"It says, 'President Issues Order to Services: Integrate—Or Else!' What do you think of them apples, Joe?"

Kugler sipped on his coffee. "I don't think. The Air Force

53

don't pay me to think. It pays me to turn kids into airmen. If you'd do the same, your flights would do better."

"Aw, Joe, you take this shit too seriously."

"Yeah. Maybe that's why I got five stripes and you got three, Roscoe."

"Maybe. Anyway, they say here that—and I quote—'Yesterday, July 26, 1948, will go down in history as the day that the integration of the several races of America was pushed forward by the nation's Chief Executive. Pentagon sources say that the new policy, to go into effect immediately, has not been met with universal acceptance within the military branches themselves.' No shit! Can you imagine old Finley's face right now? Hoo-ee! That guy hates nigras."

"Captain Finley will obey, just like all of us, Roscoe. If they tell us to do it."

"Says here there ain't no more iffn about it, Joe. Says here that from now on, colored and white will all be mixed up together. Boy. Sounds like trouble to me." Roscoe slurped his own coffee. "Hey. Wasn't you in England with the Eighth when they had those riots?"

"Yeah. Forty-four. I was at Alconbury, with the 395th. Why?"

"Well, I mean, you seen all this shit already, right? Tell me, did those colored boys really beat the crap out of the white boys?"

Kugler munched the greasy doughnut slowly. The little finger of his right hand sent a shock of pain through him, the way it sometimes did, even though it wasn't even there anymore. Frostbite at twenty-seven thousand feet had killed it on the raid over Friedrichshafen. That was the day he downed two Focke Wulfs. Not bad for a waist gunner from Idaho, the skipper had said. What the hell ever happened to the skipper, anyway? What the hell ever happened, for that matter, to everybody? To his goddamn finger? He sighed and sipped coffee to kill the gooey sweetness of the doughnut.

"No. That wasn't the way it was at all. I guess it was nobody's fault, see, except those assholes who figured the white English girls wouldn't go for the colored boys and sent them over anyway. Too many guys on that island in those days with too much money and not enough women. Really didn't matter if they was colored or white. Too many guys."

"But the riots—"

"Sure. We had big fights. Wouldn't call 'em riots. What the hell you expect? Four hundred young bucks jammed into a big

54

damn dance hall, there's bound to be some problems. White guy didn't like a girl dancing with a colored guy, next thing you know, pow. Knees and elbows, man. Knees and elbows."

"Well, I hope to hell we don't get that kind of shit around here, what with this integration crap."

Kugler sat his empty cup down, scraped his chair back from the long table, and stood up slowly. He carefully placed his campaign hat on his head, strap rearward over his burred scalp, and looked down at Roscoe.

"Like I said, Roscoe, that's why they pay us. Come on. Your babies are waiting on the quad. And today, I want to see some results from your people on the obstacle course."

Roscoe grimaced and folded the paper. By the time he had gulped his own coffee and scrambled to his feet, Kugler was striding out the door, heel taps clicking, swagger stick tucked under his left arm, every inch the pressed, starched, perfect training instructor. It occurred suddenly to Roscoe as he trotted to catch up that here at Lackland, in the Air Training Command, was where all this integration stuff was going to be tested first. He wondered if he'd be up to it.

0035 LOCAL
22 March 1949
Brooklyn, Illinois
USA

There were no streets at Lackland Air Force Base as mean as those Millard Washington knew so well in East St. Louis. Lackland was a paradise of clipped lawns spaced between blinding white buildings, of order, precision, and an overwhelming sense of direction and purpose. Where Millard Washington had lived until two weeks ago, in the Brooklyn section of East St. Louis, there was only fear, confusion, and the sense of things slowly coming apart.

He was not altogether surprised at what Lackland had to offer, nor what was expected of him. His mother had wanted him to be a preacher, but he had dreamed other dreams. Dreams of Col. Benjamin O. Davis and the famous Tuskegee Airmen, of the all-colored 99th Fighter Group, of climbing into the cockpit of a lovely little Mustang with SALLY FOURTH painted jauntily on the

55

nose and zooming up into the blue like no other colored boy ha
ever done before, Bennie Davis excepted.

Colored boys weren't supposed to dream such dreams,
course. That didn't stop him. He simply never told anybo
about it. John and Volar Washington worked like draft anima
to help him do what they could not: to escape the chains of the
lives in Brooklyn. When out-of-towners wanted to sin, the
crossed the river from the Missouri side and went to the seed
parts of East St. Louis that Mike Kelly knew. When native Ea
St. Louis folks wanted to go crazy they went to Brooklyn, whe
any semblance of law and order simply disappeared, whe
whorehouse fights, rigged gambling and reefers, whiskey an
anything else was available along any street. These were th
streets along which Millard Washington had walked without fe
or temptation every day, until he had climbed aboard the bus
Lackland.

He was not superhuman. He had wanted to taste some
those things as a boy, but the powerful religion of his moth
kept him straight. That, and the deep sense of debt he felt towa
his mother and father. John was a small man, wrinkled, be
and crooked from decades spent smiling at insults and despe
ately trying to keep his job when other colored lost theirs. H
was a janitor at Monsanto now, working double shifts. Volar di
domestic work uptown and anything else she could. But whe
the war had closed down the prosperity of the town, when th
oligarchy of thieves who ran East St. Louis decided not to inve
any of their spoils from the war in the city's industry, thing
turned bad for everyone. The chemical business, the stockyard
the steel mills, everything just ran down after V J Day.

Volar's tenacity and deep Methodism had secured her a fa
friend in a white preacher with connections at McKendree Co
lege in nearby Lebanon. So when Millard graduated from hig
school, he found himself with an hours-long commute t
McKendree, where he was the only Negro student. But th
nature of the college and the people who taught and attended
protected him, and he did well, within the limits of exhaustio
imposed by his working two jobs in addition to going to college

Washington never flinched from anything. His physique helped
He had somehow translated his mother's girth into height an
sinew. He stood six-two and weighed 190 pounds. He wa
Nubian black, with a long head, wide-set black eyes, and
strange combination of John Washington's almost mulatto fea
tures and Volar's thick lips, blunt nose with wide-flaring nostrils

56

and dense hair. Rednecks sometimes called him nigger, but only quietly, after he had passed by.

He never knew the source of his passion for flying, for airplanes. He had never been in one, not even in one of the little Cubs or Stinsons at the grass airstrip outside town. The closest he'd come was twelve feet from the cockpit of a Mustang during an open house at Lambert Field. Just getting that close had given him the sweats and the shakes. He wanted wings more than he wanted Betsy Tatum, and he wanted her so badly it scared him.

All through the war, he'd collected every scrap about the colored airmen who'd made the all-colored flying school at Tuskegee, Alabama, famous. He kept them in a special little book in the boards below his bed. When the war had ended, his heart had sunk; now, he felt, there might never be another chance. But an item on the notice board at McKendree had caught his attention. The Air Force was continuing the Aviation Cadet program. All you needed was sixty credits and the right skills and they'd make you a pilot.

He burned with the need to escape, to fly SALLY FOURTH. But the debt he owed John and Volar kept him studying and working, one job with Bud Drummond's gas station in East St. Louis, the other at the slaughterhouse, poling shrieking pigs under in the scalding vats. Yet he would not have acted unless something happened. One night, it did.

Volar was waiting for him when he got home after midnight from Drummond's. She rocked back and forth in her rocker, knitting, while soft music came from the old radio by the window. He was surprised to see her. She rarely stayed up past ten.

"Hello, Mama," he said and pecked her a little kiss. She patted him on the arm and said, "Work all right, Millard?"

"Yes ma'am. Not too bad. Is Daddy in bed?"

"He is."

"Then why are you still up, Mama?"

She stopped rocking and pulled his scrapbook out from under her knitting. "Millard. Is this yours?"

He sat down slowly on the threadbare sofa. "Yes."

She studied him intently. "Why didn't you tell us about all this, child?"

"I don't know. Mama. I guess I thought you wouldn't understand."

"I confess I don't, Millard. But . . . what does it all mean?"

"I want to fly, Mama. I want to be a pilot. In the Air Force."

Volar rested her head against the back of the rocker. She closed her eyes. When she spoke, they were still closed.

"You be colored. You know what that means?"

"Of course, Mama. But the services will be integrated soon—"

"Listen to me. That don't matter. People don't change. You always be colored, they always be white. Only God can change that."

Millard knew at that moment, suddenly, that a wall existed between him and his own mother, a wall made of what he knew, what he'd learned in school and college, what he thought, and most of all, what he wanted.

"I can't be a preacher, Mama. I just can't. God won't come to me."

"You think you can get to Him in one of these?" She held up the scrapbook.

"Maybe. Maybe not. But I have to try, Mama. I have to."

She lowered the scrapbook to her lap. Not looking at him, she picked up her knitting again. Her gnarled fingers, worn out from washtubs and scrub brushes, worked deftly. She said nothing for a long moment, then looked up at him. Tears rolled down her cheeks. "Then you got to go," she said. He leaped to his feet and enfolded her in his long arms. She weighed more than 160 pounds, but was light as a feather and fragile as a bird to him.

"I'll make you proud, Mama, You'll see. I'll make you proud."

She sobbed silently, head against his chest, and despite the pain, something inside him broke free.

1345 LOCAL
8 August 1949
Lackland AFB
San Antonio, Texas
USA

Don Picard didn't know why he volunteered to take the bottom bunk. Maybe it was because he was ashamed of the other white guys. There were nine colored in Flight 1311 so somebody was going to have to take the bunk under Washington. As the others stood around, he suddenly decided it was all hogwash. He tossed his duffel bag on the bunk and stuck out his hand. "Don Picard," he said.

Washington shook his hand. His grip was firm and dry. He

was almost as tall as Picard—who was a gangly six-three—but much better muscled.

"Millard Washington. Nobody calls me Millard. Just Wash."

"Glad to meet you, Wash. Looks like we're all in the same boat."

Washington chuckled and ran his hand over the stubble that was all that remained of his hair. "Yeah. Pretty close shave. First of many, probably."

Picard chuckled in reply and started unpacking. "Might as well get used to it," he said. Washington nodded and did likewise. Neither man saw the look that Jimmie Nelson cast across from the next bunk, nor heard him mutter, "Some of us ain't never gonna get used to it, Nigra."

They did hear T/Sgt. Joseph R. Kugler slam open the barracks door, though, as clearly as they heard his shouted "Barracks, Tenhut!" Because they were raw recruits, they were slow to respond properly. Which resulted in more clearly heard instructions from Kugler, instructions with which they were to become intimately familiar over the next thirteen weeks of basic training at Lackland Air Force Base, Texas.

They learned, as all recruits through all time have learned. They learned how to fold their clothes to avoid the wrath of Kugler. They learned how to march ten miles through the heat, to run the obstacle course at the double, then march another ten miles back again, with enough energy left to sing lustily as they clumped through the impeccable base. Among them there were those who complained constantly that if this was the Air Force, they could do without it. Don Picard was not among them. And neither, to Picard's surprise, was Washington.

The unwritten, unspoken code of conduct kept most personal questions unasked in the barracks. But one hot Sunday, while Don and Wash were sitting in their skivvies on the bunks, engaged in the endless task of polishing their boots, they traded stories. Washington outlined his briefly. Whenever he'd stop, Picard would nudge him again, and soon he had it all.

"Pre-Cadet, huh? Boy, that's great, Wash. Hope you make it all the way."

"Yeah. Me too. Got a long row to hoe, though."

"Where do you go from here?"

"Randolph, across town. You do both preflight and basic there. Seven months."

Picard whistled. "A long time."

"Worth every minute. If you make it."

"You'll make it." And Picard believed it.

"Why don't you try for it, Don? You're smart enough."

"Nah. I wasn't cut out to drive 'em, just to fix 'em. Runs in the family."

"Your dad a mechanic?"

"Was. Air Corps. Killed in a PT-17 back in '43. Hotshot instructor at Merced—that's where we live—decided to take him up to show him what the goddamn thing was doing wrong. Along the way, decided to show Dad how sharp he was by flying under a bridge on the Sacramento. Augered in."

"Sorry."

"Breaks of the game, as Dad used to say. He was a good wrench. Best on base, the skipper said. Didn't help Mom any, though."

"She making out okay?"

"Now, yeah. Married to a Portagee. Nice guy name of Joe Amado. Manager at the Del Monte plant in town. Used to be a picker, then worked up to running the canning operation. When they got married, I figured it was time to leave. You know."

"Yeah. I know."

"Anyway, Dad left Mom the ten gees in insurance and left me the best tools around. Hell, I knew 'em all anyway. Been working with him and his Snap-Ons since I was old enough to hand him a hammer. We had some good times on base, I can tell you. Real good times." Picard stopped polishing his boots and stared at the floor.

Washington felt the hurt with him. "You go to school on base?"

Picard picked up his brush again, and began methodically working the shine. "Some, yeah. Went to high school at Merced. Played guard on the basketball team. We made state semifinals, too."

"Sounds good."

"It was okay. Best part was shop, though. Mr. Feldman was a hell of a machinist. He even helped me drop a Caddy twelve-cylinder in a T-bucket."

"Damn! That thing must have scooted!"

"You bet. I love doing that kind of stuff. That's why I figured I might as well join up. There's no place better than the Air Force for a guy like me." He paused to listen as some training instructor screamed abuse at a recruit outside. "If I survive Killer Kugler, that is." He grinned.

"We'll survive." Washington smiled back. "Long as we pull together, we'll make it. All of us."

Picard didn't reply. None was needed. They fell back to polishing, their shoes so shiny that Kugler could read his watch in them, and soon the only noise in the barracks was the hiss of their brushes on leather and jangling of their dogtag chains as they worked the Kiwi polish until it was mirror-bright. They were complicitly silent, already old comrades in arms, ready for the night's real work, in which spit and polish played no part.

Both men had noticed Beatty and Clay, but because of his father's stories, Picard had approached Washington first about them, and about what was needed.

"Wash, you been watching our little troublemakers?" He'd asked it in an offhand manner that did not give away his intentions. He knew the colored boys thought of Washington as their leader, and respected him for it. But you could never be too careful.

Washington had smiled thinly, immediately understanding Picard's drift. "Sure. Got any ideas?"

Picard had returned his smile with one similarly mirthless. "Yeah. Blanket party, unless they shape up."

Washington had nodded, and agreed to let Beatty and Clay have another chance. Beatty was coal black, an ox of a man who regarded the flight as an extension of his turf on the streets of southwest Washington, D.C. He had a nasty habit of leaning on the smaller colored troops, shaking them down for favors and cash. They looked to Washington for help. His first direct request to Beatty to knock it off had been met with an icy stare and a turned back.

Cletus Clay was the other problem child. He came from a crossroads in Louisiana and worked the other side of Beatty's street. He was a huge, slow-moving, dim-witted lout who gave new meaning to the word *redneck*; his neck was literally red. He bullied the smaller airmen, dogging his duties and somehow avoiding a shower even after a long, sweaty day on the rifle range.

Within a week, both Beatty and Clay had used up their chances. Wash and Picard talked briefly, decided not to wait; they would lead the reliable men in the flight tonight on a blanket party, to try to bring Clay and Beatty in line. As the ancient recording of Taps sounded over the Lackland P.A. system and lights began to blink out all over the base, Picard nodded to Washington and whispered, "Twelve o'clock. Sharp."

Washington did not need reminding. At midnight he stood next to Picard's bunk, a huge silent shadow, holding a blanket in one hand. Picard swiftly arose and joined him, also holding a blanket.

61

Around the barracks, another dozen men slipped out of their bunks. Half moved with Picard toward Clay, half with Washington toward Beatty. Beatty was awake and sat bolt upright as the blanket dropped over his head and the fists began to pound him. Clay was awakened with a flattened nose. The beating was over in three minutes, with both men weeping and pleading for help. They ignored Beatty and dragged Clay out of his rack and down to the latrine, where they ripped his stinking slept-in fatigues from him and scrubbed him with a stiff brush and Fels Naptha.

The next day at roll call, Sergeant Kugler noticed that Beatty and Clay were subdued, and awkwardly trying to conform to the discipline of the flight. He looked at them closely as they marched to chow and chuckled when he saw the bruises. These things had a way of working out.

1600 LOCAL
11 August 1949
Lackland AFB
San Antonio, Texas
USA

"At ease, Airman Washington."

Wash relaxed slightly. He dropped his gaze from the spot two feet above Kugler's head to his eyes. The T.I. was seated behind his immaculate desk, swagger stick and campaign hat on the desktop.

"You know why I've asked you here?"

"No, Sergeant."

"It's about the blanket party."

"Sergeant?"

"Don't be cute, Washington. I know you and Picard arranged a little blanket for Beatty and Clay two nights ago. I know how, I know when, and I know why."

"I see."

"No, Washington, I don't think you do see." Kugler stood up and went to the window. The second-story office was just above the barracks classroom. It looked out over the arid drill field.

"Your flight is only the third we've had through here since integration, Washington. We don't have a lot of experience in handling mixed races."

"We haven't had too much of a problem, Sergeant."

"No. You haven't. Until now. If you and Picard hadn't held your little party—"

"Sergeant, excuse me but Clay was threatening the white boys, and Beatty was extorting money from the coloreds. They needed disciplining, by the group, not the Air Force. Their behavior was inexcusable."

"Don't interrupt me again, Airman. One day you'll be an officer—if you make it—and you'll have that privilege. But now you're a slick-sleeve airman basic."

"Sorry, Sergeant. I only meant—"

"I know what you meant, Washington. And you're right. Those two needed it. You saved us a lot of work. That's why we almost never stop blanket parties. Usually, the guys who get 'em need 'em."

"But?—"

"But this time, because you and the other colored boys from 1311 participated in working over Clay as well as Beatty, we've got a problem. The word got around, see. And when the word gets around, as you'll soon discover, it gets screwed up. In this case, what's happened is that the word now says that you and the other colored boys singled Clay out and ambushed him. With no whites present."

Washington just looked at Kugler.

"Normally, that wouldn't be too much of a problem. Normally, I'd just make certain the other tac officers and T.I.s rode careful herd on the boys until everybody graduated. But there's a snag now." He turned back to the window and stared outside for a long moment.

"The snag is the C.O. He heard the word, and called the tacs in to find out what happened. Before I could straighten it out, he let us know he expected 'appropriate steps' to be taken."

"Does that mean a court martial, Sergeant?"

"No." Kugler clasped his hands behind his back so tightly they turned white from lack of blood. "No. Unfortunately not. What it means, Washington, is that the goddamn commanding officer has arranged for a bunch of rednecks to get you. That's what it fucking means."

Washington rocked back on his heels. "Officially?" he asked.

"Christ, no. Nothing official. But Finley is Old Army. He knows how to get things done. And there's a couple of T.I.s who think like he does. They think the niggers have to be kept in their place. Unofficially."

"What will happen?"

"Probably, you'll be jumped. Probably while you're in the latrine, or otherwise by yourself. They won't go one-on-one with you. You're too big. These kinds of scum are usually cowards. Then they'll get the others in your flight. But first, they'll get you." He paused again. "And there's not a goddamn thing I can do about it."

"What about going over Captain Finley's head?"

"The colonel? That would just about finish my career, Washington, even if he did anything about it. And there isn't much chance he would. I'm taking a big risk just letting you know this shit."

"Sure," Washington said drily.

Kugler spun and glared at him. "Look, I know how it sounds, Washington. But this is all new, see? Nobody knows how to act. God knows, if I could do anything, I would. I don't give a shit whether my boys are red, white, or blue. But—"

"But your career would be finished."

Kugler shut his mouth and turned his back slowly on Washington again. "That will be all, Airman. Dismissed."

Washington snapped his heels together and came to attention. He waited a beat, did a right-face and walked out the door. He pulled it gently closed behind him.

It was worse than a slap in the face for Kugler. He winced as the latch snicked closed.

How had it come to this? He remembered those fifty-five missions over Germany, the intensity of life in the air and on the ground, the pain of sudden death and the joy of unexpected life. His missing finger throbbed and he rubbed the stump where the flight surgeon at Alconbury had sawed it off while he lay on the table with his sheepskin boots still on, screaming bloody murder because they'd run out of anesthetics. He remembered the look he'd caught through the smoking fifty's gunsight, the look on the German pilot's face when he'd seen his own 20mm rounds go wide of Kugler's body, tearing through the thin aluminum of the Fort's fuselage only inches from Joe, then seen Kugler's tracer rip through his FW-190's wingroot and understood he was a dead man.

But that was war. And this was peace. At least, that's what they called it.

1000 LOCAL
7 September 1949
Lackland AFB
San Antonio, Texas
USA

"Captain?"

Finley irritably hit the intercom switch, not looking up from his report. "Yes, Collins? What is it?"

"Sir, uh, there's a Major Williams here to see you. With some M.P.s."

"Williams?" Finley scowled, trying to recall the name. "I don't know any Major Williams. What does he want?"

"Sir, he wants to see you. Now."

Finley sighed. "Okay. Send him in."

The door to the office of the commanding officer, 3321st Basic Military Training Squadron, burst open without ceremony. A tall, tight-lipped major entered, followed by two burly M.P.s. As Finley stood up, he read the major's dress blue uniform for clues as to job and accomplishments. He washed the irritation from his face as he noted the pilot's wings, the three rows of ribbons surmounted by the DFC and the Purple Heart. "Captain Finley?" the major asked, ignoring his hand.

Finley allowed it to drop awkwardly.

"Yes, Major, ah, Williams, is it—?"

"Chester Williams. I'm with the OSI, Captain Finley. Here is my identification." He plucked a thin I.D. card wallet from his breast pocket and flipped it open. "Do you know what that means?"

Finley glanced at the card. "Office of Special Investigations. Sure. But what—"

"Captain Finley, it is my duty to inform you that as a result of charges brought against you by T/Sgt. Joseph R. Kugler and the findings of a subsequent OSI investigation, you are herewith relieved of duty and remanded to the custody of your commanding officer, who will confine you to quarters until the date of your special court martial. The charges will be conduct unbecoming an officer, inciting to riot, dereliction of duty, and failure to carry out an order. The specifics of the charges are on this sheet." He unsnapped the briefcase with a deft move and slapped a paper in front of Finley.

Finley sat in his overstuffed swivel chair. He blinked. Then a sneer erupted to twist his face. "So. I had no idea the Air Force was being run for the benefit of a bunch of niggers. And enlisted niggers at that—"

The briefcase Williams carried slammed down on the desk. The two M.P.s jumped slightly and put their hands on their gun butts.

Williams leaned over the desk. "Finley, you are being given a chance that you were not man enough to give your own troops. I suggest you take advantage of it, and remember that I will be a witness at your court martial."

The sneer slipped off Finley's face and he reached for the paper, eyes held by Williams's glare. He wanted to stand up and punch in the major's face, just like he'd always wanted to punch every other smug flyboy. Instead, he rocked back in his chair as far as he could, and glanced at the paper. Breaking eye contact gave him enough craw to sneer again after he'd scanned the sheet. "In the old days," he said, "things like this were handled differently. In the old days, gentlemen knew how to take care of things."

Williams straightened up and regarded Finley with a glacial stare. "There are two things you ought to know, Captain Finley. First, men like you are never gentlemen, even though they sometimes become officers. And second, the old days you're talking about are gone." Without waiting for a reply, he spun on his heel and limped to the door, where an M.P. pulled it open for him. He paused, midway through, and looked back. "*Forever*," he said. Then he was gone, and the M.P. was closing the door.

1100 LOCAL
17 September 1949
Lackland AFB
San Antonio, Texas
USA

"You got a goddamn problem, Washington?"

"No, Sergeant."

"Good. Then maybe you can keep your goddamn eyes to the goddamn front as I asked you ever so politely. *Comprende?*"

"Yes, Sergeant."

"All right. Now, flight, when I tell you to move your asses through this here obstacle course, I want you to move your fucking asses! You people got that?"

66

"Yes, Sergeant!"

"I can't hear you, people!"

"YES, SERGEANT!"

"Okay. That's better. Beatty. You're first. Remember, boy, this is the last time you got to run this goddamn course before graduation. If you don't fuck it up, you're home free. Got it? Good. Go!"

Beatty went. The others followed, one at a time, hurling themselves into the long corrugated tin tube that led to the first section of the course. Kugler strolled back and forth at the start line. On one pass, he felt Washington's eyes on him again. He clamped his jaw shut and pulled the black man aside.

"What the fuck's wrong with you, boy? You got the hots for me?"

"No, Sergeant."

"Well, what, then?"

"I was just wondering, Sergeant. Why you did it."

"Did what, boy?"

"Turned him in. You took a big chance."

Kugler stared hard at Washington. Sweat dribbled down his pockmarked face and stained his starched collar.

"Washington. You listen, and listen good. Someday you may be an officer. You got to understand about the Air Force. Most of the time, you can pretend it's just a job, see. But sometimes, you got to know what it's really all about. You see this?" He held up his hand with the sawed-off finger. "This is what it's all about, boy. Our job is to fly and fight. Period. Don't fucking matter what color we are, don't matter about careers, don't matter about rank. We fly and fight. We kill the fucking enemy, we take the air away from him, and we fucking win. Only way we do that is to take care of business on the ground. We all got to hang together. Guy like Finley screws it all up. Somebody had to take care of him. This time, I was it. Next time, might be you. You got that, boy?"

Washington swallowed. "Yes."

"Good. Don't you ever fucking forget it. Now get your black ass over there and run that goddamn obstacle course right or I'll kick you all the way back to wherever the fuck you came from. MOVE!"

Washington moved.

4

**1500 LOCAL
6 November 1949
Randolph AFB
San Antonio, Texas
USA**

Washington didn't mind that the training schedule did not allow him time to return home after graduation from basic. Or even that Randolph AFB, where he was slated for aviation cadet training, was just a bus ride away across the sleepy Spanish village that San Antonio imagined itself to be. He was in no hurry to renew his acquaintance with Brooklyn, and the sooner he got on with getting his commission and wings, the better. He had been on pass twice, had walked down the river paths, and visited the saloons and whorehouses distinguished from Brooklyn only by a few degrees of skin color and the sound of Latin rather than jazz music. The experiences had been chilling reminders of his fate if he failed. He never wanted to travel anywhere again except as an officer.

Randolph AFB was another world, and the World War II grittiness of Lackland disappeared in the polished "West Point of the Air" atmosphere. At first he was concerned that there was some sort of elaborate plot, for, from the moment he checked into his barracks, there was no sign, no comment, no awkward moment that suggested that he was of another race. In time he came to accept it. The six weeks he spent in academics and physical training before he went to the flight line were the best in his life, not least because it turned out that he was virtually the only one who knew anything about airplanes, or the Air Force. His knowledge came from books, admittedly, but he had a sense of what he was getting into, and he most of all saw the flight line as a passport not just to the sky but to dignity.

From the moment he entered preflight, the outside world ceased to exist. The cadets took no notice that Truman had authorized construction of the H-bomb, that Alger Hiss was fighting perjury charges, that Chiang Kai-Shek had to stand impotently in Taiwan and watch Mao Tse-Tung negotiate with Stalin. They did troop to see *Command Decision*, and seethed with anticipation at how well they would fly and how heroic they would be when the time came. They woke to the sound of engines running up, and no plane entered the pattern without their eyes following it.

The supply of cadets built up with the heat of the cold war, and each flight instructor had five or six students assigned to him instead of the usual table of four. Most of the instructors were young, only a year out of flying school themselves. Many were discontented because they were not in operational units, and had to put their lives in the hands of green would-be pilots riding the knife edge of the essence of flight instruction, which was to let the student pilot go as far as possible on his own. If you took over too soon, he didn't learn; too late, and you both bought it.

Like ten thousand before them, the cadets of Washington's flight marched singing down to the flight line to halt at the manicured lawns. They made a left-face, dressed right, right faced, and then in swift single columns marched into the classroom that they desperately hoped would be their home for the next six months. As right guide for the formation, Washington marched in first, striding crisply in thirty-inch steps past First Lt. Bennie Oliekiwicz, who watched him with narrowed eyes, then whispered to his roommate, "The spade is at my table. Three rides and he's out."

The long classroom, filled with tables and chairs and bordered with blackboards where the same mistakes could be outlined year after year, filled rapidly with smoke. The anxious cadets milled around as an officious, pimpled Airman Second Class reshuffled the assignments, trying to keep a balance between student officers, aviation cadets, and the half dozen foreign students.

Washington sat uneasily at Oliekiwicz's table. The instructor could not have been more charming. He introduced himself to the three obviously nervous cadets and two seemingly calm student officers, and assured them that they were fortunate in getting the best pilot in the Air Force as their instructor. He chatted with them individually, setting them at ease, and making no special overtures or exceptions for Washington.

The first day was mostly filling out papers, and getting their first close-up look at the T-6 trainer, their first scent of oil and burned metal and the pungent aromatic fuel. The next day, they'd get their dollar ride, an orientation flight around the area.

Washington was tight with anticipation the next morning as Oliekiwicz walked around the airplane again, pointing out what to look for, how to twist the lugs on the tank drain plugs to check

69

for water in the fuel, and how to adjust his chute and safety harness. Then he climbed in the rear seat, joshing with the crew chief.

As Washington adjusted to the front seat, the control column suddenly came alive, pounding his thighs, jerking back into his groin. He turned in surprise to see Oliekiwicz's round face contorted in anger.

"You dumb pissant," cried the instructor, "are you going to sit there all morning? Get your head out and get this clunker started." Washington's mouth went dry. He'd never started the big radial engine of the T-6 before, although he'd memorized the drill, and Oliekiwicz well knew it. He hooked the stick with his right elbow, planted his feet on the toebrakes, and reached with his left hand for the handle on the handpump to prime the huge cylinders. Before he could hit the engage button for the energizer, the stick drummed his thighs again, and Oliekiwicz's voice rasped through his earphones.

"You idiot! You were going to turn the prop without yelling 'clear'? Jesus! Just put your hands in your lap, you ape, and I'll get this thing started."

A crew chief had been watching, and he jumped up on the wing to work in concert with the instructor for engine start. Washington looked at him in misery, but the mechanic ignored him.

The routine of the pounding stick and curses was repeated several times on the way to the runway. Washington began to panic. Clearly he had not gotten the word on what to learn, or how to handle himself. He wasn't sure he could take treatment like this for six months.

The flight was an unending stream of abuse, mixed with occasional bursts of instruction. Washington was miserable, and concentrated so hard on the procedures he never felt the thrill of his first flight. If this was being a pilot, he obviously was not cut out for it. Twenty minutes into the lesson, Oliekiwicz came over the interphone and said, "That's a pink slip, mister. Three of them, and you are o-u-t out." With that he did a split-ess, leaving Washington's stomach at altitude, and flew wordlessly back to land.

They debriefed in the hut. Oliekiwicz reverted to his polite, charming self, becoming sympathetic, but firm. "Mr. Washington, you didn't seem to have your procedures down today, and you got a little behind the airplane. You have to learn the procedures so well that you can concentrate on flying the airplane."

70

A harder edge came into his voice and he said, "You have to fly the airplane. You can't let the airplane fly you. If you do, it'll kill you. Tomorrow, we'll try again, and I suggest that you spend some time learning your checklists and procedures."

There was more than two hours to endure before marching back to the barracks. Washington was too humiliated to talk to the other cadets, to find out how they did, but he could tell from the buzz of chatter and the laughter that they'd done better than he. He tossed in his bunk sleepless that night, grinding the thick flight manual and the procedures into his brain. When they marched through the gray morning, he was drawn and trembling with the effort, and it showed when he climbed in the airplane.

The next two flights were repeats of the first; he would try to respond to Oliekiwicz's commands, get halfway through, and then the instructor would jerk the controls from him. Within three flying days, he had the dreaded three pink slips.

After they landed from the third flight, Washington simply sat in the front cockpit, drained, exhausted, and numb. In the classroom, Oliekiwicz seemed to relax a little and he took Washington aside to console him after the brutal debriefing, which amounted to a public humiliation.

"Some people are just not cut out to be pilots, Mr. Washington, and it's better to find out early than late. You just don't seem to have the memory or the reflexes to learn even the basics. I'm really very sorry, but it's not fair to the other cadets to spend more time with you. I'm sure you understand, being an intelligent man."

Washington nodded dumbly. He had obviously not done well. He hadn't gotten airsick, and he thought he was catching on. His only hope was the ride with the check pilot. But Washington was too anxious on the check flight, and screwed up even the things he knew well. The check pilot had agreed with Oliekiwicz: no aptitude.

The system was arranged to handle cases like his swiftly, and a formal board quickly convened to decide his fate. It didn't occur to Washington that the instructor might have been at fault. He was living with one thought, that he had failed, and that his mother and father were going to be terribly disappointed, so when he stood before the polished table, behind which sat three captains and a major with his papers, he did not present a case for reconsideration. They looked through his record, and recommended him for navigator training at James Connally Air Force Base.

Washington saluted and left the room. For the first time in his life, the system had not only defeated him, it had demoralized him.

By chance, he would be able to begin training almost immediately, so they warned him at headquarters that it was unlikely he'd be able to secure a delay en route to Connally to take leave. He was glad to avoid having to explain what had happened to his mom and dad in person. But the letter home was still the toughest he'd ever had to agonize through. He knew they would be crushed, certain that race problems had caught up with him, certain that it was evidence he had overstepped his place.

But when their reply came, it was evident they simply thought that he had done so well that he was going to bypass pilot training for something better. He felt a combination of shame and relief and swore as he signed in with the officer of the day at Connally that here, if not at Randolph, he was going to do it right.

1000 LOCAL
6 December 1949
Connally AFB
Waco, Texas
USA

James Connally AFB was another austere collection of World War II buildings disposed randomly beside a runway complex, indistinguishable from a hundred others across the Southwest. A splash of watered green in the summer, it was named for a colonel killed on a B-29 mission over Yokohama.

Once again, Washington walked the base with the toe-stubbing caution of the first night in a strange hotel room. Once again he found himself a leader, popular despite his shyness, enjoying the training in spite of his bitter disappointment in washing out of flying training. There were other washouts, although most were there because of choice or because of some minor problem in the testing process. One thing was drilled into them: it was the navigator-bombardier upon whom the mission of the Air Force revolved. Pilots were merely chauffeurs. They tried bravely to believe it.

Washington did well at learning the trade, then began to love it, and in time began to believe that what had happened had

72

been for the best. He was not only good with the tools of the trade, he had that sixth sense that made great navigators and bombardiers, the ability to use Kentucky windage when the data weren't right, to know when and how to compensate for equipment drifting out of tolerance. There was an immense intellectual satisfaction, but always the nagging sorrow, the sense of disbelief that pilot training had been so short and so bad.

Immersed as he was in mathematics and preparation for, execution of, and debriefing from the endless flights in one of a beat-up collection of B-25s, the training year went rapidly for him. He began to forget, as the others did, what life was like as a civilian. He grew used to weekly haircuts, to the jargon, the rituals, the fraternity legends. At Connally, the life of a navigator candidate was subtly different from that of a cadet at Randolph; perhaps because of the adversary relationship between the pilot and navigator, there was no hazing, no strident he-man stuff. He excelled at it, and at the end of navigator training, he was transferred to Ellington AFB in Houston for bombardier instruction.

He whisked through the bomb course almost as if he'd written the texts. And then, suddenly, almost as if by mistake, the day of graduation was upon him. He awoke early, put on the uniform he'd prepared the night before, the dress khakis, and almost did not stare at the shiny gold bar on his left collar tab. He walked through the morning's ceremony as if in a dream, shaking the colonel's hand when he pinned the nav wings on his blouse, saluting and then simply stepping back into line. When it was over, they marched past the reviewing stand, then were dismissed. He threw his new officer's cap into the air, like the others, and felt a remote kind of elation. He'd graduated third in his class. He was an officer, respected by his classmates and instructors, treated fairly by nearly everyone, and had a promising future.

That night he went to the officer's club, like the other ex-cadets, and celebrated manfully. He drank a little whiskey, though he didn't like the taste, and stayed until they threw them out at closing. With Bernie Jacobson, a Jewish kid from Long Island who'd been shunted into navigator training by his eyeglasses, he staggered back to the BOQ and fell asleep on his bed without removing his uniform.

The next day he found himself assigned to Spokane AFB, Washington, to a B-29 squadron. The cotton-cocoon feeling began to wear off as enlisted men saluted him on the way to headquarters, as those outside the training portion of the base began simply to treat him as another officer. He began, at last, to feel the part. And soon, as he packed for his trip to Washington, he began to think about himself on squadron duty, a member of a crew, the man responsible for guiding a huge bomber above the clouds to a precise spot in time and space. The only thing that could have made him happier was to have gone as a pilot.

1545 LOCAL
8 December 1950
Brooklyn, Illinois
USA

John Washington was speechless when his son stepped through the door, creases sharp, brass glittering, wings dazzling. The old man stumbled back and grinned so wide Millard feared for his sanity. Volar wept and wept, crying happily through the special dinner she piled on his plate, kissing him endlessly, unable to tear her eyes from him as he towered over the family friends who'd gathered to help the Washingtons celebrate. Millard slept that night in his old bed, the bed over the loose board where the dreams had been stored, and felt so out of place he itched to bolt. But he owed them more than he could repay, so he went with them to church the next day and endured the stares all over again, smiling and shaking hands and standing up when the Rev. Mr. Gallows pointed him out to the entire congregation.

He spent the best Christmas of his life with them, but he was ready to go, to get to work. When he got on the train, his skin was almost crawling, he was so eager to leave. East St. Louis had nothing but painful memories to offer him. Down the tracks, across the continent, the future awaited.

0800 LOCAL
15 March 1951
Spokane AFB
Spokane, Washington
USA

It was better than he'd believed possible. The duty turned out to be wonderful. The base was a madhouse of expansion. Navi-

74

gator bombardiers were in short supply and he was brought into crew duty immediately, far faster than he would have been as a pilot. And best of all he met Louise Walsh—albeit under the worst possible circumstances.

In one wild spree after graduation from basic, Washington had returned to downtown San Antonio to celebrate. He'd drunk too much and found himself coupling feverishly with a dark-eyed girl in one of the back rooms of the bar that lined the river. It was not his first time, but early-morning reflection made him wonder if it wouldn't be his last.

Despite a thousand surreptitious checks throughout navigator training—each trip to the head was sick call—there were no symptoms, but his fears flagellated his conscience. He was afraid to go to the flight surgeon; it was obvious that he couldn't even have an inquiry about V.D. on his records. But in keeping with his determination to make his first line assignment a clean start, he decided one day soon after checking in to resolve the issue of his own physical cleanness once and for all. He fingered through the slim Spokane phonebook, and located a specialist. He made his appointment over the phone to a soft-spoken woman.

Two days later, in civilian clothes, Washington climbed out of the taxi, walked up the two flights of stairs to Dr. Leon Andersen's office. Waiting behind the desk was the soft-spoken woman with whom he'd made the appointment. He stopped in the office as he stepped in and blinked in surprise. She was colored, lovely black hair and dark skin, with flashing, laughing eyes, and long, slim limbs. In her starched white nurse's outfit, she was the most beautiful woman he had ever seen.

She greeted him coolly and gave him forms to fill out. He wanted to put down a false name, didn't dare, omitted his rank, and worried about it. She took his form without comment, scanned it and glanced up at him. "What is it you wish to see the doctor about?"

"I—ah, I'd like to talk to him, ah, personally."

"I see," she said. She smiled warmly at him, revealing perfect white teeth.

"Mr. Washington, I'm Dr. Andersen's assistant. I'm a registered nurse, and I need to be able to prepare you for your visit. I assure you, you can be frank with me."

Washington wouldn't, couldn't talk to her. She finally gave in, and left him alone for a moment. When she returned, she rather frostily told him the doctor could see him immediately.

Leon Andersen was colored too. Washington smiled reflexively as he introduced himself. By pure blind luck he'd found exactly the right kind of professional help.

Andersen, a burly man with a curly crop of white hair that contrasted starkly with his caramel coloring, listened impassively to Washingon's tale. He ordered Millard to undress, then briskly examined him. He sent him to the next room to give a blood sample, taken inevitably by the nurse. She managed the process efficiently, with a minimum of small talk. As she worked, Washington noted her splendid figure, then reprimanded himself. It was that kind of thing that brought him here in the first place. Soon he was dressed again and facing Andersen.

"Call me next Thursday, Mr. Washington, and I'll have the results of your blood tests for you."

There were days of agony until Thursday. He knew he must be punished, that he was sick, and that the nurse would know. He fumbled through the few duties he had as a new crew member getting settled, thankful for the tradition of aircraft commanders going easy on new guys like himself. The skipper was a nice guy, and simply told him to take as much time as he needed to get squared away. Finally Thursday dawned and the hours crept by until at last it was time to call.

His hands trembled at the pay phone. He felt a rush of relief when the doctor answered. He told Washington to wait a few minutes until he found the records, minutes that stretched into eternity.

"Humph. No problems here, Lieutenant. You're fit as a fiddle. It is Lieutenant Washington, isn't it?"

Relief poured over Washington like a cold shower after a hot day. "Yes sir. Thank you sir." What else could he say?

"Yes. Well, my boy, you're not the first young flyer to come in here, and you won't be the last. Lieutenant, it's none of my business, but I think you ought to know that your anxieties were perfectly normal, and you did the right thing. You can't be too careful."

"Yes sir, I'll be careful."

"What you need is a wife, young man, and no fooling around in cathouses."

"Yes sir, thank you, sir." Washington glanced at the young housewife who was standing nearby, waiting for the pay phone. She juggled a baby from one arm to the other, casting hurry-up looks at Washington. Using the phone at the PX had not been a good idea, not for this kind of conversation, anyway. He began to say goodbye, but Andersen interrupted him. "It occurs to me,

Lieutenant, that because of your race, I might be able to help you out a bit, where staying out of cathouses is concerned. Did you notice the young lady who took the blood from you last week?"

"Yes sir." Notice her! She'd poleaxed him.

"Well, I think she might just be willing to go out with you even after your little examination here. Maybe especially after your little examination. I happen to know that she found you rather attractive, so I'm going to do the uncle go-between routine and tell you to give her a call. Do you understand me, son?"

"Yes sir. Thank you, sir. I will. Now—"

"Yes, I have to go too. Don't forget. By the way, her name is Louise Walsh. Call her here during work hours."

Washington hung up and grinned weakly at the impatient woman.

Naturally, he didn't call. He couldn't conceive of asking a nice young woman for a date after meeting her like that, no matter what Andersen said.

A week went by, a week in which Washington occasionally toyed with the idea of working up the guts to do it anyway. By the next Friday, he'd given up, and work was getting more demanding.

On Monday, she called him, leaving a message in the BOQ office. When he returned her call, he stammered and uhhed and sweated like a rube. He was simultaneously excited by her and terrified of her. Nobody he'd ever known in East St. Louis was anything like Louise Walsh.

They started dating in the most restrained way. Washington felt somehow that he would soil her if he touched her. He hesitated to kiss her, and she was polite but cool to him. Her manner was cool, her skin was cool, and once, when he brushed her lips with his own saying good-night, her lips were cool. He had the feeling she had an alcohol-soaked swab at the ready, ready to dab any parts of herself that came in contact with him.

He would have stopped seeing her, except that she always managed to arrange the next meeting before they parted. It was strange, but Washington felt that the matter was out of his hands, that Louise was going to decide what would happen, and he was better off letting her do so. He surrendered himself to the process.

When Andersen asked after them one slow Thursday afternoon, Louise let her hair down with him.

"Frankly, Doctor, he's scared stiff. He's not letting himself have any fun. We go to movies, we eat out, we dance, and he's like a kid in a china shop, acting like I'm made of porcelain."

Dr. Andersen had been friends with the Walshes for years. He'd sponsored Louise's nurses' training and valued her judgment. But he also valued his own, and he was certain the two of them were right for each other, or at least as right as they could expect, being colored in a white town like Spokane. He had promised Andy Walsh that he would look after Louise, help her socially as well as professionally, and he would not go back on that promise even if he could. Andy had been with him in the Army. They'd been through some tough spots. A man didn't forget that kind of obligation. Besides, he liked Louise, and thought of her as the daughter he had never had, and couldn't have, since Cornelia was barren. He pressed the issue harder than he might have otherwise. "What do you think's wrong with the good lieutenant, Louise?"

She pursed her lips. "Well, for starters, I think he's kind of lost. He's had a tough life. He's from the Midwest, you know. His parents are poor, and he's fighting a lot of battles I've been lucky enough to escape. But mostly I think he's just inexperienced with women generally. He didn't date much in college, and since he's been in the Air Force, he hasn't had time for much socializing. Except for the little fling that brought him here."

"Going to give up on him?"

"No way. Fact is, I really like the lunkhead. He's gentle, considerate, and intelligent. He just needs a little time, and some straightening out."

"And you're the woman to do it."

"Some woman has to. Can't let a man like him go to waste."

"Is he going to make an honest woman out of you?"

"He hasn't made a dishonest one out of me yet, and I'm beginning to worry about it." She looked away from Andersen, out the window, and past the mountains in the distance. "No, we're going to get married, but he just doesn't know it. He's going places, and I'm going with him."

5

Everybody is invisible to somebody. In advanced training at Williams AFB, Kelly was invisible to Duke Brown, even though they were in the same flight shack for almost six months, with different instructors at different tables, but spending their lives within a twelve-hundred-square-foot room, bustling in and out of the same personal-equipment building and sprinting to the same lines of airplanes. And Brown never saw Kelly. He saw through him, around him, over him, past him, and under him, but he never saw him. Brown exercised the supreme luxury of not gloating, not reminding Kelly of the incident in the bar. To Kelly it was an insult. To Brown it was simply part of the program: he never saw anyone in whom there was not an advantage.

Kelly saw Brown, though, and saw in him the distillation of every threat and obstacle of the past. The instructors continued to defer to Duke, knowing very well that they might be working for him in the future. They didn't defer very much to Kelly, although the treatment was far more professional and equitable than it had been in basic.

It made it all the tougher for Kelly not to call Joan Brown on her offer, or to somehow use her against Duke. As time passed, his imagination inevitably dwelt on the incredible fact of her propositioning him. And inevitably, he began to wonder what it would be like. Had he not been sent to Williams with Brown, it would not have mattered. But they were here, in the same flight, and he even saw Joan a few times, from a distance, to be sure, but each sighting was itself enough to stir his juices.

Kelly was pleased to note that the other student officers didn't act like Brown at all; they were somewhat reserved, uncertain themselves of their new rank, but in general were friendly as puppies with everybody. And Brown held back from them, too, preferring to do his cultivating with the senior instructors.

In the flying context, it didn't matter. Kelly was doing well

79

with the program, having whipped through the T-6 portion of the training, finally dominating the recalcitrant airplane that would submit only to a sure hand. He found that the jets, the Lockheed P-80s, were not only easier, but also more fun to fly than anything he had ever imagined. The visibility through the lovely teardrop canopy was wonderful, the tricycle landing gear assured easy landings, and you could roll the airplane endlessly and effortlessly with a little pressure on the stick.

Williams was a relatively small base, friendlier by far than the stuffy imitation West Point of Randolph. He wanted more than ever to win his wings, and still wrote and muttered PDGLMWMW a hundred times a day, but life had never been better, never more filled with the promise of success and the presence of compliant women.

The government had become generous, increased the dependent allotment home, and Kelly had a little more cash to spend on girls. The cadet club was a wonderful spot to meet, with a local group named Stars and Bars, but inevitably called Whores and Bores, coming in to entertain. If all else failed, there were the telephone operators. Many a night a group of cadets would dial the town's switchboard operator, and ask if four or five operators might be available for a date. More often than not, the answer that came back was: Sure, but can you get more cadets?

With a deal like that in operation, Kelly should have had enough flying and fucking, he thought, to keep him satisfied. But as usual, the crazy streak wouldn't stay locked up. He wanted Joan.

2110 LOCAL
5 November 1949
Williams AFB, Arizona
USA

"I thought you'd never call."

"Actually neither did I. Is Duke—?"

"Gone. As you very well know, Cadet Kelly."

Kelly flushed. Why was this woman always turning him red?

Joan Brown opened the door wider. The invitation was clear. Kelly hesitated and darted a glance around, like some fugitive. He did indeed know that Duke was off on a two-day cross-country to the East Coast. He also knew he was running the biggest risk of his life. He looked at Joan silently, hungrily.

She reached out, grabbed his arm, and pulled him inside. He let himself be led in, still wondering at his own actions. He did want to lay this woman; of that there was no doubt. But the real reason he was here was Duke. If he hadn't taken it on the chin at Rosa's, Kelly knew he wouldn't be standing there. He told himself it was simple justice, East St. Louis style.

While Joan closed the door, he glanced back at her. She was playing it to the hilt. She wore a loose velvet robe open just enough to show flashes of nipples. He felt himself heat up, and she noticed.

"Well, at least some of you is paying attention," she said. It could have been funny, under other circumstances. As it was, it just made Kelly flush deeper.

"Take off your coat," she said while he stood nailed to the floor like a mannequin. He peeled it off, and checked out the place.

It was oddly sterile. Kelly was used to bare walls, even to the aluminum-window semipoverty of his family's household, but this was different. Everything was—he searched for the word— correct. That was it. Correct. Tasteful, proper, correct.

And sterile. It looked like a place nobody lived in. The little sofa with the discreet pattern seemed never to have suffered a human buttock; the small dinette table seemed never to have supported a meal. A chill passed across his shoulders as she took his coat and placed it on a chair.

"There," she said huskily. Mike turned slowly to face her. The air almost crackled with sexual tension. She reached up and cradled his face in her hands. "Were you angry?" she asked.

"What about?"

"About the slap. At Rosa's."

Kelly fought to keep his mind clear. The two beers he'd downed at the Cadet Club dueled with the whiskey that preceded them. "Uh . . . no. I guess."

"Good. I had to, you see. Otherwise . . ."

"Yeah. I get the picture. Otherwise Duke—"

"Right." She cocked her head at him appraisingly.

"Don't judge too swiftly, Mr. Kelly. It takes two to tango."

She had him.

"Do you?"

"Do I what?" Things were going too fast again. She shimmered, as if she were not in focus.

"Tango."

"You mean like the dance?"

"Yes. What else would I mean, Mr. Kelly?"

He was losing control. He sensed that crazy stupid feeling coming like a rush of hot water.

"This, maybe," he said, and stepped forward to grab her. He wrapped his arms around her and pulled her face up to his, kissing her hard on the lips.

She tasted of whiskey, but she was soft and willing. After a second, she thrust her tongue between his lips and found his, sucking it greedily. He reeled back, gasping. She laughed silkily.

"This way," she said, and led him by the hand out of the living room, down a short hall to the apartment's bedroom. One of the sidetable lamps was on, the radio next to it pulsed with soft music, and the bed covers were thrown back. She pushed him gently onto the bed and stood before him.

Kelly watched, mesmerized, as she allowed the robe to open and fall to the floor. She was the most beautiful woman he thought he'd ever seen. She placed her hands on his knees and kissed him again, eyes open. She reached out to unbutton his shirt.

"Like what you see?" she purred.

Kelly pulled his shirt off, sending three buttons flying. He tore off the rest of his clothes and pulled her to him.

"Don't hurry." She laughed. "We've enough time, little cadet."

Kelly didn't hear her. He heard nothing but his pounding lust. He kissed her breasts briefly, then pressed himself between her legs.

She opened herself, and entwined her hands behind his head.

"Oh, yes . . ." she whispered.

Kelly spent himself in a single convulsive thrust. He withdrew in haste and rolled to her side.

"What's wrong?" she asked after a moment. She leaned on her elbow and looked at him. "That's it?" She sounded half hurt and half amused.

A flood of guilt and embarrassment washed over Kelly. He lay still, feeling himself shrink, feeling his heart slow down, not looking at her.

"How long has it been since you've had a woman, Mr. Kelly?"

He didn't answer. His throat was too dry. He swallowed and tried to make his vision clear. A glint in the dimly lit room caught his eye. He stared at it blankly for a moment before recognizing it.

A second lieutenant's collar bar. The butterbar, they called it in the cadets, yearning for it to be on their own collars. As his eyes adjusted, Kelly saw that it was on one of Duke's khaki blouses, hanging in the wardrobe, reflecting dully the light of the little side-table lamp.

Something snapped inside him. He sat up and grabbed for his shorts, at the foot of the bed. "Sorry. I've got to go." He stood up and pulled on his shorts, then his trousers.

Joan looked at him in disbelief. She reached over and touched his shoulder. "Hey. don't feel bad about it, Mike. It can happen. It'll be better next time. Relax. Let's have a drink."

He heard her as he might hear someone on a bad telephone line. He struggled into his clothes, wondering what the hell he was doing there, why he was putting his own gold bar in jeopardy. If Duke knocked on the door he was done, finished, washed out. His shoelaces were still tied in knots. He fumbled with them, then jammed his heels down into the shoes with them still tied, got up and lurched toward the door.

Joan's voice froze him. "What the hell is the matter with you? What kind of man are you, anyway?"

He slowed, but made it to the living room without looking at her. He picked up his overcoat, then turned to face her. She was back in her robe, face flushed, eyes blazing.

"Look. I'm sorry. I shouldn't be here. I made a jerk out of myself. Let's forget it."

She glared at him a moment. "So. It's the same with all of you, isn't it? You get your rocks off, then it's all guilt and sorrow. Damn it, what about me?"

Kelly opened the door. "I'm sorry. I'm leaving, that's how it has to be." He hesitated, trying to think of the right thing to say. But there wasn't a right thing. He stepped through the door and pulled it closed behind him.

She drank a long time. How long, she couldn't tell. Her anger gradually became remorse. What had she been thinking about? What if Duke had come back early? What if a friend had seen Kelly coming in or leaving? What had happened to her?

Joan Beaufort Dade, the girl voted most likely to succeed at Miss Farmer's, the girl who had turned her four years at Randolph Macon into a triumph of conquest, couldn't even score with a lousy cadet.

Duke. It had all to do with Duke.

At first, ever since that incredible night in his daddy's Packard after the dance at the Point, they had made love with an intensity and a frequency that almost scared her. As much as her own daddy's being in favor of the union for obvious political reasons, it was that intense passion on Duke's part that convinced her to marry him. But after their marriage, as soon as they got to Texas for his flight training, he had cooled toward her.

It had taken a while for her to admit her distress. And even longer for her to admit that there was no one with whom she could share it. Her mother was no use; she was a prig, a woman who had stopped living as Joan understood it decades ago. They hardly spoke to each other, except in the most formal and genteel chats.

Daddy was no use either. All Congressman Dade cared about now—all he had ever cared about, really—were his deals, his markers bought and sold. And Duke's family, from his forbidding, ramrod-straight father to his arch older brother and his disapproving mother, were remote, stand-offish people with whom she had almost nothing in common, save Duke.

And Duke was the last person to whom she could speak about—well, about anything. They had been married almost a year and were still strangers. Something had changed him, something to do with flying; she knew that instinctively. Yet he would not confide in her, would not even admit that when he came back drawn and pale, covered with a sheen of sweat from some flight, he was more than just "tired."

They had all made it clear to her from the start that Duke was going places. They had made it clear, even at the gala reception after the wedding, that she had a specific function in his getting there, wherever that might be. She understood now that she was a support system for him; no more, no less. She was to make his off-duty life as perfect as she supposed his on-duty life was.

Initially, she had hurled herself into the project with enthusiasm; she looked forward to running her own household with almost girlish glee. But it soon palled; there was, after all, only so much to be done. She could have the little apartment spotless by ten every morning. And then what?

Social life at the base was awful for someone from the best of southern society. The women were dowdy, the children dreary nuisances. Compared with the girls she had known at Miss Farmer's and the women at Randolph Macon, the Air Force wives were neither competition nor stimulation.

That left the men. And increasingly, they frustrated her too.

Kelly was only the latest in a line of disappointments. She knew the code of conduct to which she was expected to adhere; the old harpy back at Randolph, wife of the deputy commander, had drunk too much tequila one night and let fall some pearls of wisdom, probably fearing Joan's attentions to her own husband.

The encounter had all the trappings of a disaster, but Joan had to admit the woman had been helpful, in her own twisted way. Joan had seen from the start of military life that there were other rules of engagement in effect here; that what worked in Nashville parlors and Virginia parties wasn't going to work here. Oh, the casual flirtation was the same, but there was some strange overlay of restraint that puzzled her. The Harpy cleared it up.

They'd been in the club, four couples, Duke soaking up all the points he could by listening attentively while Colonel Pruneface sputtered on and on about the old days, Joan stuck with the Harpy and two other women. One woman huge with child, sour-looking and glumly downing glass after glass of liquid fire as her husband's eyes roamed the room ceaselessly, and a major's wife, whose husband had given up trying to catch Joan's eye and was now splayed out in a chair next to Duke and the colonel, still casting what he undoubtedly hoped were smoking looks her way.

As the evening wore on and the drinks got more frequent, the Harpy and Joan found themselves together, walled off from the others by the noise level of the club bar. That's when the Harpy got serious about the Rules.

She'd watched Joan gazing around the twilit room and watched her avoid the major's looks. Finally she patted her thigh and leaned conspiratorily toward her. "Good girl. He's trouble."

"Pardon?"

"Oh, don't play the ingenue. I have eyes."

"Well. I'm sure I don't know—"

"Of course not. But let me give you a little advice. Never around the flagpole. Ever."

Joan was intrigued. Enough so to be a little daring. She smoothed her dress, accentuating her figure, and looked hard at the Harpy.

The older woman did not miss the nuance of youth reproaching age. She snorted and downed her tequila in a single gulp. "Don't be cute, dearie. If you try, you'll see why."

"Why, then?"

"Because this is different. This is the Air Force." She made it sound like a curse. "The men are—different. You'll see."

"I don't know what you mean. Why, Duke is—"

"Yes, I'm sure. But don't ever expect to get away with it with someone from the squadron, my dear."

Joan blinked, unsure she had heard correctly. Nobody had ever spoken so bluntly to her before. She lived in a world of sly innuendo, not straight talk.

The Harpy swiveled her watery gaze to Joan and fixed her. "It's the airplanes, you see. The airplanes. We have the men only on the ground. The airplanes get them the rest of the time. It does something to them. Who knows what? But it does something. And—remember this, when some slick joker on TDY starts playing: when he finds out your husband is a pilot, he'll change faster than you can believe."

"What? What did you say—?"

"Guns, you see. The airplanes have guns, dearie. It changes the way a man acts when he has to fly with other men who have guns. Accidents have been known to happen. Catch my drift?"

Indeed Joan had caught her drift. And despite her unpleasant frankness and obvious jealousy, the Harpy had taught Joan a valuable lesson. Never with a squadron mate. Fine. She could understand that.

But Duke. If only he would be the way he was, she could be the way she was.

How had it all gone so wrong so quickly? "How?" she cried aloud in the living room with the correct furnishings.

"How?"

Nobody answered. And she began, at last, to weep.

0915 LOCAL
8 November 1949
Williams AFB, Arizona
USA

Duke had never felt better. His last flight had gone perfectly, and the special treatment he'd worked out to survive the training had at last broken the back of his nightmares. It had been obvious when he spent the night on the two-day cross-country.

The treatment had been painful. It involved allowing his fears full control of his mind all night, every night before a flight. Instead of fighting it, he let his mind work over the awful scenes of his own fiery death until he was almost exhausted. Then he would begin, bit by bit, to create the flight as it should be, rather than as he feared it would be. He began with the preflight checklist, the conversations with the crew chief, everything, as if it were a movie and he an actor. Then he'd play the actual takeoff and mission in his mind, over and over, right up to touchdown and rollout, until at last he was back on the ground again, safe. After that, his exhausted mind would allow him some sleep. Usually, it was less than an hour to daybreak, but it was enough.

The pills helped, of course. King had been right on one score; Mothersils worked—but only in conjunction with the Dexedrine tablets he stole from the flight surgeon. Nobody except the weasly little medical orderly knew about that, and nobody ever would, since Duke had the goods on the orderly and his small-time pill-selling racket.

He'd known he'd broken the back of the nightmare when he'd spent the night at the Langley AFB BOQ. When he lay down to sleep, he fully expected to go through the usual nighttime mission. Instead, he slept like a baby. And when he took off for the next leg that morning, he felt nothing. Absolutely nothing.

Joan had been stunned last night when he'd come home, grabbed her, and had her right on that awful cold little sofa. He knew he'd been neglecting her, but he couldn't help himself. The terror had him in its grip; it had been all he could do to get through the days, let alone the nights. But last night—last night had been like the old days. She had loved it, too. That had been obvious by her little screams of pleasure. And this morning, she'd teased him awake and they'd done it again.

Duke beamed as he pushed open the door to the ops shack to check his schedule. This was it. The last flight in the syllabus. He was going to live, after all. He smiled wide, remembering Joan and the freedom from fear. His smile froze when he saw Kelly loitering near the briefing room.

Duke walked into the room, looked past Kelly, made a note of the schedule. As he turned to go, Kelly reached out and grabbed his arm. Duke looked hard at him. Kelly dropped his arm and faced him. "I hear you were quite a boxer at West Point, Lieutenant. I guess that made it pretty easy for you to clip me back in San Antonio."

"Take your hands off me, Mr. Kelly, or I'll have you on report."

Kelly showed his teeth in a tight, menacing grin. "No need to get angry, Lieutenant. What I've got in mind is a little rematch. My way, this time. How about it?"

"Your way? What would that be, Kelly? Brass knuckles at fifty paces?"

"No, Lieutenant, P-80s in Arroyo Seco canyon. Tomorrow at oh-eight thirty."

Brown's first reaction was to laugh. Then he realized Kelly was serious. His brown eyes were narrowed, and his cheeks were tight and drawn. Duke glanced round to see if anyone had overheard the challenge. His heart sank when he saw Ken Fraser, a cadet, and Capt. Glenn Ross, an ex-navigator, both about to graduate, listening intently, making no attempt to conceal their interest. They changed the equation. He had no option but to agree.

"Right, Kelly. But I won't be surprised if you're not there. As I recall, you weren't too eager at Rosa's."

"That was your game, Lieutenant. This is mine." He thumped the notice board, where their flight times were posted. "We take off five minutes apart. I'll be on Echo channel over the canyon. Check in at oh-eight twenty-nine." He looked at the other pilots.

Brown put his on garrison cap. "I'll be there, Kelly. I'll be there," he said, and shoved past Fraser and Ross.

The elaborate code of silence that surrounds stupid endeavors had worked flawlessly, even though almost everybody in their flight knew about the challenge. Both men were still on the schedule, both sat stolidly in the early-morning briefing, and both had worked out fake flight plans that they would not use. As they walked out the door, Kelly said to Brown, "I'll be coming from the west." Then he'd scooped up his gear and stalked out to the silver P-80.

As he strapped in, Kelly felt like an idiot. That same stupid streak had trapped him again. He should have ignored Brown completely. He should steer clear of him and his crazy, gorgeous wife and just get on with getting his wings. After he'd left her, Kelly had tried to erase Joan from his memory. He felt both guilty and angry about that fouled-up night. He winced every time he recalled how he felt when he'd seen Duke's collar bar.

If Brown hadn't walked in when he was checking the flight board, he never would have slapped him with this dumbass stunt. Yet here he was again, putting it all on the line because he couldn't keep his goddamn mouth shut. He knew Joan hadn't told Brown, because Brown was the kind of guy who would have to come after Kelly as soon as he found out. Joan, he knew, would go to her grave without spilling it to Duke, or maybe anyone else.

As he waved his ground-start cart away and the power built in the engine, he felt no thrill, no fear, no apprehension. He just felt stupid. But he had to go through with it.

Kelly launched at 0800 precisely, just another one of the stream of almost a hundred planes that would cleave the desert air that morning. He stooged around a while on his phony flight plan, doing the navigation problem that was the ostensible purpose of the flight. Then, when the chronometer on the panel told him it was 0820, he banked the swift little fighter into a steep turn, dove, and headed for the canyon. The adrenaline came now, and in gallons. His hands sweated through the thin goatskin gloves as he scanned the horizon for the canyon.

The Arroyo Seco canyon stretched like a wound in the desert. It opened up from a river bed 150 miles to the east, growing into a five-hundred-foot-deep, three-hundred-foot-wide canyon for twenty miles in the middle, then dwindling back to a river bed 150 miles to the west, as if the whole thing had been some embarrassing mistake, a burp of nature.

As he orbited over its entrance, Kelly realized that the guesswork would be more critical than the timing. They'd be approaching each other at two fifty or three hundred miles per hour, five to six hundred m.p.h. closing speed, so the whole affair might all too easily wind up with them sandwiched in a cube of aluminum on the canyon floor. The way to avoid that was to start on the canyon floor. That way, Brown would have to pass clean over him. And if he didn't—well, he'd figure out something else when the time came. He hoped Brown was just too chicken to play real chicken.

Brown approached the mouth of the canyon resolutely, as he had approached flying itself. He looked on the challenge as an appointment in Samara. In a way, he was relieved, for the fear that for more than a year had filled his mouth with bile was now material. This was the day. Good. He'd fly midway down the canyon, at midheight; that way he'd have a prayer of seeing and avoiding. And if he couldn't, then that eternal nightmare of flaming death and shrieking pain would end at last.

At 0829, Kelly selected Echo channel and mashed the mike button: "Okay. You there?"

"Here. Let's get it over with." Brown's voice was clear and calm in his helmet earphones.

Kelly's mouth was dry. He adjusted the rubber oxygen mask and hit the mike again. "Okay. Start your run now." He thought about adding something dramatic. But nothing came to mind. He concentrated on flying and lined up on the scar in the desert.

The two silver P-80s let down about thirty miles apart, out of sight of each other, but each in view of the brand new T-33, a two-seat P-80, orbiting above Los Felices. The flight commander was there, tuned in on Echo channel, watching to see what happened. Every man a tiger, like the slogan said, but a little common sense never hurt.

Kelly hurtled along the canyon floor, his mounting fear surprisingly matched by mounting enjoyment of the sensations of streaking along only a few feet above the ground. And of something else. Something primal, something buried deep in his ancient ancestors' hunting past. He snaked the bulletlike P-80 around the curves of the canyon, eyes opened wide to catch the first telltale glimpse of the opposing fighter, trying to stay clear of the canyon walls.

At 0831 exactly, a silver blur passed one hundred feet overhead. Both pilots pulled up in an arcing loop, both half-rolled and dove, then both sloppily pulled up again not in range to do any damage if they'd had 75 mm cannon on board.

Kelly craned his neck, looking for Brown. The fear was gone. So was Brown.

Duke flew straight and level, breathing hard, blinking sweat from his eyes, trying to get his heart under control. He had done it. Nothing would ever be impossible for him in an airplane again.

The flight commander laughed aloud at the clumsy tactics. He watched the two wander around the sky, then mashed down on his mike button. "Richthofens you guys ain't. Now form up on me over Los Felices and maybe I can teach you something."

Abashed, Kelly and Brown spotted the silver jet in the clear blue morning sky, and formed up in trail behind the commander. Brown formated last, and when he was behind Kelly's jet, punched his mike and told the C.O. he was there.

The flight commander immediately peeled off in an inverted diving turn, exhorting them to stay with him. He took them on a long, involved rat race, rolling endlessly around the Arizona desert, until both Kelly and Brown were drenched in sweat. Then Kelly's fuel warning lights flashed on, and he called, "Red Leader, I've got to go back. Low fuel." His voice was a little less than perfectly steady.

"Check your nine o'clock, Red Baron," the leader said, mirth undisguised. Kelly dipped his left wing and saw Williams's net of runways spread out about five miles away. He flushed under his helmet, glad that nobody could see him turn red.

The leader waggled his wings. "Okay, heroes. Let's enter with a little dignity, then I want to see both of you in my office at sixteen hundred hours. Class A uniforms."

After they landed, the dumb-stunt code was still in effect. Everybody knew, everybody smirked, but nobody said anything. Brown parked a hundred yards away from Kelly and Kelly was glad he did. They spent the day with their separate devils, Kelly trying to finish up the math portions of his curriculum, wondering if he had blown it, and Brown doing the same. Fear more awful than that they'd felt in the canyon gnawed at both of them.

The 1600 showdown in the C.O.'s office was an anticlimax. He didn't want to run them through an inquisition. He was delighted to have aggressive boys in his flight. What he wanted was for them to kiss and make up. They went through the motions. When they were done shaking hands, Kelly knew that he would make it, that there was nothing now to stop his wings. He also knew something else.

He was no longer invisible to Charles Kingston Brown.

1930 LOCAL
2 December 1949
Columbus, Ohio
USA

How could James Thurber have been so funny, and been born in a desolate desert of a town like Columbus, Ohio? Kathy Campbell glared glumly out her dormitory window across the campus, the wind sweeping clouds of leaves inanely from one pile to the next.

"Damn damn damn damn all men and damn all football players and damn all soldiers." She didn't cry often and would not now, though it would have helped. She was twenty years old, a junior in liberal arts, and had just been dropped by the second love of her life. Obviously, something dreadful was wrong with her. She couldn't do anything right. Except get decent grades, of course, and who the heck cared about that?

Kathy got up and went to the mirror. She might as well have been crying; her face was puffy and her lipstick smeared from Nick's rough kiss of goodbye. A red swelling blossomed on her nose, and a sty seemed to be forming on her eye. She ran both hands through her shock of blond hair, glancing at herself in rage and self-pity.

She wondered about the whole process of just getting along. She was popular enough, always had dates, but still had not come to grips with the fact that the game she had been told she should play, enticing but not surrendering, was the exact opposite of the game of those with whom she was playing. For the first two years of college she had been systematically told by every boy she had dated that she was a prude, that she should control her own body, that lovemaking was natural, and that denying them was unnatural, since it gave them the unendurable pain of the stonies. She had enjoyed the petting and hated the arguing.

Last year her own needs had asserted themselves, and she gave herself up willfully and joyously to a giant lovable oaf of a football player without any thought of the future or the past. She never dated an athlete, avoided them in fact, but Fred Rose, a big, blond, handsome varsity end, had grinned at her in class and she surrendered. She fell immediately and literally head over heels in love with him and gave him all she had to offer, her devotion and her virginity.

Once that formality was over she tried to make up for lost time, running risks to couple with him in the backs of cars, on the team bus, in the locker room, a phone booth, a stairwell, almost anywhere but a proper bed. She had broken the relationship off when she found that Fred had played end wide enough to have at least two other girls providing the same services. He regarded sex just as an extension of the training table, an athlete's prerogative. When Kathy turned on him in fury, he was perplexed, grinned amiably, and forgot about her. She was both angered and relieved. On the one hand Fred had been a numbskull and shouldn't have been able to deceive her. On the other, on the question of virginity, to give or not to give had apparently been solved.

Until this year, when she met Nick. He was a veteran, an ex-Army captain, ex-infantry, kind, gentle, and refusable. Small and dark, with a sexy shrapnel wound that had sliced a collop from his left bicep, he had every quality Fred lacked. She did enough detective work to make sure he wasn't dating other girls. Like the other veterans at Ohio State, he was preoccupied with driving the curve of the test scores up, and when he wasn't with her he was in the library. She responded to his intensity and sensitivity with the same passion with which she had responded to Fred's slavering and the eternal bulge in his trousers. Yet she had been afraid to let Nick sleep with her, or even submit while parking as she had always done with Fred. She had been afraid to let him learn she was not a virgin. He had asked her point blank on their third date, and she had unhesitatingly lied.

The pressure had built. He was persistent and demanding in his gentle style; he obviously cared for her. Yet in some convoluted way she thought she was playing it smart this time, keeping him at a distance.

But today it had ended. With his customary attention to detail he had made all the arrangements to drive to Springfield, where a friend had lent him a cabin on a lake for the weekend. No one would know where they were. He had been very firm. Either she slept with him or they broke up. It was too firm, too cold: she felt she had to resist, and she resisted with the stupidest of arguments. She said she was saving herself for her marriage. His reply had been, "I don't think Fred Rose is going to marry you." Then he'd kissed her and left. He had known all along, and she felt like a damn fool. It must have angered him to know that she had given herself to Fred and refused him. How stupid of her.

That was it. No more boyfriends while she was in college. She'd date, but not steadily. She wasn't going to go through this again. No more football players, no more G.I.s, maybe a nice quiet English major.

Unfortunately, odds were that even an English major would have sex on his mind, and she had just gone zero for two. The infuriating thing had been that her mother had been right both times. She had warned her about Fred, sizing him up in a single meeting at the beginning of the football season. Kathy had brought Nick home for the Easter holidays, and her mother gave every indication that if Kathy didn't latch on to him, she herself would try. Things were far too strained and conventional for her mother to even hint at the role of sex in courting, but she gave clear signals that Nick was an acceptable son-in-law, no matter what it took.

It had been tough to refuse Nick; she'd grown to enjoy love-making, even the rough and tumble, usually alfresco style, of Fred Rose, and she had responded intensely to Nick. But she had outsmarted herself.

There was always the possibility of calling him back; she still had a book, *Guard of Honor*, he had pressed on her. She could call him and agree to play it his way. Yet she knew instinctively that the game was over. If he came back, it would be to use her, and to move on. It was time to take a look at the long haul.

The problem was that all the solutions looked bad. The last thing she wanted to do was get married, even to Nick; she'd been born in Cleveland, and here she was going to college in Columbus. Her life was Ohio-bound. She had to travel. Some of the girls had exercised the other option, gone along with the prevailing crude male argument of use it or lose it; but she saw that they had only exchanged one set of problems for another, including the maddening risk of pregnancy. That was the only really absolute rule, don't get pregnant, because if you did it meant only one thing, marriage to whomever you could stick with the paternity. She'd heard about abortions, but only in the same terms that she heard about marijuana, as desperate and degenerate.

She looked in the mirror again. No more soldiers, no more football players. She was going to leave them and Ohio behind when she graduated.

1020 LOCAL
9 January 1950
Luke AFB, Arizona
USA

Kelly tossed his bags down on the spare little bed in the BOQ and looked around. So this was it. The life of an officer and a gentleman, a fighter pilot. He stepped to the small mirror and looked at himself again, as he had been doing ever since graduation and commissioning.

There they were. The silver wings on his breast, the little gold bar on his collar.

Second Lt. Michael McManus Kelly, USAF. He could still hardly believe it. He took the Zippo out and set it on the bare top of the metal bureau. The engraving still looked great under the little sterling silver wings.

Nobody in East St. Louis had quite believed it either. Bud Drummond had eyed him suspiciously when he'd pulled in with his brand-new Chevy Styline Deluxe convertible and asked for a fill-up. Finally he'd recognized Kelly and grinned his gap-toothed redneck grin.

Nobody at the Kelly household had smiled much. Dad was

dying, that was obvious. Mother was folding up like a card table. He saw with bitterness that the money he'd been sending home was indeed going for whiskey. Mike had wandered the streets for a week of his long leave and suddenly decided he had to get out. The only consolation he'd had was when he happened to see Francis Engle, Jr., at the Walgreen's. Engle had stared at Kelly in his snappy khakis and simply sputtered. Mike had turned to go and made sure the little twerp had seen those silver wings, then hopped in the green Chevy and laid a patch.

So long, East St. Louis.

Hello, Luke AFB, and gunnery school. The only snag was that Duke Brown was here too. But Kelly had learned his lesson. From here on out, he was going to stay as far as possible from Duke and Joan Brown. Kelly had not seen them since the commissioning and graduation ceremony back at Williams.

The commissioning ceremony had been simple and austere, the cadets being transformed into officers by a trip across a hastily built bunting-draped stage at the flight line. It was totally unlike the climactic flying scenes of *I Wanted Wings* or any other Hollywood treatment of flying school, with no long V-formation of trainers flying overhead, no passing parade of airpower. The commandant pinned their wings on with a quick-stick gimmick that required fixing later, and handed them the certificate of graduation and commission. A handshake and salute and it was over.

The officers had preceded them across the stage, and predictably, Brown's father was there, in uniform, dominating the proceeding and smiling as Joan pinned Duke's wings on. King Brown was there too, having flown in the day previously in a B-25. Kelly watched the Brown show with no envy. For him, alone and glad to be alone, the ceremony had been as pure as the ordination of a priest. He felt the weight of those silver wings as if they were a gold crucifix.

The two groups, student officers and cadets, were ranked separately. Brown, to his immense chagrin, had placed second to a laughing giant of a Texan who had dominated every aspect of the program. Kelly was delighted to have been eighth in a field of two hundred twenty. He had done well academically and in flying, but they had—correctly—said that his military deportment was less than perfect, and that had cost him. Once he had that certificate, it simply didn't matter.

Kelly savored the moments after commissioning. His first task was to separate himself from the milling crowds of jubilant ex-cadets, and find an enlisted man to give him his first salute. He had a brand-new dollar bill in his wallet, and he wanted the traditional salute from a master sergeant, not just any airman. He positioned himself outside the flight shack, avoiding the crowds of airmen who waited to pick up a few dollars from the delighted new second lieutenants, watching for fat, jovial Master Sergeant Bellapianta to appear, en route to his inevitable morning stoking of doughnuts and coffee. Bellapianta came down the steps and Kelly darted out; the NCO snapped a salute and stuck out his hand to shake Kelly's. It came back with a dollar bill in it, and both men were happy.

Two weeks before he had fulfilled the first of many fantasies of solvency at Lauterstein's Tailors. He wanted a complete set of uniforms, exactly like Brown's, before he reported to his next assignment. Lauterstein's had the great virtue of putting everything on the tab, and Kelly enjoyed the return visits for fittings. It was the first time he'd bought anything that was not off the rack, and evoked college memories of his single cheap tweed suit when he, in monumental error, rushed Phi Delta Theta. He felt foolish being measured for the enveloping blue greatcoat in the sweltering Arizona heat, but he was going for broke. In hock but for broke.

The final action after commissioning was a consecration, the consummation of thirteen months of planning, of three months of choosing, and several days of talking to Davie Costello, a Chevrolet salesman. There was waiting, for immediate delivery to Second Lt. Michael McManus Kelly, a light green 1950 Chevrolet Deluxe convertible, powered by a 92-horsepower "stovebolt" six-cylinder engine that Kelly knew very well, since it was scarcely different from the one that had wheezily powered his 1931 sedan. The car listed for a mind-boggling $2,676 but Costello had cut him a deal for $2,400 even, and the promise to buy his next car from him, no matter where he was stationed.

Mike took a single step and glanced out the BOQ window. The Chevy was still there too, parked in the BOQ parking lot. His gaze rested a moment on the little white sign with the black letters that stood like a sentry at the entrance to the parking lot.

OFFICERS ONLY, it read. He smiled and began unpacking.

Duke and Joan rolled through Riverside in silence. She stared out the windows of the Olds, fascinated by the strange scenery. California was more beautiful than she imagined, despite all that Duke had told her about it; it was a combination of austere desert plants, Spanish tiles and adobes, and the helter-skelter aggressiveness of fast-buck developers throwing up housing everywhere there was room.

Like Joan, Brown enjoyed the drive, but his thoughts were elsewhere. He was thinking of the irony of pulling down an assignment in an F-86 squadron, something that most guys, Kelly especially, would have traded their souls for. He felt nothing but numbness.

The feeling didn't change as he drove up to the ornate March Field entrance, a relic of the Depression, when it had been a major Civilian Conservation Corps resource, and the strength and energy of mobilized youth had been put to work building roads and gardens. At most bases the entry point was usually no more than an oversized phone booth; here they did things well, with a Spanish-style gatehouse guarding the entrance. Brown approved when the sentry snapped a crisp salute after he produced his I.D. card. His father had always said that the initial reception at a gate was a symbol of conditions on base. March AFB was obviously going to be squared-away.

The air policeman pulled out a mimeographed map that showed him where the BOQ was. He seemed eager to please the new lieutenant and his pretty young bride. "They have quarters for you until you're settled, ma'am. Lieutenant, there's a note here for you; looks like you were expected today." He handed a sealed envelope to Brown.

It was from Major Daugherty, executive officer to the wing commander, General Herrity. Through Daugherty, Herrity extended his compliments and requested Brown's presence at nine the following morning.

The note was another good sign. Herrity had worked for Duke's father years ago, and his brother was a staffer for Dade in Washington. Duke felt, finally, a sense of homecoming.

The BOQ was a letdown, a made-over barracks that had been

roughly partitioned so that two married couples could have some privacy, if sharing the common G.I. latrine at the end of the hallway counted as privacy. But there was no other couple in the building.

The thin walls did not keep out the raucous noise of the young pilots coming back from a duty day, raising hell, waking sleepers with loud cries of "Piss Call!" and doing all the other juvenile things they'd come to hate with more service and maturity. But Duke slept well, inured by his years at West Point, and was ready to go at six, as usual.

He took Joan to the officers' club for their first on-base breakfast, and was a little surprised that the waiter service had been suspended for breakfast. Instead they went through a cafeteria line served by a sullen woman who dispensed glares to the patrons and hairs into the scrambled eggs with equal magnanimity. It wasn't the breakfast of a lifetime, and he was glad to escape back to his BOQ room to put a final gloss on his shoes.

When he was ushered into Herrity's office at nine on the dot, Herrity greeted him with real warmth, then came directly to the point. "I'm glad you're here, Duke. I've been following your career through your brother. The fact is, I need an aide with your background, and I'd like you to be it. But there's something you ought to know before you decide."

"Whatever it is, doesn't make any difference, General. I'd be honored to be your aide."

"Not so fast! Maybe not; you're a young hot rock ready to get your hands on an F-86. This is the first operational unit to get 'em, and I know how hard you worked to get here. But frankly, the time for fighters is past, Duke. I'm going to SAC HQ in Omaha, and then I'm going to get a bomber wing. B-47s are as hot as the 86s, and they're the wave of the future in the Air Force. I want to go with them, and I'd like you to come along with me." The enormous flow of relief that washed over Duke must have looked like disappointment. Herrity hurried on.

"Look here, Duke. You're not obligated, of course. I know how badly you want 86s—hell, who wouldn't? If you want to stay on with them a year, maybe we can swing it then."

Duke sensed the need for extreme caution. He had to play this exactly right. He was supposed to want the hotrod F-86 more than anything, and bombers were supposed to be a joke to pilots like he was supposed to be. He hesitated a moment. "No, sir. If you're going to 47s, that's good enough for me. I don't know much about the airplane, but I think you're right, strategically

98

and tactically. The next time we go at it, it'll be from a distance, and the 86s are range-limited. Besides, from what I've heard from King, the 47 is one hot ship too." He strove to keep his voice brave, a soldier taking his disappointment for the good of the service.

Herrity beamed, and they shook hands. Duke could hardly contain himself through the small talk of sorting out their schedules; when they would leave, what the prospects were. He felt as if a spring had unwound in him. He was out of that goddamned aluminum coffin, relieved—maybe forever!—of having to be the eager fighter pilot having to put his balls on the bar every day. He could manage a staff job, and get enough flying to satisfy a career.

As he walked out into the radiant morning, his cheer was only dampened by how disappointed he knew Joan would be. She'd been enchanted with California. Omaha was quite a different matter. But she'd be a good soldier. She had no alternative.

1830 LOCAL
15 May 1950
Luke AFB, Arizona
USA

Kelly tossed *From Here to Eternity* on to the bed. After hearing everyone rave about it, he'd picked up a copy and was mildly disappointed. Its gutty four-letter words had caused a sensation, but he knew the language was only a shadow of the real thing. If you couldn't use *fuck* four times in a sentence, you weren't trying. Still, getting it at the base library had introduced him to a library system far better than any he'd ever known before, at least outside of college. In the old East St. Louis library a new book was a treasure; it just didn't make sense to the mayor to waste money on books when it could simply be pocketed.

He glanced around his BOQ room, surprised at the growth in his possessions. He had a radio and a record player, with a small collection of albums, mostly classical. In the closet were two sport coats, a civilian suit, and a pair of civilian shoes. Under the bed was a bottle of whiskey and a bottle of gin. It made him feel comfortable to have these things. He liked them, and liked the fact of his having them, much as he liked Luke Air Force Base, the girls in town, and the girls in the border towns. The only thing he didn't like was being an instructor.

For good reason. He was a lousy instructor. Kelly wanted to fly the airplane, not sit in the back seat and worry about some kid killing him. Worse, he was not consistent, varying from being too harsh to too lenient, aware that it was the personality of the student that drove the variation. If he liked the pilot, it was easy to be fair, and to give deserved praise or criticism. If he sensed that the pilot was a wise guy, or too self-assured, or worse of all, too rich, he was rough on him. If the pilot was unsure, diffident, and perhaps obviously getting by on his salary, he was too easy. Lieutenant Gunston settled the issue.

They had an early Friday morning mission, and Gunston had come in early and eager, as usual. He was an easygoing young Californian, hair sun bleached, full of talk about the sand and surf. Kelly had watched him on the ball field; he was an accomplished athlete, but a marginal pilot; Kelly knew within the first few flights that Gunston was on the ragged edge of proficiency, not bad enough to rate a series of downchecks, but never quite up to par. Yet he burned with the desire to fly, with the same sort of desperate intensity that Mike knew so well, so he kept him on long past the point where he should have been busted out of fighters and sent off to drive Gooney Birds somewhere.

It was the last mission in the training syllabus for Gunston, a makeup of a cross-country flight he had aborted for weather earlier in the year. Kelly's biggest concern for the young pilot was his instrument flying ability. He never seemed to be in complete control, chasing the instruments, never getting them pinned down, drifting back and forth across the heading lines, altitudes, airspeeds.

After Gunston took off, time passed slowly for Kelly. He methodically read the Pilot's Information File, a task he hated, updated his tech orders, all the busywork that never got done. Kelly kept watching the big electric clock on the wall; Gunston had taken off an hour and a half earlier, and had not checked in over his turn points. In another ten minutes, he'd be down for lack of fuel somewhere. Kelly cursed himself for letting him go; it was a clear case of neglect on his part. He had Gunston's records in front of him, and the obvious ambivalent comments— "Needs further work" or "Some improvement"—the extra flights, the repeated instruction in basics, all told the story. And now he was probably down, smeared across the Nevada desert.

"What are you doing here, Kelly? I thought all your students were finished." Crane, the ops officer, wanted to get away to an early lunch, and looked annoyed.

Finished. Man, that's the wrong word, Kelly thought.

"No sir, I've got one jaybird out there on a make-up cross country, apparently lost. If I don't hear something in the next ten minutes, I'm going to report him missing to the Command Center, and get a search launched."

Crane groaned. "Maybe he landed somewhere. Did you check around?"

"Yeah, I had them call everywhere, Williams, Las Vegas, Barstow; he hasn't checked in with anybody."

The ten minutes ran out with no word. The entire search-and-rescue apparatus began to lumber into being. Crews were alerted, aircraft preflighted, and the first search plane was on the end of the runway, prepared to takeoff, when the cancellation came in. Gunston had gotten lost and landed at Nellis, forgetting to close his flight plan. A smart line chief had spotted the Luke tail numbers when he heard the rumble that a plane was down.

On Monday, Kelly volunteered for duty in the Far Eastern Air Force, at any station, anywhere. His squadron C.O. accepted his papers with mixed feelings; Kelly was a good pilot, but a loner. He might be better off in an operational unit.

The assignment came through in four weeks to the 48th Fighter Bombing Wing at Yokota, Japan. Once again the Air Force was good to him, even if it meant putting the Chevy up on blocks for a while.

1900 LOCAL
30 March 1951
Offutt AFB, Nebraska
USA

To Duke's genuine surprise, King Brown had been furious with Duke's decision to go with Herrity.

"You're pushing it, kid," he said in his grave big-brother voice. "You should have gotten the F-86 squadron experience under your belt before becoming a headquarter's weenie. You'll be the low-time green bean in a job you got because somebody knows your old man. That's the kiss of death in SAC."

Duke felt the old resentment well up. King had told him how to do everything. How to steal third base, how to tie his Boy Scout knots, how to use a rubber, all with the same condescending tone. Would he never get away from it? He kept it all out of

101

his voice when he replied. "I don't think so, King. If Herrity gets a B-47 wing, I can jump on the jet bomber bandwagon. You're project officer on the B-47; looks like you'd want me in on them." It was the respectful taunt, part of the formula.

"It's a question of timing," King said, ignoring the taunt. "You should have put a year in fighters, maybe two, and gotten some experience. With your pull you'd probably gotten to be an acting flight commander or something. The B-47's going to be slow getting off the ground; it's just too complicated and advanced. And it's going to be around for a long time, so you could have afforded to wait. Besides, there are a whole bunch of development problems with it, and I expect the fleet to be grounded periodically for the next couple of years until we sort them out. There's no money in it for you to be a fifth wheel in a bomber unit that doesn't have any bombers flying."

As happened so often in their lives, they were arguing about two different things. King was talking careers, and Duke was talking escaping fighters. As usual, King turned out to be exactly right about the B-47s, which were already mired in production and modification difficulties.

More important, the outbreak of war in Korea had overstressed SAC's capabilities. LeMay's efforts had not yet had time to take effect when the "police action" forced the full weight of effort to be placed on dragging old B-29s out of mothballs, and old B-29 crew members out of retirement and into combat. Even Herrity himself got lost in the shuffle.

Duke saw a way out when a notice came around calling for volunteers to fly B-26s out of Japan into Korea, and Duke jumped at it. He'd heard too many stories about the problems with B-29s, and he didn't want to be a low-time B-29 copilot to some retread refugee from World War II. The B-26 had a tremendous reputation for being a safe, tough aircraft, and he liked the idea of flying with a crew, but without another pilot looking over his shoulder.

This second swift shift in career plans managed to make everyone, including his father, mother, brother, General Herrity, and Joan, angry with him. Yet he felt good that he was calling the shots at last, that he was managing his career, even if it was not the way King wanted him to.

In fact, that King was opposed to it made it all the sweeter. King, after all, had already gotten his combat ticket punched. Duke had not. And while Korea wasn't much of a war, it was, as they reminded themselves constantly, the only one they had.

Book Two

FLYING
HIGH

6

He'd always thought the worst fear would seize him in the air, in combat, but Duke's biggest scare came one night in the BOQ. The buildings that were pressed into service as BOQs were spartan, built of wood and stuccoed over with mud. They'd been hastily thrown up as dependent housing for the families of the members of General MacArthur's Occupation Force, but with the war they were turned over to the expanding combat units. The volte-face suited the craziness of the war itself, which was still being called a police action.

The tiny room Duke shared with a hawk-faced captain, John Tullot, symbolized the whole affair. Tullot had pinned up on his side of the room three items: a calendar, with each day successfully passed marked carefully with a huge red x; a photo of his ex-wife and kids, and a Bill Mauldin cartoon, torn from an old copy of *Yank*, in which Joe and Willie were sitting on a wrecked German gun, watching a line of fresh-faced troops march toward the front. Tullot had neatly sliced off Mauldin's caption for the cartoon, leaving the line drawing as a kind of enigmatic art. Duke never asked him why he put it up. Just as he never asked anybody to come back to their room and paint over the little drawing scrawled in purple crayon on the wall next to his bed, a drawing obviously put there by the dependent kid whose room this had been, a drawing overlooked in the rebuilding of the kid's house into a BOQ for combat crew. It was the last thing Duke looked at every night and the first he saw each morning. He had come to like its awkward slashes, its exuberance, its innocence. Just as he had come to know the sullen Tullot's moods.

Tullot was a retread, a reserve pilot who had been called back from a job he apparently liked a lot. Duke never asked what the job was, and Tullot never told him. All Duke knew about Tullot was that he was not a career man—and therefore not important in the long run—and that he was a fine B-26 combat pilot, with a distinguished record in the last war. Because of the former,

105

Duke was able to use the latter to his own advantage, squeezing Tullot gently for every bit of operational information the captain possessed. So even when Tullot drank too much—as he was doing tonight—Duke listened to him.

"You wanna know something, Brown?" he asked. Duke laid down his logbook and nodded.

"I made a gear-up landing today in 4581. Did you see it?"

"No, I wasn't back yet, but I hear you did a great job. Chief said they're supposed to have it back flying in two or three weeks."

"Christ, I hope not. I did the same thing in the same airplane in France in late 1944. Same goddamn 4581. Can you beat that, it acted the same goddamn way, the gear just sat there, nothing I could do to get it down, emergency system didn't work. It was locked up tighter than a drum. Same way, both wars. I hope the sonofabitch never flies again. It'll kill me in the next war."

In spite of himself, Duke was impressed. "No kidding, same airplane, same tail number?"

"Same airplane. I checked my logbook. I thought I recognized that murderous bastard. It was the same thing all over. I dumped the gear and nothing happened and I couldn't make nothing happen."

Brown wanted to make him feel better, to get his mind off the subject. Tullot was increasingly cranky lately, and as long as he was Brown's roommate, Duke wanted him either cheerful or quiet. "Well, things must be better nowadays; we don't seem to be standing short on anything, do we?"

There was a whistling sound, like a rocketing pheasant, as Tullot tossed the bottle of Scotch against the red-hot pot-bellied stove. It exploded and a flash of flame burst in a ball as the alcohol burned. Duke winced.

"You stupid shit, you don't have any idea how to fight a war the right way. We ain't got shit out here, and we ain't getting any. Let me tell you what we're missing. One: we are missing decent airplanes; we're flying clapped-out old crocks with two thousand hours on a one-thousand-hour airframe. Two: we ain't even got enough of them. In the last war you could draw a new squadron in twenty-four hours; you can't get a goddamn rudder replaced in less than six weeks here. Three: we don't have any decent forward controllers. In France those guys would call out individual tanks, trucks, and if it was dull, little old ladies on bicycles, and the goddamn fighters would have to take a number to play. Four: we don't have the engineering capability. Christ,

106

our tanks used to advance thirty miles; next day there'd be two or three runways dozed, PSP'd, ready to go, with a mobile radio unit right up in the goddamn front lines, and all the flak protection you could stand. I used to get more hits from flak droppings our guys were shooting in the wind than I'd get from the goddamn Germans. The Germans never bothered us unless they had to."

Tullot looked mournfully at the residue of Scotch drying up by the stove.

"Five, and worst of all: you young guys don't know anything about fighting a war. You're willing to make do with any goddamn thing, dropping bombs on one-horse railways, shooting up coolies. You don't know nothing."

Duke considered it. His first instinct was to dismiss the diatribe. After all, anybody experiencing the situation Tullot had just gone through would be jangled. The same airplane trying to kill you the same way twice. Who wouldn't be a little buzzed?

As he watched Tullot scowl at the stove, wrestling with his own demons, Duke began to feel a chill himself. Not because of the possibility of death in combat, but because of the implications of Tullot's analysis of their real status in Korea. It had simply never occurred to Duke that coming here, doing this, was not the right thing to do.

Yet the fact that SAC let Duke go showed clearly how low he was on the totem pole. He had known that, of course, and used the fact to his advantage, in pursuit of his combat tour in B-26s. He had avoided going back to F-86s through the pull he had so carefully cultivated with the base personnel office.

It had all been planned. Brown had taken the trouble to check out in the multi-engine aircraft down at Base Flight, flying the C-45, C-47, and B-25 on weekends. He put on the image of the pilot in love with flying while desperately trying to exorcise his fears through sheer familiarity. It all proved prudent. When he got to Perrin Air Force Base in Texas for six weeks' transition training, he had no difficulty with the sweet-flying B-26.

At Langley, during the four months' combat crew training, he discovered something new in himself, a plus factor he had never expected. He absolutely reveled in having a crew depending upon him. There was something intoxicating about the total trust the navigator/bombardier and the gunner placed in him. It was his team, he was its captain, and the pleasure it gave him more than offset the continued lurking fear of flight.

When he went to Ashiya, to fly with the Third Bomb Group,

he was proud of his two fine crew members. An easy-going giant, Lt. Jim Middlebrook was his nav/bombardier. Like Tullot he had served on B-29s during the war, and concealed his resentment at being recalled to duty as admirably as Tullot did not. Sgt. Clayton Whiteside, the gunner, was as small as Middlebrook was large, a soft-spoken man from Tennessee who'd never fire any guns but would serve for all practical purposes as Duke's flight engineer.

The Third had distinguished itself immediately when the North Koreans had stormed across the border, operating from the start in groups of twelve, later in whatever numbers could be mustered. Early on they established their aggressive tactics, bombing railyards near the 38th Parallel at Munsan, then dropping down as they turned southward, strafing targets of opportunity.

When Duke arrived, he was given a few routine familiarization flights, then turned loose. He didn't encounter any fighter opposition at first, although the flak was severe, and there were continual losses. He lost two roommates he'd never had a chance to meet, shot down on their first missions.

It occurred to him almost in passing that he was less frightened flying combat than he had been in training. The fact that people depended on him made the difference. The weather was abominable, and at the business end of the mission there was flak which varied from the annoying to the frightful, but it didn't matter; people depended upon him.

He was halfway through his combat tour when he realized that he had begun to love the physical side of flying, that combination of disagreeable things that weave into a fascinating challenge. He tried to analyze it, and concluded that it was because he was at last out from under the baleful glare of his father's inspector general's eye, and the always mildly disapproving presence of his brother.

He was bemused to find that he relished sitting at the end of the runway at about thirty-five thousand pounds gross weight, watching all the instruments settle into position, feeling the boot in the ass when the throttles came forward, and then that sweet relationship when the sky closed in and there was nothing but him, the instruments, the radio, and the mission. The checklists and the tech orders were bibles, and compliance was fulfilling. It was a discipline different from the giving and taking of markers, of watching who was talking to whom, of playing the career game, the political game he loved so well.

Even the radio process was fascinating, reassuring, his key to the passage from his crew to the outside world. You were passed from positive reinforcing hand to positive reinforcing hand until actually launched into the combat area itself. When you returned, you were again shepherded from point to point all the way back to your own sand-bagged revetment. He had seen *Fantasia* years ago, and he was Stokowski to the orchestra of the Air Force; the B-26 was his baton.

He was not so stupid as to be fully secure. He still got scared when flak suddenly ranged them, bucking the aircraft, sometimes rattling its sides with shrapnel. He was petrified, when on their fifth mission takeoff the big R-2800 engine at his left froze with a shudder that damn near tossed them into the water off the end of the runway. When the danger was over, when the fear subsided, then the satisfaction returned.

Suddenly confronted with the truth of Tullot's summary of their real position, the fear slammed home like an icy knife into his heart. He had been enjoying the war as the other pilots had, as myopic as they; in love with the flying, insensitive to the dying. But now—the sense of satisfaction he had cultivated so carefully shattered like Tullot's bottle of Scotch. He felt a profound sense of shock at the realization that he had been gullible. He, of all men!

He had never concerned himself with the morality of the conflict. There was combat; it involved the Air Force; and in the Air Force, combat equated with promotion. Period. Yet now Duke felt betrayed. How could they do this to him? He had never expected anything but self-interest from anyone, above or below him, but Tullot's truth took his breath away.

American military men always fought with the best. It was gospel at the Point, and underlay everything that was happening in the States. The jets, the new bombers, everything pointed toward that truth. Yet here he was in a kid's bedroom, and every day he flew an airplane that should have been junked five years ago.

They did not have the best. He knew it now, and saw it as he had steadfastly ignored it before. Worse than that, they not only did not have the best, they had almost nothing. They were expected to fly and die in junk. Why?

Duke lay back on his olive-drab blanket and stared at the ceiling, sweating despite the chill in the room. They were being used. They flew brilliantly, they did their jobs and didn't ask questions, and somebody was benefiting.

It wasn't Tullot. It wasn't Duke.

The Mauldin cartoon drew his gaze as he wrestled with the implications. After a moment, he thought he saw something in it, and around that something coalesced his defense against the awful betrayal.

His plan was a simple one. It took into account all the facts, including the new ones Tullot had revealed to him.

Fact one: he was trapped into being here and flying these junk heaps. Having so rashly irritated all his closest advisers and sponsors, he had to endure this until they sent him home. He could not try to get out of it. With this combat tour, he could hold his own against anyone in the coming years. Without it, he would be left behind. And the fact that everyone knew how miserable conditions were here, the fact that he would be seen to relish those conditions and excel in them would add luster to his standing.

And he needed that standing to make Fact Two work. He would not allow Tullot's final indictment of him—"You don't know nothing!"—to be true in the next war.

In the next war, he would know. He would know, specifically, that he would not be fighting in it. He would be the one benefiting. He would be the one wearing the eagles or stars. In the next war, he would be in Washington, and some other Tullot would be out here, trying to land 4581 gear-up again.

Tullot began snoring. At any other time, on any other night, Duke would have been annoyed. Tonight, he simply smiled. And the fear again dissolved.

1456 LOCAL
5 October 1951
Korea

Sky and earth merged, gray-black above and gray-green below, spliced by unending rain and broken only softly by the rolling hill horizon. A spare winking of gunfire, red collapsing into black, marked the village from the rice paddies.

Kelly kept turning, his eyes moving from the cluster of rude huts to his instrument panel to the flight of four silver Mustangs forming up in a classic bombing-range pattern. Jim Garvey was leading the strike on this worthless "target of opportunity."

Kelly systematically scanned the little round dials that showed his P-80's wings cocked at a thirty-degree attitude, his speed and altitude constant. Moisture swirled outside the canopy in contin-

110

ually diverging rivulets, parting to the left and right yet seeming to drive through the clear plastic to run in condensed streams down the inside. The cockpit was strangely silent with the radios out; he would have welcomed the imperative stream of staccato comments that ordinarily filled the headset, crisp judgments of course and distance spiced with occasional coarse quips. Instead the stupid first lyrics of *If I Knew You Were Coming I'd Have Baked a Cake* kept running through his head; the Koreans knew they were coming, and it wouldn't be a cake they would bake.

The Mustangs turned and dove, sequential seals plunging to the bottom of the pearl-gray pool. Rockets from Garvey's plane leaped out, mixing a twisting white trail with the clouds; the others must have strafed with their fifty-caliber machine guns, but Kelly could not see it. Nor did the Mustangs see the heavy concentration of antiaircraft fire—37 mm probably—which came from a copse of trees a quarter mile east of the village and sawed the last fighter in two. Kelly watched it impact, sorry to see it go, glad not to know—or be—the man inside.

He brought the wings of the jet level, then counted to fifteen as he passed the village on the left, extending his line of flight out to permit a turn to attack the guns. Without communications, he would attack parallel to the path of the Mustangs, although he would have liked to have come in perpendicularly from the east, over the rise of hills bordering the polished-tin surface of the rice fields. This was his preferred war: alone, impersonal, inventive.

He armed the six fifty-caliber machine guns, turned and dove, his tips sluicing twin rooster tails of vapor back across the wing. He missed his wingman, who had left earlier with fuel problems.

The relative position of the gun emplacement was fixed by the crimson black tombstone billowing from the downed Mustang. At eight hundred feet above the ground he fired, watching his line of tracers walk mini-waterspouts up each side of the slim dike into the forlorn trees hiding the guns.

The North Koreans, professionals, had been ready with a second battery, eight hundred yards to the south of the first. They fired as Kelly fired, and the P-80 was shattered as it began to pull up at five hundred feet. A sudden clattering and the instruments tumbled. Black smoke poured into the cockpit, obscuring the red warning lights. Kelly jettisoned the canopy as the aircraft exploded, blowing him out of his seat. He pulled the D ring of his parachute, and was watching upward, waiting for the canopy when he hit the ground.

111

* * *

Sims's voice was guarded. "Yellow leader, the poor bastard' chute didn't open."

"Roger, Yellow Two." The combat adrenaline pumping ir Jim Garvey didn't permit him sorrow for Kelly, or for Winckler who'd gone in on the first pass. Later, back in his cot, it woul come.

"Yellow Two and Three, form up and make one last pass or the new flak site. Dump everything, then be ready to join up with me. I'm going down to take a look at the P-80 pilot if can."

It would be a good practice for Sims and Peden and he couldn't let Kelly go without one look, anyway. Against all rules Kelly had flown a solo top cover, and then made an attack on hi own initiative. Garvey eased the throttle back on the Mustang and when his speed bled off, dropped quarter flaps to help him maneuver around the hill line overlooking the fields where Kell must be lying. He brought the airspeed down as low as he dared making himself vulnerable to any flak, and began a series o gentle turns.

Kelly lay flat on his back, breath knocked out of him, the water of the rice paddy submerging all but his head. He wa unaccountably alive, even though his parachute had not ever streamed. He must have hit the water just right, his still-packed chute absorbing some of the shock. A miracle of hydraulics. He saw a Mustang dropping down, and he forced himself to rise an wave his arms.

Garvey pressed his helmet against the side of the Mustang' oilfilled canopy; he saw the man moving, thinking him a Korear soldier until he caught the flash of the yellow Mae West and the frantically flailing arms.

"That lucky sonofabitch lived. He actually lived." Garve cobbed the throttle forward, picked up his flaps, and called fo his flight to rejoin him. It was too dark for a rescue tonight, bu they would be there in the morning.

The smell and the cold brought Kelly around again; he though at first he was back in East St. Louis. He lay with his eyes shut stunned but not feeling pain, aware that heaven wouldn't smel so bad and hell wouldn't be so wet and cold. When he opened his eyes he assumed he was blind; the black sky squatted righ down to the edge of the dikes surrounding him. He moved hi arms, and then his legs, and with a rush of pain sat up to look

112

around. There was nothing. He rubbed the mud from his G.I. watch; the luminous hands were stopped at five o'clock. He must have been out for four or five hours. He dragged a wet handkerchief from the zippered knee pocket of his flying suit to swab the water from his ears. If he couldn't see, he must hear, for the North Korean soldiers would be looking for him. There wasn't a sound, and he eased himself toward the viscous smear of the dike to wait for morning. Kelly wondered if he'd really seen the Mustang and waved to it, or if that was just part of the jumbled dreams he'd been having.

The wet cold cut through him; shivering uncontrollably, he voided. He tried to think what he was going to do when the Koreans came; for the first time in three years he wished he were back home. Even the rank northwest winds from the stockyards would be preferable to the overpowering scent of human waste on the fields. And his cold tent back at K-2, six cots parked around a dinky coal stove, seemed wildly luxurious.

He dozed again despite the chill, awakening to a minimal dawn, a thin glint of light hurdling the dikes. He couldn't orient himself until he realized that the rise to his west was east of the gun emplacement; his fighter must have carried him above the hill before it blew up. That explained the absence of soldiers so far. Now they'd seek the wreckage, then look for him when they didn't find a body.

Kelly flexed his arms and legs; surviving a chuteless bailout was just one more gift from flight. The war wasn't going well from an overall point of view, but it was perfect for him, turned loose with his comrades day after day to do whatever they could to stop the North Koreans. Usually it was squirting truck convoys or the occasional train, but Kelly had caught two airplanes, a Yak-9 and a Sturmovik, and he felt he'd paid for his flight training expenses. It had been a perfect war up till today, and it wasn't over yet.

He wrapped himself in his traitorous chute in a futile attempt to get warm. To his west, the top of the hill was sunlit before the fields, and he saw the thin line of Korean soldiers before he heard the rifle shot and ricochet. They'd probably flushed some poor frigid rabbit for their stewpots. It sounded pretty good to Kelly, whose appetite never failed. He watched them move, methodically, searching each clump of grass, not worried that their dead man would run. Until the sound of Merlins broke the air.

Kelly looked up as first four, then eight Mustangs dropped

below the clouds and began to set up a pattern for strafing. The Korean riflemen immediately began firing and at the same time increased their pace down the hill; the Mustangs were obviously there for a reason. Kelly felt no elation yet; the lovely silver F-51s might delay the process, but they couldn't get him out. He was probably a little over a hundred miles north of the bomb line, too far for a rescue chopper. He unwrapped the chute to see if he could walk, and to be ready to signal.

As murky dawn stretched into misty day, he saw the tiny village about a half mile away, the usual redolent swatch of mud and thatch huts, disposed about a single swampy rubbish-piled road. At the shed nearest him, a Korean farmer stood waving a rice bowl, offering food. Kelly stood up and limped toward him; he had to get some help from someone to get out of here. The farmer dropped the bowl, picked up a rifle bigger than he was, and aimed. Kelly dropped back into a paddy, cursing.

The farmer let off a few rounds, bullets sucking into the mud. Kelly took out his .45 caliber Colt, the gun he could never hit a barn door with, and fired a couple of shots just to make him feel good in John Wayne fashion. It seemed to work; when he looked next the man was gone.

He turned on his back to watch the classy strafing of the Mustangs; it was very economic, designed to keep the soldiers' heads down for as long as possible with a minimum expenditure of fuel and ammunition. He knew they could be on station for an hour or so if they didn't get called to another mission. Maybe there'd be relief by then. The Korean troops were now only about half a mile away, and were beginning to lay down rifle fire on him between the Mustangs' runs. It was cat and mouse; hide when the F-51s came in, run twenty yards in between, and shoot.

The noise of the Mustang engines and guns and the sporadic counterfire from the Koreans masked the putt-putt sound of the Lycoming engine. The shadow of the Stinson L-5's wing startled Kelly; he saw the pilot pointing to the road leading to the squat collection of huts. One of the Mustangs broke left, pickling off a napalm tank that sent a sheet of flame through the village. Kelly began hobbling through the road as the Stinson—just an elegant Piper Cub—made a slow, hovering carrier approach curve to the roadway.

The L-5's pilot touched down in a spray of mud, opening the angular side door in invitation as he braked hard to stop. Kelly plowed through the paddies, alternately stumbling on a dike which seemed solid, or painfully mushing directly across the paddies. He tossed off his jacket as he ran, feeling oddly bad about the farmer's field he was trampling.

Garvey twitched the airplane with bursts of power to encourage Kelly. The riflemen opened little lozenge-shaped holes in the wing. The fabric-covered airplane could take a lot of bullets and keep going—unless they hit Garvey, or the propeller, or a critical part of the engine.

Kelly made it to the roadway, stomach heaving and legs unfeeling, falling against the open door. Garvey grabbed him by the back of his flying suit and hauled him in, putting the throttle forward just as the first burst of machine-gun fire stitched across the fuselage. The little L-5 lurched along the rutted roadway and jumped into the air. Kelly quietly passed out, but not before reaching forward and squeezing the back of Garvey's neck.

Leveling off between cloud decks, Garvey watched approvingly as the Mustangs developed an eccentric circling pattern to keep him in sight and covered without slowing down too much. He glanced back at the unconscious Kelly, passed out and mud smeared. Even in the drafty L-5 cabin, Garvey could scarcely stand the rice-paddy smell. Kelly owed him one, he thought, maybe two.

The ambulance drove beside them as Garvey taxied into the L-5's parking spot. Kelly was awake now, complaining about a headache and an earache, but otherwise jubilant, pounding Garvey on the back, hooting, and moving his fingers and toes continually to keep check. He tried to shrug off the insistent medics who gave him a rough bath as the flight surgeon checked him over. He insisted he was going to fly his mission tomorrow. The doctor slipped the needle in his arm.

Kelly awoke the next morning paralyzed. His head pounded and he couldn't move his arms or legs. He screamed for the medic, who popped in, took one look, and ran for the flight surgeon. No mission today.

1825 LOCAL
2 November 1951
Tokyo
Japan

"Hi, I'm Lt. Jim Garvey, greatest pilot in the Orient."

"Hi, I'm Miriam Siegel, and that's the least thing that interests me. But I would like a drink, and you look thirsty."

115

For the first time in three years, Garvey forgot about flying. The debriefing from Kelly's evac had been painful for him. He'd had six victories, and was gaining a reputation for being too aggressive. He knew he should not have lost Winckler; he'd studied the situation, and decided to make the pass from a single direction because it was getting dark, and he didn't want to lose time in setting up an attack from different compass points. The crucial, damning thing was that the target couldn't have been worth it. There were no trucks in sight, and the huts could only have had a few soldiers billeted inside. But there were guns guarding it, and their mission was to attack, attack, attack. The only things saving his ass were the secondary explosions during the napalm attack on the village and the fact that he'd pulled off the rescue with the L-5.

He was tired and overdue for leave. The C.O., Stan Everts, had been trying to get him to Japan for R & R for weeks; he would go. Maybe he'd see Kelly there.

The trip to Japan made Garvey long for combat. He had waited at Kimpo for hours to get crammed into a tired old C-46. It promptly lost an engine on takeoff, and barely creaked around the pattern to get back down. It was another six hours before he wangled a seat in a B-26, slumped into the gunner's compartment, airsick most of the way. But things began to look up at the hotel.

Garvey had seen the short, raven-haired girl across the room even as he was checking in. She was dark, with the tight body of a ballet dancer, and she smiled at him openly as she stood in line at the phones. She wore a dark blue wool coat over her shoulders revealing a beige wool dress that did nothing to hide her figure, and the little pillbox hat she wore set off her long black hair stunningly. In other times, he might simply have smiled back, and wondered what might have been. Fresh from Korea, he did not hesitate. He stepped over the drowsing G.I.s waiting for transport back to the airport and put out his hand in greeting.

Miriam's response stopped his tongue. So he lifted the hand with which she shook his to his lips and kissed it. She grinned at him and did the same with his.

Garvey groped for the next move. Standing there foolishly holding the hand of a total stranger—who had called his bluff—he fell back to talk of flying, until this moment his sole passion.

Miriam wouldn't let him speak of it. She didn't want to know what he did or what he thought about flying, but she drew him

116

out on every other subject. Somehow, he found himself at the hotel bar, talking furiously. The loss of his parents in a car accident during the Depression. The desolation of life with his widowed aunt in Indiana. The allure of flight for a solo player, a kid who tried to win his football and basketball games all by himself, who barely scraped by at State until he got into ROTC.

She talked too, and amusingly; about herself, her work in the dependent's education program, her archetypical Jewish parents and her absolute determination to foil their attempts to hold her tight to the family. They talked until they had closed the bar down and found themselves again in the lobby of the hotel.

For Garvey it was intoxicating; months of combat slipped from his shoulders. Their partnership came easily; even before he had tried to kiss her lips she had suggested spending the leave together, so readily that he was disquieted.

She laughed at his discomfort. "I'm not a nympho. You'll survive. In fact, though you won't believe it, I'm a virgin, technically anyway. It doesn't matter. But I'm sure about you, and I was when you walked in the room. If I'm wrong, so what. It's worse than wartime, it's life."

Garvey wasn't sure about getting her into his hotel room, and agreed readily to her suggestion to move the next day to a newly reopened inn near Nikko, some sixty miles from Tokyo. She saw the doubts resurface in his eyes and laughed again. "Boy, are you suspicious; if you weren't with me, you'd be trying to shag some Japanese whore and probably chickening out. Relax, we're both going to enjoy this."

Miriam had connections. Two phone calls provided reservations and an immaculate 1941 Ford dredged up from somewhere. She was experienced in driving in Japan, and Garvey nervously let her take the wheel until they were clear of the city.

Garvey stared at the houses passing by, most with the blue tiles the builders hoped would fool the god of fire, making him think the home was a blue lake. How many blue tile roofs had fooled the B-29s? She drove expertly, and with care; he drove nervously, starting at each intersection, coming to a complete halt on the tiny streets when faced by opposing traffic. Finally she laughed so much that he let her have the wheel again, rode with his hand resting on her thigh.

The inn had not been damaged by bombing, but all the shortages of war showed still on the outside. The paint was worn, and the garden seemed unusually uncared for.

Inside was a different story, with polished cypress and soft

117

white paper shoji walls offset by bright flowers, chrysanthemum designs and imponderably deep lacquer work. Their room opened onto another garden, perfectly maintained, glistening under a misty spray of rain. The older Japanese couple who ran the place seemed to understand exactly what the two required: privacy, food, drink, and privacy. In Jeevesian fashion they seemed to shimmer in and out when needed, then completely disappear.

Miriam and Jim joked about the baths coming up, talking bravely, but when the time came it was almost too much for Garvey, already embarrassed by feet too large for the straw zoris provided at the door. Some curious hesitation had kept their kisses cool even as they stumbled through the bathing process. The water was too hot for him to pretend to enjoy. He was bashful, too, ashamed to be in the water naked, a little taken aback if not erect, more if he was. Miriam teased him by staring, by pretending to enjoy the bath more than she could have by finding special reasons to rinse him in special places.

The food was good, washoku, the man had said, and they had agreed, unlike anything Garvey had had before. Miriam relished popping a morsel in his mouth, then identifying it for him as raw tuna, or seaweed. He loved the role of being taught, kidded her about kosher sashimi, played at being played with. They fed each other, and the kisses became saki-warm. Miriam's dark hair stretched down over a white kimono; her breasts were heavy through the silk, and surreptitiously he watched the alternate rise of her nipples, now one, now the other, now both. Once, absorbed in the process, he reached out and gently touched the protuberance, then drew back. He had his own rise to contend with.

The paper walls seemed fragile and Garvey worried about the sounds. Miriam didn't care. She slipped down to the cotton mattress she had pulled from the wall and reached up to grasp Garvey's ankle, tugging him to her.

Garvey had expected to find himself uncontrollably excited, to leap upon her and spend himself prematurely. Miriam was in fact a virgin, but years of petting and lots of intensive conversation with her peers made her know what to expect: an intense slavering, a few quick thrusts, and exhaustion—till the next time.

It was totally unlike that, mostly because they laughed so much. Garvey was not an experienced lover, but he sought control of himself so that he could please Miriam. Their very inexperience pleased them, not knowing what moves to make,

118

ut knowing there were no bad moves. They played a long and slowly heating game. Garvey had never been excited and amused at the same time; Miriam laughed continually, and mostly inappropriately for heated passion, but with an engaging frivolity that charmed Garvey even more than the sweet scent of her thighs. He would range from tender petting to animal panting, only to collapse into giggles. In the back of his mind he knew he was violating some sort of male code which stated sternly that a fighter pilot wasn't supposed to giggle with a woman, but he was enjoying it too much to care.

She finally asked, "Are you or are you not going to enter me? If not, kindly ring for the porter, who probably knows what to do."

Garvey jumped up and rang, and the porter knocked at the door seconds later.

"I believe madam has a requirement," Garvey called through the thin partition.

Miriam giggled and pulled the quilt over her head. Outside, the porter looked blank and went away.

"The bastard was probably listening in anyway."

He dropped again beside her, kissing her breasts for the hundredth time, then swinging his face down until his chin rested on the top of her full crown of pubic hair.

"How do you like me in a beard?"

"Let's see how it looks as eyebrows," she said huskily. He dropped his head and they became very serious.

They parted with a plan: to get married immediately and then begin to learn about each other.

Garvey found the intensity of the last three days had given him two new emotions: genuine love and realistic apprehension. He felt like a new man, different in some basic way from the fighter jock who'd scored six and saved Kelly's ass. Thinking of Kelly gave him a pang. He really had intended to see Kelly, but Miriam had intervened, and she was more important. It was just that simple.

But he couldn't let the poor bastard go unvisited, so before the courier to K-2 cranked up its engines, he found Red Man Benson at Base Operations, in full swing, as usual, as the world's premier free-trade artist. A few words, a hundred dollars in scrip, and Benson had the situation well in hand. Garvey climbed aboard the shaky old C-46 happier than he had ever been, but a little bit worried. Could he feel this way, and still fly and fight?

The woman was small and attractive, dressed in a white nurse's outfit. She briskly arranged the screens around Kelly waking him, then set out a little kit of alcohol, baby oil, and powder. She didn't speak English, but she moved her hands in little clutching gestures to tell him she would massage him.

Kelly was immediately suspicious. He'd been suspicious of everyone and everything since they'd hauled him here, sedated for most of the endless trip to the hospital in Japan. When he awoke it was with an enormous thirst and immense depression. They were taking his jet horse from him, and he wasn't going to stand for it. Literally. For he not only could not stand for their treatment, he could not stand at all. He was still paralyzed, and nothing they had done seemed to help either his paralysis or his depression.

The near-barbarism of the military medicine hadn't helped. The doctors were harried, and it was a rare corpsman who gave a damn. The nurses tried, but there were far too few of them, and there wasn't much they apparently could do for Kelly.

Kelly had spent hours every day trying to coax some movement from his toes or his fingers; nothing seemed to work. The doctors had plans to move him to the United States after a few more tests; in the meantime, he was left to tough it out, alone in a ward that had become almost empty after the last air-evac flight. He spent most of the lonely time sleeping, as he had been when Red Man Benson's special physical therapist arrived.

Kelly studied her closely. He was used to unexplained, even bizarre treatment from nurses, but something about her made him even more suspicious of her than he was of most of the others. She washed his genitals at somewhat excessive length and his suspicions were confirmed when her head dropped down to cover him with her mouth.

He felt nothing but embarrassment at first; he was afraid to yell and be caught, afraid not to. Then her work began to have effect. Sensations began to return he thought he'd never again experience.

She glanced up at him and smiled approvingly. Flushed, he

smiled weakly back at her. She reapplied herself and the sensations built into real pleasure. It wasn't long before Kelly noticed
that he could at last curl his toes.

7

1830 LOCAL
13 January 1951
Langley, Virginia
USA

"Lola?" Micky called. For some reason she insisted on being
called Lola; "grandmother" was absolutely verboten.

Lola didn't reply. She was locked on to the television set
again.

Micky walked across the room and snapped the set off.

"Lola, we have to talk. This isn't working out, and I need to
know what you want to do about it."

Lola's soiled handkerchief flashed to her eyes with a practiced
gesture. She looked moistly at Micky.

"Look," Micky said sternly, "it's been great having you, but
when we talked we said you were going to come down to help
me. And you're not helping. In fact, sometimes I feel like I have
three babies now."

Lola ran the handkerchief around the course again. Micky
steeled herself and forged ahead.

"Lola, I think I know that you don't have the greatest situation
back home; Larry's told me that his dad is pretty inconsiderate.
But you can't take it out on me. If you want to stay here, and I
hope you do, because I need somebody, you've got to pull your
weight. And—I'm sorry to say this, but somebody's got to—
you've *got* to take baths."

There, the worst part was out.

Lola's eyes wandered back to the blank screen of the television
set as if to check if this were part of the drama. She hesitated a
moment, then sprang to her feet with a Jackie Gleason grace that
belied her 240 pounds.

She looked at Micky and simply nodded. "Okay," she said,
and went directly to the bathroom. The water began to run in
the tub. Micky rarely drank, but she sneaked to the cupboard
and poured a triumphant shot.

121

Another tiny step forward in the life of Mrs. Lawrence A. White. Another step taken alone. For Lola was Larry's mother, like Libby and Larry Jr. his gift to her, given, as always, in between leavetaking, in between airplane flights.

Micky grimly refused to believe that her parents might have been right all along. But what difference did it make if her wedding had been straight out of Emily Post if she never saw her husband?

What was he doing in Korea? She sipped her Scotch and pondered the letters while Lola splashed in the tub.

When Larry came back from Berlin she had been overjoyed, and they'd had a storybook reunion and homecoming. But within a few weeks he was gone again, flying all over the world. "Got to build up my flying time," was his constant refrain and apology.

She was glad when he volunteered for B-26s, not knowing that the Air Force would send them to Langley Air Force Base, near Norfolk. Was she ever going to get out of the Tidewater?

Larry had loved the B-26s and for the six months he was in training they actually had a home life of a sort. The Air Force proved to be perfectly consistent; after training him to be a first-class B-26 pilot, they jerked him out of Langley to go to Korea and fly L-5s. He was very upset at first, insulted, afraid that somehow he had fouled up; by the time he left he was reconciled, glad to be getting to Korea "before the war was over."

But she had not reconciled herself to an absentee husband. He had gotten her pregnant before he left for Berlin, and Lawrence Jr. had been born at Dover. She had carried him and given birth with a minimum of fuss and a maximum of excitement. Then, again in true Air Force style, and to the horror of her parents, she was pregnant again. She could look in their eyes and see that they considered Larry to be some kind of Bluebeard.

The second pregnancy was difficult, the more so because he was gone. She had problems with bleeding and cramps, and the doctors made her take it easy. Her mother came down and was impossible, fussing over her, crying quietly in the corner, unable to cope with her pregnancy or the oddities of service life. She never said it aloud, but she constantly signaled "I told you so."

Micky lay in bed for weeks before the delivery, thinking too much and wondering what she was going to do. Then Mary Elizabeth was born, light brown ringlets of hair glistening wetly in the harsh white light of the base hospital delivery room. The young doctor seemed tense, and she sensed a disquiet among the nurses. He visited her later, before she saw the baby again, and mumbled something about "Down's syndrome" and panic seized her heart. She clutched his arm, made him explain. She didn't really understand until he reluctantly used the term "mongoloid."

Now she had made up her mind; she would have no more children. If Larry needed airplanes, needed flying, more than he needed her, fine, but she wasn't going to spend evenings home alone, or fool away her time in the club, and she wasn't going to go on having babies. There was more than one life to be led by the family, and she was going to lead hers the way she wanted to. With him if possible, without him if necessary.

Her mother simply couldn't stand the fact that Libby was not perfect; Larry wrote that his own mother might be a change of pace, and he made arrangements for her to come down.

It was another disaster at first. Larry's mom was more than she could handle. She'd breezed down to Norfolk from Arlington on the train, hot and sweaty, and stayed that way. She'd gladly responded to Larry's request to come down to take care of the kids, but the first weekend's entertainment set the tone, and she seemed more intent on a vacation than helping Micky manage. Micky knew it was time for a talk; she was going to have to be more responsible now that her workload was increasing; then she'd have full charge when Larry came back and they had their "second honeymoon" in Florida.

Everything was awkward at first. Lola had to be reminded more than once what the arrangement was, but as time went on she got better and enjoyed it more. She shed about thirty pounds, so fast that Micky was worried that she was unwell. It was probably just the combination of responsibility and purposeful activity, and her mood changed so much that both Larry and his dad sensed it in her letters, the former with delight, the latter with suspicion. Eventually she became totally dependable, doting on the kids, particularly on little Libby, providing Micky with the leeway she needed in her business.

Micky had started working at Roy Rice Real Estate as a secretary; it galled her but it was a start. The place was a mess, and her orderly mind and energy quickly set the office tone. Old Mr. Rice rarely came in anymore, but the sales manager, Barney Green, was good, and he saw to it that Micky got to spend her weekends sitting in model houses. She was attractive, and she learned the business so well that the real-estate agents began to depend on her.

She went to school at night, working for her license. As soon

123

as she had it, Green let her start doing listings; in a few month
she was the top lister.

It was a military market, and Micky had the insider's view o
what the serviceman could and should buy. She fell naturall
into working solely for the customers' advantage, putting hersel
in their place, and she sometimes lost sales by being honest. She
grew adept at picking up a young officer, only rarely with hi
wife, at the airport, with a prepared list of five or six best buys
Almost invariably an officer would buy in a single day, flying ou
that evening. She treated them right, because she would have
wanted Larry to have been treated right, but most of all because
she was looking to the future. In two or three years, her buyers
would be rotating out, and she wanted them to be her sellers
then.

She needed the job for more than the money it provided,
although that was desperately important. Libby had cardiac problems the Air Force doctors couldn't diagnose, and she was
spending a fortune on civil medical bills. The job was primarily
a substitute for Larry, giving her what he could not, a sense of
accomplishment and satisfaction. It also gave her something he
would never know she needed, room for him to be an airplane
nut, an Air Force fanatic. If she had this he could volunteer for
all the missions, take all the bad flights, spend all his time
studying the goddamn tech orders instead of playing with the
kids or playing with the kids' mother. It would give them room
to survive.

By the time Larry was due to come back from Korea she was
earning far more than she'd ever dreamed of. She began to worry
about how he would take it. He was so sensitive about so many
things. But she was learning some psychology as she sold, and
she finally decided she wouldn't tell him anything until they
were on their second honeymoon.

2200 LOCAL
15 June 1951
Fort Lauderdale, Florida
USA

Larry had forgotten how good it was to have a woman. He had
maintained a difficult celibacy in Japan, an easier one in Korea;
the temptations had grown less as his libido had grown stronger.

124

Now he lay exhausted beside Micky, feeling spiritual and physical relief.

"Thanks, honey. That was so good. There were a lot of pipes and valves that were pretty rusty."

She snuggled next to him, thinking she'd told him a thousand times never to thank her, but for the first time not saying so. She buried her face in his shoulder. It was almost as much R & R for her as for him; she'd been hard at it, kids and work, and training Lola, ever since he had left.

He eyed the hotel room. It was the first time they'd ever traveled so luxuriously; a suite in Fort Lauderdale, even if not in the season. Why not? It was really their honeymoon. The room was warm and they had kicked the sheets to the end of the bed. He glanced down at Micky's body pressed next to him. She was still trim, but more mature, with little lines around her eyes he had not remembered. She smoked now too, and he hated it. He caressed her breasts; she had a firmer tone to her body, ironing out some of the soft roundness he used to tease her about. He inventoried himself; he was skinny, pure and simple. It was easy to get skinny in Korea.

They tried to remedy that three times or more a day. Larry would order steak and eggs, with pancakes on the side every morning, while Micky stayed with juice and coffee. They'd swim early, then lunch on huge greasy hamburgers and fries, and a milkshake. It was catch-up time. They devoted the early part of the evenings entirely to food, drowning in conch soup, stone crabs, and key lime pie. Micky drank more than Larry, which surprised him. He liked a rum and Coke in the afternoon, and maybe a couple of Seven and Sevens before dinner, but Micky had developed a taste for manhattans at noon and martinis at night, and she knew which wines to order. Best of all—and most worrisome to him—she would ice a bottle of champagne in the bucket by their bed every night.

Larry winced every time he paid a bill, and he scanned the rate card on the room every day, as if he were hoping it would change, or that there would be some new fine print about rates for war veterans. Micky had deliberately chosen the Delray, and a suite, to condition him for the serious talk to come. She'd learned in a year of real estate that no matter what you do for someone, no matter how extravagant you are, no one thinks it's too much. That was the secret of tipping clients into houses that were better buys for them, that they could really afford, but were shy about undertaking. Make 'em feel like kings. And who should be a king better than Larry?

After a year in BOQs, living out of B-4 bags, using a communal latrine right out of the Middle Ages, he felt it was great, but didn't see how they could afford it, no matter how well Micky was doing. He could not conceive that she could be making as much as he was, and he couldn't afford it on double a first lieutenant's pay, even with combat pay and flying pay on top. Micky made him promise not to discuss money until the day they left, and he readily agreed; maybe realtors got a rate.

She had been worried that he would feel bad about her making so much money; she'd earned more than twice his pay last year, and would probably do better than that in the next six months. Micky knew his flight-school mind, so she had a set of "real estate tech orders" in her bag. It was standard stuff, the first lectures in the real-estate courses she had taken, a combination of inspirational platitudes about ethics, helping the customer, the nobility of the profession, and then a series of hypothetical studies of how much you could earn. The greed factor was suppressed in Optimist Club service talk, but the greed factor was the clincher.

He was noticeably enthusiastic. Then she gave him the cold facts and figures on what she had made, listing by listing, sale by sale, showing the expenses, showing the net.

She took a risky step, showed him the medical expenses for Libby. Larry had assumed it was all being taken care of by the Air Force; it was part of his fierce belief in the Air Force that if you did your job, they took care of you, a joint maintenance agreement that extended like a blanket around all possible problems.

It wasn't the Air Force's fault; the only doctors they could attract were fuzzy-faced kids right out of medical school. The Air Force had paid for most of them to go and extracted a service commitment in exchange. They were good and bright and caring, but young, and they didn't have the experience to treat Libby's heart condition. Nor for that matter, apparently, did the Mayo Clinic, but she had to keep trying. The medical expenses were more than half of Larry's take-home pay; she thought the news would devastate him and scanned his face, watching for the tightness in the jaw and expanding rhubarb patch of vessels in the throat that forecast an argument. There were none.

He didn't mind a bit; he was touched that she had done so well by Libby, proud of her for being so smart.

She threw her arms around his neck. "Honey, I was so scared you were going to be furious."

He kissed her. "Babe, it's only in the movies where the husband gets mad if the wife makes a lot of money. You keep earning like this and you can buy me my own Air Force, and I'll stay home and play with the children's mother every evening. Or maybe two, three nights a week, anyway."

His equanimity was not solely based on his calm acceptance of her news. He had his own news to spring, which he feared would be considerably more difficult for her to swallow. He kept it to himself until much later that night, trying to judge the best moment. Finally it came.

"Pour me a little bubbly," Micky purred. As he upended the last bottle, she said, "Are you going back to Langley?"

It was a logical question; combat-wise pilots were valuable commodities, passing on what they'd learned by surviving to the new crews. She wanted to stay in the Langley area; she didn't know if she could move in view of the money, and the fact that she had an interest in the new Riverdale Estate development. It was all borrowed money, backed mostly by the banker's confidence in her ability and his hope that he could sometime—after a suitable period, when no question of ethics would be involved—get in her knickers. Micky didn't intend to sleep with him, although there had been times when she wanted to for sheer relief. She did intend to see that he got every nickel back with its blood-sucking 6 percent interest, and on time.

Riverdale was a new concept in the area, borrowed from the Florida boom days; the houses sprawled over half-acre lots, and each one backed or fronted on manmade canals and lakes controlled by a system of locks that would keep water moving. She had her eye on a marina site, too, but she wasn't sharing this with her collaborators on the project; it was going to be hers alone. The whole deal would take eighteen months to consummate. Till then she really couldn't leave.

Larry silently poured the champagne and then kissed her, and looked at her with the hang-dog eyes he always wore before telling her he was off to some godforsaken place. "Mick, don't hate me, but I've volunteered to go back and fly T-6s as a forward air controller. It's something I've got to do, they need pilots with combat experience there."

She was embarrassed by the disturbing flood of intermixed relief and grief; she hated to see him go, but knew she'd rather see him in Korea for a year than have to pick up stakes and move away. She didn't know how to play it; she sobbed, and he comforted her. Finally they found a mutual way out, agreeing that it was the best thing for Libby not to move, that he might be reassigned anywhere, and that this way they'd have time to plan what to do when he returned.

They drove back to Langley quietly, with the exaggerated artificial courtesy of a husband and wife who have avoided one argument and don't want to start another. By the time they got home, Larry's second tour seemed to them both to be more of a reprieve than a problem.

Larry felt doubly bad about the kids; he had scarcely seen them, and Libby was terribly shy of him, enfolding herself in Lola's voluminous skirts every time he came around. He had a week at home to rationalize that as young as they were, they were better off with his mom than with him. Larry Jr. caused more of a pang; he was just at the point where he could buy him some simple fishing gear. Next year, he'd make up for it.

Larry could scarcely recognize his mother; her sweet indolence was gone, and she had picked up on Micky's acid wit. He had not seen her so trim—well, maybe not trim, but at least not mountainous—in years. Micky had kept him laughing with her tales of the "Training of Lola." She'd been like an amiable sheepdog, anxious to goof off, but responding to the choke collar of Micky's demands. It was probably the best thing that ever happened to her.

The biggest surprise was his dad's visit. The newspapers had given a lot of play to his return, citing his Air Medals for combat missions, and his father was for the first time ever demonstrably proud of him. Larry thought back to the times when he'd bring some achievement home, being elected class treasurer, driving in the winning run in an intramural ball game, to have his father snort and look away as if the proffered treasure was unworthy. This time they didn't have their first argument until two hours after he arrived. It was a record.

And after years of trying, Larry won his father's heart the following day. He went out to the little fixed-base operation where they rented Pipers and Aeroncas, and checked out in a Cub. He took his dad for a tour of the coastal countryside, and the old man saw more boats in that forty-five minutes than he'd ever seen in his life. The older man didn't even seem to be aware of the airplane, but he noted where the big marinas were, and spent the rest of his visit touring them, poking around in the old-fashioned wooden boats that were his single passion.

The flight was so successful that he finally persuaded Micky to go for a ride. The airplane didn't interest her at all, but she made him fly southwest of Norfolk, and marked on her realtors' county map a number of places where it seemed the growth pattern was reaching. It was the first time she had ever flown with him, and the first time she'd ever felt kindly about her rival, the airplane.

Micky was almost sexually excited when they landed, but not for Larry; she was tingling because she had picked out a triangle of land sitting athwart two development thrusts. The point was not obvious on the ground because of the way the present street system ran, but from the air she could see the logical conjunction of the two most important commercial developments in the area. If she could get the money to pick up that triangle, she'd be a wealthy woman. Even if she could just get an option to buy, she'd be sure to clean up, but buying it was better and probably would cause less notice. It was Larry's penultimate night of leave, but she left him to go down to her office and sort through recent purchases of land in the area, trying to determine a pattern, a growth rate. It seemed to her that in two years, the trend would be obvious to anyone; in three years, the land prices would skyrocket.

She lectured Larry closely about their finances, trying to make him understand what she was doing. Like many Air Force pilots, his approach to money was primitive. If the Air Force wanted him to have more money they'd pay him more. In the meanwhile he simply sent her his check, and waited for her to send him an allowance, which he rarely entirely spent unless he bought some gifts to send home. As she explained what she was doing, he became worried about the risks. She pointed out that flying L-5s or T-6s in combat carried a little risk, too, and it satisfied him. Her preoccupation with making money was foreign to him, but the thrill of the risk was easily understood.

In a fit of helpfulness, Larry asked his dad if he was interested in backing Micky. Not unreasonably, he wanted full disclosure and some control of the deal, having been vastly impressed by Micky's acumen. She turned him off. If she wouldn't turn to her own father—a banker—she wouldn't turn to White Sr. She would have the money some other way, some way that did not involve family, and she would have the land.

There was a final comic twist to the joint reunion. Larry and Micky had come home early from a last trip to the BX with the kids; when they went upstairs there were unmistakable sounds of passion heaving from Lola's room. They turned around and tiptoed out, masking their laughter; Lola's new trimmer figure and defiant stand must have triggered some almost extinct pocket of libido in his dad.

Larry left a new family behind as he headed for Korea again. Micky was assuming a role in his mind that no one had ever had, the sustainer/confidante. He'd never loved her more, never felt freer, never felt more bound to her.

Micky watched him go and sensed a stirring within herself; Larry was never going to change, nor would she ever need him to. There was room for them both.

July 1951–June 1952
Korea

Larry sailed through the Forward Air Controller Course with honors; his flying had progressed beyond the master's stage now, to the point that it was simply an extension of his being. He flew in his mind and the airplane did what he wanted it to do, his body merely an interfacing mechanism. In a little over three years he had accumulated nineteen hundred hours flying time, probably twice as much as a busy pilot, and perhaps four times the average. The T-6, so formidable in flying training, was now the suit he put on before launching himself into the sky. His instructors had looked over his logbook and were impressed with his combat experience. They asked him to stay on as an instructor, but he refused.

The worst part of going back to Korea was the simple physical difficulty of getting there. The interminable train ride to Camp Stoneman was relieved by the obvious bustling prosperity of a countryside he'd never seen. He enjoyed traveling at ground level, soaking up the detail, taking a professional view of the targets he passed, railyards, fuel dumps, speculating on what he could do with a few five-hundred-pound bombs.

In sharp and endless contrast, the trip overseas was a nightmare of delayed takeoffs and inedible in-flight lunches—the standardization of bologna on Wonder Bread, tired apple, and near-sour milk was incredible. The boredom was compounded by minor emergencies that did not thrill, but only delayed; there was interminable waiting in strange base operations, drinking stale coffee from fast-melting paper cups. It took two weeks between Travis and Tachikawa; Korea, he thought, was going to be a rest home.

Until he saw Pyongtaek, or K-6 as it was called. The engineers had laid a short runway of PSP, but the rest of the base was substandard even by Korean standards. The airplanes were a rag-tag collection of North American T-6s, scarred, worn, and mud-spattered, far different from the polished aircraft on training command flight lines. The landscape was Korean issue olive drab, surfaces blown dry by the wind, but opening to sucking mud with the least rain and weight. If they had known of it, the British could have used Pyongtaek as a place to exile Napoleon.

White was surprised by the extent of his briefing. Capt. Ray Boyd went through the whole history of the organization of the 6147th Tactical Control Squadron (Airborne). It was forced into being when North Korean Yak-9 fighters began hosing down the slow and vulnerable L-5 liaison planes. A young turk, Lt. Harold E. Morris, brought a T-6 into Taejon and proceeded to demonstrate that it could do the job. The new group began flying as much as fifty miles behind the enemy lines, calling up fighter bombers on their primitive VHF radios, and talking them into targets. The first officially designated flights were called Mosquito Alpha, Mosquito Baker, and Mosquito How, and the name became generic. Legend embroidered the tale that the Communists called them mosquitoes because they buzzed around so low, a rumor wrapped around the truth.

The Mosquitoes would loiter for three or four hours over enemy territory, picking up targets and handing them over to the fuel-hungry fighter bombers to attack.

The new tactics were so effective that jurisdictional disputes erupted—everyone wanted their services—forcing an elaborate airground communication-and-control system into existence. Air Force forward controllers, working on the ground with the Army troops, would pass requests for attacks through a labyrinthine radio network to a joint operations center. Attack orders were relayed back to the fighter bombers in the same way.

At least that is how it was supposed to work on paper; in practice, the Mosquito had to control the attack directly, on the spot, because the hills made straight-line radio communication so difficult. They preferred it that way.

Boyd gave him a pep talk, told him of the great days when the North Koreans would be trapped by the fighter bombers the T-6s brought in, with whole companies being destroyed. For virtually nothing in resources—two squadrons of the obsolete T-6s served the whole front—the Mosquitoes had accounted for thousands of enemy troops. One man, Lt. George Nelson, had actually captured two hundred troops by dropping them a note demanding surrender, and signed "MacArthur."

The ground duty was a surprise to White; after twenty missions, he became a forward air controller for sixty days, doing no flying, not even drawing flight pay. His withdrawal symptoms began as soon as he learned of the duty.

The twenty missions passed quickly, and White soon caught on to the technique. He relished the fact that as much as 90 percent of his flying time was spent right over the enemy. And to his amazement, he enjoyed his tour as a forward air controller, even though the terrain was so rugged that he controlled only three strikes during his tour. During the rest of the time, the Mosquito pilots worked directly with the bombers.

When he returned to flying, he was senior enough to have an LT-6 assigned to him. It was a field mod of the T-6, with a bigger fuel tank for more time on station, a vastly improved radio setup, and a good gunsight for the twelve target-marking rockets they carried.

The North Koreans hated the T-6s, which called death down upon them, and fought them with everything from rifles and machine guns to cables strung between the hills. White had seen a T-6 clip its rudder on a cable; it had gone straight in. As vulnerable as the T-6s were to even small-caliber ground fire, there was no alternative to going down low, stooging around the hills, for the Communists were masters at digging in.

Once he had just finished a particularly satisfying shoot when a Chinese Yak-9, a counterpart to the F-51, dropped in behind him, wings lit up with machine-gun fire. White slowed his airplane down, dropping flaps, and turning until he was actually behind the Russian-built fighter. He fired two of his target-marking rockets which streaked past the Yak like smoking javelins. The enemy pilot broke left wildly and almost collided with a hill, leaving Larry to finish the patrol. He'd have given anything to have had machine guns, but the guns had been removed long ago to keep the T-6s' pilots from starting their own private wars.

Enemy resistance had stiffened, and the Mosquitoes rarely penetrated more than two or three miles behind the front lines. In late June, White had spent an hour looking for targets; unopposed, he pushed on eight miles inland, where he found two hills, not over eight hundred feet high, absolutely crawling with troops.

His call for fighters was picked up and relayed to the "Mosquito Mellow" airborne C-47. In minutes, two flights of Republic F-84 fighter bombers were over the target, calling for him to mark it with his rockets.

White made a careful pattern, armed his rockets, and fired into a cluster of foxholes in the center of the taller hill to the right. He moved out and watched two of the F-84s come in, just like gunnery school, and strafe right into his smoke. The dust rose, and he chose the other hill for the second attack.

The next flight of F-84s came in, strafed where he marked, with the same results: mostly dust, no apparent casualties. White made a low pass over the target, taking a couple of hits from small arms, then called in the next flight.

It was frustrating; he was going to get shot down watching F-84s rearrange the surface of the hard flint hills. The Communist soldiers were taking it as a sporting event; when he'd fire rockets on one hill, the troops on the other hill would come out to watch and fire their rifles against the attackers. Something had to be done. As he orbited, he suddenly knew what it was.

"Oboe Flight, this is Mosquito Purple, Over."

"Roger, Purple, how we doing?"

"Can't tell; looks like their foxholes go all the way back through the other side of the hill. Let's do something different this time, over."

"Ah, roger, bitty buddy, go ahead."

"I'm going to put my smoke on a target on the big hill on the right, but I want you to attack about the same place on the hill on the left."

It took a few transmissions to sort out the idea, but they got it straight.

White dove on the big hill, watching the soldiers scuttle into their foxholes; he fired two rockets into the upper-right-hand section. On the other hill, the soldiers poured out to watch the attack.

The F-84s were good. They set up a pattern that looked like an attack on the hill on the right, then jinked and dropped all they had on the hill on the left. The last one to dive had napalm on board, and there was a black blossoming of heat as a devil's tongue of flame dripped down the hillside.

"Good show, Purple; we nailed a few that time. We have to go now to refuel and rearm."

"Ah, roger, Oboe, thank you for your business."

More F-84s were inbound; White flew a low pass to reconnoiter the damage and picked up a sheet of small arms fire. He must have irritated them. The LT-6's engine began bucking; White shoved the mixture forward and climbed, asking Mosquito Mellow to send in the relief airplane.

Boyd's voice came over his receiver. "Ah roger, Purple, you're relieved; I'll pick up the trade now. Looks like a good day's work."

White nursed the LT-6 back to Pyongtaek. When he landed he counted the bullet holes. There were thirty-six of them, half in the engine cowling, the other half spread over the airplane. He'd been lucky.

Just before he left Korea for the second time, White learned that Boyd had not only picked up the trade, he'd picked up the Distinguished Flying Cross for "tactical improvisation under fire, directing fire against one enemy concentration by marking the positions in another." It might not have been a coincidence that Boyd also served as the awards and decorations officer.

8

2100 LOCAL
2 January 1952
Pusan AB
Korea

King's letter forced Duke's decision. The B-47 program was still not rolling. The radical new bomber had engineering problems no one could have foreseen. For Duke it meant a simple but hard choice: return to be a third wheel on a staff, or stay and continue to take his chances in combat. Because things had slowly improved, and because some part of him continued to be fascinated by the fact that he could actually do this, day in and day out, he decided to take another tour in B-26s. Once he had decided, no one was more surprised than he himself.

Brown switched over to the 17th Bomb Group at Pusan just as it was changing over to night intruder tactics. He wasn't long in the night war before he wondered if he had not made a mistake. The old fears began to gnaw at him, and he wondered how long he could endure it. Daily he recalled bitterly the dash with which he'd casually announced at the Tachi Club one night that Oh yes, sure, he was staying on—wasn't everyone?

There were times when he'd have been glad to have given up

the whole career, his family, everything if he could have shed the noose and done what he wanted to do. Now he again expected every takeoff to wind up in a ball of flames. He never saw a weather report he didn't hope would be a cause for cancellation.

Yet his obligation had been doubled; his crew had stayed with him, even though it was Middlebrook's second war. There was a dumb wonderful loyalty that he had never experienced, didn't feel he was worthy of. It was the only thing that compensated for the eternal feeling of fear and loneliness, keeping him going.

The sense of unity reached a high one night on the truck out to 44-43517, Jolting Joanie, a name she would hate. It was their forty-third night mission, and they were all feeling the strain. Middlebrook was slouched at his side in the truck, unusually quiet.

"Brownie,"—he never called him Duke—"did you ever look at the front end of these little hot rods? The inside of the front end?"

"Yeah, Jim, it's pretty cramped for you, isn't it?"

"Every time I ride out to these things I know they are going to crash, and I know there's no way in the world I can get out. I'd just as soon forget my parachute. I'd never be able to get out."

Whiteside, the gunner, broke in. "Shit, it's the same for me; I never come out here figuring I'm coming back, and I don't think anybody else does either. Except maybe you, Lieutenant."

A surge of something like relief swept through Brown as the truck pulled up by the sinister black B-26. He looked at them both. "Everybody feels that way; you wouldn't be normal if you didn't. And Jim, if it ever gets down to it, I'll get you out before I go."

Capt. Harvey Sunderman, the pilot for the other crew sharing the truck, spoke up. He was a perfectly anonymous man, the type whose likeness is always clipped from photographs, so his sudden announcement surprised them all. "Man, it's a question of percentages; you always have to play the percentages in your favor, otherwise the house will nail you."

Brown shrugged. Sunderman seemed always to be nearby, in the club, on the flight line; maybe it was just coincidence, but he thought he could feel a tug on his coattails. There was something wrong with Sunderman's crew, too. They rarely joked, and when they did it was usually some sort of wry comment that only Sunderman understood.

The Pusan runway ran north and south; you took off to the

135

south and landed to the north because of the mountains perched to the northwest. The base was laid out in a series of cartridgelike buildings to the east of the runway. In the summer it was hot and dry and in the rainy season the mud sluiced down from the hills and lakes opened up everywhere but on the runway.

Brown went through the tedious process of strapping in, fixing the parachute straps, the dinghy, the mike cords, the oxygen hose. He flew without the fleece-lined boots, to feel the rudder pressures better, just as he took off without gloves, against advice, so that he could tell the switches by feel and not have to take his eyes away from the instrument panel.

The big Pratt & Whitneys started easily and he eased out on the runway, slipping his oxygen mask on to start prebreathing to improve his night vision. At his side Whiteside was busy sorting through the paperwork, his eyes scanning the instruments periodically. He knew the power settings and the engine limits as well as Brown did, and Brown relied on him when the things tightened up.

Their call sign was Pacify 82. They were cleared on the runway, and Duke could feel the pierced-steel plank runways undulate beneath the wheels of the airplane as it gathered speed, as if a bow wave of mud and steel were forming. He felt Whiteside make minute adjustments in the power. At 142 m.p.h. the airplane left the ground, and Brown went on instruments immediately as the black void swallowed them. The blazing exhausts were blinding, but a nod to Whiteside started the first power reduction, and the glare became tolerable.

It was quiet on the climb out except for the studied radio calls as the B-26 departed on its assigned route.

They were passed to the Tactical Air Control Center marking their route of flight with radar, as they cruised at seventy-five hundred feet in the clouds. Brown worried about icing; the B-26 had no icing equipment—not even an icepick, he thought ruefully—and the thin airfoil ran out of lift almost immediately with even a light coating.

He called up BROMIDE, the controller who would monitor their flight over North Korea as long as they were at an altitude he could read, and they entered enemy territory at 215 m.p.h., snaillike compared to the P-80s he had flown or the F-86s he could have been flying.

The battlefront was marked by hundreds of Allied searchlights, each one shining on enemy strong points, waiting, watching. At intervals there would erupt the ripping serrated flame of a firefight.

Jim called back, "Past the bomb line," the arbitrary division beyond which it was safe to bomb with assurance of not hitting any United Nations patrol.

Middlebrook was searching the black below for signs of a road cut from the earlier B-26 attacks. If done properly, the North Korean road traffic would get backed up, making targets worth risking their lives and airplanes for.

"Red Eleven coming up; I see truck lights." Middlebrook's voice tightened. Red 11 was one of the principal highways coming south; they couldn't drive its twisting, cliff-strewn path without lights, even though they knew lights invited attack.

The whole mission of B-26s was interdiction, stopping this endless flow of troops and equipment, even though it sometimes traded an airplane and crew for an ancient Lend Lease Dodge and a ton of rice.

Middlebrook was bent over the Norden bombsight, applying corrections for wind as the B-26 began its attack. Brown scanned his instruments, bringing the pilot direction indicator, the PDI, into his cross check. At this point the mission always took on a weird silence, as if they were in a vacuum chamber; the sound of the moist wind, the engines, the static all faded and Middlebrook's voice came like penance from a priest. As Brown followed the PDI's movements, Middlebrook would establish a course to off-set the effect of wind.

"Open bomb bay doors," Middlebrook called. Brown added three inches of manifold pressure to keep the airspeed steady at 215 m.p.h. The PDI was centered with a caress of the rudder pedal.

"Bombs away!" The cry seemed ancient, an echo of a World War II film. Brown closed the bomb bay doors and counted to seven before banking hard left, away from the moutain range that menaced on the right. The bombs hit with two little yellow puffs followed by four large billowing yellow-and-red bursts, probably fuel tankers.

Whiteside punched him in the arm and yelled, "Break left!" just as the clatter of flak sprayed against the wing like golfball hail on a tin roof.

The B-26 almost went on its back; Brown watched the flight instruments tumble. He glanced outside to pick up a horizon; it was bowling-ball black. He eased against the control pressures, centered the needle and ball, stabilized the airspeed and altitude, and breathed for the first time since Whiteside screamed.

Brown scanned the instruments, watching the flight instru-

137

ments slowly struggle into usefulness. He glanced appreciatively out at the huge engine nacelles that blocked his view, but were wonderful shields against flak.

"What have you got left, Jim?"

"We have four clusters of twenty-eight-pound fragmentation bombs. I got a problem with the bombsight, though; it hasn't come back since that half-ass wingover of yours."

"Okay. Play with it for a while; if you can't get it to work, I'll pickle them off over the nose. That fire's burning bright enough for me to hit something."

"Duke, this damn thing is out. Why don't you just dump the bombs from here?"

"No, we wouldn't hit anything, they'd scatter all over hell. I'm going to make a diving attack."

Whiteside chimed in. "I wouldn't do that, skipper; you don't know what damage we suffered from that hit."

Whiteside was right, as usual. But the bile was gone from his throat, and Brown was savoring the sensation of being in command of his fears. He knew it would pass, but by then he'd be back at Pusan. He hoped.

"Okay. Get set. I'm going to come back in and dive down to about three thousand feet before dropping. I'll pull up hard to the left as soon as I drop. I don't want to come in at the same altitude they hit us at last time."

Middlebrook and Whiteside sat in silent disapproval. Brown traced an orbit around to about the point he'd started the last bomb run, eased the power back, dropping the nose to about a twenty-five-degree angle. The airspeed built up, and the yellow secondary fires grew bigger.

"I'll tell you when, Jim."

They both yelled "Now!" simultaneously, and Middlebrook jettisoned the rest of the bombs. Brown reefed the control column back into his stomach in a hard climbing turn to the left. Now they only had to go back, make an instrument approach, a GCA, and a landing on the undulating PSP. Piece of cake, as he'd heard the British exchange officers say.

It was nearly dawn when Brown tossed his debriefing forms on the pile on the weary intelligence officer's desk. His diving attack had been a dud, and when they got back they found a stitching of shell-fragment holes across the right wing, just sheet metal work to fix.

Middlebrook had already checked the schedule: they were on for an 0200 takeoff tomorrow, virtually a repeat of tonight's mission. Well, six more to go after that. Idly, Brown picked up the folder underneath his. It was Sunderman's, much more neatly filled out and far more detailed than his own. He noted the coordinates and the times; Christ, they'd been in the same area for most of the time, and Sunderman was reporting a lot more activity than he'd seen. And he never heard him once on the radio. Sunderman was faking it; no wonder his crew was distressed.

June 1952
Nellis AFB, Nevada
USA

The treatment on the Nellis AFB flight line was reversed from Kelly's cadet days. The first F-86 combat pilots were just returning, and most of the instructors were properly respectful of Kelly's combat time. He found out that Garvey had just been through the course, was married to the girl he met in Japan, and she was already five months pregnant. He was some swift dude.

Not that he was doing too badly himself. When he'd gotten back to the States, the doctors had seemed to feel that Kelly was letting them down. He'd earned a broken neck, at least a hairline fracture, but nothing showed up on the x-rays. His paralysis faded over the weeks and they began to talk about pressures from fluids and swellings. He moved about easily and had begun to exercise again as they flew him to Walter Reed to San Antonio to the Mayo Clinic and back to Walter Reed again. Finally, they signed off and he headed straight for the Pentagon to get assigned to F-86 training. He talked himself into the next class—he was, after all, a bona-fide two-victory hero, with a failed chute turned in for a new one.

He met Kathy Campbell in the bookstore. To pick up a girl in Las Vegas in a bookstore was completely implausible; to pick her up because he heard her ask for the Maude translation of *War and Peace* was irrational. Still, it happened precisely that way.

Kelly had gone into the bookstore to buy a book of instructions on blackjack and craps; he'd been losing every day at the casinos. He'd bought three books on the subject, then bought a half dozen paperbacks, the Bounty trilogy, *Northwest Passage*, *Oliver Twist*, and some Wodehouse. When he heard her request, he quickly picked up the Knopf edition of *Anna Karenina* and approached her. "Have you read this?"

Kathy started. She turned, grinned, grabbed the books out of his hand, glanced at the titles. "My goodness, I didn't know you flyboys read."

Kelly flushed with irritation. "Hey. Never call a pilot a flyboy. Besides, some of us read a lot. My name's Mike Kelly, and I'm perishing with thirst. Will you have a drink with me?"

Kathy regarded Kelly levelly. She had of course run into Air Force types from Nellis—they were impossible to avoid here—but something about this guy attracted her. She remembered her vow, made long ago in college, never even to date another military man. Until today, she had managed to make it stick. But something about this improbable encounter tickled her. And something about Kelly tickled her too.

She agreed to have a soda. And dinner that night. And soon found herself spending all her time with him.

At first, they divided their time together between talking about books and wandering the casinos. She knew how to play everything, including baccarat, all learned at her father's knee. Kelly stuck to craps and blackjack, trying out all the systems, betting the minimums.

They lost piddling amounts, wolfed down the virtually free food and drink, watched the shows, and in short order established an intimacy of the outsiders against the insiders. Both quickly tired of the compulsive gambling and unremitting neon.

Kelly took Kathy to the base a few times, to sample club life, to eye the world he inhabited. He did so gingerly, for there was a certain reserve about her when he showed up in uniform or talked about his life in the Air Force, a reserve he interpreted as dislike. But she had captivated him, with her perky good looks, her wise observations, and her wisecracks. She was younger than he by two years, but unaccountably he felt her to be older, somehow. Moreover, her self-sufficiency, her aura of inner calm intrigued him as no flashier woman ever had.

As his F-86 transition training intensified and ground toward its completion, they began spending their spare days—there weren't many—in the desert, looking for rocks and watching the surprisingly rich animal life.

The walks through the desert were times of the greatest peace he had ever known. They talked about books, ideas, the wildlife, her research project. She was working on her masters degree at UCLA, and had come to Las Vegas for the summer to do research on the effects of the gambling industry on the local

140

school systems. But best of all they could get by for hours without talking at all, content just to be together.

For one night together in the desert, he'd gotten a tiny tent from Supply, so they could avoid the frenetic atmosphere of town as well as the suspicious snooping of Kathy's landlady. They'd walked miles through the heat of the desert, absorbing the immense silences and the subtle palette of the landscape. The sunset came as he was heating up some canned rations in a battered skillet. Kathy put aside her book and simply watched the clouds change color from orange to livid purple and then deepest indigo.

She studied Kelly hunched by the fire, backlit by its snapping mesquite flames. He concentrated on getting the Air Force rations just so; he'd claimed with his usual phony bluster that he was the only man in the service who knew how to make them edible. She smiled at his back. He wore a battered old leather jacket, torn denims, and scarred combat boots.

Why was she here? There was no good reason. But then, she mused, there was no good reason not to be here. She understood, she thought, watching Kelly work intensely at cooking, why she had been so fatally attracted to Nick, and perhaps why she had been so to Kelly. There was obviously something about some military men that struck a chord deep within her, a chord she would liked to have not known about, since she was not particularly interested in war or the machines it created.

They were like priests, in a way, or particularly dedicated teachers; they felt a sense of calling, and pursued it almost—she searched for the word, and at last it came—selflessly. Not that Mike wasn't selfish; he was obviously selfish, in specific materialistic ways, ways that related to his dreadful life in Illinois. But still he had the air about him of a man wholly absorbed in something larger than himself. She guessed it had something to do with flying.

Kathy knew she was a romantic and worked hard to stay alert against being driven into ultimately fruitless liaisons. In casting this feisty Irish fighter jock-cum-bookworm as a kind of modern knight errant, driven to his deeds by some higher calling, she knew she was treading perilous ground. He had feet of clay; she'd seen that enough in his rough demeanor, his determination to "make it"—whatever that could mean in the absurd confines of the Air Force—and his sometimes appalling behavior in public.

She didn't feel used. They had of course made love; she no longer felt the silly constraints of her college years, and it had

141

seemed natural to use the desert silences for themselves all those weeks ago when he had first made clear his passion for her. But this time, there was no question of his intentions; somehow, she didn't even care. Somehow, regardless of why, or how, or what it might mean, she simply felt right with him.

Kelly lifted up the skillet, peered into it, and tossed his infectious grin over his shoulder.

"Chow's ready. Are you?"

Kathy stretched luxuriously on the sleeping bag and smiled back at him. "Any time, flyboy," she said, and she meant it.

When he proposed, later that night, after they'd made love and, naked in each other's arms, watched the stars wheel through the night, she didn't even hesitate to say yes.

Before the sun rose, they had it all planned. They would marry immediately upon his return from Korea.

9

5 January 1952
Spokane AFB, Washington
USA

Washington's introduction to SAC had been ideal; the 92nd had been one of the first units to go to Korea, and the very first to prove the practicality of SAC's "Mobility Kits," the aggregation of spare parts that could be tucked in a bomb bay to sustain operations until the transports could catch up. The word to go had come on July 2; in fifty hours the airplanes were leaving, and ten days later they were dropping bombs in combat.

Washington was eagerly accepted by the training cadre that had been left behind. They welcomed a new second lieutenant who could be pressed into every kind of duty. He enjoyed it because he was getting five years of experience in six months, in everything from protocol to supply to physiological training. The more they loaded on him the better he liked it, as long as he got to spend a few evenings and maybe Sunday with Louise.

In some ways Wash's enthusiasm hurt him. He wanted to get overseas and join the 92nd in combat, but the training unit was so shorthanded they kept deferring his departure. When he finally left, via Stoneman, Travis, and Tachikawa, it was only after he had raised a lot of hell.

And after making a little agreement. Louise was going to try to get a job as a nurse in the dependent school system in Japan. If she did, she'd join him, and they would get married.

She felt not at all bad about stacking the deck. Louise had confidence in Dr. Andersen, for he had everybody's number. He treated the famous and the infamous in his specialty, and he did it with discretion and good humor. He knew their local congressman very well, so well that his opposition would have loved to know the degree of their familiar acquaintance, and when he called on Louise's behalf he got action. He stressed from the start that she was a colored girl, but in a little more than three months she was on her way to Tokyo to work in a clinic there. Louise hated to leave the incubator security he had provided, but Wash was in Japan, and she would be with him there—and everywhere after.

Wash was delighted, even though he never knew the extent of Andersen's fiddling to get her overseas. He was still dazzled by Louise, and found when he was away from her that he missed her terribly. He loved her more than anyone he'd ever known.

Washington also loved the B-29, even if it was the plane's second war. In the first, the B-29 had been a wild gamble, second only to the Manhattan Project, a boiling synthesis of airmens' dreams and engineers' hopes, an unlikely combination of probabilities that promised either an end to the war or its indefinite prolongation. Too many new things had been jammed into the pell-mell package of its acquisition: new engines, new airfoils, new structure, new armament, pressurization, impossible speed, impossible range. If it worked it would be the absolute evocation of America, the triumph of her flight technology, production, and people. The resources allocated to its development were so great that failure would simultaneously make an invasion of Japan inevitable and fatally risky.

Failure had stalked it from the start. The second test flight airplane crashed, killing the legendary test pilot Eddie Allen and many engineers critically important to the program. Engine fires were epidemic. The fire control system didn't work as planned. Boeing's production efforts, though based on building more big bombers than anyone, were not advanced enough to match their own sophisticated design.

Conservative wisdom had called for its cancellation. The cognoscenti knew that so many ambitious development factors could not be brought together in time to fight the war. But Army Air Force chief Gen. Hap Arnold persisted, and program manager

Maj. Gen. K. B. Wolfe persisted, and Boeing persisted, and on June 5, 1944, twenty months and fifteen days after its first flight, the B-29 entered combat. Its first showing was not auspicious, but as the leaders and the crews learned how to use the weapon it became successively able, fearsome, awesome, and finally so devastating that there were no longer targets to burn.

Except two. Hiroshima and Nagasaki. Peace was born of LeMay's marriage of sufficient capability and ultimate horror. The atomic weapon was perhaps the only thing spared Korea.

The B-29 was handsome. If the B-17 had been a Cadillac of bombers, the B-29 was a Rolls-Royce. The long, slender wings supported a needle-smooth fuselage in flight; inside, the crew operated in relative comfort. Flight at altitude in the B-17 had been an agony of freezing-cold drafts, cramped quarters, frozen relief tubes, deafening noise, and the misery of stultifying oxygen masks. The B-29 was pressurized, with an almost adequate heating system.

In the B-17, the gunners were cramped in turrets or stood at open barn-door windows, with only pounding fear to force blood through cold-constricted vessels. In the B-29, the guns were remotely operated and could be controlled, like the firepower of a battleship, from a central station.

The B-29s had merged with history over Hiroshima and Nagasaki, and then they had been relegated to training duties or the limbo of storage areas. They sat for years, fuel gumming in tanks, seals leaking, windscreens crazing, wiring aging, tires cracking and flattening, spared the scrap man's torch by a hunch that they might someday be used. The B-29s' vast foundation of support, from crew members to training systems to spare-parts pools to weapons, was not treated even with this elemental care. It was simply spent in the wind of demobilization.

With Korea, the whole creaking apparatus was summoned forth, Lazarus-like. It came unwillingly, men and machines, and except for the cutting edge that SAC had maintained at the ready, took months to reach a level of efficiency that would still have been considered unsatisfactory in the last war.

The 92nd was part of that cutting edge, and Washington fell to his duties with a sense of joy. The mission was not glamorous, like the brawls in MiG Alley, and it was circumscribed by political rules of engagement which sought to avoid a third world war. In essence its task was to support the ground forces, a job it couldn't do well, to interdict the supply system, the railyards, bridges, and highways, which it did superbly, and obliterate with

144

maniacal efficiency the power systems and airfields. All with conventional bombs left over from World War II.

6 June 1952
Yokota AB
Japan

Washington had phased into combat easily; to do so, he did what almost all airmen do, disassociate the task and the explosions from the people bursting on the ground. He had missed the earlier period of fighter opposition from the MiGs; now they were coming back in ominous strength as the pressure of the B-29 operations built. The bomber missions encountered the same performance anomalies as the F-86s did. At times the MiG attacks would be flown aggressively, with precision and élan. At other times it was like watching a parade of awkward students making tentative, ill-coordinated passes, and streaking away at the first sign of escort opposition.

Back in October 1951, the Communist tactics improved and five B-29s had been lost to the MiGs on a single mission, compared to six in the previous fifteen months. It was time to adopt night bombing.

Washington had smoothed the way to his success with a joking, smiling style, kidding himself and others about being one of the few Negro officers, and Louise despised the process. She had encountered it first in the club at Spokane and flown into a rage with Washington. "Don't belittle yourself with these people! You are better at your job, better at anything than any of them! You don't have to make those awful jokes about 'nightfighters.' And I don't want you to say 'Negro,' I want you to say 'black.' You're black, damn it, and so am I and so are our parents, and we are as good as anybody anywhere, and don't you forget it!"

Wash had listened and agreed, although the word *black* seemed to bite into him. In school "You black bastard" had been the penultimate insult; the really rough guys said "motherfucker." He knew his joking, easy manner was a successful initial formula. Later, when the time came, he'd gradually drop the pose. In the meantime, it made it easier for the well-intentioned, and it defused the would-be critics.

Louise had made it to Japan with no difficulty, and with characteristic determination sorted out the process by which she and Washington could be married. It was a simple ceremony in the small chapel at Tachikawa. Like most of the hastily built Air Force chapels, it was New England-simple and changed denominations on an hourly basis, with the type of service performed.

They had a weekend for a honeymoon and, considering the tepid level of their lovemaking, it was enough. Louise, who was so bold, so fierce in so many of her ideas, was terribly shy in bed. For all her level-headed worldliness, she could not surrender herself to Washington with any abandon. She loved him, and he was tender, and he knew he could wait. In some ways the shyness pleased him.

Some of the B-29s had been repainted a sinister black for the night missions, and Washington's crew had outlined in gorgeous white enamel new nose art, a picture of a black hangman slipping a noose around a stereotypical Oriental, with buck teeth and glasses, and below was printed the legend NIGHTFIGHTER. Washington laughed when he saw it, knowing it was an affectionate tribute to his accuracy and skill. But Louise's image rose in his mind and he knew that it was time to drop the act. He had their respect; he had his own respect. It was time.

He talked with her about it that weekend; at first she was furious, and demanded that he have it removed. He persuaded her of his intention to drop the mask of friendly acknowledgment. They argued, and the argument subsided into lovemaking. Washington won two key points; he persuaded her to disrobe entirely, and to leave a small night light on. He thought she was incredibly beautiful; she thought she was incredibly wanton. Their night missions were fatiguing. He couldn't sleep well in the day, and there were too many other duties. Wash was flying extra missions as an instructor, cramped in the rear of the pressurized nose between the new navigator and the radio operator. As big as the B-29 was, the crew quarters were cramped and stacked with parachutes, lunches, folders, tool kits, ditty bags.

His twenty-fourth mission seemed to be just another rerun of the previous twenty-three. The blackness merged the drone of engines, pumps, and wind into a white noise, hypnotically boring. Just across the bomb line, where it was usually quiet, a band of searchlights reached up; the inside of the cockpit blazed incandescently, and the lead gunner began chattering: MiGs at three o'clock.

The shells burst the sides of the airplane, smashed through the cockpit, shattered the copilot's head, tore out the glazing of the bombardier's nose windows, and released the cabin pressure with

146

a vortex of maps, clothes, pencils, glasses, sandwiches, and whatever was not nailed down to drift across the Korean countryside. Fire broke out in the wing and center section as a second burst of shells tore into the aft fuselage. The interphone had died. The cockpit was a stream of misty red as the airflow sucked the copilot's blood into the cold void.

There was no panic yet, and no action from the aircraft commander, Maj. Pat Kimball. The autopilot flew the airplane, and no warning bells rang. Washington grabbed his chute and went forward. The copilot was dead. Kimball was unconscious. They had passed the searchlights now, and the red flame blossoming from the wings promised an explosion. Washington hit the bailout button, hoping the signal would clear the aft end of the airplane. He slammed down the gear lever and felt the punished airplane lurch as the massive wheels hit the airstream. If he had had time he would have lowered the nose gear alone, but it didn't matter; this airplane would never land again.

He felt a change in the airflow and realized that the student navigator and the others had opened the hatch and bailed out. He needed time. He cautiously moved the knob on the autopilot, turned the torching airplane slanting back across the bomb line, out to sea. He fumbled with Kimball's straps. Kimball was small, and had cinched his seat belt and shoulder harness tight. Washington pulled his gloves off, breaking a nail as he opened the seat belt. He dragged Kimball back, across the throttle quadrant, edging to the side to avoid the gaping hole where the entrance hatch had been. They were no longer caught in the lights, but reflected glare from the burning wings showed him that the nosewheel was full down.

Wash had planned to lower Kimball through the hatch, pull his parachute D-ring and drop him, but the bulk of their clothes and equipment made it impossible in the cramped wheel well. Instead he eased himself down into the hatch, held Kimball up over him like a rag doll, straightened his legs, and dropped, whipping back as the hurricane wind caught him.

Somehow he held on, his massive arms pulling Kimball tight to him as they tumbled, his rump staring him in the face. As they plummeted through the icy black, Washington thought of Louise, very glad that she had been with him intimately, entirely nude.

He wanted to free-fall farther, but he was afraid of the terrain and pulled his own D-ring, tightening his hold on the inert pilot. The jerk of the chute opening almost pulled Kimball from his embrace as it checked their descent. There was a glow on the horizon that gave Washington an indication of their height. He waited as long as he dared, then pulled Kimball's D-ring and dropped him. Kimball rocketed from view, but Wash caught a glimpse of the chute, enough to know that it had opened.

Washington hit the tree line before he saw it. Branches whipped across his face as his chute straps jolted him to a stop. He'd made it. He didn't know whether he was in enemy territory, or if he was ten feet or fifty feet off the ground, but he had made it.

There was no sound but the scrape of his risers against the tree. His eyes accommodated and he saw that he was perhaps fifteen feet off the ground, and that he could swing himself to a branch and get down easily.

As he dropped to the ground, a scream startled him and he reached for his holster; it was empty, his service .45 lost somewhere over Korea. He began to move toward the noise, and saw the chute spread out across the trees. It was Kimball.

Kimball had made a better landing unconscious than Washington had awake. Wash unbuckled him, and felt to see if he could find the wounds. There was some heavy bleeding near his collar bone, and he had a gash across his forehead, probably put there when they bailed out. No bones seemed to be broken, but he was deeply unconscious, moaning far too loudly for safety. When he had finished the rough examination, Washington wrapped him in the chute and collapsed beside him, nerves sandbagged into sleep.

He awoke at dawn, shivering uncontrollably. Peeling Kimball's chute back, this time he found the wound, a deep puncture that welled blue bubbles. He put a compression bandage on it, rewrapped Kimball, and began to run to warm himself. He heard the sound of an engine and dropped to the ground. There was a road to the right. He moved to some bushes and heard more noises coming.

It was a G.I. jeep. Somehow they'd made it far enough to drift across the lines. Washington ran out to the road, to be covered by the startled G.I.s.

Suddenly, it was over. He and Kimball were jolting down the rough little road to a MASH unit, then while Kimball was being prepped, the C.O. there debriefed Washington, checked him over, and sent him back downcountry via medevac chopper. Within hours, he was back at Seoul, dazed, only just beginning to comprehend that he was the celebrity they all claimed him to be. He knew as he climbed off the C-47 at Tachikawa that his life would never be the same: the army of flashguns popping as he clumped down the ramp had told him that.

Washington had never had the full public-relations treatment before, but he handled it well. Kimball had recovered, but the medics said he wouldn't have lived without Washington's crude first aid, and he surely wouldn't have lived if Wash had left him in the cockpit. The airplane had flown almost to the coast before blowing up. It had been assumed that everyone on board was lost, and then the crew had started turning up. Only the copilot had been killed.

Washington was nominated for the Medal of Honor; it came back as the Distinguished Flying Cross, but he was still delighted. Gen. Paul Chamberlin, FEAF Commander, made the presentation at a full-dress ceremony on a cloudless Sunday right on the flight line at Tachi. The bands played, the troops marched, the fighters roared overhead, and everyone cheered after Chamberlain pinned the decoration on his dress blue blouse and Kimball walked up and saluted Washington, then shook his hand.

Afterward, Chamberlin took Washington aside and said, "Well, Lieutenant, is there anything I can do for you?" He might have meant it as a gesture, to be declined. But he hadn't reckoned with Washington's lifelong desires.

Wash smiled at him, not his willing-nigger smile, but his negotiating smile, and shot back, "Yes, sir! Get me back in flight school, where I belong."

Chamberlain's eyebrows rolled up like a shade. He considered the young Negro navigator a moment, weighing the risks and benefits. If he sent Washington back to flight training and he busted out again, no embarrassment would accrue to him, only to Washington. On the other hand, if he succeeded in pilot training . . .

"Let me see what I can do," Chamberlin said at last. Wash's grin lit up the whole flight line.

It turned out Chamberlin could do quite a lot. In two weeks, Wash had his orders for flight school. His basic flight training would be at Goodfellow AFB, near San Angelo, Texas. He looked at the mimeoed orders in his hands and thought about Oliekiwicz. This time he was going to make it if he had to jam the stick down the instructor's throat.

149

10

Pauline stirred, turning to arch her bottom against him; Don slept, but his foot rubbed against her lower leg. He was the most affectionate man she had ever known, a squirming puppy of love. Odd, he had never heard a bomb fall, had been raised in the richness of California (to her it was all simply an extended Hollywood), and still he needed affection, he needed her. She raised the big alarm clock close to her eyes, squinted. It was only five thirty. She had half an hour, an endless luxury of warmth and security. She would enjoy her hunger, the haunting, ineradicable hunger that would be with her forever, enjoy it because she knew there would be coffee-milk, lots of sugar, real cane sugar, bread and tinned fruit, as much as she wanted.

Pauline Krause was twenty-two, and this was the fifteenth or sixteenth man with whom she had slept. She didn't count the rough encounters, where sex was demanded or where she used it to get a small advantage. But this was the first man she had loved. He would die if he ever found out how experienced she was; he was an angel of innocence himself.

What a funny smell he had; clean or sweaty, he smelled like an angel. When the war had ended, she was sure she would be happiest about the end of the bombing, the end of the thousand random dangers of the end of the Nazi regime, when a word of angry frustration could mean denouncement, perhaps even death. Now she realized that the worst things had been the hunger and the smell, the endless hunger, and the ever-present odor of death.

Warmth and food. And love. She loved Picard, this man-baby, so strong, so clever with his hands, so wonderful in bed with his amateur enthusiasm. And not simply because he helped her get the warmth and food. There had been others who were just—providers. Not Picard. He had sworn he was not a virgin; she was not so sure. She admitted to being raped; he would not

150

understand that sex not long ago was common currency, better than cigarettes or chocolate because the supply between your legs was ever-ready and inexhaustible. She felt no shame. She'd sold herself when she had to live; now she was faithful to him and would be so as long as he wanted her.

His wanting helped her feel secure, yet she didn't need him as she had at times needed a meal, or a night's shelter. She worked herself, at wages the Americans thought were low, and which to her were scandalously high, more than her brothers, her poor dead brothers, had made as sergeants fighting in Russia, more than her father, her poor dead father, had made as a handyman in the shell factory. Sometimes she thought she loved Picard so because he reminded her of her father before the war, before he'd been savagely wounded in a stupid explosion at the factory. He'd labored on, one leg useless, in pain; she had felt no grief for him when he died in the bombing, because she knew his shame and his pain were ended.

The villagers did not scorn her for living with an Ami. Many of them envied her, she knew; she was the little brunette who would have done well to have married a local farmer. At the Schoengarten Markt, they understood all the new facts of life. To be German now was to be practical above all else. The time for the luxury of self-delusion was long gone.

Pauline Krause did not delude herself about anything. Least of all about Don Picard. And so she considered the amazing fact of his stubborn determination to marry her with the same detachment with which she pondered potatoes at the market.

The Americans were so rich. They had fought the war with their wealth of tanks and planes and cannons, and their wonderful concept that it was better to spend money than lives. Poor Germany. She had lost so many people, brothers, friends, lovers, ultimately her parents, because of the opposite ideas, that you could throw bodies and slogans more inexpensively than guns or tanks. The results lay all about them.

She would not be a farmer's wife. She would go to America, with Picard if she could, with someone else if not. But she would go to America.

He had asked her to marry him the first night they slept together; she had been hurt, because she thought he was being cruel. She had not shown him her hurt. Instead, she laughed and said no.

It was the smartest thing she could have done, binding him to her freely and, she hoped, forever. She would have married him

151

then, knowing no more than he was a big strong American and a gentle inexperienced lover. She loved him, knowing now that he was poor for an American—could it be, he was richer than anyone she had ever known, and he was poor for an American, and inexplicably proud of it, too?—but that he had qualities she thought were German. He was proud of his work, loyal to his people; he worked as long as was necessary, and laughed with his friends about it. He was naïve, and she loved it.

She dozed, waking when Picard sprang up and went to the bathroom. She heard him brush his teeth, gargle; it meant for certain that he wanted to make love to her again. Good; she'd skip breakfast to tumble joyfully with him, bending herself against him to drain away his temptation for others, wrapping her strong legs around him to satisfy and bind him.

"Rub my back, *liebchen*, that was so good. You are so good to me." Afterward Don was content. He had worked late, didn't have to be at roll call until nine.

Pauline looked at the clock, rubbed his back vigorously, and leaped out of bed. "I must go, I'll be late," she said in her delightful, fluting, too-precise English. It was duty, they both understood that. It was her turn to open the base exchange kitchen; she would get there with the Air Policeman to unlock the doors, then set up for a busy day. She'd put the coffee on—fresh ground coffee in incredible quantity, you'd think the Americans had conquered Brazil instead of Germany—and then have some of the terrible greasy pastries the Americans liked. Maybe there would be time to boil some of the awful sausages, hot dogs, for breakfast.

Picard watched her dress, admiring the taut slimness of her body, the brightness of her brown eyes. She dressed economically—she did everything economically, he realized—in little swift motions. She had gotten out of bed his lover. She stood eying herself critically in the tiny bathroom's mirror as a no-nonsense German worker.

She was still enigmatic to him at times like these. He would think he knew her as well as any man can know a woman, then she would suddenly shift moods and become a brooding stranger. He thought he understood why; the devastation still lay all around the village and the base, and it would be years—decades, maybe—before everything was back to normal. He knew she had had to fight for her right to life after the collapse of Nazi Germany; he knew that she had slept with many men to stay alive, and he even knew she had slept with Major Kowalski to get her job at the base exchange. He knew, and didn't care.

His mother had cautioned him against all foreigners when he got orders for Germany—his mother, of all people, who had married Joe Amado, a Portuguese!—and he'd been briefed a dozen times about the dual dangers of what the chaplain called "fraternization" and the black market. He understood well enough the dangers in both. Yet he was determined not to waste his time in Europe, as so many other guys did, spending all their off-duty time hanging around each other in the club, hoping to score with the sleazy whores who hung out there too.

On the long Atlantic crossing aboard the U.S.S. *Breckinridge*, an old Liberty ship attached to MATS, Don had planned for weeks how he would hoard his meager pay to see the country. He was stunned when he boarded his first train for Frankfurt and discovered how far his money would actually go, and more stunned to see what a cigarette or bottle of booze bought him. Since he didn't smoke and rarely drank, he had found a way effectively to double his earnings just by using his Class VI store rations. It was illegal, of course, but nobody really cared. Even all these years after the end of the war, the Germans were still on their knees; without the Marshall Plan and the black market, nobody who knew Germany had any doubt that the great fear the OSI boys harbored—the fear of Communist influence—would have materialized. Desperate people do desperate things. Don had seen that for himself in the ruined streets of Stuttgart, where the rubble was piled four stories high and every man he saw was somehow physically scarred. The mental and emotional scars came out only when you got to know a German.

He was only five months into his tour when he met Pauline. Even though she worked on base, he met her in the village of Schoengarten. It was his habit to borrow a jeep for the weekend from the commo squadron boys—who had more than they needed—and wander the countryside. He was slowly picking up a little German, and he always tried to use it when he was on a weekend tour.

He got to know a lot of the local Germans more quickly than most Amis, through the great universal language of mechanics. One day he'd been halted in Schoengarten's bombed-out garden— for which the village was named, and which had been the site of a munitions storehouse—tinkering with the jeep's distributor. He'd worked in the Sunday sun, stripped to the waist, for an hour, carefully disassembling the distributor, cleaning the points

153

and checking the point gap, when he became aware of a small audience. He ignored them, having learned that Germans did not like too much ersatz familiarity.

The audience was made up of three people: an old man, a kid about ten, and a strapping young guy about Don's age, who was missing an ear and whose face on that side was hideously disfigured. People bicycled past Don and the group as he worked carefully, as was his style, not hurrying, doing it right the first time.

Replacing the distributor called for all his dexterity. He balanced on his toes and cautiously wiggled it back onto the timing shaft. As usual, the thing wobbled and almost slipped over. But just as he was about to give up, relax, and try again, a tanned arm reached in and positioned it precisely right, allowing Don the opportunity to secure it. He didn't look up as he did so. When the bolt was cinched tight, he straightened up and looked at the arm's owner.

It belonged to the deformed young man, who dropped his arm and stared hard at Don, as if daring him to flinch. Don wiped his tools silently, eying the guy, then cleaned his right hand with the rag and stuck it out to the man.

"*Tausend Dank*," Don said carefully, knowing his accent was awful.

The young guy blinked, then slowly extended his own hand and shook Don's. "It is," he said as carefully, "of nothing. The pleasure was all yours."

Don's grin infected the guy, who grinned back, stretching his face into a grisly Halloween mask, and just like that Don slipped inside the defenses of the village of Schoengarten-ob-der-Tauber.

The guy's name was Dieter, it turned out, and he worked at the only garage in town. Between them, in awful German and execrable English, they probed their mutual interest in machinery and discovered a bond that reached beyond nationality. Dieter took Don to his garage and showed him around with the pride of a master craftsman. Don responded with the same appreciation, and soon they were friends.

Dieter took to asking Don to his home for meals. Naturally, being already sick of the mess hall on base, Don accepted, and within weeks became a fixture at the Bachmeier garage and home. At home, Frau Bachmeier—Dieter's stooped mother—fussed over him as if he were simply another son, sharing with Picard everything from her ancient homilies to her strudel. At the garage, he would loiter with the men and machines, accepted for his skill, appreciated for his generosity with cigarettes and liquor, quietly coming to understand some of what it meant to be German in 1952.

It was Dieter who introduced him to Pauline. In the normal course of events, Dieter would have been a candidate for her; Don knew that. But he also knew that the British bomb that had killed Dieter's shipmates and wiped away his looks had also somehow killed Dieter's sense of self-worth where women were concerned. He had known her for years, and admired her too. But now—now all he could do was find someone suitable for her.

In his own way, he arranged for the meeting to take place at his garage. Don was invited to stay after work one Saturday, and Pauline had been asked to come by for an unspecified reason.

She walked into the garage with an armload of shopping basket, a babushka on her head, and a threadbare coat on her back, and she didn't know how to react when she saw Picard leaning on the old Horch chatting in terrible German with Dieter. All precisely as Dieter had planned it.

What he had not planned, what he could not have known, was that his timing had been perfect. Don had been too shy to fool around with the whores, and far too shy to get serious with any of the German women he met casually.

Pauline bowled him over. She stood in the door of the garage, outlined by the crisp bright sun of fall, and Don just fell in love. It was that simple. She was perfect.

Pauline was not so affected. But as she began cautiously to go out with Don—experiencing the new sensation of approval and respect from the villagers—she gradually began to fall under his spell. He was handsome in a regular-featured sort of way; he was intelligent, as his big brown eyes proved, and he was gentle and considerate. More, he was the first American soldier of any rank she had ever known who had tried to live beyond the bounds of the Little Americas of the bases, who had tried to see, taste, and feel her country. That alone touched her deeply.

Picard knew he would marry her one day, despite the constant barrage of propaganda they spewed at them to stay on guard against girls just looking for a ticket to the States. The word was out, they said, that marrying a soldier was the easiest way to the good life. Maybe so. But watching her dress for work made him certain he was right to ask Pauline—or Polly, as he called her—to marry him.

She strapped on her watch, grabbed her purse, and kissed him in a single swift motion. Then she was gone.

Don finally arose and dresssed leisurely; she'd left the coffee pot on, and there was some bread and butter. He'd grab a doughnut when the *roachencoachen*, the dreadful wagon turned commissary, came to the flight line at ten. The chow wagon was a German innovation; the Germans were quick to fill any need that provided cash.

He had four men working for him, all ex-Luftwaffe. They were supposed to do the dog work, washing the airplanes, cleaning up, but he used them for whatever he could. They were good with their hands, and would flatter him about the quantity and quality of American equipment. All except the airplanes, the Lockheed P-80 Shooting Star jet fighters. They said the Luftwaffe had a better plane in 1944, the Messerschmitt Me 262. Don hated to believe it, but it might have been true; the Germans were so damn clever, and such good engineers. Dieter and his spotless garage told him that.

Don gulped his coffee and grabbed the keys to the jeep. He was eager to get to work; he thought the P-80s were wonderful, easy to work on and reliable. The flight line was so much fun that he sometimes wondered what he was doing here in this cool green paradise, so different from Atwater, California.

He was a line chief, responsible for the C.O.'s airplane and for the work of four crew chiefs even though he didn't have the rank for it. He should have been a tech sergeant at least, but they were shorthanded, and he knew the airplane. The C.O. was a great guy; he'd come out to the airplane, return Don's salute, and ask him if it was okay, which it always was. Then he'd climb right in the cockpit, with no walk-around inspection at all—supposedly required by regs—and go off and fly. He was telling Don he trusted him with his life; Don understood it to be both tribute and insurance; the C.O. knew Don would work twice as hard to be sure it was right.

He was right about that, for it was that special camaraderie that Don relished about working the line, even more than getting his hands on those beautiful machines. He had absorbed it as a boy, as he had absorbed the skills of his father, among the old Air Corps pilots and crew chiefs. Civilians never knew the bond they shared; and even the Germans, who said they had something like it back in the old Luftwaffe, were amazed at the intensity with which Picard and his men would work.

He'd never tried to explain it to anyone, since he'd never had to. As Don jumped into his jeep, he stuffed another piece of thick dark German bread in his mouth and ground the starter, thinking about how he would explain it to Polly. Because she would have to know, since he intended to share everything with her. The engine caught and he let it idle a moment, half listening to the message of the motor, half thinking how lucky he was to have a life like this; a life off base, in which he had a woman he loved, a set of wheels, and an apartment the C.O. winked at, and a life on base, in which he was privileged to make the fullest possible use of himself and his skills.

He waved at old Frau Meissner, already on her morning shopping, and slipped the jeep's gearshift into first. If he could be this happy at the very beginning of his Air Force career, how could it get any better?

Only with Polly. And that, too, would come.

11

0910 LOCAL
19 December 1952
Nashville, Tennessee
USA

Joan looked at the figures in disbelief. She stepped down from the scales, then stepped on again, positioning her feet precisely. 138. She leaned back and it dropped to a scarcely more satisfactory 135. Duke was due home in a month, and she was fifteen pounds overweight. She'd thought she'd snap back after the baby was born; instead, reddish blue aiguillettes of flesh hung below her navel. She leaned against the sink, peering at the mirror. There were circles under her eyes outlining the puffiness that stayed no matter how much she slept. The lines around her mouth she could take care of with makeup. Her breasts worried her most; she seemed to see a little sag, and there were blue veins that reached down and almost circled her areolas.

She tucked a stray strand of hair behind her ear. From down the hall, a sudden cry announced that Charles Kingston Brown, Jr., wanted something. Joan winced and willed Millie to get to him before his piercing wail woke Duke's mother. After a second, the crying stopped. She sighed.

None of it was turning out the way she'd thought. After the

buildup Duke's parents had given her about the joys of service life, reality was considerably different. Partly it was Duke, partly it was her, and partly—mostly, really—it was the Air Force.

She had missed Duke's promotion party when he made captain in Japan, and he'd missed the birth of his own son. He'd moved heaven and earth to get onto the MARS network to talk to her in the hospital, of course, right after Charlie was born, but that wasn't the same. The hissing, noisy radio-telephone hookup was no substitute for a husband.

What was a good substitute? Joan picked at an errant eyelash and considered it anew. Not the man picked up at a bar or a party. Long ago she'd learned that lesson—as the old harpy had predicted. She was utterly faithful to Duke now, not from any keen sense of loyalty, but from sheer frustration with the pickings and the possible repercussions. The Air Force was expanding at an incredible rate, and there were new, virile men appearing every day. But in some ways it was like a small town; secrets—real secrets, not the silly military secrets they fussed about—were impossible to keep. Everybody somehow knew everything. So Joan gave up trying to find a substitute for Duke—in bed, in love, even in companionship.

She had come reluctantly to the conclusion that she would have to fit in somehow with the other women. It was not easy for her; she was too used to thinking of them as competition, not companions. Yet the way they had rallied around her when they all found out she was pregnant touched her; and God knew the problems of bearing and then rearing a child were far greater than she'd ever imagined, back when she and Duke had so casually planned a family of four or five.

Not now. She stared grimly at herself and admitted that she was thankful that Charlie had been delivered by Caesarean section. It had destroyed her muscle tone for good, but it also ensured that she would not have another baby. Perhaps some part of her had wilted at that; but another, larger part exulted.

She looked at the bulges on her belly clinically. They were too big. Of that, there was no question. She would have to do as they told her in the dispensary; she would have to exercise, cut down on the food and most especially on the booze.

The thought did not fill her with joy. She seemed only able to enjoy herself nowadays when she took a little liquor. The General—she never called Duke's father anything else, just as she always thought of his mother, Martha, as Mrs. General—

was getting to be a pain on the subject, with his coy little hints dropped broadly at every opportunity.

Well, screw him, as they said at the OWC when they'd all had a little too much and loosened up. Duke had his promotions and his buddies and his damned politicking, and all she had was a baby, some rooms in his parent's dreary old house, and the solace of her sherry.

A tiny knock sounded on the bathroom door.

"Yes?" she said, rather more irritably than she actually felt.

"Miz Brown, it's me, Millie. I gived little Charlie another bottle. You want me to stay with him?"

"Yes. Please, Millie. I'll be there in a while."

"Yes'm."

Thank God for bottle feeding. And thank God for Millie, too. How did women handle this when they had to drag the child around, hanging on their breasts, all day long? She snorted, thinking about those long discussions she'd drifted into and out of with the other wives about Dr. Spock and his notions of how a child should be reared. Obviously, Spock knew nothing about what the U.S. Air Force did to people's lives.

She ran the hot water into the sink and took out her double-edged razor, critically eying her underarms. Men complained about shaving every day. What the hell did they know of shaving? She had armpits and legs to deal with at least once a week. It would be nice to use a Remington electric, as Duke did.

She paused, remembering his shaving in the morning. It had been so long since they were together. He'd only had a week's leave from flying those bombers. They'd met in Honolulu and had a wild week of screwing and dancing and laughing, just like the old days. It had only begun to wear off the day he had to leave. She'd never felt so content as during that leave; and maybe it was no surprise that little Charlie had been conceived then.

Would it be like that again? Would she again wake up and enjoy his distinctive scent of Vitalis and sweat? When he'd called last week to tell her his great news about his rotation home and his new assignment, she'd been happy. Genuinely happy. She'd felt like a teenager again as he fought the static on the line to tell her about going to Maxwell Air Force Base for Squadron Officers' School, and then—the really big news! —that he was already holding his orders to go to the Pentagon after that. Typically Duke, he'd cut off her squeals of delight with a barrage of orders of his own: about getting a house bought in Arlington, Virginia—and who should help acquire it—about where and

159

how to meet him in California, and about getting a new car, suitable for a hotshot combat-wise captain going to SOS.

It was all a puzzle. All she knew was that she could at last leave this house and these dreadful people, and escape her own parents' often disapproving eyes. Nashville was a nice place to visit, but she had spent too long there already.

At Maxwell, she would live in married officers' quarters' —tasteless, drab, and cramped, no doubt—but they would be her quarters; she would rule there, not Mrs. General. And when finally they got to the Pentagon, she would have her own house at last, and would be able to mix with much more appropriate people.

She was enormously cheered by the prospects; by the chance that she and Duke might at last become a real couple; by escaping the somber confines of the Brown Prison, and by meeting new and exciting people.

It called for a little drink. She smiled and kicked the scales under the sink. To hell with it. There was plenty of time to lose weight.

1330 LOCAL
1 January 1953
Hamilton AFB, California
USA

HAPPY NEW YEAR—1953. Miriam Garvey read the sign over the base commander's front door with a little smile. Like the Hamilton Air Force Base officers' club, Col. Harold Kane's residence was almost twenty years old, built in the best California tradition of the pseudohacienda, a style made up of equal parts cream stucco, red tile roof, and arched doorways. The beautifully manicured base was as different from the windblown, thrown-together scene at Nellis in Nevada as she could imagine. Instead of the dusty desert lying all around frame shacks and cinderblock buildings, Hamilton was an oasis of Palm trees, sweet-smelling lawns, and immaculate Spanish-style buildings with the calm aura of a college campus rather than the barely contained frenzy of an operational fighter-interceptor base. She slipped the Chevy's gear selector into neutral with some effort, killed the engine, and decided that she liked it here.

Well, she thought ruefully as she swiveled the rearview mirror to check her make-up one last time, *here* is a relative term. Had she been lucky enough to be stationed at Hamilton, she might live in something akin to the spacious Kane home, even as a first lieutenant's wife. But since Jim was overseas, she was only attached in a loose way to Hamilton. They had decided that since he would leave for Korea again from Travis AFB, just up Highway 40 from Hamilton, she might as well relocate from Las Vegas to the Marin County area. The weather would be nicer, and she would have full access to the Hamilton commissary, PX, and hospital. So "here" for her nowadays was a dreary, brown-stucco single apartment in nearby Santa Rosa. It was little more than four hundred square feet of necessity, thrown together by some shrewd developer after the war, but it suited her needs well enough. How well it would suit her needs after Paul arrived was another matter.

She again felt the bulge under her dress and marveled at the life thumping and squirming inside her. Automatically, she ticked off the days until Jim's leave brought him home. Today was January 1, so in a little less than thirty days, he'd be home. If Paul—she knew it would be a beautiful boy—stayed on schedule, Jim would arrive within a week before his delivery. Then things would get a little cramped at 101C Petaluma Court. But there'd be plenty of time to find other quarters for the remainder of Jim's tour in Korea. And then, within only seven months, he'd be home and they'd all be together.

She blinked and realized she'd been daydreaming again. The cool winds drove crisp white clouds across a blue sky. Her smile widened. January in the San Francisco Bay Area was certainly different from January in New England. She wondered how her parents were spending the day. Shoveling snow, probably.

She tugged her dark brown wool coat over her proud tummy and carefully worked herself clear of the steering wheel. She could ill afford to do damage to the red serge maternity dress she'd splurged on at the City of Paris in San Francisco only last week. With luck, she might get to wear it again before she delivered—going out to dinner with Jim, maybe—but for now its sole raison d'être was to make her presentable at Mrs. Kane's reception. She'd grimaced first at the limited selection of even remotely chic maternity dresses available at the famous department store, and then grimaced again at the thirty bucks they wanted for it. You'd think the immense red tent with the little white collar was some kind of French original. It had stretched her budget to the snapping point to buy it, but this was a special occasion.

Getting out of the car was not easy. She finally got clear of the wheel, and then the wind pulled at the Chevy's thick door. As she struggled with the door, a gloved hand steadied it and allowed her to get out and stand up. She smiled up her thanks.

"Sure," the hand's owner smiled back. "I've been there, kid. Here, let me help with the keys." Miriam gratefully let the other woman reach in and pull out the keys from the ignition. She'd forgotten them again, and being hugely pregnant made even such a simple thing as grabbing keys from a dashboard a major operation.

The other woman closed the door and handed the keyring to Miriam. She was both taller and older than Miriam, a blonde with a pleasant, open face nicely made up, with a jaunty little feathered pillbox hat and a dark red coat. As Miriam slipped the keys into her purse, she stuck out her hand.

"Nancy Barnes," the blonde said, "and how close are you?"

"Miriam Garvey, and it should be within the month. Is yours in Korea too?"

Nancy nodded, slipping her glove back on. "Tachikawa. Flying 46s. Yours?"

"Somewhere in the South, with the Fourth, 86s." She chuckled. "I've only been in the Air Force for a few months, and already I sound just like he does, talking in numbers."

Nancy smiled. "I know. Me too. But there's nothing you can do, honey. Take it from a veteran. In a few years, it'll seem like it's the only lingo you've ever known."

Miriam nodded and started up the little walkway to the front door, trying not to waddle. Other women were coming and going, and there was the unmistakable party atmosphere around the place. Nancy joined her and they strolled slowly toward the door.

"Do you know Mrs. Kane?"

"A little. We were at Frankfurt together. Bob and Colonel Kane were in the same squadron then—on the Airlift."

"I was surprised when I got the invitation. She must be a nice person to ask us over like this."

"It's an old Air Force custom. Just like the New Year's reception the colonel is having at the club. The permanent party people go there, and the base commander's wife asks the wives of the men overseas to drop by her house."

"It's a nice custom. How do they know—"

"The base housing office. Didn't you get your place through them?"

162

"Yes. They had quite a time. There isn't much available."

Nancy grimaced slightly. "Do tell. I'm staying way out in Novato. Anyway, Carole Kane just asked them for a list of the Air Force families nearby and they got it for her. That way, she can cover most of us. Only those whose home is around here escape that list. And the club people find those."

"Escape? Surely that's not the word."

"Well . . . Carole can be trying at times. She's Old Army, you know, just like Hal Kane. He was Class of '20 at West Point."

"Oh? She must be proud. After all, here he is, base commander and all. Do they have children?"

Nancy stopped just before the porch. A woman in gray came out and waved a hello at them, which Nancy returned. From inside came the hubbub of many women chatting. Nancy looked at Miriam.

"Look. Miriam. I can tell you're new at this, so let me give you a little briefing. Carole Kane is not proud of Hal, and Hal is not proud of Hal. Most of his class got stars in the war—or even before the war—and he wound up a chicken colonel, which he still is. Nobody knows why. But he messed something up when he was a light colonel, back before the war, and somebody upstairs has never forgotten it. Making him the base commander is their way of sliding him out gracefully. If they'd made him the wing commander, that would be another kettle of fish entirely. But being base commander is like being . . . well, like being the head clerk or something. For a pilot, it's kind of degrading."

Miriam shook her head. "Seems wrong, somehow. Somebody has to be base commander."

"Sure. But all the pilots figure it should be some paper-pusher. Not one of them. You ask your husband about it. He'll tell you."

"So Mrs. Kane—Carole—is bitter too?"

"Very. Maybe more. She worked her fanny off over the years to help him make it. And now—he'll retire in a year, and that'll be it—out, into the toolies. So if she seems a little brittle, try to understand. Okay?"

"Of course. Thanks, Nancy."

"Sure, kid. Ready?"

Miriam grinned. "You bet. Onward."

"And upward. After you, kid."

Inside the door, the noise level increased dramatically. Miriam blinked as she eased through the doorway and looked around. They stood in a small foyer, a sort of half-scale replica of a real

163

hacienda's entry hall. A Mexican-looking maid appeared before them and awaited their coats, which they peeled off and handed her. Nancy grabbed Miriam by the elbow and sallied into the crowded living room.

Tasteful but slightly worn furniture of no particular distinction lined the walls of the room, which was full almost to bursting with women of all ages. Bright flowers spilled from vases everywhere, counterpointing the equally bright colors of the dresses and suits the women wore. Miriam saw in her first glance around the room that there were at least a half-dozen young women as pregnant as she. Somehow, it relieved her and annoyed her at the same time, since it stripped her of her specialness. A large crystal punch bowl stood on a sideboard near the entry, and Nancy stopped there to fill two small crystal cups. She quickly sipped hers as Miriam looked around.

"Rum," she announced, sotto voce. "Try it."

Miriam sipped hers and felt the cool fruitiness give way to a remote tingle. Nancy grabbed her elbow again and maneuvered her to where Mrs. Kane was holding court.

They hovered on the periphery of the little knot of older women chatting with Carole Kane, then Nancy seized the moment and slipped between them.

"Carole!" she said brightly. "Happy New Year!"

"Nancy! How good you could come," Carole answered. Only the most seasoned observer would have detected the tiny frost at the edges of her tone.

"Wouldn't miss it for the world," Nancy gushed, "and neither would my new friend, Miriam Garvey. Miriam, let me introduce you to Carole Kane, who knows what you're going through." She stood aside while Miriam shook hands with Carole.

Kane regarded her with deeply hooded eyes. She was an imposing woman, large-boned, with the worn look of an aristocrat fallen far and hard stamped indelibly on every feature and movement. There was about her an air of weariness and resignation that moved Miriam almost physically. She wore a beautiful silk dress of shimmering cobalt blue that should have offset her auburn hair wonderfully, but which seemed only to accuse the gray in it. She looked trim and fit, despite her height, which Miriam guessed at being nearly five ten, and her face was made up with almost Hollywood perfection, the ruby-red lipstick following lip lines so precise that Miriam, who despaired of ever pouting so perfectly as the models who graced Revlon ads in *Look* magazine, instantly felt that she had somehow smeared her

164

own lipstick on almost haphazardly. The overall effect was quite devastating; she felt immediately outclassed by the brooding, stunning presence of this woman, who had to be at least as old as Miriam's own mother.

"Welcome, my dear," said Kane slowly and carefully, her own appraisal of Miriam occurring in tiny, lightninglike shifts of her dark eyes, "and Happy New Year."

"Thank you, Mrs. Kane," Miriam replied with as much spirit as she could muster. "It was wonderful of you to invite me. One gets so lonely off base, and I don't really know anyone here yet."

A chilly smile spread those cold lips. "Yes. How well I know. Your first?" She inclined her head slightly toward Miriam.

"Yes, but not our last, I hope."

"No. Indeed not." She paused. Nancy jumped in to save the silence.

"Miriam's husband is in the Fourth," she said cheerily.

"Oh? Is he a pilot, dear?"

"Yes, Mrs. Kane. He flies fighters—F-86s now."

For some reason, it was the wrong thing to say. The eyes closed down even more.

"Ah. Fighters. Yes. Well, I'm sure you'll be glad when he's home."

"Oh, yes. Very glad."

Miriam raised the glass to her lips in an attempt to break the encounter into a manageable piece. She seemed to be dizzy already. Why should this woman be going out of her way to make her feel bad? She really had been glad to get the invitation, and she really did want to get to know everyone here. She'd already joined the local Officers' Wives' Club, but she was out of phase with the activities planning, so she was just a spare wheel until the Easter parties began. It had all seemed so easy when she'd observed it from the outside in Japan. These women were just like her for the most part; bright, well-educated, living on the edge of nameless fears as their men took off in aluminum tubes filled with bombs and guns, just trying to get by. Suddenly the hood came off Carole Kane's eyes. She looked piercingly at Miriam as if seeing her for the first time, or as if she had suddenly remembered something. Miriam caught the gaze over the edge of her crystal punch glass.

"Why yes," said Kane, "of course. Surely we've met, my dear. At the chapel, last Sunday."

Miriam swallowed and controlled her little start. So. Here it was again. Her father had warned her, but she hadn't really believed it could still be so. Not after the war. Not after all that suffering by so many Jews.

"I don't think so," Miriam said slowly. "I don't go to the base chapel."

"Oh? Where then? St. Joseph's? I hear they have perfectly lovely stained glass there."

Miriam allowed herself at last to get angry.

"No. Temple Beth-El, in San Rafael." She spat the words as if they were bullets from a machine gun.

"Oh," breathed Carole Kane, "I see." She smiled wide, as if she had just done something of profound importance. "In that case, I couldn't possibly have met you before, could I?"

This time, nobody rescued the silence. Miriam stood two paces from Kane, clutching her drink so tightly she felt her hand go numb, thinking furiously of some perfect squelch. But nothing came to her; only confused, angry flashes. None of the other women filled the awkward gap into which she'd plunged, and Nancy finally tugged on her elbow and simply steered her away, into the crowd.

Near the doorway, she leaned against a table and closed her eyes. Her punch spilled a little and she jerked. She felt tears welling up.

Nancy handed her a handkerchief. She put her arm around her and squeezed. "Hey. You did great, kid. Cheer up." Nancy's voice was husky and slightly ragged too.

"Why?" Miriam finally said. "Why did she?"

"Don't even think about it. Don't even start to think about it. It's not worth it, Miriam. Please. Take my word for it."

"But, damn it, I'm not ashamed to be Jewish. Why should I let her make me feel ashamed?"

"You shouldn't. I told you. She's just bitter. She's looking for someone to blame. They all are, all the old guard. Their world is gone, and they don't like it. Why, Hal Kane even refuses to wear the new blues. Right now, he's over there in the club in his pinks and greens, the only Air Force officer in the state, probably, who's still in the Army, at least in his mind."

"I just don't get it. We're all in the same boat—"

"No. Not quite. You're just at the beginning of your career in the Air Force. She's at the end of hers. Your husband is a fighter jock, a hot rock in the best outfit there is, with an excellent chance to make it all the way, probably. And you're pregnant and pretty to boot. Her kids are grown up, Miriam, and from what I saw in Frankfurt, they don't have much to do with her.

166

Imagine what that does to a mother, any mother, including Carole. And to cap it off, the wing commander here is a guy who used to work for Hal Kane a long time ago. When I tell you his name, you'll understand a little why she got so vicious. It's Goldberg. Bernie Goldberg. General Goldberg to Hal Kane."

"So he's Jewish. Why—"

"Look. When they were young, it was all different. I hate to be blunt, Miriam, but you know as well as I do that a Jew just didn't have a chance thirty years ago. Back in the Old Army, the prejudice was so thick you could cut it with a knife. Nobody talked about it, but it was there. Kane expected it to stay that way, if he thought about it at all. But the war changed everything. It's hard for them to adjust."

Miriam swallowed the last of her punch. She looked around at the women. They seemed different now; less friendly, less like her. "I don't know," she said, "I don't know if I can take that."

"You won't have to." Nancy took the glass from her and set it on the table. "The Kanes are the past, Miriam. We're the present, and right here," she patted Miriam's tummy, "is the future. Nobody else I know acts like Carole and Hal Kane. Believe me. Don't judge us all by them."

Miriam looked up at the older woman's candid, open face and couldn't help feeling better. She knew that the chemical changes the pregnancy was causing in her body were as much a part of her sensitivity to Kane as anything the woman might have said—or not said. Miriam Siegel had dealt with the veiled anti-Semitism of gentile society all her life, first at the private schools she attended in Connecticut, then at Barnard, where she collided with the subtlest forms of prejudice that even the most supposedly liberal of her classmates and professors harbored. It had all contributed to her self-reliance, which was a key factor in her attractiveness to Jim Garvey. She understood that slowly at first, but as she grew to know Garvey, she recognized the deep scar that his parents' death had left in him. Raised by an aunt, Garvey cherished his own self-reliance, raised it almost to a faith, and was stunned to discover a woman whose own strength matched his. She knew that he was in some deep manner transferring his yearning for his mother onto her shoulders, and knew that if she did not handle it right, there would be problems later on. But she was a victim of her own upbringing, too, and she was as much in love with him as he with her. Upon her would fall the burdens of the family. They were burdens she

167

accepted with joy, just as she had gladly accepted the burdens of life as an Air Force wife.

She straightened and handed Nancy her handkerchief. "Wait here a moment," she said, smiling, and before the older woman could respond, she was driving back through the crowd.

Carole Kane hadn't moved, and the coterie around her had not changed when Miriam hove to outside the circle. She paused, then forced a space and thrust out her gloved hand to Kane.

"Mrs. Kane, I'd like to thank you again for your lovely party. I'm afraid I must go, though, and before I leave, I just want to volunteer my services for any project that might require them."

Kane automatically took her hand, blinked in confusion, and mumbled, "Of course, my dear," and let her own hand drop limply away.

Miriam smiled her most demure smile, then turned and went one step. She halted, turned back, raised her right hand to her hat in a mock salute, and called, "Shalom!"

When she got to her car, the Chevy's door seemed much lighter. And inside her, Paul stirred aggressively. She slipped the keys into the ignition and thought, Yes, he'll be a pilot, just like his father. She didn't like to think about what Jim might be doing that very moment, about dogfights and bailouts and augering in. She only thought about the life within her and the New Year. "Shalom," she whispered again, and drove away from Carole Kane and the sign over her door that read, HAPPY NEW YEAR—1953.

12

0750 LOCAL
5 March 1953
K-14
Korea

Kelly knew he was home when he eased his eyes open. Lim Wye Koom stood at the end of the cot saluting. Lim had a comforting intuitive sense; somehow he was always there just as Kelly's eyes came open. Kelly glanced around the twenty-five-by-fifteen-foot tent, the five G.I. cots lined up on each side, the cold—but shiny—pot-bellied stove in the middle. Home again. Lim grinned

168

at Kelly's sloppy return salute and hustled out to bring him a cup of what passed for coffee.

There was the normal processing and a field checkout; Korea looked no better from F-86s than it did from F-80s, but he'd have better shooting.

He didn't see Garvey until that night in the club, but he'd heard the tales. Garvey was behaving like a maniac; wild nights in the clubs, fights, and even more reckless flying. He'd knocked down four MiGs, and lost two wingmen.

He was at the bar; Kelly threw his arm around his shoulder and offered to buy him a drink.

"Fuck off, sucker; I'll buy my own fucking drinks," Garvey snarled, not even looking up.

Kelly couldn't believe it. Garvey had rarely sworn, never used *fuck*, that common denominator of soldier language back to Roman times.

"Come on Garve, it's me! Christ, you saved my life, you can't be nasty to me." Garvey finally turned and made a small moue that he must have meant for a smile.

"Welcome back to the war, Kelly. Where you been?"

Kelly filled him in on the details. He mentioned Kathy in passing, didn't say he was going to get married. He talked for a long time, trying to pump Garvey full of information to see if he would reciprocate, if he would unload. He hadn't said a word about Miriam, and Kelly was afraid to ask. Had she dumped him?

Garvey called for another drink; he'd rarely had more than a beer or two in the past.

"Nothing much happening here, Kelly. Not enough MiGs to go around; too much paperwork. In January, we had a little baby girl, named Rachel. And Miriam died." Silent tears ran down his face; he didn't seem to notice.

Kelly didn't know how to react. He sat quietly as Garvey began to talk.

"You know, Mike, it was all my fault. I loved her so goddamn much I insisted we try to get her pregnant right away. She really didn't want to, but she went along. I was nuts; I was so afraid I'd lose her, or that I'd buy the farm, that I was insane to get her pregnant, to put myself in her and merge with her and have a kid with her forever."

He smeared his glass around in the moisture on the bar, and made a series of wet circles, interconnected. "Everything was going fine; she went into the labor room, and had some kind of massive hemorrhage. Died on the table. Went in smiling, came out dead. The baby was a girl, Rachel, perfect. We'd already picked names to please her dad, Rachel and Paul.

"Her old man was there, screaming at me; little guy, no bigger than five-two, hundred twenty pounds, I thought he was going to kill me on the spot. I hoped he would. He said I'd killed her and he was right."

He swirled the whiskey in the bottom of the bar jelly glass. Kelly waited.

"So I turned the baby over to them to raise till I get back. But I doubt if I'm going back."

Kelly's latent Catholic training stirred his ire. "Jesus, Garvey, what are you talking about? You got the baby; it's not your fault; her dying's just like somebody's going in. You didn't cause it, you wouldn't have hurt her for the world. You're taking this the wrong way. She'd expect you to be home with the kid."

"Kelly, if I want any of your half-ass advice, I'll ask for it. I'm some sort of badass and don't know why or how. But it never should have happened to Miriam. It was my fault."

He was silent, but Kelly sensed that he was a shade less desperate. He also sensed that that was all he'd get out of Garvey then, so he downed his own glass, slipped off the rough stool, and squeezed Garvey's shoulder as he left. Garvey ignored him, staring into the universe of circles on the bartop.

Kelly expected to be in combat within a few days; instead there was almost a week of indoctrination, local flights, a practice gunnery mission. A retread major, Earle Miller, was in charge of the indoctrination program. Miller, the story went, had been a victim of the classic wartime tragedy. He'd been in Japan when the war broke out, and was sent immediately to Korea. He'd been there six months when the dear john letter came from his wife. She was leaving him to marry a lawyer.

They had no kids, and Miller simply stayed on. He made himself too valuable to rotate as long as he volunteered to stay, and he provided a living historical continuity from the first days when the fighters flew out of Japan, through the first introduction of the F-86s, when the MiGs appeared, right up to the present, when the thin line of silver Sabres contained the hundreds of MiGs along the Alley. He'd started out with the 4th Fighter-Interceptor Squadron, then been transferred to the 51st when it was set up.

Kelly cultivated him; he didn't know anybody there but Garvey, and Garvey was impossible to be with. He bought Miller a few drinks, to learn what had been and what might be.

Miller's drinking was impressive. He'd sit with Kelly for hours, putting back the straight shots, occasionally freshening up with a beer, and give no sign of it except a slightly red flush, and, later in the evening, the barest tendency to slur. Next morning, he'd be perfectly recovered, able to do a good day's work. Kelly thought his liver must have been about the size of a watermelon to process all the alky.

"I'll tell you, Kelly, me boy, you're here at a lucky time; it was never better for a young guy. It hasn't changed a bit since the war started, but it's a lot different."

That didn't make much sense to Kelly, but he nodded.

"I was here when the 4th started up, with about forty-four F-86As on its strength, and maybe only thirty of them in commission. There were four or five hundred MiGs opposing 'em all the time in MiG Alley, and anywhere else the MiGs had guts to go.

"Everything's changed and nothing's changed. MiG Alley used to be a strip of land along the river; now it's a great chunk of real estate, twice as big as Cook County, and safer for them, too, the bastards—they can duck across the Yalu and we can't touch them. It'd be just like Dillinger being able to go free if he could just get across the line to Cicero.

"The big difference has been the pilots. The airplanes have stayed about the same. The early-model MiGs were better airplanes than the 86-As, could climb faster and fly higher, just like the later-model MiGs can over our Fs. But the Sabres are better fighters, better gun platforms, and they can pull the high-speed, high-G turns and not come unglued."

Miller eyed his whiskey morosely. He always approached it in the same way; he'd smell it and wrinkle his nose, then toss it down with a little shudder. Then he'd put the glass on the bar and signal for another.

"The big difference used to be the pilots. We had nothing but veterans when we started, mostly aces from the Big War, too. Guys like George Davis, Bud Mahurin, Gabreski, real pros. Not like you young guys, right out of flying school."

Kelly bristled a little, but sipped his beer. He was getting an education, and Miller meant no harm.

"The Commies were a bunch of beginners at the start, but they learned fast. They had so damn many airplanes they could do pretty much what they wanted. They'd fly a whole shit-pot full of them across the river, sixty maybe eighty, and they drop off a few sections to engage the 86s. We could only put up sixteen, maybe thirty-two at a time, usually in flights of four or six. They'd just mix with them a bit, and get them to drop their tanks and pour on the power, enough so they couldn't stick around and fight long. The rest of the train would drop down to fifteen thousand feet or so and pick on the bombers and fighter bombers.

"Then the B-29s started tearing up their airfields, and the MiGs got serious. They'd box off the 86s with one gaggle and send another flock in to hit the B-29s. They had some F-84s escorting them, but the Russians—we figure it was mostly Russians doing the aggressive flying, and once in a while somebody would see a blond guy bailing out, and ain't no blond chinks to my knowledge—would sail right through them. That's what the MiG was designed for, to chew up bombers, and that goddamn thirty-seven-millimeter could tear chunks out of a tank."

Kelly saw Garvey look in the bar, see him, and duck out. Christ, he thought. Has it come to this?

"Then they switched again, long about late '51. It was finishing school all over, with big patrols, flying high, and having a sort of graduation exercise where they'd come down and mix it up. They were probably rotating all their pilots through, just like the Germans did in Spain. We called the few tough aggressive pilots 'honchos' and the rest 'students.' It's a good thing they didn't try too hard, too, because we were on our ass at the time. We had 86s out of commission all over the ramp, and were short on pilots to boot."

He ordered a beer, sipping it daintily as if it were a liqueur.

"Things finally got so bad they established the 51st, about doubling the number of fighters we had, but the pilot pool was entirely different. We had every sort a guy coming in here to fly 86s, and mostly no time to train them. It's a good thing Gabreski and me were running it, or it would have been a disaster."

Kelly nodded; he'd heard about the way Gabreski ran things.

"You know, it was like the Battle of Britain in reverse. They always had ten times as many planes as we did, and they had a ground-control intercept better than anything anybody ever had. Our guys would have to stooge around and seduce them to fight. They'd only come down when they had all the cards. It was a dopey way to fight a war, but it was the only war we had.

"You're coming into it at the best time, kid. Old General Barcus is going to turn you guys loose one day, and then Katie bar the door. You're really lucky."

172

Kelly took it for two nights, about all the education he could stand, and more whiskey for Miller than he could afford. He tried to ask about Garvey, but Miller grimaced. "He's nuts. He won't last a month before he's killed or grounded. He won't talk to me, or anybody. He acts like he's the only guy in the world that ever had a problem back home."

Miller was right. Garvey was nuts and Kelly was lucky. On his first operation, Kelly got separated from his flight, an unpardonable sin, and ran right into a TU-2 twin-engine bomber scooting back on the deck. He blew the right wing off of it with a single burst, and came back to a disbelieving intelligence officer, who apologized when they ran the gun camera film. The same day, Garvey had led his flight into a gaggle of about thirty MiGs making their way back from an attack on B-26s operating against Pyongyang. Garvey and his element leader, Ed Gwinn, each got a MiG, but Garvey's wingman was picked off.

The days went by, and Kelly began to build his own score; the TU-2 had been his third kill, but he wanted some MiGs. Instead he hammered a Yak-9, for number four. And the victory that made him an ace was totally unsatisfactory. He'd settled in behind a MiG-15, obviously being flown by a "student" and, as he mashed the trigger button, the pilot ejected. They ran the gun camera film half a dozen times to see if they could see any hits, but there was nothing but the frame-by-frame sequence of the canopy blowing and the pilot coming out in his seat. Still, five was five, and he had nine months to go on his tour.

He was alone in his tent when the Padre came in. Kelly felt just like he used to at Holy Angels when Father Hannegan would stop him on the school ground. He always knew he hadn't done anything good, it was just a question of what bad Hannegan knew about. He jumped to his feet. "Come in, Father, sit down."

Father Borman was an airplane junkie, just like most of the flight surgeons. You had the feeling that he'd like to trade the round collar for a white scarf and helmet, at least once anyway.

"How is it going, Mike? I hear you're an ace already."

"Yeah, but I had a head start in F-80s, you know. Also, I'm shooting up the turkey farm; they're going to put a price on my head for molesting students."

Borman fenced around for a while, but soon came to the point. "You know Garvey pretty well, don't you?"

"Yeah, he saved my life." Kelly told him the story.

"Well, he needs some help. His wingman has refused to fly with him—says he doesn't mind fighting a war, but he's not going to shepherd a crazy man around."

"Pretty tough. What are they going to do, send him home? The flight surgeon can do that."

"Not when you can fly like Garvey does; we're not out here to avoid fights, and Garvey is in one every day."

Kelly winced; it was always the same, the priests and the flight surgeons and the other groundpounders were always so goddamn bloodthirsty.

"Yeah, well, what do you want me to do? He avoids me all the time, and I'm not too crazy about talking to him when he's like this."

"How about volunteering to be his wingman?"

Holy shit, Kelly thought. There go my MiGs. He'll kill me off too, before I ever get a chance to mix it up with somebody decent.

"Well, Kelly?"

Silence.

"Come on, Kelly, the man saved your life."

Kelly stalled. He really didn't want to fly with Garvey. He'd be moving up to element leader on his own pretty soon, with his own wingman to cover his ass. He'd be bound to get some MiGs, and he'd be in control of his own destiny. With Garvey, it would be funnyfarm time. He'd never get a shot at a MiG himself. But he owed Garvey, not just once but twice. First for saving his ass back in that rice paddy, and then in Japan, with the nurse who jump-started him. He sighed and realized he'd have to do it.

"Okay, Padre. I suppose you've already talked to the C.O."

"No, give me some credit, Kelly; I'm not entirely a schmuck. But I will now, and thanks. You're lucky, and he needs your luck. It's as simple as that."

Garvey seemed to take no notice of the change. They briefed and flew as if they had always been together. Kelly had to admire Garvey's flying technique; he was smooth as silk, and always landed with thirty or forty gallons more fuel than Kelly. Part of it was because Kelly was formating on him, had to make more power adjustments, but most was just the delicacy of his flying. Kelly hated to say anybody flew better than he did himself, but Garvey was a master.

In combat he was a madman. Kelly stayed with him the best

he could, but Garvey would fly right up a MiG's tailpipe before firing and twice Kelly had to fly through debris that could have flamed him out.

The more he scored, the stranger Garvey got. Kelly talked to Borman, and to the flight surgeon, and to the C.O., but Garvey would dissemble with them. As soon as they started chatting with them, he turned into Mr. Affable. It was a game, and he beat them at it every time.

Finally, late in spring, the Sabres were turned loose. Squadrons were being converted over to F-86Fs, with a solid leading-edge wing and boosted engine power that gave them near-MiG performance. The 5th Air Force began a systematic effort to bait the Communists, even offering fifty thousand dollars in Operation Moolah for anyone who would defect with a MiG. The insults seemed to work, and in May, the MiGs, mostly flown by students, came down, mixed it up, and were shot down. Aces blossomed like flowers in the spring.

The height of the battle came on a silvery blue May day. Garvey had made one pass that scattered a flight of four MiGs; he pulled up, with only Kelly still with him. The other element was chasing four others south. Garvey turned north; Kelly couldn't see anything, but he pulled in tight. No sense in talking to him. They were isolated, alone, boring straight in to the nexus of MiG Alley.

Sixteen MiGs were climbing across the Yalu, passing Uiju airfield, probably out of Antung or Sinuiju. Garvey signaled, then dropped straight down on them. Kelly slid left and picked out a target; it was a cinch no one was behind them, and they were only going to get one pass through the MiGs. He fired as Garvey fired, and two MiGs blew up, changing from vibrating smudges against the Yalu delta into a drifting pointillist flower of red, gray and black dots, fading into nothingness. They scattered the formation, and Garvey kept up his dive. Kelly tried to close, but he couldn't and he was scared. He knew that half of the MiGs would be dropping back down on them, the rest climbing slowly to cut them off if they got away.

Garvey arrowed down. Kelly saw why; there was a MiG entering the pattern at Sinuiju. It was slow, with its gear down. Garvey was near transonic when he fired and the MiG shuddered, but continued on in the pattern. Kelly checked behind him; no MiGs. Where were they?

It was like dropping into a well of flak. When they started their dive they looked down on a round earth, with a sweet blue

175

horizon for home; now they were in a green-gray pit, with streets and cliffs and hangars all registering plainly even as they ripped past at 550 miles an hour. The Sabre was stiff in his hands, a dog lunging at its leash. He overshot Garvey; one of them had to keep his speed up, and the MiGs were bound to be among them in a minute.

The MiG pilot must have been right out of basic; he took his hit from Garvey and turned final as the flak began opening up. Garvey made a 180 and bored back in, slowing down. Kelly pulled up out of light flak range; there was nothing he could do for him now.

Garvey bored in behind the MiG, dropped his own gear and flaps, fired the six .50-caliber machine guns in a barrel-burning burst that blew him out of the air. A feeding frenzy of flak followed the F-86's tail.

Above, Kelly swiveled his neck sore from watching for the MiGs.

"Come on you crazy bastard, get out of there!"

Garvey kept his descent as if he was going to land. He must be hit, Kelly thought, or completely nuts. Maybe he's defecting. They'll really be glad to see him after smearing that MiG on the overrun.

Garvey flew down the flight path and touched down; as his wheels hit he poured the power to it, picked up the gear and flaps, and began firing at the MiGs in revetments around the field perimeter. Kelly watched the crazy overlay of flak blackening the field. They were firing into their own hangars trying to down the insane F-86.

Everything was slow motion as Garvey pulled away from the field. Not one of the thousands of rounds of flak had hit him; he'd been going too fast on his first pass, all the flak moving behind him; on the second one he'd been slow, and like Keystone Kops they fired ahead of him the whole length of the field.

He climbed up and joined on Kelly's wing. Anxiety pulsed through Kelly; every smudge on the canopy was diving MiGs. Where were they? Must be their lunch break, he thought. God, what targets we are.

"You take us back as far as we can get, Kelly. I'm a little low on fuel." Kelly glanced at his own gauges; Jesus, he had just enough to get back himself to K-14, maybe. Garvey must be bumping on empty already.

They climbed to thirty-two thousand in silence; Kelly saw glints of silver that must have been MiGs, but none appeared.

"We'd better head out to sea, don't you think?"

"We ain't heading anywhere, Kelly. I just flamed out."

Kelly saw the F-86 separate as Garvey began trimming it for best glide speed. Jesus, he thought, what a pretty airplane. He could make the coast but they were too far north for Air Sea rescue. The North Koreans would be after him as soon as the radar picked up his descent. God help them both if any MiGs showed up.

"Hey, Garvey, listen up."

"Roger, Kelly, you go on; you got to be low on fuel, too."

"Ah, did you read the stunt that guy in the 4th pulled off?"

"No, I got no time to talk now, Kelly, I'm going to have to leave this thing, and I got to tidy up."

"Stick tight; I'm going to try to give you a shove past the bomb line anyway. I'm going to stick my nose right up your tailpipe, so fly smooth."

Kelly dropped back, slowed his fighter, and moved into trail position behind Garvey's slanting F-86.

"Just fly straight, Garvey, don't do anything, just keep that airspeed. I'm going to ease into your tailpipe, and shove."

"Okay. Give it a shot."

Garvey sounded like he was enjoying it.

Kelly slid in. Garvey was flying velvety smooth, so the flying would be up to him. He eased the Sabre forward, the other F-86 looming big in his canopy. He could see every rivet line, every access panel; there was a slight hydraulic leak smearing pink past the tailpipe. It looked as if the horizontal stabilizer might have taken a little flak. What a pretty airplane.

As he got in close, the airflow over Garvey's Sabre shoved him back; he'd ease the throttle forward, and come forward too fast, and have to dump the dive brakes to avoid over-running him. They were passing through twenty-five thousand feet when he finally nestled his nose section in the tailpipe, and gently applied power.

He couldn't tell at first what was happening. He pushed the throttle forward a little more, and saw their rate of descent checked.

"Hey, Garve, I'm going to set up about a two-hundred-foot-per-minute rate to try to save some fuel. I got to play with this a bit to figure out what to do."

In the cockpit, Garvey relaxed. There was nothing he could do but keep this sucker steady. He began to laugh when he thought of the damage the Chinese had done to themselves. It

177

was like the old stories about Chinese laborers running in front of the airplanes taking off for flights over the hump, each trying to get his devil run over. Maybe his devil had bought it back on the runway. There was enough flak for a few devils, even one the size of his.

"Kelly, you're looking good so far."

The nose-to-tail 86s edged across North Korea. Kelly kept thinking how he would like to run across a target like this. One pass, two victories. There wasn't much problem flying; the trim seemed funny, but the airflow seemed to suck them together now, and he hardly had to touch the power. He watched his fuel counters unwind. Christ, they both might end up in the drink. He kept running the figures, running the figures. It looked like he could push Garvey across the bomb line, disengage, and try to make K-14. Garvey would have to bail out, but at least on our side of the lines. That goddamn buttinsky Borman!

The wind must have shifted; they were crossing the line at fifteen thousand feet, five thousand better than Kelly had estimated. He figured he could push Garvey another three or four minutes, then they'd have to disengage.

"Hey Kelly, how about pulling out? I think I see an emergency strip straight ahead; I can make it, no sweat."

"I can't see it, Garve, but they are usually pretty short. Can you make a power-off approach and stick it in there?"

"No sweat."

Kelly retarded the power, popped his dive brakes, and the F-86 with the reamed tailpipe seemed to shoot ahead.

Garvey was in the bar. Kelly had blown a tire at K-14, much to the amusement of the guys in the 4th there, and it took four hours to get airborne again. His airplane hadn't been damaged except for a little sheet-metal work.

Garvey's manner was changed. He seemed totally drained but totally renewed. He was laughing and talking, like a man just released from solitary confinement. When he saw Kelly, he jumped up and slapped him on the back, beaming. "Kelly, I quit. That's enough for me. I'm going back and get Rachel and start living. You really saved my ass, you know that, don't you?"

"Well, I figured if some cat from the 4th could do it, we could too."

"I don't mean pushing me back, yahoo; I mean sticking with me until I got this nuttiness out of my system. Too bad you didn't hear me back at Sinuiju; I came across there cussing and singing, and those bastards throwing every goddamn thing they had at me and just shooting the shit out of their own airplanes. When I pulled up it was like I'd just taken a bath; I was clean."

Kelly wasn't so sure that night; he'd seen a lot of strange things happen to guys who flew combat day in and day out. But he hoped so. And so he drank and sang and threw up with Garvey that night, and hoped for the best the next morning.

The best happened. Garvey announced that he had put in for his long-delayed rotation, and the C.O. immediately okayed it. They threw a huge, beery party for him later in the week, and everybody chipped in to buy him a beautiful silk kimono for Rachel, who wouldn't be able to wear it until she was a teenager at least. Garvey cried like a baby.

Then, suddenly, he was gone back to the States, and the war still had to be fought.

Kelly had never been happier. He got his own wingman at last and was promoted to element leader.

The wingman, a young lieutenant named Harry Fish, was brand new in the squadron, and was amazed at Kelly's consideration in passing over the older guys to pick him. The weeks flying wing on Garvey had taught Kelly much more than he'd ever learned in flying school, and his biggest lesson was how valuable a wingman was. Fish expected to be hazed, given the donkey details, and made to prove himself to Kelly. Mike reversed the role, carefully briefing Fish on every mission, praising what he did well, encouraging him when he goofed, letting him fly lead whenever he could. Kelly was glad to have a chance at the MiGs again, but he felt himself brought one step closer to maturity by the process. On his last mission, he let Fish lead a perfect bounce on a pair of MiGs.

They both scored against the MiGs, and when Kelly left Korea a few weeks later, he had a fan for life.

He also left with a red silk kimono for Kathy and a hangover that lasted all the way to Hawaii, because the squadron had given him a party that made Garvey's seem like a church social. As the coast of California at last hove into view through the windows of the MATS C-54 that was taking him back to Kathy, Mike felt a chill pass over him. He looked around the cabin and realized the other returning troops felt something like the same thing.

It was more than just a homecoming. It was a return to life from the land of the dead. Once he had yearned for combat. Now he yearned only for Kathy.

13

It was cold on the desert and Duke shivered involuntarily. Damn it, he muttered to himself, do you ever get over being a kid brother?

The airmen on the bus that had brought them from the BOQ at 0600 were now busily setting up a table with a cloth—probably a bed sheet from the BOQ—big G.I. pots of coffee, and the lethal G.I. doughnuts. It was the Edwards Air Force Base idea of elegance.

About forty senior officers were standing around in small groups along the edge of the wide, fifteen-thousand-foot-long runway, talking quietly about the RB-47E and its strategic mission of poking its nose around the perimeter of the Soviet Union, ferreting out the radar secrets. They were here today to see the first RB-47E to be completely equipped with all the sophisticated "Raven" equipment.

It was going to be a long day. King Brown was due in at six thirty sharp, flying the RB-47E as aircraft commander, the culmination of his time as the program officer. He'd land and then guide them on an inspection tour of the big aircraft. Finally, they'd all be hauled to the officers' club for breakfast. Afterward there would be day-long briefings. Duke was there ostensibly because he was going to be a project officer on B-47s; the real reason was that King wanted him to meet a lot of officers who could help in his career. He had the choice, as usual, of resentment of his brother's eternal meddling or the use of it. As usual, he chose the latter. So he stamped his feet in the chilly air and gulped hot coffee, still playing the little brother.

There was a rumble on the horizon and a murmur ran through the crowd. A rasping loudspeaker called out, "Raven approaching." Duke looked for it at traffic pattern altitude; someone said "down low" and he saw it, a slim spot in the distance, the wings lifted high, a wisp of smoke appearing from each of the six engines.

A pot-bellied colonel with binoculars nudged Duke in the side. "He's doing three hundred knots at least, maybe more." Duke nodded. Of course. King never missed a chance to make an entrance.

The B-47 grew visibly in size as it raced down the desert floor at fifty feet, roaring toward the runway. Duke was flooded with the dumb admiration mixed with the resentment that he'd always felt for his brother. King had never done anything wrong. He loved to fly, and he always had the answers. He was both an eternal ideal and reproach to Duke, and Father never let him forget it.

The B-47 flashed down the runway silently, the noise following behind. The roar of the six engines reached the crowd just as the airplane reached the end of the runway and King reefed it back in a sharp climbing turn, a turn that every pilot in the crowd knew immediately was fatal.

The B-47 climbed hard and turned in a sidling lurch. Slowly, deliberately, the wings began to fold up, the slender tips reaching overhead toward each other.

Duke watched helplessly, a clammy hand suddenly gripping his stomach. The seconds stretched out as the aircraft almost apologetically showed that it was not going to fly, that the brutal G forces King had summoned with his powerful, irrational pull on the control wheel were simply too much for it. As the silver airplane continued upward, the fuselage seemed to pull backward from the wings. It shuddered, the wings touched like hands in prayer, and the fuselage exploded in a rippling flower of flame.

The fuselage plunged straight down into the ground, sending up another billowing black cloud in pursuit of the one already drifting away in the early morning breeze. The wings drifted down in an almost balletic flutter, crumpling onto the desert floor as a muffled counterpoint.

For a long heartbeat, nothing moved and no one breathed. Then pandemonium erupted. Sirens sounded as ambulances and fire trucks screamed off the ramp toward the crash site.

Duke knew the ambulances were wasting their time. But he began to run toward the wreckage with the others anyway, an airman's instinctive reaction. Then he stopped.

He stood and watched the others racing across the wide concrete runway, even the fat old colonel, and two things struck him like fists in the gut.

The first was that he didn't want to see King as he had to be

181

now, broken and burned shapeless, oozing purple through split blackened skin.

The second was that King had finally made a mistake.

As he watched the thick black smoke roiling skyward, he did not know which realization unnerved him more.

1815 LOCAL
20 May 1954
Dover AFB, Delaware
USA

Their arguments had a build-up rate as predictable as the melting point of ice. Micky White would begin the day happy, and enthusiastic, turning a little more sarcastic as the day wore on. She would start out perfectly coiffed, neatly dressed; as the time of argument grew near, her curly brown locks would go askew, and buttons would begin to pop on her clothes. Then she would go silent, breaking it only with terrible politeness. Finally she blew up.

Larry didn't believe it when Micky said she wasn't coming to Dover with him. He wasn't angry, just impossibly hurt. He had come back from Korea to be sent to the bottom of the pile, copilot on a C-124 out of Dover, and Micky was furious. She had worked through the whole cycle, and was now coming on strong. "You've let them screw you out of everything but your goddamn flying time, and now they are setting you up as a donkey copilot in the worst job in MATS in a half-ass Delaware village. And I'm supposed to give up thirty thousand dollars a year for that? What would happen to Libby? She'd be in some base hospital with an eleven-year-old doctor listening to her heart through the wrong end of the stethoscope."

Most of the rage was directed against herself. None of her schemes had gone well; the Riverdale development had gone sour when the percolation tests proved that sewers, not septic tanks were required. Micky had come almost undone when she found out that everyone had known about it but she, and that the real-estate community had let her press ahead. She was almost fifty thousand dollars in debt as a result, an amount Larry could scarcely imagine. To make it worse, she had been incautiously vocal about her hopes for development of the triangle of land sitting athwart the Norfolk growth pattern. Two old-line realtors had quietly purchased the land she had her eyes on, and it looked like the buy of the century.

Micky knew that much of her anger stemmed from guilt. As the Riverdale project developed she depended more and more on her boss Barney Green for advice. They had grown close, and Larry had been gone for a long time. At the height of her problems, when it looked for a while like there might even be some criminal liability in the way she had drawn up some of the papers, she had gone gratefully to bed with Green. She needed him for moral support, and she needed him sexually. He provided both with no demands. A month before Larry returned they had broken off their affair, and she felt desperately confused. Larry wouldn't kill her if he found out—he'd simply be hurt. She told herself that it was a one-time slip, and that she would put it behind her. But she wasn't sure that was the case.

From all of it she tried to glean the consolation of learning by experience. But her greed had been great, and the disappointment was burning. She wanted more than profit now; she wanted revenge.

As their predictable evening of argument wore on, she actually tried to persuade Larry to resign, as much to have him around to avoid temptation as for anything else.

Larry heard her out, as always, hiding his own anger, and as she persisted, he knew she was right. He had been shafted. He was still a first lieutenant, after two combat tours and the airlift, and he was starting at the bottom in MATS because he didn't have much four-engine time. His aircraft commander would probably be some junior birdman with no combat time and most of his hours logged on the autopilot.

Put in that light, his career so far had been a bust. He knew that. Yet he could not forget the side of the Air Force that she knew nothing of. There was no way to explain it to her, either; even if he had the words, they wouldn't make sense. How to capture the value of the ethereal beauty of a sunrise takeoff? How to convey the silent comradeship of an aircrew? How to articulate the rankless rewards of flying, of doing a job well that only a handful of people in the world understood? Besides, he was no dope; he well understood how he had altered his career when he volunteered for T-6 duty after flying L-5s at their command. Every pilot understood that age-old dictum of service life—"the Service comes first"—and knew that no matter who you knew, sometimes your number comes up and you do time in the barrel. The L-5 was Larry's barrel. Other guys might have gotten the hell out of FAC duty as soon as they could, but Larry had been changed by the experience of flying low and slow over the grunts, being pounded mercilessly by the Koreans and Chinese, and once even by their own 105 mm howitzers. He knew he could save people by putting his experience on the front to use; and knew that a T-6 stint would give him more satisfaction even than a tour in B-26s, which his old C.O. had urged him to put in for. The new phrase coming into vogue—"career-enhancing" —was a laugh when applied to Mosquito duty. Larry knew it, and the other LT-6 pilots did too. But that only drew them more tightly together, and made them more determined to do their best. It was no wonder Micky couldn't understand that; even other pilots had a tough time buying it. So he never even tried to explain how the mud and death and T-6s had changed him and what he wanted out of the Air Force.

Larry listened to Micky venting her spleen, hoping the kids were asleep, knowing that she was right and knowing it simply didn't matter. Even as he'd read the orders condemning him to MATS, he had seen the bright side, as he always did: flying 124s was pretty good duty. MATS air routes wove a spiderweb around the world, from Kimpo to Delhi, Hickam to Athens, Thule to Teheran. MATS airplanes plugged in and out, in every kind of weather. For a flying fiend, for a real Air Force pilot, it was a kind of paradise, not a prison. Let the groundpounders peddle themselves upstairs; he would fly forever, or as long as they'd let him. And however crassly they treated him in promotions and decorations, they never missed a chance to put him in an airplane. This was their secret lock on him, and if Micky knew it, she didn't show it.

They compromised. He'd go to Dover and see how things were; he promised her that if they didn't treat him right in a year or so, he'd resign and come back. If they did, she'd sell everything and come up to Delaware to start over.

Micky regarded him suspiciously, but agreed. She could hardly be too judgmental about his career indiscretions; she shuddered when she thought about Riverdale. There had been at least a dozen warning signs, all too clear in retrospect, from the casual laughter around the office that she hadn't understood, to the surprise on the clerk's face when she was looking into the titles. It was inexplicable that Green had not warned her. When she asked him he said he was so confident in her, that he thought she knew the risks and was going to be able to pull it off. He probably was just using her, as she in fact was using him. It looked as if she was going to be able to salvage some of the money; the rest would simply have to be paid off over time, out of the money made from ordinary sales. The anger finally evaporated as it always did, and the evening of crisis ended as it always did. Larry crinkled his tanned face into a boyish grin, held her in his arms, kissed her, and told her not to worry about things she couldn't do anything about.

Wearily, Micky realized he was right, and she rested her head on his shoulder. To celebrate, Larry gave her a rare treat that night; dinner out, and a movie, *On the Waterfront*.

The movie was a bad choice. As they drove home, she saw him all too clearly eternally cast in Marlon Brando's role.

August 1954
Wright-Patterson AFB, Ohio
USA

The Air Force had taken a virtually derelict World War II office building—Bldg. 125, the black-on-white signs proclaimed—located on a hill overlooking the Wright Field runway, and tried to convert it to a college with plywood panels and cheap prints. Dayton's weather was Midwest miserable, and Bldg. 125 was boiling hot in the summer while in the winter snow drifted in piles on the inside of the loosely applied windows. But the instructors were good and the pace intense. They called it the Air Force Institute of Technology and it served as an umbrella for degree programs in a hundred civil colleges. With salaries and careers noncompetitive with the civilian world, the Air Force was going to recruit and train engineers just as it had done with pilots.

Wright-Patterson Air Force Base was an enormous complex conceived in the Depression and blown into giant proportions by the war. It combined procurement, test, and logistics in roughly equal proportions, spreading out the functions over two complete airfields, Wright and Patterson. There was either justice or irony, depending upon your point of view, that the immense acreage encompassed the very area where Orville and Wilbur did their post-1903 flying. The base was largely made up of civilians who ranged from a brilliant few at the very leading edge of the industry to a host of almost somnolent drones putting in their time saying no to much and yes to nothing.

Kelly had signed up for aeronautical engineering, not to learn

185

how to design airplanes but to test them. Everybody worked hard; the Air Force routinely crammed four years into three, three years into two, and the grim competition kept standards high. Poor grades were more than an embarrassment; they were effective barriers to promotions and to choice assignments.

For a while he thought he'd flunk out of his old bugaboo calculus. He had worked two hundred problems by rote, not sure even when he got the right answer when suddenly the process became clear to him, when calculus became *the calculus* and he saw the immense power of the tool. It caused an immediate and fundamental change in him. If he could see this inner working of something that had so stoutly defied his understanding, he could learn anything they had to teach.

Because of his combat experience, he got to fly with the test pilots in the experimental group at Patterson, rather than with the routine base-flight effort at Wright Base Operations. The test group had one of almost every kind of airplane in the inventory, many drastically modified for test work, and, if it had not been for Kathy, he would never have been home on weekends. He flew all the standard stuff—B-25s, C-47s, C-45s, and even some leftover exotics like the XB-48 or the XF-91. His favorite was an F-51 that was still being used for some radio tests.

Kathy had met him in San Francisco on his return; they were married in Las Vegas, and honeymooned across country. His Chevy only had sixteen thousand miles on it, but he traded it in on a Muntz Jet, a homemade sports car with a Cadillac engine, manufactured from components in Los Angeles by a television-set mogul. Kathy thought it was the tackiest, funniest car she'd ever seen. She loved it, insisted on driving it. When they got to Dayton he bought her a '47 Ford convertible. He wound up driving it while Kathy drove around in the Muntz.

For someone who had always disparaged suburban respectability, Kelly embraced married life with an enthusiasm that disarmed, delighted, but sometimes dismayed Kathy. He was utterly pell-mell in his race to establish a home environment that matched his mental image of "what is correct."

He bought their house as he bought the Muntz; on the spot, without consultation, without negotiation. The owner was hammering a For Sale sign in front of the two-story nearly-Colonial-style house when Mike drove by. He rolled down the window and said "I'll take it" to the bemusement of the seller, a major who administered the base hospital and was being transferred. He seemed a little discomfited at not being able to haggle.

Kathy seethed at his side, but Mike didn't notice; he was delighted at being able to please her so.

And in fact the house was fine; nestled on a hill in one of the super Levitt-style tracts, Huber Heights, it was surrounded by a finely controlled mixture of five different designs. You wouldn't see the identical house until four doors away. Kathy had lived in rather different circumstances for most of her life, and she knew her mother would have some restrained comments to make. On the other hand, they could afford it, and when the time came to move, it would sell readily to another Air Force type rotating in.

Mercifully, he left the furniture buying and the decoration almost entirely to her. Sometimes he would bring in some godawful addition—divorce loomed over the mounted deer's head he fancied for the walnut-paneled den—but for the most part he was happily content to let her decide what to get and why. He didn't look at total price tags, only at the monthly payments. As long as these stayed at a point where they were using his flight pay for savings and entertainment it was okay, for like every pilot he carried with him the phantom fear of going off status and losing that little extra bit. Kelly had already wired an assignment to the test group he was flying with after graduation from AFIT, which meant that they would be able to stay for at least three years before transferring, a long time in the Air Force. Kathy got a job teaching school, and they happily and systematically went about the process of getting her pregnant, for that was part of the code.

The pregnancy rate was fantastic; at any party of twenty couples, at least twelve of the women were expecting. It provided the major topic of half the conversation, which was uniformly divided by sex and location into flying and babies. The men stood in tight groups, alternating between intensely serious discussions and wildly outrageous lies, while the women worked over the little gossip and bragged about their kids.

There was always a couple who were having trouble conceiving; Kathy was initially appalled at the candid level of inquiry and advice. There were no sex secrets if conception was at stake. For the men involved it was murder; one poor captain, whose secret regimen for improving chances for conception became known, was promptly nicknamed "Numbnuts," probably forcing him into premature impotence.

There were a few sex secrets, though, ranged around contraception needed for the relatively few illicit sexual liaisons that emerged. It was dealt with by silence: if it was happening, it was ignored, for like most difficulties in the Air Force, it was sure to be cured by time or transfer. It was a paradox that the apparently most disruptive factor in Air Force life, the continual moving from assignment to assignment, in many ways contributed to the stability of the family. It demanded more of everyone, parents, children, and the extra efforts made when settling in a new area cemented relations that might have slowly eroded in a single setting. And no matter what the problem—difficult boss, extra-marital fling, boredom—transfer was a clear, imminent, sure way out.

Death was more difficult, but had similar effect and was treated in a similar way. One ignored the possibility; but when it happened, everyone rallied around the wife and family—until they left. It was rare for a pilot to be killed and the wife to decide to stay on in the area; when it happened there was eventual rejection. Kathy had seen her cat reject a still-born kitten, turning it aside and ignoring it, and widows who stayed received the same treatment—not that they were any less liked, but because they interfered with the rhythm of adjustment by being a constant reminder of what could happen.

There was an exception Kathy considered macabre, but understood. A widow could rejoin the flock if she remarried, if the new husband was also a flier. The younger women were able to do this more readily, of course, and it represented an almost Easter-like affirmation of Air Force life. Death couldn't occur; if it did, you ignored it or prevailed over it.

In Kelly's line of work, death was as possible as in combat, and perhaps even more predictable. They were tasked with testing new aircraft types, new equipment, and new tactics, often in combinations that defied prior analysis—you simply had to go do it, and see what happened.

The 4360th Operational Test Unit was small, divided into Bomber Ops and Fighter Ops, but most of the twenty-odd pilots and crewmen took pride in flying all of the equipment available. There was risk in this, for the cockpits were all nonstandard, and each one, especially the newer jets, had distinctive characteristics. On the other hand the experience was invaluable for evaluation, and for detecting in one aircraft incipient signs of what had been a problem in another.

The dangerous risks were always the unexpected risks. The 4360th types somewhat resented the attention given to the Edwards Air Force Base test pilots. There the Yeagers, the Kincheloes, the Everests, flew dangerous, important missions, but they received all of the glory. At Wright-Patterson the missions were no less important, but the world scarcely knew of their existence. The risks of spin tests, of high-speed runs, the sort of things Edwards specialized in, were genuine, but fairly definable and conducted in discrete elements. In contrast, the 4360th missions almost invariably involved the strapping on of a new system, with all the attendant possibilities of change in flight characteristics, wiring interferences, or simple mistakes in installation that could be fatal. Some of the older airplanes in the test program, like the early B-45s, had so many changes introduced that no one really knew what the systems were any more; you could put in a black box and find equipment activated that had no relation to the test.

The significant element though, was that these changes had to be evaluated under tactical conditions, on bomb or gunnery ranges, or in simulated combat.

Capt. Tom McGee, a handsome, sandy-haired midwesterner who had flown A-20s in Europe, had been moaning about the endless test programs in the B-45. "That sonofabitch is going to kill me someday, Mike; I've had two engine fires in the last four flights, and there is no way to get out of that dude."

Three weeks later McGee was given a new assignment, checking out the bombing system on the new Martin B-57. The B-57 was originally a British design, the English Electric Canberra, and was being manufactured for the Air Force by Martin. It was a sweetheart of an airplane, with a huge thick wing that made it fly like a Cub, and it featured the new Martin-Baker ejection seats, the best in the world. McGee was delighted; he never walked past the B-45 without kicking it, exorcising it from his fear. The B-57 was a present from heaven, and the ejection seats were better than an insurance policy.

Kelly was flying chase when it happened. They were working the bomb range near Langley, flying simple patterns to work up a base line of data for the later tests. The program called for a simulated drop of parachute-retarded bombs from an altitude of one thousand feet, airspeed 440 m.p.h., a simple mission. McGee entered the pattern, made all the calls, set up the telemetry, and at the point he should have pulled up he dove vertically into the ground. It was over in a tenth of a second; neither crew member had time to try to eject.

Kelly had watched it happen, in silence. There was no time to think, to call, to react. One moment the airplane was perfect, with two healthy human beings inside, doing what they loved.

189

Less than a second later it had disappeared into a black smoking hole, no bit of man or metal bigger than a silver dollar, two men gone, two families destroyed. He flew back with Kathy on his mind; he rarely thought of her when he flew.

Three weeks later the same thing happened in a tactical unit, and the B-57s were grounded. The flaw was a simple transient electrical error that ran in full nose-down trim, so fast that the pilots could not respond, forcing them into an instant vertical dive. They were flying airplanes one second, missiles the next.

Yet there was never enough of danger or flying. Lt. Arlie Artilla was a diminutive dynamo; he spent the week flying fighters, and the weekend building his own racer, *My Tara*, a low-wing midget that he intended to fly in the Goodyear races at Cleveland.

It was strange watching Arlie climbing into the big North American F-100, the Super Sabre successor to the F-86. He had to stretch to get his legs into the snap-covered holes so he could climb into the cockpit; when he got in, he disappeared until he got the cushions and seat adjusted so that he could see out.

The F-100 was in volume production, but a rash of accidents had killed North American's senior test pilot and put the program in jeopardy. Artilla had run a series of tests in which the airplane almost came apart before he brought it back with a recommendation for modification of the vertical fin.

Kelly was flying chase on Artilla on the Friday when he made his final tests on the F-100. Kelly watched the airplane enter a dive, shudder, buck, begin a wildly yawing flat spin. When it passed ten thousand feet he yelled "Get out, Arlie!" into the mike, but the F-100 simply tightened up. Then the spin chute spilled, the airplane straightened out, and Arlie pulled out, three thousand feet above the ocean, with the data he needed. They landed at Langley for fuel, then flew back to Wright-Patterson in tight formation.

On the ground, Arlie explained the problem to him. The vertical fin was not only too small, the radius of the curves on the stabilator were too abrupt, and there was a mild incipient flutter that compounded the problem. Flutter had been a nightmare since the mid-1920s, and every time one problem was solved the trouble appeared in another form. It could range from a mild buzz, barely perceptible in the control column, to a wild bucking that would tear man and airplane apart in an instant. The whole approach to flutter was a complex process of balancing weights, curves, structures, and strengths. He spent the night

190

making out a test report. It was a brilliant example of why test pilots were still needed, the intuitive fleshing out of a theory, something that computers would never be able to do.

Artilla was alone the next day, getting his little 180-horsepower racer prepared for the races. My Tara was tiny, with a twenty-foot wing span, about the size of the horizontal stabilizer on the Super Sabre, a perfect scale to Arlie. When he climbed in My Tara he seemed almost oversized; Kelly thought that was one reason he spent so much time on it, lovingly tuning it for top speed.

He made a high-speed pass, and picked up flutter in the elevator, a minor mirror image of the problem he had just solved in the F-100. He landed, and with a pop rivet tool fixed a small tab on My Tara's elevator. On his next high-speed run, the tab tore loose, pulled the elevator with it. My Tara plunged straight down, just like McGee's B-57, and Arlie died, mixed among a very small pile of wreckage.

The F-100 he had flown was sent back to the factory for modification and then to Edwards for flight test. When it was approved, they'd never thought to give Arlie the credit.

Kathy and Mike lost three more friends in aircraft accidents in the next two years. He never thought about it; she, like the other wives, simply shut it out of her mind.

September 1954
The Pentagon, Virginia
USA

Duke went into the Pentagon B-47 program office just as King had arranged. Before his death, King was to have taken over a B-47 wing at Pinecastle, Florida. The timing would have been perfect. It would have been awkward with them both in the same office, but from Pinecastle, King could simply have advised Duke on what to do and how to do it. Most important, he could have told him whom to do it with. Now he was on his own, would have to depend on his instincts. He knew they were up to it; he had seen that at Maxwell, where he had completed Squadron Officers' School as top man in his class, in more ways than one.

Joan and Duke had swirled through the school tour like royalty. Duke aced the course work and used the proximity to his colleagues to test his skill in maneuvering, which he feared had

191

atrophied slightly during his long tour in Korea. The results were especially gratifying when he was easily able to outclass them all, considering that they would be among his most visible rivals for flag rank later on.

Equally satisfying had been Joan's reaction first to him, then to Maxwell. He had known she was not happy with him, even back in flight school. But he had written it off as unimportant; she, like he, was playing a role in marriage, a role she had been well versed in by her background. When Father had approved her for him to marry, Duke had been assured that she was suitable material. It never occurred to him that he was expected to be happy in marriage; it was just part of the plan. So he was more than a little surprised to note how much he cared for her, and even she for him when he returned from Pusan.

They had reached a stage of great delicacy in their relations. They made love fiercely and silently, in the dark as Duke assumed she preferred it, but they treated each other with great caution and courtesy when the lights came back on. It was an enormous relief for Duke; and from what he could tell of her reaction, she felt the same. If they were not exactly in love, they were at ease with each other, comfortable and not threatened.

As he realized how it would be for them during the first week of his leave back in Nashville, and then when they had taken a little apartment near Maxwell, Duke was able to relax and get on with the vital work of the school, confident that the worrisome notes he had received from Mother about Joan's behavior had been simple fussbudgeting. Joan's style at Maxwell only reinforced the conviction.

Joan loved the Maxwell way of life; she was gracious lady to the wives of the others in Duke's flight, and they entertained almost every week. For some reason, Duke was continually surprised at how good Joan was at making people feel at home, for injecting a genuine sense of fun into what otherwise would have been just another aggregation of people and drinks.

She had done an especially impressive job in organizing a small party for the outgoing British senior officer, a personable wing commander with a horse-faced wife who laughed at all the wrong times. The pair had discomfited almost all the other women, and it had been Joan who had made the evening sparkle. Driving home from the club after the affair, Duke realized he had no idea why or how she managed such things.

On impulse, he reached across the car and squeezed her thigh, grinning at her. "You were wonderful tonight; you made the wing commander and his wife very happy, not to mention everybody else. How'd you do it?"

Joan flushed with pleasure. He had never handed her such a compliment before. Still basking in her undeniable success, she felt a sudden closeness to him, a surge of friendship if not of love. She watched the Alabama rain shower turn to muggy steam as they slowly drove home, searching for a way to give her intuitive understanding words he would comprehend.

"The parties are the best part of Air Force life. They're more than just parties, somehow. If you do one right, they kind of make us all immortal. We lose our own problems, just for a little while, and we become . . . oh, I don't know. Bigger, somehow." She paused and listened to the wipers, thinking hard. "It's the interchangeability of people and events. That's it. You can go from one base to another, and in a few days it seems like you've been there all your life."

Duke watched the side of the road; the misty steam from the rain shower was worse than a fog. He glanced at her. Her mood had caught him; he had never felt this reflective with her before. "But don't you worry about enduring friendships? You never really get to spend a lifetime with anybody, it's three years here, three years there, start all over again."

"It's better that way. It takes three years to know most people, and you get to move before you are disappointed. And you'll see some of them again, another base, another assignment. The ones you like you can pick up with; the ones you don't you can avoid."

They pulled into their apartment's parking lot more at ease with each other than they had been since they were married. They walked up to their door holding hands, almost shyly. Neither was prepared for the distress of their babysitter. The girl greeted them tensely and said, "Don't be mad, Mrs. Brown, but I had to let Charles stay up. He was acting so strange; every time I'd put him down, he'd scream and cry, and I—I didn't know what to do."

Joan ran into the bedroom. Charles was quiet in the bed, but obviously perfectly awake.

She picked him up and hugged him; he seemed to shimmer in her arms, in contact nowhere. Duke came in.

"What's the matter, Charles? Got a tummy ache?"

Charles turned away from him. Joan hugged him, placed him back in bed.

"Linda, did he ever behave like this before?"

"No, ma'am; most times he's been good. Sometimes he cries, but mostly real soft; I don't even know it unless I happen to feel his pillow. But tonight was strange."

Joan was concerned, but Duke more than concerned. His uncle Leslie had been "unusual"; he'd never worked, had no friends, and lived his whole life out on his small inheritance in a shabby hotel almost on skid row in Chattanooga. Worse, he had never been able to escape an overwhelming depression. King and Father had always brusquely dismissed Leslie as a family aberration, but Duke had often wondered about it. He often had to fight a certain depression himself. And now Charles was not behaving well. Maybe he'd take him to the flight surgeon, get an opinion. Might be something physical. He hoped it was physical.

The incident with Charles had broken the almost magic spell, and soon after they left the semirural atmosphere of Maxwell. As Duke became once again opaque and distant from her, Joan wondered if they would ever be as happy again. The inevitable stop in Nashville was almost without incident, until Charles acted up again. She could hear Duke's father and mother fulminating, blaming her drinking. When she walked in the room to confront them they stopped, embarrassed. She let it drop. They couldn't see that Charles Jr. was just like Duke, just like King, just like his grandfather. It was as if Duke had planted the child, egg and sperm together, within her, and she had merely carried him. She felt again the icy chill of separation from them all.

The drive to Washington was made in almost total silence; Duke took one look at the house she had selected, sneered, and went to a real-estate agent. In a month, they had sold her selection and moved into the one Duke had picked. It was a block away, the same price; she couldn't tell the difference, but she knew that in some strange way the house she picked was an analogy for Charles, and Duke's house was one for a child that now he'd never have, a child who was not "strange."

She set up house almost desperately in an attempt to re-create the atmosphere, the closeness of their time at Maxwell, but it was no good. In the manicured but shuttered suburb of Arlington, Joan was simply another service wife, and Duke another ambitious captain putting in his time at the Pentagon.

Engaged in battle, Duke failed to notice the change at home. He concentrated his energies and learned within days of reporting that the whole Pentagon was a vast waste of resources. There were just too many talented people working too few meaningful jobs. Its elaborate official structure with the various services, the

Joint Chiefs, the congressional liaison, was a brilliant example of organizational overkill. As in every bureaucracy, the formal networks were for show, the informal were for go. The secret to success was in finding out who did the work, who was dependable, who you couldn't trust. It took most people at least six months, often a year, to begin to sort it out. King had been briefing him for almost three months, so Duke arrived knowing where most of the bodies were buried, and with a pile of King's chits to call in when ever he needed them. With King dead, they were even more valuable now, at least among the first-rate people.

The population was always shifting, and King had not tried to identify all his rivals for him. Fortunately Duke had an intuitive sense about so vital a matter. He felt strongly that it was not enough to succeed; your best friend must also fail. And Duke saw Maj. Harry MacIlmoyle coming—a tough, smart young cookie with a good combat record in F-84 fighter bombers in Korea. MacIlmoyle was working closely with the project engineers at Wright-Patterson to come up with a program to extend the B-47's life well into the 1960s. He was a threat; if he came to work in Duke's office, he'd not only be senior, he would be effective, the worst possible combination.

The office was saddled with the immense procurement and logistics problems of bringing the B-47 into SAC-wide service. The world's first operational swept-wing jet bomber was a strange mixture of radically advanced configuration and old-fashioned components and structural techniques. It brought a whole new capability with an entirely new set of problems, some of which seemed virtually unsolvable. Yet the B-47 was the mainstay for SAC and, combined with the advanced mix of nuclear weapons now available, it created a Pax Americana that was appreciated most in the Kremlin.

Despite its performance, superior to any bomber anywhere, and better than most fighters of the time, LeMay wasn't satisfied that it was the plane of the future. He had his eye on the B-52, a much bigger, more sophisticated airplane with the growth potential to take care of unforeseen events in the 1960s. The Soviets were catching up fast, even going ahead in missile design and deployment.

One of the big problems with the B-47 was that it was equipped with J47 engines, great for their time, but growth limited and fuel hungry. The B-52 would have second-generation Pratt & Whitney J57s, enormously powerful engines with excellent specific fuel consumption. Most important the B-52 was big, more than twice as heavy as the B-47, with a cavernous volume to fill with whatever equipment might be needed in the future.

MacIlmoyle was touting a compromise, one that would save the Air Force billions of procurement dollars and years of development work. It was one of the few "quick fixes" that looked intrinsically promising. Working with Boeing and Pratt, he and the Aeronautical System Division types at Wright-Pat had come up with a re-engined B-47, carrying four J57s instead of six J47s. Its performance matched the XB-52 in almost every area, and it would be far cheaper and much less risky than the huge B-52.

Brown listened to MacIlmoyle; he could be a real rival, maybe take over the B-47 program if it superseded the B-52. But King had said the B-52 was favored by all the SAC brass, especially CinCSAC.

MacIlmoyle had gone through his dog and pony show with Duke, riffling through his charts and Vu-graphs. It was an impressive briefing; this guy was someone to watch.

"What do you think, Duke, will he buy it?"

CinCSAC was coming in for program review, and MacIlmoyle wanted to get on the schedule to brief him.

"Sounds good to me, Harry. Are you sure about the performance figures? It's a little hard to believe that you get something for nothing. And what's in it for Boeing? It means they shut down new production and just do modifications for the next five years."

"Yeah, the figures are actually conservative, Duke, and Boeing is just covering its bets in case there is no money for the B-52. I didn't even include the fact that the B-52 will need new runways, new hangars, new fuel depots, training, everything. Will you help me get on the schedule?"

"Let me see what I can do; I'll have to bump somebody else—it's almost full. I'll try to get you on early, too."

What would King have done? MacIlmoyle was obviously a hot property, and there was room for only one hot property around the B-47 Program Office. He'd have to see if he couldn't fix him up with the general.

Duke called MacIlmoyle at home.

"Hey Harry, I've got you on; I had to bump the guy briefing on the medium transport, but that's a little further along, and I thought you could go on first."

"Thanks a million, Duke; I won't forget this."

Gee, I hope not, Duke thought.

They were in the big basement briefing room, the general sitting in the first curved row of seats, impatiently scanning the chart-bedecked wall, pulling on his cigar. Half the people in the room were smoking cigars and most were doing it more for his benefit than their own. A blue haze already clouded the light from the projector.

There was a general overview, and MacIlmoyle was on.

He made a brief introductory statement, mildly humorous as custom demanded, and called for his first slide. It was a straight comparison of the two aircraft, the proposed B-47 modification and the B-52A, with range, speed, and bomb load shown to be roughly equal, and with the comparative costs in double-sized print. The B-47 mod was shown to be about one-fifth as expensive as the B-52 program.

The general glared at it. "Major MacIlmoyle," he growled, "just how deep do I have to bury the goddamn B-47 before you dumb sonsofbitches will stop digging it up?"

MacIlmoyle turned bright red.

"Who the hell is pushing this at Wright-Pat? I've told them a hundred times the B-47 doesn't have the growth of the goddamn B-52 no matter what engine it's got. Who's your boss?"

MacIlmoyle turned white. His knees jellied, and he clutched the side of the podium. It was happening to him, the briefing crucifixion.

His boss was Lt. Col. Howard Whiting—he'd talked to him twenty minutes before the briefing, but the name was gone, vanished in his terror. Duke savored the moment.

"You hear me, Major? Who's your boss?"

"I can't think right now; it's one of those mental blocks, General."

The general turned to the colonel beside him. "Get him and his mental block and his briefing out of here. I don't want to see this B-47 shit again."

MacIlmoyle stumbled out; he glanced at Duke. Duke shrugged, crossed him off the list as a rival. The kid was no trouper.

14

April 1953
Goodfellow AFB, Texas
USA

This time Millard Washington loved flying school and flying school loved him. Goodfellow was a pretty base, and there were a few places in town where he could go with Louise and feel comfortable. They fell in love with the San Angelo–style Mexican food, with the enchiladas spread flat like pancakes, cheese drizzling across the top, and a jalapeño pepper roasted in the center. They drank Pearl Beer and listened to the cowboy music, but he always wore a uniform with his ribbons, and they always left early. No sense in pushing their luck, even in a town as pro–Air Force as San Angelo.

He only had trouble once; they were talked into going to Luigi's Steak House, a big rambling farmhouse fifteen miles outside of town that served enormous thirty-two-ounce sirloins for three dollars; you got the third one free if you ate two. Louise didn't want to go; when Wash insisted, feeling pressure from his friends, she agreed, but only if he drove her in their own car.

It was smart. They had just sat down when some comments came from across the room; a group of young guys, ranchers maybe, were talking about the good-looking coons. Washington and Louise got up and left quietly, before their friends could intervene. It wasn't worth a hassle, not with him in flying school.

Wash's position was unique; he was a combat veteran, an officer, a student pilot, a navigator, and a Negro. The first three items worked for him, the last two against him. It made him reflect on what he wanted to do in the Air Force.

It was good to have been in combat, and it was great to be a student officer, rather than a cadet. The privileges and the pay were better, but best of all was the treatment on the flight line. He now saw that the cadets were hazed far beyond the limit that might have been useful to determine their suitability for flying. It was a stupid, almost sadistic system that was blessed only by precedent.

The curious thing was the prejudice against Negroes, and against navigators. The former stemmed from the conditioning of society as a whole; if he met a southerner he could expect to

198

see a rather delicate formal friendship extended like a hot towel on tongs. The prejudice against navigators, however, was Air Force induced, a manifestation of the adolescent credo "If you ain't a pilot you ain't shit," so common in the operational squadrons.

He missed much of it. People didn't haze him about being a navigator; it might be misconstrued that they were hazing him because he was a Negro and that was bad form. But pilots would say anything to a white navigator, who was supposed to endure an entire smorgasbord of insults, formal and informal.

Formally, the navigator knew that he would be downgraded in the promotion process and in the assignment to service schools, and most of all, absolutely excluded from the command of an operational unit, the one sure ticket to flag rank.

Informally, no matter how capable he was, the navigator was the butt of all jokes, blamed for all mishaps, and given all of the donkey assignments as a matter of course.

The same was true of other nonpilot-rated slots: radar observers were coming into their own, and would get the same treatment as navigator-bombardiers. Even the new wizards in electronics, brainy types who operated electronic countermeasures equipment, or who snooped along the borders of the Soviet Union to ferret out their radar secrets, were subject to the low level of juvenile harassment.

It had its effect: navigators, bombardiers, radar operators, all adopted rebellious poses. A cheerful navigator was an anomalous prize; they had heard all the bad old jokes, and expected anything said to them to be hostile.

The thing that bothered Washington most was the banality; the jokes were the same at every base, and every level. It was a perfect counterpart to the watermelon/chicken-eating Negro jokes that never varied, but never failed to get laughs.

Sometimes Washington felt that pilot training was like passing; he was going to go beyond a barrier, but underneath he'd still be a navigator. Well, the B-47 was going to help things; LeMay wanted his crews to be "triple rated," pilot and radar observer and navigator-bombardier, and he was going to be one. Maybe he could do some good for navigators then, just as he and Louise planned the good he was going to do for black people when he got a little rank.

He did so well in pilot training that it surprised him; finally he realized that much of it was a matter of confidence. If he thought he was going to do well, he did.

Washington had been flabbergasted when his orders for advanced training said Luke Air Force Base—he was going to jets! He had assumed that with his navigator and B-29 background, the Air Force would routinely ship him off to multiengines. Louise was not too happy; she knew that the jets were more dangerous.

The switch from San Angelo to Phoenix was easy; the main difference was that the Mexican food was much spicier, and the enchiladas were rolled rather than flat.

It turned out that the T-33s were easy to fly, far simpler than the T-6s he'd trained on at Goodfellow, and he graduated near the top of his class, delighted and surprised that he'd been asked to become an instructor.

Louise was not nearly so surprised. She had been with him through all the training, and had been free to observe what was happening to him with more detachment than he could bring to bear. As involved in the social life of the various bases as any of the other trainee-officers' wives, she nonetheless inevitably felt herself apart from them all. First, because she was black, and second, because unlike most of them, she was a professional, a registered nurse. She was in the Air Force, she felt, as much as Wash—but she was not of it, not even so much as the other wives. Consequently, she developed a less charitable view of the events that swept Wash along.

She was careful not to allow him to sense her reserve about his successes; she knew his training was tough and his goals high. But occasionally she could not restrain herself. On the night Wash found out about being asked to become an instructor, she let it slip.

He sat at their tiny dinette, grinning like a fool and knocking back a bottle of beer while she fixed dinner. "I can't get over it," he said for the fifth time. "I started out in the Air Force doing everything wrong, and ever since Korea, I'm doing everything right. My luck has really changed, eh?"

Louise finally turned to him, hands on hips, and ignored the tamales boiling behind her on the stove. "Wash, listen to me. I don't believe it's luck. You're getting some kind of treatment, and I don't think it's the medal. There were a lot of men who got medals in Korea. *I* think they are ashamed, or something, and they're using you."

"Using me? How?"

"I don't know. But it's obviously some kind of public-relations thing. Maybe it has to do with the civil-rights people or something."

"Civil rights? Honey, the Air Force doesn't care about that stuff. We're integrated. Hell, look at me."

"No, I don't mean in the Air force. I mean outside. Somehow, they're using you to do something else. I don't know what. But I just feel it."

Wash scowled, drained his beer, and reminded himself to pay more attention to Louise. She had to be getting lonely, what with all the training time he'd been putting in. He promised himself that being an instructor would change it.

It didn't. He went through the instructor pilot training and took two classes of cadets through, enjoying it all the more when he realized that, like anything else, you only learned flying when you taught it. And in the process, he worked longer hours than he ever had as a student. But before the situation could get out of hand, less than a year after graduation, he came in and tossed a set of orders on their kitchen table. Louise, very pregnant and very tired, listlessly turned them around. As usual, it was all Air Force gobbledygook to her.

He sat down next to her and patted her tummy. "Everything okay?"

"Sure. What are these for?"

"You remember you said something's happening? Well, it's happening all right—we're going to McConnell for B-47s!" He beamed at her, as if he'd just killed a bear with his own hands.

She looked puzzled. "Wash, it that good? I thought you liked fighters."

He waved his hands. "Oh, I do, honey, I like them fine, but I like B-47s better. They're the main weapons in SAC, and SAC's the place to be nowadays." He paused and looked thoughtful. "I wonder what kind of Mexican food they have in Wichita?"

Mexican food was scarce in Wichita, but not Mexican weather. Washington had grown up in the Midwest, seen the tar bubble up in the streets and sidewalks so hot you could really fry eggs on them, but he had never felt the humid heat of Kansas in the summer.

McConnell Air Force Base was a concrete open-air oven, reinforcing the Kansas sun that had brick-baked the land for weeks. The heat had cracked the fields wide open, great gaping scars a foot across and a yard deep, the grass parched beyond the roots, no grub or worm alive, the rocks glazed into the dirt. But the ground was cool compared to the ramp, where the rumbling overlay from the hundreds of jet engines slung from the drooping wings of the B-47 fleet created a seething inferno.

The heat came with and of the noise; the blue-black exhausts roiled back from the aircraft preparing to taxi out, while shirtless crew chiefs darted back and forth. The exhaust rolled like a horizontal tornado, round all about but flat on the ramp, enfolding everyone in grease and heat; the lungs struggled with the mass, half carbon, half air, the noise driving the eardrums at cymbal-clashing vibration levels.

The heat was everywhere, but the noise was localized; directly behind the airplane, one heard nothing in a cone if not of silence at least of less clamor. At the sides, though, the heat and noise mixed and men were made violently sick.

The cockpits broiled under the clear plastic canopies; metal became too hot to touch, until finally a concession was made. If the cockpit temperatures rose above 160 degrees Fahrenheit, the mission could be delayed.

Wash loved it. He loved the walk through the miasmic heat to the airplane, the parachute straps cutting into him, flying suit already soaked with sweat, weighed down with checklists, navigation kits, thermos bottle. He loved it because he was there where he shouldn't be, where he never had a chance to be, where nobody from Bud Drummond to Reverend Gallows ever expected him to be, where he never thought he'd be.

He walked to the airplane slowly, working against the heat coming from the line of B-47s ahead, against the ten-knot breeze that seared rather than cooled. As he walked he savored the lovely lines of the airplane, a torpedo with drooping arrow wings, somewhat clumsy on the ground but in the air a flashing fighter of an airplane.

And in the air, cool, even cold. The big air-conditioning system kicked in soon after takeoff, sending a shower of snow through the system, blessing them with a smoky fog of delicious shivering shreds of ice particles. It wasn't long before it was too cold, and the sweat-drenched flying suit turned clammy.

He was a three-way exception to the general rule at McConnell. First, he was black; second, he came virtually straight from flying school; and third, he was the only one who had not come as a member of an existing designated SAC crew. General LeMay didn't want to waste time teaching crews to fly together after they joined their operational bases; yet here he was, and here was Maj. Harold McCartney.

McCartney was here alone too, and from the way he took Wash under his wing and helped him, apparently assigned by God to the task of bringing him along. McCartney was a first-

202

rate aircraft commander. He was a quietly competent, good-natured man, confident enough of his own abilities to let Washington actually fly the airplane and make landings. Many of the men training to be aircraft commander hogged every flight, reduced the copilot to a flight engineer's status, only allowing him to start engines and pull up the gear, but not McCartney.

Wash learned his key lesson at McConnell on his penultimate flight before graduation as a fully qualified B-47 copilot.

They had preflighted all morning, and he was ready, for this flight was special; Washington was going to be in the front seat instead of the rear, and was going to do everything from takeoff to landing.

As long as he did it well. The instructor, a wiry wild young captain named "Dad" Roberts, would be in the back seat, with McCartney riding up front where the radar observer sat in a full-fledged combat crew.

He met Roberts at the tail of their airplane, 0069. "Hello, Wash, looks like we got old lickety split today, eh?"

Washington didn't get it at first, glanced at the tail number, grinned.

"You get in, Lieutenant, and you act like you're the aircraft commander and I'm the dumbass copilot. You tell me what you want me to do, and I won't give you any advice unless I see we're getting in trouble. Okay?"

McCartney had filed their clearance and they climbed into the sizzling airplane. It was more than twenty minutes until they had finally gotten airborne, felt the cool air kicking through the air-conditioning ducts.

Roberts was as good as his word; Washington took them on the preprogrammed flight West to Denver and back then to Topeka to shoot some landings at Forbes Air Force Base. After his last touch-and-go landing at Forbes, Roberts squeezed the mike button. "Wash, let's go on home. How about letting me fly it for a while?"

Washington rocked the control wheel, said, "You got it," and looked down at McCartney. McCartney threw him a thumbs-up.

Roberts climbed westward, leveling off at about fourteen thousand feet. He trimmed the airplane, called to Wash. "Can you pick anything out on the horizon as a landmark?"

"Yeah, Captain, there's a big thunderhead out there, maybe forty miles out. Can you see it?"

"Yeah, keep your eye on it."

Roberts dropped the nose slightly. Wash felt the airplane accelerate, then begin to roll. The horizon spun as Roberts pulled the airplane through a perfect barrel roll. "That's a confidence builder for you, Wash. The secret is to pull a constant one-G during the roll. Do you want to try it?"

Washington glanced down at McCartney, who had moved back to the crawlway, and who was obviously furious. "No sir, I think I'll let that go for a while."

Roberts chuckled, turned the airplane over to him. They flew back to McConnell where he made his final landing, bouncing a little, but not badly. He knew he'd made it. He was signed off and went gladly back into the withering Kansas heat to shower and head for the club to celebrate.

At the club two hours later, Washington saw McCartney. The major responded to his wave and sat down next to him. He congratulated Washington by drinking a toast with a beer, then stared hard at him. "Wash, what did you learn today?"

"Well, Major, I learned I did better than I thought, and that you can roll a B-47."

"Son, let me tell you something. You did just as well as I thought you would, but you missed one lesson. This is one some guys never get, and it's the most important thing you can learn. Never, repeat, *never* make an airplane do something it's not designed for, not unless you are in combat and you have to."

"Sir? You mean Roberts's roll? But I thought we were supposed to take chances like that—"

"No, son. We're not. We're supposed to win wars. Sometimes that means you take a chance with your airplane—but you don't do it unless you absolutely have to. I know you have a lot of fighter time, Wash, and I know about your B-29 work in Korea. But you've got to understand how your role as a bomber pilot is different. Fighter jocks are cowboys; fair enough, we need cowboys. But SAC flies to win wars. We don't fly to impress ourselves with our own tricks. Nobody at Boeing thought that any Air Force pilot would be stupid enough to roll that 47, so they didn't design it to do that. In a fighter, you're supposed to be a hero when you play those games. In SAC, you're just a schmuck, Wash. See?"

"Well, sir, I—"

"Mark my words, Wash, Roberts is going to kill himself if he keeps that up; and the worst of it is, he'll take some innocent people with him."

McCartney finally let him off the hook and told him the good

204

news: they were going to be assigned together at Castle Air Force Base, flying B-47s in the 93rd.

Washington was delighted, couldn't wait till dinner was over to call Louise in Baltimore. She'd moved there at his insistence when he'd gone to McConnell, so she could avoid the lousy housing situation, in which many families were forced to live in substandard apartments or little trailers while the aircrew trained. Despite her protests, he wouldn't allow it; the imminent arrival of the baby decided in his favor, and her parents had been overjoyed to have her back for a while.

McCartney finally stood to go, and Wash made a beeline for the phones in the foyer. He calculated the time difference and thought she wouldn't mind his calling so late. The phone rang and rang at the other end, and Wash frowned.

"Hello?" said a male voice.

"Uh—hello. This is Millard Washington. Who's this?"

"Frank, Wash. Where've you been? We—"

Washington's frown deepened. Frank Walsh was Louise's brother. He was some kind of car salesman, and always seemed to be driving a fancy car and holding a fancy woman.

"Been? Right here at McConnell. Why?"

"Well, we've been trying to call all night. At the BOQ they said—"

"Never mind that! What's wrong? Is something wrong with Louise?" Panic tinged his voice. A passing couple glanced at him.

"No. She's fine and so is the baby. That's what we've been—"

"Baby? Did you say baby?"

"Yeah. Cute little boy. Louise—"

"When? Where? Oh, Jesus, I have to get there—"

"Hey! Hold it, Wash, it's okay—"

But Washington was already through the door of the club, headed for Operations. An hour later, he was on his way to Baltimore in a T-33. And five hours after that, he was holding his newborn baby in his arms, and grinning like a fool at an exhausted Louise. Nobody pointed out that he smelled like a horse or was still dressed in his flight suit. Sometimes it paid to be a pilot.

And sometimes it didn't. Six months later, at Castle Air Force Base Operations, McCartney found Wash in the briefing room. It was the first Wash had seen him since a few weeks after they had arrived, when McCartney had gone in for a flight physical and been grounded for an off-scale blood-pressure reading.

McCartney had been reassigned to a nonflying job out of the squadron, so Wash never saw him.

McCartney didn't return Wash's smile of greeting; he just held out a copy of that week's *Life* magazine to Wash, and showed him a picture of an arrow-shaped hole in the ground.

Wash took it and read the caption. A Captain Roberts had rolled a B-47, and instead of leveling out, it had augered in, inverted. There had been no survivors.

15

1550 LOCAL
28 April 1956
Castle AFB, California
USA

"Four no trump." Louise Washington said it deadpan, with a poker player's inscrutability.

Joan pursed her lips and studied her cards. Bridge was not her favorite game. But it was all the rage now, so you played it or you didn't get all the news. More secrets were traded at bridge games than through the hands of spies in Vienna. The cards she was dealt were not very good. As usual. She sighed.

"Pass," Joan said. She picked up her coffee and sipped it.

Louise's partner at South was Lena Randall. It was a peculiar pairing, since Millard Washington had replaced Norm Randall as Ted Savidge's copilot. There was a lot of bitterness reported about that one; people said Wash was far too junior to have gotten a place on Savidge's crew, which was one of the best in the 93rd. Randall had been taken out of the back seat on the B-47 and sent to Squadron Officers' School—almost as shocking a thing as Wash's installation in his place. Nobody in the 93rd quite knew how to take all this sudden activity. It was one reason Joan had accepted the invitation to play bridge at Maggie Savidge's.

At Joan's left, Lena clearly struggled to get her cards to make sense. It delighted Joan that somebody else found this game difficult and tiresome. From what went on at OWC, you'd think that contract bridge was the reason all the wives were in the Air Force.

"Pass," Lena finally said weakly, with a quick, apologetic glance at Louise.

Louise smiled warmly at her and Joan felt a tiny twinge of

206

envy. Although she was a colored woman, Louise was beautiful. She was the first black girl with whom Joan had ever interacted, at least socially. She'd been a little standoffish at first, but Joan had turned on the charm at Duke's first barbecue after they'd been sent here from the Pentagon, and both Wash and Louise had warmed immediately. To her own surprise, Joan had found that her charm was not all cosmetic; something about the Washingtons—both of them—attracted her. She found Wash a man of immense personal integrity, and Louise was friendly and sincere—both attributes hard to detect in the Pentagon's social world.

Across from Joan, Maggie Savidge squinted sidewise at her own cards through a cloud of cigarette smoke. She was ten years older than the others at the table, like her husband a veteran of the Air Force. He was an aircraft commander carrying spot promotions from LeMay to lieutenant colonel. She was a wry survivor of too many moves and too many wars. Her kids were about to graduate from high school and go away to Sacramento State College, where, she let it be known, she'd like to go one day too. Like most wives of the older reserve officers, she was not a college graduate. Joan, Louise, and Lena were typical of the newer wives in that they were graduates; in other circumstances, the fact might have made a difference. But Maggie's obvious intelligence, wide reading, and successful career as a SAC wife and mother more than compensated for her lack of a sheepskin.

"Not our day, partner," she said to Joan with a smile. She laid her cards down and looked at Louise. "Appears nobody can bid," she said.

Louise laid her cards down too. "How about a break? I'd like to visit the ladies' room anyway. Girls?"

They all made noises of assent.

"I'll put some more coffee on," Maggie said while they all stretched and rose.

"I'll help," Joan said and accompanied Maggie into the little kitchen. Back in the living room, where they'd set up the card table, Lena switched on the hi-fi. Harry Belafonte began to waft out to the kitchen.

"How's Ted?" Joan asked it while washing a cup.

"Fine. Duke?"

"The same. You know. He works too hard. They all do."

Maggie smiled through her cigarette smoke and popped the lid back on her percolator.

"It's SAC. How do you like it here? You've been here—what? Six months now?"

"Seven. I love it, frankly. Arlington and the Pentagon were awful. I mean, I know Duke needed it for his career and everything, but the people—"

"I know. Dreadful town. Ted hated it too. I suppose if we'd liked it more, he might be . . . well, that's all gone now."

Joan glanced down the little hall. The bathroom door was still closed. "Tell me, how does Ted like Wash?"

"Oh, he thinks he's great. Of course, I gather that Norm was a superb copilot, but it's so hard to get them to talk about all this, isn't it?" Maggie gave Joan a quick warning glance as Lena walked in behind Joan.

"Yes," Lena chimed in. "Norm only told me about SOS after the actual orders were cut. I guess he figured I'd be upset."

"Whyever for?"

"I don't know. Maybe because he had to go to Maxwell TDY unaccompanied or something. But I was glad he got off that damned crew duty, I can tell you."

"Really?" Joan's eyebrows lifted fractionally. One was supposed to consider crew duty the be-all and end-all of Air Force life.

"Really. Now, Joan, Duke is obviously not going to be stuck in a cockpit his whole career, but Norm—Norm's just a crazy airplane nut. If they hadn't made him go to SOS, why, he'd just as soon have spent his whole life in one of those things. This way, thank God, he may get out of SAC entirely when he gets back."

Unseen, Louise had joined them at the other end of the kitchen. "I'm glad to hear you say that, Lena," she said. "I feel the same about Wash. I know he's thrilled to be with Ted, but I know he's always felt bad that he got Norm's seat."

Lena shrugged. "Well, to be truthful, Louise, Norm was pretty ticked off when he found out he was being bumped for a new guy. Please don't take it personally, but you know they were all carrying spots based on crew integrity. He was afraid—we all were—that he'd lose his rank when he lost his seat."

"But he didn't, did he?"

"No, thank God. We sure need that extra pay. Penny and Jimmie go through clothes like—well, you know."

"Makes it all the more ironic, doesn't it then?" asked Maggie, who had been getting a coffee tray ready.

"What?" said Joan, her sonar picking up real news.

Maggie poured a little cream into a battered silver pitcher. "About Wash and SOS."

Joan looked at Louise, who simply blinked.

"What?"

208

Maggie stopped pouring and took the cigarette out of her mouth. She turned to look at Louise. "You mean you don't know?"

"Don't know what?"

"Well, dear, I—I probably shouldn't say anything then—"

"Oh, Maggie, for heaven's sake, tell us, will you?" Joan's frustration echoed all of theirs.

"Well. I heard from Annie Callahan—you know, Colonel Callahan's wife, who runs the thrift shop—anyway, I heard from her about the latest batch of SOS guys. Wash was one of them. I'm sorry, Louise, I thought surely you knew—"

Louise shook her head. "No. Wash would have told me. Who's Colonel Callahan? Would he actually know?"

"Sure. He's the admin chief."

They all looked at Louise, who was trying hard to take it in. Going to Maxwell SOS was a major part of an officer's upward movement; it was a treasured breakthrough for most men, and almost unheard of in SAC. Most SAC types had to take it by correspondence. Wash had been Ted Savidge's copilot for only a little while, and here he was, following Norm Randall to Maxwell. It was all too bizarre.

"Well," Louise said shakily, "well . . ."

"Yes. Congratulations, Louise," said Lena. It wasn't hard to detect the envy in her voice, hard as she tried to suppress it. Now Norm's feat was not so spectacular; she wondered, as they all did, whether it meant that he would be jerked back into Savidge's crew instead of moving on and out of the 93rd.

The news seemed unsettling to everyone. After Lena's congratulations, there was a long silence in which they thought about what it might mean, not just directly for Louise and Wash, but for them all. The rules they thought they understood were shifting rapidly. When such things happened, the fabric of pretensions they all carefully nurtured—the pretensions about how Air Force life really wasn't all that different from other kinds of life—was ripped asunder and the uncertainty of everything spotlighted anew.

"I guess Wash'll be leaving pretty soon then," Joan said finally. It broke the spell, and Maggie began clattering the cups and saucers onto the tray. Lena bustled around to help. Louise picked up the napkins.

"Yes, I guess so," Louise said.

"Well, Duke and I will throw a nice tacos-and-enchiladas party for him as soon as it's official. We'll invite the whole

209

darned squadron. We'll make it the blowout of the year!" She put her arm around Louise's shoulders as they went back out to the card table.

"Sounds great," Louise said. But her words sounded phony even to herself. Her mind buzzed with unanswered questions. Why were they doing this to Wash? He'd been accelerated through everything, and now, when they had expected a nice three-year tour and some stability, a chance to make friends, somebody Up There was rushing him along again. He was a fine pilot and excellent navigator, she knew that from his ERs, but why this?

As they sat down again and the chatter drifted into less serious channels, Louise again wondered if Wash's career wasn't more than just a career. There was great racial unrest in the South and in the industrial Midwest, and you didn't have to be a social scientist to see that a lot of powerful people were scared of it. Suppose, she thought, suppose Wash is being used as a token, a sort of Uncle Tom of the modern age, a symbol of how "you nigger folks ain't got it so bad?" Suppose he was simply being manipulated? What would that mean to him . . . and to her?

"Cream, Louise?" Joan's gentle query broke her reverie. She looked at the pale, sympathetic face and cleared the dark thoughts from her mind. She was among friends. Leave it at that, and get on with life, and the game.

"Surely," she said. And they did indeed get on with the game.

That night, when she told Wash, he went wild with excitement about his continuing incredible luck. Louise let him exult. If there was cause for her foreboding, it would show with time.

1435 LOCAL
18 June 1956
AF 3958
en route to Maxwell AFB, Alabama
USA

It had been a beautiful warm Alabama morning when they left, but now a swiftly moving cold front had piled the towering rows of cumulus into an airborne mountain range, far higher than the aging C-47 could climb, and ranging in Cannaen arc about it. Capt. Mike Kelly felt the everyday joy of flying begin to degenerate into work. He sucked on the Dutch Masters cigar he

210

smoked only to keep awake, scanning the instruments and the chart. With luck they'd be over Montgomery radio in an hour, with an easy ground-controlled approach into Maxwell. Piece of cake.

Piece of cake, maybe, he thought. Some of the clouds were ominously black, convulsed by lightning, changing from bright to light yellow like an expiring incandescent bulb. They burbled at random, with only an occasional jagged streak flung at the ground. He heard no thunder, the crackling discharges muted by the roar of wind and engines. Kelly remembered the joy he used to feel as a kid, standing in the attic and watching a wild electrical storm, wishing he could somehow fly in it. He knew better now.

He glanced over at his copilot, Steve Mason, dozing while still appearing to be examining the book of let-down plates that described the various instrument approaches available at Maxwell Field. Kelly laid his cigar carefully behind the twin throttles, and reached back for the oxygen regulator. They didn't carry masks on the C-47 as a rule, but you could suck oxygen straight from the flexible tubing. He switched the regulator to 100 percent, took several deep lungfuls to clear away the cigar smoke, then filled his lungs and held his breath.

Kelly picked up the cigar and nudged Mason. "Wake up, Mace," and as he yelled, he blew his oxygen-laden breath through the Dutch Masters. The pure oxygen surged to the tip and blow-torched a sheet of orange-yellow flame in front of Mason.

"You bastard, you scared the hell out of me! I thought we were on fire. How did you do that?" Mason was obviously glad to have the numbing fatigue relieved by the adrenaline shot. He scratched, standard occupational necessity in the sweaty flying suits, and busied himself with the let-down plates.

Behind the two, crew chief Sgt. Howard Justine watched the byplay with some disapproval. It was dangerous to fool with oxygen, and he hadn't been too impressed with either man so far; they might be hotshot pilots from Korea; but they sure stumbled around the inside of a C-47. Justine had pride in his work, and in his airplane. It was worn but clean, he knew every nut and bolt in it. Just like he knew the slight fluctuation on the oil pressure on the number-two engine wasn't normal. His eyes kept making a triangular sweep: outside, flight instruments, not to use them, just to see if they were working, and back to the number-two engine oil pressure and temperature gauges. Sure enough, the temperature was creeping up, a confirming bad sign. He was no longer sleepy, but he reached down for his thermos bottle—stainless steel, a real luxury for a crew chief, his wife had won it at bingo—and finished the dregs of the weak base exchange coffee.

Kelly wedged the bucking control column in place between his knees while he blew on his chilled fingers.

"I wish I'd stayed in bed," he yelled over to Mason, who was still studying the instrument let-down plates.

"Yeah, me too. Weather didn't mention any thunderstorms down here, and there ain't no end to them." Mason was stevedore-heavy, his neck swallowing his dogtag chain.

"What kind of approach do you want? An ILS?"

Mike considered. In a fighter he preferred an ILS; the instrument landing system was operated entirely within the cockpit, in response to automatic signals from the ground, and he didn't have to worry about the competence of the crew giving the ground-controlled approach. In the C-47 it was different. He didn't have much experience in the airplane and maybe he could use some help.

"When we get there, ask them for an ILS with a GCA backup."

"Gotcha—best of both worlds."

Kelly resumed his scan of the big round dials set in the instrument panel; zinc-chromate green when it came from the Douglas factory in Long Beach in 1943, the panel was now a worn black mosaic of chips and touch-up paint. Justine kept a clean ship, but he couldn't keep a new one. Everything looked okay but the number-two engine; he'd been squinting to see if he couldn't urge the oil pressure back up to normal, but it was slumping pound by pound, and still the temperature was rising. The airplane was talking to him but he wasn't sure what it was saying. In a jet it was simple: if the red lights stayed out, you were pretty well okay, and if they didn't, you got out. The same with weather—in a jet you were either on top of it, or you went through it so fast it didn't matter. He was beginning to feel uneasy.

"Weather like this makes me wish to hell I'd never told them I could fly Gooney Birds. How much time do you have in these buckets, Mace?"

Mason stiffened and snorted. "Shit, man, they told me you was an instructor pilot. I haven't logged more than twenty hours of piston-engine time in the last four years, and only a little of that was in a Goon."

A little stab of apprehension speared Kelly as he watched the wind whistle up over the windscreen. Older pilots had told him that all C-47s leaked like sieves, and this one had to be worse than most. Water was running down the control column onto his sleeve and his left leg was soaked. "What's the chance for some more cabin heat, chief?"

"It's doing about as good as it can, skipper; are you keeping your eye on number two?"

"Yeah." Keeping my eye on it is about all I can do, Kelly thought. He only had about a dozen hours in the C-47 and he was flying first pilot only because they were so incredibly lax at Maxwell Base Operations. Each month a new crew of pilots showed up at one of the half a dozen schools on the base, and it was almost impossible to run any kind of systematic evaluation program. The ramp was covered with planes—Lockheed T-33 jet trainers, North American B-25s, Cessna U-3As—but there were mostly C-47s and Beechcraft C-45s in which to get flying time. The senior officers scarfed up the T-33s and B-25s, and if you wanted your four hours to make your flying pay, you took what you got. They'd asked him if he was qualified in the C-47 and he'd said yes, on the sound basis that he could fly anything with wings. That was it, no check ride, no check of his Form 5, nothing. Now he had thirteen passengers and two crew members on his hands in an ailing airplane in a set of granddaddy Bama thunderstorms. Wonderful.

He glanced out his side window, watching a thin white glaze of clear ice forming on the wings. You never saw ice on a jet, and he remembered from his weather classes that clear ice was supposed to be the worst. The C-47 was famous for its ice- and weight-carrying capacity, so he wasn't worried. It wouldn't be a problem so long as both engines were running.

Nerves and too much coffee put pressure on his bladder, and he yelled to Mason, "You got it for a minute. I'm going back to take a leak."

Mason nodded and gently tugged the wheel to show he had control.

Kelly slipped back past Justine and stepped into the brightly lit, frigid passenger compartment. The two rows of passengers, all fellow students at Squadron Officers' School, were crumpled like dead rebel soldiers in Brady photos of the Civil War. Some had G.I. blankets wound about themselves, but most were just shivering, toughing it out.

When Kelly got matters underway in the bleak, chemical-smelling can, Mason began walking on the rudders, yawing the airplane back and forth, which caused him to piss on the floor, making up for the cigar business.

On the way back he stopped by Capt. Millard Washington.

"How's it going, Wash? Hot enough for you?"

"It's freezing back here, Mike; isn't there any cabin heat?"

"Crew chief says no; there's a little bit coming out the outlet, but most of it's being dumped overboard. How do you like SOS?"

"It beats Korea—sorry we haven't got together more."

Mike felt a little uncomfortable with the conversation. It was unusual enough for a Negro to be an officer, and more so to be a pilot. Washington was the only person he'd met since he joined the Air Force who was from his hometown; he was also the only Negro officer he'd had any contact with. They had worked at Bud Drummond's gas station at the same time; Mike pumping gas, and Wash, appropriately enough, on the wash rack. They hadn't been exactly pals then, and Mike felt confused about how he ought to act toward Wash; he'd been surprised and even glad that another East St. Louis inmate had escaped, but Wash's world was as alien to him as his was to Wash.

Washington probably knew he'd been avoiding him. But they didn't share classes and were staying in different quarters, so the only times he'd actually seen Washington were at the club, and Mike had never done more than have a cursory chat with the big black man. He'd felt uneasy about it more than once, but the press of schoolwork occupied his time, and every time he saw Washington, he reminded himself that he owed it to them both to get together. Like most of Kelly's good resolutions, it petered out into inaction.

Kelly shuffled past the rest of the passengers, most asleep or bleary-eyed. If they knew how little I know, he thought, they'd all be up in the cockpit helping. He buckled himself back in, then reached over and grabbed Mason's arm. "I got the airplane. See if you can get ATC on the horn and see what the current weather is at Maxwell; we ought to be there in about fifty minutes."

Before Mason could comply, the C-47 yawed to the left, shivering as the number-one engine bucked and shuddered. Kelly grabbed the wheel, booted in right rudder pressure, and scanned the instruments again. Number one was losing power fast, with the oil pressure gauge wobbling at zero. Number one? What the hell was this? He shot a glance at the gauges for number two, but couldn't focus as the press of power from the good engine goaded the aircraft into a left turn. Kelly had to

214

stand on the right rudder pedal to keep the airplane straight; he shot a glance out the side window again, to see oil streaming over the nacelle.

Justine leaned forward and said, "You'd better feather it, sir, or we might get a fire." Justine had already reached up and covered the number-two engine feather button; he'd seen more than one pilot feather the wrong engine on a practice flight.

Kelly missed the familiar stupid feeling of euphoria that he always got in combat. Just before a fight he really felt good, almost like during sex, but this was different. He couldn't dredge up the feathering procedure from memory, and knew better than to fumble through it. He had his hands full keeping the airplane straight and level. "You shut it down, Justine, I got to fly this fucker. Mason, call Birmingham for an emergency landing at the Municipal."

In the cabin there was a flurry of quiet activity as the parachutes were passed forward from the stack by the door. Each man acted as if he wasn't afraid, but all kept their eyes on the bailout signal over the cabin door. Washington began jamming his big frame into a parachute that must have last been fitted tightly on a WAF. Across the aisle, a tiny captain was trying to cinch down straps that bulged around him like linguini around a clam.

"Here, Captain," Washington yelled, "let's swap. We either got time to change, or we don't have any time at all."

The other officer grinned and exchanged chutes. He'd flown with Washington a half a dozen times out of Maxwell's Base Operations, and never got over his deep Paul Robeson voice or his sense of humor.

"I'm going to stick with you, Wash; you've done this before." The rest of the cabin passengers settled down nervously, chutes painfully tight against the groin, just like the instructors said, eyes still on the cabin warning light, ready to get up and jump if the alarm bell sounded. Except for the pounding of the engine, it was quiet.

Justine went through the feathering drill swiftly, glad Kelly had not tried to bluff it out and screw it up. The left engine shivered and the propeller slowed to a stop, blades knife edge to the wind. "Chief, keep your eye on the number-two oil pressure; it's still dropping."

"No sweat, skipper. I'll watch it but it won't do much good. If it goes, it goes, and we ain't got any more. You just fly the airplane like you been doing, and we'll be okay."

215

Mason's fat fingers danced over the buttons of the VHF set, finally punching channel 5. "Birmingham, this is Air Force 3958, we have, ah, a slight emergency. We just shut down number one, and are requesting a GCA approach and landing at Birmingham Municipal."

Kelly added power on the number-two engine, watching its oil pressure gauge build a little, knowing the temperature would follow. He trimmed the airplane to take the insistent pressure off the controls, dropping the right wing just like the textbook called for. He was trading airspeed for altitude, and it couldn't go on much longer, especially with the ice. He kept feeding in back pressure and trim, and kept the radio compass needle pointing at Birmingham with a lot of right rudder. "Mason," he yelled, "they can't hear you on intercom, for Christ's sake. Get us a goddamn approach, I can't hold eleven thousand feet much longer. Airspeed's down to one fifteen already."

Mason blushed and switched his junction box to Command, and Birmingham Air Traffic Control Center came back promptly on his next call, answering "Roger, Air Force 3958, proceed to Birmingham radio. Cleared to seven thousand feet now, and I'll have a lower altitude for you in a few minutes. We'll alert the tower and rescue; give me your fuel state and souls on board."

Kelly snorted. "What the hell does he mean, 'souls on board'? Mason, tell him we got our hands full just flying this thing, and that we want a GCA right away."

Mason shrugged and said, "Thank you, Birmingham; we got three hundred gallons of fuel, and sixteen souls on board." He toggled the intercom and said to Kelly, "That's what they always say, Mike, 'souls on board.' They don't mean no harm."

Kelly wished he was alone in an F-86; if things went wrong, he'd just pull the little handles, and whoosh, into his parachute let-down pattern. He dreaded an ejection as much as anybody—he knew how tough it was on the spine—but it now seemed simpler than fighting this wallowing beast down the next three thousand feet to level-off altitude, and then flogging it through the approach.

It was tougher keeping the radio compass needle centered now. They must be nearing the station. The ice on the wing was gone, melted by the higher temperatures of the lower altitudes. The compass needle began swinging so wildly he couldn't tell if it was because they were over the station or whether the increasingly brilliant lightning flashes were cocking it.

The Birmingham ATC operator came in, calm as controllers on the ground always are in a thunderstorm. "Air Force 3958, you're cleared for a standard ADF approach to Birmingham Municipal airport; call passing the station, and inbound on the final approach."

Kelly stiffened. "Hey, Mace, get us a GCA; I can't drive this thing through an ADF approach with this much electrical interference; the damn needle's drifting forty-five degrees either side of center. And get a reading on the weather."

On a GCA, Kelly could concentrate on just altitude, heading, and airspeed, responding to the directions of the controller. If he had to do an ADF approach, he had to guess what the needle was telling him, and do some accurate timing. He'd been into Birmingham before, and it was like flying down into a bowl. The field was surrounded by hills that sloped down gently to the boundaries.

Mason transmitted the request, but ATC came back with, "Ah roger, 3958, we'd like to give you a GCA, but our equipment's down. We've had some power outages, and there is only emergency lighting on the field. Weather here is eight-hundred-foot overcast, thin layers of fast-moving scud under that, visibility two and a half miles and falling, pooled water on the runway, with thunderstorms in all quadrants. We had some hail earlier, but that's gone now."

Thank Christ for small favors, Kelly thought.

"AF 3958, Birmingham here. Would you like a vector to another airport?"

Kelly stabbed his finger at the ebbing oil pressure on number two and asked, "What say, chief?"

The crew chief scanned the instruments one more time, leaned over, peered behind Mason to examine the number-two engine, and said, "I think we ought to try it here, skipper; I don't think we ought to stooge around on number two any longer than we have to."

Kelly squinted through the moisture-laden windshield; it was pitch black ahead, with lighter gray patches to the left. Lightning snapped in all quadrants, and the old C-47 lumbered rather than flew through the turbulence.

"Mace, tell them we'll be landing at Birmingham."

Mason reached over and slipped the approach plate into Kelly's knee pad. It was simple enough. You crossed the station at three thousand feet, heading 180 degrees. After one minute you made a 45-degree turn to the right, and as soon as your wings were level, you turned back through 225 degrees to pick up the reciprocal course, 360 degrees, into the station, letting down to fifteen hundred feet. After crossing the station, you had two minutes to drop down to eight hundred feet and track into the field. Simple enough, if everything worked right.

"Hey, chief, what kind of rate of climb can I expect out of this bucket at this weight with an engine out?"

Justine ran a few figures through his head. "If you keep your speed up on the approach, and go around early, you ought to be able to get maybe one hundred, two hundred feet per minute."

Shit-oh-dear, Kelly thought. Not enough with those hills. Why didn't I stay in bed? It bothered him to have the passengers and crew on board. If he busted his own ass in a fighter it was one thing. Taking all these trusting people with him was another.

The rain drummed on the windscreen. It sounded like hail was mixed in. Funny, you couldn't hear the engines or the thunder, but the rain pounded like gravel on a tin roof. Kelly had bled the airspeed back to 110 and the C-47 was wallowing with its nose in the air. The change in airspeed and attitude had changed the leak pattern, and the water that had been soaking his left knee for most of the flight was now running down the control wheel to soak the clipboard cinched to his right knee. There was nothing but swirls of dark clouds and lightning outside and a tight, sour feeling inside. The turbulence was picking up and his arms were knotted from keeping the wings cocked a little to the right to help him offset the asymmetric power.

"Chief, start the approach to landing checklist—don't call it out, just do it. Mason, you keep calling out my airspeed and altitude, so I don't screw up."

Kelly concentrated on the instruments. The ADF was not swinging so widely now, for the most part, but it would periodically do a complete 360-degree sweep of the dial. He had to average out the swings. As the tension built, he began to cool down; he had to do it, or they were going to drop into some Birmingham back yard.

The sky suddenly turned brilliant yellow below. Kelly was disoriented. The lightning shouldn't be coming from that direction. He glued his eyes to the gauges, keeping the wings almost level, the ball centered with pressure on the right rudder. Then he remembered the Birmingham steel mills, pouring hot steel whether it was raining or not. It might have been a good sign; there was a cluster of them near the station.

The ADF needle swung around, 360 degrees, then 180 degrees, and began arcing back and forth. They were past the station.

218

Kelly turned to a 180-degree heading, and called, "Check my timing, Mace."

Mason had already punched the little button on the clock that started the second hand going. Kelly eased back the throttle on number two and began a four-hundred-foot-per-minute letdown.

"Passing twenty-six hundred," Mason called, "and you can start your procedure turn."

Just like an indoor GCA, Kelly thought.

Kelly watched the needles wallow around. It was so different from a jet; the jet was clean, the instruments moved with precision. This was like screwing a marshmallow.

"Okay. You overshot a bit, Mike, start your procedure turn back in."

Mason was right—he'd turned out more like fifty-five degrees; no matter up here, but he'd have to watch it in closer, where there were rocks in the clouds.

Kelly turned back through the 225-degree turn, and the ADF needle seemed to fix on the station. He picked up the inbound heading and let the C-47 slip down to fifteen hundred feet.

"Mason, call high station when the needle swings again. Justine, do the landing checklist, but keep the gear up until I call for it. I don't want it down if we have to go around. I'm not going to use more than fifteen degrees of flaps until we're committed."

Justine kept nodding and grinning with each instruction as if enjoying the situation, but underneath his grimy fatigues his stomach was knotted. He knew Kelly was basically a jet pilot and didn't know his ass from a hole in the ground about C-47s. What a way to make a living, he thought; even if we make it it means at least one and maybe two engine changes for me.

Mason called Birmingham radio as the needle swung again over the station, and switched to the tower frequency. "AF 3958 inbound from the high station, fifteen hundred feet, beginning descent; requesting emergency equipment to stand by."

The tower came back, "Roger, 3958; you're cleared to land. Emergency equipment standing by. Good luck."

Kelly's sweaty hands slipped away from the control wheel. "Before-landing checklist, chief, but hold the gear."

Justine leaned forward to set the mixture and propeller, and quickly finished out the landing checklist. His hand dropped to the gear safety latch mounted on the floor at Kelly's right.

"Whenever you're ready, skipper."

Individual lights began to pick through the undercast, as Kelly

219

watched the last two minutes and seven-hundred feet run out on the panel. Mason was leaning forward, peering to the right and left, as Kelly began to level off at eight hundred feet. There were too many hills around to try to sneak a peek.

"Turn left about twenty degrees," Mason called. Kelly glanced up and saw the blinking lights of the approach to the main runway.

"Gear down, chief!" Kelly yelled, and turned the C-47, slipping sharply into the shut-down engine. "Quarter flaps," he called, kicking the rudder to straighten out to line up with the runway, and saw that they were high, way high. "Full flaps, chief, I'm dropping this mother in."

There was a strong crosswind from the left, and Kelly had to drop his left wing into it, keeping the pressure on with the right rudder. He had the number-two engine at idle now, and was trying to remove all the trim he'd put in to control the asymmetric forces.

The ground was right below him. It was like coming down a ski slope, dropping at five hundred feet a minute, and instead of getting closer, the ground seemed to keep falling away as he flew down the bowl. The airport suddenly came into view as the scud cleared away, and Kelly felt relief flooding through him. He was lined up with the runway, and he had to add a little power on number two to keep his airspeed up.

He pulled back again on the right engine, slipping off the rudder trim, then trimming off the back pressure of the stick. The C-47 crossed the boundary lights almost docilely. He kept feeding in the elevator trim as he brought the good engine back to full idle, his eyes glued to the far airport boundary. He felt the wheels touch down with an imperceptible kiss, and the C-47 flew on, slowly settling down on the extended oleo shock absorbers until finally, again imperceptibly, the tail wheel touched down. There was no sensation of transition from flying to ground. It was the best landing he'd ever made.

"You're a clutch player, Kelly," Mason grumbled, before busying himself with the radio. Justine crossed himself. In the cabin there was a spontaneous round of applause, and Washington unbuckled his chute with a laugh, playing to the crowd with, "This old black ass will fly again." It was a nervous reversion; Louise would have killed him if she'd heard him.

Kelly edged the Gooney Bird off the runway on to the first taxi-way, shutting down among a circle of fire trucks and ambulances. Grinning firemen waved, and somebody in the airport manager's station wagon was standing on the hood, waving his hands over his head in salute.

An odd mixture of relief and guilt spread over Kelly; he knew he had just had as much as he could handle. If one more thing had gone wrong—a bad airspeed indicator, radio failure, anything—he'd have probably dumped the C-47 into a flaming ball, maybe right in the city. Yet nothing had gone wrong and he'd made the landing of a lifetime in a strange airplane on a strange field, in mighty strange weather. Not bad for a fighter jock.

A shabby olive-drab bus, obviously war surplus, pulled up on the right, and the passengers straggled on board with their odd bits of luggage, laughing and joking with that intense good humor of survived danger.

"Mason, you take everybody in to get something to eat. I'll get this bucket squared away with Justine, and call Maxwell to send an airplane for us." Kelly was more than a little euphoric himself. There had been moments when he thought he was going to lose the airplane.

The guy on the station wagon turned out to be Hugh Merton, a B-17 driver during the war, and now manager of the airport. He was openly proud of the way his crew had operated under tough conditions, and he appreciated Kelly's praise.

"Son," he said in the broad accent of the region, "you did right well, too. I know what it's like to be up there in this stuff, and it's bad enough with two engines and a ground-controlled approach. Your C.O. is going to be happy about this."

He will if he doesn't check my Form 5 and find out I had no business in the airplane, Kelly thought.

Kelly was a hero for the next forty minutes, as he and Justine arranged for the airplane to be towed to the maintenance area. He visited the tower and thanked everybody, and made a phone call across the field to ATC, who told him they had their GCA back in operation if he needed it. Merton had called Maxwell, and an airplane was being sent to pick them up. To top it off the weather began to break with that sudden clearing that characterized the end of spring storms.

Kelly closed out the flight plan and told Justine to button down the airplane. He drove with Merton over to the airport restaurant, and the wizened little airport manager couldn't get enough of the real details so Mike had to begin making them up. By the time he pulled up in front of the terminal they were old friends.

The terminal restaurant was classic southern Formica and

vinyl, with iron-man doughnuts dusted in powdered sugar and piled in stacks underneath clear plastic lids. A familiar smell of frying hamburgers, indigestible chili, and hot dogs that had been on the rotating spit too long hit Mike, and he wondered if he could put anything down. A sign threatened BREAKFAST SERVED 24 HOURS and he considered some scrambled eggs. A tinny radio was blaring out the latest Presley song, something about a hound dog.

He was surprised when he walked over to Mason and found the thirteen passengers lined up on two sides of a bench table, everybody looking embarrassed. His heart was warmed by the sight, because of what they'd just been through together, but maybe they were pissed at him for getting them into an emergency. Then he noticed two policemen standing at the door.

The big copilot swung to his feet and joined him.

"What's going on? Are they out of food?" Kelly asked.

Mason leaned his mouth next to Kelly's ear and said, "They won't serve us because of Washington."

Kelly scowled. "What the fuck has Washington got to do with this?" Then he realized that Mason was talking about Millard Washington, not Washington, D.C.

The fear and anxiety that Kelly had been fighting off for the last hour now merged with his temper. Washington was a fucking hero, a DFC winner, and these redneck bastards wouldn't serve him? He whirled on the airport manager and grabbed him by his lapels. "What kind of shit is this? You won't serve an officer of the United States Air Force who just made an emergency landing on your field? This guy got shot down in Korea while you were sitting back here picking cotton, and you won't feed him?"

"Keep your hands off me, mister," Merton sputtered. "I did my own share of fighting. I don't make the laws around here. I'm trying to be as nice to you—"

"Shut up!" Kelly raged. He turned on the passengers who'd begun to mill around, and yelled, "Sit down! We'll eat or else!"

The two thick-necked cops advanced menacingly on Kelly.

"Now, Captain Kelly, I know you're upset, but don't come in here tryin' to bust our rules," Merton said, from behind the one nearest the door. The lead cop slowed and stopped a foot from Kelly, and pulled out his long nightstick. He spread his feet and slapped the truncheon hard into his hand.

Kelly felt his self-control slipping away fast. "Get this guy out of my way," he gritted to Merton.

"He's there for your own protection, Kelly," said Merton more calmly. "I can't let you create a ruckus. It's the law, son."

The cop grinned an ugly bully's grin and Kelly lost whatever shards of restraint he had left. He looked at the passengers and Mason. They stood back, spectators.

"Mason—!" he growled.

The thickset copilot flushed and stepped back even farther.

"Hey, Kelly, this is crazy. Let's just call it off, okay? Hey—"

"You fucking coward! You'll kowtow to these pissants? I ought to—"

Washington suddenly stepped through the gaggle of passengers behind the cops. He started toward Kelly, looming over all but the biggest cop, still planted four-square in front of him. "Listen," he said, "don't, Mike—"

"Don't 'Mike' me, you black bastard!" Kelly was red with fury, standing alone by the hot dog rotisserie, fists still balled, fighting mad, dimly aware that he had completely lost control, but somehow powerless to stop. He saw everything through a red haze. "You're the cause of this whole fucking mess!"

Washington, still half-reaching to him, slowly dropped his hand, spun on his heel, and stalked outside. The screen door clattered against the doorframe in the sudden silence.

Before Kelly could act, Merton grabbed one of Kelly's arms and the big cop the other. "Come on, boy," he said, "let's go to my office before you get in any deeper." Kelly struggled and then the fire went out of him. Merton led him down a shabby yellow corridor, lit with flickering fluorescent lamps, the cops following close behind.

Kelly tried to sound reasonable. "What kind of an outfit is this, Mr. Merton? Those men deserve to be fed, and you've got no right to treat them like this. They're all Air Force officers, white or Negro."

The airport manager moved behind his desk, drawing security from it. "Captain, we tried to treat you right, but if you screw with me anymore I'll throw your ass in jail. We'll feed your men, but we'll feed the nigger separate, because that's the way we do it here. That's the law, Air Force or no Air Force."

The big policeman spoke for the first time. "Listen to the man, sonny, and no more smart-ass talk or I'm going to shove this nightstick right up your nigger-loving ass."

The other cop grabbed Kelly before he could swing and slammed him down in a folding chair, pinning his arms. The first cop stepped forward and Merton said, "There's a C-47 from

Maxwell due in here in less than an hour. I suggest you sit down, shut up, eat with the first sitting, and then get out of here fast."

Kelly bit back his bile. He'd made a prize ass out of himself with these yokels, and had probably embarrassed Washington more than they had. He relaxed, and the cops let him stand up.

"Okay. We'll go. Forget about feeding anybody."

The airport manager spread his hands on his desk. "Suit yourself, son. Just don't make any more trouble for us."

Kelly stood stiff-backed for a moment more, then turned slowly and went back out the door. The two cops followed him back into the restaurant.

Except for Washington, all his passengers and crew were there, still milling around in confusion. When he reappeared, they all tensed slightly, wondering what the hell would happen next on this crazy flight. Kelly surveyed them calmly, hands on hips, cops flanking him from behind. "We'll eat," he said quietly and deliberately, "when we get back to Maxwell." The raw edge was gone from his voice. He glanced around. "Where's Washington? Anybody know where he went?"

Somebody muttered something about the Ops shack. Kelly sucked on his cheek a moment, then said: "Okay. We'll all go over there, get some coffee, and wait for the Maxwell Gooney. Questions?"

Nobody said anything. Slowly, they began to shuffle to the door. Nobody quite knew how to act. Mason was the last out, eyes averted from Kelly. Without glancing back at Merton and the cops, Kelly clapped his battered garrison cap on his head and fell in beside Mason.

Mason, red of face and neck, expression unreadable under regulation sunglasses, clumped along and said nothing, ignoring Kelly.

"Mace, listen, damn it. I'm sorry for what I said. I was, uh,—"

Mason stopped suddenly and turned to Kelly. "Shove it, Kelly," he said slowly and carefully. "It'll be a cold day in hell when I fly with you again." Then he strode ahead into the Ops shack.

Kelly felt himself deflate. The wind gusted across the wet concrete of the hardstand area, bringing the clean scent of a thunderstorm-scrubbed sky. Kelly drew a chestful and squared his shoulders. There was still Washington to deal with.

Inside Ops, they had broken into little groups, idly chatting and drinking coffee. They all ignored him when he came in to scan the crowd for Washington. He was lounging in a tattered chair flipping through the pages of a ragged copy of Life. The chair next to him was vacant. Kelly walked over and eased into it.

Washington ignored him. Kelly glanced around, catching fleeting, speculative looks hastily withdrawn. Suddenly he felt old, tired, and gritty. He needed to get this whole day over with. He leaned across and spoke in a low voice to the black captain. "Wash. I'm sorry."

Washington continued to look at *Life*. "Yeah," he grunted, and turned a page.

"No, listen. I mean it. I was out of control back there. I want you to know that."

"Yeah."

Kelly felt trapped, helpless. Would nothing work today? "Okay, Wash. I understand how you feel."

Washington lowered his magazine and looked at Kelly for the first time. His eyes were stony. "Really? I doubt it. But it doesn't matter. See, Mike, it's the old story—you can take the boy out of East St. Louis, but you can't take the East St. Louis out of the boy."

Kelly shook his head.

Washington went back to reading, and said, "Forget it. You've had a tough day."

But neither Kelly nor anyone else could forget it. In Montgomery, the six o'clock news was full of the white Air Force officer who had tried single-handedly and violently to integrate Birmingham Municipal Airport. He had flagrantly violated the law, used bad language, and roughed up the airport manager.

Col. Bart Winslow, the Maxwell base commander, groaned to himself as he listened to the news. He picked up his red phone for a direct connection to Base Operations, and told the airdrome officer, "When that C-47 lands, tell Captain Kelly he's confined to quarters and is to talk to no one. Have him report to me at oh-seven-hundred tomorrow."

Then he picked up his other phone and dialed Lt. Sam Shapiro, his brightest JAG officer.

Kelly was outside the C.O.'s office at 0630, his khakis crisp and clean except for a couple of drops of blood that ran down from his morning duel with his vicious Gillette. He was holding a piece of toilet paper against a cut on his lip, hoping he'd get some coagulation before the C.O. arrived.

The hallway was empty. Polished to a luster by endless coats of Johnson's wax and big buffers, it spoke of solidity, and said that here was one of the few headquarters buildings in the country that was sure to be around more than thirty days. Most general officers—past, present and future—had passed by the oak bench Mike was sitting on. But most did so in better circumstances.

A shuffling down the hall announced an arrival. Mike leaped to his feet, but the shuffling came merely from a bespectacled young first lieutenant wearing Judge Advocate collar insignia. He stopped in front of Kelly and looked him up and down.

"Are you Capt. Michael McManus Kelly?"

"That's me."

"You're in deep shit, pal. I'm Shapiro, JAG. Let's go into my office. We've got a little work to do before you see the C.O."

Shapiro's office was just down from the C.O.'s—an ominous sign to Kelly. In the eight-by-ten office, crowded with a desk and tired, overladen bookcases, Shapiro waved Kelly to a chair stacked with folders. Kelly cleaned it off, looked for a place to put the stack, shrugged, and finally just placed them on the floor. Shapiro settled himself behind his chaotic desk and considered Kelly over the top of his thick glasses. He looked like a ferret, thought Kelly, but at the moment it was clear he had Kelly by the balls.

"You," Shapiro finally said in his nasal tenor, "are some kind of stupid, man. If half what they say is true, it's 'Hello, Leavenworth.' You got yourself and the Air Force in a lot of trouble, and the last thing it needs down South is trouble. So for Christ's sake try to cooperate with me. I got a hangover that won't quit, so don't give me a hard time. Tell me now, did you really call them Ku Klux Klan cocksuckers? Just kidding—that's the only thing you are not accused of."

They went through a grueling hour-and-a-half session before Shapiro said, "That's it. You wait outside until the colonel's ready to see you."

An hour later, Kelly's stomach was grumbling. He was dying for a cup of coffee, and his lip had started bleeding again. He counted the tiles down the length of the corridor, and its width; there were 550 brown asphalt tiles, all perfectly polished. There were eight sets of fluorescent lights, each with three bulbs; there were eight ashtrays made out of hundred-pound bombs. It was a nice place.

The minutes dragged; he leafed through a month-old *Time* magazine; Khrushchev was giving Stalin hell, and some guy named Nasser was throwing the Brits out of Suez. It seemed like petty stuff compared to his own problem.

The door to Winslow's office swung open, and Shapiro walked out. There must be a side door, Kelly thought. Shapiro nodded to him to go in.

226

Kelly walked in across another forty yards of polished asphalt tile to a desk flanked by two big flags, a globe, and a bookcase filled with model airplanes. Back stiff, Kelly strode to the prescribed two paces in front of the desk and saluted. "Captain Kelly reporting as ordered, sir."

Winslow looked up at him. "Don't pull that cadet shit on me, Kelly. You're in deep trouble, and I'm going to throw the book at you. I've had every goddamn congressman from south of the Mason-Dixon line calling all night, and they want my head on a platter. Or yours. I'd prefer to give them yours."

Kelly stood at attention.

"At ease. In fact, sit down. I haven't had a chance to talk to a complete meatball like you since I was a TAC officer at Lackland. What is it with you? Are you some kind of pinko liberal?"

Kelly sat on a straight-backed chair and said, "Colonel, I just fucked up. I was scared shitless from the letdown and the engine failure, and the spade is an old buddy of mine from my hometown. When I saw what was happening, I just blew my cork."

Winslow looked out the window. "I'll bet you were scared. I had your Form Five pulled, and you didn't have any business flying that airplane around the pattern, much less in weather. Damn, I hate you arrogant fighter pilots. You blow so much smoke about how great you are, you believe it yourself. You shoot your mouth off about the civil rights of a Negro officer, but you were willing to kill him and fourteen others with your incompetence."

Kelly winced. The C.O. was right.

Winslow turned over the papers on his desk, and reread the notes he'd made from his conversation with Shapiro. He got up and walked over to the window, then went back and stood in front of Kelly. "It's a funny thing, Kelly, but wiseasses like you always get by. You've got me by the short hairs. If they investigate this and find out that my stupid Base Operations people let a dumb jock like you fly people around in a C-47, they'd have me up for attempted murder."

Kelly squirmed, his mouth dead dry. The coffee on the C.O.'s desk looked delicious, even with the thin film of milk curdling at the top.

Winslow walked back to the window, fury barely suppressed. He crumpled the papers in his hands and strode to the side door. He threw it open and stomped out. "Shapiro!" he yelled, and disappeared.

Kelly sat and twitched while the minutes ticked by. Ten

minutes later, Winslow came back, still glowering. "Kelly, when are you supposed to clear this base for Wright-Patterson?"

"They want me back on Friday sir. We've finished the course and I'm just cleaning up paperwork."

"Wrong. You go back tomorrow. I'm giving you an official reprimand, to stay in your file as long as you stay at Maxwell. So you stay on base, keep your goddamn mouth shut and the rest of you out of trouble. Now get out of here—and don't ever let me see you back here again."

Kelly staggered to his feet and made for the door without saluting. His legs were rubbery, and he grinned weakly at Shapiro as he passed him in the corridor. They were letting him off, but only because he had screwed up so royally they couldn't handle it.

The rest of the day, Kelly kept a profile so low he was invisible. He ate dinner by himself after dealing with the few minor paper shuffles his courses had left him, and went to the club well after dark.

Kelly slipped into the bar and noticed Washington towering over everyone, as usual. His big laugh filled the place. Kelly eased over and tapped him on the elbow. "Wash, I've got to talk to you," he said quietly.

Washington looked at him without expression. "Well, well. Here's the man of the hour, Mr. Civil Rights, USAF Branch."

Kelly flushed. He sat on the barstool next to Washington and leaned on his elbows, staring at the bar top. "Listen," he said. "About that crack—I must have embarrassed the hell out of you, Wash. I didn't mean to. I don't talk like that, see? I was just—well, out of my mind, I guess."

Washington studied him for a moment. "Thanks again for the apology, Kelly, but now you listen. You do talk like that, because you do think like that, and you can't help it. You were brought up that way."

Kelly started. "No, look, I—"

Washington raised a hand, smiling. "Hold on. Don't take it personally. It's the truth. You can't help it—and I can't help what I think either. But I'll tell you this, Mike: I don't take it personally anymore, either."

Kelly looked up at him, surprised. Washington nodded solemnly. "No shit. Really. If I went berserk every time I thought some guy was abusing my so-called civil rights, I'd be dead by now—because that's the way just about every white mother's son in this country thinks." He paused and sipped his drink. "But it's getting better. Much better. And I want you to know I appreciate what you tried to do yesterday."

Kelly flushed a deeper shade of red. "I don't know what to say, Wash. I just wish the whole thing hadn't happened. Part of it was because I knew you, I guess. How many guys who slaved for old Bud Drummond for thirty-five cents an hour wind up in the same airplane?"

Washington slapped Kelly on the back, almost collapsing his lungs. "Not many, Mike, not many. But I'll tell you what: old Bud would have been pissed off at you today for getting everybody all upset over a nigger. Bud called me that many a time, but he was still a hell of a nice guy." He looked around the room, where people avoided his eye. He sighed. "Look. Let's forget this crap, and have a drink. What say? Sit with the colored folks, will you?"

"Sure." It was all he could think of to say. He felt about an inch tall.

"Mike, what will you have?"

"Boilermakers. Not one, but two. It's been a long day."

The waitresss came at Washington's nod, and stood by. "Miss," he said, smiling, "as a civilized type, I will have a martini, very dry, with a twist, and this gent will have not one but two boilermakers."

The young woman frowned. "Boilermakers?" she asked. "I'm not sure . . . what's a boilermaker?"

Kelly opened his mouth to explain, but Washington spoke before he could. "See? It's like I said yesterday, Kelly."

Mike closed his mouth and frowned. "What?"

"You can take the boy out of East St. Louis, but you'll never take the East St. Louis out of the boy. How about a martini?"

16

1015 LOCAL
20 June 1956
Luke AFB, Arizona
USA

"Hey, Garvey, take a look at this."

Nick Kosano was a big, tall, curly haired, overweight insensitive clod with enough insight to realize that Garvey had to have some help.

Garvey grunted, not bothering to look up from his F-84F training manual.

"Come on, Garve, take a look. You're an old Mustang jock, ain't you?"

"Yeah, I got a few hours in one once. What's it to you, Kosano?"

"They're looking for some high-time Mustang guys for a special project."

Kosano ripped the announcement off the bulletin board, an unspeakable act he knew would be mentioned at next morning's briefing after Lieutenant Hartzell, the new adjutant, noticed it.

He tossed it in Garvey's lap. Garvey picked it up, scanned it, put it aside. "So what. Kosano, why don't you apply? You never flew a P-51 but you sure as shit can't fly an F-84. Maybe you can fake it."

"That so? Then who shot a hundred percent out there today, Garvey? It sure as hell wasn't you."

"Instructors don't have to be able to shoot; they just have to be able to tell people how to shoot." Garvey lapsed back into his customary silence.

Kosano watched him with his squinty worried eyes. "Garvey, you ought to see a flight surgeon. You're acting nuts, and you're going to kill yourself if you don't snap out of it. I was watching you on the range last week; you were target fixated. I thought twice you were going to fly right into the ground."

"Look, Kosano, when I want your advice, I'll ask for it. I've been flying for six years, never got a wingtip, and I'm the best gunnery instructor at Luke."

"Yeah, just ask you."

Jim Garvey lapsed into silence; he knew Kosano was being kind in his elephantine way, knew he was right. It was getting to be like Korea, except he didn't have Kelly here to shepherd him around, straighten him out.

The stupidity, of course, was that he wanted to join Miriam, even though he didn't believe in heaven, hell, or reincarnation; he wanted to join her in oblivion. Rachel kept him from it, although he was doing her a lot of good keeping her with her grandparents back East. It suited them perfectly; Rachel was getting a good Jewish upbringing, and he was two thousand miles away, almost ideal from Myron Siegel's point of view. He wrote her every week, sent presents monthly, tried to visit on each holiday he could wangle time off for.

He'd last visited six months ago; Rachel had warmed to him,

and Myron and Sara clearly had been doing their best to put her father in the best light, even though they dealt with him in private with thinly disguised dislike. He could understand why; to them, he was a killer, not just officially in his fighter-pilot role, but because he had killed their only daughter. Thank God they didn't take it out on Rachel. He didn't know how long he could continue with both Rachel and Miriam on his conscience.

"Sorry, Nick. I'm a little nervous. You're right. I'm pressing too hard; I figure I had about a ten-second margin the other day."

"I checked with your crew chief; the G meter said you pulled eight Gs; that means you had no seconds left, and you got out lucky, 'cause that sucker could have gone into a high-speed stall pulling those kinds of Gs."

"Yeah, I know, I was light. It was the last run of the day, and I dropped the bombs and was running on fumes. But you're right. You can only do that so often, and it's smear-city."

Kosano tapped him on the shoulder and left. Garvey picked up the notice. It was unusual to advertise for pilots like this; the supply of F-51 pilots must be dwindling.

The announcement was straightforward. A Major Welsh in the Pentagon wanted to talk to current jet pilots who had previous experience in F-51 aircraft, including at least six hundred hours flying the airplane.

Garvey hadn't kept a logbook for years, but he knew he must have better than seven hundred hours in Mustangs, maybe two hundred in combat.

They had a long line in the orderly room. He walked in, got the first sergeant's permission to call Major Welsh. He could have just picked up the phone and done it, but it was always smart to acknowledge the first soldier's authority, stroke him a bit in front of his troops.

The call went through the first time; now he had to be worried about being cut off in midsentence by a priority call.

"Major Welsh speaking."

"Major, this is Capt. Jim Garvey out at Luke. I saw the announcement on the F-51 pilot; have you got any takers yet?"

"We've had a couple of calls, Captain Garvey, about one every two minutes since that damn thing went out. Tell me about yourself."

"Well, I've got about seven hundred hours in the Mustang, maybe two hundred combat; I shot down about . . ."

231

"Jesus, are you Jim Garvey? The guy who went nuts and shot up the North Korean airfield, and then had to be pushed home?"

Garvey cursed under his breath.

"Yeah, that was me; don't hold it against me, I was young and foolish then."

"Well, I hope you are still young and foolish enough for a mission that should be a lot of fun."

"Tell me about it, Major."

"Can't do it on the phone; tell you what, I'll send a TWX telling your personnel people to cut orders for you to fly back here Monday; we'll brief for a day, and then you can come back Wednesday."

"What's the chance of me sticking a few days' leave in the middle?"

"No sweat on our end, Jim; you have to handle that there."

He finished up the call with some instructions on how to find him in the Pentagon, and Garvey went back to see if he could scrounge up an F-51 flight manual to see how much he had forgotten. And he had to call Myron to warn him he was coming.

You couldn't get much of anywhere from Luke, except maybe Nogales, and he persuaded Kosano to fly him to Los Angeles in a T-33 early Monday morning. The ready access to airplanes was one prerogative everybody depended on. You could get an airplane virtually anytime to go anywhere, because there always seemed to be more flying hours allocated than pilots to fly them. He knew Kosano would fly home via Vegas, dropping maybe as much as twenty bucks in a quick noon trip to the tables on the way.

Once he got to L.A. the trip back in the Connie was pure pleasure. The back end was crowded and a cute little stewardess named Joy had waved him into first class and proceeded to pummel him with liquor, food, and her D.C. address. By the time he got to Washington, eight hours later, he could scarcely walk. The time difference added three hours and he finally persuaded Joy to wait until the following night to meet. He didn't want to walk into Welsh's office hung over and exhausted.

He stayed at a brand-new motel, the Aimsworth, almost within walking distance of the Pentagon. It was expensive, six dollars a day, but it had a television set. Besides, Joy's roommate might be in town, and he wanted to have a decent place to bring her. He'd forgotten what a sleepy city Arlington was; the Jeff Davis Highway virtually shut down after eight o'clock.

It made Garvey sick even to look at the outside of the Pentagon. He wasn't much on poetry in school, but he remembered something about "the castle alone on the landscape lay, an outpost of winter, dull and gray." The Pentagon was all of that. The anxiety mounted as he fumbled down the long grimy corridors filled with an endless wave of field grade officers carrying portfolios stamped TOP SECRET. If the secretary of defense had positioned himself at the entrance and sent every other man back to field duty, the productivity of the place would have picked up 100 percent.

There were four dreary flights of stairs to cover; they changed color but not shabbiness at each landing. There was a consistency in the degree of paint peel, ground-in cigarette butts, crumpled paper, and sense of deterioration. Garvey jostled upward, thinking that the entire establishment, Army, Navy, and Air Force, prospered on the business of self-inflicted wounds. There was an underlay of civil servants who provided stability and continuity. They never got involved in the internecine bloodletting—they didn't have to—nor did they work more than forty hours a week unless it was really necessary, as it rarely was. The service donkeys put in their sixty- or seventy-hour weeks, guided to work by the red taillights of the car ahead on the Shirley Highway, leaving in the same monastic procession, bitter, yet sustained by the wearied comradeship of fellow donkeys.

He got lost and asked a harried light colonel how to get to the room where he was supposed to report in five minutes. The light colonel glanced at the room number, mumbled, and ran on. Garvey finally located a guard who steered him to another stairway which led to a series of afterthought offices created by dry-wall subdivisions. He was one minute late when he arrived; the office was empty. Thirty minutes later a fresh-faced young civilian came in, obviously a political appointee from his expensive suit and cuff-linked shirt. No civil servant ever wore a cuff link, not while Sears sold button-down shirts.

"Captain Garvey, I'm Milton Stamm, assistant secretary for special projects. It's a pleasure to meet you. Major Welsh told me all about you, and I've had your file pulled. He'll be back in a few minutes to talk to you, but I have to say that you look exactly like what we need for our little project."

Garvey hated the sonofabitch on sight. He was an Ivy Leaguer who was doing a little civic duty, straightening out the military. "Yes sir. What can you tell me about it?"

"Well, first of all, you're going back to basic flight training."

233

Garvey twitched, then subsided. He was already in flight training as instructor.

"Yes, you are going to learn to fly F-51s, Thunderbolts they called them, right?" He smirked in congratulatory self-knowledge.

"No, F-51s are Mustangs; the Thunderbolt was a P-47. And I already know how to fly the hell out of them." No sense in being easy on this striped-suit ape.

"Oh, yes, that's right. I always made models of them during the war."

"Which war, Korean?"

"Why yes,"—his yes seemed to have seven esses in it—"but I made them during War Two also."

War Two! Garvey wanted to throw up. Stamm must have heard the big boys say War Two, and was parroting them. Garvey figured him for one of the gap jumpers; always too young or too old to fight in a war, but always just right to profit by them.

"How do you feel about flying a Mustang again, Captain?"

"Okay, but I wonder why; it's got to be foreign duty somewhere, because we don't have any in the Air Force, do we?"

"Right and wrong. It is foreign duty, but the Air Force is being asked to consider buying some remanufactured Mustangs to use as inexpensive fighter bombers. You'll be doing some test work; then we have a black assignment for you."

"What's a black assignment?"

"Captain, a black assignment is beyond Top Secret; it's done in complete secrecy with a budget that is not revealed to the public. The chief briefs the heads of the Armed Services committees, and they are sworn to secrecy. You won't be able to tell anyone what you are doing, not now, not ever. Not even your wife."

Stamm flushed. "Oh, sorry, Captain Garvey; I know you lost your wife."

"I didn't lose her, she died." Garvey was ready to leave.

"From your personal point of view, you are simply going to disappear for three or four months after you complete your F-51 training and test. When you come back you'll be reassigned to another outfit, and the project will never appear on your field records."

"Is it work as a spy?"

"No, nothing so dramatic. It's basically a routine flying job, but your experience qualifies you to make some assessments that will be useful to us. I think you'll like the duty. It's something most pilots won't get to do. It's probably not as hazardous as being a gunnery instructor."

234

He smiled, glad to let Garvey know how much he knew. "Are you willing to endure this sort of life? Your father-in-law and his family will just have to accept the fact that you are okay and will get in contact with them when you are finished."

Garvey didn't say anything; as far as Myron and Sara Siegel were concerned, no news about Garvey would be good news. Rachel was still too young to know or care.

"Sure, I'll do it; will I be able to tell them roughly when I'm getting back?"

"Yes, and we'll be in touch with them periodically to let them know you are all right. We aren't complete beasts."

You ain't any beast at all, Garvey thought; you're just a goddamn paperpusher getting material for your memoirs.

The door opened and a young major walked in.

Stamm introduced Major Welsh and left, obviously glad to get away from the wild man. Welsh first swore him to secrecy, using an old-fashioned Bible and an oath similar to the one used to commission cadets. He then confided that he had called the Luke flight surgeon to check on him.

"Garvey, Doc Weston thinks you are nearly perfect physically, but damn near losing a screw or two mentally. If I'd called him first, I wouldn't have asked you to come. What do you have to say to that?"

"Well, fuck him, and fuck you for starters, and fuck that little pimp Stamm. I didn't drag my ass three thousand miles across the country to have some slick-wing major tell me I'm nuts. I've got some worries, but who hasn't? I'll bet you are worried about how you are going to get that two thousand hours of flying time in before they ground you."

It was a telling blow; half the Air Force was engaged in a pell-mell scramble to log time, to convert their "slick wings" into first senior and then command pilot wings, with a star and a star and wreath, respectively. It was getting harder to do all the time, especially for staff people like Welsh.

He grinned at Garvey. "You don't sound so nuts to me. Let me tell you about what we want you to do; if you like the idea, you have the job. But take it or leave it, you can't say one word about it to anyone, under pain of court martial. I'm not kidding, this won't be like forgetting to lock a safe, this will be a long trial, maybe for treason. So before I tell you any more, you tell me you will keep my confidence, come what may."

"Major, I just swore an oath on a Bible, I'm an officer in the USA and F, and I've been keeping secrets all my life. Shoot."

235

"Jim, we want to send you to Florida to check out in a F-51 at a civil contract school we have down there. They'll give you the whole works, transition, gunnery, everything, a fast version of what you got at Craig or Luke or wherever it was. Then we are going to send you to fly with a foreign air force, friends of ours obviously, for three months. While you are there you'll be under their orders, fly their missions, just as if you belonged to them. But you'll be doing an evaluation for us. I've got a laundry list of things for you to look into, but it's training, discipline, morale, equipment use, just the sort of thing you'd be looking at if you were giving a readiness inspection to one of our units."

"It's not a paperwork survey is it? I don't want to spend my time looking over Form Fives, requisitions, and that bullshit."

"No, not a bit of it. And we don't want you making a lot of notes; this outfit is the most security-conscious, spy-crazy group this side of the Iron Curtain. But remember everything, and when you get back, we'll interrogate you, pump you to make sure we get everything."

"Okay. When do I leave?"

"You leave from here. From now on you are under security wraps, new I.D., everything."

"Hey, I was supposed to visit my kid, then I've got a flock of students to finish out back at Luke."

"Not anymore. You can see your kid when you get back, and I've already made preliminary arrangements for your not going back to Luke. You'll have a 'car accident' while you're here, and we'll ship your battered body around to hospitals faster than anybody can visit you. Your C.O. will know you're on assignment, but that's all. Don't worry about it, we handle stuff like this all the time."

"Christ, Stamm said I wasn't going to be a spy. Sounds like it to me."

"No, you are just on a very sensitive assignment. The other guys want you there, because they think they are good, and they know an upcheck from you will help them get more assistance. But we can't let the story get around because you will in fact be in an extralegal situation. If you get lost and land at the wrong base, in another country, we'll have a hell of a time explaining who and what you are."

"Sounds good, I'll do it."

"Jim, there are risks, and there'll never be a mention of this in your official records; in effect you are subsidizing the Air Force with a few months of your time."

"Man, I've been doing that for years."

Six months later, Garvey showed up at Myron Siegel's house, tan, skinny, and still weak from amoebic dysentery. Rachel took one look at him and screamed.

17

**1130 LOCAL
28 August 1956
Arrow Pass, Idaho
USA**

Polly saw the wisp of vapor rising from the Buick's hood and cried, "Stop, Don! We're boiling up!"

Picard checked the dashboard; the water temperature gauge read 212 degrees. He eased the station wagon over to the side of the road, trying to find a place long enough to hold it and the Elcar trailer.

One glance at Polly's face was enough. She was furious with him for sticking with the expensive lemon, the old trailer. But it wasn't a question of choice, it was simple economics.

"Got-damn it Don, why do we do this to ourselves?" A little German would break through when she was angry.

He didn't say anything until he got the rig safely off the road. The top of the hill wasn't more than three hundred yards away; if he'd made it there they could have coasted into Mountain Home. He pulled into the roadside rest, let the car idle for a moment, then shut if off.

The kids were asleep. Picard shot another glance at Polly, who was still fuming, and went back to open the door for Omar, their big mixed-breed spaniel. Omar frisked along the side of the road. If only we could all be like Omar, he thought; never a cross moment.

He came around the side of the car, reached in, squeezed her shoulder. "It's okay, Polly. We'll take a little break here, and then go on over the hill. It's downhill from there."

"Yes it's downhill, all right, downhill all the time, and we were never very uphill yet. I'm tired of going downhill."

Picard leaned against her door and took his hand off her

shoulder. "Don't start it. It's a long trip, and just don't start it. He walked to the side of the road, picked off a pine cone from tree. He crushed some needles in his hand. He lifted them to hi nose, inhaled deeply, and smiled. "Smell this, honey, isn't wonderful, so fresh, just like Germany, huh?" She sniffed duti fully. "Come on, let's take a little walk, just down the roa aways. We'll keep the car in sight."

They had done this ritual so often; she'd get mad, he'd strok her out of it. She rarely used to complain; it was more frequen now. They were older, and times hadn't gotten a whole lot bette economically.

Polly got out. Her moods were mercurial; he could see he normal good humor beginning to reassert itself. The scenery an the clear, crisp mountain air helped. She looked to the north where the mountains marched away from green to white.

"It does look like southern Germany," she said after a mo ment. "Bavaria."

"Yeah, well, the map says those are the Soldier Mountains That sounds like Germany all right."

They were on their way to Mountain Home Air Force Base and the 9th Bombardment Wing, Medium, stationed there. Don was desperately working his way west, trying to get back to California; he'd gone from Germany to Ohio, down to Texas fo training, and now to Mountain Home.

Opinion about that assignment among his friends had been mixed; most people said it was a hardship assignment, in a cold and dreary land. People who had been there said it was great.

The main thing was it had B-47s, and Don wanted to work on them more than anything. They were the dominant airplanes in the air and best of all they had them at Castle Air Force Base in California, and he was going to get there if he had to work his way across country base by base.

Polly was feeling better; she took him by the arm, snuggled close. As she nuzzled him, he realized that she was still very much a good-looking woman. He took her hand and kissed it as he always did, starting at the fingertips, working down to the wrist.

She wrinkled her nose at him, now in mock anger. "Damn you, Don, you always do just what you want. That old station wagon never ran right since we bought it. It isn't going to last the winter up here. Why don't we get a decent car? And how about the trailer? Is it going to be all right? I don't want the kids having colds all winter."

238

Picard smiled. That was better. She was talking future now, not past.

"Honey, it'll be fine. And we'll leave it here. I'm going to swing a transfer to California in a year or two, and we'll just leave it here and get a nice house there."

The Buick had stopped percolating. Don whistled Omar back in, and then he and Polly climbed inside. He started it, listened for a moment, then eased it over the rise. They had sneaked along the foothills of the mountains; now ahead they could see for fifty miles, a great river-bounded triangle with the Snake running across the base. Above them, a contrail streamed. Polly shook her head. "It *is* beautiful, Don. Maybe it won't be so bad."

He located a decent trailer court a few miles outside the city, about halfway to the field, close enough for him to ride a motor scooter most of the time. That night they settled again into the familiar routine of hooking up to the sewage, water, and electric mains at the court, getting to know the neighbors, and trying to feel for the pulse of the area. As usual, a lot of the court's residents were stationed at the base, and not a few were officers.

Reporting in was a comforting ritual for Don; there was almost always a two- or three-day cushion you could take getting settled. He knew enough of the senior enlisted types to get a quick rundown on how things were run, whom to watch out for, whom to take care of. Within a week it was business as usual with the bonus of getting to work on the sleek B-47s.

It was business as usual for Polly too. She got Donna into kindergarten and found Jamie a babysitter, a nice old lady called Grom, who lived in the court. She hated to leave them with a stranger, but Grom had a good reputation, and she needed the money, so Polly figured she'd be reliable. Then she started methodically checking out the jobs in the area. There weren't many openings, but she persisted, and finally was taken on at the best restaurant in the area, the Branding Iron. She knew she could always get work in restaurants, but she hoped against her own better knowledge that Don would get out soon and she could stop working as a waitress.

The hot smell of the fuel oil stove jerked Don awake. Adrenaline pumping, he felt the clammy fear of fire before realizing that it was his own home improvement startling him. He'd rigged a thermostat stolen from supply in the trailer's heating system to start the stove on the cold Idaho mornings, and this was the first time that it had kicked on. None of the other trailers in the court had one, and the overnight drop in temperature meant all the other families would be chilled in their sleep. The little Travalarm read five fifteen; he had another fifteen minutes before hitting the deck.

The acrid stove smell had banished sleep. He knew only too well how vulnerable the "mobile homes," as they had begun to be called, were to fire; he'd seen more than one reduced to a steel frame and smoldering tires in minutes. Even in their brand-new forty-two-foot-long double-wide Olympian, one of the best built, the risk was never out of his mind.

He glanced at Polly lying beside him, deep in sleep, her hair rolled tightly in little paper bands, and felt a pang. He was twenty-seven years old, a tech sergeant, with two kids, one in a special ed program, and all he could afford to provide was trailer park living. In the early days, Polly hadn't complained. She hated the old Elcar, and he had all but promised to sell it and start renting. But it was hard to find a decent place near the base; he'd probably have had to go all the way to Glenns Ferry to get something, and then Polly would have had to drive twice as far to get to work.

They compromised by trading in the Elcar for the Olympian. Her awareness of how well his friends did when they left the service was the real problem and it seemed to boil with Jim Cagle. She had never particularly disliked Jim, but she didn't think he was very smart. Until he got out. Then he became a Solomon, the wisest man on earth. Her ordinary German hausfrau nagging took on a new virulent tone; she wasn't nagging to nag, she was nagging for effect. It was something totally new for her. In the past if she got mad she blew up and then was silent till she got over it. Now she never stopped nattering.

240

Jim Cagle and he had been together almost since they got back from Germany, and both had gone through the same service schools, learning the mysteries of the big bombers they serviced. Both had been given special training in electronics to handle the K-System radars of the B-47s, and then Jim had had an offer from Westinghouse.

As much as he liked him, there was no denying the sharp pang of jealousy that jabbed him every time Don thought about it. Westinghouse started Jim at twice his Air Force salary, with benefits that made his head swim. The troops were always talking about service "bennies," the little perks like the BX and the commissary, as if they made much difference. Cagle's benefits started out with a car allowance and went on to profit sharing. They sent him to school for six weeks back east, and paid everything for both him and his wife, Barbara. When he came back he went to work in virtually the same job as he'd had before, making twice as much and putting in only forty hours a week. It was an easy week when Picard didn't spend sixty hours on the flight line.

The finishing straw for Polly was the housewarming; as sweet as she was, she couldn't be gracious at the Cagle's new place, bought before they sold their trailer. It was a three-bedroom rancher, with a rec room, basement, even a den; Polly cried in front of him for the first time in their marriage. He was going to have to do something, and soon.

There was a thump as Omar jumped off Jamie's bed, sending a sine-wave quiver along the trailer's length. He knew that he shouldn't let the dog sleep with the boy—the Idaho fields gave Omar a rich choice of disgusting smells to roll in—but Jamie was so withdrawn he needed all the love he could get, even if it was from a fleabag. He knew that Omar would want and need to go out, so he grabbed his socks and brogans from beside the bed, scooped up his fatigues, and slipped past the sliding mirrored door. Polly stirred, but went on sleeping. She was tired nowadays; five years ago she would have been on her feet, cooking breakfast as soon as he stirred.

He let the dog out, put on a pot of coffee, and went into the bathroom to shave. It was positively luxurious, with a real bathtub, not like the three-by-four shower/toilet combination in the Elcar. There was even a half bath forward for the kids. And the water wouldn't freeze as long as the power stayed on; he'd wrapped the pipes with electrical heating tape. There were many bitter memories of mornings he had spent flat on his back under the trailer, trying to unfreeze the water and sewage lines with a blowtorch, and still not set fire to it.

He winced as the three-day-old Gillette Blueblade knicked his chin. Maybe it was time to listen to Polly, after all. Jim had been promoted and he was coming over tonight with an offer to go to work for him. He wanted Picard to take his old job, at the same sort of boost in salary. It would mean moving out of the trailer into a decent house, buying a car he could depend on, and giving Polly some of the things she always said didn't matter. He'd weighed the idea a hundred times against completing his Air Force career. He had twelve more years till he had twenty in, and could theoretically retire. But he knew that retirement from the service at twenty was an illusion. It simply meant you went to work for someone else, a green bean at forty or so, with a few hundred dollars of pension to make up the difference. Most guys stayed on till thirty; you got a little better pension, but the main thing was you could afford to take a job that paid a little less so that you didn't have to start the whole hustling competitive process over again.

He stood at the tiny sink, drinking the black coffee and poking down the last slice of Polly's angel food cake. He wondered if Barbara had told Polly about the job. He had made Jim swear not to discuss it with her until he had made up his mind, but he told her everything, and Barbara and Polly were thick as thieves. He hoped she hadn't found out. He wanted to tell her himself.

Picard dressed quickly, cinching up the brogans after he had buttoned himself into the green, freshly ironed fatigues. He looked for his cap, checked on Donna and Jamie, who seemed to be getting a cold, let Omar back in, then went back in to whisper goodbye to Polly. It was five fifty, time for him to hit the road.

Polly stirred and opened one eye as he leaned over to kiss her goodbye. "Don't be late tonight, honey," she whispered groggily, "Jim is coming over with the job offer."

Picard slammed out the door, angry not at Polly but at Jim, and climbed into the new Studebaker pickup truck. He loved the truck; it was visible evidence, with the trailer, that he wasn't doing too bad. Still it was just as well she knew. The scare from the stove had made up his mind. He was going to take the job.

Six hundred fifty air miles away from Mountain Home, at Castle Air Force Base, California, the weather was warmer. Maj. Charles Kingston Brown rolled the throttle on the green Lambretta motor scooter and felt it accelerate away beneath him. The motor scooter was one of the few Air Force fads of which he approved, because on the sprawling SAC flight lines it meant real mobility. Without it you had to wait for one of the crew buses, or depend upon a harried maintenance team to drop you off. He'd seen other fads come and go—the Japanese screens, the camel saddles, the Noritaki china—but those were fashion fads, without utility. Motor scooters were different. They allowed you to use your time wisely, and to a man in a hurry like Duke, time was more than the essence, it was the advantage. The Lambretta gave him time to be out here when everyone else on the mission was still lolling at home.

Brown checked in with the young Air Police security guard at the flight line gate, hoping as always that the K-9 German shepherd was really on a leash.

Brown sped the little scooter through the gate, and got on with doing one of the things that distinguished him from his competitors, his colleagues. He had a station time of noon, and there was to be a special briefing at 0900. He was going to go over the airplane and talk to the crew chief and the maintenance people. It made them know he cared and respected their work, and consequently they made an effort for him. The result was that he had never missed a takeoff time, no small thing in SAC; real career protection.

The chill night had given way to a warming fall morning. Earlier in the year, it would have been fog-ridden and overcast. Now the mornings were golden, and even on the flight line you could hear sounds of bird life gorged to near insensibility in the lush fields that bordered the airbase. In an hour, as auxiliary power units stuttered to life, and then later, when the aircraft engines themselves started, the hundred acres of concrete ramp would be laden with noise and noxious JP-4 fumes roiling in shimmering, expanding cones behind the airplanes. The olive-drab-clad mechanics would swarm their ladders attending to the

243

diminishing number of B-47's myriad maintenance needs, unbuttoning cowlings, charging accumulators, swapping parts, and more often than their supervisors would have approved of, resorting to brute force to close their charges back up. When all else failed, a wooden chock, swung in a wide arc, did wonders to jolt an alternator on line or force a fractious cowling into place.

Brown rode along the short row of Boeing B-47Es parked at precise intervals, admiring both the military precision of their spacing and the airplanes themselves. Once they had dominated the ramp, forty-five of them; now there were only fifteen, replaced by bigger, more powerful B-52s being introduced into the inventory. Castle was the lead base on B-52s, and was retaining its combat-ready status by not phasing out B-47s until the bigger planes were ready. He'd be going to B-52s soon, but in the meantime he loved the B-47 beyond all telling because it had made a pilot and a man of him. It was ironic, because the B-47 was supposed to be a mankiller, tougher than all others to fly. He had seen it kill his brother. No, that wasn't fair. He'd seen his brother kill himself in one.

Yet there was truth to the rumors. He'd been on the inside at the Pentagon, saw all the accident reports, knew the hazards involved. He had dreaded the day of his rotation when he knew that he would have to go to Wichita to learn to fly the most demanding airplane in the Air Force.

It had not been easy, but he had done it, as he always had. But just as in Korea, it was not by will alone. No one, not even the flight surgeon, knew that he supplemented his courage with the buzz of Dexedrine tablets. He needed them especially for the instrument letdowns, when he was coming back tired, and the weather was marginal. By sheer force of will, he had focused every ounce of his being on beating the fear and never letting it show. He had performed well; his B-26 crew thought he had nerves of steel.

Part of beating the fear was the imperative need to become a general. That was the aim of life, of education, of flying, to do what his father did, and to do it better. The pills had worried him; he wasn't sure what effect they had on his proficiency. He swore to himself, and believed it, that if his fear—or the pills—ever lessened his proficiency and endangered his crew, he would simply quit flying, no matter what the career outcome.

Nobody knew any of this. Not Joan, not his father, not his crew, not the padre, no one. Iron will and determination had made Duke, kept Duke in flying school, kept him ahead of the fear that squeezed beside him in the cockpit when the canopy closed and the tower cleared him for takeoff. He had accumulated nearly two thousand safe flying hours in the Air Force, and his colleagues all thought him a flawless, if styleless, pilot. Beating the fear had become as much a stimulant for him as sex was for others.

It was a double irony, then, that midway through his tense transition training into the B-47 at McConnell AFB in Wichita, he'd realized that he loved the airplane. He could not have been more surprised or even shocked if he'd discovered he was a homosexual. There was ample reason to hate and fear this airplane—which Boeing, and no one else, called a Stratojet— more than any he had flown. It helped somewhat that the sorrowful loss of his brother's death was accentuated later by an accident report that was so brief as to be bitter, a three-word conclusion that was totally correct: inexplicable pilot error. The airplane hadn't killed King; King had killed himself. The airplane wouldn't kill Duke.

He went to McConnell for training in almost desperate double fear. His first concern was the fear itself; the second was that, at last, people would know. It was even harder to maintain the indispensable façade of loving to fly. Yet by his fourth flight he began to think of the B-47 as a fiery mistress, a Carmen who would thrill and exhaust you with an all-giving, all-taking love— and kill you for the slightest inattention. It was the first time he had ever thought of an airplane in human terms. And the more he flew it, the more deeply enamored he became.

The B-47s sat on rather foolish-looking tandem main gears, the only aesthetically unattractive element of their design, Carmen with thick ankles. But the rest of the airplane was magnificent. A streamlined tapering fuselage, thin wings swept back, and six pugnacious engines suspended in pods. Near the nose was a fighterlike canopy, where the pilots sat in tandem. The poor radar observer was sunk below in a dark windowless cavern, mesmerized by the green arcs of his radar set and terrified by the noises above. He had to sit, blind and powerless, through inflight refuelings, where in close proximity to the tankers a boom was shoved in a receptacle next to his ear. He had to sit in his downward ejection seat on takeoff, knowing that if anything went wrong, he could only hasten, not avoid, his demise.

Brown was in love with this Carmen, but he lavished care on the B-47 because of two reasons that were founded in selfishness. The first was that he would conquer it and conquer the shadow

245

that King had imposed on him all his life. He would tame the airplane that tamed King. The second was that it was the single most important element in his career checklist. He knew, as many of his competitors did not, that it was the first weapon in history to dominate the world in such an implacably comprehensive fashion. The Strategic Air Command could put fourteen to fifteen hundred B-47s in the air at once, each armed with one or more nuclear weapons. Brown had studied the war plans with his usual intensity, and the strategy called for a closing concentric ring of devastation on the Soviet Union that would have reduced its warmaking ability to uselessness in six days. The Red armies spilling into Western Europe would have been cut off at the roots. The B-47 force would have had losses, but more from accident than combat. They were virtually immune to interception from the Soviets, and by the end of the second day the enemy radar and communication centers would have ceased to exist.

As a general's son, as a future general, Brown felt a pride that there was no chance whatever that this awesome force would be employed except in self-defense. It was a containment of power, a degree of control and selflessness that no other nation had ever exhibited. He had no doubt what would have happened if the situation had been reversed, if Russia had this enormous power, or China, or even the old adversaries, Japan or Germany.

Best of all, the B-47 was the only sure ticket into the B-52, and the B-52 would be the premier airplane for the next four or five years at least. It was bigger, better, and safer than the B-47, even if it did not inspire either the love or the hate.

Brown concentrated on keeping the little scooter at a safe speed. The Strategic Air Command gloried in its ground safety record, and the only thing worse than an aircraft taxi accident was a vehicle accident on the ramp, even with so modish a conveyance as an Italian motor scooter.

He reached the first pair of B-47s of his own 330th Bomb Squadron, noting the single toolbox placed precisely between the two airplanes. This was the Air Force in cameo. Two three-million-dollar airplanes, each backed up by several billion dollars' worth of command support structure—training bases, the entire elaborate apparatus necessary to support a weapon system—and toolboxes were in such short supply that two mechanics had to share one box. Brown had seen more than one occasion when a fistfight broke out over who was going to get to use a certain tool. With all the pressure on to make takeoff times, a crew chief wasn't going to stand idly by and watch someone else use the tool he needed.

He rolled the Lambretta to a stop at the red line that marked the boundary of the parking space near his airplane, tail number 068, and strolled over to his crew chief. T/Sgt. Ted Gallegos was engaged in a heated discussion with some electronics maintenance types. As Duke walked up, he could tell by his aggressive stance that Gallegos was winning, as usual. The dapper crew chief was no more than five feet six inches tall, couldn't have weighed 140 pounds, fatigues tailored tightly to his frame. Unlike most of the maintenance people, he didn't wear the inevitable crew haircut, but instead pasted his dark black hair to the side with Brylcreem. His face was leathery, and he wore his regulation sunglasses with a piece of foam rolled around the sweat bar to keep the perspiration from dripping into his eyes as he worked under the hot machinery. As soon as he saw Brown, Gallegos stepped back from the civilians and threw him a perfect salute.

"Any problems, Ted?" he asked, pleased with the enlisted man's punctilio. Gallegos was of the fast-disappearing old school, who didn't go along with the new convention of "no salutes on the flight line."

"No sir," Ted said. "These *cabrones* are telling me they haven't got a rectifier I know they've got, and it's just a matter of me persuading them, verbally or with a two-by-four."

"Need any help?" It was a rhetorical question; Gallegos would no more have called on him to solve this problem than he would have called on Gallegos to make a night in-flight refueling. As he expected, the diminutive sergeant shook his head. "No sir. We're under control. Thanks anyway. Here for a quick pre-preflight, Major?"

"Yes. Mind if I poke around?"

Gallegos grinned. "No sir. She's all yours."

Brown went around to the left side of the airplane where a collapsible ladder extended down from the entrance to the tiny crew compartment. He hoisted himself up, and found the aircraft log and maintenance books on the seat, right where he knew Ted would have them. The crew chief respected his interest, and met him more than halfway every time. The airplane was in good shape. Brown pored through the maintenance entries in the back of the book, looking for recurring problems. Faults got fixed and signed off, but if you found a series of similar problems, it probably meant they were either not really fixing it, or were fixing the wrong thing. The difficulty, of course, was that failures occurred at forty thousand feet, at 425 knots indicated airspeed, and at sixty degrees below zero, perhaps with conditions of intense vibration or turbulence. They were analyzed and fixed on the ground, at zero feet, zero miles per hour, and eighty-five degrees Fahrenheit. It was no wonder the real problems were often masked and often recurred.

Brown noted the entries on the fuel service and then checked with Gallegos to put power on the airplane. Ted connected the pounding auxiliary power unit, and the B-47 began to buzz with life, like time-lapse photos of a chrysalis opening. Brown went through a systematic check of the fuel gauges, radios, and instruments. In three hours he and his crew would do it all again, but then there would be no surprises—unless, as was possible, although unlikely, a failure occurred in the interval.

He got down and walked around the airplane, checking for hydraulic or fuel leaks—God knew there were enough of them, another product of temperature, altitude, and vibration cycles—and carefully inspected the drogue and brake chutes. Sometimes these got short shrift, but when you needed them, they had to work. The chutes system looked like a Rube Goldberg arrangement, a combination of ultramodern and ancient practice, as was so very characteristic of the plane.

The B-47 was so clean it was difficult to slow down, and Boeing had added a chute to deploy in the landing pattern. This enabled you to carry power farther into your landing so that the General Electric J47 engines wouldn't take so long to come to speed if you had to go around. Even so the airplane touched down so fast, as much as 140 m.p.h., that the brakes wore out too rapidly if you stopped with them alone. Another chute was the answer, this one a huge brake chute to be deployed after the front main gear was firmly on the runway. It had other uses, too. If the aircraft commander misjudged and hit with a bounce, sending the B-47 into a dangerous porpoising mode, a veteran copilot could deploy the brake chute at the top of the bounce, and the airplane would respond with a perfect touchdown. Of course if he misjudged, it could turn a bad landing into a crash, the front gear slamming down and beginning a series of bounces that could wind up in a ball of flame. Brown had seen motion pictures of a B-47 landing in England, doing just that, finally rolling up into a funeral pyre like King's. With the B-47 he had the firm conviction that it could only happen to others; it had been the opposite with every previous plane. There was something in the airplane, a combination of capability and inherent strength that suited his personality, made him feel one with it.

Satisfied with the airplane's condition, as he had known he would be, Brown thanked Ted, who now had the electronic types nodding and agreeing with him. He rode his Lambretta back down the flight line to the 330th's ready room to get some food before the special briefing. They'd had a mission briefing the day before, and done all their preflight planning, but there was always something new.

Most missions were standard canned routines—a navigation leg, a refueling, some electronic countermeasures practice while getting set for bomb runs, a celestial navigation leg, then back home for a few approaches and landings. The flights varied in length. Some were only eight hours, some fourteen, and at least twice a year, twenty-four hours long. The all-day all-night missions were killers, with little Dexedrine tablets being used to rouse you from near sleep at the treacherous hours before dawn, or just prior to one of the three or four in-flight refuelings that were necessary. He watched his intake of the Dexedrine carefully—no need to risk becoming dependent again. The twenty-four-hour efforts demonstrated the ability of the aircraft and the crews, and they raised the Soviet defense surveillance problems enormously.

As Brown was parking his scooter, T/Sgt. Don Picard was riding back to the Mountain Home maintenance shack, where there was a phone he could use in reasonable privacy.

Polly's voice was still sleepy when she answered, but she immediately launched into an apology. "I'm sorry, honey, I was half asleep. I wasn't supposed to tell you I knew that Jim was coming over."

Picard smiled. "Poll, I'm going to take the job, and you can start looking for a new house today."

There was a silence. "Don, do you mean it? Can you live without the Air Force?"

Picard peeled off his glasses and wiped his face. He was already sweating, and it was only morning. "Well, I figure we'll be in the Air Force as much as ever, but we'll just be wearing different suits."

The sleep completely left her voice. "Oh, I'm so glad, and not for the money. I don't think I could stand another separation now that Jamie's getting bigger. It's so hard to find a decent

249

school for him. And it looks like Donna is going to need braces, and—" She paused. "I think I'll go over to Meadowlake and look at those new houses, you know the ones that go for about nine thousand? We could afford that, could we not?" The hope in her voice split him to the bone.

"Yeah, I know them. But you go over to Soldier's Mountain Farms, and look at their Sierra model. It's eighteen thousand—and we'll be able to afford it. I've been reading the ads, and you get an acre and a half of ground; we could run a pony for Jamie there if we wanted to."

They talked excitedly for a few more minutes until the maintenance officer, Capt. Tony "Big Al" Perone, came in and glared at him for using the phone for personal use. He grinned and went back out to the airplane; he wouldn't have to put up with this much longer. He crawled up into the A/C's seat in the lead B-47 and leaned out to put a final polish on the canopy. The wing commander, Colonel Bailey, was flying and it wouldn't do for the C.O. to have a dirty canopy.

Inside the old World War II building, used originally as a briefing room to train aviation cadets, the crews of the 330th began to assemble.

Brown met his crew, Capt. Alan "Bud" Rosen and First Lt. Zeke Wimmer, inside. Rosen was a superb radar observer, always calm, able to extract the best even from the often malfunctioning equipment or to come up with a really funny cynical comment if he could not. He was famous at Castle as the man who had asked Duke, before every takeoff, to "roll the airplane a little if anything goes wrong," a wry and hopeful reminder that his ejection seat, unlike Brown's and Wimmer's, fired straight down. Wimmer was a professional copilot, the kind who was a contradiction in terms, and perfect for SAC. Wimmer could have been an aircraft commander; he knew the airplanes, could fly well, and was totally dedicated. If the aircraft commander had ever been incapacitated, from a bird strike or a bad in-flight lunch, he was perfectly capable of finishing the mission and flying home. He just didn't want the day-to-day responsibility of command. He didn't like the competition for crew members, the gamesmanship that was required to get noticed. He preferred to do his job so well that a smart aircraft commander would want him. And so it was. He knew he would be a copilot forever, and an extremely valuable asset; he was indifferent to the lesser prestige that drove his copilot colleagues to distraction. The decision also let him drink a little more of the potent home brew he made with a chemist's care.

The three men made up a select crew, meaning that all of their bomb runs, navigation legs, refuelings, and other missions had been done with such exemplary skill that they were at peak proficiency and were competing for spot promotions. These were an innovation of Gen. Curtis LeMay, the other side of the brusque, demanding SAC commander. It partially made up for many of the sacrifices he'd called upon them to endure. If you did well you could get promoted fast, and in the peacetime Air Force, that meant you could go from first lieutenant to captain in maybe three years instead of six or seven, and from captain to major in two instead of six. Some lucky—and skilled—crew members had "spots on spots"; there was one young lieutenant colonel who looked as if he were sixteen years old, carrying tarnished silver oak leaves where he would otherwise have been wearing shiny captain's tracks.

The briefing was easy, for the mission had been changed to be unusually simple and short. They were going to do a formation flight with the Mountain Home wing; there were no longer enough B-47s at Castle to do a full-dressed wing-sized effort.

Plans called for them to launch, fly out to Point Loma, and enter an orbital pattern while Navy jets tried to intercept them. Then they had a navigation leg across California to orbit over Tonopah radio in Nevada, where they would join eleven other B-47s, five from Castle and six from Mountain Home. It was a standard formation, four elements of three aircraft in V formation. The B-47 didn't fly formation often, and this practice flight was different because it was going to be done above twenty-five thousand feet, much higher than usual. They weren't told the reason for the variation and, like good SAC troops, they didn't ask.

The formation was sketched out on the blackboard. The first V of three—Alpha flight—was from Mountain Home, led by their wing commander. It was to form up at twenty-five thousand feet. The second and third flights of three were from Castle. Each succeeding formation was to be five hundred feet back, and five hundred feet higher Brown was leading the third element, coded Charlie. According to the new Air Force phonetic alphabet, it really should have been Cocoa, but not all the new letters had caught on. One could imagine a tail-end Charlie, but not a tail-end Cocoa. The fourth three-ship element was from Mountain Home.

"Never fear, old Ben is here," a big Texas voice boomed in the midst of the formation briefing. Ben Rinehart, a tall, lanky farmer from near Austin, and the self-proclaimed world's greatest fighter pilot, was late as usual. In an unusual move, LeMay had sought and received an infusion of senior fighter pilots from TAC for the B-47 program. Rinehart was typical of the breed. Brown didn't see how he got away with it, except that big guys, fighter pilots, and Texans seemed to charm the C.O., and Ben was all three rolled into one.

Anyone else coming in late would have gotten a blistering comment. He pounded Brown's back, grabbed Rosen's cap and tossed it in the waste basket, frazzled Wimmer's hair, moving through the briefing like a waltzing bear. His copilot, Lt. Brian Sage, had made copious notes, and briefed him on their position as number three in the second element, Bravo flight. Things were shaping up for a good mission.

Gallegos had the B-47 tuned perfectly, and the takeoff and climb out were uneventful. They circled Point Loma, listening for the Navy fighters trying vainly to locate them. A blue Panther, a Grumman F9F, finally staggered by them, obviously beyond its peak altitude and laboring to stay there, just as their time on station was running out. It gave Brown confidence for their chances in war; if the Navy couldn't find them on a prebriefed mission, the Russians couldn't find them on a combat strike.

Brown enjoyed the brief leg over to Tonopah. From the crystal dome of the B-47's canopy, he could survey California from Mexico to the Sierras to beyond Sacramento. The aircraft moved silently through the sky, a solid .74 mach registering on the instrument panel. The B-47, like most jets, was so vibration-free that they had to put an instrument in to jiggle the panel and keep the needles operating. The cabin interior was comfortable despite the oxygen mask that had to to be worn most of the time. The airplane was so utterly responsive; no racehorse could provide the direct feedback that it did from any slight stimulus. You cracked the throttles a little, it accelerated; you pulled them back, it assumed exactly the rate of descent you wanted, from one hundred to four thousand feet per minute.

Brown picked up his flight of two B-47s over Tonapah, and they began an easy series of orbits, circling the dusty valley where miners and whores had labored so long for so little. The six airplanes from Mountain Home were in their appointed lead and tail positions, but the second element, led by "Bud" Neely with Vic Clausen on his right wing, was waiting for Rinehart, the number-three man, to show up.

Just like that stupid cowboy, Brown thought; fighter pilots are always late, and always have an excuse.

Sure enough, Rinehart came on the radio, saying he'd had maintenance problems, but was about ten minutes out of Tonopah, and would join up with them.

The Mountain Home wing commander leading the first flight signaled the formation to move out, departing from Tonopah on a heading of north; Rinehart could join up en route. It was a wide formation, purposely kept loose because at the high altitudes the air was thin, and the low drag of the ultraclean B-47 made it difficult to decelerate. If they'd had dive flaps, so that they could have maintained the engine power within a decent range, using the flaps for drag, they could have closed right up.

Brown's task was easy; he could stay in trail above and behind the first two formations, and admire again the beauty of the B-47s as they pulsed along at seven miles a minute. In the air the airplane assumed a different shape; its wings no longer drooped—in fact in turbulence they sometimes flapped alarmingly in a six-foot arc—and there was a vast impression of speed, so rarely felt at altitude, imparted by the faint trails of smoke and the contrails. He watched the station keeping with a professional eye; Bailey's number two never moved an inch out of line, but his number three was moving back and forth, almost imperceptibly, but enough to get a rocket when they returned. In the second group, Neely and Clausen were maintaining impeccable formation as the number-one and -two airplanes; at their left was the number-three space reserved for Rinehart.

They proceeded north, and Rinehart called in: "Formation in sight. Joining up."

Brown looked to the west and saw the B-47 roaring in from the eight o'clock position, at a seventy-degree angle; it should have been approaching from just a little left of directly astern, matching the formation's speed and then easing into position. "Crownpoint Lead," he called to the formation leader, "Bravo Three is coming in pretty hot."

Rinehart came back: "Don't sweat it—never fear when Ben is here."

Rinehart brought the B-47 in fighter style and banked it up sharply in an almost ninety-degree turn, expecting the drag to slow it down. In a fighter, at ten thousand or even fifteen thousand feet, the drag of the additional area caused by the angle

253

of bank would have decelerated it rapidly, and a tap on the throttles would have provided the power to bring it into position, the third plane in the second V. At twenty-five thousand feet the one hundred sixty thousand pounds of bomber didn't slow down at all, and the radio erupted with warning shouts.

Time collapsed for Brown. He saw Rinehart's airplane moving vertically like a windshield wiper across his canopy. Rinehart, unable to see, unable to stop, died when the nose of his aircraft crashed into the aft fuselage of Neely's B-47. Neely's plane pitched forward, and Brown hoped the crew would eject. In seconds that seemed hours Rinehart's B-47 plunged down and to the right. Its left wing slashed through the belly of Clausen's airplane, exploding the main fuel tanks. There was suddenly a vacancy in front of Brown, with two clouds of flame and Neely's broken bird almost disappearing from sight, breaking up as it went. He couldn't see any parachutes.

"Crown Point Lead," Brown called; "we've lost Bravo flight."

Bailey's voice came back shaken. "Crown Point Charlie and Delta; return to base. Alpha Two and Three, spread out and help me look for parachutes."

Brown could hear the calls going back to the command post; he knew the whole massive rescue operation would be put into action, looking for anyone who might have made it out. The incident was so senseless, one more, one final expression of Rinehart's lack of professionalism. Six, maybe nine people killed—probably ten, because Clausen was carrying his crew chief—just because a stupid fighter pilot had to show off. Three airplanes, worth millions. And the wives and the families.

As they set course for Castle, Brown could hear Bailey giving instructions to his wingman. The wing commander was looking for parachutes, but he really was seeing his own career go down in flames. LeMay would hold him personally responsible for Rinehart's blunder, and rightly so; it would mean the end of the Castle wing commander's career as well.

Brown shifted in his seat. There would be a ripple effect. Promotion opportunities.

Rosen checked in on interphone. "What the hell happened, Duke? I was watching the formation on the scope, and that clown came out of nowhere."

"It was Rinehart, Rosie. He pulled a smartass fighter pilot trick and killed nine other guys plus himself. Makes you want to throw up."

Behind him, Wimmer was doing just that.

254

It was a quiet flight home, but he knew the base would be an anthill of activity as all the myriad drills of an accident aftermath went into play. The Air-Sea rescue teams would already have launched, and in Omaha, LeMay would already be tearing stripes off everyone he encountered. The accident investigation board would be throwing clothes in their beat-up B-4 bags for the flight down in the Command Shrimp Boat, a weary C-97 transport. The press, the vicious press, would be looking for grim human-interest stories, and if possible photos of burned jackets and empty flight boots. There would be hell to pay.

The saddest of all would be the rituals with the families—breaking news that was already broken, giving comfort where none could be given. The wives would try to be brave, the kids would try to stifle their tears, the neighbors would rally around with a week's food, but the questions would remain. Why did it happen? Why us? What will become of us? And there were no answers that counted.

Picard watched the flight line erupt. He knew the sudden swirl of activity at Base Operations could mean only one thing: an accident. He hoped it wasn't Bailey; he hoped it wasn't anybody. Maybe a civilian plane had gone in.

He knew better within fifteen minutes. The story had flashed around the base with lightning speed and remarkable accuracy. Three airplanes were down on a formation flight, and that meant a midair collision. He went to the parking area to wait, leaving the engine running on the blue Air Force pickup so that he could hear the radio calls. He was still there when 671 appeared at the end of the runway, and he knew that it wasn't Bailey who had gone in. Bailey listened to ground control on the radio as he taxied the last two hundred yards to his parking spot. There was not much more radio traffic than usual, but the voices were pregnant with emotion.

The shut-down procedures went quickly, and Picard was up the ladder and in the crawlway before the crew could unstrap. Bailey briefed him on the accident.

"Jesus, Colonel, what happened? Were the airplanes from Castle?"

Bailey nodded, jumped down from the airplane, and strode away, unable or unwilling to speak. His copilot followed.

Picard had checked over the cockpit and was climbing down the ladder when Captain Perone grabbed him by the leg. "Picard, you're going to have to take the duty tonight. Ferko was going to pull it but he's out sick, and I don't have anybody else. We have eight aircraft to launch on a unit mission, and we are probably going to get a half a dozen airplanes coming in from Bolling and Offutt."

Picard nodded, hoped fleetingly that the night missions would be called off, but knew better. If the cause of the accident had been in doubt, there might have been a stand-down to do an extra maintenance inspection, but because it was known to be a catastrophic pilot error it was business as usual. He didn't call Polly; she'd hear what happened soon enough, and know not to expect him.

Picard marshaled his people and began handing out assignments. There was far too much work to be done for the number of people available, but SAC never accepted excuses and it certainly wouldn't today, after the accident. He began assessing the jobs to be done, comparing the talent of the men mustered before him, and orchestrating the work. To do that, he had to be everywhere at once. The idea of orchestration appealed to the old trumpet player within him; he knew that he was obtaining far more work than could reasonably be expected, because he was willing to take some personal risk and authorize shortcuts in the maintenance process that wouldn't have been tolerated in normal circumstances. As the night wore on he realized that he was gaining control. He finally persuaded Mission Control to scrub the mission for one aircraft that he knew could not be put into the air in time, and the three ground-crew members freed up enabled him to handle the remaining tasks easily.

As the glow from the six engines of the last B-47 to launch winked into the hazy distance, he felt a pulse of satisfaction. No one he knew could have done what he did. He trudged back to the line maintenance shack, and found the deputy commander for maintenance, Col. Pat Deming, sprawled in the line boss's creaky swivel chair. Deming stood up and stuck out his hand. "Don, I want to thank you for what you pulled off this evening. Captain Perone told me the way you handled an impossible situation. You got us out of a bad spot on a bad day. Thanks."

Picard mumbled something, but no reply was expected. He flushed with pleasure and began to organize the last of the paperwork as Deming walked out the door.

At midnight, eighteen hours after he'd left with a lump of angel food cake dissolving in his own rotten coffee, Picard wheeled his pickup truck slowly down the lanes of carefully

256

maintained trailers, easing over the traffic bumps that could jolt a fender off. The day was a blizzard of memories; snatches of frantic conversation shouted over the whine of engines and power tools, the remembered bitterness at the slow work of the paperpushers in supply, the physical exertion of getting recalcitrant machinery to work. And then, the last, almost unreal scene with Deming. He was so tired when it happened that it seemed dreamlike. Yet he knew it was real. He savored again the nuances, the unspoken bonds between the colonel and himself, the sense of accomplishment.

He pulled up to his double-wide Olympian and was puzzled to see lights on in the trailer, and a strange Pontiac parked in front. He realized it was Jim's new car; he had waited for him. Suddenly he remembered the job offer. He hadn't even thought about it since Bailey had come back and all hell broke loose. He quietly closed the Stude's door and dragged in to the trailer. Polly met him at the door, kissing him hard, and then standing aside to allow Cagle to greet him.

"Jesus," Cagle said, "rotten news, eh?"

Polly closed the aluminum door and said, "I will leave you to talk. I know you have much to say, Jim, and you also, Don. Good night."

Picard kissed her again and watched her go down the narrow little hall and close the connecting door. After she'd gone, he picked up the bottle of Seagram's that Cagle had already diminished. He jolted down a slug, then began to poke through the tiny refrigerator.

They talked about the accident for a few minutes. Then Cagle said, "Don, I brought a contract along. I got you a better deal than I started with myself. You know a hell of a lot more about B-47 electronics than I ever will, and they've agreed to start you at twenty grand."

Twenty grand. Three airplanes down. Picard looked at the contract. His eyes were so tired the type was blurred, but he could see the numbers that said twenty thousand. He picked up the Seagram's, went to the cabinet, and got a glass.

"Polly will kill me, Jim, but I can't do it." He poured a healthy shot and sluiced it down. Cagle just looked at him.

"See, it isn't just the money. Those guys need me. The Air Force needs me. Hell, I need it. I got something today, something most guys don't get in a lifetime. You understand?"

Cagle shook his head wordlessly. Don grunted and continued. "Look. I was needed and I produced, and everybody knew it.

That's the truth of it. I need it; I need it to take care of me, and I need to take care of it. Today's a good example of why I can't get out."

Cagle didn't try to argue; Picard was emotionally wrought, and he didn't want to provoke an argument. Cagle looked over at him, half-pitying, half-understanding. "You're tired, Don, and its been a bitch of a day. A crash affects everybody. It affects me, too, even if I'm just a feather merchant now. I'll get out of here and you talk it over with Polly. I'll see you on the flight line tomorrow."

Don didn't have the energy to argue the point. Cagle waited a moment, then got to his feet, and they went outside. Don felt bad that he had been so abrupt. He waved at the Pontiac as Cagle moved to the driver's door. "Good looking car, Jim; like it?"

"Yeah. Listen, Don, you could have one just like it."

Picard ran his hand over the five bright strips of chrome that ran straight down the new Pontiac Custom Catalina's hood into the famous Indian-head symbol. It was funny. They each had five stripes. Picard had his on his sleeve, Cagle had his on the hood of his car.

"I'll see you tomorrow," Picard said, "but I'm not going to change my mind. I don't think I can."

In the dim light of the single bulb that lit the trailer-court drive, Cagle's shrug was invisible. He lit a cigarette and climbed in his car. The Pontiac started and Picard stepped back. He watched the car move slowly away, and he glanced at his watch in the glare of his door light. It was almost one o'clock, and he had another six o'clock call. He'd skip the shower tonight. He would need it to wake up in the morning.

18

July 1958
Travis AFB, California
USA

The C-124 reminded Larry White of the hippopotamus ballerinas in *Fantasia*. The huge fat fuselage with its cavernous maw sprouted dainty little wings that seemed barely able to support it. He couldn't understand how Douglas could make two airplanes so dissimilar and both so good. He'd flown the B-26 at Langley, before he got shafted into L-5s in Korea. The B-26 was light, lithe, and fast; the C-124 was heavy, fat, and slow. Both were outstanding airplanes.

The missions were different in the same way the airframes were. In the B-26 you would fly three or four hours at the most in the training he had done. In the C-124 you took off on missions that might last a month, hauling you all about the world, in and out of foreign airports, loading and unloading passengers and cargo. Now he seemed to have the best of all possible worlds; he was an aircraft commander. He was moving to California, and he was going to have his family with him whenever he wasn't flying.

He wasn't surprised when Micky agreed to move to Travis with him. She had been able to bail herself out of debt through an annealing process of endless hard work that had changed her physically and mentally. She was no longer the girl he married, but a businesswoman, whose mind ran to profit and loss statements rather than recipes. Yet she was still vulnerable, still smarting from wanting so much triumph, and then failing so visibly. What hurt her the most was that the friends who had cheered her on in her early selling successes were the very people who destroyed her when she went on to her own ventures. Larry knew that he was eternally naïve; it surprised him to find that she had been too.

Her new bitterness was most apparent in their pillow talk. They used to spend their somewhat infrequent nights together initially with passion, and then with long catch-up conversations about the kids and the family. Now she was focused on one subject only, revenge through real estate. She was determined to be a bigger success than any of the people who had hurt her.

He was bitter himself. He'd had a long tour at Dover, almost five years. He'd made captain in 1956, at the same time they'd finally checked him out as aircraft commander, long after he was ready. The main reason he had transferred to Travis wasn't to get to California; it was to get away and get a clean start. After you stooged as a copilot for five years, people discounted you. Maybe it would be different at Travis; it almost had to be.

Micky couldn't wait to move; they wanted to have a farewell party for her at Roy Rice Real Estate, and she refused. What bothered her was everyone's conspiracy to ignore what had happened. They treated her humiliation, her terror, her indebtedness as if it didn't exist; she was supposed to be as good natured and hard working as ever. The last day that she was there, she confronted old Mr. Rice himself. She insisted on telling him the whole painful story; he stayed, fidgeting, for he customarily began a three-martini lunch at eleven o'clock, and she was intruding on his time. He sat, a shriveled old man in a clean but wrinkled seersucker suit, a week-old egg spot splotched on his tie. His eyes were rheumy, and it seemed to her that he laughed in all the wrong places, as if appreciating the piquancy of her screwing.

When she'd finished, he reached over and patted her shoulder with his leathery liver-spotted hand. "Honey, you ought to go out and thank all those people who were helping you."

"Helping me? They didn't help me, they hurt me."

"Yeah, this time, but this is penny ante. You were violating the first law of real estate, the first law of business. There has to be a little sweetener for everybody. You were trying to nail everything down for yourself. If you'd spread the wealth around—or even just the prospect of wealth—you'd have had a different reaction. And you were greedy; you had two projects going, plus your regular job. No wonder you didn't get any help. I'm surprised you got off as easy as you did." He chuckled in appreciation of the clubby skulduggery; it was as if he wished he could have taken a crack at Micky himself.

By the time they were en route Micky had become reconciled to the fact that she'd been given postgraduate work in the real-estate school of hard knocks. It gave a luster to the prospects in California, where it was obvious that the boom was coming. You couldn't pick up a professional magazine and not be deluged with facts and figures on the coming California tidal wave of real-estate deals. She'd have a solid basis; many of her customers would be coming through the area, anyway.

The trip across country was as much another honeymoon as it could be, given that Lola, the two kids, a cat, a dog, and a parakeet were in the safari. Micky figured she was relocating a business, so she arranged for adjoining suites at all the motels on the way; she'd need the deductions this year. Lola stayed with the kids, and she and Larry had a bottle of champagne in their room every night.

Libby's condition had stabilized; for a while Micky considered flying across country with her, but she thought she'd enjoy the drive. They hit all the sights, from a Mississippi riverboat in St. Louis to the Grand Canyon to Disneyland to Chinatown in San Francisco. Larry Jr. liked it almost as much as Larry Sr. did, but no one enjoyed it more than Lola. She kept losing weight, and once Micky had a devil of a time finding her one evening in Dodge City; she came back to the room about 3 A.M., and Micky suspected she'd been trifling with a trucker. Fortunately, Larry was asleep; mothers weren't supposed to do that sort of thing. It was just as well his dad had died.

When they got to Travis, Larry reported in and Micky went through an elaborate process of buying a house outside of Fairfield-Suisun, the dreary little village Travis sustained in the valley. She was looking for a real-estate firm as much as for a place to live, and got a job doing secretarial work for Jerry Eatherton, who had sold her the house. It was a good way to build up experience and contacts while she was working to get her California realtor's license. Right from the start she began to look for acreage to buy all around the valley. She wanted Larry to fly her around for an aerial survey, but he'd been too busy getting field and route checks. It could wait for a while.

The family hated it when she came home tight lipped and unhappy most evenings. She was unhappy in part because she wasn't generating the income she had back in Virginia, but mostly it was because Eatherton, who turned out to be sales manager, called her honey, was patronizing, and gave her most of the office dog work to do, at the same time that he laid ambiguous flirtatious hints on her, wanting her to relate her progress in the office to his progress toward her bed. She accepted it all grimly, and Larry was vaguely aware that Jerry was joining the ranks of those who would some day pay.

It helped that the officers' club at Travis was not only more elegant than most, it served decent food. Most O' clubs around the country were disgraces, vending substandard food to captive clients. They had the single virtue of being slightly cheaper than restaurants on the outside; Larry always assumed they made up the difference with watered drinks. He took Micky there once or twice a week when he was home; if she was busy, he'd eat there alone. He wasn't much of a drinker, but the bar seemed to serve decent drinks, and the club actually had a wine list with a selection of local wines that Micky said were good. The best part for him was that Travis was the West Coast counterpart to Dover, and he was almost always sure to run into someone he knew, coming from or going overseas.

It got to be a routine that when Micky had to work late, Larry would go to the club; it was better than putting up with what Lola mistakenly thought were good old home-cooked meals. One Thursday night Larry was at the club, anticipating a rare prime rib and a trip to the new salad bar, when he spotted Duke Brown.

He was surprised when Brown remembered him; they'd met briefly in Korea at the end of White's tour. They had both been first lieutenants then, with White senior by date of rank. Now Brown was a major. It was hard for Larry to understand.

Yet he was flattered that Brown, obviously a hot property, was glad to see him. He was coming back from a tour of the Pacific, checking to see which airports could be used by B-52s if they were deployed overseas. He needed a flight back to Washington, had been bumped from one by a team of colonels, and knew a MATS insider might be able to help him get another quick flight out. The alternative, even for Duke Brown, was a long haggle with the MATS desk people, who made a career out of denial.

They had manhattans, then went in to eat. Brown insisted on buying another round at the table, and called for a bottle of Beringer Cabernet Sauvignon with the meal. It was more than Larry usually drank, and he loosened up enough to ask the question that had been bugging him. "Duke, I know you are a West Pointer and all, but when did you make major, and how the hell did you do it?"

Brown had drunk more than usual, too, and he felt benevolent. This was an old compadre; they'd fought a war together. Usually he was annoyed at questions of rank or dates of rank. Gentlemen didn't discuss things like that; they just made sure they knew them. But he felt he owed White something.

"Well, Larry, I was lucky. I made it a couple of years ago. I made it the hard way, with a lot of combat, and a tour in the Pentagon." He paused, and knew what was expected of the ace-on-base, so he added, "Combat was better." White nodded, not really understanding at all. It was clear he was only inches away from calling Duke "sir"—and that would have embarrassed both of them, no matter how militarily correct.

The dinner hadn't come, and Brown signaled for another round of drinks. "Slow service, Larry, I tell you, they don't give you rank, you have to take it."

"I don't know. It seems to me that you're supposed to do your job, and the Air Force is supposed to take care of you. I've never asked for an assignment, never refused one. I've got nearly four thousand hours flying time, a chestful of ribbons, and it seems to me that should do it." He slugged back his drink defiantly, as if staking out a claim.

Duke almost laughed, then thought better of it. This guy was serious. "Jesus, for an old Mosquito driver, are you innocent! Let me ask you, have you got a sponsor?"

"You mean like a PCS sponsor?"

"No, I mean like a job sponsor. Haven't you got someone in headquarters, here, at MATS, or in the Pentagon, who's looking out for you?"

"Man, I know everybody, but at the same time, I don't know anybody, anywhere who's looking out for me; you're the hottest rock I know. Maybe you can help me."

Duke squinted into his glass. He hadn't counted on this.

"Have you gone to any of the service schools? SOS?"

"No, never had time."

"Are you taking them by correspondence?"

"No." Larry was beginning to feel distinctly uncomfortable. Among his buddies, nobody ever talked about this stuff. You either flew airplanes or you were a groundpounder, period.

Brown talked about square filling, about watching for jobs, about being political. Then their food came; it was decent prime rib, medium rare, the best thing Brown had seen since leaving for the Orient.

Duke sliced into the meat and continued. "How are your OER's?" Officer Efficiency Reports were the colanders of the Air Force, sifting out the gifted from the ordinary for later personal selection.

"Pretty good—all above average."

Duke hid his reaction from White. This guy was a cripple, he thought. The brutal fact was, unless you are rated at least outstanding, you don't even get in the running. And to stay in the running, you had to be a "water-walker." As he chewed the beef, he thought, there's nothing I can do for him, nothing anybody can do. He's a donkey. But he couldn't let White know that. Not only was it unnecessarily cruel, but he needed White's influence for that ride back to the Pentagon tomorrow. He smiled after he finished his meal, dabbed his lips with the napkin, and said, "Do you know your rating officer pretty well?"

"Well, I work for him; we don't socialize much. He likes to play golf and I don't have the time for it. When I'm home, which isn't often, I like to spend it with the kids."

Such candor stunned Brown. He considered leveling with him. The Air Force was made up of men who worked for the Air Force and men who worked for themselves. You couldn't do what the Air Force wanted and manage your own career. In the field, 80 percent of the people worried about the Air Force and

20 percent worried about their careers. In the Pentagon the percentages were reversed. The career managers needed guys like Larry to get the work done.

Brown swirled the wine in his glass, carefully thinking about what he might tell White. Finally he decided on the party line. "Sounds like you're doing fine, Larry. I just got lucky; maybe you will too." White beamed at him, mood lifted enormously; it was obviously the right thing to say, because White wanted so much to believe it.

The evening ended with a phone call from White to the Command Center. He got Brown on an early flight out to Washington. It gave him a sense that he had made a real contact, somebody who was going to help his career.

19

0950 LOCAL
30 September 1959
Castle AFB, California
USA

"Just who in the *hell* do you know, Washington?"

Col. Rodger Pinney glared at him. Pinney, a professional southerner, was motion-picture handsome with wavy hair gone prematurely gray. He had furrows or wrinkles only where it helped. As he walked, his glance searched for every mirror for confirmation of his good luck. He carried himself with West Point rigor, even though he had come up through the ranks. Normally he was good humored; Wash thought he smiled just to show off the glistening perfect teeth. He was not smiling now, as he strode into the little rec room in the alert facility, where Wash was reading a magazine, alone.

Washington stood up; Pinney liked the courtesies.

"What do you mean, sir?" He shot his best willing-darkie grin.

"We're short of pilots, and you get yourself an assignment overseas. You got to know somebody, because *nobody* is getting out of SAC crew assignments nowadays."

He handed Washington a TWX; it was from Headquarters USAF, instructing the wing personnel office to cut orders assigning Wash to Korea as commander of a radar site. Wash looked at it, read it twice and handed it back to him. "Colonel, this is the first I've heard of this; it's probably a mistake. Let's send a TWX back asking for confirmation."

"We don't have to; I already have. You are most definitely going; but I'm going to get you back in SAC at the end of the year. You are by God going to put in your time like us white folk do."

Pinney spun on his heel and left. Washington was puzzled. From alert to Korea didn't seem like such a good deal, but getting a command, even a radar site, was a career godsend. He sat down and contemplated it; the more he thought about it, the better it seemed. Because alert duty in SAC was worse than combat in many ways.

The Castle alert facility lay like a shattered hulk in the earth, the wet concrete-walled steps a descent from humanity for the crews. Inside was an artificial code of anticipated war; they traded life and home for academy rigor and the tired horseplay of men who had been soldiers together too long. It was one more twist of the screw for the SAC crews, one more exaction of sacrifice.

Washington hated the uniform brilliance of the fluorescent lights most of all, from the smoke-filled briefing rooms, down the hallways, to the "recreation rooms" and latrines. Even in the dismally neat sleeping quarters the escape from glaring, pulsating yellow fluorescents was cloaked in a cloying sweet-sour combination of sweat and deodorant, tobacco and aftershave.

Outside, the routine of Castle Air Force Base and the world went on untrammeled; inside there were drills, classes, tests, and arguments. When the crews were not preflighting the airplanes, "cocking" them for instant takeoff, they were flying the simulator, studying the war plan, or taking self-improvement courses. In pathetic honest endeavor, some worked their ways through Squadron Officers' School, Air Command and Staff, and the War College, all by correspondence, never realizing that to do so was an indictment, not a commendation. It told the selecting officials that they had never been asked to go in residence; they were automatically inferior.

Louise bitterly resented the duty cycle of four days on alert, two days of regular squadron duty, and two days off. You couldn't depend upon the off-duty days, which shifted vagrantly through the week, making ordinary plans impossible. She was raising the kids effectively on her own. And she hated it.

"What do they gain by keeping you there? We only live twenty minutes from the base; couldn't you just get a call at home like you used to? Staying away four days at a time, week in and week out, is destroying us. Mary Louise Kemper is getting a divorce because of it, and I may be next!" She rarely complained, and never jested about serious matters. Wash knew she was deadly serious, and he ached for her. But he knew what she did not, or cared not to know.

"Look," he'd said, "Russian missiles take thirty minutes to get here. Since last year, SAC has tried to have one third of its planes ready to go on fifteen minutes' notice. If we're not off the ground, they'd destroy us—and once we're gone, the country's at their mercy. I hate it as much as you do, worse, because I have to live with the crew night and day, and nothing gets on your nerves more than being cooped up next to a bunch of hard-headed SAC crew members."

"How long will it go on?"

"I can't tell; forever, I guess, until we get some missiles of our own. There's no way around it till then." She had not been placated, but after they'd had that talk, she had settled down grimly to wait the Air Force out. From that moment, Wash had known that a clock was ticking for the two of them.

Washington despised the enforced intimacy of the alert area; you trained together, ate together, watched television, played handball. Even with the best will in the world, nerves frayed. Of course SAC, as it always did, tried to make things as good as they could be while still getting the job done. Over time, they built play facilities outside the alert area, so that the kids would have somewhere to play while the parents visited. Even the sacrosanct rules of the officers' club were relaxed, and crew members in flight suits could eat with their families. Still, nothing could take away from the fact that the separation was enforced, the hours long, the routine ultimately boring beyond words.

The fact that some of the families were less than five miles away exaggerated the artificial quality of life. It happened more than once that cars were wrecked, limbs broken, babies born, with the husband unable to come to the family's aid. For some it was more than could be borne; for others it was just another facet of service life. As he considered how it had strained his relationship with Louise, how indeed it had made him wonder about his own place in the service, he realized what a chance this assignment to Korea might be. He checked the time, and counted the hours until this stint was done; he'd refrain from calling her, and tell her in person. She'd be ecstatic.

Louise burst into tears when he told her. He stood dumfounded while she wept, both kids looking on, as wide-eyed as he. He put out his arm to comfort her and she shrugged him off violently.

"It's unaccompanied, isn't it? You'll be gone for a year, and I'll have to stay here and raise the kids. Right?"

"Uhh—right. Unaccompanied. Hey, babe, look—it beats alert duty—"

She chopped the tears as if by a faucet. Glaring at him through red-rimmed eyes, she said, "You bet your life it beats alert duty. But I'll tell you this, Millard Washington. As God is my witness, when you get back from this tour, you promise me that you will not go back on SAC alert duty! Do you hear? Promise me!"

"Hey—calm down, honey. Sure, I promise. But you know how—"

"Yes. I know all too well. But you promised. Remember that."

They had the going-away party at their house. He was gratified by the response of his crew members and the ground crew he worked with most often. The going-away presents were the usual excruciating exercises in bad taste, from a rudely carved set of wings to rough gifts that had Louise turning away in embarrassment. He noted an undercurrent of envy. A shot at command this early in his career was an obvious sign that he was on the fast track; many in the squadron resented it. Inevitably, he had to give a farewell speech. After they'd all drunk too much, he staggered to his feet and cleared his throat. Everyone stopped talking and reluctantly gave him their attention.

"Thank you all for coming; I am as surprised as you are that I'd be pulled off the best duty in the world"—mock cheers—"to go to a paradise"—groans—"like South Korea. But I want you to know that I've learned a lot"—catcalls, whistles—"and that I'll never forget all your kindness to Louise"—applause for Louise—"and me"—more catcalls and hoots. "There is no better, no nobler duty than SAC, and I want to come back as soon as I can."

This was met with boozy shouting, cries of disbelief. Pinney should have come forward and made some closing comments. Instead he quietly left, slipping out the door under Louise's hard eyes. She glanced at Washington. He'd pay them all back. And if he didn't, she would.

"Surgeon" was a smear on a mountain, twenty miles north-west of Seoul; a dirt road slanted up the side, piling Quonset huts one after the other to an apex of radar dishes. Half a Korean village seemed to grow out of it, a cancerous collection of knocked-together boxes. Some would do laundry; most would do airmen.

Wash remembered using Surgeon during the war; then it had been a friendly voice in the night. Now it looked like a stage set from Stalag 17. Below, a squatty village straddled a road, trees poking up from the sloping roofs. The Han river ran brown to the sea, a viscous thread connecting Surgeon to Seoul.

He rode up the twisting flinty road in a taxi; no one had been able to raise Surgeon on the pathetic Korean telephone system to send a jeep. The guard post was empty; he drove on, finally stopping at a rough-sided building marked OFFICERS' CLUB. In the distance he could see the runways of what had been K-14 when the F-86s had battled the MiGs.

There was music inside. He eased the door open; half a dozen airmen were dancing with Korean women. A G.I. whorehouse.

"Sir!" a voice boomed behind him.

He turned to see another Negro, as tall as he was, sporting master sergeant stripes and standing with a sloppy salute.

"Welcome to 'Surgeon,' Major Washington; I'm your first sergeant, Master Sergeant Baldwin." Wash returned his salute and reached out to shake Baldwin's hand.

"Well, Sergeant Baldwin, it seems to me that things are pretty loose here. Do you think we can straighten it out?"

"Yes sir! It's a little loose, but it's peacetime, and the men have to have some relief, sir. We don't get to Seoul too often, and almost never to Japan. I'm trying to make it as easy as possible for them."

Washington paid the taxi driver, and the big black sergeant escorted him to his quarters, half of a Quonset hut, distinguished from the others only by a private bathroom built on to the side.

"As soon as I get unpacked, Sergeant Baldwin, I'd like you to take me on a tour of the station; this evening I'd like to meet the other officers and men."

"Certainly, Major. But we don't have any other officers right now, Major; Lieutenant Naylor had to go home on emergency leave after they rotated Lieutenant Schmidt out. I've been running the place with the noncommissioned officers, and they've been doing fine."

"I see. Well, what is the mix of white and Negro airmen here?"

"I don't know; let me think. We have forty-five people authorized, and about thirty-eight here. I'd say there are twenty blacks and the rest white."

Blacks; it was obvious he was going to have to start using the word.

"How are they getting along?"

"No problem; or, well, almost no problem. We've had a few fights on payday night, but that's normal. They work together good, and that's all I ask. You get as many blacks fighting blacks or whites fighting whites as you do black against white." Baldwin beamed at him. Obviously, he thought of the situation as hunky-dory.

Washington thought otherwise; it sounded very much like a powder keg. He spent the next three days prowling the area. He checked the mess hall, pored over the accounts, checked the books at the club, which against all regulations was open to everyone, enlisted or commissioned, and especially to any Korean women who would come by. It was obvious to him that Sergeant Baldwin, an outwardly amiable man without a clue as to the mission of the radar site, was in business for himself. He had subcontracted everything out to local Koreans. God alone knew what the men had to do.

Instinct told him to delay visiting the radar shack for a while even though it was his primary concern. He knew from the looks of things that they would need time to get set, and he didn't want to create problems that a few days might solve.

He steeled himself on Friday morning and made an unannounced visit. Less than half the people on duty were in uniform; the rest were local Koreans, illegally operating the classified equipment that was the only reason for the station's existence. Millard spun on his heels and stalked out the door shouting "Sergeant Baldwin!"

"Sir!" Baldwin had materialized from behind the building, obviously shadowing him.

"Sergeant Baldwin, I want every Korean off this base by noon.

269

If you've got contracts with them, they are broken as of this minute."

"Sir, I can't do that; they do all the dirty work. Besides, they'll put another kind of contract on you and me if I do that."

"Baldwin, that's your problem. Get them off the station and muster the men, all of them, at thirteen hundred, Class A uniforms."

By 1305 Millard was furious, shifting his feet, trying to keep his temper as the last of the young troops struggled in bewilderment into their first formation since they had arrived. Their wrinkled Class A's had obviously been pulled from duffel bags. He didn't know what to say, yet. He stared at them a while, letting them stew, and then lit into them.

"Men, things are so screwed up we're going to start with going back to work; I don't want any Koreans on the base until further notice. If we have any official local contracts, we'll pay them at the usual rate, but all Koreans are barred from the base until we get squared away. Sergeant Baldwin will be setting up the new schedules. The faster we get organized, the faster we can get back to normal. But listen to this: Normal is *my* normal, Air Force normal, not what you've been doing. I hope you understand that. For the time being we are going back to basic training, starting with G.I. parties, inspections, and drill."

There was a groan.

"Silence!" he thundered. "If I want to hear groans I'll get them by working them out of you. Don't ever let me hear anything like that from the ranks again, or I'll have you marching for the rest of your tour. Don't fool with me, or you *will* regret it."

He watched them for a moment. This was unlike him, but he was doing it well. They had their eyes straight ahead, but their radars were all homed in on him.

Softly, he called, "Sergeant Baldwin, dismiss this formation."

Baldwin, furious, cried, "Group, Atten-hut! Dismissed!"

The new officer, Lt. John Wiley, reported the next morning. He was a tall, blond, handsome kid who looked like his first remark would be "Anyone for tennis?" He had washed out of navigator training, so Washington was immediately sympathetic. Wiley was right out of the radar course at Keesler, and appalled at being in Korea.

Washington observed Wiley for the next few days. He was moderately competent with the radar equipment, and within the week had formed an assessment he was willing to pass on to

Washington. "Major, we're in deep trouble. We'd never pass an inspection. Half the equipment is down, and the training is a joke. The North Koreans could send a flock of MiGs and we'd never even pick it up with this crew."

"What's the problem?"

"There's no leadership, sir." He hesitated, obviously wanting to say more.

"Look, give it to me straight; I just got here myself, I won't take offense."

"Sir, you can't get the men to do anything serious; I went through the tests they've been taking and they are all faked. Somebody has handed out the key, and they're simply waltzing through them. Most of them haven't done any genuine work for weeks. The Koreans have taken over."

Millard announced an inspection for the following Saturday; he told Sergeant Baldwin to muster an old-fashioned G.I. party and clean the place up. The laundry was carried out to the line of abandoned shacks at the base of the hill on Thursday instead of Saturday, for Millard had specified unwrinkled Class A uniform.

On Saturday morning, Sergeant Baldwin knocked on the door of the Quonset that served as the base headquarters. He was impeccable in his Class A's. "Station ready for inspection, sir."

They walked silently down the dusty, rock-strewn paths to the enlisted quarters. Baldwin swung the door open and yelled "Ten-hut!" as Millard walked in.

The men stood by their bunks. Sergeant Baldwin stood at ease at the door as Millard went down the aisles. He glanced at the floor, the beds; he checked the contents of a footlocker, and eyed the haircuts. Without a word he strode out of the barracks. "Rest," Sergeant Baldwin called, then joined him. "Mess hall next, sir."

Millard walked through the dining room, scrubbed clean but still smelling sour, tables slick to his touch. He glanced at the grease-covered stoves and put his head inside the big walk-in refrigerator; a film of mold stood over bacon boxes; and in the corner a dropped egg had frozen into a silent sun.

Wash didn't say a word; his jaw worked, but he didn't say a word. He managed to cool his fury until he and Baldwin were back outside the headquarters. Then he turned on the big sergeant and pinned him with his eyes. "This inspection is completely unsatisfactory, Sergeant. We will do it again in the morning. Please see me in my office in one hour. Dismissed." He turned to Wiley, watching wide-eyed.

"Lieutenant Wiley, please follow me."

Wiley tracked behind him into the Quonset.

"Wiley, can you type?"

"Hunt and peck, sir."

"Okay. Type this up and post it."

It was a simple memo; on Monday morning, standard tests on all specialties were going to be given; anyone failing was confined to the station until he passed. If he didn't pass on the second test, Washington said he was going to reduce the individual administratively one grade in rank. He didn't know if he could do it or not; by the time they found he couldn't maybe he'd have them back in line.

Wiley gulped, chuckled, typed it out. He had not returned before Washington could hear the scramble at the bulletin board. They were watching what he had to say pretty close.

"Well, what's next, Major?" Wiley asked.

"We're in real trouble. This place is on its ass. Have you had a chance to figure out who was worth a damn and who wasn't?"

"Maybe you ought to ask Sergeant Baldwin about that, sir."

"Christ, Wiley, Baldwin is the problem; he's supposed to be running the place for the Air Force, and he's running it for himself. What about the other noncommissioned types?"

"You have one sharp tech sergeant, Howard Walker, and one smartass but competent buck sergeant, Tyrone Bates. The other men are okay, but not leaders. The ranking tech, Palmer, is a cook and a lush."

"What do you think will happen when I relieve Baldwin?"

"You can't do that, Major; nobody fires the first sergeant, especially a Negro. You'd probably have a riot on your hands."

"That's what Sergeant Baldwin is counting on. Come on, Lieutenant, you just got out of school—tell me what I should do."

"Why don't you wait it out for a few weeks, Major? We're due to get another officer, and there will be some rotation among the men. We're not supposed to have an inspection for another few months, and maybe we can shape them up."

"Yeah, but the problem is that we are not here to pass inspections, we're here to defend the fucking airspace. And we might get an I.G. team in tomorrow on a surprise visit, and then what happens?"

Wiley had no answer to that. And Sergeant Baldwin looked nervous when he reported.

"Sir, I know you wasn't too happy, but it's been a long time since we had an inspection. If you give me a week or two to shape them up, things will go fine. Things are too touchy here to go too fast. I got the black troops under control but they won't take too much of this West Point shit."

"West Point shit, Sergeant?"

"Well, sir, you know what I mean. Inspections, G.I. parties. You know."

Washington swiveled in his beat-up office chair and looked out the dirt-streaked window at the bleak hills. When he turned back to Baldwin, his jaw was clenched in fury. "Sergeant Baldwin, you are relieved of duty, as of now. I'm appointing Tech Sergeant Walker as your replacement. I want you to work with him until you get your orders back to the States."

"Major, you can't do that! A black man can't do that to a black man! The men won't stand for Walker replacing me; there'll be a race riot, and you'll be the one who's fired!"

"Baldwin, this place is in chaos, and you are responsible. If the men riot, I'll break heads until they stop. Don't pull any of that race business with me. I'm the wrong color. I want you to go to your quarters and stay there until I send for you. If I see you outside, I'll put you under arrest and have you sent to the can in Seoul. Don't screw with me."

The big sergeant whirled on his heels.

"Sergeant Baldwin!" He stopped at the door, facing out.

"Turn your black ass around and salute properly or I'll place you under arrest."

A film of hatred glimmered in the sergeant's eyes.

"I'll remember that remark at the inquiry, sir!"

"You do that, Baldwin; you'll need to remember a lot, especially when I pull out those account books."

A few hours later, Washington called Walker and Bates into his office. "I'm totally dissatisifed with the condition of this installation, and I want you to help me change it."

Bates stirred uneasily. "Excuse me, sir, but where is Sergeant Baldwin?"

"Sergeant Baldwin is relieved of duty; he was responsible for the condition of this installation, and I've fired him."

Walker looked at Bates, then said, "Jesus, sir, we're apt to have a race riot; the colored men worshiped Baldwin; he treated them right."

"Yeah, well, *you* are going to treat them right too, but the whole unit is going to go to work."

He glanced at Bates; the sergeant's face was grim with resentment.

"Bates, are the white guys working any harder than the black ones? Be honest with me."

"No sir, I don't think so. We are all fucked up, black or white. Baldwin was doing the best he could; he had things working. You can't just throw him out. Besides, he's got connections with the Koreans; they can make life miserable for us in town as well as on the base. And they play for keeps."

"Bates, you don't know what playing for keeps is. I grew up in East St. Louis and survived, and no gooks are going to intimidate me. You can tell Baldwin that if you want. We'll go on an emergency footing; the guards will be on the gate, and we'll issue ammunition so they won't be carrying around an empty stick. I'm not going to fool around, and if you're smart you'll help."

Bates looked nervously at Walker.

"Walker, I want you to take over as first sergeant; I'll try to get you another stripe as soon as I can. Bates, I want you to work with Walker. He'll be leaving in four months, and you can succeed him as first soldier if you work out."

"Can I have a word with you in private, sir?" Walker looked very nervous.

"Sure. Go ahead, Bates. I'll talk with you later. Dismissed."

Bates saluted and left. Walker fidgeted, then said, "Sir, you might want to think this over. I can work with Baldwin and help him get straightened out. We'll have a real fight when the word gets out; Baldwin has a lot of friends, inside the camp and out."

"I see. Well, tell me what you think about Bates."

"He's good technically, but a wiseass. I don't think you can count on him to straighten anybody out. You'd be better off sticking with Baldwin. Bates is really pretty radical when it comes to racial stuff, but Baldwin got along with everybody."

"Yeah, everybody but me. You've got the job, and I'll support you. I think Bates will be okay. If he's not, let me know."

The next morning there was a delegation of Koreans at the gate, led by a short, round-faced older man named La Woon Sung, who sucked one cigarette after another into oblivion. As he put down the stub of one, another would appear lit from the taller man at his side. He spoke excellent English.

Washington greeted them with great formality. He had coffee and tea brought in, and insisted on Sergeant Walker taking photographs of them arm in arm. After toying with the tea—it was obviously not to his taste—Sung came to the point.

"Major Washington, I understand we have some contractual difficulties. Can I be of assistance?"

"Sir, we have some temporary difficulties that I can't discuss with you; I believe, however, that we will not be able to employ as many people as we did in the past. In all honesty, my men need to have their work to do to maintain their skills, and however competent the native workers are, it is not possible to let them do everything."

"Major Washington, I am not a businessman, but I do know that certain contracts are in existence, and must be honored."

"Sir, any official U.S. Government contracts will be honored; any that you have negotiated with individuals on this station will not be."

Sung attempted to hide his anger and failed. "Major Washington, you are new to Korea. There are contracts and there are contracts. If some are not honored, others are put in their place. Do you understand me?"

"Yes, Mr. Sung, I believe I do. That's why the pictures I've taken of you will be sent to the ambassador, along with a record of this conversation. There are contracts that are honored in the breach; if you wish to initiate others, be sure that you want to be in full receipt of the total payments." He smiled.

Sung considered this. Wash pressed on. "We are not going to disturb the normal flow of service contracts, Mr. Sung, but it may be that certain optional extras will be discontinued. I'm sure you understand that there is more to be gained in the long run by cooperating than by disagreement."

The Koreans left, talking quietly among themselves. Bates had been in the room; he looked at Washington with new respect.

Millard went back to basics; he canceled all leaves, put everybody on twelve-hour shifts, scheduled a G.I. party every other day, and closed the club. He kept all Koreans off the base except for those providing the essential support work that only they could do. He rescinded all the previous training tests, and established classes for everyone every evening.

The first inquiry came from headquarters in Pusan the next day. A pompous colonel somehow got through on the phone. "Major Washington, what the hell is going on down there? We just got a call from the ambassador that you were discriminating against Negro troops and Koreans. They say the damned base is supposed to be virtually shut down."

"Colonel, why don't you come down and see for yourself? This place is a disaster area and I'm trying to clean it up. The only people I'm discriminating against are loafers and thieves. The base is shut down for everything but its operational mission, and it will stay that way until it's running right or until you relieve me."

"Major, you can't handle black troops like you can white troops. Hell, where are you from, Montgomery?"

"No sir, better than that, East St. Louis. But you better know that I'm a Negro myself, and I don't need any advice on handling black troops or white troops. Sir!" He heard the colonel deflate and said, "When can I expect you, sir?"

"Ah, Major Washington, let me get back to you." An hour later, the ambassador's office called. A silky-voiced woman inquired about the problem.

"Ma'am, you tell the ambassador there's no problem; we just need to get a few things straightened out. I'd be glad to meet with him here or in Seoul, if you feel it's necessary."

The woman promised to get back to him. Everyone was going to get back to him.

Sergeant Walker stopped him at the end of the first week of the new regime. "Sir, I think you'd better let up. The men are getting pretty down, and morale is bad."

"Listen to me, Sergeant Walker. Morale is bad when the men desert or when they put a hand grenade under my bed. Nobody's deserted, and there haven't been any hand grenades. And things are shaping up. Check with me a week from now."

He watched Bates carefully; at first, Bates spent a lot of time with Sergeant Baldwin. Millard couldn't tell whether it was out of sympathy, or if he was trying to learn the ropes.

He was lying on his bunk when Bates came to the door. "Major Washington, can I have a word with you?"

"Come in, Sergeant, stand at ease."

"Sir, the men have asked me to give you this petition."

"Let's see it."

Bates handed him a sheet from a yellow legal pad. The paper demanded the immediate reinstatement of Master Sergeant Baldwin as first sergeant, and bore twenty-five signatures. That meant it wasn't a purely racial issue, although he could tell at a glance that most of the signers were black.

Wash considered how he should react. He had been a hardass ever since he arrived; and yet, this was obviously going to need a showdown of some kind. He decided to hang tough.

He glared at Bates and gritted, "Sergeant Bates, do you think this is some kind of college campus? I could call this mutiny if I chose to. Instead I want you to assemble these men in the club in thirty minutes. I don't care what they are doing, even if they are on duty in the radar shack, I want them in the club. You be there too, and make sure that Sergeant Baldwin is there."

Half an hour later, he walked in to Walker's call of "Ten-hut!" The men stirred roughly to attention. He wasted no time.

"Sergeant Walker, you are dismissed; please go back to headquarters and wait for me there. Bates, are you the spokesman?"

"Ah, yessir. The men feel you haven't been fair to Sergeant Baldwin, and that Sergeant Walker isn't qualified. I have to agree with them." Bates went on with a speech he had obviously worked on; he quoted the Constitution, and he quoted Martin Luther King, Jr. He closed with a ringing tribute to Sergeant Baldwin, and an appeal to racial solidarity. The men didn't quite cheer, but they rumbled.

Washington nodded and looked at them all, face composed. "Sergeant Bates, you are quite right. I haven't been 'fair' to Sergeant Baldwin, and Sergeant Walker isn't qualified. If I'd been fair to Baldwin, I'd have court-martialed him. And Sergeant Walker is going to have to learn on the job to become a decent first sergeant. And so will you."

He waited a minute and went on. "That was a good speech; the only thing wrong with it was the time and place. Martin Luther King is working one problem in the South; we're working another problem here. He's trying to integrate, to get some laws passed; we are already integrated, and we already have our laws, our regulations. There isn't any race problem here, no matter what you say. There's been a work problem and a discipline problem and a care problem. Those are being cured." He waited a beat then looked at Baldwin. "Sergeant Baldwin, will you come here please."

The sergeant moved forward. He seemed a broken man.

"Sergeant Baldwin; you tell me now in front of these men. Were you fired because you were black?"

His words were a whip to Baldwin. He didn't speak.

"Sergeant Baldwin, be honest; was this installation in the shape it should have been?"

"No sir."

"Did I fire you because you were black?"

"No sir, I don't think so. But you could have given me a second chance."

"Yes, I could have, if I felt I had the time, and if I felt you could do it. I don't have the time and I don't think you could do it."

Sgt. Gifford Russell put up his hand.

"Sergeant Russell?"

"Sir, Sergeant Baldwin was like a father to us. He took care of everybody. He didn't have no supervision, so maybe he didn't do it like an officer might have, but he was mighty good to us."

"Russell, he wasn't here to be mighty good to you, and neither am I. We're here to run a radar station; we're here for a year, and during that time we've got two countries and two air forces depending on us. Don't tell me we can't do it, because we can. Baldwin knew what he had to do; he didn't do it."

Russell looked sullen. "Sir, you're not being fair to us blacks; we don't often get a black first sergeant, and when we get one we want to keep him."

"Goddamn it, Russell, you got a black commanding officer; you can't have everything!" The words simply escaped from Millard before he could stop them, but the crowd laughed a little. He realized that now he had a chance with them.

"Men, I'm giving it to you straight. I don't care if you are black or white, and I don't care if the first sergeant is. In the goddamn radar shack, we are all gray-green from the goddamn screen anyway. I'm here to do a job, and so are you. Look, maybe you guys don't understand what it is we really do here. I do. I depended on this station when I was flying combat; I talked to the controllers here, verifying my position, not an hour before I got shot down. I don't want some poor guy to be flying up north and not have us to depend on."

It was the right tone; spoiled as they were they couldn't argue with someone who had been shot down. Especially a black someone.

There were a couple of more questions, and Washington dismissed them. It had been rough—and potentially dangerous—on Sergeant Baldwin to brace him in front of the troops, but there wasn't any other way to handle it.

Alone in his quarters, Washington brooded later that night. They talked about the loneliness of command, he thought, but they never told you how it would actually feel, especially when it was a weird situation like this one. Or maybe they were all weird situations. Maybe that's why command was so special. He lay down on the uncomfortable bed, listening to the Korean wind whistle through the cracks in the walls, and wondered how it would all turn out. He worried about it all through the late hours, then finally fell asleep just before dawn.

The next morning, at breakfast, Lieutenant Wiley filled him in on the results of his showdown.

"Boy, you really had them going, Major." He dug into his chipped beef on toast, universally called SOS, for shit on a shingle. Millard sipped his vile coffee and waited for Wiley to continue. Instead, the young man chomped away, oblivious to Wash's agitation. Finally Millard slammed down his cup. Wiley started.

"Damn it, Lieutenant. What the hell went on?"

"Oh! Sorry, Major. I thought you had the word already."

"No, Lieutenant, I have not had the goddamn word, as you put it. What is it?"

"Well, sir, according to Bates, the men are all in line now, ready to get serious. He said—uh, he said, these were his exact words, 'The Major really called a spade a spade!' "

Washington erupted in laughter. Wiley never did figure out why. And six months later, Surgeon passed a surprise readiness inspection with the highest rating in the Far East.

20

October 1959
Wright-Patterson AFB, Ohio
USA

It was only with reluctance that Kathy had begun to accept that Ohio was beautiful and the Air Force an intriguing mixture of contradictions that even a wife could enjoy.

There had been no little irony for Kathy in returning to the state where she had started out her romantic life with a series of debacles. How on earth could something so fundamental and so pleasurable as sex have caused her so much trouble? She eased the Muntz around the hairpin turn in Route 201 that had spun her out in the ice storm last year. Now the only trouble it caused was kids, the regular cowlike dropping of offspring that was as much a part of Air Force life as the uniform. This was the last year for the Muntz; Mike Jr. was two years old, Renee was one, and there was a lump of indeterminate sex growing in her that would pop forth in about six months.

Shopping at the commissary had always irritated her in the past; now she accepted it as a part of the social ritual, a self-flagellating punishment that like castor oil was somehow supposed to help. The graduate student in her was never far below

279

the surface, and the commissary was a rich research source for her growing list of Air Force contradictions.

The commissary and the base exchange were both examples of the way the good intentions of the service tried to take care of people, and how individuals within the system managed to divert most of the good to their own pockets. They derived originally from attempts to provide frontier troops with something to sustain their families. Over the years the grasping sutlers had turned into grotesque bureaucracies that offered the illusion of savings but actually passed, with a few exceptions, inferior merchandise that could be found cheaper at discount houses in the civil market. There were certain exceptions, sensitive items like milk and cigarettes, which were genuinely cheaper, but these were too few to make a difference.

Kathy had done some comparison shopping, with the idea of writing a research paper when she went back to school—if she could ever stop having children long enough to get back to school. Item for item, brand for brand, the commissaries didn't save the shopper anything over the civil market. And there were inequities that shocked her. She'd picked up some prepackaged sirloin steaks, marked prime, but scarcely marbled with fat, and supposedly weighing two pounds four ounces. It seemed light, and when she weighed it on a scale it was five ounces under the listed weight. She took several packages and weighed them; all were underweight. A burly butcher in a bloodstained white apron whirled out and asked in almost menacing tones if he could help. She told him the problem, and he gave her a long song and dance about shrinkage, differences in scales, and difficult customers. With sirloin going for better than a dollar a pound, a four-ounce deficit on each package could mount up.

The base exchanges had other sorts of problems. There was never any difficulty getting clothes, as long as you were a midget or a giant; anything in between was never in stock. It looked as if the buyers took seconds from the wholesalers, and pushed them off on the stores. Kathy noted that it was customary for appliances—toasters, mixers, that sort of thing—to come in boxes that had been opened and resealed with tape. They were probably items returned at civilian stores, and either repaired, or passed on in the hope the service buyer would be too stupid to notice.

The real victims were the enlisted people. The officers, especially the ones like Mike on flying status, were at least on the low end of equity with civilian pay scales. They not only had a little income to investigate buying on the outside, they had the awareness to do it. The enlisted troops were simply exploited, tied by circumstance and distance to the base, and the commissaries and the exchanges were part of the exploitation.

Perhaps the saving grace was that the two institutions provided convenient on-base jobs for the wives of the enlisted people, and that these were generally genuinely nice and as helpful as they could be in the circumstances.

The touching thing was the delusion with which the two institutions were regarded. Each year Congress came out with threats to reduce the "privileges"; each year the service fought to keep them, with the retention being presented as a victory for the personnel.

The actual value probably was the reinforcement of the sense of community even she had felt today. The commissary—big, drafty, ill laid out, vegetables dry or rotting, anything reasonably desirable out of stock—was still where people met and commiserated. Civilians were excluded, and the general economic poverty was concealed from the outside world. It was compensated for by the comradeship and the esprit de corps of the hardship and the phantom benefits.

Yet it seemed to work; somehow the prospect of doing something for the country, of engaging in the apparently purposeful exercise of airpower, appealed to the people involved, and there was very little complaining. She had made herself unpopular early in their married life by calling attention to the irregularities and anomalies she saw. It was bad form, and she soon learned to keep her observations to herself.

She drove slowly down the twisting streets of Huber Heights, the red-brick houses almost painfully well maintained, flowers and shrubs symmetrically placed, grass clipped to the precise two-inch height favored by the new crop of rotary motors. Mary Martin came over on the radio with a cloying list of "her favorite things" and she snapped it off.

When she pulled in from her social-commentary commissary run, almost submerged in the paper bags of a week's worth of groceries, she found Kelly dancing on the lawn, little Mike riding his shoulders, Renee pressed like a sword at his side. Typically, he didn't wait to spill the news. He raced up to her, kissed her, and danced around, yelling, "Pack your bags, Kathy, we're off to Edwards Flight Test!

"The big time at last! California at last! If we get there in a hurry, we can have a wild weekend at Las Vegas on the way!"

They had begun their honeymoon a little before the marriage in Las Vegas, and they both recalled it with fondness.

Still her heart sank as they hugged; it was a great thing for him, if he lived through it. She had hoped he'd get out of flight test after his work at Wright-Pat.

The next few weeks followed a familiar pattern of throwing things out, calling realtors, and farewell parties. Despite the kids and the pregnancy, Kathy was serving as a substitute teacher and had been asked to finish out the term. So Mike left her to take care of the kids, sell the house, supervise the move, and join him later. If he was lucky, he'd get a few days off to fly back and help her with the drive out.

In a last-minute switch, Kelly sold the convertible and picked up a big nine-passenger Country Squire Ford station wagon. As usual, the salesman packed everything on it he could find in the parts bin, and Kathy groaned when what appeared to be a chrome and fake-wood-finned ocean liner pulled up in the drive. Mike was totally pleased with it and was sure she was delighted.

The Muntz ran well on the way to Edwards, and for once Mike took time to chart his Air Force course. The whole country was toppling into a panic over scientific education after *Sputnik*, and the Air Force was no exception. Yet it seemed to him that piloted aircraft were going to be around for at least as long as he was. Computers were essential for discrete tasks; they never would have gotten the McDonnell F-101, the Voodoo, sorted out without a computer to solve the pitch-up problems. But the main computer was always the pilot, in flying, in shooting, in solving emergencies. And after AFIT, he had a little appreciation for his own brain's computer qualities.

The country was changing as he drove; he stopped for two days in St. Louis, where he had placed his mother in a retirement home. It was grim, but after his dad's death she had really not been able to take care of herself, and she didn't seem to notice her surroundings. He felt nothing but guilt at his relief to be on his way. He loved her as one must love a mother, but there was nothing he could do for her now, just as there was never anything she could have done for him. Two people, one family, zero lives.

West of St. Louis, the highway system began to improve dramatically; Kelly missed the buccaneer boldness of the old Route 66; the new highways were antiseptic. In the West, the wonderful old stores where you could see dragons (an aging king snake with a fake ruffle) were replaced by sterile restaurant/

282

filling-station/restroom stops. But the scenery and the air were still wonderful, every horizon evoking a memory of a flight.

Kelly's reception at Edwards was cool; if he had come straight from Korea he would have been warmly welcomed, but the tour in Dayton was a stigma. There was only one Flight Test Center, Edwards, and only one way to do it, Edwards way. Dayton was the sticks and Wright-Patterson was where they tested the obsolete stuff; or so the story went.

And in a few weeks, Kelly began to see that they were right. He was one of seventeen pilots in the class, fourteen from the Air Force, one from the Navy, one from the RAF, and one from the French air force. They were not only the best pilots he had ever seen, they were the best engineers. Squadron Leader Robin Lucas had been through the RAF Test Pilot school, so the course was a breeze. Captain Françoise-Wachter had similar experience in France. Kelly began to wonder what he was doing there.

He had no difficulty with the flying portion of the course, or with the mathematics; his problem lay in not analyzing succinctly what the airplane was telling him. At Wright-Patterson, the test reports had been more subjective; at Edwards it was a clinically objective recording of facts. Hating it, he put in a minimum effort.

There was no way to get away to bring Kathy back. He called her, glad that there were almost two thousand miles between them when he gave her the news.

"You mean I've got to drive that barge across country, pregnant, with two kids, and two dogs? Why the hell didn't you wait to buy a car until I got there? I could have flown out."

"No, it'd be worse—you can't get here from there by commercial air. Maybe you could leave the kids and the dogs at the vet, and we'll pick them up next year?"

"Very funny. It's always easy for you to be funny when I've got the short end of the deal."

She slammed down the phone. An hour later he called again and they made up.

The trip out was actually pleasant; the big Ford, a bear around town, had performed well on the road, and she was able to spread everybody out enough to keep the fights down to two or three an hour. She was carsick herself briefly, but by the time she hit Oklahoma City, she felt like a veteran traveler. One thing for sure, the Air Force taught the women to be independent.

She was only mildly appalled at the flat-top cracker box he

had rented for them. It sat with three dozen others on a little hill, where the junior officers who couldn't get base housing gathered together. The most it had to recommend it was the swamp cooler, a roof-mounted rig where water dripped through straw pads and was blown by a noisy drum fan through the house, keeping it cool and moist except at noon on the hottest days. They settled in happily, Kathy quickly learning the local drill of club, swimming pool, and shopping. Kelly was immersed in his flying. It was a relief for her not to be teaching now, as General Custer, as Mike had named the prospective addition, grew restive inside.

Mike was sitting on the metal lawn chair, still hot from the sun, when Kathy slumped in the chaise longue beside him.

"Mike, I don't want to interfere with your studies, but something peculiar is going on inside. Either I'm getting allergic to tuna salad, or General Custer is getting ready to join us a little early."

He tossed the manual aside, grinning. "Are you sure? And are you sure it's mine? I was leaving you alone a lot in Dayton."

"Yes, you swine, I'm sure and I'm sure it's yours. I can feel its knobby bulging forehead already."

"If it's my son, that's not his forehead."

They were pleasantly excited; Mike fussed about getting her kit ready. They joked about their two standard kits, his for TDYS, hers for BABYS. They flagged Elizabeth, the next-door neighbor, to babysit and dog sit and headed for the hospital. On the way they reminisced about how they had worried when they were first married; worried that one or the other was infertile, and they had begun an almost clinical attempt to do all the things *Good Housekeeping* said to do to get pregnant. It was fully six months till the first pregnancy was assured, and Mike had steamed out to the base the next day in a fit to tell everybody. Now it was so routine that a premature birth was just another event.

General Custer turned out to be Barbara, six pounds two ounces and looking almost full term; Kathy figured they must have miscounted. She went through the usual spartan military hospital drill, up the day after the delivery to make her bed. It was no-frills birthing; you came in, had your baby, and got out, to make way for the next one on the production line. In the movies, it seemed that the mother was always surrounded by white lace, soft lights, and adoring looks; in the Air Force the delivery motif was more on the order of an oil change for your car.

Kelly found a subtle mood change on the flight line when he got back. He was distanced by everybody, from the normally friendly airmen clerks to the ops officer. Something was in the wind, and it soon surfaced.

Maj. Frank Bradley, a lean, wiry little man with breath like a camel's, clued him in. Bradley ran the academic section, and he caught Kelly in the tiny library, reading *Aviation Week* when he should have been working his slide rule.

"Kelly, we've got to talk."

Kelly edged a little away.

"Listen, Kelly, your grades are good, and your flying is great, but you are going to wash out of this program in the next few weeks unless you improve your paperwork drastically."

Mike was hurt and surprised. "What do you mean, wash out, Major? I'm not having any problems flying or in school."

"You think not, but you are. You are not taking the time you need to think things through; you're trying to hustle and get ahead of the program, and you are taking shortcuts in your analysis. And you are sloppy as hell."

He tossed down a file of Kelly's recent test flight reports. "Look at this garbage; you've used a soft pencil, smeared it all over, erased it—this one has a *hole* erased in it, for Christ's sake. Didn't they teach you anything at Wright-Pat?"

"We were more worried about the flying than pushing a pencil."

"Yeah, and that's why they are Wright-Pat and we are Edwards. You can't fly a precise flight profile, then write it up like you're in fifth grade."

Kelly was chagrined. He'd never considered the paperwork to be more than a penance.

"Look, it extends to a lot of other things too. I checked your personal equipment; it's dirty, your mask hasn't been inspected, your G suit has a worn capstan. You are simply not sharp enough to be an Edwards graduate. We've got an image, a reputation to maintain, and you, my friend, quite frankly, don't fit the image. I'm sorry, but I've got to level with you now, while you've got one more chance."

Panic flooded Kelly; he hadn't been talked to like this since Holy Angels. Bradley was being matter-of-fact; there was no doubt that he was serious. Mike felt sick. He wanted this as much as he'd wanted his wings. There were no smart-ass answers in him when he replied. "Okay, Major, you win, I'll try. No, I'll do it. I'll be the sharpest sonofabitch you ever saw."

"Kelly, I'm not kidding you. You shape up in the next two weeks, or we'll have to let you go. I don't want to see that, but I've been in this business too long to let you get by. It's a waste of money, and you might hurt someone. Two weeks, no B.S."

Kelly was crushed. He had not had a failure since going to flight school. He got mad, thought about getting drunk, and then sulked.

Kathy couldn't get him to talk to her. It was her "first day back full time on the job," and she had fixed her famous rolled enchiladas. She knew he was in trouble when he barely touched them. Normally he finished off the tray with two or three beers, then lay around cursing himself for being a pig. Instead he nibbled at one, skipped his coffee and stomped into the ten-by-ten bedroom he shared with the baby as an office, slamming the door.

Kelly sat at the card-table desk; he carefully propped the wobbly leg with a folded piece of paper, and took out their checkbook. It was as if he had never seen it before. Half the stubs had no entries; most of the rest were so cryptic he couldn't decipher what the check was for.

He pulled a box out from under the spare bed, and resurrected his last year's income tax file. Kelly pawed through his work sheets; they were indecipherable.

The next morning when Kathy went in to clean up the bathroom she almost fainted. The washbasin was sparkling, Mike's towel was folded up instead of sopping wet beside the shower, the mirror had been wiped clean. It was the first time that she had ever worried about him except when he was flying.

Bradley worked with Kelly for two weeks; he reviewed every bit of paper, from performance calculations to flight plans to reports. He broke Kelly's bad habits with savage public critiques that left him squirming.

It worked. Kelly graduated number nine, precisely at the midpoint of the class; he knew if he'd met Bradley sooner, he'd have been number one.

The Edwards flight line was an endless expanse of concrete, punctuated by plain steel hangars housing the most advanced collection of aircraft in the world. The days started early, with the dawn turning the sage Zane Grey purple, and ground crews hustling to get their exotic charges ready for flight. By ten o'clock most of the day's fighter flight tests were completed; only the ones that had maintenance problems were still waiting to launch, cockpit temperatures rising to 150 degrees, the heat shimmering everywhere in glaucous whirls. The big airplanes, bombers and cargo types, got off at daybreak, and would reappear between eleven and twelve. There was a stand-down while the heat made the field unbearable, distorting performance figures, and rendering the metal too hot to touch. About four, there would be another flurry of action, preparation for the few evening flights.

Kelly got all the donkey tests, just as he expected. Mostly he flew chase, in either a T-33 or an F-86, riding herd on the crop of new fighters, F-102s, F-104s, and once in a while, on the B-52 carrier plane for the X-15. When Carl Shaftner called him in for his own first primary test assignment, Kelly thought the big, rawboned light colonel was joking.

"Mike, we've got a classified project that I can't even tell you about yet, but it involves getting the same set of data points on two very different airplanes."

"If I don't know what the project is, how can I do a decent job?"

"You'll know before too long; the clearance is so sensitive that the weenies at Air Staff want to look at the first sets of data before they decide to go on. You won't need to know what the project is unless they decide to proceed."

"Suits me. What do I fly, a 102?"

"No, not exactly. You might not have heard of either airplane; they are obsolete, and we've pulled them out of the boneyard to refurbish for these tests. One's the XB-51, and the other is the F10."

Mike knew the XB-51, a three-engine jet tactical bomber from Martin, a hot airplane. He thought they had all crashed.

"What's an F10?"

"It's a Grumman, a Navy job with a variable-sweep wing. They called it the Jaguar; tested it about five years ago, and it didn't pan out. Looks like a guppy with thyroid trouble."

"Great, two obsolete planes and both failures."

"The Martin wasn't a failure, Mike; it was a roaring success. But there were political problems. The old man, Glenn Martin, who founded the company, had sided with the Navy carrier admirals against the B-36, and Vandenberg never forgave him. It was—and is—one hell of an airplane."

"I don't see the connection between the two."

"No, neither do I, but I have a good idea, judging by what they're asking you to do. But don't worry about it, you can do the flight profiles without knowing what they are for. It's a tough program, but do-able. Incidentally, they call it 'Project Combo'; you'll see why."

They rode in silence in Shaftner's jeep to the end hangar on the flight line; a jeep for your own use was the height of privilege and prestige. Mike wondered if he'd ever rate one. A young Air Policeman carefully checked their papers before waving them on with a quick grin that said he knew them both but was just doing his job.

Inside the hangar, two thoroughly disreputable-looking airplanes were almost covered by mechanics trying to get them into flying shape.

"I'll level with you, Mike; the F10F was pulled off an artillery range; it was a static test article and has never flown. The prototype, the XF10F, had a difficult test program, and was deliberately destroyed in crash barrier tests. The XB-51 was a magnificent airplane, could have set all kinds of records, and should have been put into production. One crashed on takeoff in El Paso—pilot error—and this one was used here for test work until the maintenance problems got too bad. The last time we used it was in a Hollywood movie as some kind of advanced new fighter. Since then it's been sitting behind this very hangar, leaking fluid and tires getting flat."

"Didn't they get a lot of data on these airplanes when they were testing them? I don't see how we could learn much more given the condition they are in."

"Well. You know that statistical analysis is all the rage today, and the brilliant leadership in Washington has come up with a statistical model for a new airplane that sort of combines the characteristics of these two airplanes. Unfortunately, none of the remaining paperwork has the data points they need to complete the statistical model. That's what you are supposed to do."

They walked around the hangar. Martin had developed the tandem gear used on the B-47, and the XB-51 used the same awkward-looking arrangement. The engines were slung against the huge fuselage like teats on a bat, and a third engine was mounted in the rear, nestled under the vertical stabilizer which supported a big T tail.

Shaftner pointed up to the swept wing. "This thing first flew in 1949; it was the hottest tactical bomber in the world, and it would still be competitive. Look how the wing has a variable incidence, for shorter takeoffs and landings. The amazing thing is that they area-ruled it by accident; F-86s could barely keep up with it."

They poked around the big Martin; Kelly noted that most of the equipment bays were empty, that oil and hydraulic fluid seeped from odd places. When they crawled up into the tiny cockpit, with its F-80 size canopy, he was appalled. The instrumentation was almost gone; holes gaped where instrumentation had been, and wire bundles poked through empty sockets.

"Christ, I've seen better airplanes than this being cut up for scrap metal."

"It's not as bad as it looks, Kelly; they've removed everything from it that won't be necessary for the tests, to get it as light as possible. The only instrumentation that will go in will be the stuff you need to pick up for the missing data points. You'll understand this when the Air Staff team comes in to brief you."

If the XB-51 looked disreputable, the XF-10 was a whore. The blue paint had peeled and the outline of a Jaguar leered from behind the cockpit. It was a positively porcine airplane; the swollen fuselage was topped by a delta-shaped stabilizer perched precariously on top of the vertical fin like an afterthought. The proximity to the Martin emphasized its blimpish shape; both airplanes had wingspans of about fifty feet, but the bomber's fuselage was almost twice as long.

"Grumman was ahead of its time with this one; it had a variable-sweep wing, and they had to build this fat fuselage to contain the mechanism."

Kelly looked dubiously at the airplane; two main wheels were missing, and the cockpit was vacant—no seat, no instruments, just wire bundles lolling like hollyhock stalks.

"It looks like it will be a while before they are ready."

"No, the test program starts in three weeks; they'll be ready for what they have to do."

The Air Staff team arrived the next week. To Kelly's disgust, Duke Brown led the team, but the mathematics were being done by Capt. Harvey Sunderman. Duke had been incensed in the Pentagon when he heard who the test pilot was going to be; he tried to get it changed but couldn't. Edwards ran its own programs and bitterly resisted any interference in what it considered to be "internal affairs."

They met in the briefing room.

"Hello, Mike, long time no see. I hear you did a great job in Korea."

Duke stuck out his hand with what seemed to be obvious and honest pleasure. Kelly was nonplussed.

"I asked for you especially when I found out you were here,"

Duke said. "I remember you used to specialize in low-level work in flying school." It was part of Duke's style; if you couldn't lick them, join them, a little B.S. could go a long way. There was always another day for revenge.

Kelly flushed; he couldn't tell if he was being kidded or not. That bothered him more than Duke himself. Sunderman, a small curly-haired man who looked out of place without a beard, had a habit of sticking his tongue out. Kelly looked at him with distaste. "Yeah, well, I can hardly wait to hear what I'm supposed to do with those two revived ashcans you selected for this program."

"We didn't select the airplanes, Mike; it was just a forcing function of what we have to get. Let's get started."

They went through the formalities of checking clearances and turning the Top Secret briefing light on. Kelly watched with some detachment; they'd probably read the results of the meeting in the next issue of *Aviation Week*. The whole industry was porous; no secrets could be kept.

Brown started off with a chart showing the rise in aircraft costs; bare-bone B-17s had been built for a couple of hundred thousand dollars, B-47s for three million, B-52s for six. When you added the engines, electronics, and other equipment and spares, those numbers almost tripled. The next generation of bombers were threatening to cost tens of millions. The same was true of fighters; Mustangs had delivered for about fifty thousand; the newest fighters cost millions.

"DOD is getting businesslike. McNamara is trying to make the services think in corporate terms. He wants to develop a new fighter that will serve both the Air Force and the Navy in several missions. That way we can build them in enough quantity to get the unit cost down. The program's current designation is TFX, for Tactical Fighter, Experimental."

He paused, then turned the sheet. "Gentlemen, here's what the various companies are proposing. Douglas, Boeing, General Dynamics, Fairchild, McNaughton, McDonnell, and Grumman all had ideas on what was needed; most looked about the same. They were all big two-place airplanes with two engines and wings that pivot to about a forty-five degree sweep.

"The Air Staff wants to take it one step further, and we're working with McNaughton only. It's too hot to let out. Once the concept is developed, then we'll compete it generally."

Kelly snorted to himself. Yeah, and McNaughton will only have a two-year head start. A stacked deck.

He flicked another chart on the viewer. It showed the McNaughton entry with plugs placed in the fuselage fore and aft, lengthening it by about fifteen feet. The change made it a better-looking airplane.

Brown changed charts. The new image showed a three-man crew and a big bomb bay; the designation became TMTS for Tri-mission, Tri-service.

Sunderman started talking. "The preliminary figures show that you could introduce the bomber version on the production line sometime after the first one hundred forty-four fighters were built; this would be in about 1965, when the early B-52s will be coming to the end of their operational lives.

He flicked charts. "We'd start building one bomber for every four fighters, then as the fighter squadrons got their complement, we'll switch to one for two, and finally just build bombers only. We figure we'd save at least five years in development time on the bomber, and probably several billion in development costs."

Brown broke in. "The big savings come in tooling, spares, and training; everybody can use this, Navy, Marines. It's the only way to go."

"Why did you pick the XB-51 and the F10F? What do they have in common with this monster?"

"Good question. The main thing is the variable-sweep wing on the F10F and the variable incidence on the Martin; you can't see it on the drawings, but the McNaughton is the only one that combines these two features. The rest have only variable sweep."

Sunderman broke in. "It's also a matter of scale and weight distribution. If you melded the XB-51 and F10F weight and dimensions, you'd get about a half-scale TMTS—we're pronouncing that "Tempts" for P.R.—and we think we can extrapolate some hard data that will sell the program."

Kelly objected. "I'm new at this, but it looks like a pretty half-ass approach to me. Why don't you take one of the early fighters off the production line and experiment with that?"

"Too much lost time, Kelly, and I'm not sure any company other than McNaughton would be willing to risk it. I'll level with you. McNaughton has to win this competition or get out of the airplane business and into aluminum siding. They've got every dollar they can borrow wrapped up into this; if they don't hit it there will be twenty thousand jobs lost in Nashville. The Air Staff doesn't want to lose their capability. All the other companies have plenty of work, and plenty coming on; Boeing and Douglas are making a mint on the civil side, and so is Fairchild; McDonnell is selling their F-4 to the Navy and have orders coming in from all over the world. It's just sound business policy."

Kelly burned. He wanted to say, Yeah, and you're married to the Nashville district's congressman's daughter, but he didn't dare. Still, he had to admire Brown's poise. There was nothing to suggest that this was anything but an exercise in the best interest of the Air Force. He probably believed it.

"There's one more kicker in this, Kelly; the bomber version is going to have to have an automatic low-level capability—and I mean low, like in fifty feet or less the whole route into the target. McNaughton's developing a terrain-following system that will put the airplane down into the toughest ride possible. That's another reason we picked these two airplanes; they are rugged as hell because we didn't have all the computer design assistance to tailor parts that we do today. Most of their components are oversize, so they won't go to pieces when you are pounding across the desert."

"Terrific. One's a retired hangar queen, the other was being used for target practice, and I've got to show how strong they are."

Sunderman put his hand out. "Wait a minute. We've worked this out pretty carefully; we don't see any danger."

"No, not for you, maybe. Have you seen the pieces of junk you've picked for this?" His challenge caught them both off guard. He waited a beat, then said, "I thought not. Come with me."

Kelly led them out to the hangar; both Brown and Sunderman had the good grace to look chagrined when they saw the airplanes.

"I'll do the test program, but not until these clunkers are fixed to my satisfaction, and not until I get a few hours in each one to see what they are like."

In the next three months, Kelly finally had to admit that Brown had written a good test plan, and that the airplanes were the right subjects. It was funny about airplanes; no matter how bad they were, you got to love them if you flew them for a while. The XB-51 was a pure delight; he couldn't understand why the Air Force had not bought a flock of them, no matter what the politics. It was maneuverable as a fighter, had a terrific rate of climb, and with slightly bigger engines could probably have been supersonic. The Jaguar was different; every time he flew it he thought of the old joke about the fat girl who didn't sweat too much.

292

The bulk of the test program consisted of low-level flights across the test ranges, always during the hottest part of the day. Neither airplane had functional air conditioning, and Kelly finally stopped wearing his flying suit, strapping on the chute right over his underwear. It was stupid; if there was a fire he would regret it, but he couldn't take the cockpit temperatures otherwise.

The tests took longer than scheduled because of the maintenance problems. It was difficult to get parts for either airplane, and Kelly often had to stand down. He asked for and got a chance to fly as a back-up in the flight tests of the McDonnell F-4, the Phantom II, a big, ugly twin-engined Navy plane which was being surreptitiously evaluated by the Air Force. It was one hell of an airplane, and he wondered why the Air Force didn't go ahead and buy it.

Kathy patted her slowly flattening stomach with pride. What with tennis, swimming and riding herd on four kids—Mike, Mike Jr., Renee, and Barbara—she was getting back in shape. Their sex life had picked up again, and she was going to be damn careful this time.

Mike had never seemed happier; whatever he was doing agreed with him, and he was going through his proud-papa routine for the third time even though he finally had to give up his cherished shared office to Barbara's sole use. Somehow things were better than she had bargained for.

She had always intended to carve her own career, to be a professor in some nice college, writing. Now she saw her task as keeping Mike straight and level, peeling the pressure from him, somehow helping him to do his job. It was totally unlike her own image of herself, yet it was enough. Especially here, where the pressures were greater, but he seemed to be doing better in coming to terms with himself and with life.

Even as they had been married she had worried that Mike's moodiness would be tough to handle. It was the flying that helped, the responsibility the Air Force heaped on him. She wondered if wives of people in normal jobs felt the same way. Did an accountant's wife feel sympathetic to a ledger? She doubted it. One night she asked him. "How come you're so happy here, Mike?" She rolled her eyes and pointed around the little room, crowded with their furniture and needing paint.

"Who wouldn't be happy with you, darling, with your little round bottom and little fat stomach?"

"My God, you make me sound like a dachshund puppy. Take another look, that's a starlet's stomach. Well, maybe just a movie star's. But no, your black moods are mostly gone. I can remember days back at Dayton when I thought you were going to shoot you or me, one or both."

"It's the work, my babe; I've got to have something that absorbs me, and this is it. I wish I could tell you about it; I will someday." He fell silent, then continued. "I know it's tough on you; this is hardly Paradise Alley. But it's a big step forward for me. I'm really beginning to understand what they were trying to tell me in school. I thought I understood before, but now, every day, I learn something . . . genuine, something important. I just can't express how much that means."

She considered it gravely. "But you're beating yourself to death; you must have lost twenty pounds in the last four months, despite all that Budweiser you swill."

"You have a way with words: 'swill,' indeed, I'm just restoring my fluid levels. No, I'm doing stuff nobody else has done, and nobody else will get to do for a while, and I'm doing it well. Best of all they know it and they can't take it away from me."

It was true. For these tests, to get the right rough air conditions to make the data meaningful, Kelly would take off around noon. The XB-51 would lumber down the fifteen-thousand-foot runway overloaded with fuel, and Mike would peel off directly for the desert ranges that surrounded Edwards. On some flights he wouldn't get higher than fifteen feet off the ground until he came back to enter the pattern. In the 115 degrees of heat the old bomber creaked and groaned as it jolted across arroyos, through sand storms and dust devils, flying at 550 m.p.h., bouncing Mike around the cockpit. He was literally a hundredth of a second from death for two hours at a time. Then he'd come back and repeat the same flight with the Jaguar, a little slower, but no different in feel.

The next day he'd do the same flight, with a slight adjustment on the incidence of the B-51, and a small variation in the sweep of the F10F. Black boxes, strain gauges, and telemetry picked up the data; he couldn't make any notes because he had to keep both hands on the controls to make sure a sudden gust didn't slam him into the ground. He had a voice recorder, but he was jounced around the cockpit so much that it rarely got what he was saying.

Twice he almost bought it. The first time, he had flown across a patch of brilliant white sand that had reflected up the heat during the day; when he hit the area there was an updraft that he corrected for. Almost immediately, the sand had turned into black volcanic rock that sponged heat into a downdraft that almost coincided perfectly with his control input. The airplane sagged and the B-51's belly kicked up a trail along the ground, demolishing cactus and turning Kelly's insides into pulp as he heard the booming rush. That afternoon he looked at the underside of the airplane; the metal was scoured bright by the contact. Another inch lower and the ground would have sucked him into it, grinding the whole airplane, and him, into sintered mush.

The other incident occurred in the jaguar; he was preoccupied, working with the wing-sweep mechanism, when a vulture smashed into the canopy. He pulled straight back on the stick and rocketed up to ten thousand feet before he knew what happened. The airplane was grounded for six weeks, waiting to get a replacement canopy modified to fit.

In the interim he scrounged more flights in the F-4. It had teething problems, mainly with the automatic inlets and with the brakes, but it was one hell of an airplane. He wished he were assigned to it, rather than Brown's program.

Brown was furious with the results of Kelly's testwork. The numbers were not what he wanted to see. The variable incidence of the XB-51 didn't seem to offer a significant advantage except in the reduction of takeoff and landing rolls, and even there it was not decisive. Sunderman had worked every permutation of the numbers, desperately trying to find an advantage.

Finally, Duke got on the long line with Kelly. "Mike, we need to get some wider spreads on these numbers; can you increase your airspeed in the F10?"

"Jesus, I'm flying both of those mothers full out; the goddamn skin creaks and I'm nearly overtemping the F10. There's nothing left. Besides, I don't think there's enough aileron control in either one to go faster even if I could. They stiffen up and about all I've got left is the elevator. It's just like the B-47; I think we're getting into aileron reversal and the controls just lock up."

Kelly couldn't believe the next set of instructions he got. He was to initiate the test runs at five thousand feet, then dive to the deck to pick up another seventy-five knots airspeed. He called Brown. "Duke, are you trying to kill me? If I pick up another seventy-five knots I'll be flying a goddamn missile, and I don't know if I can even level off just fifteen feet off the ground."

"You can handle it, Mike. Ease into it; try building up in twenty-five-knot increments. If it looks bad, we'll forget it."

Kelly was scared, and he didn't like to fly scared. It was one thing to look at a bunch of points on graph paper and quite another to point a rebuilt crock at the desert floor and slam down in a dive.

He began with five-knot increments, diving from one thousand feet, then building up till the point he had added fifty knots to the top speed.

He called Brown in the Pentagon. "Duke, I don't know if it's worth it; I get about six hundred indicated in the B-51, and about five hundred in the F10, but it bleeds off in just a couple of minutes; the drag rise is real high, and it's dangerous as hell."

"Look, Sunderman says he can make some interpretations that will really help, if you can just get a few more knots out of the airplanes. We're doing our best here to get what we need with a minimum of extra flights."

Doing their best, Kelly thought. Well, shit, they both flew B-26s in Korea, so they weren't like some of the bastards who never pushed anything but pencils. But he wasn't going to kill himself for them.

One morning Kelly sat in the Grumman at five thousand feet. The test called for full sweepback on the wing; he pushed it into a dive, and watched the airspeed indicator build to five hundred knots. As he pulled out, just above the ground, cactus and sage streaming by in a never-ending belt, the airplane pitched up violently. Gravity slammed him into his seat; almost instinctively, he pulled the ejection handles and fired. The mottled blue Jaguar lurched upward, wings shedding from the fuselage as Kelly's underwear-clad body shot up. The specially installed Martin-Baker ejection seat worked perfectly, kicking him free from his seat and deploying the chute.

His legs were spread as he speared through the outstretched arms of a saguaro cactus into unconsciousness.

Kathy flinched when she saw the blue staff car drive up. If Mike's killed himself I'm going to be furious. She thought of the three kids and then felt the pain. "He's okay, Kathy." Shaftner's first words were a blanket of relief. "Mike ejected, and he's got some lacerations from getting too close to a cactus, but everything's copacetic. Let's go see him."

Kelly was in traction, his legs spread apart; his face was swollen. He was hardly copacetic. But he was alive.

"God, honey, are you okay?"

"Yeah, except for the fact we'll never have sex again, everything's fine."

The cactus had planted a dozen spines in Kelly's crotch, and another hundred down both sides of his thighs.

"Are *you* okay?" He grabbed her arm, pulled her to him, and kissed her.

She giggled. "Talk about just desserts."

The relief at finding him alive and joking set a laugh mechanism tumbling. She slumped in the chair, giggling uncontrollably.

Mike laughed too, through the pain.

"Jesus, honey, next time I'll kill myself and we'll really have a ball."

Kathy burst into tears and began kissing him. Even through the pain, Mike got signals that he would love again.

The data Mike had gotten in the last few flights were marginal, but with some assumptions, Sunderman made all the data points fit into a convincing performance envelope. The TMTS could be made to look like a low-cost worldbeater, but the timing had to be just right. The possibilities had to be announced before the TFX competition officially opened, but not so long that the other companies would have a chance to do the necessary engineering.

Kelly was glad to have the TMTS behind him, and once recovered spent his days flying the F-4 and the Vought XF8U-3. He couldn't tell which one he liked better, but they were both good. It was a desperate business for the contractors, for the winner would be fixed for life, the loser might be forced out of the fighter business. He liked the Vought as a dogfighter; it had an internal gun and an old ace liked having a gun. But the F-4 had two engines and more capability. It was almost a toss-up, but he leaned toward the McDonnell fighter, ugly as it was.

In the briefing room, Kelly was told he had a long-distance phone call. He was startled to hear from Brown, who hadn't even called to see how he was after the ejection, or when he was promoted to major.

"Mike, I want you to come to the Air Staff next week; we're briefing on the TMTS program, and I'd like you to be there to answer questions. Any problems?"

"No, I'll be there. What does it look like?"

"We're looking pretty good; we can show some tremendous savings over the life cycle of the aircraft, and the best thing is it's right in line with the secretary of defense's ideas on commonality and cost saving. We'll even be able to sell these to the Brits and the Aussies, if we can get the unit price right."

Kelly flew back east in a T-33, trying to guess what the questions would be. He didn't think the XB-51 and F10 tests had proved anything except that old airplanes would only go so fast, but he didn't have access to the data.

The secretary of defense was a remote figure of almost legendary proportions to the troops in the field, and he was there in person. It was the first time Kelly had ever seen him, and he was impressed with his cool, totally businesslike demeanor. While they were setting up the briefing, the secretary was working through a stack of papers. He read rapidly, scribbled notes, then handed off the pages to his aides.

Brown's briefing was superb. He provided enough data to give the secretary a basis for evaluation, without appearing to preach. The secretary was notoriously demanding; he wanted concise facts and no embroidery.

Brown concluded with a pitch to expand the TFX competition to a TMTS competition; his estimate was for a fifteen-billion-dollar saving over the next seven years, with a tremendous increase in capability.

The secretary didn't say anything, sat there looking at the numbers. Brown took a chance. "Mr. Secretary, I have the test pilot, Major Kelly, of the Combo program, here if you'd like to ask him any questions."

There was no response. Almost fifteen minutes went by as the secretary studied the charts and leafed through the supporting documentation Brown and Sunderman had provided. Gen. "Ham" Hamel, who had overall responsibility for aircraft procurement, looked at Brown with some disquiet; it was taking too long. If the boss was spending this much time thinking, it was probably about a problem, not a plus.

Finally the secretary looked around.

"Major Kelly?" he said.

"Yes sir." Mike hated these briefings; he'd rather be pulling the handles in the F10.

"What do you think about these figures? Is the TMTS the thing we should do?"

Kelly steeled himself. He was sending his career out the window. They could never forgive him if he didn't follow the party line. And he didn't know what the secretary wanted to hear. He was an outsider. He coughed. To hell with it. "Excuse me, sir, I have to be honest on this. Sir, I don't believe that this idea is basically sound. You can't make one airplane do six different jobs; it's like having a sports-car/ dump truck. It won't work."

He felt the room go quiet; the secretary leaned forward. This was not the party line; his boss had been the foremost TFX advocate. Kelly could sense Brown and Hamel conferring.

The secretary coughed in turn. "Major Kelly, I appreciate your philosophic views, but we've had a lot of discussions about commonality here in the past. What I want to know is your views on the TMTS aircraft proposal."

"Yes, sir, I'm going to do that, but in a minute. First I have to set the record straight on the whole bomber-and-fighter idea, at least the way I see it."

The secretary slumped back in his chair, resigned. You could see he wished he hadn't asked.

"Sir, as you know, we have problems the enemy doesn't have; we need airplanes with range and firepower to interdict their lines of supply. They defend against these with lightweight interceptors. The MiG 15 should have taught us that; the MiG 19 will, if we ever meet it in combat."

Hamel tried to interrupt; the secretary speared him with a glance. "Go on, Major, I can see I'm not going to get a short answer from you." His voice was quiet, almost metallic. His aides moved nervously; things like this could get out of control, and they had to spend the rest of the day with him.

"Sir, we're lucky that we've got an airplane that can go a long way and still be able to fight the MiGs; it just fights them differently. When we were flying F-86s against the MiG 15s, we depended upon pilot skill to beat their maneuverability. We still have to do that, but we have to do it a different way, with energy maneuverability, and fighting in a vertical plane."

"I don't know what you mean, Major." The secretary didn't say that often.

"Sir, instead of turning with the MiGs, we've got to go up and down with them; it's difficult to describe, but it's partly a new way of fighting and partly an old way. The P-38s used to do it with Zeros, in a way. I can show you some diagrams that explain it. The best way to say it is you use the energy and the power of the F-4 to do vertical maneuvers that enable you to beat the horizontal maneuvers of lightweight MiGs."

"F-4s? That's a Navy fighter; don't tell me you are recommending a Navy fighter, Major?"

"Yes, sir, that's exactly what I'm telling you. What we ought to do is buy the McDonnell F-4; you could buy it right off the line and it would do half a dozen Air Force missions."

Brown and Hamel jumped to their feet.

"Sir!" Hamel's voice had gone up a full octave. "Major Kelly is out of line; he has no authority to make a comment like that and absolutely no basis for that recommendation."

The secretary stiffened and said, "Sit down, General." The words were ice cold.

"Major Kelly, you are out of line, but you are out of the Air Force line. It happens that your thinking on the F-4 is right in my line, and I'm going to want to talk with you some more. I see no reason why the ideas of commonality and procurement savings couldn't be applied to the F-4 as well as to the TFX. But, for the sake of the record, could I get you to give me your thoughts on the TMTS program? That's why we are here, and I'm sure General Hamel is dying to learn what you think."

Even while the secretary had been talking, Kelly realized what he had done. He'd shot his mouth off, trying to be honest; it would be regarded only as disloyalty. Well, too late now.

"Sir, in the whole TMTS program, I didn't see any data that told me a variable incidence would help in any material way, given the fact that we'll almost always be operating off prepared runways of a reasonable length. I haven't been able to give the data the analysis that Captain Sunderman has, but I know if you complicate a wing sweep with a variable incidence you have the possibilities of mechanical problems that won't quit. And I've been flying the F-4 and it is superb and ready to go."

It was done. His career was over. Fuck it.

The secretary stood up. "This briefing is over. I'll see General Hamel at four P.M. Major Kelly, I want a complete report from you hand-delivered to me personally by eight in the morning. I want you to write it and to show it to no one but me. Make sure it includes those diagrams you mentioned, and that it includes a positive recommendation, with no qualifications."

He shot out of the room, a flurry of assistant secretaries, colonels, and harried aides in his wake.

Brown stood in front of Kelly, red-faced, hands clenched. "What the hell are you doing, Kelly? You are just a goddamn jock; nobody told you to volunteer any opinions."

"Look, aren't we here to get the best airplane for the Air Force? I told him what I thought, and that's what I'm paid to do."

300

Hamel leaned forward. "You're paid to take orders, Major, and you're going to be getting some soon." Then he and his coterie stalked out. Mike was soon alone in the cold little room. Screw it. He'd done his best.

The orders came a week later. He was reassigned from Edwards to one of the last straight-wing F-84 units in the Air Force as a line pilot, at Whiteman, AFB, Missouri. Well, what the hell.

Kathy didn't see it that way. She was furious, and so was Shaftner. Kelly told them to cool it; he'd stepped on his foreskin, and there wasn't any sense fighting it.

Two weeks before he was supposed to leave, an amended set of orders came through, detailing him to Langley Air Force Base for a ninety-day official operational evaluation of the F-4C for the Air Force.

The secretary had listened. And the rest of the orders were his reprieve; he was being sent to Eglin AFB, Florida, to be an armament test pilot. He'd get to fly all the goodies in the inventory. By then he would have proved that the McDonnell F-4 fighter was what the Air Force needed. Sometimes it paid to speak up. The lesson was one he wouldn't forget.

21

19 January 1960
Castle AFB, California
USA

Louise tried to read between the lines of Wash's letters. If what he said was true, he was either winning a battle that would be good for his career, or about to be plunged into a dangerous, possibly catastrophic series of fights with higher headquarters. She hoped he knew what he was doing. But she read his letters with an odd sense of detachment, because other correspondence held her attention more firmly.

The other letters were from Lyle Johnson, the California state representative for CORE, the Congress of Racial Equality. He wanted her to become politically active in the small towns around Castle. The black population was small, but relatively affluent, and he felt her status as an Air Force officer's wife would be effective.

She was torn by his proposal; at one time in her life she thought she was going to marry Lyle; they were in school together in Spokane, and he was a mercurial radical student leader. He had wanted an affair, she had demanded marriage, and their friendship floundered on undelivered sex. She had been devastated. He had killed her by being philosophically good-natured about the split; she suddenly was aware that she might not have been his only interest. Now he wanted her help exactly in the area in which she wished to contribute it.

It was out of the question for the time being. She'd talked to Wash about her old relationship with Lyle; he'd be justifiably suspicious if she went to work with him while Wash was in Korea. And, she thought with a smile, with good reason. Wash's gentle persistence had brought her a sexual maturity; she missed his lovemaking, and she might be susceptible to Lyle's charms. It was better to drop the matter for a while.

There were other areas in which to make a contribution. Linda Birdsong lived next door, with kids exactly the same age as Louise's. Her husband was overseas, at Thule, and she was a nurse, too. Linda had proposed that they go down to Springwater Hospital, and hire on as nurses together, getting separate shifts to cover the babysitting. It was ideal. Nurses were in short supply, and Louise was bored with the officers'-club life when Wash was not there.

Merced was a classic California valley town, laid out in the perfect geometry of the railroad baron's rip-offs, with giant squares on either side of the track. The hospital was at the north edge of town, situated on the few acres of "high ground" and made verdant by a small meandering stream that disappeared entirely in the summer. It was twenty easy minutes from her house, down the back roads that provided faster passage than Route 99.

Linda was twittering with excitement, eager to get back to work. Louise glanced at their reflection in the storefront window; as a child she would never have expected to be walking down the main street of a city with a tall blond girl hanging on her arm, chattering in her ear. Some things had changed.

Linda must have been nearly six feet tall, with an enormous bosom and a shock of almost yellow hair that would have to be cut short if they got the job.

Their interview was set for two o'clock, so they treated themselves to lunch at Palomina's Mexican Diner, a converted White Castle that served the food that drove Wash wild. Wash loved all

Mexican food, even the greasy stuff sold from the soft-ice-cream stands, but when he found a good Mexican restaurant he practically lived there. Palomina's was good by any standard, and Luis, the owner, fell on her neck when they came in. "Ah, Mrs. Washington, what do you hear from El Major?"

"He sends his best, Luis, and wants you to send him a care package of chile rellenos."

He steered them, as he always did, to the table by the window, his "pregnancy table."

"You sit here, you get pregnant, but you got to wait till your husbands come back." It was his story—and Louise was sure it was his belief—that any woman who ate one of his special plates at that table was instantly susceptible to impregnation.

Partly to please Luis, they shared a combination plate—two tacos whose outer crispness collapsed in spurts of grease and spice, a chicken enchilada with a curious bite of cilantro and mole, chile relleño with coarse-cut pork, rice and raisins fighting the bonds of the monterey jack cheese, green corn tamale with chicken, olives, and nuts, rice and al dente beans. Following Wash's injunction to experiment, Louise tried a bowl of menudo, the spicy tripe "hangover" soup. They desperately wanted a bottle of Carta Blanca, but decided that it might not help at the interview. After they left they picked up two packs of gum.

The chief nurse, a buxom woman who looked like she might run a prison camp, chatted with them briefly, then declined to interview them. Louise was convinced that she must have a tattoo on her forearm and another on her bottom, neither of them dedicated to Mother. She gave them both questionnaires to fill out and excused herself.

A week later, Linda was waiting at the door when Louise came home from the beauty shop, hair short, jumping up and down with excitement. "Get the mail; let's see what your letter says."

Louise ran to the mailbox. There was a letter from Wash, as always, a couple of bills, nothing else.

"No matter, it'll come tomorrow. I'm supposed to go in Monday on the seven-to-three shift. If they give you a night shift, we'll trade, on and off."

Louise tensed. The night shift for the wife of the night fighter.

No letter came. She waited a few days, then called; the chief nurse told her brusquely that all the positions were filled.

Louise wrote two letters that night, one to Wash, telling him to take care of himself, one to Lyle saying she was ready to go to work.

22

As usual, the Picards were spending his leave at home. Don took a perverse pride in the fact that he had lost leave every year since he joined SAC; there was simply no way to get off without being called back. It didn't matter where you went, or how much distance you put between you and the base, if they needed you they found you. One fed-up major, a radar observer who hadn't had a decent vacation in five years, had gone on a fishing trip to Canada, packing in miles to try to get away from the pressure of duty. It turned out he needed another bomb run to meet his quarterly requirements, and SAC sent in the Mounties after him.

So it was better to loaf around the house, if a complete redo of the fifty-by-seventy-five-foot trailer space could be called loafing. He'd brought in another truckload of topsoil for the little garden he was so fond of, and had replaced the soil in the white-painted truck tires he used to grow pansies in. The trailer was immaculate, and Picard looked at it with some affection; no matter how much Polly hated it, it had kept them warm in the winter and cool in the summer, and that wasn't easy at Mountain Home.

Polly had a totally different point of view. They were within a hard day's drive from Reno, Seattle, or San Francisco; any one of them sounded like heaven to her. She would have liked to have gone to the Napa Valley, to the wine country, and if they'd called them back, so be it. At least they would have a real vacation.

She looked at the trailer differently, too. New housing projects were springing up everywhere, and she ached to have a permanent home, one where they could store a few things and where the kids would have a chance to roam without worrying about traffic. The other women in her circle shared the same problem. The husbands got an ego boost by being needed; not being able to take leave, or being called back, affirmed their importance. They bragged about the leave they lost every year. It was almost as if you were a shirker if you took what was coming to you. It was a strange masculine masochistic logic, one that said it's okay not to pay me enough, as long as you overload me with work. The women did not understand; they shared the hardships willingly, but were unable to share in the pride of being exploited.

Picard sensed a presence and groaned inwardly; it was Airman Ed Fink, hovering as usual on the perimeter of his lot. Picard considered him well named.

"Hey, Ed, come on in; Polly just put the coffee pot on."

Fink ducked in, his usual grin missing.

"What's the matter; got problems?"

"Yeah, Don, I got big problems. I got to talk to you, you got to help me."

Picard hoped he didn't want to borrow any money; lending money to an airman was death on efficiency, and he didn't have any to spare anyway. "Well, I will if I can. Let's go inside."

The trailer leaned slightly as Picard stepped on the single metal stair; it had settled, and he'd have to slip a shim under the concrete block foundation.

They sat down at the Formica panel that folded back up into the wall between meals; no space was wasted.

Fink took the coffee shyly; he refused a piece of Polly's coffeecake with obvious reluctance. She jollied him into taking two big slabs, then ducked out the door. Don played a major role as father confessor to the younger airmen, and she always knew when to leave.

"Nothing's the matter with Emily, is there?"

Picard knew well that there was something the matter with Emily. She stayed at home in the little group of rooms Fink had rented behind the jerry-built shopping center that had sprung up on the way to the base, complaining of not feeling well, but in good enough health to entertain a stream of gentleman callers while Ed was at work. He wondered if Ed had finally tumbled to her tumbling.

"That's part of it, a small part of it. She's too sick to work, and can just barely take care of the kids. She wants a TV set and I don't blame her, it gets awful cooped up in that little apartment during the day. But I can't afford it, I'm just barely making the rent and the car payment now.

Picard nodded; as a rule if the wife couldn't work, the family couldn't make it, even with the airman moonlighting. The pay was too skimpy, promotions too infrequent.

"Between my working the line and filling in the odd hours at the dairy, I can't help her much either. But that's not it." He lapsed into silence, preoccupied with dredging up pieces of the swelling coffeecake he had dunked into his cup.

"Well, what's the problem, Ed? I'll try to help, but I've got to put another coat of mastic on the roof today."

"I'll help you; give me a brush, and we'll do it."

Picard was tempted; Fink was a natural mechanic; they always called for him for diagnosis on the line when something that should work didn't. Don knew he could be trusted on the delicate trailer roof, where you had to choose carefully where to place your feet.

"No thanks, but let's get to the point."

Fink's eyes welled up, and his voice broke.

Picard hated to see a woman cry; it made him angry to see a man do it. "Jesus, Ed, come on, don't do this. What the hell is the matter?"

"I'm in real trouble, Don. I don't know how to tell you this, but I'm in real trouble."

"Spit it out, man."

"Last night I had to go up to Hammet to get a part for my old car."

Picard knew exactly what he meant; outside of Hammet there was a magnificent junkyard, where you could walk in, find the part you needed no matter what year or make or model you drove, and take it to the counter to pay for it.

"Yeah?"

"I needed a trailing link for the suspension."

"Goddamn it, get to the point, I don't want to spend all day listening to how you find parts in a junkyard. I have enough junkyard parts in my own jalopy."

"It all fits, Don, give me a second. I stopped at a little store on the way home to get a hot dog, I didn't have a chance to eat before I went up. I was carrying this trailing link in my pocket. Somehow, when the lady handed me the hot dog, I pointed the link at her and said it was a stick-up. She screamed and gave me the money in the cash register. I ran out and came home."

"Are you shitting me? Jesus *Christ*, man, you are in trouble. Did you turn yourself in?"

"I can't do it. Emily needs me too bad. I'd get busted out of the service, and maybe sent to jail. Then what will happen to Emily and the kids?"

"You should have thought about that before you stuck that

lady up. And why tell me? I can't help you—shit, I've got to turn you in."

"Don't do it, Don, please! I never did anything like this before in my life; I was thinking about buying Emily that TV set, and I saw all those bills in the cash drawer, and I just went nuts."

"Did anybody know you in the store?"

"No, after I left, it was just like nothing happened. I jump every time I hear a car pull in, or if they come down from the store and tell me I have a phone call, but nothing so far."

The poor bastard doesn't even have a phone. No wonder he's out robbing stores. "Did she get a good look at you, or your car?"

"Yeah, she saw me, but she was awful old, and she had on these thick glasses. I don't think she saw the car, 'cause when I left she was just screaming, standing behind the counter."

"Well, I got to turn you in, Ed, it's the only thing I can do. I can't put my career on the line for you like this, I've got a wife and kids too."

"Don't do it, Don; I'll never do it again, and I won't tell anybody I told you if I do get caught."

Picard's stomach coiled. How in the hell did he get in spots like this? Fink was a good airman, a real asset on the flight line. If Don turned him in he'd be court-martialed for sure.

"Have you got the money?"

"Yeah, most of it; I spent about ten at the market, on milk and stuff. Here it is." He pushed a greasy wad of bills across the table, a couple of twenties, a few tens, a few fives. A goddamn set of lives on the line for maybe ninety dollars.

"Shut up and let me think a minute."

There was no one to whom they could turn. Even the chaplain would have to counsel Ed to turn himself in. There wasn't much prospect for any kind of mercy from the court-martial process; they'd take his youth and need into consideration, but he'd still get booted out. Maybe get off with a suspended sentence, but he'd be finished in the service, and if you tried to get a job in the civil market with a dishonorable discharge, you were out of luck.

Picard paced the length of the twelve-foot living room. "Christ, Ed, why did you come to me? I either got to turn you in and live with that on my conscience, and look like a schmuck to all the troops, or I got to cover up for you, and run the risk of going to jail myself."

Fink was crying openly now.

307

"Damn it, cut that out; you keep crying and I'll turn your ass in for sure."

Fink sensed he'd won, but he kept his tears going.

"Okay. Let's think. First of all you got to get the money back, all of it, and you've got to do it today. Mail it, don't take it. Tell you what, I'll drive down to Boise and mail it. Do you know the name of the place you robbed?"

"No."

"Shit. I got to drive you back up there, find out who to mail it to, and then drive to Boise, just to cover your ass. You are fucking up my life and my leave, and what the hell do I get out of it?"

It was a rhetorical question, and he knew it. He was closing ranks with the Air Force one more time, making up for things the service shorted people on. It was a way of life, an unspoken commitment, passed along by his father, just like those Snap-On tools.

Still, he was furious, with Ed, with himself, with the whole screwball deal. He glared at Fink, and said, "If you ever fuck up again, don't come to me. I've had it. I'm only doing this because you are a first-class mechanic."

For the next six months, Picard started whenever the phone rang. Eventually it passed; they'd gotten away with it, and Fink was working his ass off on the line, trying to please. Picard had gotten him transferred over to the Base Flight unit, and he was working on the helicopters, doing well. Maybe it was worth it.

23

2050 LOCAL
19 February 1961
Washington, D.C.
USA

The decibel level was rising. Duke glanced around the room; the few nondrinkers were beginning to look as bored as he was. Blackie's Steak House was one of the few places in Washington where you could get a decent meal and a decent drink. It was the in spot for a top-of-the-line farewell party; tonight they were saying goodbye to Lt. Gen. Carter Raven, the retiring comptroller of the Air Force. True, he wasn't going very far, just across the river to Interstat, capping a productive Air Force career, but they would be seeing him in a new, and sometimes more interesting light.

He nursed the bourbon on the rocks; he'd collected it when he came in an hour ago; it was still half full. Joan was on her third and becoming increasingly lively.

Duke looked around the room at the odd mix of couples; there was a heavy industry representation tonight, and a lot of people from the Hill, so it was a good cross section. There was really no way to tell who belonged to whom; it always amazed him to see the strange constellations that had emerged over time as smile merged into smile, deal merged into deal.

The senior man there was Lee McKendall, an old friend of Raven's. They played golf together at Burning Tree, lunched at the Metropolitan Club, shared season tickets for the Senators with trips to the Maryland eastern shore for duck hunting. Neither man paid for anything of course; corporations picked it up and passed it on to taxpayers. The funny thing was the taxpayers more than got their money's worth. McKendall and Raven wanted the country run well, wanted a strong defense, wanted to save money. They were smart, and worked well for the taxpayers. They just lived well, too.

McKendall was a former congressman and was perennially the secretary of a service or head of an agency, no matter whether the administration was Democratic or Republican. He probably had more clout with Congress than anyone since Jim Webb, and was widely rumored to be the next secretary of defense. With his leonine shock of hair and a booming laugh to match, he'd be perfect for the job. He was rich, arrogant, and competent, a tough and winning combination in Washington. His wife, Bernice, was a quiet, shapeless hulk, wracked with arthritis, always seated on the sideline with one of his aides. Brown always made a point of talking to her; it was obvious that McKendall depended upon her and liked her, even though he ignored her shamefully at the parties.

Across the room, Gen. Nelson "Dusty" Rhoades, the smartest of the Air Force's deputy chiefs of staff, was talking and laughing, his arm around a brightly beautiful woman half his age, his hand placed exactly at the point on her spine beyond which it might have been embarrassing. Norma had been his secretary, then his personal assistant; six months ago he'd dumped his wife of thirty years and married her. If he had done it two years previously, he never would have picked up his fourth star.

Norma shimmered in a gold sequined dress, her breasts barely contained by a lace net. Her eyes never stopped moving, from man to man, radaring requests for approval, absorbing the beamed-back answers, and moving on. Her feet didn't need to move, her body was unset Jell-O. Rhoades's concentration was divided, half on Frank Weiss, the congressional staffer he was trying to impress, half on Norma's wandering eyes.

The staffer was quintessential corpulence, thick from his ankles to his eyebrows, with lips that wicked bourbon from his glass and eyes that stayed stone cold. Staffers were the heart of Congress; they made it work, and if the representative or senator were stupid, or venal, or brilliant, it didn't matter, for the staffer was going to determine who saw him, whom he saw and, more often than not, what he thought. Weiss cashed his paychecks only as a matter of form; his real income, the one that paid for his suits and his trips abroad and his two homes, one in Washington with a beautiful twenty-four-year-old Iranian mistress and one in Wisconsin with his wife, came from carefully selected companies. No one ever complained about how much they paid Weiss; they complained only if he wouldn't accept their money.

Duke shifted his attention to his left, where Joan was being trailed by young Capt. Rudy Capalla and his wife Corine. Capalla was a program officer and his wife was determined to make friends with Joan. Corine had redefined the meaning of vapidity, rolling more inanity into a hello than most people could manage in a lifetime. She had two assets, well defined, hardly subtle in an apricot top that barely covered her.

"Mrs. Brown, how lovely you look tonight," she trilled.

Joan smiled at the Capallas; Duke could tell by the vagueness of her look that she hadn't remembered them, didn't think it necessary to remember.

Corine gushed. "You promised to tell me how to make those wonderful brownies of yours."

Duke took a sip of his bourbon. Joan's brownies properly rounded could be used for billiard balls.

Joan stiffened; ah—the Christmas party, when Corine had come in a stunning white dress that swiveled heads around the room.

"Ah yes, I keep forgetting. I probably will keep on forgetting." She moved away; Corine was crushed, and the young captain edged her toward the door.

There was a stir across the room; Mike Shales, the *Post*'s plague on the Pentagon, had entered with his wife Bobbye.

Shales mined the Pentagon like an army ant, snipping off bits of information and carrying them off to his typewriter to mold and grow readable fungus. Bobbye was an ardent anti-militarist given to wearing army shoes and carrying protest signs in demonstrations at the Pentagon. Six feet tall, with the grip of Big Bad John, Bobbye dominated the room with voice and aching ego. Brown wondered what in God's name they were doing here.

Shales went over to congratulate Raven, who leaned forward to give Bobbye a kiss, but she stuck out a beefy forearm and squeezed his hand in her powerful grip.

Uncharacteristically, Raven was playful; he pulled their joined hands to his lips; Bobbye flushed in what Brown thought might be a sudden heat. That old devil Raven; they didn't call him Magic Lips for nothing.

He continued his detached assessment of the crowd. The majority of the women were high-school sweethearts; it was interesting to see how they had progressed. Their husbands, then fullbacks, now full colonels or better, had been through a graduate school of flying experience, competition, service schools, even advanced degrees from civilian colleges. Some of the women had moved up step by step, perhaps even exceeding the husband in sophistication; others stayed the high-school sweetheart, with Lana Turner hairdos, bubbling sparkiness substituting for personality, and a conviction that Cherries in the Snow lipstick on cupid lips was always irresistible.

Duke speculated on the phenomenon of push-pull that seemed to dominate. Either the men were capable enough to succeed, pulling their wives along, or else the wife was the power behind the throne, thrusting the man forward. Rarely was there any synergy, where the man and the wife's personalities combined to achieve success. The tightest groups seemed to be the wives who were content to be themselves, bonded together by their stations in life and by the thousand little daily hurts they endured in the process of their husbands' advancements. Their laughter was quiet, their pauses longer, but almost alone they were at ease. There would be no divorce; there would be no heights, but the depths were endurable, for there were children, and there was retirement, when the career glitter was gone and the husbands would have the adjustments to make. It was a waiting game, one with rules that made Rhoades and Norma so out of bounds.

Joan had moved on, her gait a little unsteady, mouthing kisses to women and passing a cheek before the men, edging nearer to Raven and McKendall. She'd known Raven for years, and had met the Secretary, as he preferred to be known, despite his immediate insistence on being called Lee, at several parties. Brown watched with wry distress as she went through her charm preflight. Her hand patted her increasingly rebellious lock of Claireoled hair to another errant spot; it reached the top button of her blouse, to be sure it was open, and then swept back over her fanny, as if to drive the bulge on her waist down and out of sight. Her tongue darted over her lips, and her eyes got wide. She was ready to strike. "General," she said, her voice inquisitively sappy, "am I going to get to kiss you goodbye?"

Raven looked annoyed; McKendall was potentially a big customer for Interstat. "Yes, Joan, by all means."

He puckered up and leaned forward; Joan moved to him and tripped, her drink sloshing on his chest.

"*Godda-* no problem, Joan, I've got a handkerchief."

Duke looked away. Help like this he didn't need.

In the corner, Col. Dan Harrison had moved Raven's secretary Donna into a corner. His wife was across the room, flirting with a Navy commander on exchange duty. He knew he had a few minutes.

"Donna, I've had my eyes on you since the day I got to the Pentagon."

"Colonel, I'd never have known; you rarely come around my desk more than three or four times a day."

"Now that you've got a few days before the general's replacement arrives, why don't we have lunch?"

"Lunch? We ought to be able to do better than that."

Harrison shot a glance at his wife. "Right. I'll call you tomorrow."

Donna circled to his right, edging toward the center of the room. "You do that, Colonel."

Tomorrow Raven's replacement was coming in, a week in advance of schedule. Roger Pogue was a brand-new three star, nonrated, a miracle fast burner who had been jumped over maybe thirty of his colleagues. He'd been sleeping with Donna for the last five years, every time he'd come to the Pentagon, and whenever she accompanied Raven on field trips to Dayton. She had deftly stage-managed his advancement, funneling information to him daily that enabled him to give brilliant briefings or destroy those of rivals. Harrison would faint when he called and she told him that Pogue was quite literally on board.

The crowd seemed to shimmer; Duke knew that Lisa Abrams must be coming. She was Lt. Gen. Fred Abrams's wife, always dressed exactly like a movie star of the twenties. The wives gathered to look, and even the men were good-naturedly expectant. Lisa didn't disappoint them; she was wearing a sprayed-on sleek silver sheath, a white skull cap with a tremendous white plume, glittering rhinestones, and shoulder-length white suede gloves. Her ivory cigarette holder was a field marshal's baton.

Duke loved her; underneath the glitter she was a smart, sincere woman, who instinctively knew that she was too plain to dress plainly. Her manner—warm, genuinely interested—was such a contrast to her heavy make-up and always outrageous dress that it took a while to believe that it was real. She had time for everyone, powerful or not, but she did not suffer fools for an instant.

Joan moved in; Lisa's plume and baton bridled.

"Lisa, darling, how lovely you look."

"Yes, Joan, right out of *Sunset Boulevard*."

"No, it's marvelous. I just wish I had the courage."

"Honey, you've got your courage in your glass." She said it with a smile and a Sugar Ray Robinson move to the right that left Joan cold-cocked.

Duke left to go to the men's room. Some nights they just weren't competitive.

24

0945 LOCAL
7 June 1961
Los Angeles, California
USA

Ed Novack walked slowly past the red-brick buildings, really looking at them, seeing them for the first time. They had been peripheral to his interest for the last four years; now he wanted to impress them on his memory, for they had molded him and changed him.

He had come to UCLA a virtual parody of the adolescent: acne-ridden, thin, high voice, an eager puppy dog. The acne was mostly gone, replaced by dimpled scar tissue, his waistline had swollen to account for his thirty-pound weight gain, he didn't sound like Henry Aldrich anymore, but he was as eager as ever. The major difference was the bottle-bottom glasses, correctors for the 20/100 vision that genetics and too much reading had provided him.

His normal camel gallop had faded to a walk as the sidewalks seemed to slant up, delaying his departure from this safe and rewarding ground. The crowds of students, mostly unknown to him, yet so familiar yesterday, were total strangers engaged in rituals forever behind him.

Tomorrow Ed Novack would graduate with a bachelor of science degree in electrical engineering, a ticket to the gold mines of Southern California aerospace. He had offers from Aerojet, Northrop, and Westinghouse. The money was incredible; they were offering him as much as sixteen thousand dollars a year, right out of school. He felt like a college football player being hounded by the pros. But David had advised against it. Join the Air Force for four years was his advice.

Because Novack owed a great deal to Professor David Mahoney, he considered his advice with care. The other guys in his class all figured only a dimwit would burn that much time in the service when the real excitement and moolah was right here in Surf City, but Novack wasn't so sure. Mahoney had worked both sides of the street before he'd joined the faculty here; he'd been a bombardier in World War II and then helped design a lot of the supersecret hardware still locked up behind the steel doors in Burbank and Culver City. The guy knew what he was talking about. Besides, Mahoney had given him a job grading papers in his freshman year, and spent the next three years investing in him more time and effort than Ed would have believed possible. Novack had never had the guts to ask why. Now, today, he might find out.

The morning had the milky California opalescence when the smog is thin and the sun just strong enough to burn through. As on every trip across the campus, Ed's head was on a swivel, taking in each girl as she passed. There was a young Chinese girl—he called her China Doll, had never had the courage to speak to her—who sunned herself each day next to Mahoney's building; she sat nonchalantly with her dress pulled to mid-thigh, her head back to catch even the misted sun. Ed wouldn't have been half as eager to see her in a bathing suit as to catch this promise of illicit exposure.

She wasn't there. He picked up his pace and bolted upstairs to David's office, a ten-by-twelve hole in the wall stacked to the ceiling with books, with piles of tests growing from the floor. The door was almost bowed out with the weight of stale tobacco fug that formed a palpable part of Mahoney's being. He was one of those unfortunates whose chemistry amplified and projected the foul cigarette residue; the image was enhanced by the small red dot of an inhalation-whipped cigarette forever about to set fire to his beard.

Only one spot in his office was neat, the little typing table he used for reading doctoral theses. It was bare, except for some hopeful candidate's thesis lying in the middle, riddled with Mahoney's savage red pencil marks. Mahoney was deadly serious about most things, but most of all he was dedicated to creating genuine engineers, not slide-rule-snapping salesmen. He grunted when Ed knocked and waved him through the half-open door. "Come in, Ed. All set for tomorrow?"

"As much as I'll ever be. How about you?"

"Tomorrow's just another day; I'll be in here, sweating out another idiot thesis, trying to make some solid sense of somebody saying old facts in a new way."

Novack found a corner of a wall to lean against. Mahoney eyed him expectantly.

"David, once more, thanks for all you've done. I know I can't repay you except by doing well, but I'm going to try to do that. But I've got to ask you something, and that's 'Why me?' I wasn't the smartest guy in the class by a long shot, and I never felt that we had any special outside interests in common. We got along very well, of course, but I could never understand why you were so kind to me."

Mahoney jerked the paper he was working on out of the typewriter, balled it up and tossed it in an arc to land near the pile beside the wastebasket. "Another two points. I don't know if I can explain it to your satisfaction, Ed. You're right, you weren't the smartest guy in the class, in fact you were about number fifteen, and I'm being a little liberal at that. No hard feelings. The fact is, though, that you have some qualities that the great engineers have to have, in my opinion. I don't mean you are automatically going to be a great engineer, but you have enough brains to be one—enough, not too many—and you have a natural method. For one thing, you don't smoke a pipe. Any time I see a student smoking a pipe, appearing professorial, I write him off."

He was silent for a moment. "Just kidding, of course. The fact is that I've known very few great engineers, but they all had a few things in common. First, they would pursue the orthodox when it was adequate; they didn't strive for elegance simply for the sake

315

of elegance. Second, when the orthodox didn't work, they were game to try anything, even the absurd, if they could factor something else into the equation that would make it work. Third, they expected to succeed ultimately, so they'd work around the clock until they did. And last, they'd make things happen. If something was in the way—no money, bureaucracy, precedent— they would simply run roughshod over the difficulties. I thought I saw the beginnings of those qualities in you when we started four years ago. I know I see them now."

Ed gulped and flushed. "I've never noticed any of those things in myself."

"No, but that's another plus; you've kept your eyes focused on the problem—except when we'd walk past that little Chinese honey—and you didn't take yourself seriously. Now you are going to have to, for the competition is going to get rougher every day."

"I don't know. Somehow with companies paying what they are paying, I'm not sure there will be the same degree of competition in the Air Force. I hope you're right about all this; four years is a long time out of the marketplace."

"Goddamn it, kid, you are taking yourself seriously already, but the wrong way. Listen, when all these companies were starting up out here, engineers had real jobs to do. John Northrop wasn't even an engineer when Donald Douglas had him designing the fuel system on the Douglas World Cruisers. He went out and started building Vegas for Lockheed, then started his own company. The community was small and you had to know how to do things. Today the companies are large, and you'll be a new guy behind a drafting table, updating drawings. There is no way to distinguish yourself now in a hurry. In the Air Force you'll get responsibility ten times faster; when you get out in four years you'll be a hot property because you'll have done something, and you'll know how to do something. After four years behind a drafting board in a big company you'll be just another guy with a green eyeshade."

"I hope so. I don't go for this military B.S.; I hope I can get through OCS without busting out."

"No sweat, you'll like it. You will have a problem, though, and that is you won't be a pilot, and if you get assigned to a base where they have an operational unit, you'll feel like the second team. Don't let it bother you; they are just the drivers who have to fly what guys like you design." He held up his hand to forestall Novack's inevitable reply.

"I know, I know. You're hot after the missile thing. Well, as I've said before, you're right on the money. It's pretty obvious that the whole field is crying for improvement. The military has been shooting rockets for five hundred years, and they still aren't worth a damn. After Korea, everybody thought the manned airplane was doomed, that there would be no more gun-carrying fighters. The fact is that they haven't built a decent air-to-air missile yet. They've got big torpedos they can launch against a bomber, but nothing for fighter against fighter that works more than fifteen percent of the time. And they are damned expensive." He lit another cigarette and glared at Novack as if he'd done something horribly wrong. Ed knew it was part of the Mahoney act, a precursor to the important part of the lecture.

"And that's where you're going to have your real work cut out for you, Ed. Listen to me carefully now. The Air Force lives and breathes pilots. It's run for the pilots and by the pilots. And that's the prime reason the missile thing has been so slow to develop: pilots fear them, even though they'll never admit it. Anything that might take them out of the cockpit, or even lessen their glory in combat, is going to have to be so obviously superior to whatever it replaces that they simply cannot argue the point. This is just like the old Navy days, when the wooden-navy guys hated and feared the powered-navy types; it took twice as long to convert to the obviously better equipment simply because of that. You're an engineer, Novack, like me, and you're likely to make the same mistake we all make when dealing with this sort of thing, and that is, you ignore the human factor in pursuit of the technical factors. Don't do it, not in the Air Force, not ever. Got it?"

As always, Mahoney had shrewdly tapped a nerve. Novack had toyed with the idea of joining the Navy; the Navy guys had talked up the Polaris program, and he had been pretty excited. Then they overplayed their hand and talked about him going on board a submarine. He'd seen too many wartime pictures about submarines and was a little claustrophobic. He couldn't stand the thought of lying on the bottom of the ocean, trapped, while destroyers dropped depth charges; he couldn't even crawl under a car on a creeper without getting the willies. Give him the bright blue sky in an airplane, if he had to do some real service work. Or just a desk and a slide rule, if it was all the same. He nodded solemnly.

"Good," grunted Mahoney. "Any questions?"

Novack had no questions, exactly. But there welled up in him a sudden sense that this was a watershed moment. He shared a bond with this intense, eccentric engineer-professor who was his mentor and more father to him than his own father had ever been. Stan Novack was a proud, hard-working man, but he didn't even speak the same language as Ed, not when it came to the important things. He'd wanted his boy to be a football player, and instead got—what?

Mahoney knew, and dimly, so did Ed himself. He knew very little about the Air Force except what David told him, and the recruiting sergeants chanted. A handsome captain had come around to promote the whole thing to him, but Ed had been a little put off by the guy, who was exactly what Stan Novack would have thought proper for his son, and was exactly what Ed himself disliked; a cheerful, intelligent jock. After the guy had left, Novack had decided not to bother with the Air Force if people like him typified it, but days of Mahoney's working him over pulled him out of it. He'd never had a chance socially against guys like the jock—not in high school, not here in college, and, he imagined, certainly not in the Air Force. But David persisted, his acidic wit tearing Novack's self-consciousness to shreds. Anybody can fly the damn things, he'd said; but how many jocks can design *anything*?

He'd been doing some reading and some thinking ever since Mahoney had mentioned the Air Force and rockets. So far, all they had done was take artillery rockets, not much different from those the Chinese had fired, and made little miniature manless airplanes out of them. They had to be fired within close limits of range and G forces, or else they simply tumbled wildly out of control. He thought the process should start from scratch, building a mean little monster determined to kill, with a tiny malevolent computer brain. You should be able to snap shoot it from any point, coming in, going away, and have it latch on like some insane fox gnawing into the bowels of the target. He knew exactly what it should do. Now all he had to do was invent it.

He straightened up and stuck out his hand to Mahoney. "Well, this is it. Thanks for everything, David."

Mahoney stubbed out his cigarette ferociously and got to his feet, his twisted and gnarled leg as always making the process obviously painful for him. Ed restrained himself from lending a hand; Mahoney was proud of his ability to overcome the wound the German flak had given him all those years ago. He hobbled around the desk and confronted Novack, eyeing him gravely. "Give 'em hell, kid," he said finally, his voice huskier than Ed had ever heard it before. Then he grabbed Novack's shoulders with his strong, wiry hands and squeezed so hard it hurt.

Ed didn't know how to react. He stood for a moment, then put his own hands on Mahoney's shoulders and squeezed back.

There were no words for what passed between them. And all at once it was obvious that the moment was past. Novack blinked back the tears that blurred his vision and dropped his hands. He stepped back and threw a jaunty, completely unmilitary imitation salute to Mahoney and fled.

Mahoney smiled a bit at the empty doorway and returned the salute. The debt was being repaid.

25

1030 LOCAL
24 November 1962
Fairfield-Suisun, California
USA

She sat back at her desk, closed her eyes, and for the thousandth time imagined the scene. Micky liked to add detail, to make it so much like life that when it happened it would match the dream. In her mind's eye the sign was going up; it had cost four thousand dollars, and she didn't want the rigger to drop it in the strong Suisun Valley breeze. The riggers set it in place and the electrician came up to connect the wiring; it was like a little Hollywood, because nobody could do anybody else's job. Micky shuddered as the sign moved; then she realized it was turning, just as it was supposed to. One side, in red, white, and yellow, said TWENTIETH CENTURY REALTORS across a map of the United States; the other said BUY THE GREAT WHITE WAY. It looked good against the golden backdrop of the California hills; it would look even better in the spring when the hills turned an intense green.

The slogan was Larry's idea, and she didn't have the heart not to include it. But the map was the real message; she intended to begin a franchise operation all across the country, with standardized advertisements, dress, interconnected multiple listings, and slide shows of houses. She figured she could establish one near every base, and make sure that she not only got the sales, but got the resales.

All she needed to do was to break out of this male-dominated mold, to kick the clammy traces of Jerry Eatherton's mixture of lust and greed. He had a combination movement that gave her a Pavlovian sexual revulsion; whenever he was taking something over from her, whenever he was maneuvering her out and him in, he inevitably would find a way to come close behind her, lean over her, and press against her as if offering a flaccid penile salute to his cleverness. She would feel a reaction inside, a sucking inward of her sexual apparatus. Someday, when he did that, she'd turn around and deck him. She had another fantasy in which she dragged his inert body to the paper-cutting machine and severed forever the object of his misplaced pride.

She went back into the stained redwood building, climbing up the back stairs to her office loft overlooking the floor. Below there was a waiting area, a bullpen of eight desks, four on each side, and four small conference rooms, rather more luxuriously furnished, in which she and the sales manager, Manny Feldman, did the tougher closes. Business was so good that they could have used more of the conference rooms; there was closing activity going on all the time.

Micky watched as a 1962 Chevrolet station wagon pulled into the employee's lot. Alice Cayley, recently hired, got out. As soon as she reached the door, Micky signaled for her to come upstairs.

"Hello, Micky, sorry I'm late; the kids had to go to a ball game."

"Did you miss an appointment?"

"No."

"Then it's okay; we can cover the floor, but you can never cover for a missed appointment. Is that the family car you're driving?"

"Yes."

"I want you to take it down this afternoon to Valley Motors, and trade it for a Buick station wagon, if you have to drive a station wagon, or a Cadillac sedan."

"Oh—Micky, I'd love to but we can't afford it. I can barely swing the payments on the Chevy."

"Go down today and make the trade; I'll get Jerry to cover the difference until you start earning it—then you can pay him back. We can't have salespeople driving around in ordinary cars; it tells the customer that you're not successful."

"Jerry talked to me about that, but I think it might make them resentful that you are driving a big car and they aren't."

"Alice, you've got to learn to condition the customer's mind with everything that will expand their thinking; when they are driving around in a Cadillac, they think in Cadillac terms; if you drive them around in a plain-jane Chevy wagon, they'll think that's the kind of house to buy. It's particularly true with service people; a ride in a Cadillac gives them a buzz that makes them think like civilians do for a change, makes them think that they deserve something. All of us service types need to be reeducated all the time."

She assumed the managerial tone she felt inside. "I'm not asking you to trade cars, I'm telling you. Look out on the company lot; your car sticks out. You'll make it up in additional sales in no time. Don't worry about your husband, I'll talk to him."

Alice's husband was a navigator in Larry's squadron; he considered himself a prudent investor because he hoarded savings bonds and bought all his clothes at the base exchange. He was like most Air Force guys; for him, it was a wild adventure to invest in a mutual fund. Their main energies were thrown into stretching the salary as far as possible by watching every penny, and believing they were getting bargains at the BX or the commissary.

It was part of the greater psychology of isolation from the realities of pay and prestige. Micky had seen tired airmen, just off from twenty straight hours working to get an airplane into commission, standing in line for an hour to see if a shipment of tools or toys had come in. There was the delusion of bargains, and, amazingly, the delusion was enough, the bargain didn't have to exist. Yet when it came to real estate, to buying a house, they were convinced that they couldn't afford anything but the minimum and that they would lose their shirts in the next economic cycle. It was pathetic. And it explained so much.

She closed the door to the office as Alice scuttled downstairs, and asked the harried secretary, who responded in the same feverish way to conference calls or group gropes in Marin County, to get Bill Brady on the phone. Brady ran Valley Motors.

"Bill, this is Micky. How are you doing?"

Bill came back with his usual patter about how much he missed her.

"Yeah, Bill, I know. But a little woman named Alice Cayley is going to be driving up in a white Chevy wagon in a minute. I want you to quote her the best price you can on the biggest Buick station wagon, or a Sedan de Ville. Make sure they are

321

loaded. But cut the price to the bone, or I won't let you in on our Heathcliffe Heights project you've been drooling over."

"Micky, we'll fix her up, you know that. How about a demo?"

"No demos! I've got to get her thinking big, and with a husband like hers, my work is cut out for me. Just make sure she picks a conservative color."

It was a situation she had come to relish. She liked to give orders, to control situations. Some people thought it wasn't very feminine; Micky thought this was a crock. She was as feminine as any woman, liked to make love as much as anybody, more than Larry did now. But she liked to run things, because she ran them better than most people. It was a function of brains, not sex.

She sat doodling on her notepad, numbers, dollar signs. There was irony in the difference between her need to produce and the means she had available. Just as in Virginia, she'd made money by beating the bushes for sales, running down leads, persuading people to do what was really best for them. What she wanted to do was make money managing people and putting together packages. She might miss the selling part, for she really enjoyed helping people. The average serviceman was such a baby, so easily taken advantage of. She protected them, gave them courage to do more than they dared. The greatest cowardice, the riskiest thing in California now, was not to invest. California land was simply a money multiplier; you bought on borrowed money, with an absolute confidence that you could double the asking price in a year or two. She wanted to stop speculating in individual houses even though she was doing well. The capital accumulation was too slow, the paperwork took too much time. What she should be doing was concentrating only on developments and on picking her people.

She was almost ready. She wanted to be a Johnny Appleseed of realtors, setting good people up in their own businesses with her as partner if they didn't have any money, or selling them a franchise if they did. She liked the franchise process best, because it provided more money up front, and she had greater protection from losses. She wouldn't be like that slimy Eatherton, or the greedy bumpkins back at Roy Rice Real Estate; she would give freely of what she gained—as long as the people were busy gaining it for her.

It was November 24 already; Larry was due home tomorrow. She wondered what great godawful gifts he would bring this time. She had enough camel saddles to outfit Lawrence of

322

Arabia, and now he was beginning to corner the world's supply of ceramic elephants. At least it kept him from the jewelry counters; he'd filled her bureau drawers with cut-glass monstrosities he thought were rubies and diamonds. She never disillusioned him and wore them faithfully, even the Thai cocktail rings that dropped the settings like popcorn in a movie.

About the only thing he ever bought for himself were the self-destructing suits from Hong Kong. Four wearings and the sleeves would separate, the linings would sag, and the cuffs would give up. They must have been sewn with spit. But it was what was done; you hit Hong Kong, you bought a camera, every time, even if you never took a picture, and you bought a couple of suits, because the tailors would take you out to a gigantic Chinese dinner, on the house. It was more of the BX bargain syndrome, and generally harmless.

Larry brought no gifts, just bad news. They'd lost a C-124 in South America, flying relief supplies into an earthquake area in Chile. No one knew what had happened yet, but it probably just flew into a mountain during a storm. Maj. Gordon Peyton, the squadron operations officer and Larry's best friend, was on board.

Three weeks later they got the word; the airplane had clipped the top of a peak not two miles from the airport. There were no survivors.

Larry had been working with Peyton, and he took over as acting ops officer. He felt guilty, that he was somehow benefiting himself by taking over Peyton's work, but there was no one else to do it. And maybe it would help him. The Air Force was cutting costs with a reduction in force, a RIF, and the main target was reserve officers; he'd seen more than one master sergeant walking around looking forlorn with pilot's wings still pinned to his chest. If he didn't make major the next go around, they could very well RIF him. Then he'd have to see if he could stick out the twenty as an enlisted man. Maybe it would be the best thing; he could go to work for Micky.

Later that month he was in Base Operations at McChord, getting ready for an 0500 takeoff to Elmendorf, Alaska, riffling through a week-old *Air Force Times*. The *Times* was the Air Force's bible of optimism; it tried to tell only good news even though usually there was only bad news to tell. This one carried the promotion list to major, and when he looked down the list of names there was a White, Lawrence A. He couldn't believe it; it was right when he needed it most. Maybe he was getting lucky.

He raced to the phone and called Micky, even though it was

four o'clock in the morning. When she answered, her voice was sleepy.

"Honey, I made major! It's in the *Air Force Times!*"

Micky was ecstatic; she could sense the joy in his voice and was happy for him. She promised him a long weekend in San Francisco to celebrate.

He was boring along the Canadian coast, fourteen thousand feet, 150 knots, en route to Alaska, the sweet martini scent of deicing fluid filtering into the cockpit as the props slung ice against the fuselage. Suddenly it hit him. What if there was another Lawrence White?

The letdown into Elmendorf was endless; he snapped at the copilot, raged at the engineer. He left the copilot to shut down the engines and supervise the cargo off loading, and commandeered a jeep to take him to Base Operations. He got on the long line back to MATS headquarters. He'd forgotten the time differential, the office had just closed. He spent a sleepless, anxiety-filled night in the dry heat of the barracks, sinuses baking to the snapping point, waiting to make an early morning call.

It took three calls to get the right office; when he did he found out that it was a Larry White in Tactical Air Command that had made major. Different guy, different serial number, no chance of a mistake.

The rest of the trip was agony. He didn't know how to face Micky, it was tough enough facing himself. He'd been a jerk, one more time. He called her on the way back, from Honolulu.

Micky took the news with cold indifference. Maybe he'd see the light now.

After talking with her, White felt worse than at any time in his Air Force career. He'd made a fool of himself; he'd told a passing Travis C-124 crew the good news; by the time he got back, he'd be a laughingstock.

He went down to the club, slipped the manager a twenty and got a bottle of Seagram's Seven, drank it in straight shots, no chaser, and was dead drunk in his room when the noon takeoff time rolled around. His crew chief, Tech Sergeant Margolies, had found him. If they found out that White was too drunk to fly, there would be hell to pay; they'd probably court-martial the poor sucker.

Margolies tossed a blanket over him, made sure the door to his room was locked, and went out to the flight line. He got a starter cart, and ran-up the number-three engine, radioing maintenance that he was checking on an engine that had given them trouble on the way in. Margolies ran it up to full power, the airplane shaking and gyrating, then pulled the engine control back so that the fuel air mixture was too lean to run smoothly. He helped the process along by rapidly switching the magneto on and off; big backfires shook the airframe, pushing gouts of flame out the exhausts. The engine was bucking, so rough that the cowling threatened to fly off. The line chief was signaling frantically for him to shut it down. Margolies chopped the mixture control, and the engine died. He stuck his head out the window to the line chief. "Hey, Sarge, call Base Ops and tell them we're canceling for maintenance. We won't be able to leave at least until tomorrow." White had done a lot for him; it was a pleasure to pay him back. White would have a headache in the morning, but at least he wouldn't be court-martialed.

When Larry awoke blearily, he checked the time and sat up in panic, setting off fire alarms in his pounding brain. He lurched out of bed, head aching, and saw a note from Margolies, explaining what had happened, and telling him that their new takeoff time was next morning at nine. White knew what Margoles had done for him; he'd have to make sure he took care of the debt some way.

The homeward leg of the trip usually seemed endless. This time, the hours flew past. Larry dreaded their arrival, certain that he would be kidded unmercifully.

He was right. The news had traveled; when he walked into the Travis squadron operations room there was a big homemade sign saying WELCOME BACK MAJOR WHITE. He winced. Capt. Kerry McCuen was there when he came in. "Hey, Larry, when's the promotion party?" White tried to ignore him, walk out of the room.

McCuen maneuvered in front of him. "No kidding man, not everybody makes major like you. How do you do it?"

McCuen was a wiseguy, passed over and sour. He saw White as another loser like him; instead of banding together, he despised him for it.

"Not funny, McCuen; it was an honest mistake."

"Jesus, White, did you think they're going to promote some stupid C-124 driver when they got all those hotshots back at headquarters to take care of? You and me we sweat and slave, and those mothers get the promotions. You still owe me a drink, though, just for thinking you had a shot."

Somehow White found himself at the club, buying McCuen a drink, when all the hell he wanted to do was get home and get

325

out of sight. McCuen kept calling people over, and Larry had to keep buying. It would have been cheaper to have a promotion party. Most of the other people were sympathetic, understood how it happened. When you want something so bad, you tend to believe any good news you hear. Most of them had had similar, if not so obvious, flashes of hope. McCuen didn't make any friends for himself. But when White looked around, the people drinking with him were people like himself; not a single field grade officer had come over. He had the first real inkling of what Brown had been trying to tell him all those months ago.

The next day things were back to normal, and he was in the office, trying to catch up on the paperwork his acting ops officer job generated.

There was no ceremony about Colonel Haley. He walked into the operations room with a bright-eyed young major, who looked to be about twenty. "Captain White, this is Major Skeffington; he's the new ops officer. I told him you'd show him the ropes."

Larry took it. He always took it. He also took off a notice from the bulletin board asking for volunteers for a special project in Southeast Asia.

26

0927 LOCAL
14 June 1963
Eglin AFB, Florida
USA

Kathy glanced at the clock; almost nine thirty. The landings were scheduled for eleven o'clock; it would take them at least half an hour to shut down and line up for the big dismissal scene. She had three hours to get ready; it was enough, even though she had been waiting ninety days to do it. It was early summer now; the special group had deployed in early spring, to England, to do whatever in God's name they did there. She didn't want to know all that Mike did; she had a good idea of what his off-time activities might be. Somehow it didn't matter now, and it wouldn't for a couple of days; then it would surface, and there'd be a row, but that was all right too. Rows were a part of life, just like sex; it was just too bad that Kelly was better at rows than he was at sex. Maybe it was her fault; she was probably too romantic, even after three kids.

She didn't mind the frantic urgency when he first came in, the wild romps in the hallway were a part of Air Force legend. If you had kids, you got rid of them for that first hectic hour, or there were too many questions. But later, she'd have liked a little more finesse. How was his finesse in England, she wondered. The idea intrigued her; it would be a great way to start a fight when the time came. She poured an extra dollop of Estée Lauder Youth Dew in the tub, and set out the cologne and powder.

Seven hundred air miles away, cramped in the seat of his Phantom, Maj. Mike Kelly felt the recurring surge of lust that would build in anticipation of his homecoming. Their lovemaking had changed as his perception of Kathy had changed. When they first met, and with all the other women in his life, the lovemaking was a function of the hormones, a response of body to body. Now he knew she was a pillar of his own personality, a strengthening bow of intelligence and love, and he made love to both her still lovely body and her brains. Life had been tough; she was making it easier as he grew older. If he could ever be as wise as she.

He knew at that moment Kathy would be getting ready, probably already submerged in a bubble bath. He slipped a finger up inside his oxygen mask to wipe away the sweat; the airplane, as new and sophisticated as it was, was performing flawlessly, all the gauges were in the green, and he was running a shade better than he had planned on the fuel.

He called to his back seater, Capt. Ron Sherrod. "Be glad to be home, Ron?"

"Yeah, but I hope I don't find my wife like I left her."

Kelly didn't know Marcia had been ill. "Jeez, that's too bad. How did you leave her?"

"Fresh fucked."

Mike winced. Rough cut as he was, he had never quite gotten used to the coarse aircrew version of humor.

The line of twelve big jets stretched out for miles across the Atlantic sky, each pair creating their own small contrail as they loafed along in comfortable formation. It had been an exhilarating deployment, a selling tour for the F-4 to England, Greece, Turkey, and especially Germany. They had reveled in the mock

327

interceptions, the long low-level flights across Europe. Most of the time they had flown with foreign pilots. From all Kelly could tell, the countries were dying to buy the big Phantom. But now all the pilots were tired, and would have to watch it on the last hours of the flight. That's when accidents happened.

He was hot and grimy; last night the showers in the BOQ had been off due to a water outage, and his flying suit was streaked with sweat. He felt a momentary stirring in his groin that he knew would not last; the parachute straps, the G suit, the whole heap of life-support equipment that sustained him inhibited erections.

This time it's going to be different, he thought. We've been married long enough to act a little civilized. Kathy had been making some pretty direct remarks about their sex life before he left, and she was right. He'd gotten into a thoughtless process of satisfying himself, without worrying too much about her. She had pretended she was satisfied most of the time, and he'd been willing to accept it.

Then too, he was feeling very guilty. The seductive promise that deployments held out were usually just that, a promise. Every pilot believed the fiction, of course, and Kelly had long ago grown used to the intercom call, "Okay, crew, gear up and rings off!" But this time he had met a really nice woman, Alexandra, and they had been together for most of the last week, long past his PCOD—Pussy Cut-Off Date—but he hadn't been able to refrain. She was so beautiful, and so aggressive. He had to stop this nonsense; it was time to grow up.

Maybe he could be a little more sophisticated too; God knew Alexandra was. She appeared so proper, so typically English, well dressed, well mannered, well spoken, and when he'd met her at the club at Mildenhall, he thought she must have been the station commander's wife. They chatted for almost half an hour before he realized who she was—the station's community relations officer—or that she was obviously trying to pick him up. He was no more able to resist her than he'd been able to resist Joan Brown back at Williams, and they spent the rest of his TDY there shacking up. It had been wonderful, and now he felt miserable. She obviously simply considered it an amusing fling, and bade goodbye to him almost as coolly as she'd said hello, clearly never expecting to see him again nor bothered by the fact.

He was very bothered by it, though, and so as usual, he had a bundle of presents for Kathy; some sweaters, a brooch, perfume, and a bottle of port, which she liked and he didn't. He had some knickknacks for the kids, and even a first-class collar for Rocky, the huge, worthless mutt that had adopted them a year ago.

She'd have some champagne on ice, and there'd be martinis later. First he'd take a shower, and they'd sip some champagne, and talk a bit. Not too long, though.

Kathy toweled steam off the mirror to examine herself; at thirty-four she was still in good shape, with firm breasts, no sags, and only a few tiny stretch marks to show that she had given birth three times. Her legs were always her best feature, but her rump showed her clearly where those extra two pounds had gone. She determined to get rid of them, back down to her normal 118, somehow. She knew it wouldn't be for the next week, for Mike would be demanding big meals and lots to drink, and she couldn't stand for her not to join him. She smoothed on the Estée body lotion, working hard on her hands and her feet; tennis was great for toning, but it played havoc with skin. Then she sprayed herself with the Chanel cologne he'd brought back on the last trip. Not too much, but little extra splashes in places she knew he would dwell on.

She dressed carefully, a dark black slip, black demi-bra, no panties. Probably half the waiting wives assembled on the flight line would have no panties on, all desperately hoping there'd be no breeze and that no airplane would run its engines up behind them. She'd never heard the matter discussed, but it just seemed so logical.

She felt an inner stir, an anticipation of the rough coupling she could expect when they stepped inside. It used to bother her, but she realized it was as gallant as Mike got; he thought it was a compliment to be so in need that he could not wait. Thank God good Irma, her next-door neighbor, was always glad to take the kids for the first few hours after Mike arrived. It would be difficult, later, when they grew older and would expect to be a part of the welcoming committee.

Mike preferred her without any makeup, so she kept to a little lipstick and a touch of eye shadow. She dressed rapidly, checked the weather, checked to see that Rocky had water—the big oaf drank it by the gallon in great slurping quantities that dripped from his whiskers—called Irma to see that everything was okay, and left for the flight line.

Kathy wasn't crazy about the Air Force, but even she could

329

not resist the gaiety and the anticipation of these homecomings. Once they were relatively rare; squadrons would deploy to an overseas base once a year, perhaps less often if they weren't considered qualified. It was unusual for Mike's test unit to do it, but they had been augmented by some crews from Tactical Air Command for the special tour, and the reception was being done TAC's way.

The flight line was decorated with the usual tired bunting, and a stand had been set up for the base dignitaries. They promised to keep the ceremonies short. When the unit landed, the aircraft would taxi in trail formation and shut down, and then the pilots would form up and march in very loose order, baggy flying suits flapping in the breeze to the reviewing stand. The C.O. would review the deployment in glowing terms—particularly because there had been no fatalities or even accidents—and give a dismissal order. Then it was time for the families to surge forward for hugs and kisses and a quick trip home to the bedroom if they were lucky, the hallway if they were hot.

Kelly listened to the radio transmissions idly; he was flying wing on the unit commander, a West Point weenie named Wetzel, and merely had to keep his station and acknowledge instructions. The weather was good. He thought of Kathy and the kids and wondered if they could count on Irma again.

"Roger," he acknowledged; Wetzel had called for the formation to close in for a low pass across the field, and then to pitch up for an intrail landing pattern. The twelve F-4s in a perfect V passed across the field at one hundred feet, twin columns of black smoke pouring from the engines, shock waves of moisture peeling over the wings, then pulled up in a satisfying arc that positioned them for landing. It was good to be home.

Kathy heard the dismissal order and broke with the crowd for the line of pilots moving toward them. Mike grabbed her and lifted her up, squeezing her close before holding her back to examine her. They kissed, and then moved toward the flight line, toward their aging 1956 Thunderbird, the trouble-prone "value-appreciating classic" he had paid a fortune for and wouldn't get rid of. Mike was holding her with one arm and carrying the small kit that contained the presents. The rest of his gear would

330

be dropped at Base Operations by the KC-97s that were following them in.

They talked animatedly on the five-minute drive home; Mike pawed at her legs a bit, but wouldn't touch her more because his hands were still grimy from the flight.

Inside the hallway, Kathy put her arms up to be kissed, but Mike pulled aside. "Why don't you open the champagne and then meet me after I take a shower?"

Kathy blinked. No hallway action? England must have been sensational for him. "Okay. You'll have to pop the cork, though. Usually we've already popped your cork by this time."

Kelly grinned, patted her bottom, and dashed for the bedroom. He was out of his flying suit and into the shower in a minute, back out in two.

"Where's my cold champagne and hot woman?"

Kathy came in, carrying their remaining two champagne glasses from their wedding present set and a bottle of Moët, the most expensive champagne she'd ever bought. She hoped he'd like it. Mike had a towel wrapped around him. Very discreet behavior for him.

She set the champagne and glasses down, and whirled around and flicked his towel off. She kissed him on the lips, and began to undress.

Mike stepped over to the bed and lay down, beginning to be excited as she removed her clothes.

"I always like this part," he said. "You are looking wonderful; and what little helpless furry goodie is that I see, all pantieless and hopeful?" He held out his arms and she flowed over to him.

"Some champagne first," he said, and got up for the bottle.

Well, she thought, I asked for finesse and I'm getting it. I'm beginning to think I like hallways. Her nipples began to swell in a deeper surge of heat.

"You look pretty good, Mike, but not too excited. What's up, or rather is it coming up?"

"Ah, don't fret, my pretty angel, my pretty blond angel; you see a new man, Mike the skillful lover. We are going to drink a little champagne, and then I'm going to kiss you in places you've never been kissed before."

"The only place I've never been kissed before is Philadelphia, silly, but you can cover some of the same old territory."

She was beginning to like his mood of restraint; it wasn't the old Mike Kelly, and that almost had to be good. A year ago he

331

would have already climaxed and begun talking about dinner. This was a better approach, if she could handle it.

And handle it she did; she'd always loved to play with him from their very first date; she knew that 90 percent of the attraction had to be sex at first, and it was maybe 50 percent now. He took a sip of champagne and lowered his mouth to her breasts; she could feel the bubbles popping against her nipples as his tongue explored her.

"Give me some champagne, honey," she whispered. He took the bottle and drank from it directly, then kissed her, forcing the warming champagne from his mouth to hers in a jet. She was excited now, and began sucking his tongue, began moaning as his hands swept over her body, then sought the little trigger of her clitoris.

Mike sat up. "Roll over," he said. She obeyed, hot, puzzled, but ready to play out the new games.

"At last a decent ass; you must have gained some weight. Don't lose it. You've finally got the perfect shape that drives men wild." He bit her bottom, softly, as she laughed, mentally scratching the tuna fish diet for the following week. She reached back to fondle him, stroking him to full excitement. She leaned down to kiss him.

"Not yet, my baby; I'm going to do all the kissing and licking and nuzzling and fingering and all that until you are ready to go crazy; then I'll let you have a turn.

"Lie down on your back," he commanded, his voice different now, not trying to be funny, deadly serious. She did, her hand still reaching for him. He sprawled over her and kissed her forehead, her eyes, her nose, her ears, she tried to kiss back, but he wouldn't let her. He sniffed her skin, seeking each perfumed spot; he licked under her breasts, nuzzled her armpits, stuck his tongue in her belly button, his hands lightly stroking her. She felt a burning urgency, and wanted him.

"Come inside me, Mike."

"No, not yet," he said and continued to kiss. "Roll over," he muttered.

"No, come inside me, damn it, it's been ninety damn days!"

"Yes, and it'll be ninety more if you don't do what I say. I'm doing the kissing here, you just do the lying and the waiting."

He kissed her more passionately, wondering at the strength in her back, loving the extra softness of her bottom, wondering why he had not kissed the back of her knees more often, biting her ankle gently.

332

"Roll over," he said, more softly this time.

Kathy rolled over, spreading her legs, holding her arms to him in a peculiarly beckoning manner, her lips parted. He buried his face between her legs, slowly, gently opening her with his tongue. He pulled back to watch her unfold, gently, first one side, then the other, then more rapidly; he kissed her again marveling at the sweet wholesomeness of her scent. All the rough folklore of oral sex was so wrong; she was like the inside of an orchid.

"God what a sweet expression you wear down here, and you are absolutely delicious. I'm going to make you come by kissing."

"No, no, oh God Mike, I can't hold on, come on in me, honey, come with me, don't make we wait, oh, I'm coming, honey, I'm coming I'm . . ."

He glanced up over a black horizon to see her flat stomach and lovely breasts heaving; her head moved from side to side and a fine transparent bubbly broth of excitement coated her lips, cooling them, refrigerated by her own excitement. She was the only woman he had ever known whose lips turned cool as she came. He worked carefully now, extending her orgasm, realizing he was ready, too ready now to delay longer.

She moved her body convulsively, then reached down and dragged his head up. "Come on honey, let's go."

He kissed her mouth with her own sweet wetness as he slipped inside her. She responded to him, moving rapidly.

"Come on, honey, you can come again, come with me come with me," he commanded, leaning into her, raising up to be in most direct contact. He tried desperately to contain himself until she met his rhythm and his urgency again.

"Come, damn it, come, you can come, move it move it come, I can't wait."

Much later, they drank champagne in companionable silence getting their breath back, still touching, still kissing, legs wrapped like ivy around each other.

"That was good. I needed it badly." He stroked her nipples.

She was silent. "Mike, you have finesse. I love it, but where the hell did you learn it, you bastard?"

"Honey, I made that up for you on the leg home. I was sitting there thinking about you being in the bathtub, and I made up my mind to try to please us with a little different style. Pretty nice, if I do say so."

She looked at him. Even if it was only 50 percent sex nowadays, it was still worth it. After that session, maybe 70 percent.

"More champagne, Mike, and in a minute, I'll show you if I learned anything."

He sat on the bed, glass in hand; he normally had a sex cycle time of maybe twenty or thirty minutes, but from the look in her eyes he thought he might be able to improve on his previous record. "Ready when you are, C.B.," and he leaned back to await her lips and tongue. It was a good start, and maybe he was growing up. God, he hoped so.

27

1130 LOCAL
27 August 1963
Castle AFB, California
USA

Duke Brown eased his Continental up to the archway gate guarding the entrance to the field. The young Air Policeman at the gate saluted and waved him off, covertly admiring the car, and aware that a lieutenant colonel as young as Brown was obviously a hot customer. Security had relaxed dramatically. During B-47 days, he'd been politely asked to wait at the guard shack for verification; now the kid barely looked at his I.D. card.

The base was familiar, retaining its World War II luxury of a tree-lined oval drive leading to headquarters, but it had been filled in on both sides. On the right a new commissary/BX complex had sprung up, with a fancy multipump gas station; when he'd been here with B-47s, they had been content with a four-pump, open-bay setup. On the left the old wooden hospital had been torn down and replaced with a modern three-story concrete building. Another anonymous set of buildings stretched beyond; simulators and classrooms probably. SAC flew as much on the ground as in the air nowadays.

He parked the Lincoln carefully, so that it straddled two spots; he hated having people open doors and bump against his paint job. The club was the same patched-together collection of geriatric World War II buildings, melded with redwood siding and interconnected by small sets of stairs deadly to any survivors of the inescapable happy hour. Inside nothing had changed, from the stale-beer-charged atmosphere to the inexpensive paneling that maintained a uniformly gloomy atmosphere. The place made the Air Force statement for all of its nonofficial amenities: this is the best cheap stuff you can get.

He walked down a flight of stairs, past the bar; it was early, and some graying retirees were already drinking. Duke was beginning to be aware of the pattern in clubs around the country. As the young volunteers of 1941 crested their twenty years of service, some simply retired to the golf course and the bar. It was a shriveled, deprived existence, nurtured only by the familiar atmosphere and the lingering sense of belonging. They were as forlorn as the plastic palms guarding the end of the bar, all of them overdue for retirement too.

Duke ducked through the bar before he could be hailed—the retirees were like Ancient Mariners, bound to have known you at some point—and out to the patio. The pool was another refraction of the past. The bathing suits were skimpier, the women were older and had more to cover; doughy rolls and stretch marks had replaced flat stomachs and creamy thighs, but they had all grown older together.

Brown had been through Castle for crew training a year before, and then spent an intensive six months at Loring Air Force Base in Maine, preparing for his command. Loring had been as forbiddingly cold as the San Joaquin Valley was enticingly warm, but the crews were expert and he felt he'd learned enough to take over a squadron.

He had a quick lunch and then walked across the street to the headquarters building. Career courses ran parallel, and Bruce Patterson, his squadron commander in Korea, was wing commander here, a major general. Inflation had hit everything: pocketbook, efficiency reports, and rank. An excellent rating used to suffice for a brigadier general to command a wing; now captains had to be supremely outstanding, an officer slated to be chief of staff just to have a crew, and a major general was delighted to be given a wing to command. Now there were too many generals and not enough slots.

There were also many organizational changes; the old 330th Bomb Squadron in which he'd lost his heart to B-47s had been changed over to a 4017th Combat Crew Training Unit, and all of the Air Force B-52 crews passed through here. The 330th had been maintained for a while and then was deactivated; the 328th and 329th were still in being, keeping up the wing's war mission. Brown was to command the 328th.

Patterson greeted him warmly in the walnut-paneled room that had started life in 1943 as the base commander's office—

then, the C.O. had only been a major—for a training unit. SAC didn't think much of amenities.

"Glad to see you, Duke; hope you are going to like it here."

"Glad to be here, General; it beats Korea and the Pentagon."

They reminisced for a while, then Patterson came to the point. "Duke, we've got some real problems here, and I want you to delay taking over the 328th until we sort them out. Boeing is working on it, but I'm not satisfied with what's happening. The shift in our mission from high to low level has caused some tremendous structural problems. The airplane was designed to drop nuclear weapons from maybe forty-five thousand feet; we're pounding in on the ground today at three hundred feet, and the turbulence is killing us. We've lost a few airplanes, as you know, and the crews are getting spooked. I don't blame them."

"Got any ideas?"

"Part of it is simply fatigue; we were supposed to be flying B-70s and B-58s only now, with all the B-52s out to the boneyard with the 47s. But the Russians cranked up their high-altitude missiles and the B-70 never made it. We didn't buy enough B-58s—too expensive even though they are as fast as lightning—and they are so costly to maintain that they are being scheduled to phase out in a few years. There's nothing else but the B-52, some of them with Hound Dog missiles strapped on, and we've got to figure out a way to make it work."

"What does Boeing say?"

"They're concerned as hell and have a big program going, but the results aren't coming in as fast as we need them. I want you to take an airplane, get it instrumented at Boeing, and then fly our missions to find out what's happening. Boeing is simulating the missions, but I can't be sure they are duplicating our combat profiles."

"What do you think is the problem?"

"Two things: fatigue and turbulence. I don't think we understand the fatigue involved in flying airplanes this big so fast and low, and I'm damn sure we don't understand turbulence, particularly around the mountains. You know that a lot of our penetration routes run right across the Sierras, just like they'd run right across the Caucasus, and God alone knows what the stresses are."

Duke nodded. "It's just like thunderstorms. We used to routinely fly through them when we couldn't go around them, until they began testing and found out they could break up a steel I beam if you got in the wrong spot."

"Exactly; and we could pretty well tell where thunderstorms were, especially after we got radars. Clear air turbulence and turbulence around the mountaintops are almost impossible to predict."

"Why me, Bruce? You've got a lot more experienced men in B-52 here, and I never was a test pilot."

"I'll level with you, Duke. I can spare you. I can't spare anybody else right now. You haven't got any roots in the wing, you can be totally demanding, and last, and best, you've got the brains."

"Can I get some help? I'd like to have somebody with test experience in the cockpit, just for scientific rigor. If we do this, we ought to have data that people will trust."

"Got anybody in mind?"

"Yeah; he's no friend of mine, but he's one hell of a test pilot. Let's see if we can get him detailed here."

If East St. Louis was one end of the world, Pasadena was the other. Kelly could not believe the gently filtered sun, more phosphorescent dew than light, the twisting streets, manicured lawns, stuccoed castles, and total peace. Everything spoke in muted terms, agreeing that rich is good. The scent of oranges was overladen with a thousand other luxuriant perfumes. It was strange, but the streets were always vacant; if you saw someone it was a gardener. The tennis courts were deserted; the entire lovely place was a Hollywood set ready for shooting, waiting for the actors.

But not Cal Tech with its incredible "California-style" architecture, a swirling melding of stucco, tile, frescoes, covered walkways, and a sprinkling of classical Greek. It bustled with purposeful activity. It was an exhilarating statement that for once the bright could be also the well treated.

He couldn't get over being there. It had all been so simple; he applied for an advanced degree at AFIT; within three weeks the confirming papers had come back, as if he had placed an order with Sears for a washing machine. The Air Force never ceased to amaze him. If he'd asked for something simple, a new door on his G.I. house, it might have taken years.

Kelly was an old man compared to most of the students, and had to work harder than any of them. There were a few native-

337

born Chinese students he simply could not match, but by devoting every hour to study, he struggled day by day to a degree in thermodynamics. The old joke "Last week I could not spell ingneer and now I are one" ran through his head more than once.

They treated him well; he was an anomaly on campus, but his prestige was enhanced by the fact that he often had been able to fly Gerd von Bauman to appointments in San Francisco. There was a Beech C-45 at Burbank Airport for Air Force officers working or studying in the local area to get their time in, and Kelly had made it known he would schedule it whenever von Bauman wanted to go somewhere in California. The C-45 was too slow for anything else. Von Bauman was a legend in his discipline, as a thinker, and as a world-class fanny pincher. He obviously liked Kelly and he enjoyed the flights, often sitting in the right seat. He might not say a word the whole trip, but he'd get off, stimulated and refreshed. To have him nod in passing on campus was an honor that Kelly traded off for tolerance. With the pressure increasing in Southeast Asia, a military man wasn't too popular.

Kathy met him in the porte-cochere of the Athenaeum; she was supposed to be bringing him some papers he'd left on his desk, but he knew she'd expect lunch. She looked troubled.

"What's the matter? Are the kids okay?"

She handed him an envelope with a return address of "Lt. Col. Duke Brown, Castle Air Force Base, California."

As he always did when he thought about Duke, he flinched inwardly. For a long time, he'd worried if Joan would ever take revenge by admitting to their abortive coupling, and whether Duke would come after him. It was so long ago now that he knew the odds were overwhelming that nothing would ever come of it. But still, everything associated with Duke and Joan was unpleasant.

"Jesus," he said, holding the envelope, "what can the bastard want?" He ripped the envelope open; Duke was giving him advanced notice that he'd be coming on a special project to fly B-52s at Castle. He could expect orders in two weeks. He handed the note to Kathy. While she scanned it, he said, "Well, there goes the degree." He had another three months of course work and a thesis to write.

"Maybe they'll let you come back," Kathy said hopefully.

"Yeah, maybe." Kelly was boiling. Brown must have known what his status was, or he wouldn't have had his address; he probably enjoyed the fact he was torpedoing Kelly's chance of getting a degree.

Mike cut his afternoon class and got on the phone to Pentagon personnel. His contact there, fat, nonrated Major Smith, whom he'd only met twice, kept repeating that he knew that it was unusual, but it was "an exigency of the service," that classic cover for shafting. They told him only what Brown had said; he was going to Castle on a special mission, and they couldn't make any promises on going back to Cal Tech.

Kathy was depressed. She'd hoped Mike would have gotten an assignment to teach at the Air Force Academy, giving them three years in a decent spot, the first they would have enjoyed since they got married. Now it looked like he was back in the pilot pool.

His adviser, Professor Robin Richards, was furious; Kelly was no von Bauman, but he was a prime example of what an older man could do when he returned to school. Now it was wasted. He asked von Bauman to call Washington, but the old man declined; in too many countries he'd seen too many military operations take precedence over study to be bothered by this.

Kelly and Kathy drove to Castle over the weekend, staying at the Pine Tree Lodge, a gateway motel to Yosemite. Joan invited them to stay with them, but Mike declined firmly. "If we have a fight, I want to have a place to retreat to. Besides, we'll be seeing enough of them."

Patterson had given Duke a set of offices on the flight line. He met Kelly there. "Mike, first things first. No hard feelings about the TMTS; you did your thing, and I did mine."

"Yeah, you came out okay, didn't you? The Air Force is still going to buy some, according to *Av Week*."

"Well, you set them back three years, at least; but they still won the competition, and it's probably all for the best. Was the XB-51 the biggest airplane you ever flew?"

"No, I got to fly everything at Wright-Pat, B-47s, KC-97s, KC-135s, even a few flights in a YB-52, the prototype with the B-47–style canopy. Guy Townsend took me for a few flights in an A model, too, at Edwards."

"Good. We're instrumenting a G model for some flight tests to check out the structure in turbulence. It will take about six weeks to get ready, just time to put you through the aircraft commander course here. You'll be flying copilot to me, but I want you to have the full range of experience. You'll have to really hump it during the day, because at night I want to work with you to develop a test program. Don't worry about the academic side of it; just learn the systems, and we'll take care of the rest. You won't be a SAC crew member when you leave, so don't worry about that either."

He handed Kelly a sheaf of accident reports. A B-52G at Seymour Johnson AFB, South Carolina, had developed a massive crack in its lower wing skin; when the pilot put the flaps down for landing, the wing simply collapsed. A B-52D had come to pieces and gone in at Burns, Oregon. There were a half dozen others.

"The problem's the environment, Mike. You can fly a B-58 at three hundred feet; it has the ride characteristics to absorb and dampen the vibration. You do the same thing with a B-52, and it can shudder itself to pieces. We have to figure out what the limits are, and where the reinforcements have to be fitted, so that we can penetrate on the deck at three hundred knots."

"One thing before I go, Duke. Why me?"

"You know, I asked myself that, Mike. I think it's because you're so goddamn dumb honest and because you owe me one for screwing up the TMTS briefing."

"Well, ask a stupid question, get a stupid answer."

Kelly walked back toward the club, boiling. It wasn't a stupid answer at all. Duke wanted to use him; so what else was new. Yet it galled him. He'd do the planning, the evaluating and, if he knew Brown, the toughest flying; Brown would dance away with the credit. Yet underneath the resentment he realized that Brown was managing, that he was making use of Kelly's talent to expand his own. Maybe that's what I should get into, he thought. If I did a little managing instead of trying to solve everything by strapping it to my ass, maybe I'd get somewhere.

That night Kathy couldn't figure him out; he wasn't in a bad mood, but he wouldn't talk. They drove back to close out their Pasadena apartment in virtual silence; he seemed to be shifting gears the whole way.

The training course didn't generate much enthusiasm in Kelly's soul. The B-52 was a truck on the ground, and a family sedan in the air. It was painfully slow compared to a fighter, and the control reactions were far too heavy for Mike's taste. But as his time grew in the airplane, he came to like it. It was honest, solid, and had plenty of power.

The power was almost a problem in the B-52H. The new engines had so much thrust there was a gate to limit their travel. After a long preflight, poking through every door and every fitting of the five-hundred-thousand-pound monster, they would crawl up into the tiny cockpit, thrust so far ahead of the drooping, fuel-laden wings that it was like being at the end of a tunnel. The engine start was relatively simple, and with a burst of power the airplane would creak forward, limping on its fuselage-mounted gear, lurching toward the runway with a series of crablike thrusts as the crosswind gear was checked.

On the runway, the engines were run up slightly, but not completely; a B-52 had literally shaken its wing off on a run up at a northern base, so now they applied the power as the brakes were released. The bomber moved down the runway, the forward roll translated into shocks that bounced the wings up and down. As they gathered speed, the wings began to fly—not the airplane, just the wings—and Kelly would level the flying portion out while the fuselage lumbered on. Eventually, always at the precomputed moment, the rest of the airplane caught up with the wings and launched into the air, an instant transition from truck to albatross. The copilot quickly cleaned up the gear and flaps, and Kelly was happy with this enormous hunk of split-personality metal. Against the background of curved metal sucking support from the air there was a Stockhausian symphonic combination of JP-4 fumes, smoke, acrid sweat, sweetly sour crumbs from bygone inflight lunches, Lysol-squelched urine, aged leather, staccato whirl of hydraulic pumps, creak of metal, beeping of electronics, static, and a lover's warm response to touch. In the air, it was like every airplane, a joy.

Duke had him over every night, working out the test program. It was obvious that Brown was far from being an engineer, despite his West Point training. He deferred to Kelly on the test plan, insisting only that they get into it gradually, and build up a data base on straight and level flight before beginning to get down among the Sierras at high speed.

Compared to the test work Kelly had done at Wright-Patterson and Edwards, it was boring. They'd launch every day about 0900, fly for six hours, and come back. That night they'd analyze the data, and make out the next day's flight plan.

The data weren't speaking to them; there was nothing they found that wasn't perfectly predictable. Duke wanted to deviate from the original plan, to go lower and faster to see if they could pick up some leads. Kelly refused.

Patterson was impatient. Another airplane had been lost, this one out of March AFB, and both SAC Headquarters and 15th Air Force were raising hell with the manufacturer and with him.

He kept pressing Duke to leapfrog to the low-level work, but Kelly wouldn't budge. He knew any data they would get wouldn't be meaningful unless they had some good comparisons. Even comparing it with the manufacturer's work in Wichita wouldn't be valid unless they somehow rationalized all of the different instrumentation installations.

"Hey Charlie! Heads up!"

Charles Kingston Brown, Jr., jerked his head up, precisely as commanded. He was just in time to see the ball sail over his head. Too late, he flung out his right hand, arm outstretched, mitt extended to the limit of his fingers, straining every sinew to will the battered baseball into the glove. It didn't work. The ball arced uncaringly past and out into the farthest reaches of right field. He jarred back to the earth and stumbled after it.

He tripped just as he almost had the ball in his glovetop, letting it dribble out. Screams of protest and derision drifted toward him from the infield as Bill Johnson rounded second and pumped for all his young legs were worth for third. Panting now, Charles scooped up the ball, flipped it to his left hand, and hurled it so hard toward second base that he thought his shoulder would rip apart. He stood, gasping, sweating, hands on knees, and watched it fall far short of the second baseman. He groaned and turned his back on the debacle he'd caused. He used the tip of his Wilson Pro glove to shove his glasses back up his nose.

A roar went up from the infield. He spun and saw Bruce Kinner tag Johnson at the plate. Bill had gotten cocky and tried to make it a home run. He paid by getting tagged out. Charles shook his head and started to trot in for the inning change.

The San Joaquin Valley summer heat pounded him mercilessly. The Little League field was kept almost green by constant watering, but still, in places, it was beaten into a brittle brown mat by the sun. The shadow of a B-52 passed overhead. Like the other boys, Charles halted and stared at the airplane, shielding his eyes with one hand.

"D-Model," called somebody near the dugout.

"Nah, bullshit, Harry, it's one of them Gs. Lookit that tail gun," somebody else retorted. Charles Brown dropped his hand and thought about correcting them both, then gave it up. Nobody listened to right fielders. Especially four-eyed right fielders.

He plumped down gratefully on the hard wooden bench in the tin-roofed dugout.

"What the crap were you doing out there, Charlie? Jeez, you shoulda had that one. Even you shoulda had it."

Brown peeled off his plastic issue glasses and wiped his sleeve across his sweaty face. Harry Thurman was an asshole. Everybody knew it. But he was so big nobody told him so to his face.

"Yeah," Brown said. He dropped his mitt on the ground and kicked it across the dugout floor.

Thurman, at eleven a big kid a year older than Charles, scowled. "Hey, asshole. You don't treat good equipment like that, okay? Not on my team."

"Great, Harry. Maybe I should get off your team."

"Hey, Charlie Brown, no kidding about that. You're so bad, if your old man wasn't—"

"Thurman! Knock that shit off!" Coach Griego—Capt. Don Griego, navigator-bombardier on a B-52—glared at the burly Thurman. "Doesn't matter whose old man is who around here. Got that?"

"Yeah," muttered Thurman, staring at the ground.

"What, mister? I didn't hear that."

"I said, Yes, Coach," Thurman growled.

"That's better. Okay. Thanks to Kinner we got another chance with these pukes. We can take 'em. Got that? We can take 'em. All you guys gotta do is get base hits. No heroics, no Mickey Mantle stuff, just get some hits. Now, our lineup is, uh, Martinez, Thomas, and Brown. Jose, knock it out of here. Don, get on deck. And Charlie, come with me."

The other boys grabbed their bats and went back toward the diamond. Brown got to his feet and followed the little coach back to the wire fence between the parking lot and the field.

Griego leaned on the fence and looked out at the fields around Castle AFB. He squinted through his Ray-Ban flying glasses. "Charlie, you've had it pretty tough these last weeks. That right?"

Brown scuffed his Keds in the dust. "Yeah," he mumbled, "I guess so."

"Guess so, hell. Kid, I've watched. Listen to me, Charlie. And don't take this wrong. You don't belong out there, son. You've got more heart than any three of these goons, but you just can't do it. Maybe it's your glasses. I dunno. But you're knocking yourself out for nothing." He turned and peeled off his

glasses, squinting at Charles. The boy stood almost as tall as he.
"Why are you doing this to yourself, Charlie?"

Charles looked off at the hills. "I like baseball."

"Bullshit. Excuse me, but that's bullshit. What you're doing is
not enjoying baseball, son, what you're doing is punishing yourself. Now, this might not be any of my business, but tell
me—did your dad make you go out for the team?"

Charles leaned against the hot fence. "Yeah," he said at
length.

"I thought so. Look, tell you what. You take this turn at bat,
play out this game, and then call it quits, okay?"

"You taking me off the team?"

"No. I'm not taking you off anything. I'm asking you to drop
out, for your own good."

"And for the team?"

Griego wrapped the wire ends of his Ray-Bans around his ears
again and looked off at the bean fields. "Yeah, okay. For the
team."

A shout went up as Jose Martinez knocked a line drive.
Charles studied the scene for a moment, then nodded. He
lurched away from the fence and started for the dugout.

"Okay," he said, to nobody in particular.

Behind him, Griego watched the skinny little boy trudge back
to the dugout. He sighed and pulled the peak of his cap down
and followed him.

Somehow, they all knew about it at the snack bar. Charles
pushed his red Schwinn up next to the other bicycles parked
near the air-conditioned PX snack bar and knew that they all
knew. He shrugged inside. So what. What could he lose? He
kicked down the kickstand, made sure the backstrap on his mitt
was tightly over the handlebar, and pushed open the door.

Inside, the guys were at their usual table, near the jukebox.
Little Richard screamed something from the big speaker in the
middle of it. Charles glanced around. Besides the guys, there
were some airmen in the snack bar and one old fat NCO. He
went to the bar, ordered a burger and a chocolate shake, paid the
bored Mexican his sixty cents, and went over to where they sat.

Shithead Williams, Beano Philips, and Hound Dog Beaudry
went silent as he slid into the booth. The cool red plastic of the
seat felt good after the blast-furnace heat outside. He sucked on
his shake for a minute and ignored them.

"Heard you crapped outta the team," Beano said. His Oriental features screwed up into a malicious grin. "Heard you dropped three and fanned out."

Charles sucked noisily on the paper straw. He slurped up the thick ice cream and milk, and put it down deliberately. "Yup," he said.

Shithead clapped him on the back. "Ah, don't sweat it, Four Eyes. Baseball's a dumb game anyhow. Now you take basketball—"

The others hooted him down. Shithead was the best basketball player at their school. He was almost five foot nine already, and his old man was six three. They said that Tech Sergeant Williams was born to play basketball, but now that the Harlem Globetrotters had visited Castle, they said that about every colored guy, especially his son, Shithead, whom everybody else called William, of course. Charles sucked on his shake.

"Hey kid," called the Mexican, "your burger's ready."

Charles slipped off the seat and collected his burger. He splashed ketchup and mustard all over it, then plopped down again in the booth. An airman fed dimes into the jukebox and Elvis began moaning about his shoes. Hound Dog started to do his Elvis imitation. They ignored him.

"You gonna tell your dad?"

"Got to," Charles said between bites.

Shithead whistled. "Man, you braver than me. My old man'd whup my ass if I was bounced off the basketball team."

"Yeah, Four Eyes. How you gonna do it?" Beano seemed genuinely concerned. When he talked like that, he sounded like his mother, Tatsuko Philips. All the kids loved her because she never gave them any crap about eating too much on Saturday afternoons when they blew into Colonel Philips's place in Wherry housing to see what kind of great chow Beano and his family had.

"Dunno," Charles muttered.

They fell silent while Charles munched and Elvis moaned about blue suede shoes that Charles could scarcely imagine.

"Maybe you could say you got sick or something," Hound Dog said hopefully.

"Nah," Charles grunted. It might work with Master Sergeant Beaudry, but not with his father. Not with Col. Charles Kingston "Duke" Brown.

The fellowship of the booth lapsed into a deep silence. Charles polished off his burger and knew he should leave. The guys were trying to help. But there wasn't any help. He'd screwed it up and

345

now he had to face the music. He slurped up the remnants of the shake and jumped off the seat again.

"Gotta go," he said and headed for the door. Somebody said something in reply, but he didn't hear it.

"Mom?" He closed the door behind him and called again. "Mom?"

There was no answer. He ducked into the living room. She was there, asleep on the sofa. A glass stood empty next to her dangling hand. Two bottles of something were out of the liquor cabinet. Charles looked down at her for a moment, then bent and kissed her lightly. She stirred but did not awaken. She smelled of booze and perfume. He picked up the glass and went to the kitchen.

Isabel had already cleaned the house spotless. He pulled open the refrigerator and stared inside for a moment. He got out the jug of cold water, poured a glass, and rummaged in a drawer until he found the Fizzies. He pondered the packets and then selected black cherry flavor. He dropped them into the cold water. They mushroomed into little bombs of bubbles. He took the glass and went back to his room. While they fizzed, he got out the latest copy of *Amazing Stories* and found his place in "The Planet of Death." He sipped and read until he, too, fell asleep, lulled by the brilliant sunlight pouring in through the venetian blinds and the humming of the air conditioner trying to deal with the effects of the sunlight.

When he awoke, it was night. The hi-fi was playing some Perry Como thing his mother loved. He blinked himself back to awareness, and looked at his alarm clock. It glowed in the dark. It was after nine o'clock. Another late dinner. He got to his feet and fumbled to the door. Light poured through from the hallway and he followed it to the dining room.

Joan Brown hummed to herself tunelessly as she clattered around the kitchen. Charles stood silently in the doorway for a moment, watching her erratic movements. She was juiced again. She finally saw him.

"Charles! Did you have a nice sleep? Give Mummy a kiss."

He let her embrace him and pecked her on the cheek. She smelled even more strongly of liquor. He pulled away and headed for the dining room.

"Where's Dad?"

"Well, your father, as usual, seems to be working late. He

called an hour ago and promised he'd be home in fifteen minutes. You know what that means."

"It means an hour," Charles said. He didn't have any time left. And he had no idea what he'd say.

"That's right," she said in her mocking tone, stretching "right" into a ten-syllable word. "He—"

The front door opened, halting her in midsentence. Duke Brown, in a flight suit, carrying a flight bag, came in wearily and dropped his gear near the foyer.

"Hello the house," he called. "Anybody home?"

"Hi, Dad," Charles said, halting near him.

"Hiya, Prince Charles, had a good day? Good." Duke patted him on the head and clumped into the kitchen. Charles stood rooted to the spot, mouth dry. He'd almost blurted it out. He listened as they kissed perfunctorily and chanted their night greetings to each other. Duke went through to the bedroom. In a few seconds, the sound of his shower drifted into the living room, audible over even Perry Como.

Dinner passed in half-heard phrases.

"—absolute bitch of a test, what with Kelly refusing to do the hard stuff—"

"—Elaine was simply too tired for the run to San Francisco, so we got into the Buick and—"

"—another month and we'll be able to wrap it up—"

"—perfectly dreadful time she'd had with that doctor, you know, what's his name—"

Charles forked the cold peas and seared chicken-fried steak into his mouth, not tasting them, not even really being at the table. Joan occasionally darted a glance at him to see that he was not putting his elbows on the table, or not playing with his food, or not committing some other heinous crime. Duke ignored him, until dessert. "So, sport, what'd you do today?"

"We had another practice game today, Dad."

"Oh? Whipped 'em good, I bet." He dug into the ice cream savagely.

Charles shoved his glasses up on his nose and stirred his spoon in the ice cream. "Not exactly," he mumbled.

Something in his tone caught Duke's attention. He looked up sharply. The three triplane creases in his forehead deepened.

"Something happen, Son?"

"Sort of," he mumbled.

"Take a ball in the gut, did you? Happened to me once at the Point. Damned painful."

"No sir."

"What, then, Charles? Don't play games."

"Well . . . I sort of dropped off the team." He scooped up a big spoonful of ice cream and shoved it into his mouth. The cold hit his teeth like a fist.

"What? What do you mean, 'sort of' dropped off the team? You mean Griego dropped you? Why, that goddamn little—"

"No sir," he spluttered. "He didn't drop me. I quit."

Duke sat back and glared at him. "You quit? Just like that?"

"Yes sir."

Joan came back in and sat down. She darted big-eyed looks at Duke and Charles.

"Oh, Charlie," she said, laying her hand on his skinny arm, "I'm so sorry—"

"Sorry, hell," exploded Duke. "What the hell made you do that? Somebody threaten you? Chicken out? What?"

"I—I'm just no good at it, Dad. I'm sorry. But I just can't do it."

Duke's face seemed to darken. A vein throbbed in his temple, clearly visible next to his short hair. He laid his hands on the table and splayed his fingers. Charles wanted to run, but he knew better. He'd left the table without authorization too many times before and always paid the price with welts from the yardstick that was Duke's chosen instrument of punishment. He shivered in his seat while Duke contained his obvious fury.

"So," Duke said finally, grating the word out between clenched jaws. "You can't do it. A Brown can't do it. A Brown. Can't. Do. It. So."

Joan shrank from him. Charles felt a fear he'd never felt before. His father suddenly smiled a vicious smile at him.

"Were you afraid, little man? Afraid they'd laugh at you? Or afraid, maybe, of me? Well, you should be. Because they will laugh at you. And they'll laugh at me, too, and that's what you should fear, Prince Charles. Me. You should fear failure in my house. Because Browns do not ever say they can't do something. Not ever. So do this, little man. Go to your room. I will visit you soon, believe me." He paused. "Now!" he shouted, in a voice so barely controlled that Charles leaped from the table and ran to his room, crashing through the door and pulling it closed behind him, gasping for breath and letting the tears gush finally from their hidden wells.

Joan hiccuped, blinking impotently at Duke's rage. He glared at her with loathing so palpable she felt it as a physical blow.

348

"This is what comes of it," he said, hissing, "this is what comes of a mother like you. I hope you're happy. No Brown in five generations has needed glasses. No Brown in five generations has failed to excel in sports. No Brown in five generations has failed in anything. And now . . . now you give me this."

She rallied herself and bristled. "Don't raise your voice to me, Duke Brown. For God's sake, he's just a little boy! Can't you see that you terrify him? Can't you see—"

"Yes! I see. I see a coward, a mama's boy, a whining—"

Joan slapped the table hard and stood up. She weaved slightly as she looked haughtily down at him. "You," she said carefully, "are despicable at times. This is one of those times. I am going to go to his room and comfort him, as he so obviously needs comforting. If you were any kind of man—any kind of father—you'd be in there helping, instead of shouting abuse at him. Your own son."

She turned on her heel and left the table. Slowly, Duke unballed his fists. The red haze began at last to clear from his vision. He drew a shaky breath and wiped his face. From down the short hall came the unmistakable sound of sobbing. Brown looked around the little dining room and shook his head. As if his limbs were lead weights, he hauled himself to his feet and headed for the source of the sobs.

Midway along the hall, the phone rang. He halted and listened to it ring once more. Then he hurried back to the living room and jerked the receiver off the cradle.

"Colonel Brown," he barked into it.

"Sir? McNeil here. We've got a major problem with the data on the test article. Can you come back to the hangar?"

"Now?"

"Well, yes sir. Now. The chief says that only you—"

"Okay, okay. Look. I'll be there in fifteen minutes."

"Roger, sir."

Duke didn't hear his sign-off. The phone was already on its way to the cradle. He stood for a moment in the living room, then made up his mind. He strode to Charles's door and knocked.

"Joan? Charles? Look. I'm—I have to go. That was Ops. We've got a problem on the program. They need me there. Now. Look. I'm sorry I blew up. Do you hear? I'm sorry." He paused and tried the door. It was locked.

He stood back from the flimsy hollow-core door and considered it for a moment. Charles had violated Joan's fanatical decorating scheme by pinning a picture of a B-52 on the door. Duke stared at it. He wanted to say something, anything, to make them understand. But no words seemed to come to him. He stared at the B-52 and finally swallowed hard. "Okay," he called, "I'll see you both later. I'm—I'm sorry. Do you hear? I'm sorry."

There was no reply from the room. Duke turned and went into their bedroom. When he passed the door again on the way out, dressed in his khakis, he suddenly remembered something one of his classmates had said when they'd lost to Navy.

It's only a game, the guy had said. Only a game.

He grabbed his flight bag and hurried to the car. Far away, on the flight line, a jet engine roared into life and shook the still of the night.

Kelly had talked so much about Duke and his rank-hungry life-style that Joan's appearance shocked Kathy. She had assumed that anyone serving as Duke's wife would be Duchess of Windsor thin and stylish. Instead Joan was a balloon, at least forty pounds overweight. Her face was puffy, and the dark circles were amplified rather than concealed by the rhinestone-ringed sunglasses she wore even indoors. Polish hams poked out from her sleeves and she had given up concealing the Goodyear around her middle.

Kathy wanted to be friends with her, to smooth over any problems Mike and Duke might have, but also because she sensed Joan needed help desperately. The first time she called on her, she had dropped in at ten and Joan immediately poured them both stiff gin and tonics.

They had gone through the traditional game of trying to match up lists of mutual friends. It didn't work too well, because Joan's list was two or three ranks higher than Kathy's. There were a few though, and they spent some time getting up to speed on who was married, who had babies, who had been divorced. It was sad, but Kathy already had more friends on base than Joan, who was a virtual recluse.

There was a long silence and Joan burst into tears. "I hate you, Kathy; you look like a million." She wasn't jesting; she hated Kathy. She hated most people, especially herself.

Kathy was taken aback; she would have preferred to go, but this woman was wounded. Duke spread wounds about him, a burr of life.

"Joan, you look great, you've just been working too hard. You've got to get Duke to take you up to San Francisco for a week and just relax. And we all need to diet; maybe you and I could start one together, and ride herd on each other."

"Kathy, I haven't done any work in years; a lovely little Portuguese lady comes in and does whatever has to be done here. The only diet I need is to get off this stuff." She threw the glass—empty now—across the room.

"I'm on the sauce, and you know it and Duke knows it, and I can't stop."

"Do you want to?"

"God, I've got to. Look at me. I'm a fat old broad, look like I'm sixty. Duke will dump me if I don't get in control." She began to sob softly, her tears cutting through the heavy pancake makeup.

Kathy wondered if Duke actually would break off with her. It seemed out of character for him. Kelly had talked about Duke endlessly; Kathy felt she knew him. Duke was a lot of things, and he didn't have too many friends, but no one ever said he'd been unfaithful. He wouldn't dump her unless their marriage came to the point of gaining him reproach. In the meantime, he was gaining sympathy.

"Have you been to a doctor?"

"Yes, one of those damn resentful young Air Force doctors told me to go home and forget it, I was just part of Air Force life. He acted like I deserved to be a drunk if I was in the Air Force, just because he wasn't out in private practice cleaning up. A civilian doctor told me I'd have to be committed. Neither one gave a damn, and neither did Father Mullins; small wonder, he likes to booze more than I do."

Joan got up, walked over to the small bar that almost overflowed with bottles. She glanced at Kathy, who shook her head.

"Not now, Joan. Would you try Alcoholics Anonymous?"

Joan shuddered. She put her hands on the bar and hung her head. "Duke would kill me; the word would get around."

Kathy thought for a minute. "Look, the word is going to get around about your problem, if it hasn't already." Joan was silent. Kathy went on. "Now, Modesto's only a half an hour away, but no one from here ever goes there. We could say we were taking classes at the junior college, and drive up there. Nobody would know."

Joan jumped at the straw; it was as much Kathy caring to help as it was the possibility of a solution.

Kathy drove home, wondering what she had gotten herself into. She didn't particularly like Joan, but she felt sorry for her. She had the indefinable feeling she was doing something Mike would approve of, despite his acute dislike of Duke. The more she thought of helping Joan, the more she liked the idea: in a way, she was being Air Force as she had never been before.

There was a little problem in Modesto; the A.A. chapter thought they were running contrary to their philosophy of admission to the problem. Kathy cranked up her charm and talked them into taking Joan. She was pathetically grateful, but Kathy had another reason for helping. Mike drank too damn much, and the time might come when what she learned with Joan would be helpful. His father had been an alcoholic. The stresses were building and he didn't try to take care of himself.

There were six flights remaining in Kelly's program when Duke kicked open Kelly's office door. "Goddamn you, Kelly, can't you keep your nose out of my business?"

Here it is, Kelly thought. He hoped Duke was only referring to Kathy and Alcoholics Anonymous. Not to what happened at Williams with him and Joan. He put down his pen and stood up, face to face with the trembling Brown. "What do you mean, Duke? I'm not here to do anything but fly, you know that."

"Yeah, you miserable bastard, and ruin my career if you can."

"Colonel, I could care less about your career; it's none of my business what your wife does, and none of yours what mine does. If they've got something going together, I'd understand it if I were you. God knows we don't spend any time with them."

Duke stormed out. Mike sat down, weak-kneed. Thank God, he thought, thank God he doesn't know about the horns I put on him.

An hour later Duke came back, subdued. "Major Kelly, we are going to concentrate this program, and do the last flight on our next mission."

Buoyed by the knowledge that his secret was still secret, relieved of the threat, Kelly felt the dumb flush of recklessness spread over him. He jumped to his feet and hurled an ashtray across the room. It shattered against a wall and Duke jerked backward a foot, wide-eyed. Kelly advanced on him until they were nose to nose.

"Don't 'Major Kelly' me, you ring-knocking sonofabitch! When your ass is in a sling you call me out of the best deal of my life, a

352

degree I'd worked my butt off for at Cal Tech, make me work up a program that makes a hero out of you, and I'm not going to let you fuck it up! Well, you're a big man in the Pentagon, Duke, but in this room you're the same little shit who was scared to fly at Williams."

Brown went pale.

"Yeah, you thought nobody knew; I watched you sweat out every goddamn mission; that's why I called you out to the canyon. You haven't changed a fucking bit; I watch you in the B-52. Every time the alternator light blinks your hands are all over the cockpit like a fucking orchestra conductor. You still hate flying and the only thing that keeps you going is your goddamn quest for little stars on your shoulders."

Brown looked daggers at Kelly. But Kelly couldn't be halted. Years of venom spewed from him, unstoppable. He held the initiative and pressed on. "I've had it with you and your West Point bullshit, Brown. I've got your number and you know it. You'd rather be selling advertisements for some goddamn newspaper than sitting in the left seat of that B-52. And I'll tell you this: I'm not going to fly your fucking modified program, even if LeMay himself comes back in and orders me to. A test program has to have internal integrity, and yours hasn't got it. I don't think these aluminum overcasts will hold together at four hundred knots on the deck in the mountains, and that's what our last flight calls for. Well, guess what, Colonel: you can get yourself another boy, because this one's out."

Kelly whirled on his heel and sat down at the table again. He picked up the papers he'd been working on and glared at them, not realizing they were upside down.

Brown seemed to pull himself together in the strained silence. "You're wrong again, Kelly. I'm glad this happened. It gives me some real insight into your stability. I need reliable people on this mission, not some hood who tosses ashtrays. You are relieved of your flight duties as of right now, Major, but you are going to stay with the analysis. It's pretty goddamn ironic that the hotshot test pilot hasn't got the guts to do the tough part of the job." As he spoke, he seemed to reinflate, to regain that Duke Brown composure.

Kelly just shook his head. The flush had receded, and he felt bad afterward, as he always did. What he felt now for Brown was an odd mix of pity and contempt. He shuffled his papers and looked up at Brown. "Duke, all you see is your stars riding on that next flight. I see a smoking hole in the ground. Do what you want. I'll even fly chase for you. But you're making a big mistake, and I'm putting that down in writing for Patterson. You can go ahead and try to be the hero, but I'd preflight my ejection seat very carefully if I were you."

Duke ended the scene by smiling thinly and simply leaving. That night, Kelly reconsidered; he probably should go see General Patterson, just to keep Brown straight.

But the next day, he found that Patterson himself had volunteered to take Kelly's place. While he chewed on this, Kelly's loyalty to the mission struggled with prudence. To his surprise, prudence won. He stayed away from stupid heroics, and stuck with his determination to fly chase.

They'd brought in a T-38 for him to fly chase, with an instructor pilot in the back seat to keep him honest, since he hadn't flown one for a couple of years. At the mission briefing, Kelly approached Brown. The remorse had grown in him, and mixed with it was the guilt he felt for trying to get at Duke through Joan all those years ago. It had taken a decade for him to understand it, but that's what had happened. He somehow felt that he was responsible for Brown, despite their rank differences. It was difficult, but he decided he had to try to save the man from his own folly.

"Duke, I'm sorry we had words, and I wish you'd listen to me. You really are apt to lose this thing, and if it breaks up structurally, you and the rest of the crew might not get out. Nobody has made it out of one that's broken up in the air yet, except tail gunners riding in the back end of the old E and F models."

Brown considered him coldly, and Kelly realized his attempt had been misunderstood. Brown obviously thought he was trying to con him somehow.

"Major, you've been a big asset on this program, but General Patterson tells me we've got a job to do, and I believe him. He believes it enough to come along. If I see something coming, I'll back off. We should be all right." Brown turned to leave.

Kelly persisted. "Wait, Duke. This is your first flight with Hound Dogs on board; you don't even know what effect they'll have. I think this is the Air Force at its worst, a reversion to *Twelve O'Clock High* mentality when we should be working scientifically. If you go in, the whole goddamn test program will be worthless."

Brown wheeled on him, icily self-certain. "Get this straight, Major. I'm *not* going in. Now let's get our ass in gear."

The T-38 didn't have enough endurance to fly the entire

flight, so Kelly decided to fly chase only through the last hour, when they were going to drop down in a pass in the Sierras and crank the speed up to four hundred knots. If anything was going to happen it would be then.

Kelly launched at eleven, and was vectored to the big silver-gray B-52 as it cruised along the edge of the Sierras toward the almost perfect Bernoulli channel called Eagle Pass, through which the San Joaquin River filtered down in endless hairpin turns to the valley named for it.

"Ah, Tango Forty-four, this is Silver Fourteen, over."

"Roger, Fourteen, have you in sight. We are getting ready to run through the pass now; I'll be dropping down to about five hundred feet below the ridge line, and accelerating to three fifty, then three seventy-five, and then out. I'll come back in and make a run at four hundred, and that should be it. Over."

"Roger, Forty-four, how are things looking?"

"There's no significant change. We've had a little turbulence, and the Hound Dog seems to help rather than hurt. It must be smoothing out the airflow aft of the wing, or something, because we had a little clear air at about twenty-eight thousand feet, and it seemed like it was dampened out."

What dumb bastards, Kelly thought. They've got a new variable in the equation and they're happy about it because the stick doesn't chatter. They haven't got a clue where the loads might be routed, where tired metal would crystallize and fracture, or where high-frequency vibrations might meet and meld and self-destruct.

The run through the pretty terrain was uneventful. The mountains were still dressed with snow, and a half dozen lakes sparkled on the horizon. Kelly had walked through here on a survival course once; it was beautiful, rugged country, with a few austere cabins spotted near the lakes.

"Silver, this is Forty-four. I'm going to pull up and do a one-hundred-eighty-degree turn, then come back down the valley at four hundred. We'll gain a few more data points that way. How's your fuel?"

"Forty-four, I'm okay; if I need to, I can divert to Bakersfield or Nellis, depending on where we are. You still sure you want to do this?"

"Ah roger, it's looking okay. We had a little turbulence when we egressed the valley, but nothing spectacular. The nose of the Hound Dog does a little spiral circle; we want to check the mounts when we get back."

Duke edged a little closer. The B-52 accelerated, eight fragile columns of gray-black smoke from the engines merging into four smears across the snowy background.

"Kelly, I'm going to take it out a little farther so I get four hundred knots before I enter, and then hold that for the length of the valley."

"Roger."

The silver B-52 was straight and level at four hundred knots coming through the notch formed by two peaks on either side of the pass. As it entered, a karate chop of wind at jet velocity circled the peak and crumpled the entire vertical stabilizer and rudder into a ragged forty-five-degree angle before separating them like pieces of tin foil.

"Eject, Duke!" Kelly called, as the B-52 began to roll to the left, its nose swinging up and to the right. The nose came down as Brown chopped the power.

"Silver, we got a problem here."

"Jesus, I'll say it's a problem."

Brown seemed to be getting control; he'd added some more power as the B-52 continued its bank, still climbing. Maybe they could get it stabilized, then eject. Kelly closed in.

At eighteen thousand feet, Brown had the airplane wallowing toward stability. It was still banking, but he had it almost wings-level, maintaining altitude.

Kelly slid in close enough to peer into the B-52's cockpit. He could see Brown with his arms locked around the wheel, applying full opposite control to the direction of flight.

"Kelly! What did I lose? Any rudder left?"

"Negative. All the rudder and most of the vertical fin is gone. Not enough to do you any good. Can you maintain directional control?"

"Yeah, once we're slowed down."

"You ready to eject?"

"Ah, negative . . . I think I can stay with it for a while, maybe figure a way to land it."

Kelly cursed under his breath. "Roger, but that's doubtful. Why not get someplace where you can check it out?"

"Rog. Climbing now. Let's go to twenty thousand."

The climb took forever, and Kelly's warning lights for fuel state lit up. "Listen, Duke, I've got to refuel. I'll be back. You're talking to the C.P., aren't you?"

"Yeah. We've got a patch through to Boeing. See you later."

Kelly peeled off and headed for Castle, where they turned him around in less than thirty minutes. He was back with the bomber in less than an hour. Now there were half a dozen other chase planes orbiting with the crippled B-52. He came back on station and checked in with Brown.

"Listen, Kelly, Larry Lee in Wichita says if we lower the aft gear it will improve directional stability. Give me a visual on it, will you?"

The big four-wheel trucks came down without incident. "Looks good," Kelly said. "Now what?"

"I'm going to try for straight-in at Travis. The country to the west is vacant, so if I lose it, there's nothing to hit."

The end was anticlimactic. Brown herded the bomber around to the Travis runway heading and began a gentle letdown. Kelly watched as the battered airplane drifted over the Sacramento River delta; everywhere below, people played in the water, in power boats, inner tubes, houseboats. The B-52 passing over probably looked normal to them. But inside, the crew was once again tense.

They began their long final approach. Duke keyed the intercom. "Anybody want to punch out now?" Nobody answered.

Next to him, Patterson fished out the landing checklist. He was quiet, scared stiff like everyone else in the airplane. Brown kept the B-52 close to heading, gently easing it down the glideslope like an aged woman coming down a steep flight of stairs.

Brown kept the airspeed high. The airplane crossed the overrun hot and high, then started to drift off-centerline. He chopped the throttles and it lurched to the ground, wings flexing, three tires bursting instantly.

In the T-38, Kelly shook his head in disbelief. Goddamn! The little bastard made it! He swooped low over the ambulance and fire truck that were racing to the halted, smoking bomber, and executed a perfect eight-point victory roll. Nobody noticed.

Patterson and Brown both received DFCs. Kelly got a Commendation Medal, the sort of decoration given to clerks for three years of adequate service. He didn't mind. But he did mind losing the chance to stay at Cal Tech. Amid all the glad-handing, he put in a call to the Pentagon about going back. The colonel he talked to could not have cared less about his problems. He had his own, along with the rest of the Air Force. All of them seemed to come from one place: Vietnam. And that's where he told Kelly he was going next, with an F-4 squadron.

When she heard, Kathy urged him to call Brown and ask his help. Kelly just looked at her. "Help from Brown? Honey, help from that guy is like the monkey fucking the skunk; I don't have all I want, but I've got all I can stand."

They decided she'd go back to Washington, to wait out his year in Nam. Kathy seemed more concerned about Joan than about him.

"What's going to happen to her, Mike? She won't be able to stay on the wagon without A.A., and she won't go to A.A. without me."

Kelly reined in his anger. "That's Joan's problem. And Duke's. I need you a hell of a lot more than Joan does."

Kathy glowed. She had rarely felt more needed, more fulfilled. But she knew Mike was wrong; Joan was not going to get help from Duke, any more than Mike would. She needed someone. Someone like Kathy. And Louise Washington filled the bill perfectly. She did not tell Mike about her idea, but the more she thought about it, the better she liked it. Louise was a nurse, was intelligent and caring, and would probably be happy to help.

When she talked to Louise, she was surprised to find that Louise was reluctant to volunteer, only from fear of being snubbed. Kathy talked her into accompanying her on one of their trips to Modesto, and was astonished at the ease with which Joan transferred her reliance on Kathy to Louise's shoulders. As they ate their traditional lunch at the Heavenly Moon, the best Chinese restaurant in the valley, Kathy saw that the other women would not need her guidance to make the system work.

A week after Kathy left for Washington, Joan no longer even mentioned her to Louise.

Book Three

⎯⭑⎯

INTO THE
SUN

28

It was like Korea with heat. Larry White looked out from the hooch at a camp that could have been called K-14 as easily as Bien Hoa. The vegetation and the temperature were different, but the amenities were the same: none.

He had tried to get to Nam twice before; each time the C.O. had stopped his papers, and he'd spent another profitless year driving C-124s around the globe, an ancient mariner in Old Shaky, as the aging piston-engines plane were called. Now he was driving Gooney Birds built in the 1940s, green with corrosion, and maintained by a mixed crew of native South Vietnamese and a stiffening of Americans. He was part of a motley group of Americans—"advisers" the Army guys were called, while the Air Force types didn't call themselves anything—who were here because, well, because here was where the action was. He hadn't even tried to explain it to Micky; it had nothing to do with the domino theory of Communist takeovers, nothing to do with drawing more lines in Asia. He was a combat pilot. And the combat was in Vietnam.

The danger of Vietnam lay across the American horizon for almost twenty years, the signals of disaster there ignored as a smoker discounts a persistent cough. As soon as Larry stepped off the transport at Saigon, he'd known that the deal was as screwed up as Korea. America had learned nothing from the French, while the Vietnamese had learned everything.

The line that divided North and South also divided will and resources. One tiny nation, populations equally mixed, was cut by arbitrary planners into halves which could not exist apart. The northern half was determined to absorb the southern; the southern half was determined to have others defend it.

America eased into Vietnam as a novice slips into a Japanese hot bath, inch by inch, until the numbing shock of pain permits total immersion. Larry and the other early Air Force people

361

arrived as assistance, and weekly the signs were that the assistance itself would grow inevitably into a major military presence.

He crumpled Micky's letter in his hand. Things seemed to go well for her in direct proportion to the distance that separated them. She appeared to have Eatherton eating out of her hand—he hoped it was only that—and was launching a whole new enterprise. Last time she tried something like this she wound up fifty thousand dollars in debt. He hated himself, but he hoped she would again. He was tired of being the idiot wage slave, controlled by everybody, and her being the brilliant entrepreneur. Maybe this was the right life, him away, getting together for red-hot sex on R&Rs and then going away again. It wasn't much of a life, didn't say much for either of them.

The duty wasn't bad; he liked working with his RVN counterparts, who were typically cheerful, and far better pilots than he would have imagined. They were expert in the wild, low-level, bad-weather flying that the mission called for, and it took a few flights before White felt comfortable with their seemingly intuitive way of clipping along at treetop level to an unknown strip slashed in the jungle. There they would drop off food and ammunition, and pick up anything from ceramic elephants to crying families whose village had been hit by the Vietcong. All of his old MATS discipline winced as he watched as many as fifty Vietnamese scamper into a Gooney Bird, each one clutching all his possessions, some cloth, a chicken, pottery; they sat without seatbelts, jostled together, always munching. It took real work to keep them from lighting fires or smoking on the cabin floor. More than once he almost had to fight his way to the cockpit to take off, worried about the weight and balance.

But his worries were always in vain. The good old Goonies would strain and lumber over the trees; the engines never stopped running and they never lost anybody.

The flying was fine, but there wasn't enough of it. A contracting shield of boredom closed around the field, hedging in the palms that stretched everywhere, shutting out contacts from any ordinary life. A pyramid of Vietnamese workers swarmed the base, doing all the housekeeping jobs, and generating a hierarchical economy of their own. They were desperately cheerless, twenty years of war etched in every move. White was friendly with them all, but only the flying officers seemed capable of summoning up a smile or laugh. It was infinitely depressing.

There were some diversions; he'd spent a week in a South Vietnamese observation post, a straw-thatched, dugout-riddled fortress that reminded him more of the circled wagon trains of the American West than modern warfare. It had been a quiet time, with just a few mortar attacks, and an occasional rocket. He had grown to admire the handful of Army types who served as liaison with the RVN army, and had even become acclimated to the pungent food. Two weeks after he had visited, the camp was overrun, with no survivors.

Once in a while they got a trip to Bangkok, either for R&R or to pick up a part at Don Muang. Only a totally unenterprising crew chief couldn't manage to have a one- or two-day delay for maintenance, despite all the efforts of the local command post to get them on their way. He had been twice, and it was changing his life.

He lay back on the cot, sweltering. His hoochmate had brought back an air conditioner, and done a creditable job of spreading wood and canvas around the hooch to contain the cold. The air conditioner had promptly blown the generator, and now they were back to normal, the extra wood and canvas piled up awaiting the commissioning of the new power plant and reinstallation. The money being poured into the country was staggering; concrete came by the shipload, oil and bombs in a never-ending stream. There was enough pierced-steel planking to make a runway around the equator, and warehouse after warehouse of parts. Yet there were damn few airplanes. The wings were falling off the ancient planes used for ground attack. Larry lost two old buddies within a few weeks' time; one in a T-28, the other in a B-26. The first had been designed as a trainer, the second had been obsolete when in Korea. He knew that neither plane had any business in combat—and neither did he. That was perhaps the biggest difference between the two wars. In Korea, the war had been fought by the young, fresh-faced kids out of flying school, with just a sprinkling of older senior officers in command positions. Now the young man was the oddity; it was not unusual to find a squadron made up of graying majors and lieutenant colonels, all wondering what they were doing there.

Thoughts of Bangkok drifted into his head. And Bangkok meant Number 54. He'd been married for fifteen years, flying in and out of every country in the world, and for the first time he had been unfaithful to Micky. He was disgusted with himself, mostly because he knew he was going back the first chance he got. The Thai women were so gorgeous, and so submissive. Especially Number 54.

Micky had changed so much. She was still trim and beautiful, but she was so busy that she didn't seem to need him even for window dressing as a husband. Their sex life had once been fantastic, and was still adequate, but naturally seemed better when he was away than when he was home. For the past few years, though, he could tell that she was simply accommodating him; he pictured her running percentage points and commissions through her head as they coupled, fantasizing sales instead of sex.

Well, that was okay; her working had made the marriage secure, even though he was gone so much. He'd been in Singapore when Libby had died, twelve thousand miles away when the wire came. Micky hadn't stopped grieving about Libby, although in truth her death had brought release to her little stunted body.

And he was lying in Bien Hoa, thinking about Number 54 in the Bangkok Yellow Rose Massage Parlor. Jesus, what a swine he was.

The whole business was a joke. The fiction was maintained that it was not a whorehouse; the girls were supposed to bathe and massage you, with some attention to your private parts. The ritzy places employed a little hand vibrator like barbers used to use, but Brylcreem was the standard emollient. All the guys joked about it, a little dab will do you, all were embarrassed that they indulged themselves. Yet it was but a simple release of tension. Somehow it marked a middle course between the nervous masturbation of adolescence and face-to-face intercourse with a whore with all the postcoital distress. The distinction was slim, but easy and desirable.

He had fought off the temptation for a long time, but after four months in Bien Hoa, something had to give.

It gave on the first trip to Bangkok. The crew had joked about the prospects on the hazardous taxi ride into town from the airport, past the serried shops, the pepper trees prospering in the exhaust fumes, the endless crowds of cheerful Thais, talking, washing, and always eating.

Larry had been intent on getting to Johnny's Gems to pick up some more of the fabulous bargains that Micky loved so much. She was always pleased with his gifts, but the jewels were the buy here. Johnny's shop was a warren of cases of glittering stones, presided over by Johnny himself when he wasn't off on a buying trip, and smoothed by the laughing ministrations of the women clerks, whose eyes never wandered from the customers.

They had an excellent system of serving endless ice-cold bottles of Singha beer, and sending out to the sidewalk vendors for platters of delicious, strange food. There was a constant showering of inexpensive gifts, enameled pins, rhinestone-covered elephants, and they even played jokes on steady customers. The one they liked the best was a serving of prik soup, an incandescent solution of the hottest of the fiery Thai peppers. The American flyers would always try to pretend they enjoyed it but few could get more than a spoonful down; the salesclerk died with laughter, and then finished off the soup with lip-smacking relish to show how it was done.

Larry bought a few cocktail rings, and commissioned a necklace of his own design, a series of pendant rubies. Johnny promised to have it ready for him on the next trip. They had an expensive ivory and jade chess set that he wanted for himself, but he deferred buying it, and he knew he would continue to do so. Gifts were for Micky and the kids. The kid, now that Libby was gone.

His copilot, Charley Coleman, persuaded him to at least visit the Yellow Rose, so he'd know what everybody was joking about. It was just down the street from Chao Pyao Hotel in Bangkok, a concrete building with a glaring neon sign and a busy bar, filled with prosperous-looking Thai men, who never seemed to go into the back room. It was very different from the whorehouses in Saigon, so cheerless that they repelled him. There the women were pretty, in their thigh-slit skirts, but there was the same desperate quality that emanated from the workers on the field, the sense that they knew only war, and that you were somehow responsible for it and that their grinding thighs might contain a grenade.

At the Yellow Rose the process was relatively simple, with the Thais managing to make it romantic and therapeutic at the same time. They had a little ego-inflating routine that never failed; when you undressed they would peer at your penis and then gasp in admiration and fear. Most men liked that part even when they realized it was only a part of the treatment.

Larry was horny. When Charlie grinned and nodded his head at the door, he decided to go in. They paid up front—eighty bhat, four dollars—and were let into a waiting room where behind a glass wall the women waited in a bullpen. Larry realized it was worth the eighty bhat just to observe their domesticity; they sewed, read, and chatted as if it were a sorority social, never looking through the window. The Thai manager had said it was a one-way mirror, but Larry doubted it. The girls, mostly from the farms around Chiengmai, were simply and curiously innocent, feeling no guilt about an occupation that saved them from the fields and could provide a nest egg that would help them marry well later.

The thing that really bothered him was their apparent youth. It was difficult to tell the age of Thai women; they maintained their slender figures and unlined faces almost indefinitely, then seemed to crumple overnight into middle age. And then she turned to him, tiny, covered with a white robe with a heart-shaped button marked 54. Larry had fallen hopelessly in love with Number 54 the moment he saw her. She was small, with delicate features. Her tiny breasts barely caused her tunic to swell, and her face was the face of an angel. Coleman had already made his selection and disappeared; Larry signaled the manager that he wanted Number 54.

The encounter was almost a fiasco. The young woman had met him at the door and taken his hand, tugging him along and chatting gaily in G.I. pidgin English. She laughed and smiled sweetly at his comments, neither one of them understanding the other or making sense, but both trying to be nice. She led him down the corridors of cubbyholes, into a plywood-partitioned room that featured a coat rack, a tiny spirit temple, a bed, and a bathtub. She evaded his touch, making him sit on the bed and disrobe while she vigorously scrubbed the tub before beginning to fill it with a lukewarm water that in his mind pullulated with bacteria. It didn't matter, for testosterone abetted temptation. When the tub was full, she motioned him in, and soaped him all over with a washcloth. She smiled and sang, never looking at him directly, the scent of her perfume overpowered by the powerfully laden breath that made garlic seem like Chanel. She dried him carefully, and it happened: he had a premature ejaculation that caused her to frown. They had departed from the script.

The massage was both post- and anticlimax; she was bored by it because he had robbed her of the finish that resulted in extra tips. He was smitten with her fragile limbs, her sweet smile, her budding breasts. She was like a child, and her innocence in touching him warmed him and made him afraid. He was in love with her, he would have married her on the spot, and sacrificed Micky and the Air Force and his kid. She powdered him in a desultory way, and he began to swell again. She looked at him with pleasure and said, "Air start?"

He stretched his hand to touch her head, not understanding.

"Air start, 100 bhat, good air start."

He thought she meant a tip, and he nodded; she was so innocent despite her job, a flower.

She dropped her head to his stomach, and began to kiss him while she stroked him. Her mouth enveloped him, her hand plying up and down, and he came again, almost as quickly as the first time. He felt like a despoiler.

Yet he knew he did not exist for her, a big cheese-smelling *farang*, a foreigner who was but a ticket from Chiengmai. He was the commodity, not she; she probably went home to her lover each night, their mutual unconcern buttressed by the bhats she earned. In two years they would have enough for a proper house, on stilts, surrounded by a klong and a piece of land to grow rice on. In three they could have some water buffalo, and he could have a store.

Larry knew this, and he hungered for her. It bothered him because he realized how silly he was, and that his hunger came from the temporary dominance, the false submission. With her, for that moment, he was in charge, and both of their beings centered around the series of muscle spasms that would produce release. He was in charge. For a moment. In charge.

The next searing wave of heat woke him. He looked back into an inferno. He saw a mother grab a child and run forward, falling, holding the baby out to him. Rough hands grabbed him and he felt his shoulder separate as they dragged him through the C-47's overhead hatch. They lugged him to the edge of the field before the fuel tanks went up.

It had begun with an emergency call at Bien Hoa; an outpost was being overrun and they wanted the families evacuated from the tiny strip that was used normally by Air America Helio Couriers. An RVN major, Nguyen Le, asked him to fly in. In twenty minutes they had departed Bien Hoa and didn't climb over two hundred feet before they reached the strip, an absurd slit in the crawling jungle. Le landed the airplane, almost standing it on its nose at the end of the runway. He gunned it around and taxied to the far end of the field. He slipped out of his seat to supervise loading the families, while White moved over. He watched the instruments, eyeballed the length of the field, looked over his shoulder at the crowd increasing inside.

Le came forward, punched him on the shoulder. "Let's go, Vietcong are coming."

White pushed the throttles forward and the airplane barely moved; he checked to see that the brakes were released, then realized that the weight had shoved them down into the rain-soaked ground. The airplane began to creep forward. He bent the throttles forward—there was just enough room if he could get the tail off the ground and do a maximum-performance climb out. He dropped some flaps.

As the airplane lumbered forward a skinny red chicken flapped out of its owner's arms and fluttered to the rear. The owner screamed and followed it; a stampede chased him. The transfer of weight occurred just as the airplane broke ground. The C-47's nose pitched up. Larry pushed the wheel forward and slammed the throttles to the fire wall. He sucked up the flaps and was reefing the elevator trim wheel when he realized they were going in. People began to fall to the rear as the nose went ever higher, the props singing loud as they oversped.

White looked unbelieving as the airspeed bled off; he saw the tree line coming up, put his hands over his head, and that was it.

He watched the C-47 burn itself out. A few of the Vietnamese had gotten out the aft door; only he had survived of the crew. The Vietcong were apparently satisfied with seeing the Gooney go in. The battle subsided, and an H-19 came in to pick him up. He was furious with himself, for he'd spent the time watching the C-47 burn thinking of Number 54, wishing she was massaging his aching shoulder.

29

0825 LOCAL
22 November 1963
Minot AFB, North Dakota
USA

"What the hell are we doing here, Novack?"

It was the hundredth time Artie Clark had asked the question, unaware that the question he was really posing was tougher, one of human reliability. If his moods persisted, Ed was going to have to talk to someone. You couldn't have a launch control facility commander edging toward terminal depression.

"Artie, we're here for a lot of reasons; if you hadn't busted out of flying training, you'd be doing exactly the same thing, except in a B-52. Like it or not, boring or not, SAC or not, we're defending the country."

Clark was silent for a while, then started standard gripe number four. "You know, Ed, it really burns me about the missile badges. Every sonofabitch wears them, just for going through some half-ass staff course. You don't see logistic guys wearing wings, not unless they were pilots once, do you? The goddamn aircrews get everything, better pay, better duty, more respect. If you work a missile site, you're just a fucking dork."

"Hey, Artie, you make me feel great about myself. I got these bad eyes. I can't even go to flying school. At least you got to go, you had a chance. It's not the Air Force's fault you couldn't hack it." It was cruel, but he had to get him off the subject.

Clark picked up a manual, leafed through it, tossed it back on the shelf. Ed mentally said, "God, it worries me sometimes," just as Artie spoke.

"God, it worries me sometimes, ten missiles, God knows how many megatons, all set to shoot at some poor Russian bastards we don't even know."

Ed Novack had been through it all before; you couldn't handle him with subtlety. "Ellen and the kid still back in L.A.?"

"Yeah."

"Well, how many fucking megatons do you think the Russians have pointed at her? That's what we're doing here, keeping their missiles in their silos. It's a lousy way to run the world, but it's a lousy world. Just ask you."

Clark sighed heavily. "I'm going to try to doze off for a bit," he said after a minute.

Ed nodded at him. It was strictly forbidden, but the boredom forced it on them. They had run their complete set of checks when they had arrived, gone through some training exercises, even cleaned up the premises of minor bits of paper and dust. It was tough to sleep with the lights, the printers, the noise of the generators, but you fnally got to the point that you heard them only when they stopped.

Clark flopped out on the bunk, boots on, cravat on, everything still on, and pulled the pillow over his head. Novack flipped aimlessly through the pages of a *Time* magazine, not really seeing it any more than he saw or heard the command center. His mind was off by itself, mulling things over, stuck in what he called The Routine, which began, as always, with reflecting about his dad's reaction to his being posted to a missile site.

The essential thing was to bring his dad back down through the same hole he'd made in the roof when he found out that Ed was being assigned to a SAC missile site in North By God Dakota.

Stan Novack had started a contracting business in Pittsburgh forty years ago; for forty years he had paved the hilly streets, built brick houses, and made contributions to the local politicians, Democrat and Republican. He'd donated to everyone, year in and year out, and never asked for anything. He had chits out everywhere, and he was going to call them in for Ed, whether Ed wanted him to or not.

Stan couldn't believe the assignment; he had four daughters, beauties each one, all doing well, all married off to fine young men. His baby son, name carrier, pride, had gone to UCLA and graduated with fine grades in electrical engineering. He'd been a distinguished graduate of his Officer Candidate School class. In his first year at Wright-Patterson, he had been placed in charge of a classified missile project. And now he was *exiled?* He couldn't believe it.

Ed hadn't felt very good about it himself at first. Occasionally he mentally reproached Mahoney; instead of earning sixteen thousand in L.A. he'd be making about half that stuck off in a hole in the ground. But he was going to do his time, get out, and get back in the industry, no matter what. The only thing that really bothered him was leaving the Aeronautical Systems Division at Wright-Pat; he had been placed on a "smart bomb" project that was fascinating, and felt he was making a contribution. Now he was going to be a Missileman for real, wearing the new badge, but out of the engineering mainstream. In their third or fourth argument about it, he'd tried to persuade Stan Novack to lay off the political-pull stuff.

"Dad," he pleaded, "if I was in trouble, if I'd done something wrong, I could understand your being upset. But this is just the luck of the draw. I don't like it, but I made a deal, and I'm going to keep it. If some congressman got me a better job, it would spoil whatever I did in it—I'd never be sure what I was doing, and what the congressman's influence was doing. Christ, it could be worse, I could be on some submarine, or stationed in Alaska, something. This is still the United States, still missiles. Who knows, maybe I'll learn something."

Stan Novack doubted it, but he did lay off, and in the next

three months Ed learned a lot. About the Strategic Air Command, about Minuteman missiles, about missile sites, and about himself.

He had been happy with only one part of the reassignment: the school was near Los Angeles. He soon found that the location was academic, that training at Vandenberg Air Force Base was a total-immersion process, a torture course neatly divided into two phases; the first six weeks were spent in familiarizing the prospective missile-site crews with the hardware they would find, everything from the missiles themselves to the supporting air conditioning, electronics, and pneumatics. It was like a dull physics course to Ed, something to be ingested, absorbed, made a part of an arsenal of knowledge. He found that he could register and recall the schematics of a transformer box, a hydraulic pack, or a plumbing system with equal ease. The entire site layout, Escher-like in complexity, was exploded into small, digestible parts that he tucked away in compartments, available for recall on demand.

The end of the first phase was highlighted by a three-hour "open book" examination, with 100 percent a required score. He ignored the open book and breezed through the exam in an hour. (He didn't close the book, didn't want to call attention to himself.) Prudently, he retraced the test using the book, found two small errors. It was a confidence builder, he could feel the schematics talking to him, the procedures falling into cadenced reason.

The second six weeks was a translation of the knowledge into procedures, spending twelve to fourteen hours a day in the missile procedure trainer. He was assigned as deputy to Capt. Arthur Clark.

Clark was a gregarious, roly-poly ex-varsity wrestler, barely five feet seven inches tall, and almost two hundred pounds, all muscle. He had washed out of pilot training, and refused to be a navigator. Clark worked hard at the process, but he had problems, so they soon developed a routine that permitted him to pause at tough decisions just long enough for Ed to indicate the right move. They were smooth enough that the instructor teams never seemed to notice. Clark was a phys ed major, not geared to come to grips with the flinty SAC no-nonsense requirements for routine. They made a perfect pair, from both their points of view.

Ed regarded the course work on missiles difficult only in the quantity and rigor; intellectually it was a snap, designed to be followed by rote, with no variations allowed. Clark was quick to pick up the cry of some of his fellow students who rebelled against the premise as "checklist mentality" and chafed at the mental restrictions it allegedly imposed. Ed saw it as necessary and as a liberator for him, personally. He had other projects in prospect, and saw that he could develop a split-level mind, one functioning at the high, noninnovative level demanded by SAC, the other working on an advanced degree, and his own ideas on smart bombs.

The reality of arriving in winter in North Dakota dampened both their spirits. A forlorn billboard, lost in snow, greeted them with a pleading WHY NOT MINOT? Even Babbitt would have required more to be a booster.

Clark's first task was with his family, a wife—Ellen—and new baby daughter with him, convincing them that spring would be beautiful and that Winnipeg was only six hours away. Ellen was brave, but Novack thought he saw trouble in her eyes.

Ed got a room to himself in the BOQ. Compared to the tiny apartment he'd shared with an ever-changing contingent in Los Angeles, it was palatial. It had bookshelves, a desk, and a bed, all that he required.

As welcome as replacements always are, they were greeted with cries of joy, given a rapid indoctrination into local procedure, and within weeks were functioning as if they had never done anything else.

Training had abounded with rumors as to the boredom of the missile sites, the outrageous demands made by SAC, the weird personalities involved. Ed had listened to the shibboleths, waiting to see for himself if in fact there was only Perfection or Disaster in SAC; if the reward for excellence truly was no punishment; if trained monkeys would really be better on the job.

In six months he had formed ideas that would aid him forever. The job depended upon the people, the people depended on the commander. Artie Clark was not a missile genius, was not a military genius, but he was a people genius, and he fitted the reward of personal recognition neatly into the SAC system of doing it right the first time. He used Ed perfectly, letting him monitor the procedures, run the checklists, analyze the emergencies, and he rewarded him perfectly by letting him have plenty of time to himself to study.

Ed's first impression on entering the Launch Control Facility, the home base for a flight of ten of the huge Minuteman missiles, had been one of age and decay. The construction of the 150-missile complex at Minot was less than a year old, but the combination of subterranean construction, constant air conditioning, and firehouse sleeping shifts imparted a locker room fug that was ineradicable.

They told him more than thirty billion dollars had been poured into the construction program that dotted the West with a thousand Minuteman sites. None of the money had gone into luxury, convenience, or even aesthetics. The people factor had been forgotten, from the bunk-bed cots, steel sprung and back bending, to the temperature ranges: cold in winter, hot in summer. There were no amenities.

Things had gone well in the all too brief summer, but by fall Ellen was very unhappy, and nothing Art could do helped. The crisis came when she went to Winnipeg by herself, leaving the baby with a neighbor. In two days she spent more than fifteen thousand dollars, just about exactly ten times their life savings. He was able to return almost all the goods, including the eight-thousand-dollar beaver coat, but Ellen and the baby had to go back to her parents. Artie was desolate, and it affected the crew.

He had tried to adapt, had pushed himself through an exercise program, and squeezed a rubber ball incessantly, presumably adding strength to his already bulging muscles. Artie was the inadvertent perfect product of a lifetime devoted to athletics. As long as there were rules in the game, as long as one could play to win, as long as there were finite periods during which the game could be played, he was superb. As an officer supposed to be in charge of intercontinental nuclear missiles, it was all wrong. He understood the rules of the game, which he regarded as artificially constraining. It was the length of the game that caused him bit by bit to go to pieces. He could not cope with the concept of performing intricate duties forever in the sole hope that nothing would ever happen.

Ed watched him like the secret service men who swarmed now around the president. Like them, he had to spend his hours in alert vigilance, doing nothing. It was too much for Artie. Had the Russians assembled on a football field, or, better yet, on a wrestling mat, he would have been perfectly happy. As it was, the pressures of home and duty were pushing him around the bend.

Ed stopped scanning the old magazines; there was an article on the *Thresher* going down. He might have been on it, a missile officer on a nuclear sub, crashed on the bottom of the ocean;

there were some things worse than Minot. He mused about how his life might have been different had he joined the Navy, and almost missed the first chatter of the printer.

The printer's clanging alarm bell shook Clark out of his sleep. Then the alarm lights lit up. Ed dropped the magazine, began the verification procedure just as Clark leaped from the bed, wide-awake, and ripped the paper from the teletype printer.

"Holy Shit, we're going to DefCon Two; they shot the president in Dallas!" They stared at each other for a half second, then went to work in earnest.

It was hell for the next fourteen hours; when the pandemonium began to subside, when all the checks had been made, when all the calls had been confirmed, when there began to be some assurance that the assassination wasn't part of a larger plot to begin a war, Artie grabbed him by the arm. "Okay, Deputy; now I know why we're here. And I'll never say another word about checklists. If it hadn't been for the fucking checklists, we'd never have gotten through this." Ed had the presence of mind not to reply.

They drove back in silence from the launch facility, plunged into the national gloom; the cold truck's jolting played a counterpoint to the staccato rhythm of flashing lights, bells, and countdowns that had preoccupied them for the day. Their relief crew had been as shaken as they were, anxious for once to get on duty.

Just before they got out of the truck, Artie squeezed Ed's shoulder in a grip like a steel claw. "Ed, I'm sorry I've been a horse's ass. I've leaned on you since we started for procedures, trying to hold my end up with keeping people happy. Then I shafted you with that too. We got another couple of years together; I'll try to do my part. I promise."

Ed rubbed his shoulder and smiled. "Hey. You had a lot on your mind. Tonight, the Russians probably were as scared as we were, as much on alert. There's some poor bunch of Russian bastards being trucked back from the site somewhere, someplace probably colder and bleaker than this godforsaken dump. But they didn't shoot at us, and we didn't shoot at them." He paused and pushed his glasses back up his nose. "Hell, the way I see it, we're way ahead of the game."

30

0540 LOCAL
27 March 1964
McChord AFB, Washington
USA

The clangor of the phone sent him bolt upright. Groping foggily, he knocked it over, finally got the mouthpiece right. "Sergeant Picard speaking."

"Don, this is Major Cantwell; I'm running the alert notification roster for maintenance. There's been one hell of an earthquake in Alaska, near Anchorage; nobody knows how bad it is, but the Air Force is sending everything it can to help. You have a choice. You can either stay here and run the line maintenance as they stage in and out, or I can put you on a rescue team on the chopper. Either way, get on down to Base Ops as soon as you can."

Picard felt the fireman's thrill at the ringing bell. "Sure thing, Major; put me down on a chopper rescue team. I'll see you in twenty minutes."

Polly was awake, leaning on one elbow. He caught her familiar uxorial scent; her breasts, once so firm and luscious, sagged now, but he still felt a surge of arousal.

"What is it Don, a crash?"

"No, something about a big earthquake in Alaska. I'm going to go on a rescue team. Might as well put all those first-aid courses to use."

They had been in SAC long enough to have the alert drill procedure down pat. She started a pot of coffee and quickly made him some ham-and-cheese sandwiches. Searching through the refrigerator, she found some fruit and candy bars, tossed them in the lunch box. It wasn't enough; she was going to the commissary tomorrow. Maybe it would do. Maybe he wouldn't have to go.

Picard had shaved, put on his fatigues, and grabbed his prepacked B-4 bag, filled with enough clothes for two weeks. He tossed his toilet kit inside, hesitated, then put in a fifth of Jim Beam, and picked up his lunch box.

"Polly, will you drive me in? I may be gone for two or three days, and you'll need wheels."

Shivering, she pulled a coat over her nightgown, and pottered off to the truck in her bunny slippers.

"I hope to God I don't have a flat tire. Every time I go out like this, something happens."

They drove in silence. He was keyed up, happy, eager to be off, and tried to mask it. She was depressed and resentful, and tried to mask it. Neither fooled the other.

"How long are we going to be doing this? Am I going to be chasing around in the middle of the night for the rest of my life, taking you out to kill yourself working?"

He let it ride. It was just the first shot across the bow. There was no time to start, much less finish an argument. But she wouldn't let it rest. Before they got to the gate, she said, "I thought when we left Mountain Home you would get out. But no. They give you another stupid stripe and you stay in. They give you more airplanes, and you stay in. Well, you know how I feel, don't you? I don't care if you get to work on B-47s or B-52s or KC-135s or whatever the devil these *verdammt* machines are. I only want to stop this, Don. Do you hear me?"

He heard her, but he said nothing. It must all be because she was afraid for him. She couldn't really mean it. Not after what the Air Force had done for them both. Was it so long ago that they'd stood there in Dieter's garage in Schoengarten and fallen in love? Maybe he remembered that better than she did. He sighed and kissed her, and she hugged him tightly, longer than a hateful nag would have, but just as long as a fearful loving wife would. Then he climbed out and lugged his gear to the bustling line.

The alert traffic to the base was already heavy; he could see the winking exhausts of jets taking off, staging in and picking up rescue gear. He wished she could share the excitement; this was the Air Force at its best, responding to a civil emergency. Too bad the press didn't cover this like they covered Vietnam.

Base Operations was brightly lit; an outsider would have seen pandemonium, but in fact the whole process of briefing, getting weather forecasts, filing flight plans, and taking off was proceeding smoothly. It was the top of the hopper; the bottom was the runway, where every two minutes another airplane rolled.

There was a special briefing for the helicopter rescue teams. Seven Sikorsky CH-3Cs would launch within the next hour. Their route would take them via Seattle, Vancouver, Juneau, and Anchorage. There wasn't any word yet from Elmendorf, but it was presumed that they would stage from there. If not, they'd play it by ear in the field.

They picked up a full issue of survival gear from the Personal Equipment Office, emergency rations, radios, parkas, the lot. There were four men on each team, plus the three aircrew members. There was a small mixed cargo of plasma and food; the heavy stuff all had to be carried by the 130s.

Picard stood shivering as the crew preflighted the big helicopter, walking around with their flashlights, pulling inspection doors open, checking for leaks. The ramp was an inky smear of black moisture, illuminated with even wetter globs of yellow cadmium pooled from the portable lights. He was mildly nervous; the only time he had ridden in a helicopter before it had almost crashed. The pilot was practicing an autorotation and misjudged, smashing it into the ground and bending the landing gear. Picard hadn't been hurt, but he hadn't liked it. In a way it made him feel better; the odds would be with him this time.

Capt. Abe Greener, the aircraft commander, took a last look around, threw a thumbs-up to the young second lieutenant copilot, Bob Armstrong, and waved them on board. Picard groaned when he saw that he had drawn Ed Fink as the chopper crew chief. After Picard had bailed him out, he had him transferred to Mountain Home's small helicopter unit, and after Don had been transferred to McChord, he had never expected to see him again.

Fink grinned at Picard in happy complicity, shouted something unintelligible over the noise on the flight line, and slapped Don on the back, delighted to be in the position of host. Picard was in effect a guest, and he'd have to go along with Fink, particularly since he'd never crewed a chopper. The big General Electric T58 turboshaft engines began to wind the blades into their characteristic whop-whop-whopping. The cabin noise was deafening, and before Picard could get his headset plugged in, the Sikorsky had lurched off the ground, moving toward the runway. Greener apparently got clearance from the ower for a ramp takeoff, for the field suddenly began dropping away. On the ground it had been a fort under siege; now it was a peaceful invitation to return home. Like any good soldier, Picard promptly went to sleep.

The flight to Vancouver was uneventful, marred only by the appalling damage reports they received. The earthquake had brought a tidal wave with it, and the docks apparently had vanished. The sense of urgency was heightened. Maintenance was waiting for them when they landed, and they were fueled and launched in less than thirty minutes instead of the usual two hours or more.

Out of Vancouver, the weather began to deteriorate. Greener debated about dropping down, wanting to stay in visual contact as long as he could, but the traffic was so great he had to maintain altitude and go on instruments. Picard felt a faint surge of disquiet, hearing, as he always did when he was unsure, new sounds in the engines and gear boxes. He rested his fingers on the smooth metal side of the helicopter. Sure enough, there was something, a little rattling burr of vibration; he wished Gann had never written *The High and the Mighty*. He started to whistle the theme song, but it died on his lips.

Picard wanted to go forward and ask Greener about it, but Fink would regard it as a criticism. He was wide awake, his fingers freezing on the metal, unable to tear them away from the barely perceptible murmur. He couldn't stand it, moved forward to glance in the cockpit. He wasn't familiar with the airplane, but the instrumentation was fairly standard. There were no indications of a problem. Fink was dozing. He edged up next to Greener. "Captain, how we doing?"

"Hello, Picard. I'm not too happy about this weather, but I don't know what to do about it. As long as we don't have to go any higher than this, we'll be okay. No lower, either, unless we break out. The airway takes us roughly parallel to the coastline, but we cut back and forth over a whole series of parallel ridges. Not high, five or six thousand feet, but enough to give problems."

"How's the airplane running?"

"It's okay; why do you ask?"

"I don't know; I keep sensing some kind of funny vibration, and I don't know what it is."

"Shit, Picard, a chopper is all vibration, even a jet. As long as all those little red lights stay out, we'll be fine. . . . If I see anything, I'll let you know."

Greener was a good man; Don went back to stretch out and try to sleep.

The explosion was part of the dream; then he thought the alarm bell was the telephone; he woke with a start of fear to rough shouts from forward and the turbulent roar from behind.

He fumbled with a parachute, got the straps wrong, looked out the window to see the side of a mountain sliding past, snow-capped pine trees flamelit from the burning chopper. The alarm

378

bell was still ringing when Greener put the helicopter into the treetops. The blades snapped and the fuselage pitched over into the base of the tree line. Picard had his hand on his safety belt, ready to burst out of the escape hatch when the blackness came.

He heard voices first, then forced his eyes open. A thin gray light filtered down. He was nestled in a thick bed of dry pine needles, a parachute over him, his B-4 bag propped next to his feet. Fink was sitting by him, head in his hands.

"What happened, Ed?"

Fink's voice trembled. "Some kind of explosion; at first I thought it was a gear box failure, but I don't think so now. Doesn't matter, we're in deep shit, Picard. Greener's dead, Armstrong is close, and Carter has a broken leg. Myer and May are okay, just shaken up. Are you hurt any? I couldn't find anything wrong with you but I couldn't wake you up."

"Jesus, how long we been down?"

"We went in about three hours ago; thank God you and Carter got thrown clear; the rest of us managed to bug out before it blew up. There's not much left of Greener; Armstrong is real bad, broken and burned."

"You hurt?"

"No, not so's you could notice. How about you?"

Picard sat up carefully, then got to his feet, stumbled. They were on the side of a hill. The debris of the chopper was all about them, the ground reeking the kerosene scent of burned JP-4 fuel, molten metal, charred cloth, and crisped flesh. It was a scent that was forever familiar after one visit to a crash site.

"I'm okay."

He walked over to the hulk; Greener was still strapped in his seat, a grotesque doll burned black, gas bubbles slowly forming on the slit where his lips had been. Picard found a parachute, popped it open and draped Greener's poor form with it. He nodded his head, said an Our Father and a Hail Mary. He looked at Armstrong, prayed again, knowing he wouldn't make it. He had seen too many bodies lying beside airplanes to believe a man with his injuries could survive.

Picard realized that he was the senior survivor; he tried to assess what they could do. "Ed, did we get out a Mayday?"

"I think so, but I don't know; they both had their hands full when that fucker let go. If they hadn't gone into autorotation immediately, we'd all be dead. Greener was a good man."

Picard called Myer and May over; neither man had been to

survival school yet, but Myer was a bright young guy and May was big and strong. Fink might be okay.

"Look, I'm senior, so I'll be running things, okay? Somebody has to be in charge, and now is the time to settle it. If you have any objections, let's have them now, because I don't know what it's going to take to get us out of here."

May was scared. "I got no objections, Sarge, but ain't they going to find us right away? They'll know we are missing, and we should have been on radar, shouldn't we?"

"I don't know. The thing is to figure out what is best. I don't think Armstrong is going to live, but Carter could make it if we could get him to a doctor, or get a doctor in to him. We're going to have to figure out whether it's better to stay here, or try to walk out and get some help. I know there isn't much in the way of civilization around here. Might find a trapper's cabin or something. But the main thing is the weather. If it stays socked in like this, there's no way for them to find us. We can run the beepers, and the emergency radios, but they have to be looking for us. With the mountains all around, they won't get any signals unless they are in line of sight, overhead."

Picard ordered them to make camp for the rest of the day, mainly to keep them busy, but also to check on what their resources were, and to see if anybody was trying to reach them on the survival radio emergency channel.

He took stock of the emergency supplies; some of the food could still be used, and there was enough water. There were plenty of chutes to make tents and blankets with. The problem was keeping Carter alive; Armstrong had suffered massive injuries to his head and chest; he was breathing, but just barely. Unconscious, at least he wasn't suffering from the flames that had melted his chute harness and seared his face raw.

They had stopped Carter's bleeding, but he was in deep shock and had to have attention; there was probably something more wrong than his broken leg and his facial injuries.

The area still reeked with JP-4; Picard ordered them to build camp about two hundred yards away, to get away from the sight and smell of the wreckage.

May and Myer improvised a stretcher and brought Carter down; they left Armstrong where he was, afraid that moving him would finish him off, knowing that when he died he'd have to be moved away from camp.

The clouds seemed to lower with nightfall, and a light drizzle persisted until morning. It could have been worse, probably

380

would get worse. The temperature could drop to freezing and below, and then survival would be tougher.

Picard ran an hourly check on the emergency radios, but got no response.

Polly had just gone in to work at The Rusty Scupper when the news came that the chopper was down. The other six aircraft had landed in Juneau, unaware that Greener had gone in. There were more than 640 linear miles of coastline where it might have happened. She slumped into a chair; the restaurant's owner, Paul Thibedoux, twittered around with a glass of water, a glass of brandy, a cold cloth. She waved them away, trying to gather strength to go home and get the kids, prepare them.

She let a young busboy, Gary, drive her home in the truck; Paul following in his Volvo to pick him up. All she could think of was that it had finally happened, what happened to his dad happened to him, just like she had always known it would. He didn't have to fly, they really didn't want him to. Flying pay for enlisted men was a joke, rotated, stopped, it was never regular enough for a line chief like Don. But he flew every chance he got. He'd almost crashed before in a helicopter, swore he'd never fly in one again. Was this the end, was the Air Force going to get this last bit from him, and from her, from her kids?

There was a little crowd of cars waiting outside the trailer. She could see Donna and Jamie at one side, scared and anxious. There was already a mound of food in boxes by the door. It was a ritual out of the Middle Ages; someone died, let the feasting begin. She felt sick.

She hopped out of the truck; Gary ran back to Paul, and the crowd surged around her. The same scene was going on at as many other places as there were married crewmen down on the chopper. She put her arms around the children, whispered that it was going to be all right. Neither one seemed upset yet; Donna kissed her and said, "He'll be safe, Mother; I know he will." She said it with a certainty that scared rather than comforted Polly.

Chief Master Sergeant Shackleford was there, his rough bull face crinkled into what he hoped was a sincere smile but was an almost sinister leer. He never smiled in ordinary life, didn't have the practice to do it well now. "Polly, not to worry. They have a whole airplane full of survival gear and the whole search-and-rescue effort is under way. Don will turn up, probably bring you back a caribou for the freezer."

In a while they went away, let Polly and the kids escape to the inside of the trailer. It had never seemed smaller, emptier, or less filled with hope. The waiting began.

Armstrong died sometime during the first night. Picard hated the idea of burying the two pilots, but didn't know what else to do; they might be here for a while. There was nothing to dig with, and the ground was almost impenetrable. Finally they settled on hauling the bodies almost five hundred yards from the crash site, and covering them in a rock cairn. May insisted on bringing down sections of metal—doors, hatch covers—and covering the cairn with them.

May was a worry; he was increasingly nervous, spent his day scanning the sky. Picard ran the emergency radios only on the hour, to conserve the batteries; he caught May sneaking a transmission, and had to chastise him for it. "Look May, they'll know what we are going to do; it's all a part of survival training. They'll be listening and transmitting all the time, but they know we'll be down to hourly transmissions now. Don't take a chance and run us out of battery before they get here. We'll probably be able to hear them, anyway."

May nodded dumbly. He was scared, and not ashamed to admit it.

The weather wasn't bad; Picard estimated they could last two or three weeks on the food they had, maybe longer. The problem was Carter, who wasn't showing any signs of awakening. He had to have help, or they'd lose him too. He made up his mind to walk out.

The weather was turning colder. He got a firewood party organized the first thing, then called the other three together.

"I think I better try to walk out and get help. I'll go alone, or one of you can come with me. I hate to split up, but I think it's the thing to do. Anybody want to come with me?"

All three wanted to go. They drew straws, and May won. He scurried to get his gear.

Picard called Fink aside. "Ed, you are in charge. Keep the fires going, and don't use the radio except on the hour. Keep Carter warm and dry. I'm going to walk down the mountainside till I hit a valley. Then I'll walk downstream; if I reach a fork, I'll take the left-hand turn. I think that will keep us heading toward the coast. I'll make a careful record of how far we've come, and the landmarks, so I can lead people back. If they pick you up first, tell them what we are doing and send them after us. Okay?"

"Good luck, Don. This is getting old, and I'm really worried about Carter. What are you taking with you?"

"Rations, water, and one of the survival kits."

He had already consumed the ham-and-cheese sandwiches, and, in an excess of caution, broken the bottle of Jim Beam, which had miraculously survived the crash. He wished he had it now.

"We don't want to be too heavy. I'll take two of the survival rifles, mostly for signaling. I'll fire a shot every hour, just so you can tell how we are doing. There's plenty of ammunition." They shook hands.

Picard joined May and they started off down the mountainside, slanting first to the right and then to the left to avoid going too fast. May was almost happy, as if he was on his way to the BX.

Picard glanced at his watch; he was puffing hard and they'd only walked about forty-five minutes, downhill. What the hell was he going to do if they had to go over a mountain? Polly had been right: he was too old for this sort of thing.

He was as worried about her as anything. He felt sure they would get out, but until they did Polly's gloomy German outlook would have him dead and gone. He was going to fool her.

When an hour had passed he fired a shot; it merged into echoes, but Fink's reply was almost immediate and seemed only a few feet distant. They weren't setting any track records.

It was almost dark when they reached a dry creek bed.

"Okay, May, we'll stop here until morning. Let's build a fire."

It wasn't bad with the fire going; there was plenty of deadwood available. For the first time they heard some sounds of animal life, an owl, and what must have been a fox.

"Is that a wolf?" May asked.

"No, nothing. No wolves around here." Or so he hoped.

They walked for three more days. Picard had been dead tired the second day, but his strength came back; by the fourth day he found a quiet enjoyment in being in the woods, in May's almost pathetic dependence upon him. He knew he'd walk out just as he knew he would always be a survivor. The Air Force had trained him to do a job, and now he was delivering. The simple balance sheet of trust and performance was satisfying in a way Polly could never come to understand.

They had just made it down into a widening valley well

covered with snow when they heard the chopping of the helicopter blades. There was a break in the clouds, and the CH-3C poked through. Picard and May slipped the straps on their packs, pulled out the emergency radios.

"Ah, Air Force chopper letting down, we're down here on the right edge of the valley," Picard said.

"Roger, Picard. This is Fink. We have you in sight."

Fink pulled Picard into the cabin, and he in turn pulled May on board. Fink embraced them clumsily, and the chopper lifted off. Picard looked out the window at the pine-studded mountainside that they had just stumbled down. It was somehow the most beautiful place he had ever seen, and he felt an ineffable sadness at leaving it. On that mountain, there had been perfect equilibrium. There was no house to buy, no cars to drive, just the elemental struggle for survival. As May and Fink shouted happily at each other over the roar of the engines, he realized that he had, just for a moment, captured a tiny fragment of something terribly important, something about why he stayed with these men, with the Air Force.

They were flown back to a Canadian Air Force Base on the northern tip of the Vancouver Peninsula. Two helicopters had found the crash site by homing in on Fink's hourly call. There was no place to land, so they'd hoisted them out, just as the training manuals dictated. A special stretcher had been rigged for Carter; the first chopper had flown him and Myer directly to Vancouver. Fink had insisted on going on the second one to try to track Picard down. The bodies of Armstrong and Greener were left until a ground party could come in and haul them out.

They delivered him to Base Operations in style in a T-39; Polly and the kids were waiting, surged forward when he stepped out the door. He kissed Polly, knelt down and hugged the kids. She was crying with joy, but not too carried away not to say, "See, I told you so. You got to get out, Don, before this damn Air Force finally kills you. Promise me, now, right here, you are going to get out!"

He promised her; it was the hundredth time he'd promised her. But he remembered still, too well, the mountainside. His heart was not in the promise. It never was.

The rescue got a write-up in the base paper; he was put in for a Commendation Medal. Everybody forgot about it.

Two weeks later Picard had gained back the seven pounds he

had lost and five more. He went to his Kiwanis meeting on Wednesday, expected to be grilled on the rescue, maybe having to give a talk.

Chief Master Sergeant Shackleford was handling the program. "Where you been, Don? We've missed you the last few weeks."

"Yeah, well I was on the . . ."

"Excuse me, Don. I've got to get the speaker set up; we have a crackerjack broker here, going to give us some tips on the market."

Picard shrugged and dug his spoon into the Jell-O. Business as usual.

31

1610 LOCAL
29 July 1966
Da Nang AB
Vietnam

Jim Garvey stared across the flat expanse of Da Nang with disgust. He was getting too old for this shit, and the war was getting too old for him. He stared out at the cloud-decked hills surrounding the base, blanking out the routes west and north where they must go today.

Da Nang was nestled against the sea, the river a great alimentary canal sucking in supplies, spilling out a delta of mud and sewage that bobbed past the freighters tethered offshore. They ladled out great gobbets of supplies, a never-ending flow of tanks, guns, planes, pierced-steel planking, uniforms, medicine, food, petroleum products, bulldozers, steel pipe, concrete pipe, plywood, copper tubing, wiring, shoes, tools, barbed wire, flares, rockets, flak vests, radios, all the paraphernalia of a war being fought with as many comforts from home as possible, and above all, an endless stream of spare parts carried ashore in small boats manned by dour brown men. The eclectic assemblage of material was ferried ashore in a constant stream of every kind of craft, from standard Navy vessels to fragile slender riverboats powered by an outboard motor driving an eighteen-foot-long drive shaft and propeller. The supplies were checked, signed, countersigned, placed in bins or dumps, and then became a resource for both forces, the South Vietnamese and the Vietcong. Both had equal access, the RVN forces officially, the VC practically. Both regarded the depot as a prime resource, not to be tampered with, and both managed to live with the artfully appropriate distribution of equipment. The RVN got the bulk, the VC got the necessary. In another world, in another society, it could not have been tolerated. In Vietnam it made more sense than anything else. The acreage of Da Nang spread day by day, an urban cancer of supplies, a hardware ethic responding to a wartime need, an outpouring of wealth that was somehow to offset political incompetence and suicidal negotiation tendencies.

In eleven months Garvey had become amazed at the various ways in which fortunes were made. In South Vietnam, an estate could be created from plywood packing cases; simply remove them, set them up again, and you had instant housing. Two packing crates could become a honeymoon hooch for a G.I. and his slender rice-eating darling, or room for a family of seven refugees from the countryside. If in the process of removing packing cases, you moved some containing desirable material—television sets, hair spray, weapons—then you made your fortune faster.

Garvey knew that back in the United States you could also make your fortune these days in plywood: simply raise the prices, dollar by dollar, square foot by square foot, and you created fortunes the Weyerhaeusers would envy. There were a dozen ways with plywood: speculate on futures, buy up logs, bribe inspectors to change the grade on logs, change the grade on finished plywood, buy up contracts, there was almost no end to it. On balance even the enterprising Vietnamese entrepreneur had his work cut out for him to skim further from what six months before had been a fir in Oregon.

In South Vietnam, a native could arrange to provide the exact parts needed to put an armored personnel carrier back into operation—for the Vietcong, of course—simply by infiltrating the area, greasing the guards, and taking the equipment.

In contrast, in the United States you could make a fortune by setting up a rat poison factory in a chicken coop. There were ships and crates returning from Da Nang, Cam Ranh Bay, and elsewhere, and the rats they carried had to die before the passage was made, or else the plague might be brought to the United States. So entrepreneurs took grain, wax, and warfarin, mixed it in paper containers and sold it to the U.S. government at fantastic prices to reap a harvest of thin-blooded dead rats and profits. It took only a concrete mixer, a tar heater, the raw materials, and the chutzpah to charge outrageous prices. There were plenty of suppliers, and the rats died as programmed.

The only people not making a profit were the ones fighting. And Garvey, at nearly forty, was fighting again. God, how it hurt to suck in his gut when he shoved himself in his Nomex flying suit, strapped on the G suit, and strutted out to the lethal-looking F-4s parked in revetments around the field. His GIB—guy in the back seat—was twenty-four years old, bitter not to be in the front seat, lean, taut, and angry. Garvey simply couldn't permit his pot to dump comfortably in front, as much as he admired it, as much as he felt he had earned it with years of drinking beer.

By rights, he should be a lieutenant colonel by now, sitting in the Pentagon worrying about how to cover for not having procured adequate spares. If he was home he could attend to taking care of Rachel. Yet here he still was, an overage major, a flight commander, operating with an airplane so good that it could make a ridiculous mission worthwhile.

Garvey loved the F-4. It was his kind of airplane, big, ugly, powerful, tremendously capable, tremendously strong. He liked everything about it, except that it had two seats, and except the stupid way it was employed.

There was very little air-to-air combat for the Sharkbaits, the 557th Tactical Fighter Squadron, first into Vietnam, first at Da Nang. Garvey was satisfied that this was so. He'd seen too many movies where the old warhorse ace goes out for one more dogfight and doesn't return. He'd killed his share, and now he was content to use the immense power of the F-4 to support the ground troops. He had matured sufficiently not to need the confrontation, the suppression of air to air; he simply wanted to do his job and get out of there. He was due to go, one way or another; he had nine more missions to fly before he would rotate.

The Sharkbaits were flying the very oldest F-4Cs, scarred by use and rotting in the heat and moisture of Vietnam. Garvey was proud of the fact that he knew the man who helped to put them in the Air Force, Mike Kelly, but would have loved to get his hands on the idiot who had created potting compound that pooled like mercury in the tropical heat.

The F-4, for all its cranked wings, twin jets, and rockets, depended upon electrical circuitry, and the red-and-white plastic compounds intended to waterproof the wires and hold them in place simply disintegrated in the verdant moisture of Southeast

Asia. The wires moved and transferred their impulses to the wrong circuits. Two missions ago, Garvey had reached down to arm his rockets; the failed potting had sent signals everywhere, and he had jettisoned bombs, tanks, even the hard-to-get pylons. On another flight his wingman had transmitted his fuel state and his flaps went down on one side, sending him rolling off on a tangent until he could get things sorted out. It was an electronic roulette wheel, a random short-circuiting that could be anything from embarrassing to lethal.

What really bugged Garvey were the pseudomissions. Everyone from 7th Air Force up wanted mission statistics, and sorties were all important. But bombs and rockets were short, and it was not uncommon to launch a flight of four F-4s which, in total, carried no more armament than one might carry routinely. It was four times as expensive, four times as dangerous, and one-fourth as effective. Yet headquarters demanded it; there was another war being fought with the media and the public, and in that arena the four sorties with one-quarter armament was considerably better than one sortie with full armament.

Garvey's always-angry GIB, Lt. Maynard Hibbs, strode toward the F-4. An Air Force Academy graduate, Hibbs was exactly what the blue sky and tall mountains of Colorado were supposed to produce. Somehow the Air Force had done it right, endowing the beautiful facility with all the West Point plusses, and none of the mossback minuses. Hibbs bitterly resented not getting to fly in the front seat. But Garvey had already upgraded two GIBs to aircraft commander, and now he just wanted to survive to the end of the tour. It wasn't fair, but if he was in the airplane, he was going to fly it all the time.

He watched Hibbs roll forward in a John Wayne gait, loaded down as they all were with every sort of equipment: G suit, side arm, parachute harness, self-rescue tree-lowering device, good for a 150-foot-tall tree (and there were plenty of them), thirty rounds of tracer ammunition, flares, radio, extra batteries, water flask, knife, radio, maps, checklists, Mae West, everything but Gibbon's *Decline and Fall of the Roman Empire* for light reading. Hibbs supplemented this with his own conception of what he might need if shot down, adding an extra canteen, another .38 caliber pistol, and two big survival kits, each one liberally stocked with condoms. The latter were not for sex, but to carry water if you were shot down and forced to evade.

Garvey thought he was an optimist. There was almost no way to know the amount of opposition that would be defending the strike area, and it didn't matter, because you had to go in anyway. If they hit you with the heavy stuff, 57 mm or better, you probably were not going to get out. If they hit you only with the light stuff, you would probably be able to get far enough away to come down in a safe area. If you had to eject and landed in an area where you had just bombed, condoms made of steel wouldn't help.

Still, they outfitted themselves like arctic explorers, cramming in all of the items the experts said were necessary, and then staggering up the steel ladder to sit in the maw of the beast. Garvey was reminded of the pictures of knights in armor being lifted onto horses.

It was infernally hot. He remembered how he had hated sitting alert in the Korean cold, fingers, feet, and ass going numb just before the scramble, so that just pushing a switch was an agony. Now he sat and sweated, moisture running down from his graying hair in rivulets, the rank-smelling oxygen mask getting slick, great bands of sweat appearing under his armpits and down his back. Still, hot was better than cold, for underneath was the chill of anticipation.

He'd been flying for almost twenty years now, counting his civil Piper Cub time, and there was always the tingle of anticipation for any flight. These were best of all, for you were called to help, and would roar on to the scene like Custer's cavalry, able to save a friendly set of troops in contact—"TIC"—with the enemy.

If you were called; more often than not you sat out the time in the cockpit, starting with every sudden noise, then climbing down as your replacement strolled into sight with the same weighed-down gait. Then it was back to the hooch, or the party shack; those were the alternatives, and either one inevitably led to conversations with Hibbs.

It started on the walk back. "Well, Major, another day, another dollar, another goddamn tour in the back seat."

"Now, Lieutenant, we've been all over that; you know that this is a two-man airplane, and that you pretty well run things back there."

"If I'd wanted to be a fucking flight officer I'd have joined the Navy. And if it's a two-man airplane, why don't you let me fly the front seat sometimes? You could do your bit for your country pushing the knobs on the radar set."

Garvey said nothing, grimly determined to get unpacked and keep Hibbs off the same old subject by just not responding.

"Yeah, I know, you paid your dues in Korea, and you aren't letting any kid kill you. How do you think I feel with some forty-year-old geezer in the front seat? I never know when you are blacked out or just asleep."

Hibbs was walking the fine line between rowdy comradeship and insubordination, and he knew it. He didn't give a shit. He'd been first in his class in fighters, and they promised him when he came to Nam that he'd spend three months, no more, as a back seater, and then get upgraded.

Garvey really didn't give a damn, but his line was perilous, too; if he reacted and pulled any military bullshit, the kid won. If he let him go too far, to be really insubordinate, the kid won, even if he lost. He had to wait till he said something he could nail him with on his own terms.

Hibbs hitched up his chute harness and spat at the sizzling ramp. "Just like the last LZ extraction," he said, "if I hadn't seen the choppers coming in, you'd have fired right through them." That was it. Garvey pulled him to a halt. "The hell I would have; you read the wrong goddamn checklist. If they'd been MiGs instead of our choppers, we'd have been dead."

Hibbs grinned. The old man had him.

Next morning, he and Hibbs repeated the alert drill, except that this time they launched right after strapping in. It was another LZ mission, forty miles away. The Vietcong had been alerted when the helicopters had dropped a combat team, and they had been fighting all morning, unable to move out toward their objective. They were running low on ammunition, and the choppers were on the way back in.

Four Phantoms began spooling up, the smell of hot JP-4 sweeping across the ramp and mixing with the fetid odors from the sea. The armorers, stripped to the waist, moved around the formation like ballet dancers, bowing, thrusting, and then withdrawing, avoiding burning themselves on the stove-hot metal, even clutching a handful of the red-flag steel pins that safed the 750-pound high-explosive bombs.

Garvey was lead, as his age, rank, and ace status warranted. He booted the throttles forward and the Phantom leaped down the runway. He was Leopard One; Greg Sims was in Leopard Two; he had flown with Garvey in Korea, known Kelly at Edwards. Greg didn't approve of the way Garvey was holding Hibbs back, but he understood. He did just the opposite; he worked his back seater, Capt. Ivan Medvedev, all the time, giving him most of the takeoffs and landings, letting him refuel;

it wasn't so much that he was an altruist as he was making Medvedev into a life insurance policy. If something happened to Sims, he wanted Medvedev to be able to bring him back.

A tiny tired major, Harry Fish, was in Leopard Three. His career almost mirrored Garvey's, except he'd never been an ace, never done anything special, other than having been Mike Kelly's wingman back in Korea. He was like most guys, dependable, a steady quiet producer. His GIB was a riot, a big six-foot-four-inch fullback named Dick Kaplan who never stopped talking, and who idolized Fish. Fish was actually a little embarrassed about it, but Kaplan was so sincere and so eager that there was nothing to do. In number four there were two FNGs—fucking new guys—Garvey hardly knew. They flew in a loose finger-four formation, right out of the Luftwaffe manual, for the short forty-mile flight to the west northwest.

Garvey switched to mission frequency; the first flight was already finishing up. He saw the sea flashing in the distance, obscured by two thin low gray lines of clouds, one at twelve thousand feet, another at three thousand feet. The first would help, if it obscured them from the flak; the second could keep them from seeing the target.

The radio calls were crisp now; he could hear Hibbs breathing faster into the hot mike. Hibbs was closer to Rachel's age than Garvey was to Hibbs's. What the fuck was he doing here?

The controller, Oboe, called. "Leopard flight, go hot."

Hibbs starts through the checklist. "Sight setting?"

"Depressed, ninety mil."

"Weapons selector?"

"Bombs, ripple."

"Bomb arming switch?"

"Arm, nose, and tail."

It went on; Garvey had already set things up and merely called back the settings in confirmation.

The controller called again. "Leopard, this is Oboe. The VC is south of that line of hooches that starts with the building shaped like a T. Friendlies are north."

The Phantoms spread out; they'd dive almost simultaneously, from different directions to make the task tougher for the enemy flak.

"Leopards, go."

The big Phantom arced over, and he picked up the line of buildings in his sights, moved the nose, saw a gun emplacement. The ground lit up with antiaircraft fire; this was heavy duty.

Garvey checked his airspeed, watched the red tracers coming up, a curious weaving spiral that seemed first to veer off then track home. The target was already obscured with the intense black smoke from the flak. Jesus, were they ready for them! He hadn't seen such a variety of fire south of Hanoi before.

His helmet slipped over, the equipment tugged at him, countering the rough pressure of his harness. The F-4 was at forty-five degrees, through the first layer of clouds, the second apparently now moved off the target. Hibbs called off the altitude, seven thousand, six thousand, five thousand. The pipper didn't move; Garvey hit the release button and the bombs flew away just as the flak crunched into them. It felt like someone was beating on the canopy with a four-by-four. He reefed back on the stick, feeling the G suit compress, 6 Gs on the meter, his sweat-slick helmet sliding down.

Hibbs's voice wavered.

"Bombs on target, looks like a secondary explosion. We must have taken some fifty-seven millimeter."

Good man to look when still pulling Gs; the weight of head and helmet can grind your vertebrae right through a disk if you're not careful.

To his right, pulling out too, Leopard Three took a heavy hit; the Phantom folded; both pilots ejected. He didn't have time to see if their chutes opened.

He saw smoke coming from Leopard Two.

"Leopard Two, Leopard One; you are on fire."

In Leopard Two, Sims glanced down; the left-engine fire warning light was burning bright, the right one flickering. The dials of the left engine unwound, together, first reluctantly, then almost comically plunging back toward the pegs, registering the engine's pain and heat. Sims sensed the loss of power, the airspeed began to drop.

Medvedev called. "Ah, Sims, we got a lot of smoke coming out on the left, underneath."

The hydraulic pressure began to fluctuate, and Sims felt the controls stiffening; if the pressure went, the controls would freeze and they'd have to eject immediately. Maybe they could make the coast. The lights in the cockpit glowed everywhere.

Medvedev's breath came fast. "Don't breathe too fast, Ivan, you'll hyperventilate and pass out."

"Roger." The breathing didn't slow down.

"Did you see Three take that hit?"

"Roger—they both ejected, I think I saw one chute."

"Let's try to make it to the coast, Ivan. If I can keep this sonofabitch in the air for another ten or fifteen minutes, we'll hit the coast and get a ride back in a Grumman."

"Roger." Rapid breathing.

"Say, Major Sims"—Ivan was nervous, getting formal—"the smoke seems to be less. Have you still got a fire warning light?"

"Roger on the fire warning, but I've got hydraulic pressure, and the other engine is turning. I'm leveling off at twenty-one thousand."

Sims heard Garvey's voice. "Ah, Leopard Two, I'm just behind and below you. Over."

"Rog, Garve, how about pulling in and seeing what my damage is, over."

"Roger, stand by."

"Hey, Garvey, we're getting a lot of smoke in the cockpit now, this bastard's heating up."

"Roger, Leopard Two, you have a fire going good under the forward cockpit; you better get out of there."

"Yeah, I'm trying to hit the coast."

"Leopard Two, this is Lifeboat."

Lifeboat was the all-seeing radar station, dispenser of courses, rescue director, hope.

"Roger, Lifeboat, thanks, I read you, are you painting me?"

"Roger, Leopard Two, you're about five minutes from feet wet. Can you hang on?"

Sims felt the airplane jerk; the hydraulic pressure that powered his flight controls was failing. Five minutes to the coastline; it might as well be fifty.

"Don't know. I'm letting down to about eleven thousand feet. I can't keep my airspeed up."

Medvedev was breathing faster; Sims could sense him cinching up his parachute harness, checking his survival gear. The minutes passed, the temperature rose. Sims could feel the controls stiffening; it was time to go. "Okay, Leopard One, and Lifeboat, we're leaving this mother."

Sims checked his chute straps. "Ivan, you always want to be first, now's your chance. When I count to three, eject."

"Roger."

Garvey swung his F-4 out to the left.

"Lifeboat, this is Leopard One; the back seater just punched out, looks good. He's got a good chute."

When Medvedev left, the suction over the airplane pulled an

avalanche of heat and flame swirling into the front cockpit, melting Sims's equipment into him, melting Sims into his seat.

"The front seater hasn't bailed out yet."

"Leopard Two, bail out, bail out!"

"Oh, Jesus. Lifeboat, Leopard Two just blew up. Front seater didn't get out."

Garvey circled, watching Medvedev hit the water in the parachute, just as the remains of the Phantom's fuselage buried itself in the sucking sand of the beach in a billow of water, metal, and smoke.

"Lifeboat, Leopard One."

"Roger, One, go ahead."

"There's a junk going toward the survivor; I'm going down to take a look at him."

"Roger. What do you have for ordnance?"

"I got a twenty-millimeter pack; I'll have him if he's bad."

Garvey watched the junk; a man on the deck had a little machine gun, probably an AK-47. There were ripples of gunfire in the water near Medvedev.

"Lifeboat, he's hostile; shooting at the survivor. I'm taking him out."

Hibbs was running through the armament checklist. Garvey reefed the F-4 around, came in low, and got the junk in his sights.

The boat turned. Garvey fired, the 20 mm tore up the sides, cut the mast in two. He pulled a hard five-G turn, almost touching the water, cut back, fired again. The boat was low in the water. There wasn't anyone shooting.

"Lifeboat, I got the junk. I see the Albatross on its way in. I don't think I can stay here low much longer."

"Ah, roger, Leopard, thanks for handling that hostile. Is the survivor doing okay?"

"Yeah, he was crawling in his dinghy on my last pass. I'm going back now. Over."

"Roger, thank you; sorry about your buddy."

"Ah, roger, out."

As he climbed he saw the Albatross touching down. Ivan was safe. Poor Greg.

Garvey glanced at his fuel gauges. Just enough to get home.

"Hibbs, you okay?"

"Ah, roger."

"Okay, you got it, take us home, make the landing."

Hibbs said nothing, but took the controls. Garvey relaxed and took his hands from the stick and throttle. He leaned his helmet back and shut his eyes, ignoring his own rule about constant vigilance, about always checking six.

He needed the rest, needed the time to think about Sims and how he would compose the letter to Sims's wife. It wouldn't be easy. Nothing about Vietnam was easy. Except dying. Dying was too easy.

32

1630 LOCAL
19 December 1966
Washington, D.C.
USA

"Jesse come in here."

"Yes, Mother, I'll be right down."

He was talking funny, that was a good sign. Most of the time he was a cheerful boy, but when he was in a bad mood, he was mean. Not to her. He'd never been mean to her. But Mary Catlin could tell when to talk to him and when not to.

Jesse Catlin was six feet tall, weighed 150 pounds, and moved like Sugar Ray Robinson. His mother was very proud of him, very proud of herself. She was working at the Quality Inn, in charge of twenty women who cleaned rooms. She chuckled at the thought of the old motel in Brownsville; who'd ever believe she would be a manager? She was making good money, too, enough to put a little away each month, because Jesse had to go to college.

He looked so good, just like his daddy had, but thinner, harder. And he had done well in high school, too. Something happened to him long about the tenth grade, and he stopped fooling around and started working. He was still a smart aleck; but he worked hard. He talked different, too.

Jesse talked very different. Two things had happened to him in the tenth grade. One had been a straight talking-to by Ted Amos, a session at which Jesse paid attention. He might not have done the same for any other teacher, but Jesse respected Amos. It hadn't always been so. Midway through the first semester with Amos—he taught world history—Jesse had gotten bored and tried to put a big jive on the man. He'd written in wrong

395

answers on every single question of the midterm, but they were answers that showed Amos that Jesse knew the right ones and simply wouldn't play the schoolboy game.

Amos had called Jesse's bluff with that test. He'd given him a double grade; A over F. A for ingenuity, F for scoring. And told Jesse to select which grade he wanted in his records. Jesse had puzzled it out for a day, then come by Amos's office after school.

Amos had not been surprised by his visit. He wasn't surprised by much that happened at Booker T. Washington High School. He was black himself, had been through it all, including a stint as a pilot in the 99th Fighter Group in the Army Air Force in World War II. He saw a lot of promise in Jesse, but the boy troubled him, too, since he, like so many of the kids, had so few advantages. For starters, he was the child of a fatherless family, like most of the other kids in Southeast D.C.; like them too, he was from out of town, and was prey to all the lures of the sewer that Southeast was turning into. Amos saw Jesse's midterm as a last chance for the kid. If he used it right, he might make something of his obvious intelligence and swift wit; if not, then he would slip into the mindless existence so apparently appealing to so many of his peers.

"Mr. Amos, how can I choose one of these grades? If I choose the A, I get a good grade. But I didn't earn it. If I choose the F, I got to work my ass off to pass your course."

"Right, Jesse. But it's your problem, not mine."

"Well . . . how 'bout I split the difference with you? How 'bout a C?"

"Maybe, Jesse. But I'll go one better. How about you do your homework, take the tests like you're supposed to, and in return I'll include a special question on each test, one just for you. A tough one, one the others probably can't get. How's that?"

"Why'd you do that?"

"Look, Jesse. You're halfway through high school. If you don't settle down and get serious about this, you're going to waste it all. And then what? You thought about that? Then what?"

The 'then what?' changed Jesse. He'd never given much thought to the future before, because the past had been so awful. First, growing up in Brownsville, Texas, trying not to get caught stealing from the greasers and the honkies, trying to help out Mama and his sisters, and now in D.C., life was no fun. But something about Ted Amos got through to Jesse.

The other thing that changed him had been a pack of matches.

On the inside was an advertisement about being a TV and radio announcer. He'd sent away for the information. The company had sent him some pamphlets. And from the moment he'd read the pamphlets, he knew what he wanted to do. He practiced talking like they talked on the radio, and on television; he'd talk fast like the disk jockeys, and slow and important like the news broadcasters. He had a good voice, he thought, and he practiced making it deep and round sounding.

Jesse would have died before he told anybody what he was going to do. He was a little older now, and knew that the company advertising in the matchbox covers was a rip-off. But there were other ways. First he had to get a little schooling.

Mary had worried about bringing up the question of college. She was sure Jesse wanted to get out and get to work, doing something fancy. But it was time to talk about it, so when Jesse came downstairs, she faced him solemnly. "Jesse, you got any ideas about what you are going to do when you graduate from high school?"

"Yes'm."

"Are you planning to work, or would you like to go to school some more, maybe Taft Junior College?"

"Mama, I want to go to school, but I don't want to go to Taft. Probably a good school, but it don't have—it *doesn't* have—what I want. I want to study some special things, things I'll be good at." He couldn't bring himself to tell her; she'd think he was joking with her.

"Taft's about all I can afford, child; you can live at home, and it's not so far away, you can maybe work a little bit. It's not going to be easy for me."

"I know, Mama, and I'm going to work, but I have to go to the right school."

"Where you going to go?"

"I'm going to go across the river, to Northern Virginia Community College. They have what I want."

"What's that, Jesse, you tell your Mama now, we're talking serious, and I don't want to fool around. Why do you want to go to Virginia? You'd be the only colored boy there."

"Mama, you got to stop saying 'colored'—we're supposed to get mad about that. You're supposed to say 'black.' And I won't be the only one, there'll be some others."

"You didn't answer, Jesse; you want me to spend a lot of money on you, send you across the river, I don't know how much that'll cost, and you won't tell me."

"Promise you won't laugh, won't get mad."

"Child, if you knew how proud I was just to be talking with you about college, you'd know I won't laugh."

"I want to be a television announcer."

She laughed.

He laughed with her.

"I'm sorry, son, it's just so strange. I been picking up rooms, cleaning bathrooms, doing dirty work all my life, and you want to be a television announcer."

She slipped her arm around him, pulled him to her. "You know, you're good looking enough to be on TV, and you got a nice voice, I hear you talking all kinds of ways; maybe you can be. If you want to be you can be. Just imagine me sitting here someday and turning on the TV, and there you be talking to me." She chuckled, squeezed him tight.

"Have you talked to anybody about this? You know how to find out if you can go?"

"Mr. Amos will help me," he said confidently, and that settled it for Mary Catlin. She knew Amos and respected him.

But it wasn't that easy. Amos was furious when Jesse told him what he wanted to do. "Lord, Jesse! Are you off your rocker? What the hell are you talking about? A *television announcer*? There are ten thousand kids who want to be television announcers, and the only people making any money are the ones training them for jobs they'll never see. What's wrong with something like being an engineer, or an accountant, or a salesman? You'd be the world's greatest salesman, with your bullshit."

Jesse was devastated. He'd thought Mr. Amos would support him. "Let me try, Mr. Amos. What can I lose?"

Amos looked out the dirt-streaked window, tapped a pencil on the desk. "You're right, Jesse; two years ago I'd been afraid to bet you'd finish high school. Who am I to say what you can or can't do? But listen up, boy. You're doing it the hard way. It will be tough for you to get back and forth to school, tough for you to work and make any money. And I'm not too sure they'll even take you in school over there. Let me see what I can do."

He couldn't do anything. The Northern Virginia school was just starting up, and could handle only a local enrollment.

Amos called Jesse in.

"Look Jess, it doesn't matter. The first two years are about the same everywhere, and maybe we can get you some special classes next year. But if you start here locally, at Taft, you can take the required courses and get ready. And I've been talking to a friend of mine down at WROC; he says he'll put you on odd hours as a handyman/gofer type."

The prospect of actually being at a radio station offset his disappointment. And at Taft, he met some people who made sense to him, more sense than anything he'd heard from his mother or from Ted Amos. There was no reason for him to be ashamed of being poor; black was beautiful, and he was beautiful. Some changes had to be made; he should be able to go to any school he wanted to, not have to go to a broken-down junior college with rats in the cafeteria and the baskets hanging in shreds in the gym. He was learning, all right; he was learning that if you didn't have it, you had to take it, and you had to take it from those who had it.

33

1720 LOCAL
19 December 1966
"Leopard Three"
Vietnam

They ejected almost simultaneously. Kaplan had barely cleared the canopy when Fish went out. The ejection sequence was automatic; the seats separated and their chutes opened at about three thousand feet. Fish was unconscious, slumped down in the risers. Kaplan was terrified; a wall of small-arms fire followed him down. He looked up, saw holes opening in his chute, felt a searing pain in his thigh. He watched Fish disappear into the tree line, a lolling rag doll at the end of a string.

Kaplan grabbed the risers and felt a stab of pain go up his arms; he glanced at the ground to check his drift. His foot was hanging at a funny angle, almost as if it didn't belong to him. He was looking at it when he slammed into the ground and unconsciousness.

He awoke with his back bent forward, wrists and ankles bound in a clump; there was a rude bandage of some sort of black fabric tight around his thigh. Blood seeped down beneath. A raging thirst seemed to suck the sides of his throat together, forcing the sour taste of bile into his mouth. He looked down at his flying suit. It was soaked with blood and vomit, and his legs were soiled with urine. He must have pissed in his pants while he was out.

His canteen was gone; there was not a single bit of survival gear on him.

Fish was stretched beside him, still unconscious, a trickle of blood from his ears and nostrils, tied to a rude stretcher. He had been stripped of everything, too. Kaplan couldn't turn his head far enough to be sure, but it looked like Fish had a major wound on his forehead. There seemed to be a crumpled, bleeding line just below his scalp. His jaw was slack, his breathing was ragged and irregular.

It was almost night; it took a moment for him to realize he was in a bamboo-shuttered pen, about seven feet long and four wide. He wanted to shout, to demand to be released. His leg was throbbing, and it felt like his back was badly injured. He was scared, and Fish was unconscious. Fish would have known what to do. The jungle seemed silent except for a rise and fall of harsh voices; the smell was overpowering, a rank combination of dead vegetable matter and himself.

Dang-Duy Hien had authorized the mild celebration. Two Phantoms for the price of less than a ton of rice scattered by a direct hit, and two wounded carriers, was a bargain. They had been prepared to break off the attack any time, but had deliberately stayed engaged to make sure the Phantoms were lured into the flak barrage.

The company commander had released some tins of fish to be issued as a reward to the gun crews who had sweated packing the 57 mm weapons down from the North, and had set them up almost overnight. They had held their fire during the first series of attacks; when the second group of Phantoms came in, they were ready. If they had fired on the first group, the second would have been warned, and been wary. As it was, they were able to disengage from the ground forces and haul everything, including the prisoners, away before the next wave of Phantoms came. No one worked as hard as they did. That was why they would win.

The result had been like a page from the textbook. The Phantoms had flown into a wall of antiaircraft fire. Later two squads were sent back and combed through the wreckage of the Phantom that had blown up and crashed only a mile away. There was not much of value, except for two 750-pound bombs that had not been dropped and somehow survived the crash. They would be turned into mines. The first Phantom to be hit had

400

limped away, trailing smoke. He heard it had crashed into the sea.

The prisoners were a problem. Neither man could walk, could not even be forced to walk. They had hauled them along, feet dragging, when they retreated. Now the older man was near death; he had not been conscious at all. The younger man, a giant, had a broken leg, made more dangerous by the wound in the thigh. It would take a cart and as many as four men to get them back to Hanoi.

Hien would have liked to have simply killed them; it would be easier. And he would like to have questioned the big man, but there was no one who spoke English well enough. It was better to terrify him with silence and brutality, soften him up for the experts in Hanoi.

He walked to the cage. The big man was conscious.

"Can I have some water?"

Hien didn't understand. He took a length of bamboo, shoved it through the pen, and jabbed the American's leg where the bandage was. The man screamed and fainted. Hien shrugged; there would be much pain for him before they got to Hanoi. If they got to Hanoi. The other man hadn't moved. Perhaps he would be dead by morning. Serve the filthy bastard right. What business did they have here?

The French were bad enough. Why were the Americans here? They had fought the Japanese together. All over the world, the countries that had fought were made free. Except here, where the French came back for nine long years. Now it was the Americans' turn. It would be the Chinese next, perhaps, and they would be more of a problem. They understood the country and the people, and they would not be impatient, and they would not worry about how many were killed. Then maybe the Americans would fight for us; Hien smiled to himself. Stranger things could happen over time.

34

Washington glanced in the rearview mirror, tapped the brakes. Eighty miles an hour was too fast for a black man driving near East St. Louis. He imagined that a state patrolman or a county sheriff would get a great deal of enjoyment out of throwing the book at a nigger officer driving an Olds 98. Next to him, Louise dozed, exhausted by the almost hyper antics of the kids. He checked them in the mirror; John slept with his head on Antoinette's lap. He smiled.

Running his finger across the dashboard, he sensed the little chrome script that spelled out "Oldsmobile 98." It was just like a Cadillac in most respects, but less expensive. And he wouldn't have driven a Cadillac even if he could afford one, for "that nigger in his Cadillac" was a phrase too easy to say, too difficult to endure.

On almost every long trip he still recalled grimly that he hadn't learned to drive until he was seventeen, when Bud Drummond needed a backup driver for the tow truck. Bud had given him a few lessons and turned him loose, figuring he'd win any arguments with a small car, driving the big red Dodge truck. That old Dodge, with its balky gears, no heater, and noise, was a far cry from the Olds. He could honestly say that he had never even contemplated owning a car until after he was commissioned, when it came to him with a shock that he, Millard Washington, could probably afford his own car.

Once he realized he could buy one, he did so with exaggerated care, trying to ensure that he satisfied not only their family transportation needs, but his sense of propriety, of how he ought to be regarded on base. It had worked most places, because he was a good judge of such things. As the miles thrummed under the Olds's tires, he recalled the cars, linking them with where he had been, what had happened to them, what he had flown.

None in flying school, of course. Nor in nav school at Connally. The first car had been that two-year-old Ford at Ellington. He'd

402

courted Louise in that old black sedan with the mohair uphol-stery. He smiled at the memory.

Then in Japan, nothing again. But when he'd landed at Hamilton en route to San Angelo, he'd bought a brand-new Studebaker Champion. That had made him feel good; the bank really owned it, of course, but it was *new*. It was also a lemon, so he'd reluctantly sold it when they'd moved to Castle. The damn thing had given Louise no end of trouble when she went back to Baltimore and had John while he trained in 47s at McConnell.

Castle. What memories lay there! Antoinette showing up unexpectedly. Squadron Officers' School. Surgeon. And the Buick, that fabulous Roadmaster hardtop. Louise had argued for a four-door, but that wonderful two-toned green-and-white just won his heart. He had to have it.

It was a good car, too. It lasted him three years, right up to his transfer to Stewart AFB in New York. As old Colonel Pinney had promised, they had kept him in SAC after his tour as a C.O. of Surgeon, and he paid his dues, flying B-52s out of the base by the Hudson River. But he'd loved the duty, and so did Louise. They'd visited the Adirondacks, seen places he'd only read about. And they weren't far from her parents in Baltimore, so they'd driven down often in—he shuddered, remembering—the VW Kombi bus he'd somehow been conned into buying.

A great idea at the time, as they said. Thrifty, spacious, ingenious—and a consistent hangar queen. If he hadn't bought the '57 Chevy as a second car—which turned out to be the first car, most of the time—they'd never have seen anything in the East.

Luckily, the '65 Olds 98 solved all their problems. It was a hell of a car; solid, fast, spacious, comfortable. Suitable for a lieutenant colonel on his way up.

Washington was only beginning to dare the issue of how far that might be, and then only with Louise. He'd been amazed to find himself promoted at Stewart to deputy squadron commander, again over the heads of other, older guys. And when they'd asked him—asked, for Christ's sake, not told!—if he would like to go to Command and Staff College, he'd been flabbergasted. Natu-rally he'd taken it, even if it meant letting Louise take the 98, and borrowing a beat-up Beetle from her father while he at-tended the college.

Ahead lay the so-familiar territory of East St. Louis. And yet, now, so unfamiliar. He had found many excuses not to visit his parents with Louise over the years, each more contrived than the one before. But now that he had at long last been assigned to a B-52 combat squadron at Andersen AFB, in Guam, there were no more excuses. Col. Jim Fitzpatrick, the guy in the Pentagon who seemed to pull all the strings for him, had told him that his assignment after Andersen would be to the Pentagon, so Wash and Louise decided to use the thirty-day leave he had coming before he left for Guam to go places and do things they'd been putting off for years. Inevitably, heading the list was a visit to John and Volar Washington.

It was increasingly difficult for him to understand his parents' refusal to move from the little shack where he had been raised. East St. Louis was disintegrating around them; Brooklyn was a disaster area. When he had been young, it was a tough, broiling workers' town, secure in the white areas, and with crime only of stratified convention in Brooklyn. You could be beaten up, of course, or robbed in passing, but killings were reserved for revenge or for major transgressions like skimming on a numbers collection. If you were somebody, or if the killers wanted to impress somebody, you got the single contribution of East St. Louis to American culture; you were killed, stuffed in the trunk of a Cadillac—preferably yours—and sent to the junk yard for compression into a tidy tin box. When the dope came, and as the city declined, the variety and intensity of serious crimes flourished.

Wash had wanted to buy them a home on the outskirts of the city; near Belleville, maybe, or even in Lebanon, where he had gone to school. He could afford the down payment, and could send them enough to supplement their retirement and Social Security to live. But they wouldn't leave. Volar—it had been an affectation of hers, picked up from a Unitarian pastor's family for whom she had worked, to have him call her Volar rather than Mother, yet he always called her mama in his heart—had her church work, and to his dad the house was what it had always been, a symbol of defiance to everyone.

It was curious that crime had become so bad that it passed them by; their neighborhood was so poor, so denuded of people and resources, that it was not worth picking over. Yet Washington was filled with fear when he crossed the Mississippi on the crumbling Eads Bridge. He glanced in the mirror, caught the look of horror in Louise's eye. He shouldn't have brought her. She came from another world.

Driving down derelict Collinsville Avenue, the main street, he was appalled at the destruction. The most solid temples of his youth, the two big banks at the Missouri Avenue intersection, were shuttered. Even the dime stores, where he had passed many an afternoon stalking the counters, lusting after the toys, aware that every clerk's eye was on him, were boarded over. City government offices were everywhere vainly trying to take up the slack of productive businesses with rambling nests of bureaucrats.

With a start, he realized that he was passing the once imposing Majestic Theater, marquee forever dark, burned and shuttered with plywood. In his youth it had been a richly tapestried film temple, softly stanchioned with cushioned ropes to keep the orderly crowds in line. It had been a gold-leaf-stuccoed film palace so grand that he had never been allowed entrance except to work as part of a clean-up crew scrubbing gum from beneath the velvet seats. To this day films meant nothing to him; now he could go freely, but had no interest. A few years ago he would have killed to have a seat in the Majestic.

Over Louise's objections, he drove them northwest to Brooklyn through abandoned stockyards that had once fed the East with the best beef in the world. He became disoriented: so many buildings had been burned down, so many blocks leveled, that he couldn't tell where he was. It was a smoldering, brooding ghetto, with no possibility of return; the tax base was gone, and the people lived on welfare.

East St. Louis had become the quintessential black city, the blackest of American cities, and it lay in ruins, almost without services, as poverty and the race war compounded the evil of three generations of white despoilers. The city had been run by an oligarchy of Catholic political families for seventy years, and they drank deep of its resources while it was still a brawling, drinking rail town, a chemical-plant town where wastes could be spilled freely, the odors to compete with the stockyards and the sewage dumped with disregard into the Mississippi. If a street was to be built, twelve inches of concrete were specified and four inches poured, the saving funneling into the pockets of the mayors and commissioners. If an eight-foot sewer was needed, a ten-foot was specified and a four-foot installed, the difference gone before a shovel turned. There were always enough for jobs for every relative, from bogus engineer-paid-for studies that never materialized to simple gardeners planting roses in Jones's Park.

The smoldering fires of resentment burst forth, stoked by the summer wind. The slogans and the aims had spread across the country, embroiling Washington, Detroit, St. Louis, and, in an almost futile expression, East St. Louis, a city where there was so little left of consequence to damage that the harm done by the black population to itself was only an affirmation of despair.

The white families were long gone, scattered, around the surrounding bluffs, or in Florida or California, no longer able to wrest a workman's wages from the city, no longer needing an alliance with the lampreylike gangsters who consumed the proceeds of gambling, prostitution, and drugs. The children of politician and gangster alike were established in legitimate businesses, for an era had ended, and if the city could not be gentrified, the offspring could.

As they rode, Louise became more and more pensive, withdrawn. He could see her conclusions forming, knowing what they would be. She would say that they had not been radical enough, that this was too much for any race to bear, that it was up to them to do something. And yet she had seen only the surface, the knockabout end results, not the daily suffering. He wondered how she would react to Brooklyn, to his parents.

That trip, only three years ago, seemed like a vague remembrance of the past. In the meantime, the city had gone under, and worse, his mother was not well. Her once roly-poly frame, swelled by a diet of beans and cornbread and exaggerated by her lifelong habit of eating laundry starch straight from the box, was gaunt. His father was hardy and taciturn. They were still adamant about staying in the house he grew up in.

Finally the drive was over. They climbed out of the car stiff and tired, the kids boiling with energy, oblivious to the misery all around. His parents were delighted to see them, brought them into the house whooping and hollering, even though Volar seemed scarcely able to walk. She held the kids one at a time, trading back and forth with their grandfather.

Like most visits home, it turned into a disaster. Louise was terribly uncomfortable, as protective of the kids as if they were wandering a leper ward. She had known Wash's parents' circumstances were, had to be, modest; she knew that East St. Louis had suffered in the past years. But nothing Wash had said—and he had conscientiously tried to warn her—had prepared her for the destruction, the smell, the poverty overcome and absorbed.

Within two days, she admitted defeat, recognized that they had to go, that the visit was indeed a disaster. The end came at dinner one night. John was telling the kids a story while Volar insisted on spooning out mashed potatoes with Louise hovering helplessly by, when a spate of shots erupted down the block, followed by screaming, more screaming, and then a terrible silence into which no sirens came. John and Volar ignored it all, and Wash caught Louise's eye, signaled. She nodded. In bed that night, in his old room, they planned their escape the next morning like convicts whispering to each other.

John and Volar were not disturbed by his sudden decision to leave early. They knew their son, and while he stumbled through an explanation at breakfast, they simply smiled gently and made him feel worse.

While Louise was packing, his father took him to the wall of photographs. "Millard, I never thought I'd see pictures like this, see you in the Army, see you driving a big car, living all over the world." Millard winced. John had never allowed the services to separate in his own mind. "We be very proud of you. You help us a lot. But can't help two things bother me about these pictures. Two things are real bad." He gestured vaguely at the wall of smiling faces, gleaming teeth.

Wash looked at his father. He was half Wash's size, his hair frizzled white, his shoulders stooped but still ringed with loops of wiry muscle gained at the end of Monsanto's brooms and shovels.

"It didn't bother me at first, but your mother saw it. She saw it right away."

Wash looked again. "What is it, Father?"

"Well, it bothers your mother that there isn't one photo of you in church. That's not how she brought you up, Millard. And it bothers me that you and Louise are the only colored people in any of the pictures. That's not how I brought you up."

Wash cringed inside. He could have arranged the first, for he and Louise did go to church, regularly, and for a while, at Castle, there was a black pastor on base. And he could have sent pictures from Korea of his troops, he even had one of Sergeant Baldwin before the blow-up. But for the most part, he was still alone. It was not unusual to meet another black officer, but there were still not so many that you got to work with them.

"It's not as bad as it looks. I've got some at home, and I'll send them. They will make you and Mother feel better; you be proud of me then."

"Son, we proud now; just want to be at peace, too."

Suddenly the bags were packed and the kids were kissing their grandparents and Louise was fluttering around in the let's-go mode. He didn't know what to say to them; they were so tiny, so helpless against the tide of evil that threatened to swamp them every day of their lives. He stood while Louise hugged them both, emotions surging through him that he knew he must at all

407

costs contain, emotions that not even she could share. When it came time for him to kiss them goodbye, the determination that had driven him to go where no black men had gone and succeed at what none had succeeded at did not let him down; he smiled and promised to come back and told the lies he had to tell, and when he was done he knew that this was the last time he would see them alive. The look in his mother's eyes when he at last set her gently back in her rocker on the porch and turned to go sliced him to the marrow. But in the car, Louise and the kids were waiting. Each step he took through the pathetically tidy oasis of their front yard was an eternity, the ground itself seeming to pull at him, trying to tell him what he knew; that his place was here, protecting these gentle, faultless people who had made whatever he was possible. But he knew his part too well, and he kept walking.

As they drove away, his father picked up a hoe and began weeding. Louise began crying, softly, looking out the window, her hands drawn together so tightly that her nails were cutting into her palms.

"Wash, why didn't you tell me?" He felt suddenly a sense of annoyance and frustration; why did she make life so complex? He was a poor black boy who had made good, it was simple enough.

"There was just no way to make you understand. But I told you. You know that. I told you."

"I feel so ashamed. I've lived so well all my life. They—you—" She choked back a sob.

He reached across the seat and patted her hand. "Hey. It wasn't so bad here, once. You're seeing it at its worst." He glanced in the mirror and saw that the kids had caught their mood; both looked wide-eyed out the windows, silently clutching each other as the blasted streets and dead-eyed people slid by outside the thick, tinted windows of the Olds.

They drove in silence for a while, until, predictably, Louise returned to what had become their main topic of conversation on the road. "I'm so mixed up. I want to be mad at you because you're not more radical, because if anybody should be radical it's you. And yet I understand what the Air Force means to you, what it's done for you, and I keep wanting you to quit, to give it up."

They were out of the city, almost at the point where they entered the interstate. Wash pulled over to the side. He took a moment to contain himself, to bring his voice under control.

She watched his hands continue to grip the wheel as if he intended to bend it in half. "You know, Louise, you're so smart, and so sensitive about most things, but you've always missed something important about me. In a way, you've been discriminating against me, telling me I'm not like a white man, that I've got to look for something else."

She reached to him. "No, Wash, don't say that, God, don't say that. I don't know how you can say that. What do you mean?"

He relaxed on the steering wheel, checked the rearview mirror. The kids were quiet.

"You've never had a clue that I love the Air Force because I love flying; that I'm a pilot and a damn good one, and that, like all the white guys that love flying and devote their lives to it, I'm ready to die for it. There are no black pilots or white pilots, only pilots that make it and pilots that auger in. I'm lucky to be flying and be good at it, damn good, and the Air Force is treating me well. But you've always assumed I'm just a buck-ass nigger trying to getahead. You're wrong. I'm a *pilot*, not a black pilot, not a white pilot, a pilot, and when I've strapped my bottom to an airplane I'm happy. Do you think you can understand that? Do you think your goddamn tea-drinking, grass-smoking Lyle Johnson can understand that? What did that sonofabitch ever fly?"

Without waiting for her response, he pulled the lever down to DRIVE, accelerated out into traffic.

Louise sat stunned into silence. The truth of his monologue struck her like a thunderbolt, stilling the angry response on her lips. He was right. Not only about what she thought he ought to do and be, but about Lyle. Somehow, he knew about Lyle.

As Wash threaded the big Oldsmobile through the suburban traffic, she tried to imagine Lyle in the cockpit of a B-52, in any airplane, and failed.

Wash was the pilot. And Lyle was—what?

35

It really annoyed Garvey to see how these smartass young captains could get familiar with general officers, and get away with it. It was the new Pentagon, the computer-and-missile whiz-kid systems-analysis Pentagon, and Garvey had had a bellyful of it. If he had ever talked to his flight commander—a captain—when he was a shavetail lieutenant like that bullshit artist Ed Novack talked to General Glaser, he'd have been thrown in the goddamn stockade.

It was Glaser's own fault; he'd break some poor briefing colonel in half if a slide stuck, and here was this punk kid, right out of a North Dakota silo, kidding him about the lousy record the Sparrow had in Vietnam. Jesus Christ, next thing they'd be having spot promotions for nonrated goddamn engineers, and he'd be working for the kid.

He caught up with Col. Wayne Dillon, plunging along the hallways to another meeting.

"Slow down, Wayne; you going to the Council meeting?"

"Yeah, and I'm late. How you doing, Jim?"

"Well, slow down. The meeting's canceled. How about dropping back to my temporary abode?"

"Canceled? Great! I'll stop by for a little while, but then I'm going down to the gym and work out."

Dillon and Garvey went all the way back to Korea; Dillon had one MiG to his credit when he lost an engine taking off out of K-14. He was just high enough to eject, and was glad to get out of it with two compressed disks. It ended his flying, but he still figured he was ahead of the game.

Garvey closed the door, brought out a bottle of Jack Daniel's.

"Just a short snort, Jim; if I have a good belt, I won't feel like working out." Garvey nodded, poured, and they drank in companionable silence.

Garvey ran his eye around the tiny office, the Navy gray paint peeling, a window looking directly into the concrete wall of the next ring. Dillon followed his look and smiled. "Nice place you got here, Colonel Garvey. Glad to see you're living in the lap of luxury, like the rest of us."

Garvey snorted. "Beats Da Nang, believe me. They told me on the same day that I was on the short colonel list and that I was coming here to do my time on the fighter tactics team, and I didn't argue a bit. I've never liked this damn place, Wayne, but I needed a rest after flying with the Sharkbaits."

"Yeah. Heard about it. Understand you bagged a few."

"A few. They weren't worth it."

Dillon heard the warning tone in Garvey's voice. He understood; he'd put in a year as a supply squadron commander at Takhli. He slugged down his whiskey and placed the glass on the metal desk as a way of changing the conversation. "How's the kid? Rebecca, wasn't it?"

Garvey brightened considerably. "Rachel. And she's just fine. Still in Boston, with her grandparents. Making me proud. How about Bobby?"

"Dumb shit got kicked out of Tech. Probably get his ass drafted any minute." Dillon grinned.

"Hey. What did you think of that farce this morning, with the boy wonder Captain Novack setting us all straight on missiles?"

"He's a nice kid, Wayne; I don't agree with everything he says about using laser-guided or TV-guided bombs. Christ, we've been fooling with them for years, the Germans had TV bombs in World War II, so did we, and nothing's ever replaced going in straight down, putting the goddamn target in your pipper and pulling out as low as you have the balls to. I'm sure there are some special applications, but I don't think we could stand the expense of equipping with all smart bombs. I know you agree with me."

"No, that's what really pisses me off. I hate the little bastard, not because I know him, but I hate all these fast-track bastards. Problem is, I think he's right. We're losing too many planes in Nam, swapping F-4s for trucks or coolies, not to try something new."

"Yeah, but that's my point; I don't think you can laser-bomb a goddamn truck, or a guy carrying a sack of rice. The problem is the kind of war we're fighting. We try to pick off sixty-kilo bags of rice as they're humped along under a jungle canopy, instead of sinking the goddamn ship in Haiphong harbor that brings it in by the ton."

"Sure, I know, but that's not the argument, that's not what the

411

kid's talking about. He's talking using small flights of four or six aircraft, with big protective flights to take care of any MiGs. He claims the four airplanes can be so accurate that they can do what a whole flock of F-105s have been trying to do for years' take out the big bridges around Hanoi."

"Well, maybe, but I don't like it. What time's our next briefing on Novack's project?"

"We have a small briefing in our program office conference room at nine tomorrow morning. If everybody buys off, it goes to the Air Staff Friday."

To Ed Novack, the Pentagon proved everything the recruiters and David Mahoney had said were true. He'd enjoyed his tour at Minot, and had damn near completed a master's degree in aero engineering. He had also designed, on his own, one of the simplest yet most sophisticated laser bombing systems anyone had seen. Or so they told him. He'd been a little embarrassed even to put his ideas forward, figuring that at Wright-Pat, or Andrews, or somewhere, other people would be way ahead of him. He'd received permission to brief the Minot Air Force Base commander on his idea; the balding Col. Riley Smith, whose giant size was in inverse proportion to his intellect, had not understood a single word—he rarely did, on anything—but he was impressed enough to get Novack a TDY trip to the weapons lab at Eglin. It had been the middle of winter, and to go from Minot to Florida for any reason was a plus, and Colonel Smith had made sure to accompany him. The weapons people went crazy over the simplicity of his concept, and within a week, he found himself saying goodbye to Artie Clark and heading for the Pentagon.

Along the way, he found himself doing something that neither he nor Mahoney had ever envisioned; he signed up for another tour in the Air Force. He couldn't exactly say why when Stan Novack almost begged him to reconsider; but it had something to do with the way this project had him moving through the Air Force. Mahoney had told him he could cut a wide swath if he had a good idea and the guts to make it work, and it was true. He didn't have to look far on the outside to see that engineers his age, although paid twice as much, didn't get to do half what he could. Besides, he had come to like the ordered, predictable life-style of a bachelor officer, and the new Corvette didn't hurt a bit either. There was a certain young lady at Eglin who thought

hat both he and the 'Vette were aces, and who actually liked the
dea of dating an Air Force officer, despite what the media were
pumping out about alleged atrocities in Vietnam.

Novack had a professor's manner, and his briefings were already polished beyond the usual Air Staff style. The next morning, Garvey sat with Dillon, watching him work through the flip
charts, pointing out the lack of effectiveness of iron bombs on
most of the critical North Vietnamese targets, on the poor CEPs,
circular error probable, of fighter attacks against heavily defended
targets, a whole foundation leading to a discussion of his invention.

Garvey grudgingly had to agree with him as the briefing
unfolded. He realized that the thing he really didn't like about
the idea was that it shifted responsibility for the bombing—and
the victory—from the front-seat pilot to the weapon systems
operator in the back. The F-4 had started out as a two-pilot
airplane; the expansion and the loss rates had forced the Air
Force to adopt the Navy's concept of a weapon systems officer, a
nonpilot for the back seat.

The idea had been, and still was, bitterly resented. But it was
an idea whose time had come, and like it or not, Garvey realized
that if he had to fly again in Vietnam, it might be with some
four-eyed dude like Novack in the back seat, with Novack calling
the shots.

Still, Novack's briefing had a thrust and a logic to it, one that
Garvey had to agree with, right up to the last chart.

Novack knew he was treading on dangerous ground, but he
persisted, and concluded, "Finally, gentlemen, I'd like to take
the liberty of a little look at the future. If bombs like those I've
proposed are developed, the next step will be to drop them from
RPVs, remote-piloted vehicles, and the days when we lose pilots
in combat will be over."

Garvey gagged. "Lose pilots in combat" was a groundpounder's
euphemism for "We won't need pilots anymore."

It was too much for Garvey. In spite of briefing protocol, he
stood up, leaned over to Novack, and said, "Look, Captain,
you're a bright young guy, and you've got some good ideas. But
you've never been near a fucking war, never dropped a fucking
bomb, never shot a fucking gun. If you think your little toy is
going to change things, you're just flat mistaken. I'd like to have
your ass strapped in the back of an F-4 for a few weeks, and then
have you take another look at who's going to be doing what to
whom."

Novack was embarrassed. He hadn't wanted to offend anybody. He looked over at Dillon; the old colonel smiled, gave him a small thumbs-up. Novack couldn't figure it out. He tried to stammer an answer to Garvey, but Dillon cut him off. He closed the meeting and asked Novack to forward his materials for the Air Staff review.

In the end, after the briefing broke up, Garvey sought out Novack and apologized. He promised to take him for a flight in an F-4, as soon as Novack got a physical and the altitude chamber training. Novack was pathetically grateful, not for the ride, but for Garvey apologizing. He wasn't used to the Pentagon infighting yet. He would learn.

36

0800 LOCAL
April 1968
Andersen AFB
Guam

Col. Duke Brown was in an exceedingly strange position. He was deputy commander of operations for a B-52 wing, engaged in combat, doing exactly what he had trained to do, in exactly the manner he had advocated, and he knew it was completely wrong. When he had been at the Pentagon he urged a build-up in the B-52 sortie rate, convinced that a maximum effort in the South would dry up the North Vietnamese and Vietcong strength. It was an expensive approach, but he believed it would be less expensive than sending the B-52 over Hanoi. He did not believe so now. Not after ten months of duty on Guam, not after seeing what he had seen on his missions over Vietnam.

He had used the South-directed argument brilliantly in the Royal College of Defense Studies in London; the Brits, holdovers from the Bomber Harris school of obliteration, couldn't understand the American tactics. Great Britain could not have afforded to establish the enormous system of supply and logistics, nor to sustain it over time. To do so and then to administer a series of pin-prick bombing attacks seemed to them to be the height of folly. Their view permitted Duke to be a statesman, to take the long view, to point out the dangers of escalation, the pump-priming effect the war effort had on the economy, the statistics showing how many Vietcong had been killed.

His NATO colleagues had not been impressed, but it had not hurt his standing there. They treated him with great deference, and made his tour at the Royal College wonderful, a tonic after the fierce infighting in the Pentagon.

London itself had been glorious, made more so by Joan's amazing recovery. Although the college was a short tour, he arranged for her to accompany him, while Charles Jr. was at summer camp, being looked after by his grandparents. So he and Joan were alone and they clicked as they had not for a long time.

Much of it was because she somehow avoided liquor. In a land where drinks were the order of the day, where everyone seemed to be continually sucking on a Scotch, a cigarette, or a sweet, or all three simultaneously, she stayed sober, drinking endless quantities of the bland but bitter orange-squash-and-lemonade concoctions the British forced on anyone who didn't want gin or beer. She had slimmed down and regained her youth and vitality.

Joan loved everything about their tour; she charmed the British as much as they charmed her. They were able to travel on official status a great deal, and they spent many weekends hurtling down the wrong side of the road exploring the unexpectedly dreary Lake Country, the gorgeous Cotswolds, immaculate, appealing Devon, wherever they could reasonably reach in a few hours' driving.

It was more than a second honeymoon, although their sex life had blossomed with her good health and his relaxation. They both seemed secure in their lives, and, even better, secure with each other. It was refreshing for Duke to feel no pressure; the school was not a competitive situation for him, although it virtually assured his making brigadier general.

Joan loved English churches, and they toured them from one end of the country to another, from tiny villages, where the graveyards were studded with indecipherable headstones, worn smooth from centuries of moss and moisture, to the great cathedrals where the most famous names in history rested beneath tiny crypts, their small stature emphasized by the great swords clasped in marble hands. Duke had gone willingly to a few and then began to rebel, but Joan persisted and added a new facet to his appreciation of her. Over the years she had read widely of English history, and she was able to bring life to the architecture and the stories. She would inevitably dredge up the vicar in a small church, a docent in a larger one, and dazzle them with her knowledge. Usually they were delighted to find someone who was interested, and before the day was out, Joan and Duke would be invited in for tea or an evening meal.

Duke really never came to like the churches, but he did like the churchmen, and he regretted in a way that he had not followed up on a childhood impulse to enter the clergy. The appeal was still there; the peace, the removal from competition, the less aggressive colleagues. He would dismiss the idea, and then return to it. He had another five to ten years in the service, maybe slightly longer; then what? His family expected him to join McNaughton Aircraft. He had always expected to, McNaughton or someone, even though he dreaded it.

As a former flag officer, you came as a glad-handing front man, a stalking horse to get the professional aircraft people into the right offices in the Pentagon. If you were good and learned the trade, you might be kept on and have a satisfying, positive career. If you outlived your usefulness, if your contacts left, or the administration changed, you were either dumped or shoved off laterally to greet and entertain the small-fry visitors in a humiliating round of eating, drinking, and if necessary, procuring.

He'd been on the opposite side long enough to know how it worked. When he was young, picking up B-47s from the factory, he and his crew were always met by corporate vice presidents, older men, ruddy faced with great French-cuffed shirts and huge gold cuff links, stomachs sagging, the archetypical retired generals or admirals, who would take them out for drinks and dinner, and whatever. The whatever could be whatever you wanted, and although Duke had confined himself to an evening meal, some of his friends had not.

Later in his career, when he was conducting procurement negotiations, it was the same. Duke would take a bargaining team in to a manufacturer to negotiate a contract. They'd be met at the airport by a laughing bunch of public-relations types, hauled out to a multi-martini lunch, then brought back for the first session with a stone-cold-sober platoon of experts. The USAF team usually consisted of a major, a captain, and two or three GS-12 contract types, competent enough, but not brilliant.

The contractor would have an endless supply of experts, half a dozen vice presidents, general counsel, and relays of engineers. The poor Air Force group would try their best, but would wind up getting exactly what the manufacturer planned to give. They were outsmarted, outgunned, and undermartinied. It had happened to Brown only once; he never drank again with a contractor.

The manufacturer simply executed a pragmatic hard-sell approach, and the prices they charged were usually only at the upper end of reasonableness. Yet it was a desperate way to earn a living; he would have to do better. The church tours with Joan made him realize that.

Now, a year later, in combat, retirement began to seem desirable, because the mission had become unsupportable, even though it was indisputably saving American lives.

The Marines had moved in to Khe Sanh determined to create, on their own terms, a Dien Bien Phu in reverse. The Vietcong were determined that it should be merely a Dien Bien Phu.

Three Marine regiments and their Vietnamese Ranger allies had been surrounded by a growing number of regular North Vietnamese army units, perhaps twenty to thirty thousand troops, marshaling their forces to overrun the camp that blocked Giap's invasion route through the Northern provinces. On January 21, 1968, the North Vietnamese attacked; ten days later the Tet offensive erupted.

At Andersen, Brown had watched the call for sorties mount, heard newer and more glorious mission names invented. General Westmoreland called forth Operation Niagara, in which B-52s flew almost three thousand sorties, dropping seventy-five thousand tons of bombs around the perimeter of Khe Sanh, some within nine hundred feet of the camp itself. The attack broke the back of the North Vietnamese offensive, but at an enormous material cost. Brown managed the increase in sorties from eight hundred per month to eighteen hundred by the middle of February. It was effective at Khe Sanh, but Brown realized the resources of America were rolling down a tiny foreign forested drain in a single spot. What would happen if there were two Khe Sanhs at once, or a Khe Sanh and a Lebanon? Not even the United States could afford warfare on such a basis. The knowledge shook him.

Brown flew as little as possible. He was no longer afraid to fly, but he no longer cared to fly, and he cared even less to simulate the great desire that was the inescapable convention among pilots. The long missions were stupefyingly boring, and he managed the process of appearing too valuable, too essential, to fly as much as he could have, as much as he was supposed to want to. He got some combat time, but it was not like Korea; not like those night B-26 raids; it was more like an intensely choreographed aerial workout. The B-52s met little resistance from SAMs or fighters when they bombed the rice paddies from their high altitudes; the North Vietnamese only got serious when their really important targets were threatened.

The whole process of gamesmanship annoyed Brown, yet he played it to remain inconspicuous. He could not reconcile the inanity of the Peter Pan enthusiasm with the coldly calculated careerism necessary to do the job. He went along, unsure how many felt like himself, certain that there were not many.

Brown knew that the targets were not right, and the level of effort still not great enough. There was only one solution, the one the Brits had proposed: Hanoi and Haiphong must be taken out of the war in a single concentrated effort, even if it cost half the B-52 fleet. He did not believe it would be so costly, but anything was better than the mindless squandering of resources, the hemorrhaging of men and matériel that the current policy called for.

His tour at Andersen was not wasted; he met many useful contacts, learned a great deal in his busy job as DCO, and collected more punched tickets, more chits. He found that the previous year's tour in London was somehow more real than this endless shuttle of bombs from Andersen, this strange little island. He seemed to be packing his B-4 bag to get on the C-141 back to the Pentagon for the tour he'd carefully arranged only days after he'd arrived.

Whatever else happened, he was determined to try to get the strategy changed. He had enough experience to be listened to by the phalanx of generals who had not yet fought in the war. He left Andersen with a clear sense of mission, and the knowledge that his career path was absolutely perfect.

When he got back there was bitter bloated evidence that Joan was drinking again.

The vicious February wind swept across the North Parking Lot; Duke had been lucky to find a space only half a mile from the covered entrance into the dingy gray walls of the Pentagon. The contrast to Guam was absolute; no leaves, no sun, no sand, no smiles, but plenty of glaze ice, a wind-chill factor of minus five, and sullen expressions. The hunched shoulders of men and women in blue, brown, and black greatcoats, hats pulled down low, fat briefcases clutched in issue-gloved fingers, bustled through a miasma of tired resentment.

Almost everyone hated the Pentagon, and with reason. It was the greatest self-inflicted wound in military history, a gigantic

418

concentration of highly motivated talent grinding away in a competition that fed on bogus tasks, long hours, and manipulated achievement.

It was home for Duke, who was one of the few who understood it well enough to enjoy it. There were too many people for too few jobs, but that was part of a winnowing process. No one complained about how many cardinals it took to make a pope, how many vice presidents were necessary to make a chairman of U.S. Steel. The same logic applied here; the Pentagon was a gigantic corporate convulsion, a seething, grinding mill that extracted the juices of the ordinary people to use as lubricant in polishing out the hard core of top leadership.

It was difficult to predict, even as you watched the process. There were certain necessary credentials in all the services. In the Air Force, you had of course to be a pilot, preferably with combat experience, and you had to have led troops in the field. An advanced degree was at last becoming essential, a master's preferable to a doctorate, oddly enough, for too much schooling was suspect unless you were a bona fide genius in the field. Senior service schools were mandatory—the more rarefied the better, with the Industrial College of the Armed Forces becoming preferred, but none so good as his own foreign experience.

Then there was the politicking. The future chief of staff could not have offended too many on his way up, but it was acceptable to have bucked some, if they themselves ultimately lost out.

Another factor was the wife. The Air Force did not go so far as he had heard the Navy had gone, where formal fitness reports were made on the wives of fast-track comers. Yet a wife could have profound influence. The best was smart, bright, seductive but pure; a woman who people would like to seduce but would not dare to proposition.

He knew that he had a problem with Joan. So far he had finessed her drinking with a martyr's role. He had just about played that string out, and only her remarkable recovery in England had spared them both the misery of a divorce. He didn't want to keep her, but he didn't want the messy agony of breaking up, either. As long as he could get credit for handling her problem while handling his career it was all right. But she was forcing him to the wall.

A touch with Congress was essential. It was necessary to project an eager-pilot image combined with a statesmanlike demeanor, and it was essential to have a self-deprecatory sense of humor. The congressional staffers were most susceptible to this;

419

they liked humble generals who could poke a little fun at themselves, men quick off the mark with a witty response to a loaded question.

Tall, handsome men did best, but the short drivers also prevailed. On balance, it became a question of personality management. The candidate for full general, for chief of staff, metered out his personality facets with the precision of a fuel injector, giving just what was necessary—steely coolness, ingratiating warmth, indifference, even lust—exactly as required by the recipient. It drove or begged, decided or queried, all couched in the terms necessary for the moment. It was corporate role playing, acting for which there were stars instead of Oscars.

Despite all the editorial cartoons of bloated flag officers feasting stupidly at the public trough, none were lazy, none were dumb. The dumb and the lazy sometimes persisted as spear carriers, as lackies, but they were never genuine contenders. Among the contenders, there were merely the sharp and the sharper.

Duke knew all this, and knew he had it all. He knew another quality was needed, the centuries-molded determination of a ship captain to sacrifice whatever and whomever was necessary to the safety of the ship. In the Air Staff, the ships were programs of advocacy, and the advocates lived and died with them. He had seen some promising officers derailed when they let loyalty interfere with career. It wouldn't happen to him. He would not let the Air Force down, he would not let himself down. The services survived on the heat and hardness of the selection process, and individual needs were secondary. There was a congruency between the stewardship of the Air Force and the stewardship of a career; if there was not, then the entire system would collapse.

He turned in to the basement door, showing the bored guard his identity card. Once past the second set of double doors the classic excess heat and tired smell that characterized the Pentagon hit him. It was a synthesis of perspiration, urine, bulk waste paper, stale food, roach and rat droppings, cheap cosmetics of aging secretaries who had come as Pearl Harbor charmers and stayed on as vintage harpies, all melded in the burned overlay of laboring fluorescents and electronics. He stopped to inhale, to get set; it was what the British would call vintage pong, a stale mixture that smelled and tasted of human aspiration, greed, sacrifice, and venality. He loved it. It was going to be a tough four years. At the end of it he would be a general, and there

420

would be a new bombing policy in Vietnam. He, the Air Force, and the country would benefit.

Duke pushed on through the crowded corridors. The night shift was coming off, tired people with glazed eyes gone red from watching screens or reading teletypes. There was a twilight-zone strangeness to the endless groups surging past him, all familiar, identical to those he had passed six years before, but without a single recognizable face. No wonder; every four years saw a complete turnover of the military personnel, except for the occasional diehard who stayed on for unfathomable reasons. Usually finances or family health problems dictated a stay; most people were too burned out to take consecutive tours. The zest of competitiveness would be lost in the seventy-hour weeks, the intrigues, the bewildering undulations of programs appearing, disappearing, and reappearing—blessed in one budget, axed in the next.

The civilians stayed on, and Duke realized he was searching for the face of Gil Lodge, a man who had worked for him and whom he had had to sacrifice. He didn't want to see him, for Lodge never understood the need, had in fact resented him.

It had been on the TMTS program; Lodge was in charge of estimating the program costs, based on long experience in knowing what the research-and-development and production costs of other programs had been. Lodge kept coming up with a unit cost of about thirteen million, far too high. Duke told him to go back and come up with a nine-million-dollar figure. Lodge protested gently, but did as he was told, projecting an incredibly smooth development program, and a learning curve for production that dropped off the board.

Duke had carried the figures to Congress and been mouse-trapped at a hearing. A smart young staffer, Jeremy Gorton, had led him down the pike; he could remember every word.

Gorton, a Westerner, spoke softly. "Ah, Colonel Brown, you've quoted the TMTS airplane as having a unit cost of about nine million for the production program of two hundred forty-four airplanes, isn't that correct?"

"Yes sir, that's what our figures show."

"Colonel Brown, what if I showed you figures done by an outside source that show that you could get an airframe for about that price, but if you want engines and electronics to go with it, it would be about thirteen million apiece?"

"Sir, I'd have to check those figures." He felt the ice crackling beneath him.

"Well, Colonel Brown, I have them right here. They're from McNaughton Aircraft itself, and I have no reason to believe they would overprice their own airplanes." Gorton had him.

Brown sweated. Jesus, how could McNaughton have done this? There was a colossal screw-up somewhere.

"Did you prepare these figures yourself, Colonel?"

"No sir, I had a very experienced staffman prepare these. Gilbert Lodge."

"Is he still working for you, Colonel?" There was menace and hope in the question.

"Not anymore, Mr. Gorton."

When Brown got back to the Pentagon he explained to Lodge that he had had to sacrifice him; Lodge was a career civil servant, he'd simply be moved to another project. Brown was surprised at his fury. Lodge had been upset because he would be cited in testimony as having provided figures grossly in error. He simply didn't understand the politics of the situation.

Brown pushed on; there seemed to be more stairs to get to the fifth floor now. When he'd been a young major he went up the steps two at a time, came down four at a time. He was content now just to move up briskly.

He wanted to change bombing policy, and he knew how to do it. A less experienced man would have sought to work in Strategic Plans and Policy. Brown had known better; he'd been on the bottom of the pile, and it would have been a matter of chance whether he could have influenced anyone. Besides, there had always been a vocal group of hawks that had advocated obliterating Hanoi; he didn't want to be identified with their old ideas. His concept was for preannounced surgical strikes, one that would take out the missile defenses first, then systematically reduce the industrial capacity of Hanoi and the shipping capability of Haiphong. The B-52 could knock out the installations with a minimum of damage to the populace and to religious and cultural sites. There would be losses, but no more in the ten to thirty days it would take than would be incurred in the endless years of bombing coconuts.

So instead of Plans and Policy he asked for the Office of Congressional Liaison. It was better for a double set of reasons. He could promote his own career far better there, get the visibility he needed, have access to the chief. He would gain a great advantage with some of the other leading manufacturers, too; McNaughton was locked up for him, but who knew where they would be in five or ten years? The industry was becoming too volatile and a relatively small—less than a billion a year in sales—producer like McNaughton was vulnerable. He didn't want to hitch his stars to an ailing concern.

And for the bombing problem it gave him a tremendous advantage. The congressional staffers were hungry for inside information, for new tacks. He could salt them with the need for a new policy which would be fed back not in the hearings, where there would be a record, but in the interpersonal dealings with the members of the policy groups in the hearings. He had a better chance of making his ideas come into effect than did an action officer in Plans, and without running any risks. If it was successful, he could let it be known how it happened—and there were many ways to make memos for record in the process. If it wasn't successful, he wouldn't even need to disclaim it.

Brown enjoyed working with members of Congress and particularly with their staffs. He knew many of them personally, and was widely regarded as a comer sure to surpass his father's three-star rank. Again, all the cartoons were wrong. Congressmen were rarely stupid, except perhaps for the personal moral transgressions that surfaced from time to time. They were only human. But in the handling of their business, they were incredibly shrewd, given that they saw the nation's business as their business, and vice versa.

It seemed to him the Congress was a Pentagon in microcosm, or perhaps the Pentagon was merely Congress with a thyroid problem. The same identity of personal interest and national good prevailed. The staffers of the representatives were at once the most difficult and the easiest to deal with. Their jobs, and their bosses' jobs, were up for grabs every two years, and unless the member was so entrenched that he knew he would be reelected, regardless of what the issues were, the first, the only concern was reelection. This meant you could deal; if you could find something that enhanced reelection, you could get support. If you had something that didn't affect the reelection, was not of concern, you could get support in return for a chit for future help. But if what you wanted looked like it might impede reelection, even if it was clearly in the national interest, forget it.

So he entered into the same massive double-entry bookkeeping system of markers given and markers received. The appearance was often more important than the issue; to get an astronaut to a Congressman's office for a photo session was sometimes much more valuable than ensuring that a contract was funneled to a plant in his district. A C-140 from Andrews sent to pick up the member for a crucial vote was more efficacious than bailing one of his constituent's sons out of trouble at the Academy. Personal perks were dangerous, though; as soon as you did it for one, you could count on another's staffer calling with an identical request. It was all personal personnel management, and he was good at it.

Brown was lucky to have a secure pipeline back to Andersen, so he could stay current with what was happening in the field. The biggest danger of the Pentagon was its isolation, its parochial sense of values. He talked to Millard Washington by radio at least once a week, keeping posted on what was happening, and setting into gentle motion the build-up of forces that would ultimately be necessary. Washington was a bit troubling, though. He had strange ideas about bombing the Vietnamese. Brown suspected a racial backlash in this. He also differed slightly from Brown in the choice of techniques for bombing Hanoi. Wash was inexperienced; he thought that the opposition would be tougher than Brown; this was natural enough. But the black pilot was very useful. He, like everyone else, would eventually see it the right way. That was why Col. Duke Brown was here.

He swung open the door to his new office and smiled. Home again.

37

1745 LOCAL
14 February 1969
Fairfield-Suisun, California
USA

It was a small cream envelope, engraved, and would have been beautiful if Larry White had not opened and examined it half a dozen times, bending it and smearing it with ink spots from his hand. He walked on air, alternately punching the wall and waving the envelope. It was a good thing everyone had already gone home.

The goddamn thing was in his mailbox! He'd picked up the usual pile of junk he found after a three-week trip—additions to the Pilot's Information File, notification of physicals being scheduled, the usual, and right on top was this little envelope that looked like an invitation.

Inside was a handwritten note from Col. Charles Kingston Brown, which said only:

Larry:
I just had a peek at the Major's List. Congratulations, you are on it for sure. Please don't tell anybody I told you, because the list won't be released for another two or three weeks.
All best wishes, and keep up the good work.
Duke.

He thought how happy Micky was going to be; and that goddamn McCuen, he was going to invite him to a real promotion party this time. He wondered if McCuen was on it; no, probably not.

He dropped by Valley Liquor and asked them for the best bottle of champagne they had. It was something called Dom Perignon, and it cost thirty-seven dollars. He wouldn't have cared if it had been three hundred and seventy dollars. Tonight, they were going to drink well.

He was still in a daze as he drove up the long winding drive toward their house; they lived better than anyone on base, thanks to Micky's eye for real estate. She'd picked up their house for a song from a poor woman whose musician husband had run off and left her with two kids, a big mortgage payment, and no money.

The lights were on all over the big adobe-style ranch house, but Micky's car was not in the drive. She must have been home and gone back to the office. Good; he could sneak the champagne into the refrigerator.

He tucked it on the highest shelf, so that it would chill faster, and wandered down the octagonal-red-tile hallway. The cost of the house—forty-five thousand dollars—had frightened him, but she said it was a steal and she could sell it for more, and he really liked it. Upstairs there was a sunken bathtub, and if he played his cards right they'd have a sunken-bathtub, champagne-besotted orgy.

There were letters on the table; he recognized Larry Jr.'s handwriting. He must want money.

It was the standard letter; he was finding the true meaning of life in Haight-Ashbury, his father was a warmonger, his mother was a money-grubbing fool, and he needed three hundred dollars to take care of some bills he'd run up.

425

They'd gone down to visit him only once since he dropped out of school. He was living with an Asian girl, a pretty thing, but none too clean, and smelling strongly of tobacco or, probably, marijuana. She'd been so sullen. At least he was living with a girl; across the hall in the old Victorian boarding house were some queers. He didn't think he could have taken that.

They really hadn't done too well with children. When they started out, they wanted to have five or six. Poor little Libby stopped that; she demanded so much time and effort that it would have been cruel to have more. And with him gone so much, and with Micky so wrapped up in real estate, it would have been tough.

His being gone so much was probably the boy's problem, too. It's tough to move around the country even if your dad is there to help. It's a lot worse if your dad is off flying all the time.

But he had made major! Just in time, but he'd made it! For a while, he had been worried about being RIFfed, thrown out before he had his twenty in, not even getting to retire. Then he worried about retiring as a captain. That would have been humiliating. But a major was a field grade, a good place to retire, and something to show for busting your ass for the Air Force for twenty years.

He hadn't expected them to load him down with medals and promotions after his tour at Bien Hoa, but he did expect better than to be put right back into the MAC pilot pool, flying the line as a copilot. It had actually taken him a long time just to adjust to America again, and to Micky. Korea hadn't been half so tough on his system, physically or emotionally, as Nam had been. He'd thought his experience there might have been valuable to somebody upstairs, and had offered to submit a report on what he'd learned in the jungle. But the buildup in Vietnam had been so swift, so dramatic, that he and the other guys who went in before the Tonkin Gulf incident just kind of got lost in the stampede. Nobody wanted to hear what a Gooney Bird pilot thought about the war, tactically or otherwise.

And then there was Number 54. It took two years before he stopped dreaming about her, and more before he forgave himself. Naturally, he'd never told Micky about her. So in a way, coming right back to Travis to start another three-year tour was a good thing; it gave them all what passed for stability when they were all distracted: Micky by ambition, him by Number 54, and Larry Jr. by just trying to grow up. They weren't so much a family then as a collection of strangers who sometimes met for meals, or smalltalk, or, in his and Micky's case, occasional sex.

He wondered how he was going to break it to Micky. He wanted just to grab her and yell "I made it!" but he also wanted to play it cool. Maybe he'd offer to fix drinks, then just bring in the bottle of Dom Perignon, or whatever it was. She'd know it was expensive; God knew she'd drunk enough champagne over their lives, and she knew what was good. This stuff was French; he hoped she wouldn't mind. He should have thought about that, she liked California wines.

He was debating going back to the liquor store when he heard the crunch of Micky's Cadillac rear bumper bottoming on the curb. If you didn't come in slowly, it happened every time, and Micky never came in slowly.

"Where are you?" He could tell by her voice she was excited. Did she know? Could Colonel Brown have called?

She ran up to him, kissed him. She was dancing. "Hungry, darling? I got some steamed crabs, right up from Alioto's, and two big, beautiful, luscious filet mignons. How does that sound?"

"Great. What's happened? You look like the cat who ate the bald eagle."

"Oh, nothing, nothing, just let me go start the fire and fix us a drink. We can eat the crabs on the patio while the charcoal's getting set."

"I'll fix them."

She pushed him back down in the chair. "No, I insist, it's my turn."

Well, we'll have the champagne later, in the tub, he thought. He went out on the fieldstone patio; he couldn't wait to tell her, she'd be so pleased.

"You read Larry's letter?" she called in.

"Yeah, let's send him the money. If we don't he's apt to come home. I don't mind being called a warmonger once in a while, but I hate to have it around the house."

Micky laughed and sang. She came in with a silver tray, a bottle of champagne, and two glasses. It was the Dom Perignon.

"You found it?"

"The champagne? Yes, finally. I looked all over before I found one at that big liquor store on the main drag, Valley Liquors. They said they hadn't sold a bottle of Dom Perignon—it's French, Larry darling—in months, and they sold two today. I hope whoever bought the other one has as good news as I have."

He grabbed her, kissed her.

427

"How did you find out? I wanted to surprise you."

"How did I find out? Jerry told me; I was pretty sure I was close, but with all the listings, and the other things, I went over the Million Dollar Sales mark today, and it's only June. Don't you just love it? Toast me, the hottest little saleswoman in the Valley!"

He looked at her, suffused with pleasure. It was just like the old O. Henry short story, but upbeat. They both had good news; he decided to let her enjoy hers to the fullest, and then he'd spring his.

"Congratulations, my smart, beautiful, sexy darling. Here's to the hottest little saleswoman, and a little later, I hope the hottest wife, in the Valley."

She pressed against him, happy.

They talked for a while; she recounted her sales coups like a golfer going over the last eighteen holes. He was amazed at her memory; she not only knew every sale and every dollar, she could remember the ones she thought she should have made and didn't.

They worked through the crabs methodically; Larry always thought they were a waste of time, but Micky loved them for their evocation of San Francisco.

They finished the bottle with the crabs; she put the steaks on. "Larry, do you want a drink, or would you like a bottle of red with the steaks? We have some of that case of Souverain Cabernet left, don't we?"

"I'll get something."

He went in the kitchen, pulled his bottle of Dom Perignon out. Seventy-five dollars' worth of champagne today; they were living high on the hog. He removed the foil and the wire cap; the goddamn cork wouldn't budge. He worked it with his thumbs, tried to twist it with his hands, edged it against the top of the sink.

The cork was still tight when she walked in behind him, surprised him. "The other bottle of Dom Perignon? You were the one? Did Jerry tell you what happened?"

The cork popped out, spraying them both with foam.

"No, honey, goddamn it, I made major today. Can you believe it? I made major."

She kissed him, then stepped back. A frown creased her face. "Oh, Larry, are you sure?"

"Positively, Duke Brown wrote me and Duke never makes a mistake. Hell, he's almost a damn general."

Micky squealed like a teenager and grabbed him. A little later, the steaks burned, they splashed water out of the hot tub, and they found out that two bottles of Dom Perignon were enough to make them both slightly ill. It seemed they weren't such strangers after all.

38

Jesse Catlin raced down the dark, hazy street, heart pounding, lungs sucking in the smoky air in painful gulps. Fear and hatred welled from his humiliation at breaking and running from the helmeted, club-wielding policemen. The pigs had simply materialized in front of them, stepping from the menacing shadow. Claude had tripped, fallen, been overrun and snatched up; he heard Claude's cries of fear submerged in the triumphant shouts.

He slowed, turned the corner into an alley, pressed his back against the wall, and took in great slobbering gasps of breath. His body ached and his legs trembled. Jesse dropped to one knee, cautiously peeked around the corner. No one had followed him. He couldn't have started running again; there would have been no choice but to submit.

He wondered how Claude was doing. Poor Claude, he hadn't even wanted to come along, and now he was probably spread-eagled, handcuffed, waiting to be thrown in a wagon and hauled down to jail. His mother would die.

A siren wailed nearby; Jesse slumped to the ground, crouched behind the rusting garbage can and the fifty-five-gallon drum leaking some rotten-smelling fluid. He hoped it wasn't acid; he'd pressed against it when he heard the siren. The car passed; maybe Claude was in it.

Mary Catlin would be furious; she'd told him to stay home, not to go down where the trouble was. He'd almost obeyed her; they'd only gotten to 16th Street when the fighting erupted around them. The cops had stopped two black boys carrying BURN signs; they had been surrounded by fifteen or twenty youngsters, who had in turn been ringed by three carloads of

429

police. The whole thing turned into a battleground when twenty or thirty high-school kids suddenly burst out of their school and fell on the outer ring of police. Rocks were thrown, windshields knocked out; the police finally fought from each side to the center, and then back out again, this time forming a cordon that moved to the right, using clubs to drive all the kids into the schoolyard.

Claude and he had watched the whole thing; each time they intended to intervene, to help the black kids, more police showed up. They finally turned and ran—right into the arms of four more cops. If they had gone another two steps, they would have been apprehended right there, but there was an abandoned pickup truck jutting out of the alley, halfway onto the sidewalk. Jesse and Claude had cut right behind it, and run. Claude tripped, and they caught him.

Now Jesse had to get home. The fires were spreading fast, and he could hear sirens all around him. He was still sick from running, the greasy chili dog he'd had for supper racing around his stomach. He turned down Dorand Street, down past the small shops where his mother could get things on credit toward the end of the month. Halfway down the street he noticed the windows were broken out, the glass spilled on the street. The lights were out in the shops, but in the reflection from the red-hazed sky he could see people moving. He quickened his pace. The streetlights were out. He could hear sirens in the next street, sounded like fire trucks and ambulance, not police.

He turned down his street, Garland Court. There were fire trucks blocking the entrance. Down the street, near his house, there were flames and fire.

Jesse moved forward; he was grabbed roughly by a huge white fireman in yellow raingear. "Stay out of there, nigger, we got enough trouble without you."

"That's my house down there; my mama's down there. Please, mister, let me in."

"You hear me, boy? I said no. I don't give a damn if your house burns down and your mama with it, you ain't going down this street." He grabbed Jesse, slammed him in an arc against the red panel truck. Jesse felt the door handle grind into his back. He broke loose, ran back down to the corner, up Dorand Street. If he couldn't get in this way, he'd get in another.

The spotlight blinded him.

"Hands up, you black bastard!"

430

Jesse couldn't see, felt another person run past him. He put his hands up.

The policeman grabbed him, tripped him. "Spread your arms and legs, nigger." The policeman pawed his arms and legs, jerked his hands back, cuffed him. "Get up," he barked.

Jesse had turned to get on his hands and knees, raised up when the kick came driving him headlong into the side of the police car. Another pair of hands spun him, forced him into the rear seat. There was a frightened older black man, gray haired, trembling, already there.

The cop picked up the microphone. "Central, this is thirty-eight; we got two looters here down on Dorand Street. I think I better bring them in and then go back. I don't want to get caught down here with them."

Jesse was terrified. Looters? They shoot looters. "Hey, mister, I wasn't looting, I was trying to get to my house over on Garland. It's on fire, and my mama's there."

The driver kept his eyes straight ahead; the policeman who had grabbed Jesse and kicked him, turned, and laughed. "Sure kid, then who was it I just collared coming out of the store with a TV set in his arms? Must have been Alfalfa."

The old man was crying. Jesse tried to talk to him but he wouldn't answer, just cried and wiped his eyes.

There were too many people for the jail and Jesse was trundled, with another three or four dozen kids, all his age, into a schoolyard basketball court, tall wire fence on three sides, brick wall on the other. They asked for identification; Jesse had none on him, and said his name was George Jackson; he didn't know why. They removed the handcuffs, said they needed them for the next batch.

He was clammy with sweat and fear. What had happened to his mama? What was going to happen to him? Would they shoot him? The people in the basketball court had coalesced into small groups. He didn't seen anyone he knew, so he edged close to the brick wall and sat down. It was going to be a long night. And the morning would be worse.

Mary Catlin stood in her powder-blue robe, one slipper on, the other lost in the wild flight from the fire. She stood watching the old house burn, burning up her new sofa, the dinette set, everything but the Bible she clutched under her arm.

Thank God, Jesse wasn't home. She wondered where she could spend the night; probably the church was the best spot. The church would be expecting people tonight.

The flames were diminishing, and one of the fire crews was frantically rolling up its hoses, anxious to get going to another part of town where another row of houses was burning.

Mary approached the one man who was standing in the middle, directing the others. "Mister, is there any way for me to get a message to my boy?"

He looked at her. "Ma'am, I just don't know how. We won't be here for more than twenty minutes, and as soon as the fire is out for sure, the other company will be leaving. I wish I could help."

She nodded, turned. Jesse's smart; he'll know I went to the church. Maybe he's already there.

It was cool, not cold, but cool enough that Jesse had to get up and move around. Most of the people were lying down now, on the hard asphalt, trying to get some rest. Jesse made a circuit of the lot, came back near where he started, sat down next to a basement window, half submerged in a window well.

He glanced around. No one was looking. He stretched out, reached down, tested the window. It moved. He moved to sit on the edge of the window well, reached down, strained, brought the window full out. He could squeeze under it, if he moved like a snake, and drop inside. To what?

He felt around the edge of the window well, found a piece of gravel. He reached under the window ledge, dropped it. It hit the floor with a bang that seemed to shatter the schoolyard. The drop wasn't much; when he was inside he could figure out what to do next.

Jesse slithered under the window, turned, scraping his back and his belly in the process, and slipped back down into the inky blackness of the basement. He reached forward, pulled the window closed, then eased back, holding the edge with his hands. His feet were not touching the floor. He dropped about six inches, stumbled backward over a chair, fell to the floor. He waited, sure that the noise would raise someone.

There was no light at all in the basement; he had no idea where the door was, or where the door would lead to. He tried to remember what time it was. It must be after midnight. The dawn was a long time away, and he was afraid to wait.

In about fifteen minutes his eyes grew acclimated. There was a reflection on the far wall that must be the glass in a door. He edged his way over, moving his legs in a smooth arc so that he would sense an obstacle before tripping on it, made his way to the door.

432

Jesse stepped out into the hallway; it was like a tunnel, a teardrop of black, with a round gray dot at the end. He moved to the center, walked as silently as he could toward the gray. As he got closer, the gray turned to yellow; it was a stairwell, with a single weak bulb burning at the top.

He sat down and listened. There was no sound at all from above; he remembered the building was Jefferson Grade School. There shouldn't be anybody in the building, unless the cops were using it.

He had to relieve himself, went back down the corridor to where it was dark. Jesse felt wicked, but he didn't know where the boys' room was, couldn't wait, especially if he had to run again. His arms and legs were sore, but he had his wind back, and if he had to, he would run till he dropped.

Jesse went up one stair tread at a time, easing his weight down, trying to stop the conspiring boards from creaking. At the top he could see two corridors, both leading to a set of glass doors, both well lit from streetlights outside.

He pressed against the wall, moving down the corridor. He bumped into a white porcelain water fountain, bent down, drank.

The water barely moved, the pressure was so low, but it was the best thing he'd ever had.

At the door he looked out. There was no one about. He couldn't go home. He wondered if Ted Amos was home, would come get him if he could get to a phone booth. Jesse planned his route. He would leave the school, walk, not run, down to the corner, then turn up 25th Street and try to find a phone booth. He felt in his pockets. He had some change, a quarter and two dimes.

When he pressed the brass bar to open the door the alarm went off. Jesse shot down the steps and up the street, racing away from the building, away from the police station. He ran all the way up to 25th, faltering after about a mile, his feet aching in his worn Keds. There were no cars, nobody around, it was as if he had the city to himself. The sky was still red, and he wished he could run to his mama, make sure she was safe, take care of her.

There was a filling station, a phone booth on the corner where 25th ran into Alabama. He got Ted's number from information, dialed.

A woman's sleepy voice answered. "Who is this? You know what time it is?"

"Ma'am, this is Jesse Catlin. Is Mr. Ted Amos there?"

He heard her drop the phone. "Ted, some fool named Jesse Catlin's calling you. You know him?"

Amos came on the line. "Jesse, what's the matter? Why are you calling at four in the morning?"

"I'm in trouble, Mr. Amos, and I need some help."

He spilled out the story.

"Jesse, stay right where you are, drop down in the phone booth if you can to stay out of sight, or hide yourself around there somewhere. I'll be by in about fifteen minutes, maybe less. I'll be driving a Dodge Dart, black; when you see me, you come up and get in and let's get out of there."

Ted picked him up with no trouble, and brought him back to his apartment. There was a nice-looking middle-aged black lady there. He didn't know if Ted was married, or if this was a girlfriend. Ted introduced her only as Amy.

"Jesse, it might be a good thing that you didn't give your name. But is the policeman apt to remember you?"

"I don't know; I told him I lived on Garland Street when he first picked me up. I've seen him before. I think he has a regular patrol in our neighborhood—at least I think so. They all look alike to me."

Ted laughed, a little grimly. "Okay. Try to get some sleep; I'll see if I can find out about your mother in the morning, and then let's figure out what to do about you."

"Tell me one thing. If we are mad about the way we are being treated, why are we burning our own homes down? Why don't we go over to Virginia, to one of them nice white plantation neighborhoods, and burn a few of them down?"

"Good question, Jesse; best question is why anybody has to burn anything down, but it sure as hell doesn't make sense to burn ourselves up. You get some sleep."

Ted located Mary at the church the next morning.

Mary enfolded Jesse in her arms as she had so many times in the last nineteen years. He held her tight, wasn't embarrassed to kiss her in front of Ted. Finally she held him at arm's length and stared solemnly at him. "Jesse, there's something I want you to do. You got to get out of here, you got to get a trade, something you can do until you can be a TV announcer. I want you to join the Army. Don't join the Navy, don't want you fooling around with all those foreign gals, but join the Army, like Ted here did."

"Your mama's right, Jesse; there's no sense in you getting picked up here on a phony looting charge, especially since you busted out. But she means the Air Force, not the Army. I know some guys down at recruiting. Let me see what I can do to help."

Jesse didn't have the heart to argue. The last thing in the world he wanted to do was join anything. But he sure as hell didn't want to join the county farm, busting rocks somewhere for five years. Besides, he knew it was just a matter of time before he was drafted anyway. It didn't look like he had much choice.

39

2000 LOCAL
12 May 1969
Andersen AFB
Guam

For Washington, life at Andersen was a symphony of boredom, orchestrated around the ageless service command, "Hurry up and wait." He waited a lot. He waited to get breakfast, to get transportation down to the briefing area, to get a ride out to the airplane, to start the engines, to taxi, to takeoff. Everything operated to a Daliesque rhythm, a strange protracted stretching of time and compression of events.

But it was all synchronized, and despite the agony of human waiting, airplanes inevitably got off on time, tankers were met on time, bombs were dropped on time.

The flying itself was filled with long intervals of almost decaying boredom. The airplane flew on autopilot for most of the route with a minimum of attention. For much of the mission, there were not even radio transmissions to break the monotony.

It gave everyone too much time to think.

Wash was twelve thousand miles and thirty degrees of heat away from the States, and he had problems that were deeply bothering him. He was exactly where every pilot in SAC wanted to be, a squadron commander in a B-52 unit going into combat; at his age and in these times it would be difficult for him to avoid becoming a general officer if he did as well as he knew he could do.

But he knew the cause was wrong.

Washington had done as he always did, read up about his assignment as soon as he knew he was going somewhere. He had

435

been reading about Southeast Asia since Dien Bien Phu; he had felt then that American involvement was bound to come. Since then he had felt a growing admiration for the hardy Vietnamese, plugging on in their twenty-year war against the French. It had seemed somehow essentially American, as if Dien Bien Phu were a Yorktown, a victory of the natives against the invaders. There was an undesirable Communist texture to their politics, but how could it be otherwise? They were taking aid from where they could get it, just as Americans would have done in the same situation.

He was not basically a political person, and didn't feel the tug even of the struggle for racial equality. Yet he admired a country that could muster the will to resist the Japanese for four years, and then roust the French. And he saw a parallel between the North and South Vietnamese and the North and South Koreans. In both cases the will seemed to lie with the Northern forces, those with Communist leanings. The Southern nations were democratic, weak, dependent upon foreign—that is American—support. The peoples were not racially different, more homogeneous in Korea perhaps than in Vietnam, but not significantly so.

He was ashamed that he was prejudiced against Koreans in general, South Koreans in particular. His experience at Surgeon had made him wary, so much so that he kept an eye on the Guamanians around him, even as he realized the irony of his bigotry and became distressed. He knew that Louise would be furious with him if she was aware that he checked his liquor to see if it had been watered, left precise amounts of change out to see if any was taken. In town he was certain that he was being cheated even when he knew the prices were right. He thought he saw contempt in the Guamanians' eyes, and this bothered him too, even though he'd seen it often in white men's eyes. No matter how much he achieved, he expected a white man to look down on him. But a damn gook, a foreigner, to do the same was intolerable. He practiced eye contact, determined never to roll his eyes away from a native, just as he had practiced with his peers.

He wished he could have talked it over with Louise. She was more and more an activist, even though she tried to conceal it from him. It came through in her letters. It suited her, and he hoped she was smart enough not to embarrass him, for she had seen earlier than he that his career could do much for blacks as a whole. She would not jeopardize it now. And yet, he might; if

436

he openly questioned what they were doing, if he made a single mistake in judgment that could be interpreted as political commentary, he would be shunted aside. His life would not be bad, it would simply be off the fast track, and he might expect to retire at best as a colonel. The Air Force had treated him magnificently; it did not expect him to bite its hand.

It was hard to excel in a group as professional as the SAC B-52 squadrons. He had done it with some natural talent, by working twice as hard as others, and by catching the ground swell of guilt that was surging through the wave of Air Force integration. He did not kid himself any longer that his good fortune had been by chance; he was identified as a comer, a black officer who could do well and serve as a token of the Air Force's progress. His career had been accelerated from the day he was a B-47 copilot until the now legendary day when he made the first takeoff as the first black B-52 aircraft commander.

If Louise had known how he treated that day, she would have been incensed. But he had felt that as the first black B-52 AC, he had to say or do something to let them all know he understood the importance of the fact. So on that first takeoff with his crew, he signaled his copilot Jerry Bader to raise the landing gear, mashed down on his intercom, and said, "Okay, crew, the Jig is up."

The line had raced through the command, enhancing his stature even more, but it was the last time he ever put himself down. Now he was a squadron commander, another first, and his task was essentially racial oppression, no matter what it was termed politically, no matter how it came about. One black man leading perhaps eighty whites and ten other blacks into combat with a fearsome mission, to drop bombs on yellow men.

The final savage irony, of course, was that the yellow men they were bombing were living in the country of the yellow men they were supposed to be defending. It was the first war in history where the ally was systematically bombed into oblivion, while the enemy's country was considered a sanctuary.

Wash's distress was shared. Many of the crew members felt bad that their enormous resources were being used so unprofitably, that their lives were being squandered if not in casualties then in boredom. It was precisely controlled nonsense, a parody of warfare. Every target, the bomb loads, the routes, the size of the attacks all were directed and monitored from above. Command and control were exercised by means of new and extraordinary communication systems.

Wash knew that they were as much a curse as a blessing. In all previous wars, the lack of communication had been one of the greatest problems. Lee might have won at Gettysburg if he had shared a walkie-talkie with Jeb Stuart, Napoleon might have survived at Waterloo if his scouts had field telephones. And if Hitler had had the communications afforded the Far Eastern Air Force, he could have lost the war in 1943 rather than 1945, exercising on every front the headquarters control of individual squads. The latter parallel extended to Andersen.

Arc Light was the great code name conjuring up piercing, well-directed illumination, yet it was only a metaphor for an endless freight train of five-hundred-pound bombs blindly off-loaded in the dark. It had started in disaster. There was supposed to be north of Saigon a sizable base of Vietcong forces, well dispersed and a threat to the city. Smaller bombers had hit the area, but there was no evidence of destruction. The B-52s were to come from Guam, in sufficient quantity and sufficiently often to establish patterns of bombing, which even though random would be mathematically certain to damage the enemy.

On the first raid, two B-52s collided during the midair refueling; eight crewmen were killed and four rescued. The battle damage was inspected by ground forces and found to be negligible.

Within a few months, however, the B-52 began direct support of ground forces. The nuclear long rifle became another version of the rolling artillery barrage of the Argonne Forest, infinitely more expensive, inevitably less effective.

Washington had come at a time when things had become abnormally routine, where all the mindless struggle resolved itself into a simple conveyor belt, a bomb from the United States brought half the way around the world and dumped in a friendly jungle with the order, precision, and impersonality with which sticks of gum were created and dispatched at the factories of Wrigley. He had been able to slip effortlessly into the numbing routine of planning, flying, bombing, resting, planning, flying, bombing, resting. His sense that he was somehow a traitor to his causes was eased by the thing that bothered other crew members most.

What they were doing was ineffective, and caused little human damage. It was wasteful, it harmed the countryside, but it didn't kill many people, and that was something in itself.

Being a squadron commander was a godsend, for his job occupied every spare moment of his time and kept him from brooding. Everyone was busy but there were frequent rest periods, and occasional stand-downs for weather or training, which might have been intolerable if he didn't have to attend to a thousand demands. The officers were not much of a problem; their careers were on the line and they had been disciplined too long and too routinely by SAC to make major mistakes.

There was a curious, unpredictable morale problem. Most of the men had grown up with the concept that the Air Force had been a moral force for the right in Europe. It had hammered Nazi Germany to its knees, and the young men fought and died for a good cause, with universal approval at home. Now the crew members learned from the press that they were the bad guys, that they were fighting a bad war, that the B-52 was not the wholesome harbinger of peace that the B-17 was, but was instead a loathsome extension of imperialism. It was hard to reconcile a lifetime of dedication and sacrifice with being warmongering killers, despoilers of peaceful Asians.

Working with the enlisted men was the most demanding and the most rewarding. Under the SAC concept, the squadron C.O. was responsible for everyone all the time, on base or off; if an airman third class got drunk and had a fight, the squadron C.O. was brought into it directly. If there was an emergency at home, a child sick, or wife ailing, the C.O. became part of the loop to solve the problem.

The press of the duties suited Wash's natural bent; he was outgoing and able to give of himself. But a Saturday off from combat became an ordeal for him, for he knew that there would be trouble downtown, fights in the barracks, a taxicab with G.I.s smashed against a telephone pole, something disagreeable, and he would have to deal with it.

He was amazed at the reckless inclination of the young airmen to get married; he even set aside a "marriage day" each month to deal with the problem. The airmen were fresh from the States, often away from home for the first time; many had never had a girl until they found one in a bar, a professional, who gave them synthetic affection and sexual expertise. It was love at first sex, and the girls wanted to be married, to go to the United States. It was Wash's job to dissuade the airman until he gained a little maturity, or found another girl, or both. By setting one day a month to discuss it, he outlasted most of the romances; those who demanded permission to be married were deferred from month to month, until they either forgot about it or until it significantly affected their work.

Pay problems were the next most severe; for family men, even those with the maximum allotment, it was tough to maintain themselves without abject denial. Most had always moonlighted, working in filling stations and supermarkets, the extra proceeds going to pay for credit-bought necessities of life. Now they were overseas, and not only unable to moonlight, but incurring double expenses, for they had to live and entertain themselves as well. Back home the bills came due, and letters from angry creditors surged across Wash's desk, threatening repossession and lawsuits. The wives were often no more than children, unable to handle their finances, subject to threats of violence from the bill collectors who were little better than the juice men of Wash's hometown.

Boredom compounded the problem; once the attraction of the tropic island had passed, once the Orient was no longer exotic, the men became rock happy. It was difficult to work them sixty or eighty hours a week, month in and month out, and be able to offer in exchange little more than supervised beaches and athletic equipment.

Yet he had a talent for it. He was present; he made the rounds of the guard posts every week, stopped in the mess halls at least once a day to take a meal, made sure the chaplains were available and aware of his interest in their degree of interest, and paused to take a hand in whatever kinds of activity were going on. He kept a set of coveralls in the car, and in the course of his tour changed tires, loaded bombs, fueled airplanes, working for an hour or two at a time, getting his hands dirty, finding out what was happening. The troops believed he knew everything; they were unguarded in their talk around him, and he quickly established a performance profile on his noncommissioned officers. He saved much time because no one dared to bullshit him; he got the straight word, first time, and it made a difference. Especially to him.

The flying was mechanical, concerned more with the problems of getting allocations of fuel and bombs, or with coordinating with the KC-135 tankers than with handling the airplanes. Sometimes the weather posed fearsome problems, but the forecasting was superb and there were real-time reports from ships and planes that recorded the passage of storms on an immediate basis.

The missions were long and grueling; he flew as often as he could, either in the left seat in the lead of the mission, or just riding along in the crowded cockpit. He hated to dead-head; the boredom was intolerable, unrelieved even by the mechanical pleasure of flying. Inflight refueling was an absorbing task when you did it yourself; when you watched someone else, especially when you weren't sitting in an ejection seat, it was an exercise in horror.

The Big Belly B-52s were pigs to fly, and obscene to refuel. Waddling through the air with their huge pylons laden with the drag-inducing bombs, they had to first find, then formate with the indefatigable "Young Tigers," KC-135s from Kadena, Okinawa, or elsewhere. In daytime, in clear weather, it was not difficult to put the airplane into refueling position; at night, in a storm, it was a sweat-splashed, muscle-numbing nightmare.

The whole operation was carefully planned, with carefully coded charts, elaborate call signs, careful monitoring by onboard radars, and great attention to the details of altitude, courses, and airspeeds. These were but preliminaries. The heart of the problem was flying a ten-year-old airplane, long past retirement age, weighing close to four hundred thousand pounds, in coupled connection with twenty tons of highly explosive fuel gurgling around in what had started life as a near relation of a Boeing 707.

Two jet airplanes, a mass of some six hundred thousand pounds were linked together at perhaps 250 knots by a slender cylindrical telescoping boom guided by an enlisted man who earned twelve thousand dollars per year. The tanker led, its crew tired and bored by the endless round of identical missions, flying a course and an altitude, conscious always that an untoward movement upon the part of their receiver could tear them to pieces, sending them plunging in great gouts of flame toward the bottomless Pacific below. In the bomber, the tanker loomed ahead, the air invisibly washing back over it, creating a tide the bomber had to burst through, seeking the pendant-winged penis of the boom.

The checklist and drill for the refueling was surprisingly simple: electric switches released doors and opened valves, and a gaping round mechanical vagina clasped the boom in mechanical compression until the mission fuel was received.

The sexual quality of the event was used by the crews as a tension reliever; some of the bomber receiver receptacles were ornamented with thighs and hair, and the same ribald jokes were always conjured up by the act.

Under ordinary circumstances the refueling could be routine. The bomber identified the tanker, moved into position behind it, completed the standard checklists, then moved forward, within range of the boom. The bomber pilot's task was then simply to formate within a prescribed envelope while the boomer, the refueling operator, actually flew the patented Boeing boom into the receptacle. When the boom was engaged, switches were thrown and fuel poured into the bomber in a torrent. The very fuel flow itself introduced a new element into the flying equation. As the tanker lightened, the bomber grew heavy; it became easier to fly the tanker, more difficult to control the bomber.

If the weather was serene, the task was not difficult; more often it was turbulent, and then it became a matter of muscle, skill, and anticipation to keep the bomber in formation. The swept-wing planes embraced and became two partners in a massive dance connected by the boom, moving in random directions, the tanker the leader, the bomber following, but the bomber also pushing, disturbing the wall of air. If kept focused on each other, the effects of the random gyrations were minimized. If they were permitted to compound each other, the airplanes could merge together in a flash of fire, or break away to start the process all over again. There was a constant interplay of control and throttle, the movement of both always in response to a movement of the planes, the movement always controlled so that it did not exaggerate and amplify the twisting. It was like threading a needle attached to a pneumatic jackhammer.

Wash enjoyed refueling, and the more difficult the better; he was strong and accomplished. He could manhandle the bolting, bucking B-52 with precision, keeping its blunt nose poised within the boom's envelope for as long as it took, watching the green marking stand steady, glancing up into the glass bay windows of the boomer, noting the approval in the nod of his head. A good refueling mission was characterized by silence; two professionals simply did their job.

It was entirely different to sit slumped between the two pilots' seats on the upper deck, plugged into the spare intercom position, and watch some ham-handed youngster plunge into the refueling fray. It took iron nerve not to take charge, to throw the pilot out of the seat when he was having trouble, to avoid checking too often the fit of the parachute. It was largely a matter of experience; a natural pilot might be able to fly all refuelings well, but most were not natural pilots, and they were making aircraft commanders with less and less experience as the war droned on.

The noise level was the key. When Wash refueled, the only sound was the gurgle of fuel and the quiet recital of checklists.

When a new man refueled, under rugged conditions, there was a clattering and a banging as the boom was dribbled across the top of the fuselage, as the boom operator's voice would begin to rise with anxiety, as the pulse of the engines quickened and lessened in increasing cycles. Under the next to worst condition—the worst was a collision, and if that happened, nothing else mattered—the pilot would get fatigued, get out of cycle, and be forced to break away from the tanker. The concern and fatigue in the boomer's voice, or the tanker aircraft commander's voice, could scarcely be concealed.

But he flew with every crew, and it made a difference to them, and to him. He found out who his best people were, and he put them in the critical positions; he tried to schedule the best crews for the toughest missions, although often there was no option. He was their flying leader, and it never even occurred to him to joke any more about being black.

After the refueling, the mission became an exercise in boredom. They were denied even the pleasure of acquiring a target in the radar and flying precisely to it, to choose when and how to toggle off the bombs against a specific object. Instead they were wended to a set of coordinates, and Combat Skyspot, a mobile ground-control radar-guidance system would direct them to the drop point, give them their headings and speeds, and then signal to drop. It was more accurate—if accuracy could be applied to bombing "suspected targets"—but it was yet another degree more impersonal, a step closer to missile warfare. Yet Wash came to prefer it. His personal skills made no genuine difference; they would have gotten any B-52 to the same spot, and the same drop would have been made. It was a denial and he knew it, but it was one he was glad to take.

40

January 1970
Tinker AFB, Oklahoma
USA

Tinker AFB was a new experience for Picard. He had been on the line all his life, working with his hands, managing people who worked with their hands. He was assigned to the Oklahoma City Air Material Area, OCAMA, a giant supply and repair depot. Most of the work force was Hispanic; they called it, with the counterpart at San Antonio, the "Brown-eyed AMAs." The other bases, spread around the U.S. were of course the "Blue-eyed AMAs."

He didn't have to get a line full of airplanes ready to fly every morning; he and apparently several hundred other people, at Tinker, Wright-Patterson, Andrews, and elsewhere were all engaged in a gigantic project that seemed to have no beginning and no end.

The biggest difference was in the work discipline. People drifted in when they chose and out when they chose; there were endless coffee breaks, long lunch hours, happy hours after work. Most of his coworkers were civilians, G.S.s, who had never done anything else.

He thought back to Mountain Home and the B-47 crash, to Alaska and the helicopter rescue. Work had been an addictive wine, calling him every waking moment, broken airplanes waiting for him as patients wait for doctors. He had the magic touch, too. Now work hung in dead shards across his desk, mountains of computer printouts. The supply and maintenance system was generating more information every day than could be processed in a month; fresh information in reams of perforated paper would be rolled in on special carts every morning. The reports from seven days ago, still not read, were carted out and destroyed. He tried to glean information from the endless printouts; it was hopeless.

In time he began to understand that his job was to establish a relationship between maintenance techniques and supply levels, so that both could be kept at a minimum. Costs were zooming, and every dollar spent on spare parts was one that couldn't buy a new weapon system. There was always pressure to keep the purchase of spare parts at a minimum, to have procurement money for new equipment, but the Air Force had grown so large that it was impossible to ensure that every base had what it needed when it needed it. Picard knew that when a part wasn't available an airplane might be grounded. He and all the other crew chiefs he knew had kept their own private inventories of hard-to-get items. Now their practical solution was a major part of the problem.

It took him about six months to learn the place, to realize that about 20 percent of the people did 90 percent of the work, and that the rest were just overhead. He found out who could say yes and make something happen, and who would defer a decision on principle. He worked for a young captain, nonrated, a believer in the computer, but smart enough to listen to what Don had to say. His name was Gordon Chalkley, and he was working on a program to analyze the data in real time, to let them know exactly what the workloads were, what the real maintenance problems, either people or parts, were. But he was inexperienced, didn't trust his conclusions. Part of the problem was the data; a savvy crew chief, tired from eighteen hours on the line, would fill in the reports with a minimum effort, saying just enough to cover his ass in case someone checked the paper against the day's events. But that never happened. Everyone was too busy, and the real problems were buried in a sea of bogus data.

Don sifted through the paperwork. Captain Chalkley would call him in periodically, to try out some ideas.

"Don, look at this. If you analyzed the Mean Time Between Failure rate for B-52 instrument inverters for Fifteenth Air Force, you get a totally different picture than for Eighth Air Force. Yet the maintenance procedures are the same, they fly the same number of hours. Statistically it's impossible, but there it is." The inverters were a perfect example to work on, for they were normally reliable, rarely gave trouble, but were absolutely essential for the safety of the airplane, as they converted the electrical output of the aircraft alternators to a current suitable for the flight instruments. It was a textbook case.

"Captain, give me two days on the telephone, and I'll get you an answer."

He spent the morning at the Comm Center, poring over telephone books, calling the bases. At most of the bases he knew someone on the flight line; where he didn't know someone on a base, he got a referral from somewhere else. Then he started calling individual line chiefs, even crew chiefs, asking questions about how they serviced the inverters, how often they changed them, how they ordered the spares.

The men who knew him couldn't understand why he was calling; they knew Picard knew as much about the care and feeding of airplanes and their inverters as anyone. The ones who didn't know him thought he was some headquarters weenie and would try to fob him off with smartass answers. He would go along for a moment, then stiffen them with a few well-chosen comments that let them know he was serious. Then he would get the answers.

In the end it was simple: 15th Air Force was still using stocks of a lubricant that had been designed for the previous series of inverters; it wasn't adequate for the newer models, which were more common in their inventory.

Chalkley was delighted. "Goddamn it Don, I'd never have figured that out, but it proves my model worked this time to pinpoint a problem. Let's try it again."

Don dropped his regular office work, dropped the regular routine. He was at the office at all hours, calling bases all over the world. The communications officer came around to investigate, to see if the calls were justified, or if Don was just some kind of phone freak. Chalkley straightened him out.

It was a breakthrough for Chalkley; he could sharpen his computer program, make it more sophisticated, and get an empirical verification from Don from a few phone calls. Picard didn't have to make as many calls once he began to determine who was reliable. The crew chiefs he called got into the spirit, made suggestions. Within six months they had a statistical analysis system that turned the mountains of data into meaningful pages of instructions and did it directly in the computer. The printouts came out in sheets of four or five instead of thousands, and the answers were underlined.

The first time things moved swiftly was when Chalkley briefed the short, totally bald Maj. Gen. Everett Lobart on the new program. The AFLC deputy for logistics sat sour, taciturn, a bristling bundle of energy. When Chalkley was through, he commented, "Great; we'll do it. Captain Chalkley, I am going to have you reassigned to my staff. Great job." With that he swirled out of the room.

Within eight weeks the system had been refined and implemented, given a new acronym: FFF, for Fast Fault Finder. The resentful field called it Fast Fuck-up Finder until they began to see it work.

Chalkley left, going to Air Force Logistic Command Headquarters at Wright-Patterson, and Don went down to the main work area where one B-52 after another was put through a rebuild line for maintenance and repair. He was happy there, doing what he knew best, away from the paperwork.

41

A warm mixture of pleasure and guilt seeped through Kelly; it was like drinking the stolen sacramental wine back at Holy Angels. The Connaught was definitely different from East St. Louis's Broadview Hotel; he wondered what he would have received if he'd asked for high tea at the Broadview. Probably a knuckle sandwich.

He had enjoyed the experience from the moment he'd been able to drag Kathy out of the old Jesuit church. Kelly realized as he walked up Carlos Street to the Connaught's unprepossessing entrance, he was exorcising many demons, making up for many things. Kathy was excited; she was not a gourmet cook but she was a gourmet eater, and the prospect of blowing a bundle at the Connaught was one she appreciated. He had spent many days and nights away from home, and there had been many a bad meal grabbed on the road, expedient sustenance, not eating out.

They were ushered into a plush, warm-wooded parlor. She sat, immediately absorbed in people watching, one of the things that bonded them. Despite mental reservations about English bartenders, he ordered two martinis, took a nibble from the tray of slightly stale nuts before them. Around the room, studded like faded flowers in long-neck vases, were thin and regal English-women, all wearing high-collar flowered dresses, all with pearls, cigarettes and double whiskies. Each one gazed at a mystic spot on the wall opposite her, impervious to glances, unseeing, preserved by the smoke and the alcohol and the permanence of the Connaught.

A group of businessmen came in as they were served their martinis. The leader was a young American, long haired, stomach slightly too large for the Pierre Cardin suit he was wearing. There were four of them, dominated by a tall, ruddy-faced Englishman with a leonine shock of white hair, an ancient Savile Row suit, pinstripes wide enough to have been applied by a tennis-court line marker, and the usual scuffed and run-down

447

English shoes. His twit attended him, a slack-jawed blond young man with eyes that seemed to pop out over his glasses. But the pivotal figure was a tall, dark Japanese who scarcely spoke or smiled, but who followed everything with radar attention. He was dressed in the customary gray sharkskin suit, a choice appropriate to his apparent role.

The martinis were excellent, cold, large and subtly vermouthed. Kathy's eyes sparkled as an ancient archetype of an English gentleman tottered across the room to one of the nearly embalmed waiting ladies. He kissed her hand, she rose, and they glided into the dining room as if on ball-bearing shoe soles. It was the grace that intimidated the whole Victorian world.

The maître d'hotel appeared at their side, escorted them in past a long buffet table of wonderful-looking appetizers. Kelly made his choice on the way, a lobster half.

The shimmering crystal in the dining room gleamed with a patina of age that shut out the rest of the world. Kelly glanced around, wondered about the pecking order of the busboys, servers, waiters, and others, invisible here but doubtless vital to the functioning of the place. Everything was perfect politeness and formality to the diners—thank-you-very-muches churned out in endless streams—but among the workers there was the unending cut and thrust of class distinctions.

Their waiter was old, his black suit turned by time into the myriad shades of oil spilled on water, but very friendly and patient. Kelly had long ago failed menu French, but Kathy had schooled him so that he knew what the dishes were. The waiter left them to study the lovely choices a little more.

Kathy opted for a quail mousse in a pastry puff; he stuck with the half lobster for starters. They always ordered separately, shared tastes, sometimes to the bewilderment of others. Splurging, guilt-ridden, he ordered a half bottle of champagne with the first course.

The next decision was agonizing; she chose a mixed grill and he the lamb in pastry. He consulted with the waiter on the wine, settled on a Pomerol, 1967; he was familiar with it.

Kelly glanced around the almost silent room, filled with intent eaters. There was only one noisy table where what must have been a reunion of estranged parents and son was taking place. It was joyous, and even the older English couples paused in their creative mounding of layers of food on the backs of forks to look on with favor.

What a long way he had come from the Parkway Inn, where he would splurge on their barbecue sandwiches when he'd saved enough. Kathy had worked with him on the niceties; it no longer bothered him to be confronted by an array of knives and forks, nor did the endless fussing the English waiters did with cutlery put him off.

He sipped the wine. Virginia Dare Red had been the vintage of choice in East St. Louis; he could have bought several cases of it for the price of this liquid ruby.

Kathy had been following the progress of the dessert trolley, squealed softly when it was rolled in their direction. She vacillated among the fruit gateaus, chocolate mousse, flan; finally she settled on trifle, as she always did. In a spirit of self-denial, Kelly waved the desserts away, asked to see the cheese board.

The selection was marvelous; he had them pull a wonderful chèvres up from an olive-oil filled bottle, took an unknown but marvelous creamy Belle Etoile, and a huge piece of Stilton. The waiter looked on approvingly. He had judiciously kept not only a glass of the red in reserve, he had some of the rough-cut French bread put aside to use instead of the proffered biscuits.

He was sipping the very last drop of wine when Kathy said, "Mike, go ahead. I know what you are thinking."

She was right. He signaled the waiter, asked for the cigars. He selected an Upmann, a deadly brown, torpedo-shaped confection. They both had Armagnac.

Kelly steeled himself when the bill came, didn't look at it, simply thrust his American Express Card inside the case. Then he reconsidered, thought about the waiter's courtesy. He pulled it out, gasped quietly, added another 10 percent and relaxed. It was worth every cent.

Being in England, even for six months, was worth almost anything. Even if he hadn't had so much fun, done so much flying, England would have made up for it.

He'd been called over to work with 111 Squadron of the Royal Air Force, flying the F4-M version of the Phantom. The Brits called it the FGR.2, and had specified that it be reengined with the Rolls-Royce Spey. Mike's task was to fly with them, and provide them any insight he could into the airplane's operation.

It had been an easy, pleasant tour. The one thing that struck him about the RAF pilots, as it had struck the Germans more forcibly in two previous wars, was the utter contrast in their officers' mess behavior, which ranged from icy reserve to almost degenerate horseplay, with their slashing ferocity in the air.

449

Chaps who seemed mildly addled, or at best dilettantes on the ground, in the air turned into raging tigers. It was a good combination.

His tour was supposed to be only for three months, but the deputy wing commander at RAF Mildenhall had a heart attack. Kelly was asked if he would substitute until a replacement could be found. Ordinarily he would have turned the job down, for he would barely have time to learn the ropes before leaving and it was usually dog work, with a minimum of flying.

But it meant another three or four months in England, away from the Pentagon, and he grabbed at it for himself and for Kathy. They'd grown closer together in the three months in England than they had ever been before. The timing coincided with the end of the school period for the kids; Kathy's parents had moved into their Arlington house to monitor them for the first three months. Now they'd bring them to England for a vacation.

Twenty minutes after he arrived at Mildenhall he was sorry he had accepted. He was briefed by a rough, rude, Maj. Gen. George G. Lowey, who had the wall behind his desk covered with pictures of himself and various military celebrities.

"Colonel Kelly, I'm not sure you're the man for this job."

"Well, General, why don't you just send me home? I didn't ask for the job; I thought I was doing somebody a favor."

"Yeah, well, be that as it may, we need somebody with some tact. I've put a few calls around about you, and they say you are a hell of a fighter pilot, but nobody mentioned tact."

"How much tact do you need to run a wing? I have to say you haven't exactly been long on tact with me."

"Generals don't have to be tactful with colonels, Kelly, you know that. Still, I'm sorry, I don't mean to be rude, but we're sitting on a racial time bomb here, and I'm not sure somebody with your track record—East St. Louis, Birmingham—is what we need."

"I can see you've done your homework. But like Laurel used to tell Hardy, I'm better now. Let me give it a whirl. But first tell me about it."

"I don't have time to tell you about it; I've got a bottle-cap colonel named Homer Kisling coming over to brief you. But do me a favor. If you don't think you can hack it, or you don't want to, let me know, and we'll fly somebody over from the States. Don't worry about your extended tour—I'll find something productive for you to do for three months."

"I understand. Thanks." Kelly saluted and left.

Outside the door a balding, moon-faced lieutenant colonel was waiting. "Colonel Kelly?"

"You must be Colonel Kisling. Glad to meet you."

Relief swept over Kisling's face. "Colonel Kelly? Thank God. You took the job, then?"

"Yep. Why?"

Kisling brightened, took him down to a conference room. "Well, the reason the previous deputy had a heart attack was that he couldn't handle the tension between the troops. The entire base has polarized, at the enlisted level, and we're afraid we're going to have the same kind of trouble that was going on in the States a couple of years ago. And there's a lot of dope being used. We have the OSI and everybody else looking into it, but we know there's a lot of marijuana around, and we suspect other stuff too."

"Jesus, you don't have to be too smart to know they're using marijuana. They come right from the mainstream of American culture, and they are doing what every other kid seems to be doing at home."

Kisling's eyebrows shot up.

"Are you defending marijuana?" He had visions of Kelly taking a hit on a roach.

"No, goddamn it, but it's not just an Air Force problem. We'll have to handle our problem our way, but it's not like some secret sin of ours."

Kisling absorbed it dubiously, then plunged ahead. "The main problem's in the fuel dump; the POL people." He pulled down a screen and switched on a slide projector. "Let me show you some of the numbers."

While Kelly was learning more than he wanted to know from Kisling, a half mile away T/Sgt. Leo Lopez was scanning the duty roster for the night shift. He stared at the innocuous, poorly typed list until his eyes hurt, but the names didn't change. Lieutenant Fulton had put Catlin and Keene on the same shift, for the next ten days. Lopez stroked his mustache, trimmed precisely to the letter of AFR 51-3. The ball was in his corner, he was the noncommissioned officer in charge of the shift.

Technically, he had the authority to change the roster, but the problem was Fulton. He was a proud black dude, still smarting

451

from having been dropped from flight training, and extremely sensitive to any suggestion that he might have made a mistake.

What really puzzled Leo was that Fritzie should have known better. The POL—petroleum, oil, and lubricants—squadron was really run, as most similar ones were, by its first sergeant. Fritzie was trying to take care of Fulton, to bring him along, but he couldn't do it unless the lieutenant allowed it. Most young officers were glad to depend on the first sergeant until they learned the ropes. Fulton was different, and maybe even an old grizzled master sergeant like Fritz Harter couldn't handle him.

Lopez decided to call Harter before changing the roster. The thought of Catlin and Keene on the same shift made his blood run cold, because sure as hell, somebody's blood would run hot if they had to work together for ten nights, pumping JP-4 or avgas or liquid oxygen in bad weather to itinerant aircraft. POL was a crummy business, ranking down with cooks and military police, the bottom of the Air Force heap where test-score requirements were lower. It served as a dumping ground for the dipshits and dumbasses. Lopez didn't like it, had fought to avoid being transferred, but now that he was there he'd make the best of it. The work itself was bad, days or nights spent in filthy, fuel-soaked coveralls, alternately frozen or sweating. They were shorthanded, as well, and the men were working ever longer shifts.

Catlin had come in as a mystery man. When he interviewed with Lopez, he had worked a soft sibilant Hispanic note into his voice, very sympathetic in tone. Leo had been born in El Paso, knew Brownsville slightly, and the two of them chatted for almost an hour. Catlin impressed Leo as being intelligent, and even charming. There was a curious discrepancy in his records, though, and that bothered him. In any tests of native intelligence, Catlin had the highest marks that Leo had seen in a long time. But in the aptitude tests, he had done well in nothing, as if he was deliberately trying to fail.

At least he made a good appearance; like most of the black troops, his uniform was immaculate, his shoes gleaming, afro hairstyle subdued to just within the requirements of regulations.

One thing troubled Lopez above all else; after basic training, Catlin had been in almost continuous hot water. He had a letter of reprimand still in his file, and an Article 15 had been proposed and dropped on the notice of his assignment overseas.

The really deadly bit of news was a letter Lopez had received a week before from the first sergeant of the school squadron at

Amarillo Air Force Base, Catlin's last assignment. Lopez knew the writer, Will Rector, and trusted him. Rector said that there were some pretty good indications that Catlin was mixed up with what appeared to be Black Panther type of activity. Nothing had happened but talk, but the book on Catlin was that he could cause trouble.

"Airman Catlin, it looks like you've been having some disciplinary problems. We don't have time for that here; there's too much work to do. You are not going to cause me any trouble, are you?"

"No, Sergeant Lopez, I was just a young kid away from home and scared. I'm okay now. I promise you."

Leo had turned him over to Staff Sgt. Mario Shields, a smart young black who ran the personnel section. As he walked away, he overheard Catlin shift vocal gears.

"Shit, bro, wha's happening?"

Catlin did a diddibop dap routine that left Shields, a Vermonter by birth, and formerly a chaplain's assistant, bewildered. Leo stopped to watch. Catlin had changed from a friendly Tex/Mex drawl into a hipster. The kid was clever; he could be trouble.

Lieutenant Fulton hadn't helped. In the weeks that followed, Catlin had made some respectful overtures to him, sounding him out, and Fulton had given him some classic young know-nothing second-lieutenant stuff, stiffing him. Fulton obviously saw Catlin as a reproach to what he was trying to do.

The whole thing might be solvable if it weren't for the indomitable stupidity of Billy Keene. The huge kid was from some little town no one had ever heard of in Arkansas; he hated niggers, Mexicans, Catholics, and Jews with equal and impartial vehemence. He finally figured Leo out after his third consecutive KP assignment, and didn't mouth off about pepperbellies any more. But he was a loose cannon on the flight line. The only thing that kept fights from breaking out was his size and enormous physical strength. He was a bully who enjoyed his bullying.

Leo had watched the tension build, watched the shift in friendships, even in bunking arrangements. Three months ago, the barracks all had a roughly proportionate mix of blacks and whites, a random assignment that reflected the two-to-one ratio of blacks to whites. Now the two barracks were divided by race, one solidly black, the other black on the first floor, white on the second.

Both Leo and Harter had been at Travis for the big riots there; everyone had been spooked, and the Air Force was dealing nervously with the problems at other bases. The problem was no one knew what to do, for the blacks were calling for societal changes, not just Air Force changes.

There were the usual spate of "people" programs, conceived by white liberal arts students in far-away headquarters, and usually studded with slogans like "Up the People" that the blacks instantly converted into ribaldry.

Leo left the orderly room, squaring his overseas cap precisely, wondering about the certain trouble Fulton had put in train. On the white gravel of the squadron walkway he nearly collided with Fritz Harter.

"Jesus, Leo, what are you thinking about, tequila? Or Maria?"

Lopez grinned up at the huge first sergeant, whose pug nose and cauliflower ear showed that his life had not been spent in prayer meetings.

"No, Fritzie, no tequila for me anymore, I can't handle it. But I do spend a little time thinking about Maria." Maria had left him because of tequila; he'd left tequila because of Maria. He was thirty-four before he found out he was in love with the woman he'd been married to for fifteen years.

Lopez frowned. "Listen, I just saw the new duty sheet and Fulton has Catlin with. . . ."

"Yeah, with Keene, I know."

"You know? Why didn't you do something about it? Will you change it?"

Harter shrugged. "Nope. I gave the lieutenant a new roster and a little talk. He listened, and then in polite lieutenantese told me to go fuck myself. He actually tore up my new roster and dropped it in the waste basket in front of me. He informed me he was running the squadron, and that when he wanted my advice, he'd ask for it."

"So?"

"So I said what I always say when some young asshole officer gives me a hard time."

"What's that?"

" 'Yes sir.' " He paused and grinned. "Works every time. They start to get worried right away, sure they've made a mistake if you agree with them. Thing is, with Fulton, it's hard to tell; he's so fucking arrogant. Anyway, I'm afraid you are going to have to handle it, lad."

Lopez moved the toe of his glistening shoes in the white chat. "Looks like. Not much choice, huh? Thanks anyway, Harter." Leo took a breath and squared his shoulders. "Well, I survived

454

El Paso, and I survived Nam, and I'm surviving you here. So I guess I can handle a damn redneck and a crazy nigger."

Harter slipped his arm around his shoulder, suddenly dead serious. "Leo, we've both got to do better than survive. We've got to break this crap up. I know what's going down at the barracks; the white guys are running a gauntlet just to get up to bed, the black guys are afraid to be caught with less than three or four of their buddies around. It's a minefield there, and out on the line. There's too many ways to hurt people out there, from running over them with a fuel truck to freezing them with liquid oxygen. The goddamn hippies and yippies and commies have scared the piss out of everybody, so that the brass won't do anything, afraid they'll miss out on a promotion. We can't let these punks fuck over the whole goddamn Air Force! You let Keene kick the shit out of Catlin, or let Catlin cut Keene, and we'll have a riot that'll make Travis look like a piece of cake. You hear me?"

Lopez was shaken. It was the longest speech Harter had ever made. "Jesus, Fritz, they didn't cover this at the NCO Academy."

"No, not at West Point either, but they fucking well better get started, or we'll all be out here with small arms and dogs, trying to keep the fighting down."

They stopped talking as a pair of camouflaged F-4s lit off their burners on the east-west runway and drowned their conversation with the crackling roar of jet fuel exploding into thrust.

"Looks like a tough ten nights ahead, Fritz."

"Yeah, good luck, call on me if you need me."

It was after midnight when Billy Keene eased his way into the walled-off section of the POL shack optimistically called "Recreation Lounge." Jesse Catlin sat sprawled in a beat-up plastic chair, drinking the hot battery acid that passed for coffee. He was flipping through the pages of a tattered *Rolling Stone*, oblivious to the noise competing from five portable radios spewing at least four different kinds of rock. There were a dozen men, all clad like him in oil-blackened olive drab fatigues and scuffed brogans. Some still wore the yellow baseball caps that were intended to instill esprit. A huge Grundig combination radio and cassette player sat next to Catlin's ear, a giant woofer rocking the room with Jimi Hendrix riffs. Catlin undulated, head to toe, to the beat.

Suddenly a huge fist smashed the Grundig, knocking it to the

455

floor. Billy Keene grimaced—the metal knobs of the radio had hurt his hand, made him angry.

He'd just come off the flight line where a turn in the foul British weather had left them all in freezing rain. He still wore his cold-weather parka, whose ruffed collar made him seem even bigger than his six-foot-four-inch, 220-pound frame.

Catlin looked up; he knew it had to be Keene, knew that this was probably it, that Keene was going to break him in half, as he'd threatened to do a dozen times in the past.

The pain in his hand caused Keene to wince, twisting his face from a sneer to a grimace. Above his chunky cheekbones, small, very bright, and very blue eyes glinted down at Catlin.

"Hey, homme, you knocked my radio down; looks like you broke it. You'll have to pay to get me another one."

"Like shit I will. You've been playing that fucking thing just to annoy me, and I won't buy you fucking anything but a bust in the mouth. Stand up, you little nigger bastard."

"Well, sheet, oh dear, I am sorry, Mistuh Keene, suh. Forgive this old black ass for living." Catlin's hand moved down outside the arm of the chair.

The edge in Catlin's Uncle Tom impersonation brought the room to silence. The other men edged away toward the walls, eager to watch but not wanting to be involved.

The senior man in the room, Staff Sgt. Bill Thornton, knew he had to do something. He was deputy NCOIC.

"Here, men; let's knock this off. I want you to both cool off." His voice was weak.

Keene turned to him, sneering. "Fuck off, Sarge, or it's you next." He snapped his attention back to Catlin.

Thornton blushed, watched the room begin to shift into two groups, black and white. There were eight people left, five black, three white.

Thornton spoke again, tried to put some authority in his voice. "Knock it off, Keene, or I'll put you on report." His voice had quavered; he felt sick.

" 'Knock it off Keene,' " Keene mimicked Thornton's high-pitched voice.

Thornton tried again. "Keene, this is an order. You—"

Keene shoved him into the wall. "Get out of here, fucker, or I'll break your fucking face."

Thornton fled.

Keene turned back to Catlin. "Now, shit-for-brains, stand up or I'll pull you out of the fucking chair."

456

Catlin rose; in his right hand was a Louisville Slugger, taped handle, thirty-six-inch length, twenty-two ounces.

"Come ahead, Keene. Come ahead. Try it, my man, and I'll break your fucking face and legs with this, you stupid Arkansas cocksucker."

Keene stopped. Catlin picked an easy stance, open, about the way a slugger would crowd the plate.

"Come ahead, white boy, and let me stuff this up your white ass."

Keene looked behind him. The five blacks had moved to his rear; the three whites had edged toward the door.

"Put that down, Catlin, or you are in real trouble." Keene's voice lost some of its power.

Jesse swung the club in a flashing arc, demolished the table in front of him, stepped back into his batter's stance.

"This feels pretty good, motherfucker; you get your ass out of here, now, or I'm going to lay the next one upside your head."

The white airmen bolted from the room. Keene looked behind him, ran for the door. Jesse picked up the radio, hurled it after him.

The five blacks crowded around Jesse, excited, cheering, dapping. He felt good. And troubled; playing roles was one thing, starting wars was another.

Staff Sergeant Thornton stood uncomfortably in front of Lopez in his office.

"Well?"

"Hey, Leo, it wasn't my fault. Those guys were out to kill each other. That Keene is nuts."

Lopez looked expressionlessly at the younger man. More than one stripe and five years separated the two. Thornton was a product of the "new Air Force," the sensitive Air Force. He hadn't been to Nam yet. He hadn't been anywhere, and yet they gave him those four stripes, those same stripes Leo had had to sweat years for, those stripes that supposedly meant you were a leader of men, more than a technical specialist. A noncommissioned officer, maybe, but an officer.

"I want a written report, in a half an hour, Thornton. I want names, and I want to press charges. These guys were fighting on duty, using deadly weapons. We can't let this pass."

"Come on, Leo, nothing happened; you can't press charges on this."

"Nothing happened this time; next time we can have a head split open or a throat cut. Keene is a brute; Catlin is dangerous. You should have controlled them."

"What was I going to do? That fucker is ten feet tall, and the nigger had a baseball bat. Do you think I'm Superman?"

"No, but I think you failed, and I'm preferring charges against you too, for dereliction of duty. You abandoned your post."

Thornton went white, half from rage, half from fear. "You can't do that! You're just a fucking E-6!"

"You just watch me. And I want that report in thirty minutes. Now get out of here."

Lopez kept his hands below the desktop, clutched in anger. He had the option of letting it all drop, but it bothered him. You led by leading, not by following, and the tension on the base resulted as much from a failure of leadership as from racial conflict.

His thoughts went back to El Paso, where he had mixed it up with the gringos in high school, hung out with the baddest cats he could find, driving a chopped and channeled Mercury with a chain and a knife tucked underneath the seat. He thought he understood something of the young blacks out there, because he had once felt the same sense of impotence and rage. The only time he felt good was when he was beating the shit out of some redneck Texan in a dusty parking lot.

One day his mother had caught his attention; he didn't do all the work in the parking lot, and he was nursing three broken ribs and a badly mashed nose. She started as she always had, with the suffering she and his father, Manuel, had endured to get across the border to the promised land. She recalled the jobs she had done, the hours she had worked, the fact that Manuel was in his grave from overwork. And now Leo was a street hood, and not a very good one at that.

The shattered ribs tooks three weeks to heal to the point that he could walk. He spent them thinking about what his mother had said. When he could move about a bit, he got a haircut, put on his best sport shirt, and went down and enlisted in the Air Force.

The kids in the POL dump weren't there because of their mothers; they were there because they didn't want to be wasted in Vietnam, drafted fodder for claymore mines or punji sticks. The word on the street was the Air Force for four was better than Nam for one, because in Nam you had VC to worry about. In the Air Force you had guys like Thornton. The difference was large.

＊　＊　＊

Catlin sat exhausted on his bunk, arms dangling at his side, the bat underneath the folded blanket. He'd really boxed himself into a corner.

Down at the end of the open bay, sixty feet away, the communal stereo rasped out one of an endless inventory of James Brown songs. It was pride, Black Pride, to keep the music going continually, day or night, as long as someone was in the room.

He was exhausted, physically and emotionally. He'd spent the night dragging the massive fuel lines around, handling the immense fixtures, getting soaked in the sickening JP-4. He slumped back against the bed, closed his eyes.

He felt a tug at his sleeve. Keene! He leaped forward, looked into the face of Marcus Freeman. Freeman skirted the edge of regulations with his afro, his manner; he was a mean dude, for sure.

Freeman was wearing nothing but O.D. skivies and a gold chain from which dangled his dogtag. He was almost albino in color; his hair ran from reddish to reddish black. Jesse figured he dyed it. Freeman grinned wolfishly at him and sat down on his bunk.

"Shit, blood, you look booked."

"Say that again, Marcus. How 'bout you?"

"Shit, man, I'm tired of this fucking place and the fucking Air Force. Tell you what, though. I hear you nearly coldcocked Keene with a baseball bat tonight. That right?"

"Got that right. He was leaning on me, so I scared him off. This time. That's one honky big as a house."

"Shoulda nailed the motherfucker. He be leaning on everybody. I say, Hey, don't care what he does to the white mothers, but I'm tired of him facing up on the brothers."

Freeman looked around, went on. "But tell you what, blood. We be glad you didn't. We got something hot coming, something we all got to do together, and if you'd put it on him, might be trouble."

"What you mean, 'hot'?"

"I mean big shit, man, big shit." Freeman rocked back and forth to an inner beat, eyes constantly moving.

" 'Big shit,' huh? What's that mean, man? You talkin' garbage."

"No garbage. We all tired of being fucked over. We get the worst jobs, the worst barracks, the worst everything. You know that. You a smart dude, talk good, everything; so what are you

459

doing? Shit. You pushing JP-4. Well, me and some people gonna start pushing back, homme."

Catlin began at last to realize that Freeman was serious. Something was going on; something bigger than a bunch of bloods getting stoned and throwing a ruckus.

"So you gonna push back. How?"

"Man, they call it 'get whitey'; I call it a motherfucking revolution. We take over the barracks, hold the white guys hostage. Way I see it, we bring everybody over here, our guys, the white boys, then set fire to the other barracks. Then we demand amnesty, and honorable discharges for everybody. That's the way we see it. Me and my people."

"You nuts? Ain't no *way* they give in for that. And if they did, they'd get revenge as soon as they got the people back."

Marcus looked at him coldly. He stopped swaying. "Look here, little brother. You better hold on to that baseball bat; you don't help us when the time comes, you need it worse than you do now. We got outside connections, the same thing going down at bases all over Europe. We got to make a statement, man, and this is it. As the main man say, if you ain't part of the solution, you part of the problem. Dig?"

He stuck out his right fist to Catlin, who automatically dapped it.

"Remember, Keene bothers you, let me know, but we ain't doing nothing until we be ready."

He got up, went back over to his bunk.

Jesse lay back on his bunk. He felt for his bat handle.

Big shit, he'd said. Big shit.

As he had done every evening for the past three weeks, Kisling came in to talk things over with Kelly.

"Jesus, Homer, I used to think the Air Force was for airplanes; it's just a goddamn paper factory in the field."

"It is here, Mike. Lowey is a micromanager, running everything and running nothing. But here's a little billet doux for you. I got it this morning, ran a check on it." "

The envelope was marked "For Colonel Kelly. Strictly Personal."

"Another mystery admirer, I guess."

He opened the envelope. On a battered sheet of paper, torn from a spiral-bound typing tablet, was a single sentence. "We need to talk, in private. Jesse Catlin, A2C."

"Do you know this guy?"

"No, but I ran a book on him. Smart guy, basically pleasant, but a troublemaker. He's had a run-in with a big white guy, almost got killed if he hadn't had a baseball bat with him."

"So this is racial."

"Yeah, sure. More than that, though; he wouldn't write you unless it was very serious. Matter of pride—he'd handle an ordinary racial beef himself."

"Should I see this guy?"

"I think you should; it's like chicken soup, it can't hurt."

"What will we get out of it? Am I supposed to hold his hand, tell him I'm sorry?"

"No sir, we think he may have a lead for us on bigger things. There've been rumors of a blow up, a riot, for weeks. All the signs are there—it's just a question of when. He might know when."

"Okay. I'm sure he won't want to come here. Find out where he wants to meet, and I'll be there."

"Roger sir, and out."

Kelly watched Kisling depart. Groundpounders always said "roger" and "out," flyers never, except on the radio, when it was appropriate. It was part of the curse of being a nonflyer in a flying world: trying harder.

The next morning, Kisling said, "He says he'll come here, sir. He figures he's run out of time and luck, anyway, and he might be better off being open about it."

Three hours later, Catlin reported in military fashion. Kelly got out of his chair, came around, shook his hand. He walked him over to the couch; there was coffee and the leaden round things the British bravely called doughnuts.

Catlin took a cup of coffee, declined the doughnut.

"Can I call you Jesse?"

"Yes sir." Catlin seemed highly strung, tense. Mike leaned back and tried to be cool. "Jesse, you said you needed to talk to me. I want to help if I can. Why don't you start?"

Catlin sipped his coffee, slurped, apologized. He put it down, making sure not to spill it, angry that he cared. He tried to be tough, but he couldn't. Too much was going on, too fast. "Colonel, I got to get out of here, because just coming here has put my life in danger. I'm not kidding. I hope you believe me."

"Well, tell me more, Jesse. I want to hear the whole story."

"Okay, Colonel. You know there's lots of racial problems on base. Lot of it comes from brothers going down to the Smoke—to London. See, these English girls go crazy for black dudes.

461

Dunno why. But no blood's gonna turn 'em off, right? So the white dudes get mad when they see us steppin' out with some dolly birds. What you got then is this pot boiling already, and then these other dudes come in and stir it all up. They're talking riots, man, not just here, but on every base. And a lot of the bloods is listening."

"Go on, Jesse."

"Well, shit, Colonel, we got problems all right, but I can tell you, they ain't nothing like the problems I had back in D.C., so it don't seem right. These dudes are callin' for race riots. Shit. I seen race riots. I seen 'em burnin' houses and cars, and there ain't no percentage in that. Ain't nobody wins that one."

"Yeah. Nobody."

"So I come to you, Colonel. I feel like a fuckin' pimp comin' here, but I can't just let 'em bring this shit down on us all. See, I know that they're lyin'; they say the blacks will win, but I know better. I seen 'em burning my own Mama's house down. Don't nobody win when blacks burn their own houses."

He looked at the floor, looked defiantly at Kelly. "Man, if I want to burn homes down, it should be white homes, not black."

"Well, Jesse, it doesn't seem to me that burning anybody's homes down is a solution."

"No, but burning your own sure as hell isn't. And that's what's going to be happening here, we're going to burn our own goddamn homes down, and I'm not sure for what."

He poured out the whole story, starting with Keene and ending with the latest word from Freeman. The riots were scheduled for July 14; they planned to take hostages and set the barracks on fire. There was talk of setting a fire in the fuel dump.

Kelly took no notes, kept grunting sympathetically to keep Jesse talking.

"That's it; I told you all I know. I hope to hell you can do something, and I hope I don't get killed." Catlin looked miserable.

Kelly felt a wave of compassion sweep over him. This kid came from a place he understood all too well. It could almost be him sitting there, taking his life in his hands to defy the gangsters who wanted to run his life. He had to do something for a kid like this, something more than P.R. bullshit. No, he corrected himself as he saw Catlin straighten up under his gaze: this was a man. A kid would never have come here.

"Tell you what, Jesse, what kind of a job would you like if you had a choice?"

Catlin darted a suspicious look at him. Kelly sympathized; he could imagine the young man thinking, What kind of shit are they pulling on me now?

"Well, Colonel, you ask, I tell. I'd like to be an announcer on Armed Forces Radio; I've always wanted to get into announcing." He looked almost defiantly at Mike, as though he'd confessed some secret sin.

Mike smiled. "Look, Jesse, I'm just a colonel, and I don't run things. But if what you tell me proves out, I'll see to it that you get to school, and that you wind up with Armed Forces Radio, somewhere, somehow."

The interview ended awkwardly, and then Jesse walked out, feeling miserable. He wasn't halfway down the walk from the headquarters building when Marcus Freeman swung into step beside him. They walked along together for awhile, headed for the east gate and Mickey's Tea Bar just outside the fence, where all the young guys hung out. Outside the fence, Freeman swung Catlin to a halt. "What you doing at Headquarters?" There was a clean steel menace in his voice.

Catlin spit at the ground. "Shit. Tell you what, my man. Look like the Man gonna court-martial me for threatening Keene with a baseball bat. 'Assault with a deadly weapon' or something they called it."

Freeman gripped his arm, tight.

"Bad news, homme, bad news. But now I tell you what: I hope that's right, little brother. Cause if me and my people find out otherwise—just remember. Big shit. You dig?"

Catlin wrenched free and pulled his jacket straight.

"Yeah, I dig, all right. I dig."

The next morning, A3C Marcus Freeman found himself bundled on a C-141, bound for the States, with orders cut reassigning him to K. I. Sawyer Air Force Base, Michigan. As he was boarding the airplane the Security Police K-9 dog that was designated a "sniffer" singled him out of the line of troops. He was taken to a room in the Mildenhall main terminal building, searched, and found to be carrying a kilo of marijuana. His orders were amended. When he next got on a C-141, he was headed for Fort Leavenworth.

On the fourteenth of July, a base alert was called, and the troops were kept busy for almost twenty-four hours. And on the fifteenth, Jesse Catlin got orders to go to a communications course.

42

U-Tapao was a jungle-locked island, a miasmic marsh reclaimed by the simple expedient of cutting off the top of a mountain, piling it on the swamp, then bulldozing it flat. The surging jungle had at first recoiled, even the insouciant banana trees dying in the harsh crushed lava the mountain had provided; then it had rebounded and was now crowding in on all sides, springing up in the middle, ready to reclaim the area once the endless flights of B-52s had stopped.

From the air it was beautiful; the Gulf of Siam was varicolored and lovely. Postcard fishing villages dotted the coastlines, boats drawn up on the beach, the houses a variegated patch of corrugated tin roofs and palm thatch. Farther out in the shallow sea were long V-shaped fences through which fish were driven to box traps. The omnivorous jungle was blue-green, slashed at intervals by fire for village gardens, punctuated by gold-and-red eruptions of Buddhist temple roofs.

The base was a model of transplanted efficiency; laid out in great concrete swatches, the runway itself almost eight feet thick, designed to cycle bomb-laden B-52s with the regularity of beer bottles passing through a brewery. They entered at the end of one runway, taxied off to the refueling pits and then into wide revetments crowded with trucks, test vehicles, ground power units, oxygen carts. A stream of bomb trailers rolled under them, stuffing their Big Bellys with eighty-four bombs; while they sat, their wings drooped further as their armpit pylons were laden with another twenty-four. Maintenance was performed, crews were briefed, six bombers were launched smoking and straining down the runway every three hours, bombs were dropped, the cycle went on endlessly.

Behind this primary parade of loading, dumping, and loading, was an enormous network reaching to Japan, Okinawa, Hawaii, San Francisco, everywhere in the United States, as bombs, fuel, all the magnificent, numbingly stupid machinery of war fed through a pipeline that never stopped disgorging. Yet the relationship between the effort and the capacity was so close that not only were individual shipments of bombs monitored, to make sure there was always a supply to stuff into the bombers, but even crates of dog food for the K-9 corps were plotted as they crossed the ocean from the Purina mills to the U-Tapao kennels. Nothing could interfere with the *Modern Times* efficiency of dropping bombs.

Each means bred demands. The truck fleet that brought the bombs from the Thai ports to depots needed spare parts; the spare parts required catalogues, the catalogues required printing, distribution. The fuel pipelines, tank farms, tank trucks, all needed men and maintenance. The airfields, highways, railways, ports, all had to be built by engineer teams, who had to build houses, garages, maintenance facilities, recreation facilities for themselves. It was an endless, costly chicken-and-egging.

The one great facilitator was the dollar, and the dollar gushed in lavish streams that transformed Thailand. Just the spin-offs, the laundries, the furniture, the restaurants, even the massage parlors, created an invasion of cash the country had never experienced. Millionaires were created by the hundreds, hard-dollar millionaires, Swiss bank millionaires, and skyscrapers sprang up in the spongy soil of Bangkok at the rate of one per month. More was probably stolen than had been spent legally in any previous year, for there was an unseen tariff at every point. Grease was a way of life, salaries being too small to support a family.

Duke had experienced the grease on the base. He had swung his jeep in to be refueled in the motor pool garage; he handed over his credit card, signed the receipt, noting that it was blank.

He waited a few seconds, started forward, and then backed into the fuel lane. He got out and asked to see his receipt.

The Thai worker pretended not to understand. Duke walked over to the pad of receipts, found his on top, signed, with one hundred gallons penciled in. The Thai was furious, and he called in a shrill voice to the Thai supervisor. Duke palmed the receipt, got in the jeep, and drove off. He turned it in to Base Security—nothing was ever done about it. A ninety-gallon gain on a ten-gallon transaction—it was easy to make money in Thailand.

So there was a skim at every level, from the gasoline in the Thai Mercedes to the steaks marked U.S. GOVERNMENT served in the resort hotels. And for the Thais, the best of all was that everything eventually was to come back to them; every runway, fuel dump, barracks, store, radar shack, everything.

Duke was aware of the planning and work that resulted in the efficiency of the bombing process; he was appalled that it was almost all wasted on the only end that counted, the point of impact. The B-52s had been relegated to flying heavy artillery, supplementing the work of ground troops, pounding hundreds of shrapnel-riddled swimming pools across South Vietnam. The process might never end; the Vietcong could breed faster than they were killed by the bombs, the forest could reclaim the land. It could become a permanent nightmare.

He'd come to U-Tapao as a brand-new brigadier general, his Pentagon maneuvering in the Office of Congressional Liaison having paid off with new rank—flag rank, at last, even if only the bottom rung—and he thought that here, he might make a difference. He had found his ideas slowly percolating through the command and staff people at the Pentagon, but there still was not enough force to make the change from sending bombs into the jungle to sending them in waves into Haiphong and Hanoi in preannounced strikes. As U-Tapao's Deputy Commander for Operations, there was a possibility he would be able to put the final push into the scheme.

He made his first mistake within the first hour of his arrival, within the first ten minutes of meeting his new boss. He was hustled straight from the C-130 that had brought him down from Don Muang into Maj. Gen. Dave Hobart's office. Brown knew Hobart's file well; he had opposed the TMTS from the beginning, and was known to believe in the current bombing theory. He was also short, wiry, impatient, unfriendly. He barely looked up from his desk when Duke went into his spartan office. Duke greeted him warmly. Hobart glared at him. "Well, you're my hotshot new deputy, they tell me, fresh from the Pentagon. How are you going to win the war?"

Brown waited. So. It was going to be like this. "Well, General, I just got here, so like General Eaker told the British, maybe I'd better do some fighting before I do any talking."

"No no, be my guest, I'm eager to hear your views." He obviously was not anxious to hear Brown's views. But they had to play it out.

"All right, I'll tell you." Duke sketched out in about two minutes the complete change in the style of the war.

"Well, thank you for your views, General. You happen to be full of shit, but that's all right, I need a man like that. As of now, you're off the DCO job, and are my special assistant for Thai relations. I'll call on you when I need you. You were great at slinging B.S. back at the Pentagon, and experts are in short supply here. Mostly we have bomber crews, guys working hard for the Air Force; we need somebody to handle our local friends. Just check in every morning and find out what I've got for you."

Brown opened his mouth, but nothing came out. He closed it.

Hobart smiled wickedly. "You'll get to fly; I'll get you on one milk run a month, just enough to cover your flight pay. And let me tell you, if I hear you make one protest about this, if you go over my head one time, like you've done to a dozen guys in the past, I'll have your ass, I promise you, I'll have your ass." Hobart picked up another file folder and looked down. Then he looked up again. "That's all, General. Thanks for your time. Oh— welcome to Thailand."

Brown was stunned. He knew Hobart didn't like him, but he didn't expect not to be used in an operational capacity. He left Hobart's office seething and buzzing with angles to change the situation. But the irony was that Hobart's flanks were too well protected; he was the darling of SAC, another West Point man, and would be more than a formidable adversary if Duke got into a pissing contest with him. For the first time in his career, Duke knew that he had a problem that could not simply be turned around into an advantage. He had to take his lumps.

By the end of the first week, things had relaxed a little; Hobart was shorthanded, couldn't avoid using him, but it was with obvious distaste. The only bright spot, the eternal salvation of the service, was that Hobart would be rotating in a few months. Brown determined to outwait him, do his jobs, whatever they were.

But it was deadly boring; the days dragged by. It was the first time in his life that he had time to think, to feel, about anything but the immediate operational problems and their effects upon his career. He drank a little more than ever before—it was hard not to with booze this cheap—and he went to church more. The worst thing, the crushing thing, was that he was not needed; he had always been a mover and a shaker, and Hobart had relegated him to an observer's role. And he was older, too; things he might have done in the past were no longer feasible. He'd intended to pick up the language, but the Thais were so determined to learn English, and did so well at it, that he soon gave up. It was a twelve-hour day, six-day work week for everybody, and he had to go through the motions. It was humiliating for a general officer to be seen spending so much time at the library, but at least he stayed away from the club and the pool.

And Hobart did use him effectively for the Thai relations. The Royal Thai Navy Air Force owned the base, and there were endless bits of protocol to handle. It was customary for the poorly paid Thai officers to operate businesses on the side to supplement their income, and much of Brown's time was spent sorting out who should have the taxi concession, who the bar girls, who would control the soft-drink vendors. It took time, for the matter of business could not be discussed directly with the officers involved because of the loss of face. Instead he spent hours in long, elliptical discussions with their aides, trying to sort out their own fierce internal competition for the dollar.

The soft, warm tropic nights affected him; he found himself eyeing the waitresses in the club, spending more time joshing with his hooch girl who cleaned the rooms in his BOQ. It was the first time since leaving the Point that he wasn't overstressed in his work; he felt sexual stirrings, a sense of deprivation that had never bothered him before. At home Joan began to be surprised at his letters; she was surprised that he wrote about his sexual hunger for her.

Thais loved to string lights in trees for their garden parties. They had converted the grounds of the Royal Thai Navy officers' club at Sattahip into a glowing forest of tiny white and blue dots, swaying with the lush breezes from the Gulf of Thailand. Brown glanced around him at the mixture of types; he hadn't expected the Thais to be so egalitarian. A full admiral in the Royal Thai Navy had just introduced him to a giant in a perfectly tailored Savile Row suit, his huge tanned head crowned with a white tonsure, broad spatulate fingers—eight of them, both thumbs seemed to be missing—lustrously manicured. His name was Damrong, and he was a pirate. The Thai admiral had laughed, and so had the pirate, who noted politely that he was now "a retired pirate."

The crowd was nervous; the queen mother was going to make an appearance soon, and Brown was amazed at the devotion shown to her and to the whole royal family. Pictures of the king and queen were everywhere, always bedecked with sweet-smelling ropes of flowers. They had the English love of royalty, proud, possessive, protective, and always filled with a fierce enjoyment of belonging. And yet in her presence there was stress, as if a royal gesture could sweep off a head. The Thais, normally so relaxed and smiling, watched her with icy vigilance.

Brown had been presented to her that morning. She was a charming grandmother, simply dressed, as familiar and as enduring as her English counterpart. She had come to open the new base exchange at U-Tapao, had received the lovely offering of knotted strands of flowers, dutifully toured the aisles, even picked up items from the shelves—cologne, aftershave, Q-tips—to hand to her horde of men- and women-in-waiting.

The close-cropped grounds were lovely, studded with topiary elephants and pheasants, bordered by long tables of food and drink arranged as carefully as the flower garlands. White-coated waiters passed with drinks; Brown stuck to the wonderful Singha beer, icy cold, formaldehyde-laced (according to the flight surgeons), but delicious.

There was a commotion across the lawn; he thought the queen mother might be coming. Instead it was a beautiful young Thai girl, the same who had presented the flowers in the BX. She was taller than most Thai women, slender, and with a more pronounced bustline. Her hair was short and curled, probably at the beauty shop, and her eyes were lustrous almond jewels. She was with a Royal Thai Navy captain, a flyer. He brought her over. "General Brown, may I present Boon Mai? She manages the base exchange."

Boon Mai put out her hand; it was incredibly fine, with long tapering fingers, but surprisingly firm and strong. "Ah, I saw the young general this morning, I think." She smiled.

Brown was smitten. "Yes, you presented the flowers; they were lovely."

The Thai captain was gone.

"Do you like Thailand?"

It was always their first question; they loved it, expected you to love it too.

"Yes, it is very beautiful. And you are very beautiful."

It had just come out; it might be a mistake, she might be angry.

She laughed, her hand covering her mouth. "Young general is very kind."

A colonel from the base came up, excused himself, and dragged Brown away to meet a visiting Thai air marshal. Brown hated him.

As they talked the crowd grew restless; it was past the usual dinnertime, and the Thais were as serious about their eating and drinking as they appeared carefree about everything else.

A small dog wandered onto the lawn. Brown saw it out of the corner of his eye. A Thai officer stepped up, kicked the dog screaming in an arc toward the sideline. A waiter moved with soccer-playing timing, kicked it again over a small wall bordering the lawn.

It was an incredible split tableau; every American was horrified, staring toward the shrieking barks still coming from behind the wall; the Thais had not noticed. To them the whole incident had been like brushing away a fly from your face. Human life was cheap in Thailand; there was no concern for animals.

The noise picked up again, then quieted, as the queen mother made her entrance. There was no receiving line; the Thais surged around her in a crowd, then separated to let the American guests be steered toward her. She acknowledged meeting Duke, and went on, indefatigable, reserved, regal. She sipped a glass of what looked like lemonade, then swept out. The crowd broke for the tables.

Brown had learned to love the Thai food. Even at buffets like this most things were served cold in temperature, fiery in spice. He washed the food down with more beer, and saw Boon Mai talking to a small group of Thai and American pilots across the lawn. He wanted to go to her, decided against it.

He'd have to see her soon, anyway. Hobart had given him a tough assignment and indicated he was going to determine his efficiency report on how well he did with it. It was impossible. The base exchange, even in the old building, was losing something like nine hundred dollars a day in stolen merchandise, and no one could figure where it was going. They had the FBI, the Thai police, the Air Police in the store, checking packages, but they never caught anyone. How Brown was supposed to figure out what was wrong was ridiculous, but it put Hobart in a powerful position.

Boon Mai was the first Thai store manager; the last two were Americans, and neither had lasted long. The first had had a contract placed on him; he was executed in his Pattya Beach house bedroom. Rumor had it that the Americans had brought inflation; in 1969 a hit man wanted only twenty-five dollars; and now it was one hundred fifty. The second BX manager had received a note, advising him to leave, or else. He left the same day.

And Brown was supposed to solve the problem.

He called at the base exchange the next day. Boon Mai was in her office, supervising the bright young Thai clerks. She shattered him with a smile. "Oh, yes, I know why the general is here. We have a big problem. I don't know how to solve, but maybe you can. We have bad problem with thieves."

470

She briefed him on their procedures; he was amazed at the clarity of the bookkeeping; the pages of the account books looked like they had been illuminated by Benedictine monks. She went on and on with information. Brown felt tired.

"The general should also go to Bangkok, to our main BX office; that's where our paperwork comes from. We have very good people there, American and Thai. I go with you, introduce you to everyone."

To this idea, Hobart played the classic horse's ass; he accused Brown of wanting to boondoggle to Bangkok while a war was going on. Brown asked for orders, Hobart insisted that he take leave. A staff car was out of the question, and when Brown went to Base Operations to get a ride on a base C-47, he was told there were none scheduled. It really pissed him off; Hobart gave him a job, and wouldn't let him do it.

He dropped by the BX and asked Boon Mai the best way for him to get to Bangkok.

"No sweat, young general, I pick you up tomorrow morning at the BOQ, eight o'clock sharp."

Next morning he stood on the balcony of the two-story concrete-block BOQ; and a bilious-green Toyota pulled up in front. Boon Mai stepped out and waved.

A squat Thai was driving the car.

"This is Lek; he's a berry good driver." Sometimes Boon Mai would lose her v's.

Lek grinned, gunned the engine. Brown got in back, separated from Boon Mai by a huge cooler and a number of the multistory tin lunch pails that carried the Thais' enormous lunches.

The ride to Bangkok was an education. The Toyota had one speed, flat-out, and how fast it went depended upon the surface of the road. On the old country lanes, pitted, filled with ruts and rocks, Brown watched the speedometer peg at 120 kilometers. In the first village they whirled through, Lek ran over a chicken, drove an old man on a bicycle into the wall of a hut, and damn near ran under a huge two-and-one-half-ton truck that loomed out of nowhere.

Brown was gasping with fear; Boon Mai didn't seem to notice. "You want soda?"

Brown shook his head. She opened one of each, handed the soda to Lek. He ordinarily drove with one hand; when he drank the soda, he steadied the steering wheel with his knee.

At the coastal road, they had to slow down; a massive road builder was moving along, straddling the entire road, laying down streams of asphalt and smoothing it out. Ahead of it moved almost fifty Thai women, wrapped from head to toe in robes, carefully hand placing rocks to build the road bed, the speed of the modern machines tied to the antiquity of the handwork. Lek passed the entire group on the outside, picking his speed up to 140 kilometers.

The countryside was gorgeous once Brown could tear himself away from watching the on-coming traffic which was equally fast, equally daring. On the many waterways, small farms, no more than an acre in size, were intensely cultivated. The bamboo and palm houses, teetering on stilts, looked like random cones of pick-up-sticks. In front of each house were two or three dip nets; the fishermen moved leisurely among them, raising them dripping from the water, occasionally with a flashing silver fish in the bottom.

After a while they tired of their stilted English conversation; you can only indicate your happiness and pleasure so many times. They would look out the window, and Boon Mai would reach over and touch his arm to point out a pretty view, or a typical Thai scene. It seemed to him too that she always managed to touch his fingers when she handed him a drink or some food. All of his stored-up longings began to unfold. He realized he was idealizing this young Thai girl, giving her qualities that didn't exist, imputing to her virtue, charm, and appeal that no one could ever have, but after an hour in the car he was hopelessly lovesick, as beguiled with her as a high-school quarterback with a cheerleader.

Lek stopped in a little village; Boon Mai haggled with a fruit vendor, bought some small things that looked like hairy grapes, a huge yellow melon or squashlike fruit, and some pomelos, the native grapefruit. The hairy grapes had a delicious woody sweet flavor; Brown realized the melon must be a durian, or jackfruit. It smelled terrible, yet Boon Mai obviously thought she had a rare treat for him. She took a knife from her handbag and plunged it into the fruit; a dense sewer odor rushed out. She sliced off a piece and handed it to him. It was delicious. Boon Mai was fair; she divvied the durian evenly, slicing off a piece for Lek, one for her, and another for Brown.

She and Lek never stopped eating; she passed out tray after tray of food, bits of fish, spices. Lek would balance the dish on his lap, eating with the big spoon the Thais favored, occasionally spilling it as he rounded a blind corner on two wheels. Brown sampled everything; most was good, some a little too exotic for him.

They dropped him off in front of the Chao Phya hotel, the standard military hotel in Bangkok; Boon Mai promised to pick him up in the morning at eight. He felt lonely; he had expected to spend the evening with her. Maybe the night.

He ate in the spotless, air-conditioned restaurant dining room; after the spartan club at U-Tapao, it seemed elegant. That night he lost ten dollars in the quarter slot machine, never hitting even two cherries, wandered around the lobby for a while, looking for a familiar face, found none, and went to bed.

She was there at eight o'clock the next morning, framed by the two giant elephant tusks that guarded the entrance. They elbowed their way past the white-shirted, blue-shorted Thai kids standing outside as guides, procurers, whatever, and she led him through the most boring morning he had spent in twenty years.

The base exchange office was a monument to twin bureaucracies; it combined all the American red-tape efficiency with the carefree approach of the Thais. Boon Mai introduced him to everyone, dragged him through every step of the process of getting a can of hair spray from the warehouse to the BX. She seemed absolutely exhilarated by it; Brown had difficulty keeping his eyes focused.

By eleven o'clock, he signaled he'd had enough; they drove back to the hotel and he was surprised to see his B-4 bag sitting on the sidewalk, guarded by a young Thai.

"Ah, young general, we go back now, have lunch in Pattya Beach."

Lek drove even faster going back, down the crowded streets, along the klongs, past the endless shops selling gold chain, Thai silk, carved elephants, and garnets touted for rubies. The city teemed with life yet was totally dedicated to the internal combustion engine. The acrid fumes blanched the leaves of the palm trees, caused the old men pedaling the battered cycle cabs to gasp; yet nothing was more wanted, nothing was more honored, than a car.

Duke decided he had been missing too much, trying too hard; he would have to find a way to spend some time in Bangkok, exploring it from one end to the other.

The plunge down to Pattya took two hours; he was starving by the time they pulled up at the beautiful golden beach. Thailand had long strips of the world's most beautiful beaches, usually bordered with a combination of palm and pine trees, with an incredibly soft pillow of pine needles to rest in. And almost no one used them. The Thais hated suntans, and only foreigners

473

could be found on the beach, eating the vendor's sun-dried squid arranged on long sticks like a peacock's feathers, and drinking the delicious, tooth-jarring cold Singha beer.

Boon Mai steered him to a long narrow boat; they cast off, and in twenty minutes were dropped on an off-shore island. There was a restaurant, a collection of palm leaves and bamboo sticks, loosely held together with vines. They sat down at a bare board table, and two ice-cold quarts of Singha appeared by magic, followed by a bowl of steaming hot rock lobsters, drenched in a buttery lemon sauce. There was rice, a noodle dish, some other things, but Duke concentrated on the juicy lobster tails.

The breeze was soft from the ocean, a sweet mixture of salt, seaweed, and earth.

"Do you like to swim, Boon Mai?" He wanted to see her in a bathing suit, see if the roundness of her chest was real, or padding.

"Yes, a little; I'm not too good."

"Do you sunbathe?"

"Sunbathe? Sunbathe? No, I take shower."

Brown explained what he meant.

"No, too much sun, get too dark, be like dum-dum there." She pointed to some laborers, as dark black as Melanesians.

He was reaching for his third rock lobster when she grabbed his arm. "No, young general, too much. Wait just a minute."

The waiter reappeared, with two more beers, and a huge clay pot, almost three feet long, and half again as wide and high. Brown could tell it was red hot by the way the waiter carried it. He handed Brown a wooden mallet, motioning him to strike the top of the pot. Brown hit the pot; it didn't even crack.

Boon Mai laughed, made a gesture like a judge swinging a gavel. "Hit hard, young general, hit hard."

He swung the mallet hard; the top of the clay pot cracked in two almost perfectly equal parts, and a cloud of spice-scented steam roared out. Underneath was the largest lobster Brown had ever seen, at least six or seven pounds.

"From Phu Ket, specially for you."

Phu Ket! Phu Ket was south, almost to Singapore. If she could arrange something like this, Boon Mai must have influence.

He expected the lobster to be tough; it melted in his mouth. The waiter and the cook came over and sat with them, enjoyed their share of the shellfish. There was enough for five more people.

It was almost five o'clock when they rolled back onto the

beach; Boon Mai smiled and said, "It's too late to go back now; too dangerous to drive in Thailand at night. We leave nice and early in the morning."

Duke agreed docilely, hopefully. In any other job he had ever had, he would have walked back to be there in the morning, damn the traffic. Tonight he felt the Air Force could wait.

The hotel was a series of little bungalows, each with a bedroom, bath, and kitchen, used first by the construction companies that had built all of the military installations, then by the military dependents. This one had apparently gone back to Thai ownership. His bags had been placed in his room, opened, toilet kit laid out. He showered, and used the bottled water to brush his teeth. He always suspected that the bottles were filled at the tap, but it wasn't worth risking. Then he lay down for a nap.

The dark room swayed with the gentle knocking. He glanced at his Seiko: it was nine o'clock. He had slept for three hours. Slipping on his trousers, he went to the door. Boon Mai was there dressed in a native costume, a sarong folded like trousers, with a towel-covered tray.

"Did the Singha and lobster make the young general sleepy?"

Embarrassed, Brown motioned her in, put on his shirt.

She had turned on the light; on the tray were small bottles of Scotch, a tub of ice, some sandwiches carefully cut in quarters.

"You hungry." It was a statement, not a question.

"Yes." He didn't say more because she came to him and kissed him on the lips. Brown jumped back, knocked over a table.

Boon Mai laughed, sat down on the bed. "Don't worry, young general; nobody saw me come here. We just have a little snack, then I go. Okay?"

Brown walked over and sat down on the bed beside her. He held her, kissed her on the cheek. He didn't know what the hell to do; for reasons he didn't understand he'd always been faithful. And Boon Mai was the most beautiful woman he had ever seen. It had been a long time since he'd been with Joan.

She began breathing hard. He watched her for a second. She was simulating passion, breathing as if she were violently excited. He kissed her on the lips, and her hands reached up to unbutton his shirt.

She left after midnight, moving quietly down the darkened stairway across to her own little hut. Brown was filled with contentment and doubt. She had excited him wildly, but he sensed that she was under iron control. Her orgasms were too

475

conveniently timed with his, her manner always searching, never surrendering. Still he was pleased. She was so beautiful.

They drove back in silence, surreptitiously holding hands away from Lek's baleful, watchful eye. Like Thailand, she was a confection of contrasts. Brown never failed to be amazed by the gorgeous blue bays, roiled brown with sewage outflow, or the beauty of the forest broken by the sulfurous smell of the tapioca factories. Boon Mai was an equally intoxicating combination of the beautiful and the earthy.

Remorse hit him the next morning; he went to the flight surgeon, asked for and got some "No Sweat" pills, guaranteed to be good for what ailed you, no matter what secret Asian problem that was. The flight surgeon was sympathetic, and asked no questions; he was living in a cardboard-and-plywood hooch in the village outside the gate with two bar girls. He told intimates it was the first time in his life he'd been happy, even when he woke up with a rat on his chest.

Hobart was vicious; he wanted a full report on everything Brown had done, hinted he might press AWOL charges. It was all talk, and the fact that Brown had to write a report turned out to be a good thing. As Brown dredged his memory of the days' events—he was going to pass over the stay at Pattya—it became apparent to him that Boon Mai wanted to use him and probably had some connection herself with the thefts.

Yet he couldn't stay away from her, couldn't keep her from coming to see him at night. She'd appear about eleven o'clock, always with some Thai delicacies; he'd have Singha and Scotch, and they would make love. He had champagne for her one night, Dom Perignon from the liquor store, terribly expensive at thirteen dollars a bottle, compared to Johnnie Walker Red or Courvoisier V.S.O.P. at two dollars per liter. She didn't like it, wouldn't drink it.

Brown loved her as he had never loved any woman—if he had ever loved any woman. She was always pristinely clean, as if she had just stepped from a shower, and her breasts were not only larger than other Thai girls', but different from those of any woman Duke had known. When he first saw her he stared; instead of nipples she had little crosses.

Boon Mai had laughed. "Don't be worried, you suck them, I have nipples inside."

And she had; he had kissed her breasts, sucked them hard, and from within them had emerged two lovely erect nipples. At rest they disappeared.

Boon Mai was complaisant, appreciative, inventive; yet he was certain he never had control, except perhaps for one evening. She had brought a poisonous Thai pudding, a dessert that she loved, some sort of tapioca-and-banana mixture with an overlay of a purplish sauce. Lying in bed he had playfully spread the pudding on her breasts, then licked it off, sucking noisily to call her nipples forth. She laughed, was a little excited, took some pudding and spread it on his penis, reached down and with little hot licks, made him clean. Then she reached over, took a double fingerful of the pudding, spread it down her belly, through her pubic hair, between her legs. She looked at him in invitation; he complied, and seemed for those moments to own her.

Hobart wouldn't let him fly more than one mission a month; he gave him his flight pay and that was it. Brown began putting more and more effort into finding out what was going on at the BX; it was making Boon Mai nervous.

One night she came to him with a tape recorder. She begged him to record their lovemaking, to tell her he loved her. "You go away, soon, I not have nothing. If I have tape, I play it back, and remember you, my young general. And I make one for you, you can keep it and remember me, maybe come back to me."

Brown laughed, declined. The next night she did not come back.

At 13th Air Force, a sleepy Capt. Nick Brady looked at the envelope on his desk. It was addressed to "Commanding General, 13th Air Force." There was no postmark on it.

Brady was the C.G.'s aide; he ripped the envelope open. "Holy shit! Here goes a guy's career."

Maj. Gen. Howard de Viers was not in a good mood; no one in the Pacific Theater was, for Bullet Shot, the build-up for the bombing offensive, was taking every man, every dollar, and every moment they had.

Brady handed him the letter.

Dear General:
You have a bad man here, Brigadier General Charles Kingston Brown. He is making love to my wife. She is the BX manager. I am going to kill him.

It was signed "Lek."

477

"Jesus, what is Brownie up to? Brady, I want you to cut orders for General Brown to report here immediately; send a TWX to get him on an airplane today. Somebody else can clear out his stuff and send it to him. And make sure you keep your mouth shut."

Duke was on a C-130 headed for Udorn that afternoon. He was puzzled and apprehensive. The orders had been peremptory, and there had been no one he dared to ask what they might mean. Brady met the airplane and took him to the general's office.

Brown saluted. "Good afternoon, General."

"Don't bullshit me, Brownie; are you screwing some Thai BX manager down there?"

An odd mixture of relief and anxiety flooded over Duke. He was appalled at being caught like this. Yet it seemed to offer relief from the mindless journey he had begun at West Point, a pursuit of his father's goals that left him unfulfilled. Maybe it was all coming to an end. Here and now. "Yes, sir," he said calmly.

"For God's sake, man, how old are you anyway, eighteen? Can't you keep your pecker in your pants? What do you think they have the goddamn massage parlors for?" He tossed him the letter.

Brown licked his lips, looked at him.

"Brownie, your dad did a lot for me. I'm going to save your ass on this one. Stick around here for a few days, until I can get you some orders back to the Pentagon. And for Christ's sake keep your mouth shut about this." He whirled and yelled, "Brady!"

"Sir."

"Anybody else know about this dumb shit?"

"No, sir, nobody but Lek."

De Viers burst into laughter. "You smartass sonofabitch, no wonder you're still a captain. Make sure that no one knows. If they find out, I'm holding you responsible. Get General Brown a hooch, and work up a TWX I can send that will get him reassigned to the Pentagon for some plausible reason. *Don't* sign it 'Lek.' "

Three weeks later, Brown was back in Alexandria.

It had been worth it, no matter if she was faking.

478

43

November 1971
Bien Hoa AB
Vietnam

He enjoyed running his fingers over the crudely carved wooden sign on his desk. Against a background of command-pilot wings complete with star and wreath, the first line read: MAJOR LAWRENCE A. WHITE, USAF; the second, OPERATIONS OFFICER; the third, 32 AIR TRANSPORT SQUADRON; the fourth, VNAF.

It was damn near a command. He'd never been so happy, reliving the role he had played the first time he'd come to Vietnam. They had been sent over to supplement the Vietnamese efforts to defend themselves, to train them. By 1965 the Americans had taken over, reduced the Vietnamese to a subordinate role. Now "Vietnamization" was in full swing, and Larry was back training Vietnamese. This time, though, he was a wheel, with an office.

The Vietnamese had almost reversed their roles. Then they'd been young, terribly eager but relatively untrained. Now they were older, no longer eager, but excellent pilots. He flew as many missions as he could, sometimes as instructor pilot, sometimes just along for the ride.

The airplane was better too; he'd loved the old C-47, but now they had Fairchild C-123s, twin piston-engine high-wing transports fitted with a J47 jet engine under each wing. The jets gave plenty of power to get in and get out, and the way the flak was building up in the South, you had to have speed to survive.

He wondered how many wood, screen, and corrugated tin shacks exactly like his own dotted Vietnam. It didn't matter, here he was king, this was his castle. In the corner were two more ceramic Vietnamese elephants to mail back to Micky; she had plenty, he knew, but they were great gifts, and she always loved anything he sent. Nowadays the system was so pat he just put an address on them, didn't even wrap them, and they'd get through, unharmed.

The mission today would be like the missions yesterday, the missions for the past week. The North Vietnamese had a garrison surrounded at Kham Loc. The only supplies the garrison could get were parachuted in from the C-123s and C-130s. The planes couldn't land anymore; the fire was too hot. A mixed Vietnamese and USAF ground control team had been calling in the support fire from the F-4s, A-1s, and B-52s. They were supposed to have been evacuated last night. Hulks of burned-out transports lined the wretched pierced-steel plank runway, too damaged even to merit mortar fire from the enemy. When they air dropped supplies at least half landed in enemy hands, but it didn't matter. Time was running out; it was Stalingrad, Dien Bien Phu again, on a smaller scale.

He met the mission commander and his copilot at the airplane; he glanced at their mission folder. Their call sign was "Victor One," another of the war's little ironies. The two pilots said they had preflighted, but White walked around it just the same, just checking. He'd stayed alive a long time, just checking. He spent some time in the cavernous fuselage, making sure everything was rigged right for a quick release. The Vietnamese airmen were quiet, surly; they resented his looking.

The two Vietnamese pilots were in their seats, starting engines, when he crawled aboard. Their methods were strangely similar, strangely different from the U.S. types, who were less precise, more relaxed, but exacting. The Vietnamese formally parroted the checklist and response, but seemed indifferent, aloof, apt to overlook something in their coldness. He watched them, sometimes reaching surreptitiously down to place a switch in the right position after it had been called and responded to, ignored. He had to do it covertly; to call it out would cause a loss of face.

The flight to Kham Loc was easy except for the radio. The VC were making a final attack, and the air was filled with cries for support from fighter bombers and B-52s. The Vietnamese pilots looked worried; the flak was reported to be heavy.

There was a circus of aircraft on station. Some had already dropped; he saw a C-130 trailing off in the distance, two engines out on one side, streaming smoke. Black smoke boiling off the end of the runway showed where something had gone in; it was JP-4-type smoke, so it was either a fighter or a C-130.

The radio chatter was intense; suddenly a voice familiar from their past few days' missions came on. "Hey, anybody, this is Golfball, we're still here, over."

"Roger, Golfball, this is Hector Two. Where are you?"

"We're holed up here down by the second C-130, the one

with the fuselage burned out, about fifteen hundred feet from the south end of the runway."

"Roger, stand by."

"Victor One, go to Echo channel."

Larry watched as the pilot switched over. He tapped him on the shoulder, waved his mike; this was no time for a language barrier.

"Roger, Hector, Victor One."

"Did you hear Golfball?"

"Roger."

"Look, I'm too heavy to make a stop and go there, the strip's too short. By the time I taxied back and turned around, they would have nailed me with mortars. Do you think you can do a short field landing, take Golf on, and get out?"

"Let me look."

There was about four thousand feet of runway, according to the chart, but it was pockmarked with shell holes. Still, if he offloaded the cargo, flew right at the stall, and used full reverse just before he hit, it might be possible. Provided they didn't shoot him out of the air.

"Hector, Victor One. I'm just going to jettison this stuff at altitude; if I make a low pass and they hit me, I couldn't make a try at it. Then I'll try. You transmit to Golf to watch and run to get in about a hundred yards from where they are now; I won't be able to stop any slower than that. Tell them it's a one-time deal; if they don't make it I wouldn't be able to try again, because they'll be alert. First time we might surprise them, over."

"Roger, Victor, good show. We'll watch what you are doing and try to divert some more fighter bombers in to suppress the flak."

Larry had been watching the VNAF pilots; they understood what he had said, and didn't like it. They argued about jettisoning the supplies at altitude, saying the troops needed them. Finally they gave in, flew a pattern at eleven thousand feet, dropped the cargo. It spread out over the jungle; probably 10 percent or less landed in the drop zone.

Larry said, "Let me in the left seat."

The VNAF pilot shook his head, reefed the control around to leave.

White pulled his .38 pistol out of his pocket, jammed it against the aircraft commander's head. "Get your ass out of that seat or I'll blow your fucking brains out."

481

The copilot moved as if to intervene and Larry cocked the pistol. "Move you bastard, I don't have time to fuck with you."

The man slipped out of his straps, and went to the back of the cockpit.

"Hector, Victor One."

"Ah roger, Victor, go."

"Hector, I'm going to put this mother in the stall mode and drop straight down off the end of the runway, as straight and as slow as I can. When I get low I'll pop the gear and try to stick it on the end of the runway. Is Golfball ready?"

"Roger, they're ready; Charlie's been probing for them with mortars."

White went through the drill of lighting up the J47 jet engines; he slowed the C-123 down, bled the airspeed off, dropped full flaps. Unused to the treatment, the airplane groaned, and all the sounds of air whistling changed; it felt different in White's hands, flying only reluctantly, ready to fall.

The Vietnamese aircraft commander had disappeared, back into the hold; he was probably lying down next to the landing gear area, looking for protection from the spray of flak he knew was coming. The copilot looked more angry than scared.

White pulled the throttles to idle; as the nose dropped, he kept trimming back to keep the nose from pitching forward. The C-123 began to fall like an elevator, and now the flak picked up and began hammering it. He could hear the hits, but all the gauges looked good.

The jungle came up like the bottom of a roller-coaster track; he thought he was too low, added power, fought the trim that bucked the nose upward, realized he was too high, jerked the throttles back. The copilot had turned his head away. A hailstorm of small-arms fire rose up; it was like flying into a shooting gallery.

At the tree line he poured on power, dragged it over, chopped the throttles, and hit the runway hard; he threw the engines into reverse, blowing up a cloud of dust and smoke. Ahead, mortar rounds came toward him. He heard the back door open; the aircraft commander ran forward, called, "All aboard, we go!"

The engines, shuddering from the hard reversal, worked back into full thrust. He saw a line of mortar shells walking down the side of the runway, straight toward him. The C-123 broke ground between impacts, the mortar burst bracketing it nose and tail.

"Good show, Victor, that's a fucking Medal of Honor if I ever saw one!"

482

The trembling set in on the way back. The crew from Golfball, two USAF officers and an enlisted man, along with two Vietnamese, came forward. The Golfball C.O. slapped him on the back.

"Goddamn it Major, you saved our ass! They aren't going to be able to hold for the rest of the day. We'd have been on the way to the Hanoi Hilton tonight." Even the Vietnamese crew was jubilant.

When they landed, White walked around the 123. It was ripped with shrapnel; the fuselage was punctured with two rows of holes that must have been 20 mm, but hadn't exploded on contact, entering high on the right and leaving through the roof. There were small-arms hits everywhere, and some skin torn loose by shrapnel of some sort, probably from a mortar round. But there wasn't a hole in anything vital; the plane could be fixed with sheet metal and rivets. It was a tank.

He spent the afternoon getting congratulatory calls and telegrams. He got a personal call from General Martell, the Seventh Air Force commander, telling him he was being put in for the Medal of Honor.

Next morning some different calls came in.

"Major White? This is Colonel Hansen at Seventh. Let me congratulate you on your rescue yesterday; it was brilliant."

"Thank you, sir."

"But I've got a problem; I've got a complaint from the commander of the VNAF that you pulled a gun on Major Ky, said you'd blow his brains out."

White gulped. "Yes sir, I believed I specified his 'fucking brains.' "

"Don't screw around, White, this is serious. They want you court-martialed; word around here is that Ky claims to be some kind of distant relative of Nguyen Cao Ky. I don't know what we can do to stop it."

White was furious. "The man should have been shot; he was preparing to fly away, desert the scene of combat."

"You have any witnesses?"

White blanched; he had been the only American on board when it happened. He hadn't even told the Golfball team about it; he didn't want to blow his own horn.

"No, sir, but that's what happened. Why else would I have to use a gun?"

"You sit tight, son; I'm putting you under house arrest right now. There'll be a team in a chopper in about forty minutes. You pack your gear."

White slammed the phone across the room. He didn't even know who would do the court-martialing, the USAF or the Vietnamese. He could win the USAF fight, but if they let the Vietnamese do it, he'd be in a tiger cage on some godforsaken island prison.

The chopper came in, complete with two security policemen in chrome helmets. Hansen was with them, wearing a sidearm, waving a warrant.

They threw White's bags on and scrambled away in less than ten minutes. Hansen reached in his pocket and pulled out a pint bottle of Jack Daniel's. "Take a pull on this, Major, you've been through hell in the last twenty-four hours."

"What's going to happen to me, Colonel?"

"Well, we're going to land at Ton Son Nuit right next to a Navy P-3. You are going straight to Clark Field, and then you are going home. Fuck those guys and their court martial. You are a goddamn hero, and if we can't get you a Medal of Honor, General Martell says he'll personally get you an Air Force Cross."

Relief swept across White; the only thing he regretted was losing the nearest thing to a command he ever had. Well, he had his wooden nameplate tucked into the B-4 bags; the ceramic elephants were lost, but he knew Micky would understand.

44

1105 LOCAL
21 November 1971
Fairfield-Suisun, California
USA

At one moment, everything had seemed so ordinary; the dog was scratching to get out, the musty fug from the refrigerator clearly indicated it needed defrosting, and the sun filtered down through the overhead screen to the patio. Then there was the knock on the door, and the wire from Vietnam.

Micky was sure that Larry had been wounded or killed. Her hands trembled as she opened it; she closed her eyes, sat down, then read:

484

Headquarters 7th Air Force
Ton Son Nuit Air Base, Republic of Vietnam
171171

To: Mrs. Lawrence W. White
3819 Oakwood Terrace
Maj. Lawrence W. White is returning to the United States
as of this date; itinerary will be Clark Field, P.I., 23/11/71,
Hickam AFB, Oahu, Hawaii, 27/11/71. Major White requests you meet him in Hawaii, will advise further from
Clark Field. William H. Hansen, Col., USAF

Was he all right? The wire didn't say. It would have said,
surely if there was something wrong with him. She'd have to ask
Jerry if she could get the time off; Alice could handle the
Osmont closing. Everything else would have to wait.

Two days later a wire came from Larry.

Darling Micky:
Will be home early, explain all later, but looks good for
me. Meet me Royal Hawaiian Hotel on 27th. Wire hotel
what your plane will be, I'll meet you at the airport, or if you
get there first I'll come to hotel. Anyway, I love you. Love,
Larry.

Micky wondered what had happened; it must have been sensational if Larry would spend that much on a telegram.

Larry was at Honolulu International at noon on November 27
to greet her, grinning, carrying an armful of leis and wading
through the crowd of luau-shirted travelers. She had traveled first
class, was first off the plane, and swept into his arms.

"My God, honey, you look wonderful!" He held her at arm's
length, brought her back in; she was crying with joy.

"Larry, you are so skinny; we'll get you fed soon. How long do
you have for R & R?"

"It's not R & R, it's leave. I'm not going back. I'll be going to
fly C-141s somewhere, but I report to Scott in thirty days. We
can stay here as long as we want, then go back to Fairfield to get
ready to go."

There it was; Micky stiffened. She'd have to give up everything she'd built up, again, for another three years of Larry flying

off around the world. They'd talk about it later; it was so good to have him back.

She had never seen him like this; he was confident, ebullient, talking about making colonel before he retired. He spilled out the whole story on the way to the hotel.

"Did you really pull a gun on him?"

"Yes, and I would have used it; we were there helping his people, and he was going to cut out."

"Thank God you didn't have to. You would have hated yourself afterward."

"Yeah, I know; but maybe not. The bastard deserved it. Anyway, he got out of that seat like lightning, and the other guy was quaking. They thought I'd gone nuts. Maybe I had, maybe I'm always nuts."

Larry tipped the bellboy ten dollars, the biggest tip he'd ever given in his life, and told him to bring a bottle of champagne.

The bellboy was back in fifteen minutes. Larry caught his breath long enough to yell out to leave the champagne in the hallway; he was attending to first things first.

They had embraced when the doors closed, and literally torn each other out of their clothes. Larry felt rampant, a tiger on the prowl; Micky couldn't believe he was the same man. She loved his authority, his driving insistence.

As always, want was greater than need, and by three o'clock they were both temporarily sated. He told her the story in detail; half of it, the power settings, the flap settings, the flying technique in general, made no sense to her, but he loved the detail, savoring it in the telling. And he had a sense of worth from it that had been missing for so long.

"They were going to put me in for the Medal of Honor, but the Vietnamese government wanted me court-martialed, so I guess I'll get the Air Force Cross instead. Still, that's not bad for a tired old major in a C-123."

"Hey! You're not tired; you tired *me* out this afternoon."

"Yeah, and after a steak, I'm going to tire you out again. It's been a long time, darling."

They walked the white beaches of Waikiki that night; Micky always liked it better in the evening when the swirling crowds had gone. Yet there were too many little private parties scattered here and there. It was no longer the Waikiki of the Bing Crosby movies; now it was Coney Island—crowded. They wandered down to Fort de Russy, just to gain a little breathing space, into the happy hunting grounds of the officers' club bar, where TDY troops and local belles gathered to meet.

He was ecstatic about going to C-141s, the big four-jet Lockheed cargo plane.

"And with my experience as ops officer, and the Air Force Cross, I figure I'm a cinch to make light colonel next time. And they'll have to consider me for a squadron C.O.'s job, and that would put me in line to retire as a full bull. That wouldn't be bad, honey, we could do all right on that, and you would be able to give up the real-estate business if you wanted to."

Micky smiled, pressed his hand. It was tough for her to talk. A full bull earned maybe twenty-three thousand in retirement pay; she earned that every six months, and she was just getting going. If Eatherton really went along with her ideas on franchising she'd make a lot more than that. And retirement was the last thing she craved; it was like talking to Edmund Hillary about a walk in the park. Sometimes she wondered how much Larry really knew about what she was doing; it seemed that he just shut it out, made it a small thing like working part time as a nurse, or teaching. He didn't seem to want to address her success.

But she wouldn't spoil it for him. They'd have to talk about it. He could retire now, go to work with her. They wouldn't have to move, and there wouldn't be that much difference in the retirement pay. Maybe they could set up a little flying school at the local airport; he'd like that, and if she ran the books, they might even make a little money. Meantime, she and Jerry could get their ideas into practice.

Jerry had been good to her, and once he got used to the idea she wasn't going to sleep with him, he had let her do almost anything she wanted. And he listened to her.

Bouncing around the country had been good for her real-estate career, even if it had been bad for their pocketbook. She had a sampling of what people wanted and needed, what stress they were going through either buying or selling. She had worked at seven different real-estate offices, some for only a few weeks before she realized that there was some unethical stuff going on, and was amazed at the lack of consistency. She wanted to implement her long-held dream of a standardized office, with the highest ethical standards, blazers for the sales people, and connections across the country, so you could sell a house for someone in one area and sell to them again when they moved to the next. There would be advantages in training, advertising, name recognition.

There was some risk, for they'd need about one hundred thousand to invest in the first two or three offices; once they were established, they should be able to sell franchises and recoup their money. Jerry was still lukewarm, but she felt he was coming around.

As always, she didn't bring it up until the last night of their second, or fourth, or seventh honeymoon; she'd forgotten how many times they had met halfway between his base and home, to couple joyously for a while, making up for lost time, and then to have real time, real problems close in on them. Was it better to have one long, uninterrupted period of dullness, as most married people seemed to, or to have these aching separations followed by the spice of reunion? With their personalities, this was probably best. It must be, it was what they did, and she had learned that most people do exactly that, what they feel is best for them.

Larry was looking 100 percent better; he'd had a cold for the first part of the stay, the usual result of swapping the germs of one country for those of another, but the sun had baked it out of him as they traveled around the island, trying out beaches. They never tired of the flashy Waikiki restaurant fare even though there was more imagination in the dishes' names than in the dishes, but that didn't keep them from stopping at the little noodle shops that dotted the countryside. Larry had switched from Mai Tais after the first day—three of them had demolished him that night—but was drinking plenty of beer. Micky had gone on an Oriental kick, and they finally converted to sashimi in a little Japanese hillside restaurant. As they toyed with chopsticks, they commented simultaneously on how far they'd come from Virginia.

She moved around on the tatami, snuggled up against him. "I hate to go home," she whispered.

"Me too. But I'm dying to see the house, even"—he grimaced—"Larry Jr."

"He's not so bad since he started working. I think we'll get him back in college pretty soon. Nothing like eight hours a day in an office to make school look okay."

"What happened to his girlfriend?"

"He won't say. I think she may have gotten busted. When he showed up last month, he was plenty scared. I'm not asking any questions, and don't you either."

"Not me. I'm just glad he's coming around."

They were quiet for a while. Then she broached the main subject. "Larry, can we talk about what you are going to do?"

She felt him tense; he knew something had been coming. How many times had they done this?

"Sure."

"Are you sure you want to go to Scott? You could retire now, and we could start a little flying school or something at the airport."

"Don't you want to go? Is it your business?"

She told him her plans, what she hoped to do, what she had invested for them in land around Fairfield.

"I hear you. I know what you've done and I appreciate it. I think you are probably the smartest woman in the world, and the best looking too, and a great lay. But I can't do it. I've got one last shot at doing something in the Air Force, and I've got to take it. I'm sorry, but we are going to Scott."

"Okay. You're the boss."

The words seemed to surprise him.

"Yes, I guess so. I'm the boss."

She was hurt and a little bitter; she'd put in a lot of hours building up her local clientele, and some of the development deals, particularly the new townhouses, were going to be tough to close out without a loss. Once again she faced the contradictions inherent in her life: the opposing forces of being an Air Force wife and of being a successful businessperson. Half of her wanted to leave this life cold and devote herself to her business; but the other half—the half that had been brought up in the Tidewater, that had read romantic novels and listened dreamily to "Frankie and Johnnie" being lovers—wanted to be Larry's wife. She had long ago steeled herself not to expect total satisfaction in this life, but at times like this, the disappointments were hard to take. Yet, as she drifted off to sleep, listening to him snore, she realized she was more his wife than she was a real-estate whiz. He was her man, she was his woman, and that was that, even now, in the era of burned bras and female liberation. She sighed and went to sleep.

When they got home, they found Larry Jr. had thrown a party for them. He even wanted to find out about the last flight in Vietnam. Larry was particularly impressed by his father's using a pistol; this was John Wayne stuff he could understand. It bothered Micky; it wasn't at all like her husband to be brutal, and the handgun incident was completely out of character. But it seemed to be a pivotal thing with him, gave him an assurance he hadn't had before, one she liked.

At the office, Jerry was completely understanding. He did everything to salvage her deals, made arrangements with other agents to take over, promised to protect her interests. On the last day on the job they had thrown a big party for her. She had taught a lot of the salesmen and women what she knew, and they were appreciative. There were lots of gifts, some just tacky jokes, but most thoughtful things that showed they cared. Larry was there only for a while, then had to leave to attend to the movers.

When the party was over, Jerry asked her to come into his office. He had a present for her: it was a solid silver tea set. "This is from me, not from the company, not from the gang, from me."

She was surprised; Jerry was not known for his generosity. He must really have liked her. She kissed him. "Jerry, this doesn't have to be the end. We could work the franchise deal from both ends. St. Louis isn't exactly the real-estate market of California, but it could be a start."

"I wanted to talk to you about that. You keep that in mind, and maybe we can work something out."

The move across country was typically dreadful; Micky spent a frantic four weeks in a motel room until they finally located a house they could stand to rent. There wasn't any point in buying until Larry found out where he was going. It wasn't what they wanted, but the whole thing proved her point about an interrelated real-estate network, one that could serve both ends of a move.

She wrote Jerry that night, pressing the idea.

The answer floored her, even before she opened the envelope. The outside read TRANSAMERICA REAL ESTATE: WE COVER THE COUNTRY.

The letter wasn't from Jerry at all; it was from his lawyer, Bob Newcome, and it was a form letter, offering her a chance to purchase a franchise in TransAmerica for only seventy-five thousand dollars. Gerald Eatherton was listed as the president and founder. Her name didn't appear. Jerry must have figured he'd bought her out with a tea set.

Eatherton wouldn't return her phone calls; when she got hold of Newcome he was cold and told her that Jerry had copyrighted an idea he had had for a long time, and if she wanted to sue, sue.

She cried. Larry came home and she spilled out the story to him. He held her. "The way I see it, Mick, this is just part of life. I'm terribly sorry for you, but you'll come out of it okay. You haven't lost anything but an idea, and you wouldn't want to be associated with anyone who'd do something like this anyway."

She felt better. She realized it was this decent strength that kept Larry plugging in the Air Force and that made her love him. She'd given up nothing, lost nothing. She had him and their son. She also knew she would somehow have revenge on Jerry, one way or another. Maybe just run him out of business someday. It was a good fantasy.

Larry had reported to Scott AFB with anticipation. There was nothing he wanted to do more than fly jets, especially the big C-141s. He loved the base, with its distinguished old buildings, tall trees, and quiet bustle. They made a fuss over him at headquarters, told him the assignments were being prepared, and to take it easy. The base newspaper ran a story on his last flight, omitting the details on his having to use a gun. The story was run in the local newspaper, the *Metro East Journal*, and picked up by the wire services. He got letters from all over the country from people he'd served with.

He drifted around making sure that he got wired in at Base Operations so he could do a little flying. After about three weeks he dropped by Personnel. A worshipful young staff sergeant was there. He knew all about Larry, had him tell the full story of his adventure. After the kid stopped ooohing and wowing, Larry asked, "Did you, uh, see anything in the records about the recommendation for a medal?"

"No sir. Why don't I wire PACAF and check on it?"

"Roger, that would be great. I've had stuff like this drop through the cracks before. Send a copy to Colonel Hansen at Seventh, too, will you? He's a good guy, and he'll follow up on it."

"Sure, Major. And I think I saw a message on your assignment, too. If you can wait a minute, I'll riffle through this stuff and find it." He did as he promised, and came up beaming with a flimsy. "Good news, sir; you're assigned here at Scott, to fly C-9s."

"What the hell is a C-9?"

"It's a Medevac version of the McDonnell Douglas DC-9, sir; they tell me it's a great airplane."

Larry was furious. It wasn't a C-141, and he'd been virtually promised a C-141 tour.

The young sergeant read his disappointment. "Do you want to talk to the personnel officer about it, sir?"

"You're damn right I do, Sergeant."

The personnel officer was a big, heavyset man, crinkling with good cheer. He adopted a sympathetic tone; he'd check into it.

He called him the next day. It was the same old story; the pipeline was full of C-141 pilots and they needed C-9 copilots. That's where he was going. Period.

"Look on the bright side, Major; you won't have to move, and the C-9 is a great airplane." It turned out to be true; the C-9 was a dream airplane, probably more fun to fly than the C-141. But he was back in the right seat, a copilot, and as he went through the simulator training he realized that he'd been kidding himself about being a light colonel, about making colonel before he retired. He was going to wind up a buck-ass major, flying copilot to some green kid. And he'd made Micky give up a fortune and a career for this.

Micky ached for Larry when she found out. He had been down for so long; Hawaii was the first time in years that he had really begun to appreciate himself. And now they'd done it to him again.

"Larry. It's time to get out."

"You're right. I'm going to learn to fly this airplane, and then get out and see what I can do. I need the jet experience. Let me put in a couple of years, and then we'll get out."

She sighed. A couple of years could turn into five if there was another war he could get into, or if they gave him some carrot like becoming an aircraft commander. She reached over and picked up the phonebook; the Yellow Pages were filled with real-estate firms. She could do it again, but it would be tougher.

Typically, White enjoyed the C-9; it was a good airplane flying a good mission. He even liked his aircraft commander, a young captain who treated him with enormous respect, first because of his combat experience, then because he was obviously master of the airplane.

There wasn't any word from Personnel on the medal.

45

**1330 LOCAL
February 1972
Pleiku AB
Vietnam**

It was an absurd situation. The old soldier had behaved like the recruit. There was one inviolable rule of survival in the military, and that was never volunteer.

Picard had volunteered. Out of sheer ennui, he had exchanged the numbing twelve-hours-a-day, seven-days-a-week stint at Andersen for the total hazard and twenty-four-hour discomfort of Pleiku. It was wonderful.

The boredom of Andersen had become unbearable. It was monotonous on the flight line, even though he had a premier job in Charlie Tower. He had grown to hate the fact that though the emergencies changed, the basic problem of too many airplanes in too small an area flying too many missions did not.

There were very few intratheater transfers, and SAC never liked to give up prime personnel assets, but an emergency call had come in from Pleiku for an experienced line chief to supervise the maintenance operations. Pleiku was on the western edge of Vietnam, almost on the latitude of the division between Cambodia and Laos. At one time it had been an important part of the war, with a variety of piston-engine aircraft—Cessna 0-2s, A-1s, Spookie Gunships, even, sometimes, F-100 jets—all cooperating with the American ground forces. Now the ground forces were gone, and the remaining force was airpower stiffening for the South Vietnamese troops.

Picard could tell that things were almost luxurious nowadays; he lived in one side of a two-room hut that was protected by a brick-and-concrete blast wall to guard against rocket attacks. It had been officers' quarters once, when the scale of operations at Pleiku had been grander; now they were down to a few scratch outfits, and there was ample room for all. Only a few years ago, before the Corps of Engineers Red Horse teams had gotten into full swing, everyone stayed in the Quonset huts, targets for any VC who would sweep past Camp Holloway with a bazooka.

It wasn't pretty country; the ground rolled in small hillocks, building to the beginning of the foothills. The red earth was hard and sharp with flinty rock during the dry season, viscous and pulling during the wet. As everywhere in Vietnam, the pervasive heat and humidity contributed to the dour, unfriendly manner of the Vietnamese in the camp.

He'd come because he wanted to escape the endless routine of Guam, but also to actually get to Nam; he didn't want to fight an entire war at a distance, unaware of what the countryside was like, what the people were like. He wanted to see where the endless serried rows of bombs had gone. Within a few days he had; they'd gone into mindless craters that turned the landscape into a microscopic view of an aging whore's pores.

He'd never have been transferred if he hadn't made a personal appeal to Colonel Washington; he was far too valuable on Guam to be released. But he knew that Colonel Wash, as he was called by all the enlisted troops, had sympathy for the Vietnamese and plenty of clout at 13th and in SAC. Picard had stressed how much he wanted to become involved in the local civic action groups, to put to use the practical experience in first aid and health care that he had gained as a volunteer fireman. This was more important to Washington than the fact that he was one of the few men who had extensive piston-engine experience, especially on the cranky big round Wright R-3350 engines that powered the Spads. The Spad, known technically as the Douglas A-1 Skyraider, was the workhorse of the war. A relic of the Korean conflict, the Skyraider could carry tons of bombs and absorb enormous punishment. But when it was back on the ground, it needed many hours of maintenance for every hour of flight.

The novelty appealed to Picard; the B-52s had come by in bewildering sequence, an endless melange of identical airplanes. He was detached from them, directing not the maintenance, but the maintenance people. Here he was hands-on, changing jugs, troubleshooting, swapping engines, all with so few airplanes that he came to know each one personally.

The ad hoc unit had a phony name and a phony mission; it was called the 101st Search and Rescue Squadron, but its real mission was to pick at the Vietcong tightening the grip around Pleiku. There was very little search and rescue to do anymore, but the Vietcong were like the sea, relentless, coming ever closer. The main goal of the 101st was to protect the few remaining Lockheed AC-130 gunships which were America's fleet in being. The converted transports carried side-firing arma-

494

ment like a British ship of the line of the nineteenth century. Through gunports in the side, everything from tiny 7.62 mm machine guns to huge tank-busting 105 mm cannon fired. They would fly a tight circular pattern, illuminate the battlefield with searchlights, and then like defenders from a medieval battlement, pour down a stream of lead instead of boiling oil, drenching an area with fire. It was the only answer to mass attacks on encampments, and was by far the most effective means of stopping tanks at night.

Picard had found what he was seeking, a positive counterpart to the endless toil of the flight line, in ministering to the tribesmen who garrisoned the camps on the perimeter line around Pleiku and Camp Holloway. It was family-style warfare; each warrior brought his family with him, and somehow they adapted to the ceaseless danger, the endless fighting.

Picard was amazed at their combination of brazenness and timidity. They fought in a land as alien to them as Maine would have been to Picard, yet they established an immediate tribal integrity and had made the camp their country. Their personal concept of honor was mixed by Western standards; they would accept willingly anything that was somehow out of their ken—medical treatment, dental treatment, medicine, even, after lots of persuasion, vitamins. In return they wished, demanded, to share their food and, if not their companionship, their presence. Both were hard for Picard to take; he worried that the food was not sanitary, and his inability to communicate was physically wearing. Yet he felt he had made contact, that he was doing more good on his weekly visits to the tribesmen than he was doing with a week on the flight line.

He enjoyed the illusion that he was a medic. The tribesmen were used to receiving treatment from U.S. Army corpsmen before the big bugout, and they accepted his help uncritically. A U.S. Army major, a military adviser, still served with them. He was a Texan with the appropriate name of Tom Roper, in for one last shot at filling his squares for light colonel as the Army moved out. He was dubious but let Picard go; it was all he had. Two years before he could have called upon air-evac to fly someone seriously ill to field hospitals. Picard was sensible, didn't try anything beyond his skill, but didn't mind lancing boils, sewing up cuts, or passing out ointments and powders to reduce the skin problems that were so prevalent. They needed a dentist badly, but there were no more in-country. The ground power of the United States, with its incredible communications, firepower, transportation, medical corps, and endless luxuries, had ebbed away. Now everything depended upon airpower and the faltering South Vietnamese troops. The tribesmen were fatalistic in their acceptance of the decay; they knew that when the war ended as it must end, with a North Vietnamese victory, their lives, way of life, even tribal identity would end. In the meantime, they must fight, endure.

They lived inside the perimeter of a crude but effective fortress. Barbed wire and claymore mines encircled the camp, and they walked with their guns at the ready. Yet the family note predominated; women suckled their babies, children played at war, cooking pots boiled. Like any dying organism, the vital elements were centralized, protected for as long as possible against the final inevitability.

Picard sensed their friendship, but was unable to communicate enough to really establish a bond with any individual. He was amazed at first that a people so proud could accept the paternal role provided by first the Army and now the Air Force. Eventually he realized that their entire concern was fighting and survival, and the source of the rations and the ammunition troubled them no more than the source of a banana on a tree. It was there to be used, to live by, and the vendors were immaterial.

The VC attacks were becoming more persistent, more daring, with a far heavier presence of North Vietnamese soldiery. There were half a dozen veterans back for a second tour at Pleiku, and they assured Picard that it was easier in the old days. The VC would move in, set up a few mortars and rockets, throw a few rounds in, then leave in haste. Now they fought almost leisurely, moving in a great variety of firepower, and expending far more ammunition.

Picard was glad he had not tried to be an infantryman. He preferred fixing to fighting, especially these tired old clunkers that remained to fight the war with. It was a funny thing about airplanes; most pilots regarded them as mere machines on the ground, tendering them personalities only in flight. For Picard it was just the opposite; as long as they were flying, they didn't belong to him. But on the ground, he owned them.

There were so many signals. He had not been on the line more than two months before knowing, almost at a glance, at the nuances of an engine starting, the relative state of the equipment in his squadron. He was like a physician with too many patients. The airplanes that were running well would get only minimum attention, but he could sense the ones that were beginning to develop problems, and concentrate on them. As a result, he kept more aircraft operationally ready than had any of his predecessors.

Sometimes the demonstrations of his skill were dramatic. He had been working on Capt. Skip Elmore's A-1E all morning; every time he checked it everything was just barely normal. Picard didn't like it; there were signs that something was incipiently wrong, but he couldn't pin it down. He hated it because he liked Elmore, who commanded the 101st. It was a scratch outfit suited to a passed-over captain who was only happy in an airplane. Men like Elmore were a mystery to Picard; they epitomized everything the Air Force said it wanted in a pilot—someone who knew he was there to fly and fight and would never forget it—but often they were passed by for promotion. They didn't market themselves, discounted the extra things that seemed to matter, and as a result were overlooked.

He stood and talked with Elmore under the wing of the Spad, seeking a little relief from the heat. Elmore had done his customary thorough preflight, pulling panels, getting his hands greasy, checking the armament carefully. He was a pro. They chatted about the latent symptoms, and Picard climbed up on the wing, stood on the step to peer into the cockpit as Elmore went through the starting drill and run-up preflight check. The oil pressure was just over the lower limits, the temperature just under the upper.

"Captain, why don't you scrub this mission? We can get another airplane ready for you within the hour. I already checked, and the spares have gone."

"I don't see how I can, Don. I'm scheduled to launch in fifteen minutes, and it just looks marginal to me. I can't afford to wait to rearm and launch another airplane."

Picard scanned the instruments. The captain was right; there was nothing to suggest that the flight shouldn't go except for his gut feeling.

Picard had plenty of paperwork to do, but he stayed on the line, following Elmore's progression down the PSP taxi-way, to the runway. The sun was hot, and he could see heat waves shimmering off the end of the macadam.

Elmore did the briefest run-up—Picard figured his temperatures must be rising, because he was obviously shortcutting the checklist—then advanced the throttle for takeoff. The A-1 had just lifted off the ground when the engine seized, sending the propeller whirling across the flight line into an abandoned Quon-

497

set hut. There was nothing for Elmore to do but land straight ahead. He didn't even try to jettison his ordnance; momentum would have sent the mixture of bombs and rockets tumbling after the airplane.

It was like running in slow motion. Picard saw the prop leave the A-1, the airplane shudder nose-up, then abruptly nose down as Elmore fought the stall. A line of trees at the end of the runway shattered like a pane of glass as the airplane macheted through them. Picard began to run toward the emergency equipment, waiting for the explosion and black mushroom of smoke.

He jumped on the side of an ambulance that raced down the runway to the crash site, abandoning it when the jungle got too thick. He and two medics pushed and shoved their way to the foliage; the task was easier when they broke into the final sheared descent path of the airplane.

The Skyraider sat in a pool of fuel, smoking, with bombs and rockets spread around like confetti. Elmore was seated two hundred yards behind the airplane, holding a pressure bandage against his leg.

"Picard, you smart old bastard, you were right again. I barely got that mother off the ground—and when it seized and sheared the prop off, all I could do was land straight ahead, sweating, praying, and cursing."

They looked at his leg; it was a superficial cut, probably obtained when he jumped out of the cockpit, but it was bleeding freely.

"Next time I'll listen to you, Don. And this means you have to take the civic action team out tomorrow; I don't think I'll be walking on this."

One of the tents on the road to the communal mess hall had been converted to a nondenominational chapel; Picard had begun dropping in at odd hours of the day, and he was always surprised to find a few people there, praying or thinking. Today he went in to pray for a lot of things. First he prayed because Elmore had lived through the experience, wasn't forever seared on his conscience by a spark and puff of fire. He prayed because the bombs hadn't detonated, the fuel hadn't caught fire. Then he prayed that the next time he'd have enough information to ground an airplane, not let it fly when it shouldn't.

Polly would be glad to know he was praying; she had always been religious, and was more so now that they were older. There was irony in her increasing fervor, for her life had been spent praying that their son would get better, establish some contacts.

He had not, and yet her faith never deserted her, not during the big war, not after. She joked about it, said she stepped up her trips around the beads while he was overseas, but she was very serious. Her faith had undoubtedly kept her to him through the long periods when the Air Force had demanded more of him than she had to give.

He stepped out of the tent, musing that it always seemed hotter when you went under canvas, and hotter when you came out. He wondered what Polly was doing.

She should have been sleeping; instead she was staring at the ceiling of the trailer, wondering how she was going to tell Don about his son.

Jamie had always been withdrawn; for the first years they thought he was retarded, but he was intelligent enough, especially with mechanical things. He simply didn't have the ability to establish human contacts, to interact on any but the most limited basis with anyone. She had sometimes gotten through to him, when he possessed a sudden sad awareness of his condition, and sought a link with her. But for the most part his capacity to love, and even more poignantly, his need for love seemed just to be missing from his personality.

She wished they had been able to afford better medical help. The Air Force was so good about so many things, but there were limits on what they could do for dependents. The nice dentist, Dr. Russ, had gone way beyond the limits in taking care of Jamie's cavities, but when Donna needed braces, she had to go to a civilian doctor. If Don had ever found out that she had traded her services as a cleaning woman to the dentist's wife for the braces, he would have died. Air Force doctors did the best they could, but there simply wasn't a mechanism available to help. If he'd been terribly ill, no expense would have been spared; they would have flown him to Walter Reed, done whatever was necessary. But help from a psychologist or a psychiatrist just wasn't in the cards.

The doctor at the base had assured her that Jamie wasn't autistic, he just wasn't completely normal. That was no help at all.

He was a nice-looking boy, tall, not muscular but trim, with a good complexion. She had a difficult time making him keep himself neat and clean; baths were still a problem. She was lucky to nag him into taking a shower more than once a week. The problem had compounded when he began to become seriously interested in cars, wandering the junkyards, bringing home bits and pieces to disassemble. She was ecstatic that he had an interest, did everything to foster it.

Jamie could communicate his needs without ever verbalizing. It was almost as if he had willed her to purchase a 1950 Chevrolet for him to work on. The rusting black clunker was derelict, undrivable, and she had to talk long and hard to Old Man McAteer to let her have it towed to the back of the lot. He rarely relaxed on anything, but he had had a troubled son too, a slow learner, cheerful, but car crazy. Polly knew how to play him.

She had put off the question of Jamie learning to drive; he could read well enough, and his coordination was good, but he had never even suggested that he take lessons. That was mistake number two.

He'd kept a spare carburetor disassembled on the hood, and she didn't even dream that he had the engine running. The truth came out when he got in the car, started the engine, and plowed through the back end of an empty mobile home at the far end of the lot. He hadn't been hurt, but McAteer was furious, and there was no insurance on Jamie or the car. It looked like as much as two or three thousand in damages, maybe more. But that wasn't the worst part. Jamie had changed; from his normal placid silent self he had become sullen and angry. He wanted his car back, and in the few words he mustered for her, he blamed her for not sending him for driver's training.

So she lay still and felt guilty, resentful, and not at all like praying. Don had been more fortunate than most in being able to stay at bases for relatively long periods of time, even though he put in long hours. Yet whenever a crisis came, he was away, overseas, TDY, something. It was a common complaint, a joke among the wives, that the husbands had some sort of trouble calendar that they used to get out of town when problems were coming.

She had been furious when he volunteered for Vietnam; he was too old, too wise, and too near rotating home to do it. Yet it was part of the stupid male instinct, the desire to be where the action is, to work harder in more difficult surroundings, to support the Air Force out of one's hide. Polly knew that he was lonesome, that the food was bad, that there was an increasing danger from the VC as the defense of the airfields was turned over to the South Vietnamese. Yet he was storing up psychic capital, working harder, repairing airplanes in hours rather than days, plucking spare parts from the air, making things happen. Years later he and his buddies would joke and laugh, and it would be worthwhile. To them. In the meantime, she had to figure out where the money was going to come from to pay McAteer, who wasn't being unreasonable. He just needed his money.

To Jamie, the problem was a simple one. There was a spring on the carburetor he had hooked up backward; when he pressed the accelerator past a certain point, the spring had taken over and run it to full throttle. It took him a little while to figure to turn off the ignition; otherwise he might still be driving.

He missed his Dad. Dad would have been able to work with him on the car, wouldn't have let him put the spring on backward. And Dad would have taught him to drive. Mom didn't understand.

Now he didn't know if he would have a car. He was sure it still ran, he'd just have to fix the radiator, some stop leak maybe. Then he'd pull the fender off the tire and pound it out. Maybe Dad would be home in a little while, and could teach him to drive.

He felt sorry that he'd been mad at Mom. In the morning, he'd try to make up. He'd take a shower first thing, then give her a hug. And he would try to get a job in the service station. He could do a lot of things, clean up, fix tires; maybe they would pay him.

The siren jerked Don awake, just as the first mortar shells began falling along the flight line. He grabbed his shoes and his M-16 and dove into the slit trench. The attack lasted only twenty minutes, but he could see fires on the flight line that could only be A-1s going up; the AC-130s were on a mission. He hoped to hell it was 59981, the ramp queen; it was probably old 435, the best airplane on the line. Goddamn.

There was a sudden further flurry of fire from the direction of the tribesmen's camp. It was intense; it was more AK-47 fire than he had ever heard. The mortar explosions started, and there were some bazookas coming in, too. It was lasting longer than a hit-and-run attack. Picard shouldered his way into the command post. Elmore was limping around, talking to Major Roper on a field phone, the only communication remaining with the camp.

501

Roper was frantic; it looked like a regiment-size attack, and he could hear tanks in the background.

"Look, Elmore, you get me a gunship in here, or they are going to overrun us."

"Roger, Tom; I've put in an emergency recall for our two AC-130s, but they are at least an hour out, and I don't know what their armament state is."

"Well, goddamn it, get something, or we'll be kissing our ass goodbye. I can keep them off for a while, but if they send in the tanks, that's it."

"Roger."

The AC-130Es had responded to Elmore's call. In less than forty minutes Spectre 05 was over the camp. Spectre 14 was still half an hour away.

The field phone jangled.

"Elmore, where's that goddamn gunship? I can see the goddamn tanks."

"Roger, you should hear them now."

'Oh shit, here they come. You tell Spectre to fire right on the camp. The bastards are busting through the wire now."

Elmore switched to the AC-130 pilot. "The camp commander says they are across the wire. Shoot right into the camp."

"Ah, roger, we got them illuminated. It's a squirrel cage down there. We're dumping all we got left."

The landline was dead. Picard and Elmore went outside the command post, stared to the east. There was a glare above the tree line, and they could hear on the wind the shredding sound of the AC-130's gunfire. An airman came out and grabbed Elmore's arm. "We got the Spectre on the radio, Captain."

"Roger, Spectre 05, go."

"Ah, Base, we don't see any activity down there; there were two tanks, both are burning, and we don't see even any small-arms fire. There were some small secondary explosions, but it looks quiet. Are you talking to them?"

"No, we've got no contact."

"Ah, roger, no contact. We're out of guns, fuel, and ideas. We'll be coming home. Anybody inspected the runway?"

"Roger, runway is clear; we got two hulks burning, but the wind is carrying the smoke clear. Thanks for coming back. We'll try to find out what happened."

Spectre 14 called in confirming 05's report that there was no activity in the camp. It came back to Pleiku.

It was late the next afternoon before Picard had things squared away on the flight line. Just as he had feared, they had burned out the best airplane on the ramp, holed several others. The only plus was that the worst airplane was also destroyed, its propeller, wingtips, and tail disposed forlornly around a gray-black mound of foam-smeared ashes.

The trip to the camp was ghastly; it had been overrun. Everyone had been killed—men, women, and children. It looked like there had been fierce resistance, but the North Vietnamese had taken the recognizable portions of their own dead away. The gunship had minced everyone into small parts. He saw a torn torso, evidently saved from the Spectre's chopping fire by being thrown up against a hut by a mortar blast. It was still wearing a bandage he had attached the week before. He tried to remember the face of the person he had helped; he couldn't, and now some knotted bloody linen was his only link to what had been a worthy human. There was no trace of Major Roper. It was time to go home. The next time it would be Pleiku itself.

He was in a profound depression for the next week; there had been no mail, and he was desperately lonely. When the mail came there were several letters from Polly; among them one was marked "The Good News" and one "The Bad News." He read the bad news first. The accident didn't bother him; he was proud of Jamie for getting the wreck going. The good news was so good he almost cried when he read it. Jamie was working in the filling station. Picard couldn't believe it, couldn't wait to get home. He could teach the boy things, bring him around. Life wasn't all bad. Life wasn't all Vietnam.

46

July 1971
The Pentagon, Virginia
USA

It was the first time Duke had returned to the Pentagon without the warrior's relish for combat. He had been caught at Hickam with TDY orders for SAC Headquarters at Offutt, and had spent four months there briefing on what he'd learned at U-Tapao. It was ironic, for he had learned damned little firsthand, but he was able to integrate the little he had seen with the greater amount that he had heard from people he believed in. He was

503

also able to weave in what he'd learned from Washington's experience at Andersen. He'd spent each day dreading the sound of the telephone, sure that each ring was a summons to explain Boon Mai.

He was certain that the word would have filtered back to the Pentagon by now that he'd been fired, caught in a bit of hanky-panky with a Thai girl. Gossip traveled with the speed of light, especially anything with the seriocomic overtones of his affair with Boon Mai. It was grist for any rival's mill, and anyone who stumbled on it would put well-amplified rumors in full circulation.

He was philosophic; he knew what he'd do with a similar juicy morsel on one of his competitors, so perhaps he had it coming. He felt a vague pride in not being remorseful about it. If his whole career went down the tubes—and that wouldn't happen— Boon Mai was still worth it.

He wondered if he were in love with her; there had been no thought in his mind of a permanent relationship. He never expected her to come back from day to day, even early on when he realized that she was seeking a hold on him for reasons of her own. When he had refused her last obvious ploy, to indict himself on tape, she had not returned. He had understood perfectly that she realized that the game was no longer worth playing, and cut her losses. The only regret he had was not seeing her one more time, to somehow reassure her and himself that he didn't mind her insincerity, that the sharing of her body had been worth it.

His sense of her insincerity probably helped; he would have felt much worse if he had really been Lieutenant Pinkerton to her Madam Butterfly. Instead, they each got pretty much what they deserved, only he had enjoyed the process much more. He had surrendered fully to lovemaking, without concern for the partner, with full pleasure for himself. When things had been right for Joan and him, he had been driven by a desire to perform and to please her. Later, when her drinking began to take hold, it was just a mechanical function borne of morning pressures, abrupt, and not vastly more satisfying than elimination. With Boon Mai, it was abandoned pleasure, highly seasoned with the flavor of the risk he knew he was running.

Joking in the Air Force was never subtle, and he would know soon enough if there had been a leak on the affair. The jesting was raw and often corrosive, a superheated locker-room style in which cruelty was prized. The cutting edge of the humor stemmed from the profession being so dangerous, so that one had to steel oneself against losses.

It was also because you were constantly being reviewed and evaluated. Few people had to take as many checks in the course of their professional lives as pilots. The checks were run with painful rigor, as they had to be, and mistakes were pointed out with clarity and without regard to sensitivity. There was a grim "gotcha" satisfaction in failing someone on a check ride. It was especially prevalent in the Pentagon, where one would go out to Andrews Air Force Base for a check after a ninety-day layoff. The stern instructor pilot would pile event on event, emergency on emergency, until the beleaguered pilot would screw up. There was an element of sadism perhaps, but it made you work, and pilots boned up on their procedures in a way they would not have done otherwise.

It had become accepted that the stress of a check flight was a simulation of the stress that might be encountered in a real emergency, and was therefore not a bad thing. As a result, flyers developed a case-hardened resistance to sarcastic criticism which carried over to joking.

As he climbed the last flight of stairs he ran a few lines through his head to prepare himself for a comeback. The jokes probably wouldn't come from his superiors or subordinates, just from his peers. They'd say something like "I understand you picked up a case of something at the Thai BX," or "There's a guy named Lek been calling for you." Nothing too subtle, nothing too hilarious, just pungently to the point.

Nothing happened. Apparently Brady and the general had kept a lid on things.

At his request, Duke had been assigned to Plans and Programs as project officer on the TMTS, now known officially as the FB-113. He was amazed and proud to see how far the program had come. The original order for 244 had been expanded to 380, and it looked as if orders would be coming in from Australia and England.

He was a little miffed that he hadn't been able to get in to see his boss, Lt. Gen. Jerry Page; he knew he was in the building, but his secretary had said his calendar was full. That might or might not be a signal. Even back when he was a colonel and Brown a major, Page hadn't supported the TMTS program. Still, the program was in being, and doing well; Page ought to be happy with it by now.

He spent the day at his desk, going over the production

program and the R&D effort. It gave him a great deal of satisfaction to see the capability that the airplane now possessed, but major problems were evident. A lack of quality control in the manufacture of the wing swing mechanism had caused a rash of accidents. Worse, the first unit of FB-113s deployed to Vietnam had simply disappeared in combat, victims either of the wing problem or of failures in their low-level-terrain-following systems. The press had picked up on it, and there was severe opposition within the Congress and even parts of the Pentagon. Old Congressman Dade was horse trading to keep it in production, was actually seeking an increase in the total number to be built, in order to provide two squadrons to Australia and two to England. It was audacious to ask for more in a time when none was the more probable number, but Dade played the congressional system perfectly.

Still it was entirely possible that the program might be canceled, and McNaughton forced out of the airplane production business. They could continue on as subcontractors for other major firms, but the probability of their winning a major production contract was nil if the FB-113 was canceled.

He jumped when his intercom rang. "General Page will see you now, General Brown."

Page's secretary, Muriel Scott, was one of the 1941 vintage, here since the building opened, filled with a sense of important permanence. Her desk was cluttered with the mementos of the years, and signs saying things like IT'S NICE TO BE IMPORTANT, BUT IT IS MORE IMPORTANT TO BE NICE and WHAT, ME WORRY? Lacquered platinum blond hair was piled in a classic beehive above plucked penciled eyebrows and waves of wrinkles. Her figure was full, with sharp pointed breasts always accented with sweater or open-button blouses. He wondered how many men she had had, literally and figuratively, over the years. Her voice had a missile's vernier calibration; she could tune in exactly the right amount of whatever she wished to convey—friendship, flirtation, disapproval, uncertainty—in a simple "Yes sir." Insiders would make bets on promotions or reprimands, based solely on how Muriel addressed a person. She had one saving grace; she never confused herself with the general for whom she was working, as so many of the younger women did with their bosses.

He walked into Page's office; by the time you had three stars there were a few perks—rugs on the floor, flag, chrome water bottles—but it still didn't compare to the digs of a junior V.P. at Lockheed or McNaughton.

"Come in, Brownie!" Page jumped from behind his desk, and came around, grinning, his hand thrust out. He was a big man, former fullback at the Point, jogger and racquetball player now; his hair was a curly blond Brillo pad, stretched over his skull like a swimming cap.

"Good to see you, General."

"Good to see you, Brownie; you've come back at a good time. You sort of got us into this, and maybe you can get us out. We need a strong program advocate for the FB-113, and you're it. It's having all kinds of problems, from structural to range to the fact that the goddamn Navy is coming up with a submarine-launched cruise missile called the Bolide that they say will do the FB-113's job. The problem is they are not too far wrong; with the FB-113's limited unrefueled range, and the missile tracking capability, they come pretty close."

"But they've had cruise missiles since the Regulus; never been worth a damn, have they?"

"No, but now they have a little itty-bitty jet engine that runs forever on a pint of JP-4, and a terrain tracking system that is a computer miracle. And they are cheap; you can buy a few dozen of them for the price of one FB-113."

"Anybody got any ideas?"

"No, that's what you are here for; I want you to go to Nashville and talk to McNaughton as soon as you can. They have people on the problem already, but the only thing they've come up with is stretching the damn airplane again, putting another plug in the fuselage and stuffing more fuel in. That might work, but it makes the airplane more expensive, and rolls out production until the 1990s. I'm frankly worried about the structural integrity; we've already stretched it once. I don't want the damn thing to bend in the middle like a banana. You've got to do better than that, and you have to be able to sell it."

"Roger. I'll leave in the morning. It's a coincidence, but I had to go to Nashville anyway, on family business, so this is no hardship. Okay if I drive?"

"Sure. Muriel will cut the orders any way you want."

Brown had reached the door when he heard Page chuckle, and call to him.

"Sir?"

"Say, Brownie, how is that Thai poontang?"

"Couldn't say, sir." A weak reply, for all the anticipation.

"Come here, Brownie, sit down. I got something for you to read."

Brown's knees were weak. No wonder the bastard was so jovial; he had him nailed to the wall.

It was a thick OSI report, marked TOP SECRET. There was an abstract.

Thefts in the Base Exchange System in Thailand, File A 399815.

Over a period of several years more than seven million dollars in material has been stolen from the base exchange system in Thailand. Intensive surveillance and audit of the individual exchanges failed to reveal the cause of the thefts. There was no evidence that the material was being stolen from the warehouses or the base exchanges themselves. However, a paid informant, a Thai national, has revealed the modus operandi. The actual thefts occurred at sea, while the ships were at anchor at Sattahip, prior to any material being delivered ashore. A complex confederacy of accomplices saw to it that the paperwork, from ship to individual base exchange, was impeccable. A number of arrests were made, but many individuals were protected by the Thai government, and as a result the case can be considered only partially closed. A close parallel to this exists in File A 198175 "POL Thefts in Thailand."

Page reached over and closed the document when Brown started to turn to the full text.

"Don't bother with the rest of it, Brownie; you can come back some time and have Muriel check it out to you. You aren't mentioned anywhere in it by name, although there is a reference to attempts by the Thais to subvert responsible American officers to provide some cover-up."

The fact that a crime was involved didn't surprise him; he was just amazed at its complexity and sophistication—and his stupidity.

"Don't sweat it Brownie, they don't have anything on you; I'd never have made the connection if some guy in 13th hadn't forwarded this to me, with a cover note. Your secret's safe with me. Just make sure we get along."

Brown shook his head. It was blackmail of the worst sort, unspecified in demand, uncertain in time. And he was hooked.

"Yes sir, I get the message. And now, I guess I'm off to Nashville."

"Have a great trip, Brownie, and bring back a solution."

Brown went back to his offices, locked the safes and signed

them off. He'd arranged to pick up his orders in the morning; in the meantime he had to get Joan ready, and do some thinking.

The drive back to Ridge Road was lovely; it was one of those rare July days when the temperature and the humidity dropped and Washington seemed livable. Duke felt guilty that he enjoyed driving the Toyota so much. But it handled so much better than the Buick he'd traded in on it. He was happy for another reason; maybe Boon Mai had stopped seeing him because she was afraid he was part of the OSI. It was a comfort.

He found Joan right where he expected, in the Florida room, a pitcher of screwdrivers by her side, the television set turned on. She was dozing. He looked in on her, still in her robe and fuzzy slippers. She was forty pounds overweight and in repose her stomach was a cascade of fat. Her hair, once perfectly coiffed, streamed down. She made the classic picture of the neglected lush.

Something had to be done; she was no longer just an embarrassment, she was a hazard. He could afford her drinking as long as he was seen as struggling toward a solution. There was no solution now, and if he kept her on, his own judgment was in question. That was the last thing he needed.

Fortunately her family had remained sympathetic as long as they could keep their distance. The congressman shifted the sauce with a right good will; he thought his daughter was no trouper not to be able to handle it. He suggested that she be taken west to a clinic in Arizona, but the flight surgeon had highly recommended one near Nashville, and Duke was determined to at least keep her within surveillance distance of her family, in case he were sent overseas. She had to dry out; she couldn't continue drinking like this and live.

Duke packed bags for both of them, then went around and systematically closed the house. It was as sterile as a model home in a new development. Part of that was a tribute to Joan: drunk or sober, she saw to it that the place was fanatically clean. Another factor was the abnormally quiet life their son led. He knew that the latter was due somehow to his own personality, yet was powerless to change it. Even when he worked hard to be a good dad, it somehow didn't work. Charles Jr. seemed to be growing up without reference to Joan or Duke. It was just as well he was away at the private school Duke had picked out. This scene would be too painful otherwise.

Joan had awakened. "Duke, darling, what are you doing home so early?"

"We're going to Nashville. How about hopping up and taking a shower and getting dressed while I get the car gassed up. And please, don't drink any more; I'm going to need your help."

Joan nodded; something told her things were far more serious than just another argument. She moved upstairs, took some aspirin, showered. As she soaked in the hot streams of water her eyes began to focus.

Dressing was an agony; everything had become two sizes too small, and she had to layer clothes in a way that did not reveal the various open buttons. She didn't want to go to Nashville; what she wanted was for Duke to get the hell out of there and leave her alone. She picked up a travel case, checked to see that her shampoo and rinse were inside, that a fifth of Johnnie Walker Red was secure in the bottom, underneath a layer of Kleenex boxes.

Duke waited patiently for her. The trip would take at least one overnight stop, maybe two. There was no sense in having a scene here.

In the course of the drive, she sobered up. "Duke, can we stop for some coffee? I've got a thundering headache. I don't suppose you'd want me to take a drink?"

"We'll get some coffee. There's a Stuckey's up ahead. Joan, let's try to tough this out for a day or two; we're going to meet your family and I know you want to be sober. But you are going to have to get treatment. I can't let you go on the way you were doing, drunk every day. It's not fair to you, and it's not fair to me. Or to Charlie."

She burst into tears. "Are you committing me?"

"No, no, honey, it's a treatment, just like going to the hospital. But you need help, and I can't give it to you. I'm probably the reason you drink, and I know I can't make you stop."

"Duke, you are the reason I started drinking. Now you don't matter, but the drinking does."

They didn't speak again except for polite noises.

The clinic was unexpectedly pleasant; it reminded Duke of Greenbrier. Even Joan seemed pleasantly surprised.

Her family had been perfect to all appearances; they showered her with love. Duke was quickly made to understand that they regarded Joan as his problem to solve, and that while they would try to keep things quiet, word was bound to get out.

He left her in a room overlooking a garden and some tennis courts. She was checking over the program of activities; it read ike a Girl Scout jamboree. He loitered a while in her room, uncertain of what he should do next.

Finally she glanced up at him. "Duke, I want you to go. I'm really hurting, I need a drink badly, and I don't think I can keep up this pretense of being civilized for long."

"Goodbye, honey. I'll be back to get you soon."

"Listen, Duke, if I can get out of here, I'm going to get out of you, too. If I can't, it doesn't matter."

Duke spent the night in downtown Nashville, constantly analyzing the problems that confronted him. He pondered the mixture of emotions he felt about Joan; he was concerned personally about her, but vastly relieved to have her drunkenness at least temporarily out of his life. The problem of Joan merged into his own career uncertainty. Had he really spent more than twenty years plunging after the wrong things? He ate lightly, drank not at all, and still had trouble sleeping.

The next morning he drove the twenty miles south to the McNaughton plant. When he went in the receptionist was all smiles, and had his identification badge ready, his sign-in sheet filled out, waiting only for his signature.

A buzzer sounded and Bob Cranston, the McNaughton V.P. for the FB-113, burst through the door. "General Brown! Good to see you, sir. We met in 1970 at the AFA convention in the Sheraton."

He took him down the long, highly polished corridors to the executive offices. Inside the conference room, with its fifty-foot-long oak table, the best and brightest of McNaughton were there to greet him, including the Air Force plant representative, an older lieutenant colonel named Dale Dysinger.

There was coffee in great silver pots and trays of danish, but they got down to business. The McNaughton engineers didn't mince any words; they accepted the Navy cruise missile as a genuine threat to their program, and they didn't attempt to diminish any of the claims for it. This told Brown the claims were probably on the conservative side.

The FB-113 team went through slide after slide. The principal problem was the airplane's short range.

"Bob, what's different now from when the concept was sold in the first place? The airplane hasn't lost any range, has it?"

"Sir, there are some major differences. In the first place the airplane *has* lost some range capability. The original estimates were a little optimistic, like always, but there are three main problems. One is that the empty weight has gone up by four

511

thousand pounds, and there's simply less room for fuel. When they couldn't pinpoint what was wrong they added size and strength to the wing swing mechanism. They simply beefed it up, and the weight skyrocketed. The second is that the engines are not delivering the specific fuel consumption promised at low altitude. We can go all day at altitude, but when we go low, the fuel drains away. And the third thing is the tanker fleet; it hasn't expanded with the FB-113 build-up. Worse, with the B-52Ds converted to conventional bombs, they have a greater tanker requirement than before. So we can't count on the last prestrike refueling as we did before. It's essentially become a one-way mission."

It wouldn't be the first time. There had been one-way missions before in SAC, in B-50s and B-47s. But it was a hell of a way to fight a war, and a worse way to sell more airplanes.

The briefing droned on. Some of the proposals were pipe dreams. One called for the Air Force to buy half as many KB-113 tankers as bombers; the tanker would fly out with a pair of the bombers, and refuel them. The bombers would fly on to the targets, and the KB-113s would then get refueled themselves by KC-135s, and loiter waiting for the FBs to come back out. It was expensive, cumbersome, and had the sole advantage of selling more airplanes. Another proposal called for the FB-113s to tow high-speed gliders filled with fuel behind them; the bomber would transfer the fuel when it reached the enemy border, drop the glider and press on. Great.

They broke for lunch in the plush pecan-paneled McNaughton executive dining room. Duke went through the formality of offering to pay for his filet, and McNaughton went through the formality of explaining it had no bookkeeping system to accommodate him. Duke then went through the formality of promising to reciprocate when McNaughton came to Washington. The souls of the GAO were satisfied.

Duke asked for an hour's delay and a line to Washington. He was put through to Page.

"How is it going, Brownie?"

"General, if that Navy missile is as good as McNaughton says, we should probably cancel out. There isn't anything obvious that they can do to keep the FB-113 competitive without a radical revamp in thinking."

"Like what, Brownie?"

"I don't want to talk about it over the phone, even though this is probably as secure a line as there is. Will you give me carte blanche on asking them for a proposal? It could cost a few bucks."

"Go ahead; tell them to submit an unsolicited proposal for whatever you've got in mind. They are hurting; they won't mind eating a few dollars for something that might keep them alive."

At the end of the meeting, McNaughton had not yet come up with an idea that would stand scrutiny. In essence they were asking the Air Force to ignore the evidence and stick with the current airplane. Congress would never put up with it.

Brown asked for a short meeting with Cranston and a few of the top engineers.

"Bob, I'm sorry, but I haven't seen anything today that will sell. You are talking a lot of extra dollars for very little extra performance."

"But, General Brown, you forget the investment in tooling, facilities, spares. It would cost a fortune to replace these."

"Let's face it, those are sunk costs, and we can't consider them. You know that. The only thing that counts is what we are going to buy in the future. And right now it would be tough to argue on finishing out the present buy, given the Bolide's performance."

They were silent.

"But I think we might be receptive to an unsolicited proposal from you that might help."

They were alert.

"Suppose you fitted cruise missile stations to the wing and the bomb bay of the FB-113; you could cruise in with the wing swept forward, and fire the missiles in a stand-off mode. You'd keep your nuclear weapon capability in the bomb bay, for delivery, or you could stick a big tank in there, and refuel right after takeoff if your gross weight was limited."

There was a noise of the whirl of computers.

"Can we take about thirty minutes, General, and get back to you?"

Duke waited in Cranston's office. He called Joan's dad; she was getting on okay. He wanted Duke to drop by and talk to him. They knew Joan had been drinking, but were surprised by her condition. He said he'd drop by that night.

When they reconvened, the McNaughton engineers were ecstatic; the first spread sheet of figures showed a radically improved capability.

Cranston walked Duke out to the car. "We won't forget this, General, you've given us a new lease on life."

"Good, Bob. One more thing before I go: You might have problems mating the Bolide to an airframe; it looks to me like you could come up with your own cruise missile without too much effort."

Cranston smiled. "Way ahead of you, General, for once." He pulled out an artist's conception of a tiny winged missile; underneath was written "Brownie's Baby."

The glow from the thought of "Brownie's Baby" got him through the evening. Congressman Dade was furious with him for letting Joan go so far with her drinking. "Hell, I knew she drank, Duke, anybody living with you would drink. But her liver's bad, her white count is way down, she's got coronary problems; you've just about killed her with neglect."

In the end he didn't try to explain, didn't apologize. Dade drank far too much himself; it probably ran in the family.

Late that night, alone in his motel, he argued with himself, endlessly, driven by the sense that Dade was right, defending himself for doing what the other contenders had to do. It was not something he could live with easily. As he dropped off to sleep, the words "Brownie's Baby" kept appearing in his mind's eye on a photograph. But the photograph was not a picture of a missile. It was a portrait of Joan.

47

October 1972
Ubon RTAB
Thailand

Kelly wondered if he was too old for all this. The physical stress didn't bother him—though he had had to cut down on his drinking and begin jogging, because the kids were all too mean and lean around him—but the sophistication of the missions did. Ubon was an enormously busy base, used, as all the Thai bases were, jointly by the Thai military and the Americans. A gigantic unsinkable aircraft carrier, situated in the middle of Thailand, it provided support of every sort for the combat grinding through Vietnam, Laos, and clandestinely in Cambodia.

He had a dream assignment, command of the best F-4 outfit in the world, but he shared Ubon with a strange mixture of transports, reconnaissance planes, tankers, gunships, relay planes, and covert activities. There was a bewildering variety of tasks to master, most keyed to the elaborate electronic devices used to try to track the enemy movements, to slow down the transport of supplies that ran in fluid profusion from Russia and China to the outskirts of Saigon.

The classic fighter pilot one-upmanship, the don't-fly-in-my-sky attitude, had some virtues. It reduced everything to one dimension, a dimension he could still compete in. Air-to-air combat was still the be-all and end-all, and killing MiGs was the only genuine aspiration, no matter how important the other missions were. It was the ultimate line in the pecker-comparison contest, and it was the one mission he still felt comfortable in.

The other missions dismayed him. He had a Fast Fac flight, a high-speed forward air control unit that made visual reconnaissances of all the target areas. The pilots had to be in superb condition, flying low, pulling constant high G turns for four or five hours, taking on fuel two or three times, and they were constantly vulnerable to every sort of fire. The pilots and their observers had to be immensely intelligent, to draw correct inferences from the slightest change in appearance in the foliage, to call down the right sort of strike at the right moment. Their losses were higher than anyone else's, and it was usually an anonymous death, a simple disappearance of two fine young men and a three-million-dollar airplane.

Then there were the Night Owls, the 497th Tactical Fighter Squadron. They flew night after night in the dark, pitching over from twelve or thirteen thousand feet into the death-black night, diving through the orbit of the AC-130 gunships, dropping bombs and pulling out in the hope that they wouldn't be hit, that the instruments wouldn't tumble, that they wouldn't fly into a hill.

There were other missions, equally demanding; the Igloo White mission called for F-4s to streak along the ground and at mathematically precise intervals drop acoustic or seismic sensors at predetermined points. The sensors, disguised as plants in the teeming jungle, could pick up the sounds of trucks or the smell of the soldiers, and then bombers would be sent in. Over eight billion dollars had been spent on this equipment, whose target was essentially two-ton trucks and one-hundred-pound men carrying their weight in rice.

But Kelly and his Cougars of the 444th were MiGCap men, dedicated to clearing the skies of the MiG 17s and 21s that tried to stop the marauding F-105 fighter bombers and the B-52s. It was not unlike Korea, except that the cards held by the Koreans were nothing to those played by the North Vietnamese. The Asians had become better warriors as the Americans became more inept politically.

It was not easy to provoke a fight on terms that yielded kills. The MiGs were completely subordinate to their ground controllers, and their mission was to frustrate the bombers. It satisfied them if the F-105s simply dropped their ordnance outside the target area; they would make a pass, and when the 105s responded by pickling off their tanks and bombs, to ready themselves for combat, the MiGs would disappear. It was a sound strategy—from the point of view of a ground controller.

Kelly had been appalled at the standard of training he found in the Cougars. This was supposed to be the premier squadron in the USAF, and there was nothing but trouble, stemming from a dozen sources. He had status—he was a Korean ace, and there were wild rumors, all incorrect, about his test work and particularly his maverick testimony to the secretary of defense, so he could ask questions right from the start.

Kelly knew that if you ran your squadron by the book, you ran it off the rails. You had to sniff around, see who the people were, see what they thought the problems were, and then you had to find out what they really were. All the textbooks, all the novels, all the films were so unidimensional. In reel life, in *Twelve O'Clock High*, Gregory Peck just gets to be an iron ass, and everything is cured, and they love him. In real life the reasons given are all fluff and frosting; the real problems lie underneath.

He called in his flight commanders, one by one, poured a little Jack Daniel's in them, and got them talking. Then he called in the pilots, and the back seaters, and the maintenance types. In three weeks he had canvassed the wing, talking to armorers, cooks, even to the genuinely fluent Thais. A picture emerged, one that he couldn't cure immediately, but which he'd handle in his tour.

At least 80 percent of the problem was ego involvement. There were half a dozen reasons why the crews could not feel good. Most of them emerged in a talk he had with a cocky young captain, a three-victory pilot named Steve Nealon.

"Come in, Captain Nealon. Like a beer or a drink?"

"No, sir, early mission tomorrow."

"Can I call you Steve?"

"Yes sir, you're the C.O., you can call me anything you want."

"Steve, I'm not satisfied that things are as they should be. I don't want any pointless bitching, but I'd like your assessment."

It was like pulling a plug.

"Sir, there's a lot that's good, more that's bad. Are we off the record?"

"Rog."

"Okay. First is the airplane. It's a great airplane, but it has three fundamental flaws. It smokes, you can see the sonofabitch a million miles away, and with their radar, that's all they need. We need smokeless engines. Second are the rules of engagement; we give everything away before we get there. Nobody's ever fought a war like this, where you hand the enemy your ass on a platter, then have to snatch it away and hit him over the head with it. Finally, there's one too many bodies in the airplane. We need single seaters; a back seater is nothing but a drag, particularly the kind we're getting now." He reached over and took a beer.

"What's the matter with what we are getting now?"

"Shit, you know that; they aren't even pilots, just goddamn navigators with a course in the F-4 thrown in. And the bastards get to share in the kills!"

Ah, the secret was out. "Yeah, but you each get a victory, don't you?" He knew it was the case.

"Sure, but I can see a situation where the leading ace will turn out to be a fucking back seater, a guy who sets up the radar and tells you when it's safe to fire. The flying and the fighting is done by the guy in the front seat, just like it's always been. You don't see any fucking two-seat Russian airplanes, do you? They are too smart for that."

He paused, obviously aware that he was revealing as much of himself as the problem, shrugged and went on. "I can see it now. Some ragged-ass four-eyed back seater will get three victories with some poor SOB of a pilot doing the work. The pilot will get pulled out to go to some half-ass school or something, and the navigator will fly with another guy that gets two; all of a sudden the back seater is the first ace, a hero, and all the hell he did was twiddle buttons."

Nealon drained the beer, picked up another, put it back. You could see him shifting gears of discontent. He went on. The UHF radios were lousy, the gun was too long in coming, the training was bad. The Air Force was so damn anxious to be

517

democratic that it was rotating tired old bomber pilots through fighter training and sending them to Southeast Asia.

Kelly couldn't help liking him; he was like Kelly had been a hundred years ago in Korea. All he wanted to do was shoot down more planes than Richthofen, more planes than Hartmann; everything else was rubbish. And he had a point.

The next night he called in Nealon's GIB, who had shared in the three scores, a tall, polite young man who spoke slowly and never failed to call him sir.

He was Capt. Ralph De Pinto; turned out he had washed out of flying school, and couldn't believe his good luck in winding up in fighters.

"Do you think we need a single-seat fighter, Ralph?" It was an academic question.

"Sir, the best way to answer that is to ask if we'd rather be flying MiG 21s than F-4s. The answer is no way. The back seater offers a whole new dimension. He can keep track of the fuel, the SAMs, the fighters, home plate, the tankers, the armament; a single-seat pilot simply couldn't handle it alone, no matter how good he was."

Kelly went on and on, talked to everybody. At the end he knew the answer and it was not anything anybody had said. The problem was that warfare had matured faster than the men and the airplanes, and the training and the equipment were not up to it. When he got back to the States he was going to try to see that a whole new training program was established, something serious, where you practiced what combat was, not what you would like it to be. They could even get some Russian planes from the Israelis, and practice against the real things.

In the meantime, there was a war to be fought.

The periods of quiet were so elusive. Kelly awoke to the silence. Normally there were sounds of engines being run up, trucks rumbling by, the clatter of pilots suiting up for an early mission. Pilots were more considerate now; in the old days they never worried about waking someone up, either coming in late at night drunk, or getting up early in the morning for a mission. But then the hours were only mildly crazy. Now they were an abomination, with people flying at all hours, in all weathers. You had to be considerate of others when you were close to the ragged edge yourself.

The multitoned calls of the birds, all strange to him, could be

518

heard rolling from one edge of the field to the other. They probably always called, but could be heard only when the turbines ceased turning. This momentary stand-down, this oasis of quiet, was an accident, an inconsequential result of the way the frag orders had happened to lay on missions. Later the noises would pick up, and run without interruption for a week or a month.

In the silence he heard someone's radio, playing the only station, the Armed Forces Network. Kelly listened to the music; it was *Symphonie Fantastique*, one of his favorites. He was amazed it was being played on the Network any time, much less this early in the morning. He lay in bed and listened to it, remembered he'd heard it the first time in San Francisco, just before he got married. It made him think of Kathy, but everything made him think of Kathy.

The symphony ended and the announcer came on, a smooth, Nat King Cole voice, but somehow familiar. He waited. The announcer signed off with "Remember who keeps the records rattlin', your friendly sergeant, Jesse Catlin."

Kelly sat bolt upright. Catlin was the kid starting the revolution in England! He'd gotten the job. Jesus, sometimes the Air Force did things right.

Later in the week he put in a call to the station; Catlin worked only part time. He left a message for Jesse to come see him when he got a chance.

Catlin showed up that afternoon, fatigues sharply creased, grinning from ear to ear.

"Sergeant Catlin, glad to see you. You're looking great and sounding great."

"It's real nice of you to call, Colonel. I knew you were here, but I didn't want to bother you. If either one of us were going to ship out, though, I'd come see you, because I owe you a lot."

"Man, you don't owe me anything, I'm just glad the Air Force didn't renege on my promise to you. Sometimes that happens."

"No sir, it was meant to be. I went back to the States, and there was a big drive on for trainees. I auditioned, got selected, and here I am. And I work in the base Public Affairs, too, got to have two specialties nowadays."

They chatted for a while; Kelly was pleased to learn that Catlin was taking six units of credit at the University of Maryland extension campus on base. As they talked, Kelly could see that Catlin was running something through his mind.

Catlin's normal flow of conversation seemed to dry up as he

steeled himself to ask something. "Sir, I'm thinking about OCS. If I apply, would you give me your endorsement?"

"Out-fucking-standing, Catlin! Absolutely. Any time. Hell, we've been through the war together, right?"

"Yes, sir. Two wars. One here, one in England."

After Catlin left, Kelly felt more content than he had for a while; sometimes it paid to take a chance on people.

As the missions ground on, Kelly learned more about taking chances on his men and his airplane. He had thought he already knew as much as could be known about flying the Phantom. Now he had to learn to use it as a commander. He was in a large way responsible for its being in the Air Force at all, and he had almost fourteen hundred hours in it. He knew its strengths and weaknesses well enough. The airplane was immensely fast and powerful, capable of maneuvering in a vertical as well as a horizontal plane, and this was the only thing that permitted them to engage and defeat the agile MiGs, which could turn on a dime. But now he was learning about it as a fighter squadron commander, and every day something new became apparent to him.

He'd always been a single-engine, single-seat man, and it had surprised his colleagues when he advocated the big twin-engine, twin-seat McDonnell fighter. Now events proved him correct; the environment of electronic warfare had advanced too rapidly for one man to handle. Reduced to its essence, the scientists had been able to make better computers on the ground than they could yet put in the air. The offset had to be a better human intelligence using the airborne computers than was available to use the opposing computers on the ground. You needed an extra set of hands and eyes to watch the radar set, monitor the SAM launches, check for fighter opposition, keep in mind where the tankers were, what the route home was. The term they used was classic jargon: "situational awareness"; it meant your ass depended upon having eyes in the back of your head. A single pilot, not under ground control, would simply be saturated. And the Phantoms came home time and again with one engine shot up and shut down, the other turning out more than ample power for escape.

His own still good situational awareness had added to his personal score; he had eight from Korea, and two more here made ten. He was a double ace, not bad for a kid from East St.

Louis. The two victories had come on a single mission, after so long a dry spell that he was feeling embarrassed, aware that "over the hill" was the kindest thing being thought about him by the eager young troops.

He had been pulling alert duty—he insisted on being on the regular schedule, even though he was the C.O.—with his back seater, First Lt. Harold Molloy, a brand-new WSO. The WSOs were what Captain Nealon had complained about, navigators given special training and thrown into the back seat of a fighter.

Kelly had worked with Molloy and found him perfect for the job; the thing he liked best about him was his apparent determination to stay alive by knowing all there was to know about the airplane. Even though he wasn't a pilot, Kelly checked him out on everything from refueling to back-seat landings. Molloy was not gifted as a pilot, nor could he be proficient, but he had enough skill to get them back if something happened to Mike.

The war seemed curiously out of synchronization to Kelly. The feelings of confidence and eagerness he had in Korea were gone; perhaps he knew too much, had seen too many people killed. He was not afraid; he still wanted to engage, but the sense was different. In part it was the armament.

Korea had followed the classic pattern set in the first two world wars in the air. You engaged your enemy, turned with him, fastened on to his tail, and pressed the button that fired the machine guns or cannons. He took hits, began to burn, perhaps bailed out. It was impersonal, plane against plane, although sometimes dogfights were extended to the point that the sense of fighting against another human became a factor.

Now it was different; he was flying an F-4D, which had not been fitted with an internal cannon. It was all missile work, heat-seeking Sidewinders and radar-guided Sparrows, detached, and designed to be armed and fired in a peculiarly delayed fashion that was difficult for Kelly to relate to. The sense of delay was heightened by the elaborate choreography of battle, the gut-wrenching Gs pulled in directions apparently away from the enemy, but with evolutions that brought you into missile-firing range. It was a ballet danced on stilts.

They had been scrambled to take up an orbit near the Laotian border. Kelly and Molloy were in Razor One, Maj. Bob Pittman and Capt. Bo Taggart in Razor Two. Pittman and Taggart had been flying together for more than a year, had two victories, and were very eager to become aces. Pittman was a superb tactician, obviously destined for flag rank. Taggart was probably the second or third best GIB in Southeast Asia. They were both Academy graduates.

The radar ship Red Crown acquired them on the ship's radar, gave them vectors for a flight of Blue Bandits—MiG 21s—approaching.

"Razor, Bandits 060/30 Bull's-eye."

The MiGs were northeast, thirty miles from a North Vietnamese ground reference point.

"Molloy, what's our fuel?"

"Eleven point two."

Kelly nodded; five tons, enough for a long time in cruise, but a pittance in battle. But it was enough, if they got in and got out.

Kelly and Molloy went through the tight drill preparing for combat. Kelly followed Red Crown's instructions for course and distance until, fifteen nautical miles away, they acquired the target on their own radar set. Kelly couldn't see the MiG embraced by the tubes and sensors of his radar. At twelve miles still invisible, the MiG was in position to be hit by the cranky radar-guided Sparrow missile, the huge "big bullet" of a rocket that the Phantom fought with.

"Here's where we should shoot, Molloy, and not hassle with that tricky little bastard."

"Roger, but you have to have a visual identification. I wish we had TISEO."

TISEO was a new optical device that extended your vision out so that you could see what the enemy was, far enough away to keep an advantage that the rules of engagement had forfeited to the MiGs. It was another example of research-and-development money being lavished on technical devices to offset obvious and blatant political stupidities that even when recognized were not foresworn.

Kelly and Molloy watched as they moved to the target, still flying a course toward them.

Kelly acquired the MiG in the gunsight. "Visual contact!" he yelled for the record, hit the auto-acquisition switch on the left throttle. Molloy confirmed that he was locked on. He counted to four, the agonizing time needed to settle the radar and match up the missile system, an endless, dreary stretch emphasizing the delay and distance feeling, and fired. The twelve-foot-long, five-hundred-pound Sparrow leaped off the track, snaking out in front of the Phantom, moving off to the left of the target.

The MiG had seen the attack coming, was turning hard, pulling lots of Gs, trying to break the missile lock.

"You sonofabitch, it's over there!"

"Easy, Mike; you can't talk it in."

"The hell I can't; look at that bastard track!" The MiG pilot continued his desperate turn, the fight no longer between two planes and three men, the fight between G forces and the electronics and gyros of a mindless missile, loaded with thirty pounds of high explosives, and five hundred pounds of death flying at twelve hundred miles per hour.

The missile won; the Sparrow made a hard right turn, hitting the juncture of the delta wing and the circular fuselage, and the silvery blue MiG disappeared into a huge orange-red and black fireball. Kelly was amazed how the fast-moving MiG suddenly transformed into a stationary mass of smoke and fire, dribbling pieces to the ground.

"Red Crown, Razor One; splash one MiG 21."

"Roger, Razor One, he's gone from our screen."

"Molloy, where is Razor Two?"

"He broke off to the right, chasing a pair of 21s."

"Red Crown, Razor Two." Pittman's voice came over the UHF.

"Roger, Two, Crown here."

"Roger, splash one MiG 21; the other one got away."

"Break break, Razor aircraft; we paint two pop-up flights at our six o'clocks."

Kelly reefed the Phantom into a hard right turn; he could hear Molloy's gasp as the Gs hit him.

"Roger, Crown."

The pop-up was a favorite maneuver; the North Vietnamese ground controllers would lead the MiGs in behind the Phantoms at very low altitude, below radar coverage, building up energy—"smash" was the pilots' term—at supersonic speed, then send them climbing for a rear attack with their Atoll heat-seeking missiles. If they got close enough to fire, they launched the Atoll and split S for the deck; if not, they simply peeled back into the protective arms of their SAM defenses.

The pair of MiGs had already passed behind him; if Crown had not called, they'd be wearing Atolls now. Kelly saw that he was overshooting the trailing MiG, began a high yo-yo, rolling away a quarter turn from the enemy's track, and pulling up. He could see only sky ahead as the Phantom climbed and the energy decay bled the airspeed off.

The MiG was turning tightly; Kelly kept his nose up, and rolled toward it. It was highly polished silver, most unusual. He

523

kicked in the afterburner to begin closing and pulled his nose down to line up with the MiG's tail. Molloy was on the ball.

"Full system lock-on, skipper."

Kelly didn't screw around; he pickled off two Sparrows in ripple fire, from a range of about forty-five hundred feet and an angle of twenty degrees. The first hit the MiG's wing and exploded, the second went through the middle of the fuselage and the silver disappeared into a ball of black and red.

"Red Crown, Razor One, Splash Two." His voice was exultant; he turned, scanning for the other MiG, now lost in the ground clutter.

"Roger, Razor One. We lost that one on our scope too."

Pittman's voice broke in, jubilant, cocky, highly stressed. "Crown, Razor Two, I got Splash Two, too; I'm going after his wingman, over."

Kelly could see Pittman diving to the left after his fifth airplane, his acedom; Pittman didn't see the flight of six MiGs—three 21s, three F-6s, Chinese versions of the MiG 19—coming down on him.

"Hey, Pitt, break right, you got six at six o'clock."

"Roger, I'm going to nail this dude first."

The F-6s were rude, ugly little airplanes. Kelly turned in toward them, saw the winking fire from their 37 mm cannon, watched the missiles leap out from the 21s and snake to impact Pittman's Phantom. The wing folded and the airplane rolled wildly; he saw one man eject before it blew up.

Then as it happened so often, they were alone in the sky.

"Red Crown, Razor One."

"Ah, roger, Razor One, where'd everybody go?"

"It looks like Razor Two got two MiGs, then took a heat seeker and went in."

He felt bad; there was no way he could have helped, but Pittman shouldn't have been hit. He was so crazy to get that fifth airplane, to be an ace, that he stayed just a fraction of a second too long. The same lust had killed pilots in every war so far. He wondered who had made it out, and if he'd survive.

The combat had run them short on fuel, and they picked up a tanker just over the border. He let Molloy try a refueling, but the kid was too high from the combat, couldn't handle it. Kelly took on the fuel, then pulled away from the tanker and set a course back to Ubon.

"Jesus, Colonel, what's that make for you?"

"Make what?"

"How many kills?"

He knew all along what he meant. "That's ten in two wars."

"I hope I don't have to go to two wars to get my ten. I got two now, goddamn, I got two now!"

Kelly grimaced. They were all alike; pilots, navigators, weapon systems officers, priests, doctors, cooks; everybody wanted to be an ace.

"This will really piss Nealon off; he can't stand anybody but him getting any kills; two more flights with you like this and I'll be a frigging ace before he is."

Without warning Kelly rolled the Phantom hard, pulled a 6-G turn.

"Got your attention?" he snarled.

"Yes sir." Molloy was startled, wondered if they were being attacked.

"Now listen to me, you stupid bastard. It doesn't matter if you get five of them or eleven of them if they get one of you. It's not fair exchange. Never, and I mean *never* give them a shot. Make them earn it. We lost maybe the greatest officer of the war back there, just because he was a little greedy."

"Yes sir," Molloy mumbled; Kelly was sure he didn't agree.

Kelly didn't score again, air to air. There was a different target bugging him, one that had eluded hundreds of bombers before, the bridge at Than Binh.

The bridges were another part of the war Kelly didn't understand. It made no sense to send Light Brigade charges of aircraft into cones of flak that the North Vietnamese called fire boxes. They had a name for the bridges, too, "bomb pockets," targets so attractive the Americans had to bomb them, no matter what the cost.

And the cost had been outrageously high. Flight after flight of F-100s, F-105s, F-4s had flown against Than Binh in more than a thousand sorties. Thirty F-105s had been lost, as well as dozens of other aircraft. The defensive ring of antiaircraft and surface to air missiles was simply too dense.

And yet Than Binh was the main artery out of Hanoi; the tons of supplies that came south came over the steel structure built by Chinese. It had to be hit, and the Vietnamese knew it, girdled it with radar, flak, and missiles, then let the Americans fly in on their silly known routes, hampered by their rules of engagement. Kelly often wondered if the enemy laughed about it in the mess

525

at night, drinking whatever they drank, waiting for the next round of slaughter. In the meantime, the goods flowed over the bridge, down the trails, keeping alive an army that was more like a cancer than a fighting force, an ugly draining disease that never stopped pecking at the vitality and the morale of the South Vietnamese.

Kelly had been an early advocate of the smart-bomb concept in his days at Edwards, and later at the Pentagon. He knew his own limitations as a pilot precluded the accuracy necessary when you had to use iron bombs against hard targets, and he considered himself to be the best pilot in the world. An ordinary pilot simply couldn't fly a supersonic jet through intense flak and place a half a dozen five-hundred-pound bombs on a railway span at precisely the place necessary to bring it down. The bridge at Than Binh was a special case; it had been dramatically overbuilt, so that a single bomb hitting a span or a support did nothing. It had evidently been designed to stand up against a nuclear attack; it wouldn't have, but the attempt made it impervious to any conventional weapon.

He hadn't been surprised when Ed Novack turned up at Ubon; he was surprised to find him a lieutenant colonel, carrying a piece of paper that said he was qualified in the back seat of an F-4.

"Jesus, Ed, I didn't know your dad was Hap Arnold, or was it Wilbur Wright? You're the youngest goddamn lieutenant colonel I've ever seen, and a fucking groundpounder at that!"

Ed grinned. "Well, Colonel Kelly, when we used to talk back at the Pentagon, and that seminar back at Edwards, you were a lieutenant colonel, too. I figured if you could do it, anybody could do it."

Kelly took him into his tent. "Seriously, Ed, I know you are a smart young guy, but lieutenant colonel in nine years? Out of a missile silo? You sure you didn't just buy that insignia and bolt it on?"

"I can't explain it, Mike; I've been lucky as hell. I had one dumbass Colonel named Riley Smith, a big bald bastard—I used to call him the black hole of boredom—who got bemused by my ideas and touted me to some guys on the Air Staff and at Eglin. I think it was 'cause he used to like to fly down from Minot to Eglin, in the winter. Anyway, it turned out I had something they wanted, and every time I turned around, they promoted me. It's a little embarrassing at times, but I just back up to the pay window and let them hand me the check."

"And now you are here to dazzle me, eh?"

"Yeah, and I'm not alone. There's a whole team coming in today on a C-130, bringing a new bomb system, manuals, the whole works. There will be a flight of four F-4s, just out of IRAN, fitted with the system, ready to go. You'll probably have to send four of your other birds back to the States, but it's a good deal. These are virtually zero time since overhaul; I have to admit they did it right." He paused, looked around the hooch. "Best of all, I get to fly with it, and I'm hoping you'll pick some pilot who won't bust my ass."

"Jesus, if you are going after bridges with this thing—it's got to be a bridge buster—any pilot will be glad to fly with you if it gives him a chance to get in and get out."

"It does better than that; they don't have to go in, at least not so far. With this little beauty, they can sort of lob it in and it will go down a pickle jar, not a pickle barrel."

"Yeah, well, seeing's believing. Are we going to do some test runs?"

"I wanted to, pleaded to, but they made me do them at White Sands. They are security crazy, but the Vietnamese probably know all about it already. That's why they are bringing in airplanes already fitted out. And that's why they trained a groundpounder like me to fly in the back seat. How about flying with you?"

"Gee, I'd like that, Ed, but I've got better bombers than me here. Let me send you in with Roy Lehnert. He's a hell of a pilot, and he's had two attempts at Than Binh himself, without any luck. If this thing works, he deserves the chance to knock it down."

That afternoon, Novack gave a briefing to the aircrews on the new system, called Pave Strife. The internals of the system were still so highly classified that he glossed over them.

"It's like the old Norden bombsight; you can use it, but you can't learn why it works."

Smart bombs weren't new; Paveway had been in use since 1969, and Kelly was eager to see what Novack had that had given him a four-year jump in seniority, combat status, and a special test group.

Novack was a decent briefer; he went through a very short history of guided bombs, from the old German Fritz X that had sunk the Italian battleship *Roma* in 1943, through the long, almost painful series of weapons that had been developed since. Pave Strife was a hybrid using laser guidance and television, plus a small rocket engine for some extra range. The same type of components were being used in other systems. A laser-guided bomb used two airplanes, one to designate the target with a laser beam, the other to drop the bomb that followed the beam into the target. Another system used a small Sony television set, camera in the bomb, screen in the back seat. The GIB simply flew the bomb in like a radiocontrolled airplane.

So far Novack hadn't said anything startling, and he was losing his grip on the aircrews. "Now, these are the things that distinguish Pave Strife. The first is the television; it's miniaturized, and it operates at a greater distance—twelve, fourteen miles out when the air is clear. The second is that the laser designator is internal. As soon as the GIB picks up the target on television, he targets with a laser beam for the bomb to follow. Third, if you are confident about the target location, if it's big enough, you can launch from thirty miles out, pick up the target on television at fifteen, lock it on laser at fourteen or twelve, depending on how fast you are, and that's it. It will fly into the target, no jamming possible."

He paused, aware that he had their attention again. "One more thing; you can drop one, two, three, or four bombs, using the first one as a master, and the rest slaves. They'll follow the lead bomb in just about the same distance apart as they were dropped from the racks. Or you can put a fudge factor in, and have them hit at precise intervals apart."

The murmurs from the crews were a combination of elation, disbelief, and anticipation. Kelly knew he would have problems selecting the other pilot to go with Novack's sidekick, an ex-F-4 pilot back seater named Jerry Bright. There wouldn't be much complaint about Lehnert; he'd paid his dues. But he'd have to be careful about the other choice. He wanted to do it himself, but knew it would be bad for morale if the old man creamed off what looked to be a glory flight.

In the end he let them have a card-cutting elimination contest to see who would fly with Bright. Steve Nealon won, and there was a round of good-natured protest. He was the man Kelly would have picked to go.

There weren't going to be any training flights with the weapons, but Kelly insisted that the crews fly three training missions together to settle in. The weather boffins were consulted and it looked like they could attack any time in the next three or four days with a good chance that Than Binh would be clear.

The frag orders came down from headquarters for a Friday

launch; it gave them two days to plan and get nervous. Kelly decided to send a MiGCap flight of four with the two bombing aircraft. If they didn't have to enter the flak "fire box" at all, it would be a piece of cake. The crews wanted to pull off some scheme, to fly in like F-105s, like they had done in Operation Bolo years ago, in the hope some MiG 21s would show up.

"Man, that's the last thing we want, even if we get the bridge. Our job is to get the bombing airplanes there, take out the bridge, and get them back. If MiGs show up, we'll engage, but we won't look for any trouble. There and back, that's all we want."

Kelly flew lead with the MiGCap; if warfare was being revolutionized, he wanted to be there.

Just before they taxied out they got incredible news; a Jolly Green had picked up Taggart. He had evaded the North Vietnamese for twenty-three days; the word was that just before the Jolly Green got him, he filled his canteen with the local ground water, so they could analyze it and see what bugs he'd been drinking. What a man. The flight was so jubilant that the raid was almost anticlimatic.

Six F-4s, four MiGCaps and two carrying the weapons, steamed in over a half-cloud-covered landscape. The MiGCap birds were call-signed Mercury 01 through 04; the bombers were Lincoln 01 and 02.

As they flew in formation, Kelly studied the Pave Strife bombs. They looked contrived, like the superweapons that used to appear in Hollywood serials. The center body was a standard USAF bomb, but there were ridiculous-looking fins at the back, and a bulbous, goofy-appearing bulged set at the front. At the very nose of the bomb was something that looked like a taillight from a '37 Pontiac, the television camera lens.

The flight had gone in with complete radio silence. Kelly was nervous, because there was a heavy undercast that the forecasters had missed. But less than four minutes out, the weather began to break up. As they drove on in, the clouds parted to reveal the bridge. Preprimed and ready, the bomb carriers dropped. Eight bombs, four from each aircraft, began a fifteen-mile flight into history.

Kelly took a look around, granted himself the luxury of watching the bombs. The target ahead could have been a Chinese screen, an arched bridge reaching out across a river, green hills, and mysterious misted sky. He followed the flight of the bombs until they disappeared in an ominous waiting. There was nothing for an endless period of time, and he wondered if they'd all been duds. Then the bridge erupted in two columns of smoke and crazy gyrations of steel. A moment later, at the bottom of the bridge, a series of secondary fires started, probably trucks accidentally caught en route. Kelly's headset erupted with cheers.

The bombs had guided themselves in like homing pigeons to take the bridge out. Two airplanes had done what a thousand couldn't do before.

"Sierra Hotel, Lincoln aircraft; Mercury flight, let's form up and lead 'em back."

Nealon's voice came over the air, wild with elation. "Merc One, we're going to make one pass, way out of range, to get some pictures. We'll form up in a minute."

"Negative, Lincoln Two; get your ass back in formation."

The two Lincoln flight aircraft had already started a turn; they had to do 360 degrees to get back on course, and they'd take their pictures on the turn. Kelly laughed; with wild men like Nealon and Lehnert an extra 360 wasn't too much to expect.

"Mercury leader, Crown."

"Roger, Crown."

"There's two MiGs popping up at your six o'clock."

Kelly pulled the F-4 around; behind Lincoln flight were two silver arrows, MiG 21s, coming almost straight up from the jungle green. He saw the Atolls launch.

"Break, Lincoln flight; you got Atolls coming at six!"

Nealon's aircraft went hard right. Lehnert's hesitated, began a turn, was hit by an Atoll. Kelly watched the missile merge with the bottom of the F-4. Lincoln 01 burst into flames; the airplane began to tumble and break up. He saw the wing break away, the nose tuck under. Two flaming trajectories broke away from the fuselage; Lehnert and Novack had punched out, or had been blown out by the explosion.

Kelly had instinctively turned to attack the MiGs; they had half-rolled after firing, diving away to the jungle deck, out of range already. He turned back on course, Lincoln 02 now on his wing.

He restrained himself from raging at Nealon; he and Lehnert must have planned this from the start. There would be an inquiry.

"Anybody hear any beepers?"

It was Lincoln 02, wondering if the chutes had opened.

"Yeah, Two, I think so, I heard something very weak. Could have been them."

On the way back Kelly was desperately sad. He was glad the bridge was gone, glad to have seen a new technology validated; but the price had been high, gratuitously high. The MiGs should never have gotten a shot in if the Air Force had installed the proper airborne control systems. Instead money had been frittered away on numberless projects like Igloo White, the idiot electronic fence on the ground.

The Air Force had lost—maybe forever—the services of two brilliant officers. He hoped they'd got out.

And he hoped the airplane had been completely destroyed. The North Vietnamese would know that something special had been done to them; they wouldn't pull any punches to extract it from either man if they survived. They might be better off to have been killed.

Later he was sad for yet another reason. The raid clearly portended the end of the manned fighter bomber, perhaps even the manned strategic bomber. Today they had done nothing a slightly smarter missile could not have done. The F-4s had merely carried the bombs to the target, simply providing an airborne navigation system. A missile could be built to do the same thing cheaper, and pilots wouldn't have to come within five hundred miles of the flak. The aerodynamics had been available for a long time, from the German V-ls to SAC's Hound Dogs. It was simply a question of stuffing the right computers and electronics into a smaller robot package. Maybe no more Pittmans would have to die, no more Taggarts would have to evade, no more Novacks and Lehnerts would have to be shot out of the sky. He hoped so; he was getting too old even to watch it much longer.

48

2200 LOCAL
17 December 1972
Andersen AFB
Guam

Washington didn't know which war to fight. He wished Brown was still at U-Tapao; he was tired of arguing with him on the long line from Washington almost every night. And for the first time in his life he hated to get mail from Louise. He couldn't

531

believe the letter he had in his hand. Arrested! His wife arrested. She'd been booked and released immediately for protesting at the Pentagon, but she had been arrested. Her letter had been a torrent of apologies, of assurances that no one had made the connection between her and her B-52 pilot husband. But she had been arrested.

His skin crawled at the thought of her being manhandled, bundled off, frisked. She had said it wasn't too bad; what did that mean? And where was that goddamn Lyle Johnson? He hadn't been arrested—like all good generals he was well behind the lines.

With every absence she had become increasingly militant, almost making a point that if he was going to go away to fly, she was going to stay home and protest. Worse, she was asking him some hard questions about Vietnam that he couldn't answer. When he had left home last time she had clung to him, swearing that she would stay out of politics. It must be a matter of proximity. Her need to express herself, her belief in equality, surfaced as soon as he was not there to hold her in his arms. For all her protests, she'd gone right back to working with Lyle Johnson, even though he had expressly forbidden her to do so! Nervous fatigue hung on him, sodden with his sorrow and concern.

And then there were the fucking Vietnamese. No matter what happened at the negotiation table, no matter what happened on the battlefield, they just kept coming on, never changing their strategy, never changing their demands, and he had to keep on worrying about fighting them. It was the greatest training process in history; the Americans were training the Vietnamese how to fight, and the Vietnamese were training the Americans on how to negotiate. The Vietnamese were winning both struggles.

It seemed to Washington that they had maneuvered Robert McNamara and Henry Kissinger expertly, conning them politically and militarily until there was no option but nuclear war or defeat. After hobbling the U.S. air forces with artificial rules of engagement, McNamara had supervised the build-up of ground forces to more than half a million men. He avoided winning the war with airpower, and then turned around and poured billions into the fight on the ground. Strange. It was the process of a man for whom all small things can be reduced to logic, if the large ones are ignored. It was left to Kissinger to create the straw-man framework to move them out again. Month by month the combat troops left, dropping from more than half a million to just a handful of support types. In one of the singularly unfortunate catchwords of history, it was the "Vietnamization" of the war.

After years of taking over more and more of the fighting from the reluctant South Vietnamese, propping them up with troops and air support, taking over more and more of their responsibilities as they bombed the bejezus out of their countryside, the Americans were saying, "You got it." At least there were two elements to the flow; as the American troops left, immense quantities of material goods were sent in to stiffen the South Vietnamese fighting capability. Millard was sure most of it would wind up in North Vietnamese storehouses, to be sold around the world to help pay for the war, a preplaced "economic miracle" for the future.

The troops came up with a better catchword than Vietnamization, pithier, to the point. They were "bugging out."

At times Washington thought he was going crazy. He had always been confident in his judgment, but everybody couldn't be wrong, and he was disagreeing with everybody.

Louise hurt him the most. In her early years she had guided him, counseling patience, telling him to wait, to work from within for his people, to accept the good fortune of being on a fast track to flag rank, and to not jeopardize what he could do as a general officer for what he could do on an ad hoc basis on the way. She had seen the path, pointed it out to him, made him believe he could do it. And sometimes it had killed him; he wanted to force issues, to speak out. Now he was on the verge of their joint dream; he was sure he'd make brigadier general in a year or two, and she may have thrown it away in a cheap gesture that meant nothing. She had brought him along and now she had put his career on the line. Worse, even in her apologies, she was demanding that he throw it away, asking him to make an official statement that he wouldn't do any more bombing, even if it meant a court martial. If she really meant it, he might wind up saving his career and throwing away his marriage. He wondered about this Lyle Johnson guy; it was a good ploy if he was hustling Louise, the sensitive black concerned about civil rights and justice, and the hawk nigger killing Asians. And he was there, with her. He couldn't believe that she would be unfaithful, yet there she was, and here he was. Anything was possible with the heat of the war and the heat of the racial strife.

He sat with a half-empty soda in his hand, oblivious to the noise and confusion in the hallway outside his tiny room.

Yeah, it had to be him, that slick pomaded Johnson and his ditty-bopping button-down agitators, that got her going. If he didn't know her better, he'd think she was balling Johnson; everything the man said got repeated in the letters to Wash. He wondered if the kids knew about Lyle; he wondered if they had thoughts on the war. They were in a pressure cooker at school, striving to do well while their peers called out for rebellion.

The crushing problem was that despite his training, despite his love for the Air Force, despite the fact that he wanted to be a pilot more than anything, he basically agreed with Louise. The war was an abomination, a stupidity that never should have been started, and once started should have been ended as soon as possible. It had been the worst of all worlds, an expensive half-ass intervention in the wrong cause in the wrong part of the world. It would have been better to do as the Joint Chiefs wanted in 1965, take out ninety-five essential targets in North Vietnam and blunt the country's power to make war. By now we would have rebuilt it with Marshall Plans, and the North Vietnamese would have won by ballot what they wanted in the first place. They would have been better off to have surrendered and worked from within, it would have been cheaper for everybody. Or we should have surrendered, and let them take what they wanted; they never would have had the vision or the gall to demand the billions that had been poured forth in wasted fuel, ammunition, equipment, and lives. Shit, we should have put them all on pensions, pay every mother fifty thousand a year for life, it would have been easier and cheaper.

He had felt Louise was running too close to the edge; she had given a lecture at Berkeley and not identified herself as the wife of an Air Force colonel, a B-52 pilot at Andersen; somehow the papers had missed it. Now, with the arrest, goodbye Air Force, goodbye helping blacks from the inside.

He thought he had turned her around after the trip to East St. Louis, made her see what he was really thinking. The problem always was that she was right, and he knew it was not the way to go. He agreed with her 100 percent on the moral issues—immoral issues, really—yet he had a larger goal.

God knew it wasn't personal ambition; he was ready to get out now, to teach, to do anything but submit to the soul-shriveling anxiety of doing the best he could at what bothered him most. He couldn't be a good radical; it was not within him. Something had to give, and it was going to be Louise.

Wash shook his head, took a drink of the soda. It was warm, sickeningly sweet.

Brown was almost as big a problem. The crazy bastard was convinced that you could take apart the North Vietnamese defenses on demand with a series of preannounced saturation raids. He was more concerned about public opinion on Vietnamese civil deaths than he was crew deaths.

The problem was it wouldn't work. Brown was talking about fighting in a place he had never been. When Duke had flown his missions in a B-52, he'd flown only against the South. And no matter what Brown thought, the fact was that the North Vietnamese had created the most fantastic ground defense environment in history around Hanoi and Haiphong. The older commanders, who had been there, said it made Berlin or Vienna look easy.

First of all, they picked up on the bombers from takeoff, from the Russian spy ships sitting offshore at Andersen, or from the "plane watchers" holed up in the mountains overlooking U-Tapao. They had the most modern effective radar system in the world with veteran ground controllers. They had hundreds of SA-2 missiles, the flying telephone poles designed especially to bring down bombers. The fighters had been able to deal with them by jinking, flying outside their envelope, but the B-52s were forced to depend upon electronic countermeasures, sending out a massive barrage of jamming interference, for mutual protection. And Brown was insisting that the B-52s attack in measured waves, at precise intervals, with turns off the target carefully calculated to permit the attack to be coordinated with the support aircraft. It would be murder.

Washington knew by now how Brown worked; he took care of both ends, advocating his ideas in the chief's office, where they would come down as instructions, and simultaneously preparing the ground work at Andersen with Washington and God knew who else.

The worst part of that was dealing with Sunderman. He didn't know how Brown did it, but Sunderman was here commanding a B-52 squadron, and according to the Stan Board troops he could just barely get it on and off the ground. Wash had never known how Brown could manipulate the system so well, even though he had profited personally from it. It was a cinch he wouldn't be here, Assistant Deputy Commander for Operations, if it hadn't been for Brown helping all the way from being a B-47 copilot. And now he was going to be the Airborne Commander

535

for the first raid in Linebacker II. He should appreciate Brown—but Brown was wrong and Brown might get him killed.

It was obvious that Sunderman was just doing what he was told, Brown's man at Andersen. Wash always thought that if brains were dynamite, Sunderman couldn't blow his nose. But he parroted whatever Brown said and made it sound convincing. Wash hated to see him, and ignored him as much as it was possible to ignore Sunderman.

Washington lay flat on his back in his sweltering BOQ room. It was the one refuge in the vastly overcrowded base, and he was grateful to have enough rank to get some privacy. Most officers were crowded two or four to a room; the enlisted men were sleeping twelve to a tent in the "Canvas Courts," tent cities, or two hundred to a hot tin hut built for eighty in "Tin City." These were the lucky ones. More were clustered in crowded cots in the base gym, the theater, everywhere. It was a build-up of men and matériel that dwarfed all the previous efforts.

The war had proceeded like the old grade-school game of best knucks, where you traded blows on the arm. He'd been good at that; you made a fist, extended a knuckle, and struck a glancing blow on your opponent's bicep. Then it was his turn. The trick was to keep hitting a little bit harder without anyone getting mad, biting back any tears, and finally to get the other guy to quit. If you got mad and hit too hard too soon, you lost pychologically; if you stayed in, smiling through the tears, you got a bruised muscle, but you were a he-man, what they'd call macho nowadays. The Defense Department had been playing best knucks for years, calling it graduated response, and now everybody was close to crying.

The build-up on Andersen and in Thailand looked like the Americans might finally be getting mad. As the U.S. troops had pulled out, the North Vietnamese regular forces had built up staggering amounts of tanks, artillery, and ammunition handouts in equal proportion from both Russia and China. In March they had rolled across the demilitarized zone, steamed in from Cambodia, and erupted in the central highlands. Then they came from the coastal provinces. It was a four-pronged attack intended to drive the remaining Americans into the sea, using twelve divisions, hundreds of tanks. The goal was clearly Saigon and a unified Communist Vietnam, without regard to any negotiations. The South Vietnamese were overwhelmed.

The U.S. responded with the only thing available, airpower, in an offensive given the presidential football-fan codeword, inebacker. B-52s began pouring into Guam, while F-4s and -105s returned to Thailand. The whole Air Force logistic system strained at the seams as planes, people, and equipment poured back into bases abandoned only months before. The units had left bases fully equipped with radar sets, plumbing, air conditioners, maintenance facilities. They came back to find nothing but concrete and cinderblock; everything else had been stolen and sold within days of the initial departure.

The Navy sealed off North Vietnamese ports with mines. Hanoi was bombed systematically with sophisticated combinations of fighters and electronic-warfare aircraft that were able to do what had not been done before, knock down the vital bridges leading from Hanoi to the South. The Navy mounted an equivalent effort.

By June, the air attack had blunted the offensive. The North Vietnamese came back to the negotiating table in Paris, and by October Linebacker was over, and, according to Kissinger, "Peace" was "at hand."

In the isolation of his room, Washington wondered why no one saw it. The North Vietnamese were at the table because they had been beaten; when they felt they could win, they'd leave the table. They left in late November.

Now Linebacker II was coming, and it looked like Duke had prevailed. It was to be a textbook exercise, cells of three B-52s bombing in waves, protecting each other, maintaining formation no matter what happened with the SAMs.

Washington knew what would happen with the SAMs. The waves were to be separated by four or five hours each; Washington knew just enough time for the hustling professional North Vietnamese missile crews to rearm and move them, tuning to the established routes of the predictable, methodical Americans, to do all the things they had been trained to do so well in this maddest of wars.

There was going to be plenty of support—fighters, the SAM-suppressing Wild Weasels, F-105s and F-4s, electronic countermeasure airplanes—everything, but it would be up to the B-52s, the BUFFS, to win or lose the ball game. If the North Vietnamese could knock down five or ten airplanes in each raid, the war was over. If they couldn't, the war was over. In the first instance, they got a clear-cut victory and the Americans suffered overwhelming humiliation. In the second, they would get bombed to bits, but still be able to win at the negotiating table and the Americans would get a transparent face saving.

537

Well, it was late December, and they were going to give them best knucks in earnest.

He went to his desk, pulled out the BX stationery.

Louise,

I can't write all I want to say. I can't believe your last letter. My wife, arrested! What were you thinking of? Doesn't our family, my name, my career mean anything to you?

It's hard for me to know what to do. We've always agreed on everything in the past, and you know that mostly I agree with you now. I wouldn't be where I am today if I hadn't agreed with you, listened to you, believed in you.

But this has to stop. I've come to a decision, and you are going to have to listen.

This will be a funny letter for me, for there won't be any love stuff in it, no practical stuff, nor any messages to the kids.

I'm sitting here with a bone in my throat. I've got to do something I don't believe in, because I believe in something else more. I believe I can help blacks, help everybody, by getting a senior command. I could be the first black three star, maybe the first black four star, maybe Chief of Staff. If you go to jail, it's all over. If I sound off about the bombing, it's all over. Do you want that? Do you want our kids to go to state schools if they are lucky instead of being able to send them wherever we want?

I want you to stop being active in the rights movement right now. I'm not asking you, I'm telling you. Stop today, as soon as you get this. If anybody gives you any static—and I mean that Johnson guy—tell him I'll come back and deal with him personally and physically. I'm not kidding. You know I'm not.

When I get back, we can argue about it. You know I love you. Kiss the kids for me, pet the dogs, but stop.

I do love you. Trust me.

XXXOOO

Wash.

P.S. Honey are you okay? Did they hurt you? I'll be back home soon and you can tell me all about it. W.

He folded the letter and put it in an envelope, addressed it, and put it in his pocket to mail at the BOQ desk. Then he reached in the drawer and pulled out another letter to Louise, already addressed and sealed. There was a note attached to it, saying "To be mailed in the event of my death. Col. Millard Washington." There was some love stuff and some practical stuff and some stuff for the kids in this one. He propped it up against the G.I. table lamp and left for the briefing.

The island hummed and vibrated. There were 155 B-52s on the ramp; the jokesters said ten had to be kept taxiing at all times, because they were out of parking places. All the rules were being varied to accommodate; they had created "Charlie Tower" for the Wing Deputy Commander for Operations to supervise the field, to smooth out irregularities, to give instructions to crews in trouble. Washington had excelled at this, really enjoyed it. It was a mental challenge to juggle the whereabouts of one hundred airplanes on the ground and another fifty in the air, keep them all fueled, maintained, bombed up, analyze their problems, but most of all extend confidence to the crews. He was helped by experienced commanders, pilots, and enlisted men to analyze difficulties on the spot, and to keep everything moving. They even had a long line back to Wichita, at the Boeing plant where Larry Lee could draw on the Boeing resources to solve any emergency.

In the control center there was a tradition that gave him some problems. Besides the instructor pilots there to advise the crews, there were two maintenance officers, one to hustle help to anybody needing maintenance, called "Uncle Ned," and the other directing the taxi and towing operations—called "Uncle Tom." They laughed about it only once with Washington; he'd come a long way since the "Jig was up."

Charlie Tower had tougher decisions to make because greater risks were being taken. The "Press On" rules were strict: if you could get over the target and drop your bombs, you went on, no matter if the radar was out, or you had to shut down some engines. If you could keep formation in the cell, you went on. The bombers were too interdependent for electronic countermeasure coverage to be allowed to split up.

The rules were tough on the crews, for they forced them to violate the basic safety concepts they'd learned over the years. Worse, they were a departure from common-sense tactics.

He dressed quickly, went down to the briefing room. The big hall was filled with battered furniture, the beige-painted walls turned a sickly yellow-gray from fluorescents and cigarette smoke. The crews were excited. Half of them expected to be told they were going home; the other half expected to be going north.

Washington could tell who thought what by the way they acted, by their small talk. The guys going home were happy and laughing, pulling the horseplay that goes on in locker rooms after the big game. The guys going north were serious, quiet, not talking, checking their watches every five minutes.

There was a rustle of expectant noise, muted joking, then silence as the briefing officer, Col. Jerry Robinson, walked across the little stage to the podium. He was direct, but the effect was straight out of Hollywood. "Gentlemen, your target for tonight is Hanoi."

Washington watched the group coalesce; home was out, they all became quiet. Harvey Sunderman, looking worried but not surprised, winked at him.

The instructions were explicit; if the crews didn't have the target specifically identified, they were not to drop. The major concern of headquarters was not to hit civil targets.

The main concern of the crews was evenly divided between the MiGs and the SAMs. The mission itself was relatively simple, once the refueling had taken place; it was go in, drop, turn, and exit. It looked easy on paper. Washington knew it would be a disaster.

Washington was in Bronze Two, the second aircraft of the first three-plane cell off. The BUFFs—Big Ugly Fat Fuckers to the crews, Big Ugly Fat Fellows to the press—creaked and groaned like ancient circus elephants, angling down along the taxi-ways. They were crowded nose to tail, lights winking, wings drooping under the weight of fuel and bombs, the tip gears castering as the airplanes turned. There was a deafening roar of engines accelerating, brakes squealing, and the endless clanking of tired metal. Unable to back up, barely able to turn, the whole B-52 formation was as vulnerable to a flat tire as the evening commuters were to an accident on a crowded city beltway.

Andersen's runway was swaybacked, with a hump in the middle, and Washington agonized at the slow acceleration of the four-hundred-fifty-thousand-pound plane. The first three planes were off; twenty-three more were to follow. At U-Tapao a similar formation was getting ready; all Southeast Asia was launching, EB-66s, F-4s, F-105s, F-111s, EC-121Ts, the whole expensive, complex, sophisticated gearing required to drop bombs and not be slaughtered by SAMs. And the rescue units tuned up their C-130s and Jolly Green choppers, to harvest the emergencies. The Navy was mounting a parallel effort in concert with them.

If Washington forced himself to look at it technically, it was

540

uperb, a miracle of organization and improvisation. Morally it educed to the factor that Louise burned in his brain: he was a lack man going out to kill yellow men. He was an American, nd America knew better than this; it gave him strange comfort o know that he was as wrong for being an American as for being lack.

And he was as black as the Pacific night through which they lew. There was no moon, and a thin high cirrus obscured the tars. There was no sense of motion forward, only a rocking ibration that hammered them toward sleep despite the anxiety.

The motion became apparent with the first sight of the lights f the KC-135s. They had to refuel before the strike. The tankers rbited, booms dangling, a covey of passive cock pheasants vaiting to cover the hen bombers. The tankers were picked up n radar first, then visually, their lights initially an elusive vinking dot in the distance, then becoming arbiters of space and ixers of time as the bombers drew near. The refueling brought he first crisis. His copilot was a young captain, Phil Edwards, all, lean, terribly eager, always wanting to hand fly the airplane. Ie did a good job on the refueling but when they dropped off he boom they were twenty thousand pounds short, exactly the eserve required when they were back over Guam. There must ave been a foul-up on the tanker loads. In peacetime it would ave meant an abort.

Washington was the airborne commander; he would decide. The decision was easy, foreshadowed, inevitable. It was simply Press On. They would worry about fuel when they got back. If hey got back. When they got back.

He was glad they were flying a D model; it was tough on the ail gunner, stuck way back at the end of the fuselage, but he :ould keep watch on the MiGs better back there. And the D had a lot better electronic countermeasures. It didn't have the G nodel's range, and you had to refuel more often, but it was afer.

They droned on in silence until they hit the entry point for he target area. They were exactly in position, exactly on time, to he second. The first SAMs were already in view, first suffusing he low clouds with an orange-red hue, then roman-candling up n the distance at the fighter bombers sent in to suppress them.

Wash wondered at the insanity that brought this precise and killed armada through thousands of miles of airspace to come ogether against targets that in another war would probably have been ignored. The same insanity infected the ground; a starving people were forced to fight a lifetime for an imported doctrine. Both sides did it well.

All the old movie thoughts came into his head. "Enemy coast ahead," "One of our aircraft is missing," "Coming in on a wing and a prayer." At the briefing earlier he had noticed that no one skipped the benediction, no one acted bored. He made a last quiet check of the crew. Then they were on the bomb run.

It was as they had done a thousand times before, on practice runs and in the eternal paddy-cratering combat in South Vietnam. Except this night erupted in a cloud of SAMs. The ground was alive with the yellow smoke of their firing. Washington could hear the Electronic Warfare Officer, Capt. Eddie Sachs, mumbling into the interphone with clinical detachment, noting the firings, the uplinks, the signals to the missiles, the downlinks, the signals back. He had only done it in practice before, and was looking at the signals with a curious professional interest.

He called Washington on the intercom. "Skipper, they've fired three—no four—SAMs at us."

Shit. Washington flew straight and level. "Radar, how far out are we?"

"Ten seconds, skipper . . . five, four, three, two, one. Bombs away. Start your turn . . . now, AC."

Washington reefed the B-52 over, not seeing the other two B-52s in his cell, knowing they were there, knowing if they didn't turn precisely as he did they would merge in an orange-black ball that spelled death for them all.

The first SAM tracked to their left; the intercom flooded with chatter.

Edwards called "I've got a SAM!"

"EW has an uplink!"

"Roger, uplink."

"Okay, he's gone, but I got another uplink."

Edwards' voice went up a notch: "SAM, visual SAM, two o'clock. Looks like a goddamn silver doughnut."

Then the sky erupted in front of them. They could see a B-52 illuminated from the flames in its belly, suddenly going much slower, its wings folding up in resignation. There was a violent explosion.

"Holy Christ, Bronze One just blew up."

"EW, uplink."

"Look out your window, skipper, there's a SAM."

Washington turned in time to see the SAM, a huge thirty-five-foot-long, five-thousand-pound monster, explode, sending shrapnel the length of the B-52. The airplane depressurized in a quick white mist.

Washington scanned the instruments; the one and two engine fire lights were on, the power was bleeding off. He pulled the fire buttons, shut down one and two. He watched the airspeed slow down, edged the other throttles forward.

"Phil, you okay?"

"Rog."

"Get a crew report."

"Rog. Crew report."

"Nav and radar okay, but the equipment's out. I'll try to get it back on line. Let me know where you want to go, and I'll get you a heading."

"EW okay; we must have flown out of range; no uplinks."

The gunner Bill Pupek's slow drawl came on. "Skipper, they winged me; I got some shrapnel in the forearm, and I'm bleeding a little, not bad. But it sounded to me like we took hits along the whole left side. I don't see any flames."

"Roger, keep me posted on how you're feeling. Be sure to stay on oxygen. Everybody check their oxygen. We've lost pressure. Phil, check the tanks, see how we are on fuel."

There was a silence as everyone checked their gear, their ejection seats. If there was a fire burning aft in the fuel cells they might not know it till it blew up.

"Nav, give me a course for Da Nang; if we are still okay there, we'll see if we want to go to U-Tapao."

"Roger, pick up a heading of one forty; I'm going to have to come up and see if I can get some position. Can you contact Red Crown?"

"Not yet; I want to get the hell out of MiG country before I tell anybody we got problems."

The airplane stabilized, flew well on six engines. Over Da Nang the plane looked okay; they hadn't lost any fuel to speak of and Wash decided to go on to U-T for maintenance. He'd try to get a ride back to Andersen for the mission the following day.

Washington had to hold at altitude at U-Tapao for a local emergency. They circled aimlessly, desperately tired, anxious to get on the ground while waiting for one of the local birds. It had been shot up and was almost out of fuel. When they landed they were silent and morose, nerves shot.

The debriefing officer told them there was a KC-135 scheduled for a dawn takeoff back to Andersen. In a GI mess hall looking not too different from the Birmingham airport restaurant, Wash watched them wolf down ham and eggs. They waited in the Young Tiger briefing room, spread out on benches and the floor, until it was time to go out to the KC-135. It was with relief that they crawled into the back of the tanker. They shoved chutes and B-4 bags together and slept all the way home to Andersen.

Wash walked into a well of bitterness when he went to the command center. The squadron commanders, all but Harvey Sunderman, were demanding a change in tactics to give freedom for the bombers to maneuver on the run in to the target from the initial point. Sunderman was insisting that the mutual electronic countermeasure coverage was the only thing that counted, mouthing Brown's ideas. Washington couldn't believe it; the man was putting his life on the line. Later he heard that Sunderman had threatened his crews with court martial if they broke the cell integrity to evade SAMs.

The losses had been high; two B-52Gs from Andersen and a D model from U-T had gone in; Washington's and one other D model from Andersen had been extensively damaged and landed at U-T.

It was tougher than combat for Wash to sit in the command post on the second night, listening to the chaotic reports. The first wave of bombers, twelve D models and nine Gs from Andersen, repeated the route and tactics exactly, and the Vietnamese were ready, mixing SAMs and heavy 100 mm anti-aircraft guns. The flak was thick, but not as accurate as on the previous night, and by a miracle, they all got through.

So did the second and third waves. Wash watched Sunderman smirk; it was a standoff on the tactics. The first night three losses, the second night none.

The frag order came down for the third day: same tactics. Washington couldn't believe it. The same routes in, the same cell formations, the same turns off the target. And Sunderman was playing the future general role, telling everybody what an iron ass he was, how he made damn sure his troops were adhering to doctrine.

"Hey, Harvey, knock that shit off. Brown talks to me most nights, too, and I know where you're getting that stuff."

"Yeah, and he knows you're stabbing him in the back, Washington. I think it's pretty shitty for a guy like you to take everything that Brown handed you, and then the first chance you get you stick it to him."

"Look, Sunderman, this is no goddamn party; there's a lot of people can get killed up there, and I'm one and you're one. Brown's back in the goddamn Pentagon. He did his flying over South Vietnam; if I stuck him in the lead airplane tonight he'd change his tactics pretty fast."

Wash felt foolish; maybe he was crazy. Everybody couldn't be wrong everytime. "Sorry, Harve; we got to do it tomorrow; maybe we'll find out who's right."

Sunderman smiled, stuck out his hand. It was wet with sweat.

The third day had all the tedium of the first for Washington. The decision had been made to go with the same tactics, and the routes were almost identical. It was handing a battle to the enemy for no reason. The only good news was some procedures worked out in the past forty-eight hours in Florida, using captured Russian equipment, which promised to do a better job of jamming the SAMs.

The fatigue was cumulative. Washington was glad to let Edwards fly, insisting that he use the autopilot to avoid wearing himself out. The crew was quiet; only the new tail gunner, Pete Parmley, came on the line once in a while, betraying his nervousness with quips, mostly bad quips.

The mission went effortlessly until they'd crossed over the coast. Edwards leaned over and grabbed his arm, pointed out to the eleven o'clock position.

"Jesus Christ: there's a MiG 21 flying formation with us."

Washington blinked; a beautiful little MiG was sitting just off their wing, lights off, a helmet glistening in the cockpit.

"What's he doing?"

"Don't know, maybe giving our course and airspeed to the ground. Altitude too. Jesus, I hope he hasn't got any Atolls."

Parmley came on. "Speed up, skipper, and let me shoot at that doll."

"Jeez, don't make him mad."

The MiG whipped up on a wing and was gone. They were almost at the initial point.

Washington pressed the intercom. "What kind of activity do you have, EW?"

"Nothing, skipper; maybe they are out of SAMs. They shot enough of them off the last two nights."

Wash wondered what Sunderman was doing; he was in the lead plane in the cell behind them. Well, Brown would hear about the MiG tomorrow.

Halfway into the target a forest of SAMs appeared, launched from the left and right in pairs.

"EW, any signals?"

"No, skipper; they are shotgunning those things up our ass."

Washington felt a clammy fear; the Vietnamese weren't playing by rote. The jamming must have been effective, so they were launching them cold. Pretty clever.

The SAMs detonated; the sky was smeared with wild yellows and reds laced with white and black. There was a rattle along the fuselage.

Another pair of SAMs appeared to the left. Washington moved the airplane left, skidding as much as banking; the SAMs seemed to respond. Neither exploded.

"Radar, give me a signal so I can get wings level before we drop."

"Roger, we're about fifteen seconds out."

Washington steadied the B-52, planted his foot on the rudder, kept the ball in the center. His PDI centered.

"Bombs away."

Parmley's voice came on. "Skipper, they got a hit on the lead B-52 behind us. Looks like they blew away the starboard outer wing. He's sliding off."

Sunderman was flying Yellow Three.

Sunderman had seen no MiGs; he was sure the enemy was out of SAMs when the outer part of his right wing was blown off.

He grabbed the wheel, forced it to the left, popped the spoilers to slow down, retarded the power on the left, desperate to halt the relentless turning. The airplane was dying, its systems trembling and jerking like a mortally wounded animal, bleeding fuel and hydraulics, filling with smoke and a smell of death. The stricken B-52 picked up twenty, then forty degrees of bank.

"AC, this is NAV; we got a fire in the forward fuel cell. We better get out of this mother."

"Roger." Sunderman reached up and hit the abandon-aircraft switch; the red light glowed and the bell clanged.

There was a boom as the navigator ejected; a swirl of air rushed past him filled with maps and debris. The instrument-panel lights glowed and darkened. A snapshot flashed through Sunderman's mind of an old film of the *Titanic* going under, electrical systems failing.

He heard the next three seats fire, as the other crewmen left, short cannon puffs and more shrieks of wind. He looked at Bell, his copilot, who nodded, moved his hands on the ejection-seat handles. Bell disappeared upward in a blur of smoke and wind, hurled outward into the cold hostile night. The hatch above his seat yawned in open invitation.

Sunderman dropped his hands to the ejection-seat handles, those red-and-yellow-striped agents of escape. Freed of the control pressures, the airplane rolled violently. He pulled the handles. Nothing. He screamed, "Oh Mother of Christ," pulled the handles again, squeezed the triggers. Were his seat safing pins in? He pulled again, the airplane was breaking up, he was almost inverted. Nothing. Sunderman slipped his seat belt and safety harness, scrambling to reach over and pull himself up, fling himself out of the copilot's vacant hatchway, now somehow below him. The wings had parted, the fuselage was falling inverted in a fire-shredding arc to the ground. G forces tugged him, bound him to his seat. He was straining on the throttles trying to pull himself upright when the airplane hit, smearing a cascade of fire down the rugged karst hills.

The command post was a demented morgue, small groups of doleful people talking quietly, others running wildly with papers in their hands; the low undertone of talk was punctuated with ringing phones, teletype clatter. The glistening yellow fluorescent light that never varied, night or day, gave everyone a dead man's pallor.

Washington saw Colonel Robinson. "How bad was it, Robby?"

"Wash, we're on our ass. We may cut and run after this. Everybody's standing by to hear what CINCSAC decides; the JCS has handed it to him. We lost four Gs and two Ds; one D is out from battle damage. There's other minor damage. We had two hundred twenty confirmed SAM reports, and there were MiGs out there too."

The big black man shuddered. Six airplanes; thirty-six men dead or injured or captured; thirty-six families to be tortured with either certain knowledge or uncertain fear. Six airplanes out of seventy attacking, almost 10 percent; it was worse than Schweinfurt on a percentage basis.

The problem had largely been with the G models; they simply didn't have the electronic countermeasure capability necessary to penetrate as a cell. This is where people who thought like Brown had been most wrong; they used the older D model as a basis, and it simply didn't work.

An assessment was going on of morale and matériel; the number of SAMs fired had fooled everyone; the North Vietnamese were supposed to be running low on them. And the way they were fired, without the customary radar signals, was troubling, too.

Wash knew that the wires were burning up between the command post, SAC headquarters, and the Pentagon; the finger was being put on John Meyer to make the decision. He was Commander in Chief of SAC and he would earn a career salary with a single decision. If he decided to press on, and the other batch of crews was lost, he would have personally lost the war, become the sacrificial target that everyone, the public, the Congress, the Air Force, could turn on. If he didn't, he lost the negotiations, to be second-guessed by everyone through history.

Air Force doctrine said you could never turn back a determined air attack; it also had a history of never turning back because of enemy action. Meyer took the unprecedented step of asking the opinion of every man in his command post, then decided himself. The decision was Press On.

The Andersen B-52s had farther to fly than those at U-Tapao, and the original plan had called for a stand-down from operations over Hanoi on the fourth day of combat. It was needed relief.

The D models from U-Tapao kept up the pressure and developed new tactics. Andersen crews operated in the South. Both bases welcomed the Christmas Day rest, though some crews were worried that the North Vietnamese would use the respite to replenish the SAM site inventories. The base was a confused mixture of pretend Christmas cheer and genuine sadness.

On December 26 there was a massive strike.

Wash and his crew rode out in silence to the drooped-wing D model.

Whalen got out, stretched, looked up at the tall tail; it was aircraft 55-681.

"Colonel Washington, was this old turkey built in 1955?"

"That's when the contract was let; probably didn't get delivered until '57."

"Jesus, I was only four years old when it was built; I sure hope it holds together tonight."

They preflighted in silence, rolled through the long taxi procedures, finally got rid of the ground, bored on toward the refueling. Washington felt strangely content. The briefing tonight had been totally different, was what it should have been the first night. They were going to put 120 B-52s over Hanoi and Haiphong at virtually the same instant. The bombing was going to be compressed into a single lightning stroke.

The North Vietnamese knew as always that they were coming. But they didn't know the routes in, nor the intricate patterns that

548

would weave them in criss-crossing elements over the ten targets at one moment.

There was early traffic from the support aircraft; more than one hundred fighter bombers and electronic-warfare aircraft were preceding them to the target, and would be on stand-by later, to be ready to escort out anybody who got hit.

The timing was controlled by a maze of courses just prior to crossing the coastline; the navigators could slide the BUFFS around a series of arcs that saved or lost time as necessary to put them on the coastline, inbound on time.

Washington could hear Red Crown calling out SAM and MiG warnings to the friendly aircraft over Haiphong. He hoped they would divert attention from the G models assigned to hit the port city. Only Ds would be bombing Hanoi.

"Skipper, nav."

"Roger, nav, go ahead."

"Skipper, we got hundred-mile-per-hour headwinds, smack on the nose. The SAMs will love us tonight."

Wash hammered the center of the control column with his gloved hand. Damn; their groundspeed would be down to no more than three hundred knots, turning them into sitting ducks.

Ahead the missile firings raged. It was just like watching for midairs with the little Cessnas flying over Los Angeles; if the missile seemed to move across the windscreen, it was no threat. If it seemed locked in one position, it was headed right at you.

"I.P., skipper; we are about a minute out."

"Roger."

"Colonel, I got four, no six, SAMs, headed right at us."

"AC, this is gunner; I got three coming back here."

Wash flew on. There was no way to outjink nine of them.

Edwards's voiced cracked a little. "I have three more on this side."

Wash listened to the final checklists going on; it sounded like a stateside bomb run. It was hell to be sitting in the belly of the beast, unable to see out, nothing but radar sets and red lights, and people upstairs counting SAMs over you.

The cockpit lit up; it was the yellow flame from a SAM that passed by, fifty feet away. Its proximity fuse must have failed; if it had worked they'd be dead now.

"Ten seconds, skipper, straight and level."

"Roger."

"Bombs away."

Wash flew on. The SAMs had somehow missed.

He heard Amber Three transmit.

"Amber Three is about five seconds from bombs away. We are going to take a SAM. Adios."

Edwards looked over in dismay. "You hear that?"

Wash nodded; on their right there was a red-orange blossoming of fire. It must have been Amber Three. A burst of beepers verified that some had gotten out.

The trip back to Andersen was quiet. Very quiet.

Wash's crew stood down the next night; there were two losses, but the indications were that the North Vietnamese were losing cohesion. There were far fewer SAM firings. Morale picked up visibly.

The last trip was a piece of cake. The SAMs had been beaten, suppressed, as Lee had called for Pope to be. Wash felt the old surges of guilt as sixty B-52s ranged over Hanoi and Haiphong virtually without opposition. In eleven days, the B-52s had flown 729 missions against twenty-nine targets; the North Vietnamese had fired more than twelve hundred SAMs and brought down fifteen airplanes. The loss rate was about 2 percent, acceptable for everyone but the crews involved. And the North Vietnamese came back to the negotiations. This time, peace, the very peace the North Vietnamese had always sought on the terms in which they sought it, was truly at hand.

49

July—December 1972
Hanoi
Vietnam

Nothing he had ever heard, nothing he had ever imagined, had prepared him for the insistent consistency of the pain. Rabbit had tied the torture ropes in tight half hitches about his arm, from wrist to shoulder, running in three-inch intervals like a native necklace. Each time a loop was made, the bastard stood on his arm, cinched up the ropes, bulging the thinning muscle and flesh into pomegranate-colored welts. He wrapped the flesh in the dirty, bloody rope as if he were sending a package that had to arrive intact. When both arms were bound, Rabbit had jerked them elbow-to-elbow, standing on Ed's back to pull them together, binding them again from shoulder to elbow.

Novack had vomited when his left shoulder was pulled out of its socket; the nexus of the agony was in his chestbone, pointing through the skin like an evil adam's apple, about to rupture.

Rabbit had jerked him around, a side of beef on a string, and tied his legs in the same vicious loops, ankle to knee. Another rope, running from his ankles, was looped around his neck, twisting him backward in an arch of agony. If he relaxed his self-inflicted arch for a moment, the rope ground into his throat, choking him.

He had a semi-detached vision of himself as Rabbit worked to get his package right. Novack could see himself, bound and bleeding, Rabbit working seriously, never changing expression, pulling, punching, making sure that every spot was covered. But he was there too, on the floor, contorted with agony, smeared with his tears and vomit, suffused with pain and fear.

He wanted to pass out, thought that he must at any moment, but the high tide of pain endured, rending him everywhere, never slackening, not even, after a point, increasing in intensity, just a sheer hot flame of searing agony.

He tried to pray, couldn't, tried to think of his parents, couldn't. The only person who would stay in his mind was Harry Fish, and he knew Harry Fish only through the abrupt tales told in code by Dick Kaplan. He thought of Fish because Fish, broken and sick already, had died like this. And he would too, unless something was done.

There were moments when he almost lost consciousness; his back would relax and the rope would press into his throat, gagging him back to the full measure of the pain.

In the end, he submitted. He agreed to talk. Rabbit walked out of the room in triumph, and two guards came in to untie him. They could not; they had to cut him free, the blunt edge of their knives bursting open the blood-welled bunches of flesh as they cut upward on the ropes.

They took him back to his cell and threw him on the floor. He lay there, rubbing his fingers first to get feeling so that he could massage the pain. He drank half of his water in a single gulp, waited, vomited it up. Then he waited to take the rest, sip by sip.

In a moment he heard the knocking from Kaplan's wall. He didn't have the strength to reply. Kaplan was knocking in the primitive tap code, where one tap followed by another stood for A, five taps followed by five taps stood for Z. He heard U OK tapped, wished he could answer. He fell asleep on the floor, in a pretzel position. When he woke he couldn't move, had to resort to the finger rubbing, then massage again. Eventually he got to the primitive shelf that served as a bed and wrapped himself in the thin cotton sheet that served as a blanket. It was strange that as soon as he agreed to talk, they brought him to the cell and left him alone. Now he knew why. The anticipation of repeating the rope torture was almost as bad as suffering it; they knew the waiting, the remembering, would work to soften him up.

Novack had never been able to determine if they knew he was part of the Than Binh raid or not; the words were about the only thing he might have understood in Vietnamese, and he'd never heard it mentioned. When they interrogated him, they asked him standard questions about airfield location, units, strengths.

When they came he was going to give them all they wanted to know about unit and locations, all made up, because he scarcely knew more than that he had been at Ubon, with the Cougars. The wreckage of the F-4 had probably thrown them off that trail, because it still had no unit markings, just the standard USAF markings it had had at Eglin.

The guards took him to a tiny interrogation room. Elephant Ears was the interrogator, a squat, swarthy man with large wens and huge ears.

It started routinely. Novack gave his name, rank, and serial number, declined to answer further.

Elephant Ears looked at him. "We know you were in an F-4. We know you took off from Ubon. We know you weren't the pilot. And we know how to make you talk." He slapped the mass of ropes on the table; bloodstained and matted with flesh and vomit, it was the set used on him yesterday.

"You're right on all four statements."

"What?"

"Yes, I took off from Ubon, yes it was an F-4, no I'm not the pilot, and yes the ropes will make me talk."

The interrogator looked at him. "Here is a tablet and some pencils. Here is a list of questions. Take the first question, and answer it. Take as many lines or pages to answer as you want. Then take the second question, and so on. Understand?"

"I understand, but I don't think I can write. You dislocated my shoulder yesterday, and my hands were tortured. I need medical treatment. I'll write, but I need medical treatment first."

Elephant Ears left the room, shouted in Vietnamese.

In a moment two orderlies came in and hustled Novack over to the Las Vegas Area of Hoa Lo prison, the Hanoi Hilton that he had never expected to see. They took him into the medic

552

oom, helped him strip out of the thin pajama-style uniform. He vas herded into the showers, handed a rough towel and a chip of rown soap. The December-cold water felt like heaven. He ouldn't bend to soap all over, but he reached as far as he could, etting the water sluice off the dirt and blood.

The guards kept agitating him to hurry, so he turned his face o the shower for one last shock of cold water, then stepped out. le couldn't towel himself off, either, and one guard finally took ity, grabbed the towel, and roughly dried his back. Without Iressing they herded him into the medic's room and had him lie Iown on the rickety table.

A man in an officer's uniform prodded him with an extended inger; the pain in the shoulder area was incredible. The medic poke to the guards, who grabbed his body. The medic took his irm, pulled, and somehow the shoulder seemed to slip back into ts socket.

He handed him an envelope; inside was a single pill, plainly narked Bayer. The medic motioned to his mouth; Novack asked or water. It seemed to cut a cord of violence in the man; he wept his hand forward, slapping Novack's face, knocking the ispirin into the corner.

Without another word, they took him back into the cell.

That night, Kaplan called again, and Novack was able to eply. Kaplan was a virtuoso with the code; he'd been at it for a ong time, and he could tap more fluently than he could speak. Novack could receive fairly well, but it took him a long time to ransmit.

Kaplan's boyish enthusiasm for life came through even in the orimitive code; he had sustained Fish for almost a year before the orture had combined with his unhealed ejection injuries to carry him away. He had sustained himself for another four, and 1ow he was prepared to sustain Ed.

He had told Ed the full story of Fish's torture and death not to frighten him, but to prepare him. Fish had spent almost a year recovering from the effects of the ejection, with Kaplan taking almost that long to get himself mobile again. Then Harry had uffered a nervous decline, had talked about suicide. The Viet-1amese had ignored them both, Fish probably because he was so 1ear death so long, Kaplan because he served as Fish's nurse.

When they had healed a little, though, the torture started, the standard beatings, the "pipe walking" where they would lay a found two-inch pipe, a yard long, over their shins, and standing on it, walk it up and down their legs. Finally, they had used the

553

ropes on Harry, and he had died, simply ruptured internally and died on the spot, blood welling out of his mouth and rectum. A husk of a man.

In the imponderable way of the Vietnamese, they had not done the same to Kaplan. He was large, and they might not have wished to get that close to him, even when he was tied. Something intimidated them, something kept them from it.

That night Novack was moved to another cell; it was larger, and there were three men in it, Kaplan, and two others. He sensed it was Kaplan immediately, there was something in his presence even though he knew him only by the tap code. The other two men were Navy pilots, one an F-8 driver named Jerry Gonzalez, the other an A-4 pilot named Wendel Buckley.

They were formally forbidden to speak, but conversed in low tones. The two Navy men had been in prison since 1969; Novack felt like a freshman.

Kaplan whispered to Gonzalez, "Why do you think they moved us?"

"Either they have a lot more captives coming in, or they are having some sort of visit from the Red Cross, and don't want to show that we were in solitary. Maybe it'll be a TV crew, or Jane Fonda coming to blast us."

Buckley had been badly injured on ejection; the treatment had been poor, and he had a terrible slur in his voice. "Thurr scurred; I cantell. Like lasApril."

The Americans had bombed Hanoi in late April, starting a worldwide furor, giving the inmates of the Hanoi Hilton a lift.

"What, scared? Christ I hope so; I'd like to scare them with an F-8 one more time."

After supper they were lying on the four shelves, no longer talking. Suddenly the lights went out and Hanoi's air raid sirens began to shriek.

"Thusis it." Buckley moved upright, shot a thumbs-up.

Outside the jail, the sky went phosphorescent white; there was a pattern of noise that sounded like an endless train going off a cliff, one tremendous series of explosions following another. They couldn't hear any aircraft sounds, just the pounding anti-aircraft artillery, and occasionally the whooshing takeoff of a SAM missile.

Buckley was counting "Morne hundred in a row; got to be B-52s!"

In twenty minutes it was all over; the sky had changed from white to grayish red and black, and from all quadrants of the city could be heard the boom of secondary explosions.

The guard force was paraded and extra weapons issued. An elderly Vietnamese officer stood on a porch and exhorted them harshly, shrilly.

It began again, precisely one hour later. Cheers ringed the prison yard; the guards were unusually restrained and polite.

The next day, gruel that passed for breakfast came without comment; the air raids started again, and they could see from the sharp upward angle their single window allowed them that these were Air Force and Navy fighter bombers, F-105s and F-4s, pounding in from every angle.

Elephant Ears did not come back to interrogate Novack. It was barely perceptible, but rations got better; rice and greens mostly. A second blanket was issued.

The B-52s came back for the next seven nights, never seen, the whistling of their jets lost in the percussion rumbles of the bomb trails. Discipline relaxed in the camp; the prisoners talked effortlessly in front of the guards, who seemed increasingly stressed.

There was a change in the noise level; the bombers came in more concentrated formations, and there was less flak and no SAMs being fired. On the sixth night they came, and Rabbit suddenly appeared in the compound. He came straight to their cell, walked in the middle of the room, stood there defiantly. "They will not bomb here," he said.

Novack looked at Kaplan; they could take Rabbit, kill him while the bombing was going on. Then he decided against it. Just having him here was victory enough. Ed decided that he would live through this, no matter what it took. If Kaplan could go five years, he could go five and then another five. But if the B-52s kept coming, maybe he wouldn't have to.

50

5 October 1973
Sebat Airfield
Israel

The bitter hot desert wind swept across the airfield. Jim Garvey sat silently in the jeep as it pulled around the well-secured airbase perimeter. The last time he had tasted this wind had been seventeen years before, when he had come screaming in to land from fifteen feet off the deck, heart in his mouth and

555

Egyptian telephone wire wrapped around his Mustang's tail. He'd come home from that war sick and discouraged; in one of the greatest turkey shoots in history, he had one lousy kill.

There weren't any old F-51s parked here today. Garvey counted a half dozen McDonnell Douglas F-4Es spotted in camouflaged revetments, sandbags stacked well up each side. Two more Phantoms sat in corrugated iron demi-hangars just off the end of the dusty runway. Those two were apparently cocked and ready. Helmets were slung on the canopies, oxygen hoses dangling down the fuselages, with bare-backed ground crewmen fussing under the wings with rockets.

"My God," Garvey groaned into the wind, "everything changes, and nothing changes."

"Sir?" The bronzed young Israeli lieutenant was unfailingly correct, but Garvey could tell from the moment he'd saluted him at the door of the Transall that he wasn't too happy to be detailed as his escort officer. Tough.

"Sorry, Lieutenant. Just musing."

"Sir." It was apparently the Israeli kid's word for all occasions. Jim ruefully recalled that he had been much different when he was younger. Full of curiosity, if he'd been escorting some old crock from a distant war around the base, he'd have pumped him for all the war stories he could. But USAF security was always lax, while the Israelis were fiercely protective. God knows they needed to be. Without that ferocity, this young officer— Bodasky, his name was—would probably never have been born.

The jeep ground to a stop before a small cantonment of tents, aligned with military regularity, but with good spacing between them; just as veteran combat troops marched with good interval on the road for protection, so the Israeli air force had learned to protect itself on the ground. The tent flaps were open to gain whatever breeze there might be to mitigate the Sinai heat. Even the lieutenant's creased khakis were sweat-ringed and dusty, but Garvey felt embarrassed about his own dirty flying suit and beat up B-4 bag. The canvas and zippered bag was a survivor of three wars. Inside it were half a dozen changes of underwear, some socks and handkerchiefs, and a single khaki uniform. The rest of the space was bulging with his personal flying equipment: helmet, oxygen mask, G suit, the works.

His thoughts ran back to Miriam and another war; he'd been so proud to be fighting for Israel, he had a half-Jewish child. What must Rachel think of him, think of the Air Force, with him bouncing from war to war, continent to continent.

The Air Force wanted him to compare the Israeli capability with his recent experience in Nam. It made sense to the Air Force, even if it forced him farther away from his daughter.

"Sir, this is Colonel Levy's tent. I'll announce you." Bodasky started forward but Garvey grabbed him by the shoulder and spun him around. "You stand at ease, Lieutenant. I'm going to announce myself."

Bodasky looked as if he were going to swing, but stopped and followed him into the tent. Frowning, he snapped the flap loose on his pistol, not knowing what to expect from the American.

"Levy, you short sonofabitch, are you ever going to be smart enough to get out of this fucking desert?"

The diminutive, swarthy Israeli colonel was seated at a small table covered with paperwork. At Garvey's words, his closely cropped bulldog's head snapped up, his black eyes narrowed in an expression of expanding fury. Then, squinting against the glaring desert that outlined Jim in his tent opening, his eyes widened, he jumped up and knocked his table over to grab at him. They thrashed around on the dusty canvas floor like two fifth-graders until they both began middle-age gasping.

Lieutenant Bodasky watched the scene with his hand on his pistol. It must be a joke, he thought, because the two men were cursing each other so fondly. But he didn't like the American's manner, so he stood at the ready, uncertain of what to do but prepared to do it—whatever it was.

Levy surfaced first. "Jim, I knew you were coming, but I didn't think you'd pull a Six-Day War attack on me." The colonel stood up, grinning and short of breath, and dusted off his flight suit. "Lieutenant," he said, pointing to the American who lay sprawled on the floor, "Colonel Garvey is my old wingman, who owes me everything because I saved his life with my superior leadership back in '56."

Jim groaned and staggered to his feet. "Bullshit, Rocco. Your fat ass would be pushing up daisies if I hadn't knocked that vampire off your tail."

Bodasky, flushing, moved to pick up the desk and set the papers straight. The tent was absolutely functional, as harsh and sterile as the desert. There wasn't even a picture of a wife or child to detract from the joyless efficiency. Levy watched with amusement twinkling in his dark eyes.

"Mike, we have to let the lieutenant off the hook. He's one of the new breed, not used to seeing old bastards horse around like

557

this. Sorry, Lieutenant Bodasky, this beat-up American colonel and I go back a long way."

Bodasky straightened, clutching a sheaf of papers, and tried to smile appropriately, as if he understood. "Sir," he said.

Levy winked at Garvey. "Let's go to the club, and let me buy you a drink. It's early, but so are you by two days. What happened?"

"Just lucky, Rocco, like always."

Bodasky looked at them with double disapproval. Senior officers should not act like this, and it was squadron policy not to drink until the last mission had been flown, and an official stand-down had come from wing headquarters.

The two old soldiers walked across the squeaking sand to an identical tent, undistinguishable except for a battered stirrup cup hanging over the door, a souvenir stolen from some RAF club. There was no one in the bar, just a handful of dusty tables and chairs and a locked liquor cabinet, fabricated from two personal equipment lockers bolted together.

Levy stuck his head out of the tent flap, telling Bodasky to stand by and keep everybody out until he'd finished talking to his guest.

Garvey sat down while Levy fiddled with a key ring to unlock the cabinet. "Well, you're looking good, Rocco, except for that gut. How do you stay fat out here in this godforsaken hellhole?"

Levy swore under his breath at the padlock, then grinned back at him. "Jesus, no one's called me Rocco for years. Around here I'm strictly Colonel Levy. But thank God we're not around here all the time; you'd go stir crazy with the heat." He jerked the lock and it came free with a reluctant, grinding snap. Levy smiled in satisfaction and swung open the cabinet doors. "I've earned this paunch," he said, poking among the dusty bottles, "eating whatever Sonia puts down in front of me. When this tour is up I'll take you back and let you see what that means. She's been dying to see you ever since I told her you were coming."

Jim was surprised at Rocco admitting to a security leak; even Sonia, a fighter from the old days, shouldn't know that he was coming. After his mission was over, he could drop in.

"You got enough for a hell of a party, Rocco. Do you cart this stuff around everywhere?"

"Yeah. It's a tradition from the Six-Day War. Every time somebody scores a victory they buy a bottle and stick it in the cabinet. But nobody drinks much. It all came from the time when we were flying combat every day, getting victories, but never being able to drink because we had to fly the next day. It's sort of a half-ass idea, but most traditions are." Levy scowled and pulled out a half-full bottle. "Still drinking Scotch? Hope so, because that's all that's open. You can have it one of two ways, in a glass or straight out of the bottle."

Garvey took a long pull from the bottle; he could feel the little "more" signal go off in his throat.

"I'm too old for the sauce, Rocco, the old prostate can't take it." It never could; he wasn't drinking any more, nor any less, but he knew it was too much. "I don't like those G forces too much anymore, either, and I finally learned not to fly with a hangover."

He handed Levy the bottle; the shorter man took a quick drink and plopped the bottle down on the table with a sigh. "Me too, Garvey. What the hell are we doing still pushing iron at our age? Can you imagine what we would have thought of old guys like us flying and fighting when we started out?"

Jim let the notion sink in, realizing that they both had indeed grown old, and realizing how close they had been, back in 1956. He had first come to the desert because of a memo posted on the bulletin board at Luke. He'd volunteered for a "black assignment" as much to escape Miriam's loss as perhaps to find her again in death. He realized he'd been doing the same things for years.

It had started out well, for the P-51 they gave him to fly was a delight. It was the best piston-engine fighter of World War II and he had saved Kelly's ass with it in Korea.

They'd shipped him out in an unmarked Constellation on a flight direct to Tel Aviv. He'd been attached to Levy's squadron in the spring, when Nasser began implementing his threats, and flew the wildest-ass combat mission he'd ever been on in the early dawn of D-1 of the Suez campaign.

In 1956 it had become clear that the Arabs were gaining arms from the Soviet Union at a far greater rate than Israel could get them from France. Nasser, seeking to establish primacy in the Arab world, seized the Suez Canal. Israel was courted by France and England and an elaborate plan was created by which a concerted attack would be made by the three parties. But Israel still did not trust the English, and insisted that the attack be made in such a way that it could be dismissed as a mere reprisal for one of the numberless Fedayeen raids if France and England wavered and did not intervene.

The heart of the attack was a parachute troop strike to seize

559

the Mitla Pass, through which the Egyptian forces would have to either retreat or advance. Prior to the drop, Israel launched a flight of four F-51s to cut the extensive Egyptian land communication lines using their props and wings. The Egyptian radio communications were not secure; with their land lines gone, Israeli intelligence could read their plan of battle easily.

Garvey, younger and leaner, and far less prudent then, had flown on Levy's wing. The pair were never higher than thirty feet off the ground from the time they crossed the border, and were often lower, kicking up a swirl of dust as a heron kicks up a spray on its last few wing beats before takeoff. Jim had hated the whole business. There was no one to shoot at, and he expected the wires to wind around him like a shroud and spin him in. But the operation went off like clockwork, with no Mustangs lost, and with various Egyptian headquarters isolated from their units, their radio transmissions easy pickings for Israeli intelligence.

The following week the campaign began to degenerate from military brilliance into political idiocy as John Foster Dulles recast Anthony Eden's historical image as a brilliant number two to Churchill and a hopeless, vacillating number one on his own. It didn't matter to Garvey and Levy, off in another flight of Mustangs. The original pair of F-51s were in the shop for repairs to canopies, skin, and control surfaces, but Jim was again on Levy's wing, this time in loose formation at a comfortable fifteen thousand feet. He wanted a swig from his canteen, so he swung out farther, cocking his head around in time to see a single Egyptian Vampire sweeping in behind them.

He spilled the canteen as he punched the transmit button and yelled, "Break port, Rocco!"

Levy had snapped into a hard ninety-degree turn, but the Vampire, a twin-boom single-engine jet obtained from the Royal Air Force, tried to slide in behind him. Garvey had scissored out, and then cut back and squeezed the trigger. The six fifty-caliber guns sawed through the Vampire and it blew up, spinning in pieces down to the desert below. He had never let Rocco forget it, either, and as the raw trickle of Scotch burned down their throats, that moment flashed through both their memories. In the way of fighter pilots, neither man fished for the deeper emotions it produced.

Garvey waved his hand at the pathetic officers' club. "You do yourself well out here, Colonel," he said, wiping a hand on the grimy table.

"Yeah, you can get used to anything, I guess. God knows I

ought to be used to it. I've been flying out here for almost twenty years. And you know something? It used to take me twenty minutes to fly across Israel in my Mustang, before we had conquered half the deserts in the world. Now it takes me twenty minutes to fly across in my Phantom, and I'm still sleeping on a hard cot, waiting to go out and let some young Arab nail me." Levy ran a big hand across his nearly shaven pate. "What's it all mean?"

"I don't know. I been through Korea, I been through Nam, I been through Israel once; this makes twice. It's better flying each time, but worse fighting. In Korea it was a kick. You would have loved Korea, Rocco. After we got serious we had the hardware and we could wax their ass every day, ten to one. Everybody got excited about the MiG 15, how great it was; we only had one problem with it, not enough to go around. And the rules; goddamn, we were told we could fight them over the Yalu, but only in the air."

Levy handed him the bottle. "Go on, I heard this story in '56; I want to see if you tell it the same."

Garvey took a longer swallow. "I was hassling this MiG all the way back over the Yalu, when I looked down and saw an airport. The MiG I was chasing broke off, so I split-essed down to the traffic pattern, and picked up a guy on a short final, gear and flaps down. He must have been scared shitless when and if he saw me. I was all set to shoot just as he was about to touch down, and I remembered the rules. I couldn't hit him on the ground. I yelled 'Bounce, you sonofabitch!' and he did. He must have been nervous, and I squirted him on the bounce. Blew up." He handed the bottle back.

Levy smiled. "Good story. In '56, he didn't bounce, and you went home mad. The stories get better, anyway."

Garvey smiled too. He hadn't told the story in a long time; it made him feel better to tell it, just as it had to do it. He wondered why he told it wrong the first time. He sat, smiled at Rocco. "Yeah. Well, Nam was worse. We had better planes but the most half-ass rules of engagement you ever heard of. We had to have visual contact to shoot the mothers, and they were launching Atolls and SAMs at us from anywhere they could."

Levy nodded. "I was back at Nellis and got the story. It must have driven you crazy. We got some problems here, but there's usually no trouble in air-to-air. We always have them identified, and if you see him you got him. Bombing's different, though; we really have to be careful not to hit any civilian targets. It's tough when the bastards put the bomb dumps by the hospitals."

The Scotch brought back more memories to Garvey, memories long buried; combats, wild nights, squadron mates. Especially squadron mates. He frowned into the tent wall, trying to remember them all. "Whatever happened to Mazer? He was a good guy, played the violin, didn't he?"

Levy's expression went blank. "Dead; shot down by antiaircraft guns in 1967; they had some 57 mm batteries that were pretty good."

"How about Barer? He was a real pisser."

"Not after the silly shit flew his Phantom into the Canal. The Gypos got him during the war of attrition. And man, did we attrite. They were knocking our ass off until the ceasefire in '70."

"Jesus, did anybody but you survive? How about Hirsch? Richard, wasn't it?"

"Hirsch was smart; he got invalided out on a physical and went to live in the States. I think he's a writer or a reporter or something. But he got shot up, too. They put a round of 37 mm flak into his cockpit, and damn near sliced his hand off. Cut all the tendons. He flew back with one hand, the cockpit a goddamn sea of blood. Enough to make you puke. I don't see how he types with one hand."

Levy took another pull of the bottle, and they went on until they ran out of names they both remembered. Most had been killed or wounded.

"It's a funny thing, Garve, this whole deal is a little like the old German Luftwaffe. The old guys keep flying until they get knocked off. Fortunately we have good young pilots coming up. I don't know how we do it, but we got the best kids in the world willing to put up with this crap."

Jim glanced out the tent door. "What's it like out here now? Any action?"

"No. It's quiet, but it's screwy. We get the word from our intelligence pukes that the Arabs were so demoralized by the Six-Day War that they'll never take us on again in a full-scale war. I don't believe it. It's the party line, but I don't believe it. They were getting better and better during the so-called war of attrition. I think our problem is that we get more like you guys in America all the time. We get to figuring that the Arabs are going to think like we do, just like your brass thinks Russia is going to think like you do. And what happens if we're wrong, and they do some thinking on their own? We get our clock cleaned, that's what happens."

He paused and scowled at the sandy floor. "They keep us on alert here on this godforsaken strip, because the Gypos and Syria have mobilized, but they keep telling us it's all a bluff. Then there is the whole razzle-dazzle philosophy of 'We will find a way.' Shit. It's not supposed to matter what the odds are, how many MiGs, how many SAMs—we're supposed to go in and do it. In a way it's our fault; that's what we did in the past. But it wasn't working for us over the canal last time—they got smarter and smarter, and it got tougher and tougher to find a way. I don't know if there is a way to play heroic Davids' to their Goliath when they're sitting there with every SAM in the book and an endless supply of MiGs and Sukhois. What do your guys say?"

Garvey blinked; his guys hadn't said anything except they wanted him to get a reading on Israeli morale and tactics. But they'd pulled the same cloak-and-dagger routine on him as in '56, so something might be up.

"Well, I'm here, and they sure aren't just sending me to the biggest beach in the world for a vacation. They must think somebody is going to pull the plug."

Levy looked worried. "If they ever try what we did, a sneak Sunday punch to take out all the airfields, I don't know if we can handle it. Sadat is a smart sonofabitch. I wish they still had Nasser. We're really overextended, and they've been getting a lot of training from the Russians, in country and out. We hear their transmissions all the time. I don't think it's going to be the same, when they finally get their guts sucked in and their kids psyched up. Anyway, Yom Kippur starts tonight, so we should have a breather."

"What? Why the hell would they give a shit about that?"

Levy grinned. "Easy. Golda would never forgive them if they screwed up a holiday."

Garvey laughed. "Of course. You can piss off everybody else, but you better keep clear of a Jewish mama. Hope Sadat buys that." He checked his watch and yawned. "Listen, Rocco, I got maybe two hours sleep in the last twenty. How about giving me a quick tour? Then I can grab some chow and rack out."

"No stamina. Lemme lock this hooch up and we'll taste the delights of Sebat, home of the quick and the dead." He paused. "Before we go, Garvey, tell me about Rachel."

Jim turned, sat down, spilled his guts for an hour.

*　　*　　*

Levy's tour of the squadron impressed Garvey more than he showed. It turned out that Bodasky's first name was Jerry, and he had an older brother, a captain, named Seffy—for Joseph—with him. The Israeli airmen were younger than the men of a typical USAF unit, but they were a tough, disciplined crew, and the American winced at the suspicion in their eyes when they learned he would be flying with them. It was the same old story; you had to prove yourself every time, everywhere, to everybody.

"Jerry, you've spent some time with the colonel. You fly a familiarization flight with him tomorrow as back seater. I'll fly lead, just for old time's sake. Jim, you and Seffy here can spend the evening briefing on our call signs, frequencies, and the usual stuff." Neither Bodasky looked thrilled.

Dinner was spartan, the best that could be done in the primitive conditions of the field. The table crosstalk was incomprehensible to Garvey. It was in English, in deference to their guest, but it was another English, a young man's combat argot that didn't play to him. The squadron maintenance officer, a myopic captain named Lerner, sought to draw him out, but it was simply a polite gesture. After a couple of hours poring over maps and frequency cards and taking a security briefing the younger Bodasky had insisted on giving, Garvey was glad to escape to the field latrine for an inadequate shower, and then to his tent to turn in. He lay down on an ancient iron cot, probably British from the big war, and thought about his house in Alexandria, with its air conditioning, fruit trees, and pool. And they call this the land of milk and honey, he mumbled before dropping off. He finally had Rachel with him, and here he was again. Jesus, what Myron must think. It's a wonder he wasn't fighting for the Arabs.

Next morning Garvey moved in an aura of other people's stares. He scrupulously preflighted the big, ugly Phantom, knowing almost every rivet and access panel, but politely checking with Bodasky when he came across some equipment or installation peculiar to the Israeli birds. Bodasky fussed along after him, rechecking everything until Jim had had enough.

After Bodasky ceremoniously checked the wheel well area Garvey had just left, he called him on it. "Look, sonny, I got fifteen hundred hours and two MiGs in these hummers. I think I can get you there and back okay."

Bodasky flushed, and from that point communicated to Garvey only with the required responses to the checklist. Jim felt bad; he didn't want to singe the man, but enough was enough. It was no way to go to war, and he hoped he could mend the fence before his tour was over.

The two ran through the start procedure. Garvey was impressed with the crisp, businesslike responses of the maintenance and armament people. Clearly, they were skilled professionals. He taxied out behind Levy, listening to Bodasky handle the radio procedures, so much like those of the USAF's, but different enough to make him wish he had had a more routine transition into the process. The Phantom was fully armed, as always, and he might need all the knowledge he could get.

The two humpbacked, dump-winged fighters stood side by side at the end of the runway. Garvey could sense rather than hear the windup of Levy's engines as he brought them into afterburner. The first F-4 seemed to lean forward against starting blocks as power built up, then leaped down the runway. Jim had his own throttles coming in so that he could maintain the precise interval favored by the Israelis, and in seconds they were rolling, then airborne.

He looked back to check his wing, and saw black holes erupting in the runway he had just left. The fleeting shadows of a pair of sweptwing fighters wrinkled over the dunes. Curiously, he felt nothing, even as he realized the meaning of the attack that had so narrowly missed them. Sadat had taken the chance on pissing Golda off.

Bodasky transmitted, matter-of-factly: "Blue One, base under air attack, acknowledge."

Levy had already slammed his Phantom into a left-hand vertical bank, hard enough to wring thin contrails from the dry desert air. He scanned the horizon, and low to the left was a flight of MiG 21s making another run on the base. Two more were farther out, but he couldn't tell if they were inbound or outbound. The first pair were long gone.

"Garve, let's nail those guys coming in from the west." Even Garvey blinked at Levy's violation of the iron Israeli radio discipline. It should have been a simple "Blue Two, attack." He reached down to fumble with the arming switches even as he shoved the throttles forward to keep up with Levy. One of the few faults the Phantom had was the layout of the arming switches and the short control column; you had to crawl around in the cockpit while G forces slammed your helmet down your sweaty forehead. It was like trying to jitterbug in a suit of armor.

Things began to jell as Levy led them into good position to engage. Jim could hear Bodasky's breathing coming faster in the hot mike. It reminded him of Hibbs and made him feel good to know something could excite the kid. The MiGs streamed in, saw the two Phantoms, and pickled off their bombs in the desert before breaking. Levy and Garvey closed, fired missiles, and both missed as one MiG jinked down toward the deck and the other peeled upward, its big jet popping it skyward like a shell out of a cannon. The missiles, Israeli versions of U.S. AIM-9 Sidewinders, were heat seekers, and they had corkscrewed off just like their U.S. counterparts did when malfunctioning.

Levy's back seater yelled, "Break starboard!" And sure enough, there were two more streaks coming in from the west, flying so low they almost merged with the delta shadows that identified them as MiG 21s. Both Phantoms were at combat speed, but the MiGs got to their drop points to dump their load at the edge of the runway. The Israeli planes moved in behind them. Two heat-seeking missiles leaped from Levy's wing—he was taking no chances this time—and went right up the lead MiG's tailpipe. It exploded with a orange-redblack burst that covered Levy's plane as he went through the fireball.

The second MiG, lustrous silver, almost pearlescent in the early morning light, reversed its heading and went for the sea. Garvey followed. He yelled at Bodasky, "Are we locked on?"

"It's breaking lock! I can't get a lock on it!" Garvey swore into the mask. The bastard is a smartass on the ground but he can't get the fucking radar to work.

Garvey brought the Phantom into position above and behind the MiG, all the Vietnam savvy coming into play, grappling again with the armament switch to get his cannon ready.

He yelled, "I'm going to eyeball this one, Lieutenant," into the open mike, and sprayed 20 mm cannon shells at the MiG, now just above the deck. The line of shells passed over the canopy. Panicked, the MiG pilot slammed his stick forward to duck and disappeared vertically into a geyser of seawater.

Garvey chortled into the mask. "That's how the big boys do it, sonny. You don't need radar if you've got skill."

"Bullshit, sir. You are the luckiest sonofabitch I've ever seen. Sir."

Jim looked over his shoulder, broke right, then came to level flight. The airplane he'd seen was Levy, joining up with them.

"Good shot, Blue Two; that's really what I call splashing them."

"Roger, Blue One."

"Blue Two, let's take a look to the west. Give me your fuel and armament state."

Garvey ran his eyes over the gauges, waiting for Bodasky to reply.

"Blue One, we have about nine thousand pounds and four missiles. The radar wasn't locking on, but I'm getting positive indications from it now."

"Roger, Blue Two, so who needs it?" Garvey grinned in his oxygen mask. Levy would never change.

The two Phantoms lifted up, trading their residual combat speed for altitude. While they climbed, the radios had suddenly come alive with combat reports.

"Blue Two, this looks like a full-scale attack. We'll take a look west and see what we can find out. We'll make one pass at the border, hit anything incoming, and go back to Refedim to rearm."

Refedim was an emergency base, even less well provided than the one they'd left, but it was closer, and they were going to be on fumes if they had another combat engagement. The big J-79 engines in the Phantom could turn five thousand pounds of fuel into black trails of smoke in a little over a minute in combat conditions.

Garvey keyed his mike button to respond. Levy was talking too much; it wasn't like the old days. Maybe the Israelis had loosened up. That's what he was here to find out. It was okay to have a little crosstalk on the intercom; it relieved the tension. But you had to keep the air-to-air channels free. The thought struck him that maybe Levy really was getting old and tired. Then it hit him if Levy was, so was he, probably. No wonder Bodasky looked worried.

The airplane felt good. Garvey was proud of himself. It was better than Nam, more like the old days in Korea. Good iron in your hands, an obliging opponent willing to get his ass shot off, and then back for a cold beer.

As the minutes passed, though, Jim felt a familiar chill of anticipation come over him. He was usually scared before combat, but this morning he'd been thrown into it and shot an airplane down before he was psyched up. Now it was coming, and he felt his stomach begin to tighten, and his balls draw up tight in his scrotum. His mouth was dry.

"Blue One, Agar control." It was a new voice, a ground controller.

"Roger, Agar, Blue One."

"Hostiles, flight of eight, about twenty miles, due south, one

567

hundred eighty degrees your present position, your altitude. You are cleared to engage."

Holy shit, Garvey thought. Eight what? Mig 21s, probably, and we were clear to engage. "We will find a way . . ."

"Agar, Blue One. I got a lock on them. Now I got them visual."

Jim could sense the joy in Levy's voice. What a warrior.

The two opposing flights had swept toward each other at better than twelve hundred mph; the MiGs broke up into two sections, one moving to the right, one to the left, in classic late Vietnam War tactics. The two Phantoms had rumbled back into afterburner, burning fuel at a prodigious rate, but accelerating to 590 knots, the best fighting speed for the big F-4.

"Blue Two, attacking port element, go."

Both planes leaped head-on into the incoming flight of four MiGs. Behind them, the other four MiGs accelerated to attack.

Garvey and Levy launched Sidewinders at the same time. The wait during the firing sequence between the time the radar locked on the missile, acquired the target, and left the rails was unbearable. Levy's missiles began to corkscrew in a wide arc, then settled down to fly directly into the lead MiG.

Jim had launched just as Bodasky yelled break; the attacking MiGs had salvoed their missiles, and he whipped the F-4 into a dive, trying to avoid the flurry of Atolls. He went supersonic, and pulled back up in a yo-yo maneuver, arming his cannon as he climbed. He came over the top, grunting against the Gs, ready to engage, but all the MiGs were gone. It was always like that in combat, one minute a skyful of airplanes, the next, nothing.

Three black puffs hung in the sky, with wispy trails of gray leading down to burning smears on the ground. He couldn't see any chutes.

"Blue One, Blue Two," Garvey said into the silence.

"Blue One, Agar control."

"Stand by, Agar, this is Blue Two. Do you have contact with Blue One?"

"Negative, Blue Two."

"Blue One, this is Blue Two," he said again. Sweat trickled along the mask line on his face while he scanned the empty sky.

"Blue One, Blue Two."

"Blue One, goddamn it, Rocco, answer me."

Bodasky spoke softly into the intercom. "I think they went in, sir."

They. "Who was Levy's back seater, Lieutenant?"

"Sir, he was my brother."

Shit. Garvey made his stick hand relax and blinked away the sweat from his eyes. It had to be sweat. I'm too old for this shit.

He keyed the mike savagely. "Agar control, get us a steer back to Refedim, this is Blue Two."

The flight back was short. It had to be, since they were down to their last thousand pounds of fuel when the Phantom entered the pattern with a dozen strays all milling around trying to land. On the way back they'd seen many aircraft, mostly Egyptian, streaking in and out of Israel, with Israeli fighters engaging where they could.

On the ground at Refedim, there was ordered pandemonium. Their F-4 was rearmed and reserviced in a revetment while he and Bodasky reported to the intelligence section set up at an open bench, without even a tent to keep the sun off. As Levy had guessed, it was an all-out attack and the Israelis had been caught napping. There was no word on Levy.

After the hurried debriefing, Garvey was slumped with his back against a fifty-five-gallon drum of kerosene when he felt a hand on his shoulder. It was Bodasky. "Sir, we're ready to go. We're flying with Able One."

Garvey slowly stood up. Everything changes and nothing changes. He shook himself and moved on out to the flight line, following Bodasky. Nothing changes and everything changes.

51

17 April 1975
Washington, D.C.
USA

The drive across the 14th Street Bridge was the usual telescoping of lanes around an accident; in the middle of the bridge a huge red-faced man was leaning his head on the roof of his 260Z; the Z looked perfect from the rear until halfway down the sloping hood line, where it merged with the steel bars of the dump truck. The dump truck driver seemed embarrassed to see a grown man cry.

Kathy rarely felt like crying nowadays. She was forty-seven years old and for the first time in her life doing what she wanted to do in a cause she believed in, independent of her father and of Mike, independent even of the children. It was unlike anything she had ever done before; unlike teaching, supporting Mike when he was heading toward one of his periodic career digressions, making sure that the family's end was held up in school functions. She had identified something important, and she had an important role in it.

It had started when Mike was in Thailand; Louise Washington had asked her to come to an organizing party, sending wild alarms of apprehension through Kathy's brain. Louise had been acquiring notoriety as a black activist, and even though Kathy was sympathetic, she didn't think she had a role to play in Louise's battle. But Louise knew better than Kathy how little she could do in the struggle for racial equality; instead, Louise shrewdly sensed that Kathy might fit in with Wildlife, Now, a West Coast conservation group that was modeled along the lines of the Sierra Club.

Louise had been disconsolate when Wash made her stop working with Lyle Johnson; it made it easier if she told herself it was jealousy. Yet she had a desperate need to serve, to belong, to do something for the world. Wildlife, Now had been her escape valve. And Kathy found that it was to be even more for her.

The yellow daffodils were just coming up in the planted areas ranging around the Lincoln Memorial; traffic was halted on 17th Street. Most people hated the commute, but she enjoyed it, particularly now that she had the most eloquent of Washington symbols, a parking place.

It was all part of being in the right place at the right time. When she and Louise met with the founders of the Washington chapter, exactly six people were involved, including Kerry Bayer, whose name could only have been improved for the association if it had been Teddy, and whose rumpled exterior concealed a razor-sharp mind and aggressive drive. Bayer was the Washington chapter founder, and he was determined to shift the focus of the organization from the West Coast to Washington, on the reasonable assumptions that this was where the legislative power was and that this was where he was. Now they had a staff of forty, and were growing every day. Kathy luxuriated in the realization that she was a major reason for that growth.

The start-up meeting had been a little like Robert Benchley's *Treasurer's Report*, until they began dividing up tasks. Louise had opted to do the speechwriting, the only thing Kathy felt qualified for. The one task no one wanted was fund raiser, and

Kathy got it by virtue of being the last to arrive. She told Bayer she'd take it if she could have carte blanche to raise funds where she could; he told her that anything, including robbing liquor stores and 7-11s, was fine with him.

At the next meeting she scandalized the group; she had pledges of support from the National Rifle Association, the National Education Association, and the Teamsters Union. Even Louise was shocked; Kerry simply got up, walked around the table, and kissed her.

From then on she hadn't looked back, and Wildlife, Now was beginning to have a planning problem in using the money she had raised. Louise had begun a quarterly newsletter; it had blossomed into a monthly magazine, only sixty-four pages, but getting rave reviews and a ton of glorious photos pouring in every month.

She behaved in a thoroughly Machiavellian manner when it came to raising money, reveled in the delicious sense of danger and evil it gave her when she skirted the bounds of conservation propriety. She would have been glad to get a grant from R.J. Reynolds, Seagram's, the Nuke the Gay Whales Society, as long as the funds kept coming. She simply took money from wherever she could get it, on the sound theory that it was all green. The wild level of her success had precipitated an open breach with the West Coast headquarters, culminating in an exchange of bitter letters when WILDLIFE, NOW—COME TO MY PARTY stickers were embellished by bumper-sticker pirates with a long series of obscene parodies. It hadn't mattered—they were spelling the name right, and the money was pouring in.

Kathy rolled the Celica into the Colonial garage—she loved the car almost as much as the old Muntz jet—past the somnolent but still sinister attendant. As usual, someone was parked in her slot; she parked in the next available one. A fight for later in the day.

Bayer was already at work, as usual; he came early and made up for it by leaving late. She had just poured the first cup of coffee when he came over, waving a sheet of papers. "Kathy, the West Coast mafia has capitulated; they've agreed to have a motion introduced at the next convention to move the headquarters here. It's just like when Goebbels kicked Strasser out and came over to Hitler's side." It was one of Bayer's worrisome anomalies; this nature lover was a student of the Third Reich, tried to employ some of the organizing techniques to Wildlife, Now.

She squealed, got up, and hugged him. He didn't let her go.

"Kerry, that's great—but you can release me now."

He turned, kicked the door shut, came back, and embraced her again, kissing her hard, and not with companionable pride.

She pushed him away. "Look, Kerry, you are out of line."

"Kathy, I don't care. You've given me the money to do something with this outfit, and I love you."

"For Christ's sake, Kerry, I'm ten years older than you, I'm married, and I've got kids. Don't be ridiculous. You're just on an upper, and need to get laid or something. Now open that door, or the word will be out that we're an item. And we are not, definitely, we are not."

He was shaken, embarrassed, left the room.

She sat at the desk, troubled, a little embarrassed herself, and a little pleased that she could still stir a reaction in a younger man. After thirty minutes she went into his office. "Kerry?"

His back was to the desk. He called, "I'm sorry," over his shoulder, then turned slowly to see her.

"Kerry, I'm sorry, I didn't mean to be rude. But let me tell you a little about myself, and you'll understand better. It has nothing to do with you—you are an attractive man even though you dress like a bag person."

Kerry ran his hands down over his rumpled plaid coat, patted his bouncing locks.

"Look, at one point in my life I might have responded to you, or to someone like you, who has so much going for him. The thing that attracts me to Wildlife, Now, and even to you, is the cause. We are doing something worthwhile, and I know a lot of people aren't getting rich from it. I know where the money goes, we all do, and you only have to look at our Kerry Bayer to know he's not getting rich. And we are getting results. Do you have any idea what this means to a woman who's spent her life supporting a man whose idea of a good time is to strap himself inside of ten tons of metal and have somebody shoot at him? I've never understood the Air Force, never understood my husband. You've met him, and I know you couldn't understand him. All I've understood is that it was my job to make things possible for him, to take up the slack, to carry the kids, to buy the houses, to find the goddamn lipstick on his collars when he came home from overseas. Sure, I taught, and it was important, but it was woman's work again, approved style."

Kerry seemed to relax; he'd been worried that she was going to quit.

"There were ways I could have spiced life up; I had a lot of opportunities, a lot of invitations to fool around, and maybe I should have. But I didn't, and I don't really regret not doing it.

"Still, I'll bet you and I could have a good time; we like the same things, you are young, we're probably going to travel a lot. But the timing is all wrong. You've got me hooked into something more important than I've ever done, something I see the results of. I go home at night convinced I've saved half the wildlife in the world, even when I know we are just the first step in a bigger process. But this place, from the dinky shared desks in the shopping center when we started to this lush association palace, has become the focus of my life."

She waited, to see if she was getting through. He'd reached down and was rolling a Mont Blanc pen back and forth between his fingers, the ink smearing as neatly as if he were to be fingerprinted. Kathy went to his desk, opened a drawer, and tossed him a tissue.

"It's just this simple, Kerry. I am a whole human being here, not a feminist woman, not a supportive wife, I am whole! You have the utter insight, the kindness to listen to me, and so does the staff. I am somebody here, not just some body to do what ever is required, from cleaning the cat litter to dropping the car off for service."

"Kathy, I'm sorry. I am in love with you, but I'll not lean on you again. I hear what you are saying; you are articulating the reason our movement succeeds at all. It's the goddamn propinquity; I see you moving around, and I want you."

"Look, you can't save all the wildlife; you ought to be having a little of your own. Why don't we get you an appointment down at Lewis and Saltz, and start out with buying some clothes that don't have plastic belts and polyester in them? And we'll get you a decent haircut; I hate to tell you this, but the Mario Savio look is no longer in. Then we'll start sending you to the watering holes, Clyde's, wherever, and see if we can't find you a little native wildlife."

She went back to her office; she was really becoming a conservationist. First the animals, then the nerds. But then, Kerry wasn't a nerd; he just needed a little social nudge.

What would Mike think about all this? He might have laughed at Kerry, the antithesis of all the men he'd worked with through the years. He might have laughed at her for trying to save Kerry. But probably only after decking him.

Mike had his own tensions now. Paperwork disagreed with

573

him, and he hated the Pentagon. He was drinking too much, exercising too little, and flying far too little. As she pondered Mike's lot across the Potomac, she asked herself the question that was increasingly on her mind lately: If this was middle age, what would it be like in ten years?

52

**30 April 1975
San Antonio, Texas
USA**

Rachel heard the pop and the tinkle of glass in the living room.

"Are you all right, Dad?" she called. She ran into the sprawling living room of their San Antonio Spanish hacienda, one of three hundred identical models spread out over fifteen brand-new housing developments that encircled the city, binding retirees to it forever.

The television set had sprouted an andiron.

"Sorry, honey, I'll get a new one. I just couldn't watch anymore."

She nodded; Garvey had watched the almost gloating television coverage of the North Vietnamese sweep into Saigon. On the tenth repetition of the searing scene of frightened Vietnamese fighting up to the embassy roof, grasping at the skids of the last helicopter, Garvey had hurled the andiron like a Sparrow missile into the Zenith.

"Jesus, what a debacle; after all we spent, after all the kids died. And the bastards are getting a country pumped to overflowing with equipment."

He remembered taking off from Da Nang in the F-4s; the supply dumps spread for miles around, filled with billions of dollars of equipment. All gone.

At least the prisoners were home. He had a letter from Kelly.

"I'm sorry, kid. I'll go out this afternoon and get another set. This one was four years old, anyway."

She leaned over and kissed him. Her scent was Miriam's, exactly, it came back like a wave each time she was near him. She moved like Miriam, walked like her, but talked with far greater assurance.

But he knew Rachel had missed so much. Even now he saw

her only when she bounced home from school, tan, tousled, full of tales of boyfriends and her pussycat, kept in secret against the wrath of her landlord.

"Come here, honey, let me read you Colonel Kelly's letter. It's about a guy I knew back in Nam." He unfolded the letter. "I'll skip over the insults and the fighter pilot talk; old fighter pilots can't write each other without bringing up how great they were. You'd think Kelly had saved my life. Ah, here it is."

He moved his glasses down; they were an abomination, a reproach to him. For forty years he'd had the eyes of an eagle, and now he used bifocals. Rachel sat on the arm of the chair and ran her fingers through his thinning hair.

The letter was in Kelly's rolling scrawl. Garvey squinted to read: " 'Hey, did I tell you that I've been working with a hot rock engineer named Ed Novack on some missile programs? He's about half my age and a damn colonel already. He's got some good ideas that I wish we'd had in Nam earlier, or in Korea. Anyway, he developed the self-contained laser that took out the bridge at Than Binh—didn't you make a couple strikes on it in 67?—and he got his ass shot off, knocked down by a pop-up MiG 21 and an Atoll. Anyway, the point I'm getting at was he was in the Hanoi Hilton with Kaplan, who was with you at Da Nang. Do you remember him? Great big guy, according to Novack, and with a big heart, took care of all the guys. I remember seeing him get off the airplane at Travis, on TV. He was about eight feet tall, it looked, and they'd starved him down to under 140 pounds, the bastards. He's got permanent injuries from the torture, shins all shot, joints bad. Novack gave me his address, which I enclose in the envelope.' "

"Do you remember him, Dad?"

"Yeah, just barely. I remember his front seater, Harry Fish, a lot better. I wonder what happened to him. I've got to write Kaplan and find out. Jesus, I'm retired six weeks, and I'm acting like an old soldier already. I'll probably be going to reunions soon."

Garvey had deliberately set up in San Antonio before trying to look for work. He knew if he got a job offer somewhere else, something he couldn't refuse, he'd be off again, and the one thing he wanted, the one thing he wanted to give Rachel now, was permanence. He'd find something to do, and with his pension, almost twenty-four grand, he could get by until he did. He'd like a flying job, but had few illusions about the prospects for an aging fighter pilot.

575

Rachel went out, came back in with a tray of lemonade and cookies, homemade. She made every effort to create a family environment, copying much of what she'd learned from her grandparents Myron and Sara. Myron was a big lemonade man, and Garvey was coming to love it. He couldn't drink much anymore, didn't have the taste for it. It was funny, but after almost thirty years of shifting the sauce, he found that he really preferred soda or lemonade.

He watched Rachel and her Miriam moves. She was in her last year at the University of Texas, the fourth college she'd attended. The bouncing around had cost her credits; she had been in school almost five years, was twenty-two. God, she was beautiful.

She handed him a lemonade and waited until he lifted the glass to his lips, then said, "Dad, can we talk?"

"Sure. Need some money?"

"No, but I'm going to need a lot of moral support."

Jesus! She was pregnant. He'd kill that spic bastard she'd been seeing. "What can I do?"

She took a deep breath, and spoke as if she'd rehearsed the lines a thousand times. "Dad, I'm going to join the Air Force, if I can get into pilot training. It's opened up for women, and I'm going to try. If I don't pass the physical or something, I won't join, but I'm going to fly." She looked defiantly at him, jaw set.

"Be a military pilot? You must be joking! That's no life for you. It's dangerous, you're sent all over the world; they won't ever let women fly in combat, but it's nothing for a feminine, beautiful woman like you to do." The words came tumbling out before his mind was really engaged.

She glared at him. "You know, you are hopeless! You've spent a life doing exactly what you want to do, and when I want to get in on the action, you tell me no. Well, you don't have a whole lot to say about it; I'll do it, with or without your blessing, you know me well enough for that. But don't be cross; I could use all the help I can get, recommendations from your buddies, that sort of thing. And tips on what I can expect, and on flying; I want you to check out an Aero Club plane, and give me some pointers."

Garvey was speechless. He just looked at her for a while, until she got up and collected the lemonade glasses, put them on the tray, and took them into the kitchen. His mind whirled and sought a place to get hold of the thing. She came back in and sat down again, looking determined.

576

"Babe," he said at last, "I don't know what to say. But I do know what to ask. Why? Why do you want to do this?"

"I've missed a lot, Dad. I don't blame you; you couldn't help doing what you had to do. But it took me three years away from Grandmother and Grandfather—and you—to begin to understand who I might be and what I might want.

"Please don't take this wrong, but what I wanted most, I finally figured out, was a mother and father. No—don't misunderstand; it wasn't so much an ache in me as a void, I guess. The other girls live lives I barely comprehend, somehow. When I got to thinking about all this, really thinking, I saw that it had to do with whatever drove you to fly.

"When I saw that, it suddenly became very important for me to do it too. So here I am. Asking your blessing to do it. Will you give it to me?"

Garvey felt emotions he couldn't name. Tears welled into his eyes, but years of practice forced them back. "Damn, kid. Damn. I've been so bad to you. So bad."

"No, you haven't; you did what you felt you had to do. It had to be worthwhile; you are a good man, even Myron says that nowadays; Sara always said it. But you had a wild bug in your tail that made you do it; I want a shot at the same bug."

He smiled at her choice of words. "It's not very feminine, Rachel."

She laughed out loud. She stood up, stretched her arms behind her neck, popped her leg up on the coffee table.

"I'm not feminine? Listen, Pops, I could be in a space suit and I'd be feminine. Feminine is not what you do, it's what you are, and I don't have problems in *that* area."

"I know that, but flying is so masculine, so filled with coarse guys, dirty talk, drinking. The whole thing revolves around fighting, and that's bound to cause problems. I wish you would reconsider."

"Well, I might reconsider. I might join the Navy, fly off a carrier, how would that be?"

"Don't even say it, Rachel, baby. Those guys are nuts. I never knew a Navy pilot who wasn't bonkers. Have to be, to be cooped up on a ship all day, and then come back and land on that postage stamp. If you are serious, I'll help in any way I can." He paused, realizing that they had passed the point of no return. He had given her his okay. "When do you want to go in?"

"I've already been filling out papers at the recruiter's; they think I'm hot stuff because of you. I'm going to take three months off after I graduate, travel a bit, and then go in."

Whatever he might have said was interrupted by the phone. She frowned—another look directly from Miriam—and grabbed the receiver. "Garvey quarters," she said crisply. He grinned. This girl was obviously not cut out to be a civilian. He should have seen it before.

"Hi, Len. Sure. Now? Well . . . yeah. Okay. Meet me at the front door in fifteen minutes. Don't be late, because I won't be. Bye." She dropped the phone back in the cradle.

"Len Knowles. Guy from Austin. Wants me to go out. Okay with you?"

Garvey lifted his hand in assent. "Christ, I've just been informed that my only daughter is going to become an airplane driver, and now she's asking for my permission to go out on a date? Get serious. What time will you be home?"

She was suddenly once again the beautiful young woman getting set for a date, the would-be fighter pilot gone with a dazzling smile.

"Who knows? Maybe midnight, maybe later. You be okay, Pops?"

"Sure," he said, but she had already disappeared into her room. He heaved himself to his feet, feeling those old-age pains, and wandered out into the kitchen, with its walnut cabinets and almond-finish appliances, pulled a beer from the refrigerator. He drank it looking out the kitchen window. All this San Antonio domesticity, and she was going into the Air Force.

He shrugged. It wouldn't have mattered, she'd have gotten married, found a job elsewhere, moved away. At least he would be here, there would be a semblance of permanence; she'd have a place to come home on leave. The idea was beginning to grow on him; his Rachel, a pilot.

He scruffled through the junk drawer, pulled out a box of stationery. He'd write Kaplan, find out about Fish. Then he'd drop a note to Kelly, tell him about Rachel. Kelly would eat his heart out; his kids all wore glasses. Garvey chortled; you can't call your friend's kids four-eyes, but you can tell him your daughter's going to be a pilot. An Air Force pilot.

Miriam would love it.

53

All things good and bad seemed to come in threes. Brown slouched in his decrepit swivel chair, one caster of which was always threatening to fly off and catapult him to the floor. The Pentagon was a grungy place even for major generals, but there were compensations.

The first good thing had been getting the FB-113 back on track. With its troubled career, the range problem could have finished it. It was basically a good airplane, but all the controversies had stretched the production schedule out so long that it was almost obsolete by the time it hit the squadrons. That goddamn Kelly! If he had kept his mouth shut, they would have gained three years on the program, and the airplane would have been delivered at a peak of effectiveness.

The second good thing was Brownie's Baby; he'd had the sketch dated and framed. Its official name was "Pathfinder" now, a good P.R. combination of a hint at its technical qualities, an historical association, and not too threatening. He liked "Brownie's Baby" better. In a few years, when the cruise missiles were churning off McNaughton's production line, he'd be able to point to his seminal role in the program.

He had a feeling the third good thing was coming when Daphne buzzed him on the intercom.

"General Brown, General Lawton is calling. Are you in?"

"Absolutely. Gary is an old friend of mine." He grabbed the phone from the cradle. "Hello, General, how the hell are you?"

"Just a moment, General Brown; I'll put him on for you."

Brown grinned; the old put-you-on-hold one-upsmanship. He never did it, always made sure he was on the line when he called someone. It was a cheap shot, but maybe Gary was busy.

"Hello, Brownie, this is Gary, how are you?"

They chatted a few minutes; neither man mentioned their wives. Lawton had just divorced, and he was probably aware that Joan was still in the detox center.

579

"Duke, I shouldn't be doing this, but I need your advice. I'm heading the brigadier general promotion board, and we've got fewer slots this year than ever. We've got three colonels we could promote in good conscience for every opening. One of the guys who looks very good is an old friend of yours, I think, Mike Kelly. You know him, don't you?"

"Sure, I know Mike, he's a great guy; we went through flying school, and we've worked together a couple of times."

"Yeah, he's got a good track record, top OERs, the usual, and he's been to Edwards flight test and had a good combat record. But the competition is tough, and I've heard a rumble or two that he was a little rough cut. Also, he's never been to a senior service school. That's about the only thing against him. What do you think?"

Duke paused. This would have to be done right. "I wish I knew his competitors. Mike deserves it, on the basis of the combat if nothing else. He's got MiGs in two wars. He is a little rough hewn, I'll admit, very upfront. He was a little wild when he was young, did some chasing."

He paused. He had to play this right, screw Kelly and also get some information on himself; find out if the word was out on his own peccadilloes in Thailand.

"The competition is really tough. These guys not only walk on water, they do it faster than a speeding bullet while leaping over tall buildings at a single bound. It's really a shame we can't promote them all. We've got to get the best ones, the four-star material."

"Well, that worries me a little, General. Mike is a little impulsive, and I think he's had a little trouble with the sauce, too."

"Ah, Christ, we don't need that; there's enough to drive you to drink after you get a star, you don't need a head start."

"He's good, though, Gary, don't discount him. But as we talk I'm beginning to wonder; considering all the other guys out there, I'm not really sure I could say he was flag officer material."

"Okay; I really appreciate your objectivity; it's tough not to give a friend an upcheck."

"Yeah, I'm going to need all the help I can get myself."

"Don't sweat it, Brownie; you are a cinch for three star at least, and with the breaks you can go all the way."

"Thanks; I needed that, General; sometimes you begin to wonder."

They chatted for a few more minutes while a glow blossomed

through Duke. It was the best of all worlds, to succeed while your best friend failed. Mike wasn't a best friend, but just having an enemy fail would do. This would teach him not to fuck with Duke Brown. Three in a row. It would do for a while.

He was still basking in the Lawton conversation the next morning when Daphne rang. "There's a Colonel Washington here to see you, sir."

He jumped from behind his desk and went to the door. "Come on in, Wash, I heard you were coming back. Where are you working?"

They shook hands, Duke grinning, Washington looking worried. "That's what I wanted to see you about, Duke, they stuck me in a goddamn P.R. job. I'm supposed to work over in SecDef in the assistant secretary for Public Affairs' office. I won't do it. I'll resign first."

"Hold your horses, Wash, that's not all that bad. You can make a lot of points over there, meet a lot of people who can help you."

"Yeah, and go nuts doing it. I know we didn't always agree on tactics, but I know one hell of a lot about bombers and bombing, and I'm not going to be some goddamn Uncle Tom colonel going around to the Rotary Clubs and giving talks."

They chatted for a while. Brown didn't mind that they had locked horns on tactics in 1972; he didn't even mind that Washington had been right and he had been wrong. It was an honest effort on both sides, and Washington had had the advantage of being there. It had worked out all right in the long run; he had covered his bets well enough that he had been able to shift gears with the tactics, and no one had ever raised the issue. It might be smart to make use of Washington, for a number of reasons. He was capable and he was black, and both could help.

"I'll tell you what we need over there, Wash, something you can really help with. The B-2 program has been on its ass for almost twenty years; the design has finally matured into something worthwhile, and we need a fresh face to go to Congress with it. What do you think?"

"Man, I'd love it. What would I do?"

"They need a good program manager, Wash, with strong credibility at SAC and able to deal with Congress and OMB. You'd be a natural."

It took some doing. Personnel had already lined up a program manager, a capable combat-wise colonel who was finishing up a short course at the Harvard Business School. Duke had to go all the way to the Vice Chief to find the right string to pull.

Washington was pathetically grateful until he got home.

"Louise, come down here, let me tell you about the job Duke got me."

She ran down the short flight of stairs from their kitchen; she hated the townhouse, with its narrow rooms and screwed-up arrangement. Who ever heard of having the kitchen and the dining room on the second floor? But even with Wash's colonel's pay, they couldn't afford to move back into their old house in Annandale. So it had to be a townhouse.

"What is it honey, chief of staff?" She kissed him, pushed him down on the sofa, plopped on his lap.

He kissed her back, felt her stir. From being a shy young girl in Spokane she was increasingly a tigress; he hoped he could keep up with her for a few years.

"Honey, I'm going to be program manager for the B-2."

She jumped to her feet, rigid with anger. "What happened to the public-affairs job?"

"I don't have to do it, I've got something I know something about."

"God, you disgust me. You just get back from dropping bombs all over some helpless people, and you want to start a new airplane to do it all over again. And if you were in public affairs, you'd get to do some speaking, you'd be setting yourself up to do something for our people when you get out."

He was stunned.

"Wash, we talked about this a million times. You were supposed to get yourself promoted so you could do something to change things. It looks to me like you are just working for yourself. When are we going to do something? We've watched the civil-rights movement pass us by; we haven't paid our dues."

He was silent. He thought about the dues he'd paid in flying school, in Korea and in Vietnam. He'd paid dues all right, but not the dues Louise thought important.

"Louise, I'm not ready yet. I'm just a damn colonel. I can't begin to do anything significant until I'm a two-star, anyway."

"Yeah, and you'd be a lot better off in the secretary of defense's office in public affairs if you want to do that. I don't know anything about airplanes but I know the B-2 has been around for years and gone nowhere. I'll bet that damn Duke Brown just sidetracked you because he figured you were in competition."

"Now Louise, Duke is a sharpy, but I'm no threat to him. He

needs me, he needs the B-2. And believe me, I can learn a lot from him about taking care of myself."

"Seems to me you take pretty good care of yourself already; maybe that's the problem." She stormed back upstairs, ran up another flight into the bedroom, and slammed the door.

Washington began a series of briefings to get himself up to speed on the B-2. He went out to Andrews Air Force Base and talked to the AFSC people, and spent three days at Wright-Patterson talking to the Aeronautical Systems Division troops. The B-2 extended back into history almost twenty years, and had more aliases than James Bond. It had started when the Russians shot down Gary Powers's U-2 with a guided missile, spelling the end of the high-altitude bomber. The same missile that shot down the U-2 had also shot down the XB-70 program, and forced the conversion of the B-52 to a low-altitude mission.

The initials had changed as each proposal for the new bomber was killed off. It started out as SLAM (Subsonic Low Altitude Mission), then changed to ERBA (Extended Range Bombing Aircraft), before becoming LAMB (Low-Altitude Manned Bomber). There were others, AMB, AMBSS, as the technology progressed and a supersonic capability was deemed necessary, leading finally to the ASMA, the Advanced Supersonic Manned Aircraft, which became the swing-winged B-2 proposal. Four big jet engines powered the airplane, which had a blended fuselage and wing design to minimize its radar signature. It could go supersonic at low or high altitudes, but was designed to loaf in at low speeds, climb to high altitude for a supersonic dash, then drop back in for the run over the target at either subsonic or supersonic speed, depending on the tanker availability. It was one hell of an airplane, and the Air Force needed it. He knew only too well how old the B-52s had grown.

He was shocked by the field offices. There were civil servants who had spent almost a full career preparing studies on an airplane that was never built. They had drifted into a never-never land where the dream was the reality.

He pored through the years of congressional testimony. It was evident to him that all the predecessor studies had tired the advocates, while sharpening the congressional staffers who torpedoed the airplane. No matter how good the proposal was, they wouldn't buy it simply because of the history. Wash determined to change that.

He flew out to the General Aircraft headquarters in Los Angeles and got a totally different impression. The company had gone through various reorganizations through the years, and the team running the B-2 program was relatively young and excited. He took the vice president of engineering, Jack Stenger, aside, and confided in him.

"Jack, I don't care how good an airplane you have, I'm afraid the system will screw it up."

"Colonel, you have your finger on it. We are so tired of battling the bureaucracy on this. It takes us ten times as long and costs us ten times as much to do what we want to do. The irony is no one ever changes anything; we send in a proposal, Wright-Pat studies the hell out of it and approves it, they send it to AFSC, who studies the hell out of it and approves it, and they send it back. Once, just for a gag, we sent through a modification with an obvious massive error in it, we specified the wing-swing mechanism would be made out of 4016 aluminum. They studied it and signed off; as soon as they did we sent through the change order, they studied it and signed off. Nobody said anything. I've never seen anything like it. I've dealt with the Air Force for twenty years, and always had respect for the people. Something's happened through the years with this project. They think it's snakebit. They don't think it will ever get built, so they aren't serious. We've got to do something."

Washington flew back to the Pentagon and briefed Duke. They got an appointment with the Chief of Staff for one week later.

The Chief listened quietly. "Well, Colonel, you've identified a problem. Have you got a solution?"

"Yes, sir. Let's go to a Kelly Johnson, Skunk Works, approach. We'll put a team in Los Angeles with full authority, and bypass ASD and AFSC entirely. If we do that, I'm convinced we can telescope the program by eighteen months, move the first flight date up, and save a hell of a lot of money."

The Chief was impassive. "Makes sense. It will cause a storm at AFSC and ASD; there are a lot of people with years of experience on this. But we have other programs coming along they could be shifted to; maybe a little shakeup like this wouldn't hurt. What do they say at General Aero? This will cause a shake-up with them, too, you know."

"No problem, sir; they are desperate enough to shake loose and get some metal cut. I can personally guarantee to you that they will go along."

"Give me a couple of weeks to set things up. I'll be back to you. And thanks."

Two weeks later the bombshell hit. The B-2 program was scrapped as it stood, and a new office set up in the General Aero plant for the ultra secret XB-3. It was the latest name in a long line.

Washington told Louise they were moving to Los Angeles. It was the first time in three weeks that she smiled.

Duke shuttled back and forth between Washington and the McNaughton plant. He had to do it to keep up with the FB-113 and the missile programs, but it also gave him a chance to visit Joan. She had left the sanatorium and was at home with her family. He asked her if she was ready to go back to Washington.

He knew the answer, knew he always had to ask. It was a bittersweet invitation to help offset the exclusion he suffered from the happiness Joan found in her recovery. She was contained, as if she had a new meaning in life, a meaning that eluded Duke. If he asked her to come home, it served to put Joan on the outside and simultaneously open an avenue for himself into her happiness.

She answered slowly, enjoying the sense of self-control her answer brought with it. "Not for a while, Duke. I'm not strong yet, and you know that Dad doesn't keep any liquor around the house. It's not easy for me to get out here, and that's all for the good. I'm feeling fine, but I don't want to go back to the Ridge Road house yet, not till I know I'm ready. I never want to go back into the hospital again. Besides, you don't need me, and Charles is at school. I'm better off here, safer."

Their relationship was formal, correct; he knew she had seen a lawyer. He left her as he found her: cool, distant, and not at all interested in him.

He had an office in the corner of the office of the Air Force plant representative, Colonel Dysinger. Dysinger was a smart man, but far too severe on McNaughton in Brown's mind. He worried about the quality control and the configuration control a lot more than he worried about maintaining good relations, which was his primary job, in Brown's view. Dysinger was one of the old school, gung ho for the Air Force, regarding the contractor as the enemy. You couldn't get airplanes built that way.

He opened the door to his office to find Clay Miller sitting in his chair. The cheeky bastard had retired as a lieutenant colonel, after twenty years. But he was a good test pilot, and McNaughton was paying him twice what Duke earned. Some justice.

Old habits die hard. Miller jumped to his feet, damn near saluted. "General Brown, glad to see you."

"Call me Duke, Clay. No formalities with me. What can I do for you?"

"Sir, I know the FB-113 is your baby, but it's really got me worried, and McNaughton is not paying any attention to what I say."

Oh Christ. "What's the problem, Clay? I thought we had this mother well in hand."

"It's the same problem it's always been, sir. They've had weight control problems since day one, and they've carved all the metal away from the swing-up, the wing-swing/variable-incidence mechanism."

"Yes, but that's all been done pretty scientifically. They changed the specs on the metal being used, and ran a whole series of life-cycle tests, cold weather, altitude, the whole bit."

"I know—but I also know I'm getting feedback from the mechanism that is not normal; it's telling me things are going on that we are not instrumented to detect. I get little shudders and vibrations that drum along that tank of a fuselage. I know something's wrong. To tell you the truth, I don't think we have any idea of what the fatigue life is on the mechanism."

"Well, they are quoting fifteen hundred hours as you know, and then it's only an inspection. It's supposed to be able to go three thousand hours before they have to pull it apart and magnaflux or x-ray it."

"I know that, too. I also know we lost some F-113 fighters early on, due to the failure of the mechanism, and there were some lost in Vietnam for God knows what reason."

"Well, what do you think the problem is?"

"It's got to be in the quality-control process. I believe the engineers know what they are doing, but when the business types get a hold of it and start going out for low bids on the parts—that's when something happens."

"That's a strong statement, Clay. You are accusing a whole discipline of failure. The quality-control manuals stack a yard high, and every contract has specific instructions on how to sample. I've worked with these people before, and they know pilots' lives are riding on their decisions. The whole missile program, the whole space program, rides on quality control, and look how successful they are. The people in the field are as dedicated as you are. I've got a lot of faith in them."

"I wish I did. All I know is that a dozen sets of the wing mechanisms were drawn down from Logistic Command spare inventory to keep the production line going. I don't have any idea whether or not they get the same treatment."

"Sure, has to be. But I'll check on it. In the meantime, thanks for giving me an alert."

Miller was just like Kelly, a little old lady. Duke had been sincere in his praise of the quality-control people, both Air Force and McNaughton. They had a tough, boring job to do, and it seemed to him they did it well. It wouldn't hurt to check the spares, though. Better safe than sorry.

He called Dysinger in. "Colonel, I want you to assign someone to do a check on the quality control of the procurement and manufacture of the swing-up mechanism."

Dysinger grinned. "Right. I've been wanting to do that ever since I heard where they were coming from. I'll get out to Oklahoma City tomorrow."

The component builder, Jensen Aerospace, was located in a long series of Butler buildings just outside of Tinker AFB. When Dysinger got there, the main office was a pile of smoking ruins; a trailer was parked outside as a temporary office. The harried owner met Dysinger at the rubble. "Thank goodness you've come, General, I'm going to need some help getting started again."

"It's Colonel, and when did this happen?"

"Last night; we must have had a short circuit. It's a good thing the fire department got here or the rest of it might have gone up."

Dysinger looked in through the burned-out office at the long rows of machinery sitting on metal floors; not much could have gone up in there. In the office, the twisted pipes of the sprinkler system were pretzled on the floor. "What happened to your sprinkler system?"

"I don't know; it's like everything else, it worked fine until we needed it."

It didn't take long for Dysinger to surface that all of the Jensen quality-control records had gone up in smoke. Pretty damn convenient; somebody from McNaughton must have tipped them off. He'd put in a complaint through the Tinker office to start an arson investigation. He got a list of Jensen suppliers and went back to McNaughton.

Duplicate records had come in with the swing-ups. They were not complete, but it was a start. Dysinger worked through the

587

night, tracing what company made what parts. The material he really needed to find related to the forging and machining of the main pivot, and the associated bearings. All he had was the vendor's name, Wahatchee Forge, a foundry north of Seattle. He called his secretary to cut orders for the trip.

Miller liked the money, but production flight test was really pretty boring, even in the FB-113. The only part he really enjoyed was the final check of the terrain-following system, which had a roller-coaster ride that he loved. He and his copilot, whoever was on the duty roster, would take off from the McNaughton field, and fly southeast until they were well out over the Gulf. Then they would turn, drop down to sea level, engage the terrain follower, and fly a course across Florida, up through the Georgia Piedmont into the Appalachians, never more than fifty feet off the ground, never touching the controls. It took iron nerves the first few times, until you gained confidence in the electronics. When they were well past Atlanta, they would pop up to fifteen thousand feet for the flight back to McNaughton. The whole thing took less than four hours, but it was exhilarating because they flew it in daylight, and could see the ground whistling by from the flat Florida seashore to the jagged Appalachian peaks.

Brown got the call just before he left the Pentagon for another canned Dinty Moore beef stew dinner at home. It was from Bob Cranston.

"Bad news, Duke: Miller is down."

"Is he okay?"

"No, he and Morgan, the copilot, are both dead. The airplane had just finished the terrain following and was popping up to altitude. The swing-up must have failed; the goddamn wing was almost intact, fluttered down, the fuselage went straight in like a bomb. We didn't recover much of either man, the usual blood and teeth."

"I'll be right down."

He put in a call to Dysinger in Seattle. He'd already had the word on the crash.

"It looks bad, General, worse than we thought. We've been getting the spares and the production material from two different sources, but all the forgings have been done up here, in a little-bitty goddamn plant that shouldn't be making red wagons. It's no wonder they were low bidders, there's no goddamn overhead to this place. Half the machines are out in the rain. They've got no idea what went into those parts; they just put down on paper whatever was required."

"Didn't we have any inspectors there?"

"Yeah, two guys who've spent their life inspecting uniforms and electronics; they tried, I think, but they just weren't smart enough to see what was going on."

"Was it sabotage?"

"No, Christ, these guys think they are doing a good job. They are insulted that I'm here questioning them. I've got no choice but to get contracts to cancel them out. The real problem is how many are in the fleet already? We'll have to pull every goddamn F-113 and FB-113 in the inventory and rebuild them. We can't take a chance."

"Right, Dysinger, thanks."

Duke sat down. It was the end of the program; Congress would never buy another airplane. They'd be lucky to get the money to rebuild them. Jesus. It's a good thing they had the guided missile coming along. McNaughton was no longer big enough to compete for full-sized aircraft contracts.

Good things came in threes; so did bad. Miller's crash was one. Dysinger's unbelievable story about the foundry was two. He didn't know if he could stand number three.

He buzzed Daphne. "See if you can get me in to see Congressman Dade."

"He's on his way over to see you, sir. He'll be here in about twenty minutes."

The congressman stormed in, tiny, wrinkled, dressed as he had dressed in the thirties, and still wearing a commanding aura. "Duke, what the hell is going on?"

"It looks like a swing-up problem, sir."

"What the hell are you talking about? I got a call from Joan; young Charles has tried to kill himself. They found him in a car, half dead from carbon monoxide, a suicide note and everything. Didn't you know he was having problems?"

Duke sat down, stunned.

"I'm not surprised you don't know what's going on in the Air Force if you don't know what's happening with your own son."

"What do you mean?"

"Mean? Mean? Goddamn it, I mean that the goddamn guided missile program is a sham. I just found out this morning from

589

the congressional liaison people. It's Top Secret, so don't blab, but you should have known already. The Air Force doesn't intend to buy any production guided missiles from McNaughton; the whole thing is a fraudulent goddamn bargaining chip. They are going to give this one away to the Russians for stopping deployment of the SS-16. Don't you have any contacts? Don't you know what's going on?"

Daphne buzzed him. "It's the headmaster from St. Chad's, sir." Her voice was steady, but distressed.

Brown picked up the phone, waved the Congressman to the extension. "How's my son?"

"He's going to be all right, General Brown. We thought for a while that he wasn't going to make it. The doctors think we have to be a little concerned now about possible brain damage, but I thnk he's okay. His vital signs are good. He's awfully strong and I hope we can get out of this without any lasting problems. When are you coming down?"

"I'll be there tonight."

Dade went on about the guided missiles. When he subsided, Brown shrugged. "I don't give a damn about the missiles or about the airplane. I've got all I can handle with Charles."

"What's the matter with the airplane?"

"Don't tell me you didn't hear about the FB-113 going in? Killed both pilots."

Dade went white. "Lord, that's the end of McNaughton."

Brown called the vice chief personally, explained his problem. He told Duke to solve the boy's problem first, not to worry about the McNaughton difficulties. By the time he got to his car, Duke wondered if he could solve anybody's problems.

The word on the shift in the XB-3 program didn't take long to get out. Washington was mentioned in the *Aviation Week* January 1 "Laurels" column, for turning the program around. Unexpectedly, the Soviet Union helped in Congress by demanding that the program be canceled as "destabilizing."

Wash had dropped in to see Brown once a week, anyway. The man was going through hell.

"How are you doing, sir? Is Charles getting along?"

"I'm okay, Wash. How are you? Charles is coming along okay, a little slowly. He seems to have some problems with his speech and with his right side. We have him in therapy."

Wash shook his head in commiseration. "How's Joan taking it? Must be rough."

"Yeah, but you know I think it helps her. She's at his side almost fifteen hours a day; she really feels needed. Hell, she is needed."

They talked about the XB-3 for a while. Washington wanted to see if McNaughton would furnish the data on the cruise missile installation. Brown winced. "Wash, this is Top Secret, but you if anybody has a need to know. There isn't going to be any McNaughton cruise missile. The whole thing is a bargaining chip to toss to the Soviets next May when the arms talks start. Unless you are willing to work with the Bolide, you might as well forget it. Certainly not much that McNaughton has done will help, except maybe the way they handled the pivoting racks."

"Are you kidding me? Not a day goes by but there's a story in the paper, and it's a budget-line item for the next five years, anyway."

"It's a hoax, Wash. Nobody minds it more than me."

He opened a drawer and pulled out the framed picture of "Brownie's Baby." It was too painful for him to keep it any longer on the wall, a daily reproach.

"Jesus, this makes the XB-3 indispensable, doesn't it? It's the only thing we have left besides some twenty-year-old B-52s. Any chance you coming on board the program? I'd love working for you, and there is plenty for us both to do."

Brown sat at his desk, rolling a dearmed .50 caliber cartridge back and forth.

"Wash, to tell you the truth, I'm afraid to, for the Air Force's sake. I think I'm snakebit. I haven't had anything go right for the last year, either business life or personal life."

"You're too hard on yourself, Duke; you just spread yourself too thin, and things came unglued. It happens to us all. I'm lucky if I can get Louise to talk to me three times a week, nowadays."

"What's the matter?"

"I don't know if you'll understand, but she wants me to become more active in the civil-rights movement. She's a believer, and she wants me to speak out."

"Pretty risky, Wash; anything you say will get twisted out of context, and be used against you. I'd lay low for now. You're in the running I'm sure for the next BG list."

"Man, I hope so. Those two stars look pretty good on you, Duke."

"Yeah, it's funny, I was expecting to be court-martialed with all that's going wrong, and they came back and slapped the second star on me. I'm not sure I deserve it. I never had any doubts before this year that I'd be chief of staff someday; now I wonder if I shouldn't turn these back." He brushed his hand across the two stars pinned to his shoulder strap.

Duke winced, changed the subject. "When's your first flight?"

"This airplane is something else. The country needs it and not just a hundred of them, but a fleet of three or four hundred. It can do anything, and I don't think the Russians can touch it. We have rollout scheduled for August, first flight in September. I hope you'll come out for both."

"Couldn't keep me away."

They called it the Wombat Works, not because the XB-3 looked anything like a wombat, but because they couldn't think of anything else. Wash had a cot in his office, and spent at least twenty hours a day at the factory. So did Stenger, and so did the rest of the key people on the engineering and production team. He was amazed to see the giant airplane take shape in front of his eyes. The key was a combination of informality and rigor. If a decision had to be made by an engineer, it was made on the floor in the production area. The new computers helped; the engineer could draw a rough sketch, and with just one or two dimensions fed in, the computer would turn out a finished drawing. There was a team feeling; the manufacturer and the Air Force worked as one, without any of the usual turf problems. It was live or die for Aero General as an airframe manufacturer; it was live or die for the Air Force to get another manned bomber. They had to work together.

Wash reported directly to the Vice Chief, Terry O'Rourke, once a week on the scrambler phone, once a month in person. O'Rourke, a fighter jock, loved the program because it was doing so well. In a job where most of the news is bad news, he would interrupt whatever he was doing to hear from Washington.

"Wash, this thing is going sensationally well. We've got to get a management expert out there to analyze your program. I don't think Kelly Johnson could have done it any better." It was the highest praise O'Rourke had ever given anyone, the highest praise that Washington had ever received.

There was a funding problem because things were going so well; they were spending faster than the conventional R & D

urves had predicted, and Wash needed some funds to get
overtime money for long-lead-time items.

"Don't sweat it, Colonel. We'll get the money. It's been so
long since the Armed Forces Committee has had any good news
they'll authorize whatever we need."

When the briefing was over, Wash gathered up his briefing
books and started to leave. O'Rourke looked up. "Hey, Colonel.
Here." He tossed him a little box. Wash opened it. Inside were
two small silver stars. Wash just looked at them, blankly.

The doors to the room burst open and Muriel wheeled in a
cart filled with champagne bottles. "Congratulations, General; I
predict this is the first of several stars."

Wash had a fleeting memory of East St. Louis. His mom and
dad would have been so proud.

Louise wasn't too happy when he rolled in an hour late,
obviously having been drinking. She didn't even notice the stars
until he danced around her, dipping his shoulders in an exaggerated rhumba step, flashing his stars. Then she burst into tears.
And later, she was very warm and sympathetic.

"Honey, I don't know if I can take another promotion party
like this. I'm getting to be an old man."

She stirred luxuriously, almost purred. "You just wait for those
major general stars; I'm going to turn you every way but loose."

"Mercy, mercy, honey; I'm just an old man, trying to get along."

He reached over and stroked her. "And I think I'll get along
over you again."

The disarmament talks in Geneva had been stalled for months.
The Soviets were militant about the XB-3 even though they had
unveiled a similar prototype at an unusual open Tushino flyover.
It was almost 50 percent larger than the XB-3, and it carried two
tank-car-size missiles under each wing hinge point. The West
came up with one of its usual terrific code names, Beaver, to the
merriment of the aviation press.

Duke was going through the quarterly program reviews of the
FB-113 when Daphne stuck her head in the door. "It's Congressman Dade, sir."

Duke jumped for the phone; they hadn't talked since Charles
had tried to kill himself. Dade spoke cordially; he asked if Duke
could meet him for dinner that night. They met at Harvey's,
where Dade had his usual two manhattans, oysters on the half
shell, and filet. He'd eaten the same meal at the same table every

night that he could for the last thirty years. They treated him well at Harvey's; the table was arranged so that no one could see them or overhear them.

The wily old congressman had a lot of chits out to the president and he thought it was time to call them in. He had helped him to the State House, and then had masterminded the nomination efforts. McNaughton was a heavy contributor as well.

The old man had pulled out every trick in the bag to get Duke to help, from pity to threats to virtual bribes. Duke owed him a lot, no question. And he agreed with what he was trying to do.

Dade was making a last-ditch effort to save McNaughton, and he thought he had a shot with the deficit rising like it was. There had to be a cut in the defense spending, and the only vulnerable big-ticket item was the XB-3.

"Sir, the XB-3 maybe vulnerable, but so am I; if I go against policy like this, and I'm caught, I'll be finished in the Air Force."

"You won't get caught. It will be strictly between you and me. I won't even tell my staffers where I'm getting my figures. This whole thing will be off the record; the president isn't going to want any more record of it than you do. He wants it less. It's got to look like statesmanship. And what can they do to you? At worst you retire as a two star instead of a three star, that's all. And you walk into a vice presidency at a healthy firm." In the end, he prevailed. He always had.

The next day Duke shelved the FB-113 material and went deep into his files and found the report that Kelly had made when he got back from Nam on the efficiency of the Russian radar and missile systems. He added to it some classified material he had obtained from the Israeli air attaché on the Egyptian use of missiles during the war of attrition, and updated the material with everything he could find in the intelligence files.

The results were pretty convincing. You could develop a scenario in which a mass saturation raid by cruise missiles stood a lot better chance than a raid by one or two hundred B-3s. The Russian look-down shoot-down capability was improving all the time, but they couldn't handle five or six hundred Pathfinders streaking in from around the horizon. The B-52 could go in after the first strike to pick up anything the missiles missed. And you could get the missiles into being two to three years ahead of the XB-3.

Dade had worked the economic side. You could buy enough Pathfinders to equip the whole B-52 G and H fleet, as well as the

594

FB-113s, for less than fifty of the XB-3s. That meant half of the XB-3 program could be deleted from the defense budget. There were political considerations as well. The Pathfinder was simpler than the XB-3, and the subcontracting could be spread further around the country. The president was fighting rising unemployment as well as inflation, and he could use the help in the northern tier of states. California's unemployment rate was already low, and it was a cinch to go for the opposition, anyway. Besides, General Aero could subcontract for McDonnell Douglas and Boeing.

On the international scene it worked equally well. If the XB-3 were canceled, the Russians would have to go back to the SALT talks; if they didn't, the president would be seen as having done everything he could.

Duke had worked only with Dade, wouldn't even talk to a staffer. It had to be kept secret, or he'd be in real trouble. Dade was a quick study, picked up Duke's points, converted them to his own style of argument.

"Duke, regardless of what's happened in the past, I won't forget this. You are helping your country and your state, and I think you are helping the Air Force, too."

"I agree, sir; that's why I'm doing it. It's too bad we can't have the cruise missiles and the XB-3 too, but those days are gone forever. Good luck at the White House."

A few days later, he was putting on his overcoat to go down to the River entrance to meet the chief when Daphne came in and pointed to the phone. It was Dade. "Duke, you better listen to the president's press conference at ten; there's going to be a special announcement."

The phone slammed into the receiver. Duke glanced at his watch; it was nine forty-five. The car was supposed to pick up the chief at ten for a ten-thirty hearing.

Duke flinched. It was the worst possible timing. He considered momentarily pleading illness, but he'd have to have a bone sticking out of his leg before the chief would let him out of being there. He was the only one who knew the FB-113 well enough to be able to answer—or waffle—the questions.

Congress was finally up in arms over the FB-113 program. The chief of staff had to testify, and Duke was along to provide the details. It was going to be a bloody session; almost three billion dollars had gone into the program and the one hundred plus airplanes remaining in the fleet were grounded.

Brown dreaded the hearings. The airplane had been a basically sound original design, flawed by a change in mission roles, and by changes introduced to either save weight or money. McNaughton had tried to do a good job. Yet Duke had a lingering doubt; maybe Kelly had been right in the first place. Through the years all the problems had centered around the swing-up mechanism. It was a shame.

They met on the esplanade; the car was already there. "Sir, I've had word that we better listen to the radio at ten. The president is making some sort of an announcement."

They sat in stony silence through the 14th Street Bridge traffic. The chief didn't have many perks, but a chauffeur-driven car was essential; he became so absorbed in his thoughts that he would have been a hazard behind the wheel. At five to ten, Brown leaned forward and asked the driver to turn the radio on. They sat listening to the endless commercials until Peter Hackes came on and announced the president of the United States.

The thin nasal voice grated; it projected weakness.

The two men listened; the first part of the talk was on domestic issues, the need to balance the budget and fight the soaring inflation now threatening to run 20 percent per year. He began the second part with a reference to the stalled SALT conference.

"We have a unique opportunity to assist both our financial crisis and to further our negotiations with the Soviet Union. It will take courage and vision, but it is my firm resolve that we proceed along a course that will be, I hope, warmly applauded by thinking people, just as I know it will be condemned by those with special interests. To this end, I announce today the cancellation of the XB-3 strategic bomber, which is unnecessarily expensive, and is viewed by the Soviet Union with some accuracy as destabilizing the arms race. In its place, we will begin full-scale production of the Pathfinder cruise missile, arming our existing fleet of B-52s and FB-113s with these excellent weapons."

The president was drowned out in the chief's cursing. "That sonofabitch didn't tell me anything about this. He knows the McNaughton missile is a placebo, a fake. If we give away the XB-3 we're giving away a weapon system. The Russians will just take it and raise the ante. What a . . . ." He stopped, to turn and glare at Brown. "Brown, you slick bastard, you knew about this!"

"Honest to God, no, Chief; I wouldn't even have known to listen to the radio if my secretary hadn't told me to."

The chief looked hard at him, then stared out the window.

When they got to the Congress, they found the hearings had been canceled because of the new developments.

They rode back in silence. Brown's emotions were mixed. On the one hand he knew he had to convince the chief that he had had no part in this. If he didn't, his career was at an end. On the other he exulted that Dade had pulled McNaughton out of the hole with an almost unbelievable political coup. It couldn't have happened in any other administration. And he was amazed at the security of the issue; normally a ploy like this would have been well known in the Pentagon, and leaks would have occurred. There had been nothing. He wondered how many people at McNaughton had known that the charade they were working on would come to life.

At the Pentagon the chief turned to him, face contorted with suppressed fury. "Brown, I've got to believe you in spite of your political cronies and your father-in-law. But if I ever find out that you knew anything about this and didn't tell me, by God, I'll court-martial you."

"Sir, I didn't know anything about it. When I find out—if I find out—how it came about, I'll tell you the full story."

The chief swirled out of the car. Brown waited for a while, then tapped the driver on the shoulder. "Take me back to the Congress, please." He had to make an appearance of digging out the facts.

He walked down the marble halls, past the endless droves of smart young congressional staffers and the gorgeous women who flocked to work on the hill. He could hear the noise before he rounded the corner that led to Dade's office. The hallway was filled; inside Dade was surrounded by laughing, cheering Tennesseans. He'd just saved eleven thousand jobs, and he was the man of the hour. Duke turned around and walked back. This was not the time to be seen talking to him. He was arrogant anytime; today he'd be impossible, no telling what he would say. At least one of the jobs he saved would belong to Duke one day.

Wash's first reaction was disbelief; he tried to get Brown on the phone, but couldn't reach him. Then his phone began ringing; every congressman from California wanted to know the story. He couldn't tell them a thing. He walked through the plant in misery; the workmen had stopped. He nodded to them; there was nothing to say. Some believed he could save the situation; some thought he knew all along that it was coming. General Aero had called a special meeting to get a press release together. He hoped they knew more than he did.

597

Daphne looked up when Duke walked in. She wore a haggard expression. "Thank God you're here; you've had more than ninety calls. I've got them listed in some sort of priority on your desk. And I've got you reservations for Nashville on the nine o'clock Delta flight from National."

The top message on the pile was from Phil Prandle, the McNaughton project manager for the cruise missile. It said simply: "What do we do now, pal? Punt? Cheers."

That was a good sign; security had been good if Prandle didn't know. There were guys at McNaughton who might like to get him, too, and he couldn't afford any leak from anywhere.

The rest were about evenly divided between reporters and congressmen. He gave the reporter's names to Daphne. "Refer all these guys and any other press that calls to Public Affairs. Let them figure out what happened."

"I did; they don't know anything, so the reporters keep coming back."

"We don't know anything either, kid; as soon as we do, we'll tell Public Affairs and let them handle it. In the meantime, start working on the congressionals. The guys from California are going to be bears."

He opened his drawer and took out the drawing of "Brownie's Baby." He hung it carefully back on the wall.

54

1630 LOCAL
14 September 1977
Alexandria, Virginia
USA

She ran her nails deeper and deeper into the thick wallpaper that surrounded the old-fashioned niche for the telephone, amazed at her voice was still normal at the end of the conversation. Kathy had waited until she heard the triumphant click on the other end of the line before slamming the phone into the cradle. That bitch!

It had been Helen Markham; she'd phoned to say how glad she was that Ronnie Nordeen had made BG, and wasn't Kathy just thrilled about it? It was a simple bitch code for "Well, Mike didn't make it," for if they knew about Nordeen, they would have known about Mike. Nothing travels faster than bad news about a promotion.

She knew how he would take it; indifference, pleasure in one of his pals making it, an argument over something totally unrelated, then a bottle of wine with dinner and nipping on Jack Daniel's or cognac all evening until he fell asleep. Mike was drinking more than he should now that he was flying less. It was almost as if there was a hormonal balance between his need to fly and his need to drink.

She walked out on the deck; it was cool enough now to sit and enjoy the back yard. The humidity and the infernal midges of the Virginia summer were gone, and she enjoyed sitting on the rough-hewn deck Mike had built two years ago. They'd bought the house from a retired general; he must have been in the camouflage corps, for the house was a sea of disguised distress. The first time they had put a chair on the deck, a leg had gone through the fresh paint. Underneath the paint was putty, rot, and termites. Mike was of the overstrength building school of craftsmen; he never used a two-by-four where he could slip in a four-by-four. The deck could have supported a tank, but it was roughly finished, with nail marks showing and nothing perfectly plumb. It was just like him: overstrong, nail marks showing, not plumb.

She was furious. Mike deserved to be a general more than anybody she knew. That goddamn Duke Brown was a two-star, and he had been wrong every time that Mike had been right, from the FB-113 to the B-52 gust studies. He spent his time managing his career while Mike worked for the Air Force. Maybe he was smarter, after all. Mike had saved the Air Force millions in procurement dollars over the years, and would have saved more if they had listened to him on the FB-113 as they had on the F-4. But he ruffled feathers, no matter whose, if he thought he was right. Not Duke; even if he disagreed with somebody, he never let him know, had somebody else do the dirty work. That was part of the problem; Mike was a confronter. It worked for the Air Force's interests, but it hurt him. The Air Force was lucky that there were a lot more Mike Kellys than there were Duke Browns.

He'd been productive on his current assignment. He'd helped to get the Red Flag combat training going two years ago, and kept getting more funds for it each year. But he was submerged in paperwork now. Maybe that was a hint; he wasn't running a major project, just shepherding a group of them through the involved multiple budget cycles. He'd explained it to her once; it was unexplainable.

He had taken it well last year when Washington had made it. He believed Wash deserved it and was truly happy about it even though Wash was junior to him as a colonel by two years. Besides, last year hadn't been the crucial year, the watershed year. He needed to make it this year if it was ever going to happen. It looked like it wasn't going to happen.

She wondered at her own calm. It probably had to do with her work, her fulfillment, but it also spoke of the hope that Mike would get out, at last, and they could count on being somewhere for more than three years. Kathy had grown to hate the sight of a moving van, any moving van, recalling the times she had watched a slick truck driver with missing teeth inventory her furniture as it was carried out, marking everything "worn, scarred, torn, marred," even if it was brand new. Then there was the hassle of the drive wherever they were going, and on the other end, usually after a two- or three-week wait, the same guy, this time dropping the furniture, bumping the appliances, all the time telling her how soon he had to leave. It was always a horror.

She sipped a cup of decaffeinated coffee. Ah, they were growing old; time was she would have slipped a shot of rum into high-test perked coffee to get over something like this.

The real irony was that he'd done some fighting, was a double ace, a hell of a test pilot, a troubleshooter they always called on when they were in a jam, and now he was passed over. The Air Force was always talking about flying and fighting; why didn't it count for more when promotions came around? It was time for him to get out.

Yet she knew he would have the same problem in retirement; the business world was no different from the Air Force when it came to politics and politicking. It was getting that way in Wildlife, Now, just because there was a critical mass of people in the office to brew up the trouble.

She'd watched the contractors over the years, big ones like McNaughton, small ones too, and for every ten Mike Kellys doing the work there was a Duke Brown to smoothly grab the credit. It was probably the same in the church; she could imagine a bunch of priests sitting around complaining about who was made bishop, bishops doing it for cardinal selection, and the cardinals really raising hell about who was pope.

Still it was time for him to get out. He was too old, thank God, for a flying job, but he had a lot of friends in the industry. He also talked about going back to school to get enough credits to teach. The retirement pay was good, perhaps the only equitable arrangement in the whole cockamamie service system. With retirement, and whatever a teacher made nowadays, they'd do well.

She heard the door open, the two stupid dachshunds racing to it yapping as they did every time the doorbell rang. It was about the only exercise they took. She followed Mike's progress through the house by sound; the usual curse when he knocked over the Thai candlestick by the door, the quick trip to the bathroom, the refrigerator and liquor cabinet doors opening and shutting. That was bad news, meant he was making martinis—this was going to be serious drinking. He stopped for a moment to pick up the mail, then barged out on the deck.

"Great news, honey! Ronnie Nordeen made BG! He really deserves it. Jake Morantz made it too, and so did Brian Foley. This is the best news I've had since Wash made it last year."

She burst into tears.

Mike came over, put his arms around her. "Come on, Kathy, you know I don't care. There's always next year, and who the hell ever thought I'd make colonel, much less general?"

They sat quietly for a while; she took a martini not because she wanted it, but because she didn't want him to drink the whole pitcher.

After a while, he spoke. "It is a little hard on me, honey. Makes we wonder what you have to do. You know, I've had a good career, but I just haven't got the personality to be political. I've punched most of the tickets by accident, and I've never cultivated a sponsor. Now it's coming home to roost. I've got nobody to blame but myself. And it's been one hell of a career from a flying viewpoint." He was quiet again, then added, "I know I'm not everybody's cup of tea."

"Mike, do you want to talk about it now, or should we just go out somewhere and get something to eat? The grill is fixed, and I've got steaks here."

"I don't care. I'm just going to sit here with these anesthetizers and think a bit. I've got to call Wash around six; he's in town for a few days. They're finishing two of the XB-3s for test vehicles, and he still has a lot to do."

The phone rang; Kathy ran to get it. It was Wash. "Kathy, Duke called me earlier; would it be all right if I dropped on over?

I know he must be down in the dumps, and maybe I can cheer him up."

"Sure, Wash. Did Louise come with you?"

"Yeah, we'll be over about eightish, if that's okay."

When she got back out on the deck, Mike was on his third martini.

She reached down and lifted it out of his hand, pretending to take a sip. "Honey, Wash is coming over about eight, to talk; maybe you better go light on these."

She saw the little flash of temper.

"Wash knows I take a drink or two. It won't surprise him."

"Mike, it might surprise you to know I think that drinking is the problem. You've always been a drinker and it might not have helped."

He sat up, knocking the pitcher over. "What do you mean? Most everybody drinks in the Air Force."

"Not the contenders, Mike, not like you do. I'm worried about you. Your dad couldn't handle it, you know. I don't know if drinking problems are hereditary, but I don't want to find out."

It was out. She'd wanted to say that for years.

"You really know how to hurt a guy. That's the support I need on a night like this."

Kathy flinched. It wasn't the right time, but it was out. She waited for him to boil.

He was stunned. As smart as he was, it had simply never occurred to him that his drinking was not his own private business. He'd never drunk on the job, never missed a meeting, never missed a flight. But he had partied.

It was also a plausible excuse.

"Kathy, you're usually right. Goddamn it, that's it. I'm stopping tonight, now."

She felt a wave of relief; she'd happened to time it just right; one martini less and he would have laughed it off. One martini more and they would have had a hell of a fight. It had been by accident, but the timing was beautiful.

Right after she had the call from Helen she'd gone down to Safeway and picked out two enormous Porterhouse steaks. The fire was ready, and in fifteen minutes she had Mike stabilized with a steak and a glass of Chilean cabernet. When he asked for a second glass she shook her head and he laughed.

"Okay, okay! I may not be general officer material, but I can take a hint."

Wash was there at eight on the button; promptness was a

disease among Air Force types. If the invitation said seven, they rolled up at seven exactly, not six fifty-nine, or seven oh-one. It drove civilians crazy; more than one party found the Kellys there with the hostess still in a robe.

"Hello, General! Old Bud Drummond would be mighty proud of you."

"You too, Mike; remember, he wouldn't let us make change or get near the cash register, and here you are an ace and a wheel in the Pentagon."

He kissed Louise dutifully on the cheek; Kathy was hugging Wash tight, whispering to him.

"Here's a little something for later, Mike." Wash handed him a bottle of Courvoisier.

"Thanks Wash; maybe we can turn this one into a last man bottle club."

Kathy had to bring Louise up to date on Wildlife, Now; Louise was having trouble getting the movement started in L.A., where there were almost more organizations than people.

Mike and Wash went down to the cherry-paneled den.

"Great news about Nordeen, eh?"

"Yeah, and Fred Lomax made it too. Did you know him?"

They went through the painful litany. Finally Wash said what was on his mind. "Mike, I'm really sorry. You deserve it more than anybody I know, more than Nordeen, more than me."

"Yeah, well, them's the breaks. I may just get out of this chickenshit outfit, you know. A colonel can get out in sixty days if he wants to; there's too damn many of them around. I don't want to wind up like some of these old gray-haired sixty-year-old guys, doing the same thing every day."

"That'd never happen to you, Mike." He paused. "How about coming out to the plant with me? I could use you as a trouble-shooter, and a senior flight test supervisor; you'd like flying this dude."

"The XB-3 is just a test bed; I doubt if there will ever be another manned bomber. I don't want to hurt your feelings, but it sounds like a dead end for a washed-up colonel. I'd be better off getting out and teaching school."

"Come off it. You'd go crazy. The first time you hammered some wiseass young kid for shooting his mouth off, they'd have you in jail. Get serious."

"Yeah, you're right. Me teaching somebody is an illusion. But damn, I hate to go into the industry. I've hated it ever since I found out there was a sort of revolving door. It just doesn't seem right."

"I know how you feel, but it's not all bad, and it's perfectly human. You can't expect some guy who spends thirty years flying airplanes to want to go out and become an aluminum-siding salesman. Besides, most people feel it's time to make a little money. They have kids in school, no estate, no house, no nothing. It's pretty hard to kiss away an honest career on principle."

"You're right about no money. The guy next door to me lives in the same house, bought it when it was new for nineteen grand. He has about two more years of payments of ninety dollars a month. I bought this sucker for a hundred and fifty thousand; took every cent I had for a down payment, and my payments are still twelve times his. He's always bitching about my retirement, and I haven't even retired yet."

They were silent for a while.

"Besides, who the hell would have me? I don't know anything but flying and the Air Force, and there are damn few flying jobs around for an old crock like me."

"Mike, General Aero would hire you tomorrow as a trouble shooter, a manager. Hell, everybody knows you've got the best judgment in the business. Who called the shot on the FB-113 before they ever cut a bit of metal on it? Who fought for the F-4? They want guys with some savvy, who can think and plan. I don't think you'd be worth a damn as a salesman or P.R. guy, but you sure as hell could rationalize a production problem. They know that, all of them. You've got a hell of a reputation, and getting passed over just might enhance it in their eyes. They know you've never sold out."

When Washington left, Mike was feeling a lot better. He hefted the Courvoisier in his hand, tucked it on the top shelf of the bookcase.

Charles was terribly frail, but he was walking more easily. She watched him take his daily stroll down the flagstone path to the lake. Each day of his recovery was a joy and a sorrow to her. As he got better, as his mental acuity improved, he had more insight into what he'd done to himself. He was getting sadder as he was getting better, and she knew she had to do something about it.

They were growing stronger together. She had been worried for a while that she needed his need for her. Now she thought

604

she could stand on her own. The idea of a drink was not just no longer desirable for her; it actually repelled her.

Drinking had cost her so much. She might have lost her youth and whatever beauty she had simply to aging, but she wouldn't have lost it in a morass of sad memories, blurred ideas, and forgotten friends. And Charles might never have tried to kill himself if she had been available. Doctor Wendell warned her not to dwell on this, that it could hurt her own recovery, but she couldn't help it.

She watched him come up the porch steps, one at a time. Two years ago he would have taken them in a single leap. His good hand clutched the railing; the bad arm dangled.

He sat down next to her. "Mom, I've been thinking."

His voice was slurred, but less so than last month, much less than a year ago.

"Yeth, you know this isn't all bad. I won't have to go to West Point now, will I?"

"No, Charles, you just get better, and you can go wherever you want to school."

"Yeth, I was thinking, maybe I'd like to go to Georgia Tech. It's not too far away, and it's a good college."

They spent another hour talking; she was amazed at his outlook. She stroked his hair. He played with the collie puppy, burrowing his nose deep into the dog's fur.

It was the best time they had spent together since his attempt on his life; no, it was the best time they had together in more than ten years. She was getting better and he was getting better. They would get well together.

55

March 1978
Modesto, California
USA

The mystery was that Don had never left the Valley. Half an hour ago he'd been dropping a Cadillac engine into a Model T Ford, and Joe Amado was coming by to court his mother. Now he was twenty-six years older, Joe was dead of a heart attack, and his mother had remarried. It was just the valley that hadn't changed.

He looked with pride at the sign he'd painted himself.

DON PICARD AND SON
AIRCRAFT RENTALS, SALES, AND MAINTENANCE

It was mostly maintenance. They had a beat-up Cessna 150 to rent, and could only afford to sell airplanes on consignment. But the maintenance work was picking up. "General aviation," as they called private flying now, was becoming big business. And best of all, Jamie was learning as fast as he could teach him. It was as if he compensated in mechanical ability for his shortcomings elsewhere. And he was overcoming these, too. He would chat briefly and cheerfully with customers when he had to, and at lunch, over at the Poison Palace, he would talk to Don about the day's work.

The pace was just right. After the years of flight-line pressure in the Air Force, pushing gangs of people to get airplanes ready, Don relished the ability to simply drop his tools and postpone a repair for a day. Most of the planes were only used on the weekends, anyway, so it didn't make any difference to the customer. They were so delighted to have him work on the airplane they would have accepted delays. Within a few months of opening, he had established a reputation for quality work and fair prices, and now he had enough business for the two of them. He hated to expand, to bring in some hired mechanics, because he'd have to oversee their work.

The money wasn't terrific; he made enough added to his senior master sergeant's pension to be at about the same level of income he was before he retired. At least he had had enough to buy a big new trailer; they called it modular housing now. Polly was happy about that.

Pauline sat in the veneer-and-plastic modular home, graced on the outside with prefixed trellises, and inside with, of all things, a sunken tub. She thought it was the sunken tub that sold Don, on the spot. They had to dig the hole in your lot, then bring the home in and set it up, then work the tub through the doors to put it in place. It was red marbelized composition material, and Don never went past it without looking proud; if she was nearby, he'd look lascivious.

She went over the accounts with some exasperation, worried because Don was carrying some of the young guys too long. And there was a doctor and a lawyer with big bills on a Beech Bonanza that he really had to collect. He hated that part of the business. Maybe she was going to have to do it. She wanted to do something more than this, but she didn't know what. Maybe she would go back to school, secretarial school. Or maybe she would open a restaurant. They could use one on the flight line here; the snack bar was an atrocity.

She got up and put a cassette in the stereo. It was Peggy Lee singing "Is That All There Is?" It had become her favorite song, matching her melancholy. She had a memory for each phrase, a want for every line. Polly was amazed at the speed with which her youth and the service career had passed. It had been deceptive; good things were always just over the horizon: a tour in Europe, a tour in Japan. They never came. It was sort of like being at a reception, where the waiters with the drinks and the canapes never quite got to you. Just when you were next in line, the platters were empty and they disappeared. The Picards' platters had usually been empty.

But only of the frills; she had to admit that she had enjoyed the Air Force immensely when they were young, when the parties were simple beer busts, and there were innocent flirtations. It was only when she began to see how far behind they were falling in pay and opportunities. What would they have done if either child had really wanted—or been able—to go to college? In a way, they were lucky that Jamie was perfectly suited to working with Don, and that right after high school Donna had married that nice young fellow who worked at Sears. Polly would be a grandmother soon. The prospect filled her with swirling emotions.

She thought buying the business was the last straw; she had wanted Don to go see Jim Cagle, and get a decent job with a big avionics company. Cagle had done well, and he knew Don's work. He wouldn't because of Jamie, and that turned out to be right. The improvement in the boy in the last few months had been miraculous. But the last straw *really* came when he bought the new trailer. He called it a modular home, but it was a trailer to her. It saved them money to park it on the field, and it made it easy for Don to work as much as he wanted, which was all day every day, but it was hell for her. She had wanted a normal home with normal neighbors. She had told him exactly what she wanted, and he hadn't even heard her.

No doubt it was her own fault. They had woven a marriage of submission to duty and to common sense; there was no way to survive enlisted life in the Air Force if you did not. If she were absolutely truthful to herself, she had to admit that she had

607

calculated as much from the first day she knew he would marry her.

Schoengarten. How far away it seemed now. The stench of death, the horror of the Nazi war. She had visited Germany all by herself three years before, and it had stunned her. Dieter Bachmeier was now a wealthy car dealer, selling Mercedes Benz cars, happily married to someone from Stuttgart, with four strapping kids. The village was prosperous beyond anything she had ever known there, even when things were best in the thirties. Sometimes—not often, but sometimes—she would lie awake and wonder if she had made a mistake in leaving with Don, in becoming an American citizen. She was proud to be American, but down deep inside, she was never going to be Polly: she was Fraulein Pauline Krause, of Bahnstrasse 32, Schoengarten-ob-der-Tauber.

But she was also Polly Picard. She was the woman who had fought overwhelming fears of rejection, of what they now called "culture shock," when he'd brought her to his home in California to meet his mother, who'd grimly become as American as the most American wife, who'd raised Jamie and Donna mostly alone, who'd helped to set up the German Wives' Club, who'd worked endlessly in restaurants until finally SMSgt Donald Picard had added "Retired" to his name.

The Air Force was behind them, but the style, the tastes, the appetites were not. Don divided his days into two sections. He worked at his business from the time the first airplane took off, or seven o'clock, whichever was earlier, and worked through till four-thirty. He always had lunch with Jamie at the diner, rather than coming home. Someone had told him a joke once about a wife saying "I married you forever but not for lunch," and it was somehow part of his code to stay away during the day. Polly thought it was because Jamie would talk more at the diner.

The second part of his day started after dinner in the trailer. He'd go back to the shop and begin working on the restoration of a Stearman biplane. He was going to refinish it exactly like the one his father had been killed in, right down to the tail numbers. Polly felt uncomfortable with the idea; it was macabre, but it seemed to fulfill him in some way.

His workmanship was beautiful. He hadn't done nearly as much wood and fabric work as he had done on engines, but his skill showed. The Stearman became sort of a rallying spot for local airplane buffs; scarcely an evening went by when there were not two or three people helping him. She noticed that

Jamie really enjoyed the evenings; Don was letting him rebuild the engine. She hoped he got the carburetor spring on right.

The six years Larry White had spent flying C-9s were the happiest of his life, and it had started out as just one more shafting. He'd come back from Nam expecting a decoration and a responsible job. They'd placed him at the bottom of the Military Airlift Command totem pole again, a buck copilot in a C-9, but some twist of fortune had landed him in the best airplane he'd ever flown.

And they had given him a break on being an aircraft commander; he'd flown the C-9 for less than a year when he transitioned into the left seat. But finally the time came to pull the plug. They'd given him his silver bottlecap on retirement, so he'd gone out as a lieutenant colonel then.

He was proud that Micky's success didn't bother him—too much. She had built up her own business, sold it, built up another. They had no financial worries; he could even buy his own airplane if he felt like it. But a little airplane just wasn't the same; after you flew a jet like the C-9, it was tiresome to chug around in a Cessna. You took off, and an hour later if you looked back over your shoulder you could still see the field.

The retirement ceremony had been marvelous; the Air Force had begun a policy of doing it right, with a reviewing stand, a parade, the whole bit. It was a collective process, of course; there were half a dozen people retiring, from a senior master sergeant to a major general. But it was moving. It was strictly against regulations—flyovers were considered too expensive—but his squadron had put together three C-9s for a flypast over the field, just as the troops passed in review. He had tears in his eyes, and Micky cried openly. Larry Jr. had come all the way from California to be with him.

He wished his mother Lola could have been there; she had enjoyed life with them to the fullest, and one day, without warning, simply stopped living. There was no transition; she had gone from enjoying life fully to not being there. It was as she would have liked it. He wondered if she was with his dad. For both of them, he hoped not.

Larry spent the first week of his retirement catching up on things around the house. By the Monday of the following week he was going crazy. "Micky, I've got to find some work to do."

"There's plenty of time for that, Larry. Why don't you take it easy for a while?"

"No, I'm going down to Lambert Field today and nose around. There's bound to be something going on."

He came home that night bubbling over with excitement. He'd been hired as a simulator instructor in C-9s. There was a training operation at the airport that maintained a variety of flight simulators for the smaller airlines.

He took a three-week course, passed his exams with high marks, and started to work.

Micky was delighted. It was the first time in their life when he was home on time, every day, and when every weekend was free. She needed him at home now; she drew strength from his character and his unselfishness. Coming home after a day in her office was like a vacation. He usually had drinks ready, and they ate out two or three nights a week.

Sometimes she wondered what would have happened if their ambition quotas had been reversed, if Larry had had her competitive drive, and she his sort of sweet equanimity. He'd probably be a full colonel, maybe a general now, and she'd be sitting at home, waiting for news from the officers' wives' club.

There was a fox gnawing at her stomach. The outfit she had hoped to start, the one Jerry Eatherton had stolen from her, TransAmerica Real Estate, had moved its headquarters to St. Louis. Eatherton was no longer with them; but Newcome the lawyer was, and he told her that Eatherton had been eased out years ago. It was Newcome who wanted her to come to work as an executive vice president, responsible for opening new territories. She couldn't believe the pay; they were offering her seventy-five thousand a year, and a share of the profits from new franchises.

If she took it, the spousal positions would be neatly reversed. She'd be on the road much of the time, working weekends, on call for help from whomever needed it. And she and Larry were just getting started for the tenth time, it seemed.

"Okay. What is it?" he demanded.

"What do you mean?"

"Listen, when the music is on, there's champagne in the ice bucket, the grill is going, and a shakerful of martinis is on the table, I know I've got problems. But when you add a plate of salami, cheese, and paté, it's gangbusters. Did you sell the business?"

She explained the situation to him. "I'd have to travel a lot;

probably be gone at least every other week for four or five days. You'd be stuck with taking care of things here."

"Suits me, darling. We can always make up with mini-honeymoons when you get back—we got pretty good at that in the Air Force. It's only fair; I got to go everywhere, see everything for the last twenty-nine years; you can do it for the next twenty-nine."

She hugged him.

"It won't be twenty-nine; let me do it for a year or two, see how we like it. It's not like joining the Air Force, I can quit any time I want."

Something she said made him look at her sharply. He got up from the sofa and walked around the living room, hands in pockets, obviously deep in thought. He stopped pacing and beamed at her. "Micky, I've got an idea. Are you going to sell the business?"

"I think I have to, or at least convert it to TransAmerica; otherwise it would be a conflict of interest."

"Okay. Sell it. Then, let's do this. Let's buy the simulator outfit out, and buy or lease a Learjet. I'll bet I can save you money and time by having a Learjet on hand for the important trips. And I'll get to do some flying. In between your flights, we'll charter the thing out."

She was doubtful. Larry had never run a business, and she had no idea about the economics of the Learjet. But she was going to make a lot of money on the business, and she either had to reinvest it or pay more taxes than she could stand.

"Let's start with the simulator company; if we can handle that, then we can think about the Learjet. Okay?"

Larry swept her off the sofa and kissed her, and the kissing led to other things. Later that night, she worried; shouldn't he have been a little more upset about her being away so much? She realized he'd never really retired from the Air Force in terms of expectations. He expected to work all the time, to not be able to be with the family. This was just more Air Force to him, and it suited him. It suited the competitive side of her, too. But not the woman side. Maybe after a year, she would pitch the whole thing, and just stay home with him.

And maybe she wouldn't.

56

The word was definitely out. Brown could sense it in the way he was greeted. In an earlier war, in a gentler world, they called it "being put in Coventry." Here they talked to him, but they rationed what they said, and they said nothing important.

The chief was smart; he knew better than to make an issue of something that might be tough to prove. But the Air Force was shutting Duke out just as the body shuts out the cold. It was closing down the capillaries, reducing the circulation; he was dying on the vine.

It was time to get out. He had hoped to retire at least as a lieutenant general, as his father had, perhaps as a four star. There was a point he was riding so high that the chief of staff position had seemed attainable. What a joke now. He'd join the hundreds of other two stars around the country, each aware of the other's discontent at having missed the one big rung in the ladder that meant anything to them. He knew that there would be jokes made, wry comments, serious assessments of his leaving as a two star. Well, so be it.

His workload had dropped to almost nothing. The Pentagon was a place of strife and work; no matter what your rank, you handled emergencies all day long, you stayed long hours. Stress was an ethic, and if you didn't have enough, you created some. Until you were marked as Brown was marked: snakebit, frostbit, unlucky, not to be seen with.

Well, it was time to get out. He was fifty-two years old, had thirty years in. He had done one hell of a job for the Air Force, in combat and out, flying those old buckets when he didn't want to, saving the B-52, maybe saving the fleet by getting information no one else had. What had it gotten him? Two stars, some medals, and a pervasive emptiness.

Yes, it was time. And McNaughton needed him. The process of converting a fake weapon to a real one was much harder than the president or anyone else had imagined. The Pathfinder had doubled in size since his meeting with Bob Cranston, and the guidance systems were still not achieving the accuracy necessary. But that wasn't the main problem. McNaughton was just caught flat-footed. It had not built up the base of engineering and production expertise to build a cruise missile, and despite all the pirated hiring from other companies, it was still vacillating. The production schedules were already scrambled.

They needed him. He was going to retire and go to work. But first, he had to talk to Joan.

She had seen a lawyer, but not proceeded. Now he had to find out what she wanted, what they could do. The last thing he could endure would be a divorce suit while he was getting on board with McNaughton.

There was no trouble getting leave; once it was hell to get away, now he could have signed up for six months and probably Page would have signed it off.

In the old days, he'd have called Andrews Base Ops, and either gotten a plane for himself, or had someone fly him out. In those days the ramps were covered with airplanes, barely at rest before taking off for the next destination. Now the ramps were empty, and the Base Ops scheduling board almost vacant. The Air Force had found that proficiency flying was just too expensive. So he flew commercial, in civvies, glad to be anonymous, able to stare out the window and think about what might have been, dare to think about what still might be.

The Dade place hadn't changed. Joan was waiting for him on the porch with iced tea; it was like an early scene from *Gone With the Wind*. She was bubbling with excitement. Charles had taken a sudden, almost miraculous turn; his limp was gone, he was getting strength back in his arm, and his speech was almost unimpaired. He'd started studying with a tutor they'd brought in from Georgia Tech. She related it all to him with a clear voice and laughing eyes.

Duke was delighted. The boy's problem had been an endless reproach to him. He had wound up a two-star general, but he had been a zero-star father. He sipped the tea and said, "Joan, I'm going to retire. I'm not useful to the Air Force anymore, and it's time to make way for some of the younger guys. Besides, if I'm going to work in industry, it's better to start now."

"That's fine, Duke. Whatever you want."

"What are your plans?" he asked. "Do you think we could get along if I got a place down here, something small so we could handle it?"

She smiled gently at him. "I don't think so. I'm not up to it. Come on down and get settled. I won't do anything until you are secure. Then let's get a divorce. There's no sense going on like this. I don't want to remarry, or date, or even see anybody. I especially don't want to be married to you, even as a formality."

It was like the flat of a sword blade across his face. He blinked. "Joan, you can't mean that. We've had some very rough times, and it's been my fault, but we have Charles, we have memories. Don't just toss it all away."

A tiny frown creased her face. "Charles is almost grown. The memories I don't want. Don't kid yourself, don't kid me. We were never married in any physical or religious sense. You were married to your ego. I was one arrow in your promotion quiver. My arrow is bent. Let's give each other a little peace." She looked over his shoulder, at the tall oaks across the lawn. Her expression was that of a woman intently searching for someone, or something. Finally she said, "Please, just give me some peace."

Mike had given more farewell performances than Sarah Bernhardt. Every time he made up his mind to retire, he'd get some piddling assignment that he couldn't turn down. He reminded Kathy of a persistent life-insurance salesman, who never stopped calling clients no matter how many refusals he had.

Part of it was the new energy boiling through him. He'd stopped drinking and started jogging with the same manic intensity that he did everything. He started out with two miles a day, and within a few months had worked up to six. His legs ached, he had shin splints, but he never stopped.

He took an adolescent's delight in his progress; Kathy expected him to start wearing a beanie and singing college songs again. If he told her, and anyone who would listen, once, he told a hundred times that he had dropped thirty pounds, weighed what he did as a cadet. Worse, he had become an impossible crusader, making Kathy feel guilty if she had an evening drink, virtually jerking drinks out of guests' hands.

Kelly trotted puffing into the living room, sweat steaming off him. Kathy recoiled from his hug. "Come on, give me a break. You're too sweaty! How about taking a shower before you get affectionate?"

He slapped her on the bottom. "I thought you liked me earthy."

"Earthy, not rock bottom. Hey, Wash called. I put his number on the pad. But take a shower first; it will wait."

Mike came down in his shorts, his finger holding the waist line out.

"Look at this, I need all new underwear. I'm just waisting away."

He tried to explain the joke, gave up, and went in to call Wash.

"Mike, how ya doing?"

"Fine, buddy. What do you need?"

"This is pretty sensitive. Will you promise not to tell anybody about my role in this?"

"Sure, what is it?"

"I don't know what the Air Force rules are on this," Wash said, "but I've been asked to offer you a job."

"You mean with General Aero?"

"No, that's the strange part, and that's why you've got to keep it secret. I've been approached by McNaughton—yeah, Brown's pals—to offer you a vice president of production planning job. It's worth one hundred grand a year."

Mike whistled. "What the hell do they want me for? Why are they going through you?"

"As I read it, they're in trouble. They have some Pathfinder launches coming up, and it looks like they have the technical problems solved, but they have, so they tell me, a production nightmare. They think you can help."

"Jesus, that's Brown's baliwick. I'm not going to work for him. He's shafted me too often in the Air Force; I'm not going to spend the rest of my life checking six to see if he's on me or not."

"That's why they had me call, Mike. They aren't going to hire Duke. I think Old Man Dade's blown the whistle on him or something, but he's o-u-t, out."

"I don't know, Wash. What do you think?"

"Look, I don't know anything about it. You've got to decide. They must need you or they wouldn't be offering that kind of dough. And it's not a sales or P.R. job; they aren't buying your contacts, they're buying your savvy. I'd take it if I were you. And not just for your sake, either. If we are committed to that little sucker, we better have somebody who can get it in the air."

"What do you think it means for you? I understand you're in line for a production contract after all."

"Yeah, but for a down-rated airplane. We'll need the Pathfinder **too,** or something like it. Mike, at least agree to talk to them. **And** keep this quiet, please."

"Okay, Wash. I always said I wouldn't work for industry, but this sounds pretty intriguing. It would be better than the pissant things I'm doing now. Thanks for calling. I'll be in touch."

He didn't have long to wait. Sherman Scheffer, the Mc-Naughton chief executive officer, called him the next day. "Colonel Kelly, I understand that you had a conversation with General Washington. Is that correct?"

"Yes sir; I told him I'd be interested in learning more of what you had in mind."

"Could you come down to the plant? I can have the company plane at National anytime you like."

"Let me set up some leave, sir, and let's plan on doing it the day after tomorrow."

"Right; there'll be a McNaughton 640 at the Butler terminal at nine o'clock; call me if you have any problems. And would you be good enough to keep this confidential?"

"Yes, I'd prefer it. I hope to see you on Thursday."

Kathy was ecstatic. "Mike, this is what you need. You have to get out of the Air Force rut, and go somewhere you'll be appreciated. They need help and you can give it to them. You have to have a challenge; you'd go crazy teaching school, or selling something. You couldn't sell *anything*."

He grabbed her. "I've sold you a bill of goods for more than twenty years now, me beauty, and I'm going to sell you a little loving now."

His jogging showed.

Brown tendered his resignation without regret. He'd done the best he could for the Air Force, and if it wasn't what the chief thought best, that was his problem. He'd heard of a medal once, Austrian, he thought, called "The Order of Maria Theresa." It was awarded only to those who showed valor while disobeying orders. He thought he'd earned it.

The papers went through without a hitch but there was a chill in the office. Daphne was miserable; finally, on his last day, she took him out for a drink. The word had gone out: no retirement party for Duke. He was shattered.

He had been calling Scheffer and Cranston for two weeks, trying to set up an appointment. Finally, he called Dade. To his surprise, he was put right through. "I'm sorry to bother you, sir, but I've been having some troubles getting through to Scheffer, and I wondered if you'd have him call me."

"What for, Duke?"

The sonofabitch. He was going to make him crawl. So he'd crawl. "Well, I've put my papers in, and I want to go to work. The Pathfinder's in trouble, and I can help."

"Duke, I'm sorry, but I understand they've hired Mike Kelly for the job. I don't think they've got a spot for you."

The relish in his voice rolled through the phone like an Elgar concerto. Dade loved his work.

"Duke? Duke? Are you there, Duke?"

Brown let the phone slide down the side of the couch.

Kelly had thought it would be hard to get out of the Air Force, but he put his papers in and six weeks later was taking his processing-out physical at Andrews. It was a bright new hospital, a lot different from the wooden shacks he'd processed through at Scott when he came in. But there was one thing of unyielding permanence, something that never varied, and that was the sense of total unease he felt sitting in his shorts, waiting for the flight surgeon to come in and do unspeakable things to him.

The door opened. A small, obviously Middle Eastern man was there, wearing captain's tracks and a white coat. "Colonel Kelly."

"Yes."

"I'm Doctor Sahmad. Pleased to meet you." His voice was sibilant. He sounded like a Pakistani merchant.

Kelly went through the process he'd undergone so often, the annual stripping down, prodding, poking, pressing. Dr. Sahmad looked at his papers. "It seems you are in good health, Colonel. Any problems?"

"No, I'm in great shape. But I think I still have to have an EKG, don't I?"

Sahmad looked through the paperwork again. "Ah, yes, I think it is working now, I'll get someone to call you if it's ready."

He left; a harried nurse came in, took him to the EKG room. He winced as she smeared the cold gray gritty paste on those mystic spots that spoke only to the machine. She ran the drill quickly, examined the readings. "Excuse me, Colonel, let me try that again; I must have not had one of the wires fixed quite right."

Kelly felt his heartbeat surge. "Nothing wrong, is there?"

"No, I'm sure not, but I just want to get another set of readings."

She worked rather more slowly this time, taking care with the electrodes, checking her settings. When she finished, she frowned.

"Everything okay?"

"I'm not supposed to even try to read these, Colonel, you know that. I'll take them to Dr. Sahmad. But—" She bit her cheek and hurried out.

Kelly dressed and went back in to see the flight surgeon. The nurse's demeanor had captured his attention. He sat down on the green plastic chair and rather too casually asked, "Any problems, Doctor?"

Dr. Sahmad adjusted his thick glasses and barely looked up from whatever form he was filling in. He gave the impression of being simply too busy for all this body work. "No, Mr. Kelly, Colonel Kelly, you are in fine shape. You keep up what you are doing, you will live forever."

It was exactly what Kelly wanted to hear. He didn't press the issue.

He'd arranged to retire even before he'd visited McNaughton to check things out. He felt confident the job would come through; if he didn't like it, there was always something else down the line.

At McNaughton they rolled out the red carpet for him. He was shown an office twice as big as the chief of staff's; it had a bar, a small dining room, beautiful furniture. There was a limousine for his use at all hours. They would help him find a house, finance it, bring Kathy down as often as necessary until she was satisfied.

The setup looked very promising to Kelly. He was going to have full say on the production methods. But the calendar was against them. They had a series of four test firings scheduled in September, and it was already April. A bigger problem was the production schedule. They were supposed to start delivery eight per month in October, thirty in December, eighty in January, and one hundred per month after that. They couldn't risk waiting until the four September flights to freeze the design.

He talked to the new vice president for production, Phil Prandle. They had one missile, virtually hand built, ready to go. They wanted to test fire it soon, and if it worked with 80 or 90 percent efficiency to lock in on it and start volume production. The changes would be costly if there were many, but not so bad as missing the production schedules. Kelly decided to take the job.

He had insisted on retiring without fanfare but there had been a big party for him anyway. He had tried to soft-pedal what he was going to do, embarrassed about going to work for McNaughton. He wondered what Brown thought about it. He was tempted to call him, but talked it over with Kathy and decided against it.

"I don't know if I want to commiserate or gloat. The bastard retired as a major general and I'm just a piddly-ass colonel, so I guess I wanted to gloat. But he'll get a job. He probably had one, passed this one over. He's never stood short."

There was an unexpected bonus to the job that McNaughton had inexplicably failed to tell him about; perhaps they assumed he knew. Kelly couldn't believe it. McNaughton had leased a mint F-86 from a Mojave operator to fly chase on the Pathfinder. It was a Canadian-built airplane, with less than a thousand hours flying time on it. It fit Kelly like a glove. He went out to Mojave to check it out, for he was determined to fly wing on the missile on the first flight. If something went wrong, he wanted to know.

Mojave was a bizarre airport; located at the edge of the Edwards complex, it had more exotic airplanes, half of them derelict, than Kelly had ever seen. He stayed at a miserable little motel, air conditioned by a leaking and shrieking window unit, and got up every morning at six to jog in the cool desert air.

Their F-86 was like an old friend. He stood at its side, glancing down at the silvery smooth curves, and thought about the days in Korea when this was the glittering edge of America's sword, and he was a hot young pilot privileged to be there. He opened the bays, sniffed the scent. All airplanes smell different, and this was not like the 86s he remembered; probably hydraulic fluids and oils had changed specifications since then. He read the manuals, walked around the airplane, caressed it. He would have taken the job for nothing if he knew he was going to be reunited with a Sabre.

He took two rides in a T-33 with the company test pilot, and they turned him loose. It was like graduate day in flying school. He wrung the F-86 out. When it was time to land he came in over the runway at thirty feet and did a sixteen-point roll. When he landed, nobody mentioned it. This was Mojave.

The work on the Pathfinder was completely absorbing. Ed Novack had joined McNaughton more than a year earlier, when they had made him an offer he quite literally would have been a fool to refuse, for an entirely different program. When the Pathfinder suddenly came alive, he moved over and was project manager. They were dead set to get the first test done on time.

The test firing was so critical that Scheffer was with Prandle and Novack at the launch site. They were going to drop it from a bailed B-52. The drop would take place at fifteen thousand feet, west of Mojave. The test missile was supposed to fly through the Mojave area, turn north, track through Nevada and finally self-destruct near the Tonopah range. Kelly figured he could stay with it for an hour, then come back to base.

He got up early on the morning of the flight, and cut his jogging to four miles; he was having some problems with a charley horse in his thigh and didn't feel quite right. He wanted to be set for the flight.

Kelly went to the little motel restaurant, had his usual ham and eggs and three cups of coffee. Takeoff was scheduled for eleven, so he had plenty of time. He thought he'd call Kathy, then decided against it. She'd just worry about the flight. He'd call her later.

The takeoff was uneventful. He rendezvoused near Palmdale with the big B-52, remembering the flight tests with Brown, and was flying only two hundred yards away to watch the launch. It was beautiful. The Pathfinder dropped out of the bomb bay, and its little stubby wings snapped out. A moment later, before it had lost much speed or altitude, a puff of smoke showed that the tiny Thompson jet engine was running. It accelerated, and the B-52 turned away to return to Edwards.

Kelly slid in to within ten feet of the Pathfinder, flew formation with it as it dropped down, down to the deck, below radar coverage, snaking along only feet above the terrain like a mad-dened roadrunner. That would have been a better name, he thought, Roadrunner, and they could have put a little bird with Beep Beep on the insignia.

Novack and Prandle read the missile's moves through the telemetry shack. The thing was functioning perfectly. Scheffer came in. "What do you hear from Kelly?" he asked.

Novack glanced up and waved at the radio. "We can't hear him at his altitude; he's only got line-of-sight communication."

They went back to monitoring the Pathfinder.

The pain was sudden and severe. Mike felt the squeeze on his arm and chest, reached down to switch to 100 percent oxygen, and blacked out.

The F-86 flew with the missile for a moment, then gradually

banked, its left wing lifting higher until the nose dropped and the lovely Sabre merged in billowing smoke and flame with the rough California desert.

The missile flew on, comparing the terrain with its microchip map.

The news of Kelly's death spread across the Air Force like a ripple across a pond. Kathy collapsed and went into the hospital, under sedation. She had always expected it to end in a ball of flames when he was flying combat; she didn't expect it when he retired. As she drifted in and out of consciousness, she wondered at herself. She always knew of the possibility, always thought she'd be stoic. When she had heard, her legs had given way, collapsing her into a void she knew now would be endless.

Washington got the word almost immediately, flew first to Mojave, then back to Alexandria, to see if he could help Kathy. On the way he thought about Bud Drummond, about Birmingham, and how young they once were.

The time had passed so quickly. Wash went to the mirror. His cropped black hair was no longer black. It was almost half gray, grayer than his dad had been at his age. It was the first time he had noticed.

The Public Affairs office at the Pentagon dug for Kelly's biography for the official obit. Capt. Jesse Catlin came over and pulled the paper from his ranking sergeant's typewriter. The sergeant looked up in surprise. Catlin was uncharacteristically tense.

"I'll write this one, Sarge," he said. "I knew the man."

Garvey was in the club at Randolph when the news filtered down. He'd run into General Lawton in the foyer. Together they were drinking, and remembering. Crashed in an F-86? It was like a time warp. He must have had a heart attack. Maybe it was a misprint, an F-4, more likely. He sipped the martini morosely. The important question was, What was Kelly doing flying, anyway? Garvey looked around the club, and thought the old thoughts. No. The important question wasn't about the hardware. It was about them. The important question was always the same: Why wasn't Jim on his wing, where he belonged?

Duke's contacts let him know within two hours of the accident. But Joan called Duke about it anyway. Her voice was unmistakably accusatory. Somehow, she held him responsible for Kelly's augering in. Joan closed by announcing that she was flying up to help Kathy. It seemed strange to him—they hadn't corresponded for years. But he knew now he had never understood Joan. No more than he had understood Kelly.

He remembered, suddenly and with startling clarity, the details of the day Kelly soloed. As he'd watched the arrogant young cadet accelerate down the desert strip, he'd wished mightily that Kelly would crash. Now, finally, three decades later, his wish had come true. But he felt no sense of revenge. He felt only emptiness. When Kelly went down in his Sabre, he took something of Duke with him.

McNaughton would have to call him now. They had to. He stared at the phone.

EPILOGUE

✦

CREW CHANGE

Johnson Space Center
Houston, Texas
USA

"Houston, we've got a problem."

"Roger, *Constitution*, go ahead."

"Ah . . . we have an anomaly here; we have different readings on OMS burn length. The instrument panel has some random lights; I don't like it. Over."

"*Constitution*, everything looks nominal here; you are down to 16,465, just where you should be."

"Control, I don't like this; if I believe what I see, one of the orbital maneuvering system engines did not have a full burn. Over."

"Roger. Understand, *Constitution*, Ah—we're looking at it here; looks like there is a computer degradation."

"Rocky, this is Jack."

"Go, Jack."

"Ah, Rocky, we're reading it now that your position is nominal but that you are getting some sort of attitude control failure. Over."

"Yes, I think that's right. I'm going to have to override."

"Not yet; you have a few minutes to the blackout; let's work on it together and see if it's readings or real."

"Roger, Jack. Understand. Anybody got any ideas down there?"

"We're working the problem, Rocky. Same as before. Looks like a hand job from here down to Vandenberg."

"Understand, Jack. We've got to decide pretty soon."

"We're showing you at seventeen thousand, *Constitution*, that's just a little fast, maybe you ought to be thinking about override soon."

"Ah, Roger." There was silence.

Jack Behrens, the flight director, shook his head. If ever ESP should work, if ever there should be psychic communication, it should be now, between this control room full of people concentrating their will upon success, and that group of five explorers who were once again supplementing the frailties of science with human will.

Rocky's voice came on, calm, positive. "I'm overriding, see you."

"You'll be going into blackout soon, Rocky. Good luck."

"Roger, Jack. See you on the other side."

A sterile artificial white noise filled the comm line. The controllers looked at one another. On the consoles, the relentless mathematics played out, a phosphorescent mimicking of the poignant thought processes of the controllers who had been through other emergencies at other times, always with the same sense of helplessness.

The space shuttle was coming home, but not according to the mission plan. It was coming back without the precision of multiple computers in agreement, but with a human mind supplementing the computer process.

In the cockpit of the *Constitution*, the crew went through the drill of checking switch positions, inflating G suits, watching the transition from thruster control to elevon control, conscious that their lives were controlled not only by the bulk of the plunging orbiter but by the judgments in the brain of the pilot and the skill with which these judgments were transmitted to the controls. There was nothing to do or say to affect things; there was only the routine.

A single tiny error would not only cause them to miss their energy window, leaving them little chance of making the runway, it could leave them tumbling out of control, flaming like a meteor across the sky.

A controller pointed at his screen. "They made it through the blackout!"

"They've got a chance! Call 'em. Now!"

"Houston, *Constitution* calling." The voice was faint through the static of the fiery envelope that was diminishing about the shuttle like an extinguishing match.

"Go, *Constitution*, you've got some very happy people down here."

"And up here, Jack. We're looking good up here, what do you say?"

"Same, Rocky. You are absolutely nominal. I can't believe it—on course and on time. You got good hands, Babe!"

The minutes passed as the huge shuttle—the world's biggest, fastest, and heaviest glider—slid down a prescribed path like a winged stone toward the earth, racing across the Pacific sky until at last the coastline of California loomed under its still-glowing nose.

"*Constitution*, looking good for touchdown as planned."

"Roger, Houston."

"You are right on the marks, *Constitution*, four twenty-four at thirteen thousand feet."

"Good luck, Rocky. This is it. We're all with you."

The controllers crowded around the consoles, watching the airspeed dropping from its orbital heights of seventeen thousand five hundred down to mere airliner range, 358, 308, 268 m.p.h. They could sense the subtle change in orbiter attitude as the nose came up. At ninety feet, the gear snapped down; the *Constitution* touched down at 215 m.p.h., a whisper of smoke trailing from the tires.

"Houston, *Constitution* is down at fourteen after the hour."

Along the consoles, wild cheering broke out.

"Welcome home, *Constitution!*"

"Glad to be here, Houston. Say, where do you guys want us to park this thing?"

"Anywhere you want, Rocky! Anywhere you want."

Behrens peeled off his headset and wiped the sweat from his face. He grinned at the crew working the consoles. Each of them was unplugging and pushing back from the computer screens that lined the ground floor of the huge building. Far above them, the servos and hydraulic jacks that gave the simulator its many degrees of motion freedom whined and whirred to a halt. The gigantic mock-up of the space shuttle fuselage that was cradled in the web of jacks stopped moving. After a little while, the access door swung open and the crew emerged.

Cheers and whistles from the floor greeted them, and they hooted back. Behrens waited at the console for the pilot to come down and get the traditional handshake.

"Well, shit, Rocky, I guess you by God did it! That was one hell of a fine flight." He reached out his hand, still grinning widely.

Lt. Col. Rachel "Rocky" Garvey took his hand and shook it. Her blue flight suit was drenched in sweat, and her close-cropped hair was matted to her forehead, but she beamed, made the traditional comment, "Thanks, Jack. Jim did all the work."

"Bullshit," barked Cdr. Jim Hollis, who slapped her hard on the back. "Rocky pulled the thing off. I got lost in the routines, trying to set up the initial—"

"Shut up, Jim," Rachel said, "don't ever let the IP know when you've screwed up. Don't you guys know anything in the Navy? Let 'em think it was perfect."

They all laughed. Behrens ceremoniously plucked the mission book off his console and signed it with a flourish. "That's it, folks. Rocky, you're now officially checked out in this baby. When you gonna take us for a ride?"

Rachel laughed again. "Check back in five years, Jack. I understand the waiting list's a tad long."

"Well, you'll be ready, Rachel. That was as fine an approach as I've ever seen and you made the perfect analysis of the emergency. There's not time to talk that one over—you either do it right, or you burn. Simple as that. You did it right."

"You bet, Jack; she's a winner. Hey, let's get a picture of this. Shit, this is a historic goddamn occasion, right? I got my little disk camera right here. Jack? Rocky? What say?"

"Okay, Jim, but you gotta be in it too."

"No sweat. Hey, Bill. C'mere. Yeah. Push this button here. Right. Even a goddamn groundpounder like you oughta be able to do that—no, don't throw that sucker at me—"

The photo wasn't too good; the three crew members leaned on one another as flight crews through all time have done, hamming it up for the camera, obviously still high from their exhausting and exhilarating simulated flight. The colors were off tone, turning Rachel's black hair slightly purple, and she herself was a little blurred, because just as Bill had snapped the picture, Jack had pinched her.

But when Jim Garvey got the picture in her letter, he couldn't have cared less. As he stared at his little girl, who would someday command a space shuttle, he realized at last that he was looking at himself, at Kelly, Duke, Washington, at them all, past, present, and future. It was for them that he gave the little picture a whole page in her album—more space even than her graduation from flight school, from college, even more than her marriage and master's ceremony—he inked a little block of type carefully under it. One day he would explain it to her, if she ever asked. Being Miriam's kid, she would.

EVERYTHING CHANGES, AND NOTHING CHANGES.

About the Authors

WALTER J. BOYNE, a retired Air Force colonel and recently retired director of the National Air and Space Museum in Washington, D.C., is the author of nine books on flight. Born in East St. Louis, Illinois, he was commissioned in the U.S. Air Force in 1952 and retired as a colonel in 1974. During his service career he became a command pilot, with more than 5,000 hours of flying time in a score of different aircraft. He lives in Alexandria, Virginia.

STEVEN L. THOMPSON, the only son of a career Air Force pilot, was educated in Japan, the United States, and England. He served in the Air Force from 1969 to 1972. A motorcycle and road racer as well as a pilot, he is the author of three previous novels: *Recovery, Countdown to China,* and *Bismarck Cross.* He lives in Bethesda, Maryland.